The Lost Casebooks
of Sherlock Holmes

D1409907

The
Lost Casebooks
of
Sherlock Holmes

THREE VOLUMES OF
DETECTION AND SUSPENSE

Donald Thomas

PEGASUS CRIME
NEW YORK LONDON

THE LOST CASEBOOKS OF SHERLOCK HOLMES

Pegasus Books LLC
80 Broad Street, 5th Floor
New York, NY 10004

First Pegasus Books edition July 2012

Interior design by Maria Fernandez

Library of Congress Cataloging-in-Publication Data is available.

ISBN: 978-1-60598-512-1

10 9 8 7 6 5 4 3 2 1

Printed in the United States of America
Distributed by W. W. Norton & Company

Contents

Contents

I

The Secret Cases of Sherlock Holmes

The alleged bigamy of King George V . . . The theft of the Irish Crown Jewels in 1907 . . . The bizarre circumstances of the death of President Faure of France . . . Such dramas are not fiction but historical reality.

'It would have been astonishing,' wrote Dr John Watson of these cases, 'if the skills of Sherlock Holmes had not been employed by those at Scotland Yard.'

The investigations described in this volume relate the part played by the great detective in seven major crimes or scandals of the day, some of them too damaging to the monarchy, the government or the security of the nation to be fully revealed at the time.

Compiled in narrative form by Dr Watson soon after Holmes's death, the notes have been kept under lock and key at the Public Record Office in Chancery Lane.

Now, seventy years later, we can finally open the secret cases of Sherlock Holmes . . .

To Ben and Pet
In gratitude for Mrs Carew

Contents

A Letter to Posterity
from John H. Watson, MD

I

Those who have read my narrative of the Brixton Road murder, made public under the somewhat sensational title of *A Study in Scarlet*, will recall the events which led to my first meeting with the late Sherlock Holmes. For any who come new to this story, let me recapitulate the circumstances as briefly as I may. Having taken my medical degree at the University of London in 1878, I had attended the required course of the Army Medical Department at Netley. When my time at Netley was over, I was attached as Assistant Surgeon to the Fifth Northumberland Fusiliers. I will not repeat in detail how I landed in Bombay when my regiment was already in action in the Second Afghan War; how I joined it at Candahar only to be wounded in the shoulder, my active service career terminated by a Jazail bullet at the battle of Maiwand.

It was not the wound received in battle that alone decided my fate. Enteric fever contracted at the base hospital of Peshawar so weakened and emaciated me that the medical board had not the least hesitation in ordering my return to England. A few months later I was endeavouring without success to lead a comfortless existence at a private hotel in the Strand upon my invalid allowance of eleven shillings and sixpence a day.

The weeks of summer passed in 1880, and I watched with dismay as my little stock of capital ran lower. I had no family in England, no expectations, no one to whom I could turn for immediate assistance. My state of mind may easily be imagined, as I contemplated the loss of both health and independence.

In such gloomy circumstances I had taken a turn down Piccadilly one morning in July. That fashionable avenue was busy with swan's-neck pilentum carriages drawn by glossy bay geldings, here and there a coach with armorial bearings upon its door and a hundred hansom cabs. Among these symbols of imperial prosperity, I reflected that walking costs a man nothing. The clocks had struck twelve as I began to make my way back from the trees and carriages of Hyde Park Corner, where the pretty horse-breakers and their escorts rode under the leafy branches of Rotten Row.

In the course of this stroll, I had decided that my first economy must be to leave the private hotel where I had been living. I would seek cheaper lodgings. With that, I felt a little richer and entered the old Criterion Bar in Coventry Street. It was a chance in ten thousand that, as I stood at the bar, I should have been tapped on the shoulder by young Stamford, who had been a surgical dresser under me at Bart's Hospital. To him I described my situation and my new resolve as to where I should live. He it was who mentioned his acquaintance Sherlock Holmes, a man also in search of diggings. That very day Holmes had been bemoaning to Stamford that he could not get someone to go halves with him in a nice set of rooms which he had found but which were too much for his purse.

I recall, as if it were only a week ago, my excitement at this chance of solving my own problem so easily. I turned to Stamford and exclaimed, 'By Jove! If your friend really wants someone to share the rooms and the expense, I am the very man for him. I should prefer going halves to living alone!'

As yet, I had not set eyes upon my unwitting partner.

This is not the place to draw a complete portrait of him who was to be my friend and companion for so many years. I must say, however, that in all the time I knew him the appearance of

Sherlock Holmes seemed to alter no more than his demeanour. He was a little over six feet in height and throughout his life he remained so lean that he looked, if anything, taller. His eyes were sharp and his gaze penetrating, his nose was thin and hawk-like, making him seem always alert and decisive. His jaw was firmly set, square and prominent with a look of resolve and determination. If I were to compare his features and behaviour to those of public figures, he had the stance and manner of Sir Edward Carson QC, that most vigorous and astute of prosecuting lawyers. In his style, he had something of the combative and self-assured manner of Lord Birkenhead, the former Mr F. E. Smith. Perhaps I do him and them a disservice by such comparisons. There was never any man who was a twin for Sherlock Holmes.

My first meeting with him, when Stamford introduced us later that day, was in the chemical laboratory of Bart's. His fingers were blotched with acid and stained a little by ink. Surrounded by broad low tables, shelves of bottles, retorts, test-tubes, and Bunsen burners with their blue flickering flames, Holmes seemed in his element. He quite ignored me in his excitement at explaining to Stamford the success of an experiment on which he had been engaged. He had discovered a reagent which was precipitated by haemoglobin and by nothing else. In plain terms, it would now be possible for the first time to identify blood stains long after the blood had dried.

I was soon to see for myself a curious antithesis in my new friend's character. He alternated between periods of fierce intellectual excitement and moods of brooding contemplation. There were days of torpor in which he appeared to see little or nothing of the world about him. I had yet to discover that the last of these states was often produced by his use of narcotics. Life cannot always be lived at a pitch of fierce excitement. There are days, weeks, and months of tedium. Other men might have turned to drink or sexual vice. Sherlock Holmes preferred the less complicated palliative of cocaine. I deplored his use of it and protested to him—but in vain. I came to see that the drug was not his true addiction, merely a substitute for a more powerful enchantment. Cocaine, he said, was his protest against the tedium of existence. When his powers were fully occupied, he showed not the least need of it. The excitement of discovery, detection, activity, was everything to him. I firmly believe that cocaine was a make-do for the greater stimulant of adrenalin. The syringe provided for his needs when his adrenal gland failed to do so.

The world knows so much about the reputation of Sherlock Holmes that I need add little here. He pretended to be the dedicated student of science, yet from time to time one caught a glimpse of the great romantic. When I first met him, I noted that he had a profound knowledge of chemistry, an adequate but unsystematic acquaintance with anatomy. He had a good practical knowledge of the English law and was unrivalled in his reading of the literature of crime. From botany and geology he took just such information as seemed useful to him. Whenever necessary, he could make himself expert at a new subject in an astonishingly short time. When the new science of morbid psychology came into its own after 1880, he mastered it with such skill that neither Krafft-Ebing nor Charcot could tell you more of his own works than could Holmes.

At first I noted that he appeared to have little knowledge or interest in literature or philosophy. I was to discover that, when it suited him, he could show a degree of familiarity with writers like Edgar Allan Poe, Charles Baudelaire, or Robert Browning, the analysts of human darkness, which lifelong students of literature might envy. There were days when he exercised his brain as other men would have used a chest-expander or a set of dumb-bells. In such times of idleness he set himself the task of confronting the great unsolved problems of mathematics. If he did not find solutions to Fermat's Last Theorem or the Goldbach Conjecture, I believe that he understood at length the nature of those abstract impossibilities better than any man living.

There was something not quite English about Sherlock Holmes. Having played rugger for Blackheath in my younger days, I found he had no sense of sport in his physical activities. You could not imagine him among 'the flannelled fools at the wicket and the muddied oafs in the goal'. His physical exercise was Continental rather than Anglo-Saxon. Like a French or German student, he was an expert swordsman, boxer, and single-stick player. Though far from burly in his build, he demonstrated a grip that was the strongest of any man I have ever known.

He cared very little for society, let alone for politics or public men. Early in our friendship he assured me that a nation was better led by a rogue than by a reformer. In more recent years, he abominated Mr Asquith as leader of the government but openly admired the style and complicity of Mr Lloyd George. As the result of services which he had rendered to the Crown in the years before the German war, I was with him once at the Reform Club, when Mr Asquith spoke after dinner. Sherlock Holmes had attended the function reluctantly and sat with eyelids drooping and an air of ineffable boredom. Intending to compliment or instruct his audience, the late Prime Minister remarked that he owed much of his success in life to an endeavour to associate only with those who were his intellectual superiors. To my dismay, I heard Holmes rouse himself and say loudly enough for all those around him to hear, 'By God, that wouldn't be difficult!'

He was once at a soirée of the late Mr Oscar Wilde, an occasion which he would have avoided if he could. The unfortunate playwright was at his most self-satisfied and paradoxical, preening, praising his own works and genius in every nuance, while his sycophants chortled and encouraged him. As the guests prepared to depart, Sherlock Holmes stood up and the faces of the company turned towards him. He fixed Mr Wilde, the serene egotist, with those glittering eyes and seemed to bow a little towards him. The breath hissed slightly between his teeth.

'Master,' he said with expressionless irony, 'before we leave, could you not perhaps tell us a little about yourself?'

It was cruel and it was deadly. For more than an hour, Mr Wilde had seemed to talk of nothing but himself. This egotism would have justified Holmes's sardonic reprimand. Yet there was something more about the playwright which Wilde knew and Holmes had guessed, but which remained hidden from the others. Holmes, as I have said, was well read in the literature of morbid psychology. From this knowledge he had divined a pathological truth behind the mask of the *poseur* and he let the unhappy victim know it. A smile touched Wilde's lips, the worse for its ghastliness. The truth which Holmes inferred was one that the rest of the world was soon to hear in three trials at the Central Criminal Court.

I believe it was as well that Sherlock Holmes remained a private and secretive man. His tongue would have destroyed him in public life, though not before it had destroyed a good many other men. Among several instances of his savagery, his brother Mycroft told me, after the funeral, of young Sherlock Holmes's first brief acquaintance with formal education at a great Oxford college, whose master was something of a household name. It was the master's custom to take each of the new men out for a walk alone, from Oxford into the countryside and back again. The great scholar would keep an absolute silence as the pair walked to Headington or Godstow. The hapless undergraduate would feel the strain of this and would compel himself at last to make some nervous and banal remark, often about the weather or the meadow scenery. The master would either crush this by his retort or would continue the walk without reply, as if the observation were beneath notice. In either event, the poor young man would have been put securely in his place for the next three or four years. The stratagem had not been known to fail.

When Holmes was taken on this solitary freshman exercise, it was he who maintained a silence. Keeping step with the master of the college, he walked over Magdalen Bridge, through Headington and up Shotover Hill. Unused to this resolute behaviour but enjoying a natural position of superiority and eminence, the master himself broke the silence at last. It was a laconic and patronising inquiry.

'They tell me, Holmes,' he said, 'they tell me that you are very clever. Are you?'

'Yes,' said Holmes ungraciously.

Silence returned, unbroken, as they walked grimly back into Oxford and at last reached the college gates. Holmes turned to face the offended master with a slight bow, expressionless otherwise.

'Goodbye, sir,' he said courteously. 'I have so much enjoyed our talk.'

Mycroft Holmes assured me that his younger brother thereupon shook the illustrious dust of that college off his feet and found a humbler institution, where he was left to live pretty much as he chose. Sherlock Holmes himself had told me that Victor Trevor, son of a Norfolk squire, was the only friend he made during the two years he remained at college. Holmes was never a very sociable man. By his own account, he was always rather fond of moping in his rooms and working out his own methods of thought. His line of study was quite distinct from that of the other fellows, so that they had no points of contact at all.

In the long vacation he would go up to his London rooms, where he would spend the summer weeks working out a few experiments in organic chemistry. At first he had rooms in Montagu Street, just round the corner from the British Museum. Then, as he spent more time in the chemical laboratories of the great hospitals, he crossed the river and found lodgings in Lambeth Palace Road.

II

Those who have followed the published adventures of Sherlock Holmes in the past thirty years will know something of these matters. Let me now explain how this further collection of narratives has been compiled.

From time to time, during the years when I shared rooms with him, he would lug from his bedroom the famous tin box which was half filled with bundles of papers tied separately with ribbon, each bundle representing a case now closed. Some of these which occurred before our meeting, like the case of the Gloria Scott or the Musgrave Ritual, have already been published from the documents and my friend's own recollection of them. Others were not so readily given to the world.

They included services to the state, matters of personal confidence, and investigations upon which Sherlock Holmes had been engaged before our meeting in the chemical laboratory of Bart's in 1880. In almost every instance, a delay was necessary before the facts of the case could be published. I may safely say that by the time you read these pages, Sherlock Holmes and I, as well as every other person mentioned in them, will have been dust for a good many years.

I have written often in the past of my friend's success as a 'consulting detective' to private individuals. Once or twice, in writing of the Naval Treaty or the Bruce-Partington Plans, I have hinted at something more. The reputation of Sherlock Holmes was such that his services were increasingly in demand by officers of the state. The Fenian dynamite outrages, the blowing up of post offices and the Metropolitan Railway in the 1880s, led to the setting up of the Special Branch at Scotland Yard. The safety of the Crown and its representatives was no longer a matter which could be left to an amateur police force and the good sense of all the people. Later still, as the threat of war with the German Empire approached in 1914, the Crown and government gave authority to the organisation of Military Intelligence. From Queen Anne's Gate, almost in the shadow of Parliament itself, such operations were undertaken by various divisions of this service. Two of its branches were of paramount importance. The fifth division of Military Intelligence was to supervise security at home against intrusion by our enemies, and a sixth division was to control our espionage against foreign powers.

It would have been astonishing if the skills of Sherlock Holmes, though he was well in his middle years, had not been employed by those at Scotland Yard and in the government who were already indebted to him for his assistance in other matters. The question is whether the history of these operations is to remain, for ever and literally, a closed book. That secrets of this kind should be revealed immediately after the events is unthinkable. There are men and women alive now whose reputations and safety would be compromised. The security of the realm itself might be undermined. In the present decade, it is by no means likely that even the great war with Germany will prove to be the last conflict of its kind. Enemies to our way of life may easily be identified in other quarters. A lifetime must pass before such narratives as mine can be made public.

I confess I find it a relief that the decision of publication or suppression is not mine alone. After the death of Sherlock Holmes, the question of his unpublished papers was immediately raised by Sir Ernie Backwell, Permanent Secretary at the Home Office. Sir Ernie would, I believe, have been happy to make a bonfire of them. Such a measure was out of the question. Moreover, the papers were not all in the Permanent Secretary's hands, so that he was obliged to barter a little. After long discussion with Mycroft Holmes and the legal representatives of the estate, a compromise was reached.

The private papers of Sherlock Holmes were to be deposited with the MEPO files of Scotland Yard in the Public Record Office at Chancery Lane. Files in this category remain sealed for fifty or a hundred years or even for ever, at the discretion of the government. Their very existence may be denied. However, before they passed into limbo, I as his literary executor was to have access to them in a special annexe of the Home Office library, overlooking Whitehall. Drawing upon these papers, I was to compile a narrative of the events described in them, taking much the form of the earlier adventures. The narrative was to be read and approved by Sir Ernie Backwell with his legal advisers.

It was not, of course, to be approved for immediate publication. When the manuscript was complete, it was to be deposited in the public records of domestic state papers. I asked that it should be released after fifty years. Sir Ernie assured me that His Majesty's ministers would not settle for less than a hundred. So it would have been had not Mycroft Holmes and the Attorney-General both been members of the committee of the Diogenes Club. After further argument, a period of seventy years was agreed. This would amply cover the probable remaining lifetime of any person mentioned in the narratives. It would remove any risk of exposing secret matters to a possible enemy of the state. Of what possible use can the confidences of a previous century be to present adversaries?

By this means stories are preserved of the fateful visit of King Edward VII to Dublin in 1907 and the truth attending the disappearance of the Crown Jewels from Dublin Castle; of the mysterious death of Herr Diesel in 1913 as the secrets of his famous engine were about to pass into British hands.

Other confidential matters may now be revealed which, though they do not threaten the safety of the state, could not have been made public at the time of the events without a great breach of private trust. Even in the volumes already published a certain latitude has been taken with names. If you have read the adventure of Holmes and the blackmailer 'Charles Augustus Milverton', for example, you will recall my caveat that the story could not have been told in any form without disguising the events and persons to an extent which gave the narrative more fiction than fact.

It can do no harm now to reveal the fictional character of Milverton as in reality that of the blackmailer and thief Charles Augustus Howell, born in Lisbon of Anglo-Portuguese parentage in 1839. He was secretary to Mr John Ruskin and agent to Mr Dante Gabriel Rossetti, the artist. You may read, in Mr Thomas Wise's *Swinburne Bibliography*, as you might have heard it from Mr Oscar Wilde, the manner of Howell's death in 1890, his throat cut outside a public house, a half-sovereign wedged in his teeth, the slanderer's reward.

Mr Howell's customary method of extortion was to obtain indiscreet or confidential letters from his dupes, paste them into a large album and pledge this volume to a pawnbroker on a plea of poverty. The dupes would be informed that the compromising letters had been pledged, that Mr Howell had not the money to redeem them, and that they must be publicly sold unless their authors would buy them back. Victims and their families hastened to retrieve these items only to be met with bills for many hundreds of pounds, divided afterwards between Mr Howell and the confederate pawnbroker.

It was so neatly done that, though the act was blackmail in fact, it was hard to establish the crime within the law, even had the victims been prepared to endure the threat of disgrace. The Rossetti family, Mr Swinburne the poet, and Mr Whistler the painter were among those ensnared by Howell's craft. To this catalogue might be added Mr Ruskin and the Reverend Charles Dodgson of Christ Church, known as 'Lewis Carroll' the world over. Such investigations carried out by Sherlock Holmes were sensitive in the extreme. They could be related only in a most indirect manner at the time.

State secrets and private confidences were not quite all that awaited me when I listed my late friend's papers as his literary executor. If you have read my account of our first meeting, you will recall that Holmes had been what he called 'a consulting detective' for some while. As he said, his services had already been of assistance to Inspector Lestrade of Scotland Yard when that officer had 'got himself into a fog over a forgery case'. The reference was to the so-called Bank of England forgeries in 1873, when the Bidwell brothers came within a hair's breadth of having the Bank's funds at their mercy.

Among the papers left by Sherlock Holmes were several of his 'reports' upon these investigations which preceded our first meeting. Yet a story-teller's narrative is far preferable to a mere report and I make no apology for attempting to interpret the nuances of the original. If I speak of Holmes as a student of analytical chemistry or human conduct, it is merely that he was a student of such things all his life. When I first met him, he was certainly far past the age at which a man normally walks the wards or reads for the bar.

At the time of the 'Smethurst Case', with which I shall deal first, he had his rooms—'consulting rooms', as he grandly called them—in Lambeth Palace Road, just south of Westminster Bridge. These lodgings were convenient for the chemical laboratory of St Thomas's Hospital, to which he had occasional access on the basis of grace-and-favour. I have written elsewhere that his origins lay among the English squirearchy. The indulgence shown him by the governors of the hospital stemmed from a bequest made by one of these kinsmen.

Those who know London at all well may recognise the handsome terraces and tree-lined vistas of Lambeth Palace Road as a favourite abode of our young medical men and students. Here it was that Holmes returned each evening from his methodical labours among test-tubes and Bunsen burners. All day he gathered information and much of the night he passed in restless calculation. How often did the night traveller or the policeman on his beat glance up and see the familiar silhouette against the drawn blind of the first-floor room? It was the shadow of a man pacing rapidly to and fro, his hands clasped behind his back, his sharp profile bowed by a weight of thought.

On other evenings he would venture out to eat his supper and then walk the streets of the great city until he seemed to know the landscape of London as accurately as the mirrored image of his own face. The young Sherlock Holmes was a lone observer as the hum of day ceased, the shops darkened, and the gin palaces thrust out their ragged and squalid crowds to pace the streets. The homeless and the destitute grew familiar with his passing as they huddled in the niches of the bridges and the litter of the markets. The wretched women shivering in their finery, waiting to catch the drunkard who went shouting homewards, watched him from a distance.

Sometimes this young student of humanity would stop to speak to a shoeless child crouching on a doorstep. Then his strange apprenticeship led him to join the conversations of a ragged crowd smoking or dozing through the night beside the glow of a coke fire, where the stones had been taken up and the gas streamed from a pipe in the centre of the street in a flag of flame. On summer nights, as he turned for home, the streets were already growing blue with the coming day. Church spires and chimney pots stood out against the sky with a sharpness seen only before a million fires cast their pall of smoke across the city. The early workers were gathered at the street corners, round the breakfast stall, blowing on their saucers

18

of steaming coffee drawn from tall tin cans with the fire crimson beneath. As he crossed the river by London Bridge, the first ragged girl with her basket slung before her screamed watercresses through the sleeping streets.

Such was the practical education of Sherlock Holmes. Small wonder that in later years he could assume the appearance or speech of common men, so that even his friends did not penetrate the disguise. On other nights he would turn to his books, threading some obscure avenue of research whose result would bring success to an investigation in a manner that astonished all who heard of it.

No man had so curious a library as Sherlock Holmes. You might look in vain for volumes that were in half the families of England. But if you sought industries peculiar to a small town in Bohemia, or unique chemical constituents of Sumatran or Virginian tobacco leaf, or the alienist's account of morbid individual psychology, or the methods by which a Ming is to be distinguished from a skilful imitation, he had only to reach out his hand for the answer. In far more cases, however, that answer was carried in his head.

On a shelf of the break-front bookcase, between works on the manufacture of paper and a set of the Newgate Calendar, I noticed that a number of volumes and two finely bound essays lay on their sides. They had been disregarded and gathering dust for some years. Their contents had been abstracted and stored in that precise and ordered mind. The slimmest volume was by Dr David Hutchinson and it had won the Fiske Fund Prize of the Rhode Island Medical Society in 1857: 'What are the Causes of that Disease incident to Pregnancy, characterised by Inflammation of the Mouth and Fauces, accompanied by Anorexia and Emaciation?' Next to it were works of a similar kind by Abercrombie and by Professor Stoltz of Vienna, as well as fifty-eight accounts of related fatalities in Cartaya's 'Vomissements incoercibles pendant la grossesse'.

In these volumes lay the clue to what Holmes called his first investigation, whose outcome meant life or death for its subject. By his pursuit of that inquiry, he brought his skill in scientific analysis to the notice of Scotland Yard. You may read a fuller account of Dr Smethurst's ordeal in the Notable British Trials volumes and in the newspapers of the day. Holmes, however, shunned the limelight. He preferred to remain 'behind the scenes', for fear of embarrassing his patrons or revealing too much of himself.

His report, as I read it, had been drawn up for Mr Hardinge Giffard, whom history now knows as the great Lord Chancellor Halsbury. If that investigation of Dr Smethurst's crime did not bring public fame to Sherlock Holmes, it surely placed his skills before the nation's rulers. To that first case I now turn.

The Ghost in the Machine

I

As Holmes described the scene to me, it was a blazing Sunday afternoon at the end of May, a high sun beating hard on the still and empty length of Lambeth Palace Road. He readily confessed that business had been poor. After lunch on Saturday, he had shut himself in his room and set himself to work there until Monday morning, when he might have access to the laboratory again. The idleness of 'Sunday observance' always made his active mind fretful and the time of which I write was one when a rigorous Sabbath was much in fashion. Among such pieties in the homes of Westminster, Holmes was pursuing the subtleties of murder by poisonous perfumes at the court of Louis XIV.

He was just then absorbed in the fate of the young Madame de Brinvilliers, who had not been permitted execution until she had first undergone the ordeal of the water-torture. Such vindictive aberrations of the human mind were irresistible to him. Yet he was not, as the phrase has it, lost to the world. Standing at his oak reading-desk, turning the crisp pages of a seventeenth-century folio volume, Holmes nonetheless heard the wheels of a solitary hansom cab in the quiet sunlit street outside. Without ceasing to read of Madame de Brinvilliers, he heard the same wheels stop beneath his window.

There came the jangle of the bell and the voice of his landlady, Mrs Harris, in conversation with a female visitor. There were words of surprised recognition.

A door opened and closed on the lower floor. Ten minutes later it opened again and footsteps sounded on the stairs. There was a knock at Holmes's sitting-room door and Mrs Harris entered in response to his summons.

The good lady was flushed with apology at disturbing her lodger on a Sunday afternoon. Only the assurance that this was a matter of life and death, that it concerned her oldest and dearest friend, that speed was of the essence, could be offered in excuse. Her friend, Miss Louisa Bankes, would see Mr Holmes—and would see no one else.

Holmes listened, laid a silk marker in his folio volume, and closed the cover.

'Dear me,' he said gently. 'At all events one can't refuse a lady, and such a positive one at that. If she will take me as she finds me, I am at her service.'

'She had heard of you from your notice in the column of the paper and, seeing your address was here, must have your opinion,' Mrs Harris assured him.

'And no doubt she has heard a little from you, Mrs Harris,' Holmes said kindly. 'Well, we must not keep her waiting. Will you not show your friend up?'

It had seemed to him better that their interview should take place in his sitting-room, where he might more easily discuss the troubles of Miss Louisa Bankes without inviting Mrs Harris's presence.

The landlady returned a moment later in company with a slight but pretty woman, auburn-haired and about thirty-five years old. Her high-boned face was animated by the glance of quick grey eyes, though she looked at that moment flustered rather than animated.

'Thank you, Mrs Harris,' Holmes said courteously, in just such a manner as gave the landlady no alternative but to withdraw. He looked again at Miss Bankes and thought that she was possessed of the prettiest face he had seen under a bonnet for many a month.

'Mr Holmes?' she said before he could offer her a seat, 'I beg you to excuse my arrival in this fashion. I have read your notice in *The Times* on several occasions and had half persuaded myself to communicate with you some weeks ago. Now I fear it may be too late. It would have been more proper, I know, to write to you. But a letter could not reach you until Tuesday and the matter cannot wait. I knew I could reach you by way of Waterloo or the White Horse Cellar every half-hour and that I must do so at once.'

'By all means,' Holmes said gently. 'Pray sit down, Miss Bankes. Try the sofa, and tell me what it is that cannot wait until Tuesday. Pray, take your time.'

Louisa Bankes swept across the room. The sofa was the only article of furniture that would comfortably accommodate such full, cream skirts, a tribute to the crinoline still somewhat in fashion. The day was warm and yet she shivered as she drew about her the rose mantle edged in crimson. She faced Holmes, as if undecided how to begin, sitting with her back to the window.

'Mr Holmes,' she said at last, 'you will think me melodramatic, I know. You may even think me hysterical. I have come here because I must have your help on behalf of my sister. I believe she is being murdered.'

She paused and Holmes looked at her keenly but not unkindly. He crossed to the window and stared down at the hansom cab, which still waited outside. For a moment he said nothing. Then he turned to her.

'I take it,' he said gently, 'that your sister is living with her husband at Richmond or thereabouts. You believe that for some time he has been poisoning her. She is, I assume, married to a doctor.'

Louisa Bankes looked up at him with something like fear in her eyes.

'Then you know!' she cried.

'I do not know, Miss Bankes. I deduce certain possibilities from what you have just told me.'

'But I have told you nothing!' she protested.

Holmes settled himself in the chair on the opposite side of the fireplace.

'On the contrary,' he said, 'you informed me that you might have come at any half-hour to Waterloo or the White Horse Cellar in Piccadilly. The Richmond bus comes at the half-hour to the White Horse and the Richmond train every half-hour to Waterloo. Their routes do not cross elsewhere, except Richmond. Your demeanour suggests that you have come directly from a scene of great distress. You do not tell me that your sister has been murdered or is *going* to be murdered. You say that she *is* being murdered. A murder which is part accomplished surely suggests poison. When a woman is being poisoned and even her own sister is unable to prevent it, the guilty hand is very close to her indeed and is in all probability her husband's. It is true, of course, I cannot swear that your sister's husband is a doctor, but that is far the most common profession in such cases.'

The poor young woman bit her lip and then looked up.

'You are right, though, Mr Holmes. He is a doctor.'

'You had best tell me the circumstances,' Holmes said quietly.

Louisa Bankes kept her eyes steadfastly upon him, as if to convince him of her sincerity and, indeed, her sanity.

'My sister Isabella is a little older than I, Mr Holmes, but was also unmarried until December. Up to September, we had lived together in Notting Hill. The house was mine. Then she suggested that it would be better for us to live apart. There was no quarrel between us. I made no objection, though I feared there might be an association of which she was ashamed and wished to keep from her family. From September until November she lived at a boarding-house in Rifle Terrace, Bayswater. Among the other guests was a medical man of about fifty, Dr Smethurst. I cannot tell you whether his presence was the reason for her moving there. After some weeks, the familiarity between them grew so scandalous that the landlady, Mrs Smith, asked my sister to find other accommodation. Bella moved to Kildare Terrace, nearby. On the twelfth of December, she married Dr Smethurst at Battersea Church and they set up home at Alma Villas, Richmond, in furnished rooms. Bella became ill soon afterwards, first with biliousness and then with dysentery. It is his doing, Mr Holmes.'

As she paused, Holmes asked, 'May I ask, Miss Bankes, whether your sister is a wealthy woman?'

'Not wealthy, Mr Holmes, but she has a comfortable income on capital of eighteen hundred pounds. It is the interest on a mortgage.'

'I see,' Holmes said. 'Pray continue. What of your sister's health in the past?'

Louisa Bankes shivered once more and then composed herself.

'My sister had been in good health before her marriage, except that she sometimes suffered from bilious attacks. They were not frequent and never severe. I had no suspicions of Dr Smethurst until last month. Then, on the eighteenth of April, I received a letter from him telling me that Bella was really very ill and that she had asked for me to come to her. See here.'

She opened her bag and drew out a folded sheet of notepaper. She handed it to Holmes. He glanced at it, repeating aloud the phrases which caught his attention.

' "You will greatly oblige by coming alone . . . breathe not a word of this note to anyone . . ." Curious instructions, Miss Bankes. Did you visit your sister?'

The woman gave a half-sob at the recollection.

'I did, Mr Holmes, on the very same day. She was lying in bed, looking so pale and weak, scarcely able to move. She saw that I was alarmed at the sight of her and she said to me, "Oh, don't say anything about it to anyone. It will be all right when I get better." '

Holmes frowned. 'A very singular caution, Miss Bankes. And have you seen her since?'

Louisa Bankes shook her head and drew several more folded sheets of notepaper from her bag.

'Everything I received afterwards was written by Thomas Smethurst,' she continued. 'In the next letter, on the following day, he tells me that Bella passed a very bad night. The excitement of seeing me had brought back the vomiting and purging. A doctor had been called and had forbidden any further visits. A few more days passed and then he wrote again, saying that I might see her in a week's time. But, when that week had passed, he sent me these.'

She handed the other letters to Holmes, who once again read out the ominous phrases.

' "Dearest Bella begs of you to wait a little longer before calling upon her . . ."; "I much regret the state of the case will not yet admit of your seeing her . . ." '

Louisa Bankes broke in upon the reading.

'How can it not admit of my seeing her, Mr Holmes? Until last autumn, when this wretch stole his way into her affections, we had lived together. Sickness or health was all one in our sisterhood. Today he writes again and warns me that I had best take lodgings close to them but must not come to the house. What does it mean, except that she is to die and I am not to see her until the end?'

Holmes studied this last letter, a look of concern in his sharp eyes. Then he handed back the pages.

'You have reason for suspicion, Miss Bankes. However—'

' "However", Mr Holmes? Before you say "however", let me add this. I myself have done everything to see my sister, without avail. Then I begged him at least to let our family physician, Dr Lane, examine her. He refused to have Dr Lane in the house. In desperation, two days ago, I lay in wait and spoke to Susannah Wheatley, the daughter of the landlady at Alma Villas. I asked her how Bella was. She told me that she feared for my sister and that Bella had signed a will drawn up by Dr Smethurst. Miss Wheatley had witnessed it. Surely, Mr Holmes, he has imprisoned her there to take her life as a means of possessing himself of her money.'

Holmes said nothing for a moment, then he looked up at his visitor.

'During an illness of such length and gravity, your sister has been seen by other medical men?'

Louisa Bankes looked back at him wide-eyed in her despair, 'Dr Julius and his partner Dr Bird have both seen her. But Thomas Smethurst is a doctor too. Do you not think he could make poison appear as some disease? Dr Bird and Dr Julius are both led to believe that she has dysentery.'

Holmes said nothing for a moment, then the keen eyes settled upon her again.

'Answer me one question, if you please, Miss Bankes. If all is as you say, why have you come to me?'

'Where else should I go?' she cried.

For the first time there was scepticism in his eyes as he studied her. Yet he was still gentle with her.

'Come, now,' he said. 'You would surely have done better to take your story directly to Scotland Yard. The Metropolitan Police can do more for you than I may. They have powers of investigation far beyond mine. You may walk there in fifteen minutes from here. I will give you the name of the very man whom you must see. Ah, there is something more, is there not? What is it that you cannot tell them?'

For a moment the young woman looked at her hands and said nothing. Then she breathed deeply and spoke. It was, Holmes later told me, as if she had expected to have the secret forced from her but knew not how to yield it.

'Mr Holmes, when my sister met Dr Smethurst, he was already a married man.'

'Do you mean that he deceived her by committing bigamy?'

Louisa Bankes shook her head.

'No, Mr Holmes. He did not deceive her. When Bella lived at Rifle Terrace last autumn, Dr Smethurst and his wife were guests in the same boarding-house. They have been married many years, and Mrs Smethurst is quite twenty years older than her husband. She is now a woman of seventy and more. My sister knew all this, knew that he was already married.'

Holmes's keen eyes narrowed a little and he now stared at his visitor with fascination.

'What possessed your sister to abet a wilful act of bigamy? It was almost certain to have been discovered before long.'

Louisa Bankes lowered her head until the frame of her bonnet almost concealed her face. Her words were now punctuated by sobs.

'He told her it was to be their secret marriage and that there could be no harm in that . . . When old Mrs Smethurst died they would be man and wife in fact and law. Until then, if he and Bella should live together, a married name would protect her reputation. She believed him, Mr Holmes, and now she pays the price. You ask me to go to the police? The law would condemn the scoundrel who has ruined her but it would condemn my sister as well. If I could save her life in no other way, I would do it. You, Mr Holmes, are my hope that there is some other way.'

It was not a matter to which Holmes gave long thought. He stood up, as if to indicate that his mind was made up and the consultation at an end.

'Very well, Miss Bankes. You may rely upon me to do everything I can. I must tell you that I can do little for your sister's reputation. However, if all is as you say it is, I will go down to Richmond at the first opportunity and call upon Dr Smethurst. I, at least, have no reason to spare your sister's feelings or his and he will know it. I shall give him the choice of leaving your sister at once and never seeing her again, or of being exposed as a bigamist. The law may or may not proceed against your sister; I think it may not. It is Dr Smethurst who is twice married. Against him, the courts are empowered to pronounce a sentence of fourteen years in a convict settlement. If what you tell me is correct, we may yet have him on the hip.'

II

Despite the urgency of Miss Bankes, Holmes did not go down to Richmond until he had satisfied himself of certain facts. On Monday, he walked as far as Battersea Church and there paid the clerk a shilling to read an entry in the parish register for the previous year. It recorded the marriage of Thomas Smethurst and Isabella

Bankes on 12 December. Next morning, after a visit to Rifle Terrace, Bayswater, he summoned a cab for St Mark's Church, Kennington. Another shilling won him access to the parish register for twenty years earlier, from which he copied the record of a marriage between Thomas Smethurst and Mary Durham, now an elderly lady whom Holmes had seen an hour or two before at Rifle Terrace.

With copies of these two entries in his note-case, he took the half-hourly bus to Richmond from the White Horse Cellar, Piccadilly.

Dr Smethurst and Miss Isabella Bankes had set up their home in Mrs Wheatley's rooms at 10, Alma Villas, Richmond. Holmes had gathered from his visitor that theirs was a modest apartment of bedroom and sitting-room, in the latter of which the meals were served by the daughter of the family.

In answer to his knock, the door was opened by an aproned maid-of-all-work. Holmes handed her his card.

'Dr Thomas Smethurst, if you please,' he said. 'It is a matter of the greatest urgency.'

Holmes was taken aback to see that, when Dr Smethurst's name was mentioned, a look of consternation bordering on terror convulsed the girl's face.

'You can't see Dr Smethurst,' she blurted out presently, ''E've gone.'

'Gone?' said Holmes, 'And what of Mrs Smethurst?'

'You can't see her,' the girl said hastily. 'She's better since he went but the poor soul's still very weakly.'

'And who is looking after her?'

'I am,' the girl said proudly. 'And Mrs Wheatley and Miss Wheatley, of course, and Miss Bankes—that's Mrs Smethurst's sister. And Dr Julius and Dr Bird both been and left.'

From the shadows of the hall behind the girl, a man's voice called, 'Mr Holmes!'

The man appeared, a well-built ginger-headed policeman with a broad-boned face and a clipped moustache. Robert M'Intyre, Inspector of the Richmond Constabulary, was just then in his 'private clothes' of frock-coat and sponge-bag trousers, a pearl-grey stock at his throat. Holmes recognised him from an earlier confidential inquiry, a matter of domestic robbery.

'M'Intyre?'

The inspector waved the girl away.

'What brings you down to Richmond, Mr Holmes?'

'Miss Louisa Bankes is my client. Where is Dr Smethurst?'

M'Intyre cleared his throat discreetly and stepped out into the May sunlight.

'We may talk outside, if it's all the same to you, Mr Holmes. It's not convenient indoors with only two rooms and the poor lady in the state she is. Just down here a little way, if you wouldn't mind.'

The two men walked a short distance along the pavement of Alma Villas.

'Where is Smethurst?' Holmes demanded.

'In a police cell, Mr Holmes, where he ought to have been weeks ago. He stands charged with the attempted murder of his wife. I think Dr Bird half suspected it last week. Yesterday they took samples of what she brought up in her sickness. They sent them to be analysed by Professor Taylor. He found arsenic, Mr Holmes. No two ways about that. Arsenic enough to kill her, if that sample was repeated throughout the vital organs. Dr Smethurst was arrested last night to appear at the police court this morning. Since he's been out of the way, I hear she's improved a bit.'

Holmes stood tall and gaunt in the sunlight for a moment.

'Indeed?' he said thoughtfully.

M'Intyre turned back towards the house.

'You know your own business best, Mr Holmes, but if your interest in this case is what I think it must be, you'd be wasting your time down here. We've got him, sir, and the lady is in the hands of doctors who will do all that can be done for her. And that's all about that.'

III

If ever Sherlock Holmes had reason to feel that a case had escaped him, it was during the hours which followed his return to Lambeth

Palace Road. Thomas Smethurst had been removed from his investigation, or so it seemed. Mrs Smethurst—Isabella Bankes, as she was in truth—would recover or not, as the strength of her constitution and the skill of her physicians decreed. Whether the crime of bigamy would come to light, and whether Isabella Bankes would face prosecution as well as disgrace, were matters for others.

The best cure for his disappointments in life was always to be found in work. Holmes returned to the curious affair of the poisonous perfumes at the Court of the Sun King. He proposed a monograph upon this macabre subject. History records that the monograph was never written. He was meditating its contents on Thursday evening, two days later, as he walked back from the chemical laboratory of St Thomas's Hospital. Letting himself in at the front door, he sensed a chill silence about the house in Lambeth Palace Road. Having gone up the stairs, he had scarcely closed the door of his sitting-room and removed his coat and gloves when there was a knock. It was Mrs Harris. Her face was pale and, though the tears were now dry, their recent passage showed in her reddened eyes and haggard cheeks.

'She's dead, Mr Holmes,' the landlady said abruptly, 'Mrs Smethurst—Miss Bankes, that was. Passed away this morning. I heard from her poor sister just now.'

'Then Dr Smethurst must stand trial for murder,' Holmes said softly.

'They let him go back to her before she died, Mr Holmes.'

'Let him go?' The tall sharp-profiled figure advanced a step towards Mrs Harris, as though he might seize her and hold her accountable for such judicial stupidity. 'Let him go?'

'At the police court, Mr Holmes. Dr Smethurst swore his wife was so poorly she might die that very day. He vowed it was inhuman to keep him from her in what might be her last hours. They bailed him to go back to her. She was better after he'd been taken away. They all said so. The doctors, Miss Louisa . . . And the day after they let him back, the poor soul was dead. They caught him again—but too late for her.'

Seldom, perhaps on no other occasion, had Sherlock Holmes been at a loss for words. That a man accused of attempting to murder his wife should be released to go back to her was beyond belief. Yet it had happened.

'So now he faces the gallows in earnest,' he murmured.

'And no worse than he deserves, the devil!' said Mrs Harris bitterly.

The letter that Holmes was now obliged to write to Miss Louisa Bankes was, he always maintained, the most difficult of his life. He had failed her and would accept no fee, of course. She had come to him very late. To prevent the tragedy which occurred had been well-nigh impossible. But it was his profession to triumph over impossibilities—or rather it was his temperament. 'Failure' was the word that now sat heavily in his thoughts during the warm summer, like a raven on his shoulder. He did not, as in the tedium of inactivity, resort to cocaine. In his gloom, he spent a week or more confined to his rooms, sometimes brooding, sometimes stirring the air with passages of Haydn or Mendelssohn on his beloved violin.

IV

London's summer season with all its frivolities had come and gone by the time that Dr Smethurst stood trial at the Old Bailey for the murder of Isabella Bankes. Sherlock Holmes could give no simple reason for his determination to witness the proceedings. He had, of course, never set eyes on Thomas Smethurst and was fired by a curiosity to see what manner of man this might be. There was, however, a less commendable reason. Holmes was a 'gourmet'—I think the word is not too strong—for the sight of human beings in bizarre and desperate straits. To see the prey struggling in the toils of the law, a law that would surely tighten a noose round the man's neck, was a stimulation of his nerves to rival music or opium.

Better for him, perhaps, had he stayed away. What Holmes found in that courtroom was not at all what he had expected.

Smethurst himself was an unprepossessing man in his early fifties, square-set with ragged brown hair and a moustache. How any woman could have contemplated such a wretch, except with feelings of compassion for his shabbiness, was beyond comprehension.

Those who remember the Central Criminal Court before Newgate was pulled down and the area rebuilt may recall how like a theatre it seemed. The jury sat in an opera-box on one side, the defendants on the other. The stage was occupied by the judge, his chaplain and the sheriffs. Where the orchestra might have been in a theatre were benches for counsel and spectators. Here it was that Holmes, with a keen appetite for such living spectacles, watched hour by hour the destruction of the man in the dock. In those days, a defendant was still not permitted to give evidence in his own case. Smethurst stood at the dock-rail, wild-eyed, and watched his own death meticulously prepared.

Holmes never denied that he had gone there relishing the prospect of sport. Minute by minute the presumption of guilt grew stronger. Smethurst had bigamously married the dead woman. No sooner were they lodged at Alma Villas than her violent sickness began. He had refused the assistance of any other doctor until he could hold out no longer. In his own hand, he wrote out her will, summoned a lawyer, and stood over his victim while she signed it. Of that will he was the sole beneficiary. He then found repeated reasons for preventing her sister coming to see her. It was reported that 'Mrs Smethurst' was seen to look at her husband in terror.

There was a murmur of disgust in the court when Dr Bird described seeing Smethurst place small quantities of prussic acid on scraps of bread, throwing them out for the sparrows, seeing what quantity was enough to kill them and what was not. Dr Bird, who had been summoned by Dr Julius for a second opinion on the ailing woman, concluded after a few days that the patient was not suffering from biliousness nor from dysentery. Her symptoms were not those of any natural disease but of slow irritant poisoning. Three days before her death, samples were taken. Analysis by means of the Reinsch Test showed quantities of arsenic in her body sufficient to kill her.

Worse still, at the post-mortem, Dr Todd discovered the presence of the corrosive poison antimony in the kidneys. True, the quantity was not great but it could not be explained by any medicine that had been prescribed. For good measure, Dr Todd swore that he had never before seen on the face of a corpse such an expression of terror as that in which the features of Isabella Bankes had frozen during her death agony. Her entrails had been in an advanced state of inflammation and ulceration. Death had been brought on by exhaustion from vomiting, and from starvation caused by inability to keep a mouthful of food in her stomach, so long as Dr Smethurst tended her.

By his own admission, Smethurst alone had administered food and medicine to the deceased. When he was first arrested, she had improved in his absence and was even able to retain a little food in her stomach. When he returned, she died. At the post-mortem, it was also discovered that the woman was between five and seven weeks pregnant. He had killed not only his 'wife' but their unborn child.

Holmes watched keenly the examination and cross-examination of the witnesses. Smethurst was defended by Mr Parry, of a famous Welsh legal family. Parry was a well-fleshed man whose wig sat as tight on his head as a soldier's cap. He was eloquent in speech but failed everywhere in his attempts to pierce the armour of evidence against his client. When Dr Todd said that there was no arsenic found in the body at the autopsy, Parry thought he had him. But Dr Todd retorted that there was no arsenic because the organs were heavy with chlorate of potass, given by the murderer deliberately to flush the poison from the body once it had done its work. The unfortunate defence counsel was now left with the charge that Smethurst had not only killed Isabella Bankes, but had done it in the most devilishly cruel and cunning manner. Mr Parry, as Holmes remarked, had sewn up his client tighter still.

The damage inflicted by the witnesses for the Crown was made infinitely worse by those whom Mr Parry called for the defence.

Dr Richardson and Dr Rodger swore that, if Isabella Bankes had died of the poison, arsenic would have been found at the post-mortem. Unfortunately, as the Crown proved at once, Rodger and Richardson gave such evidence as a paid profession and had both testified in similar terms on behalf of Palmer, the notorious 'Rugeley Poisoner'. Dr Richardson, indeed, had once inadvertently poisoned one of his own patients.

The sight of Thomas Smethurst's destruction was more ghastly than any melodrama at the Hoxton Britannia. The Lord Chief Baron informed the jury that the case against Dr Smethurst was circumstantial. They were not to convict him on one piece of it alone. They must add one at a time to the scales of proof and see on which side they came down. Yet, after such a trial, there was no doubt that they must come down on the side of guilt with a crash like the gallows trap falling open under the accused man's feet. The jurors brought him in guilty half an hour later.

Smethurst made a long rambling plea for his life, only to hear the Lord Chief Baron tell him that he would be taken to the roof of Horsemonger Lane Gaol in a week or two, where all the world might see him, and there be hanged by the neck until he was dead. The wild, unkempt figure in the dock, broken by the ordeal of his trial, cried, 'I declare Dr Julius to be my murderer! I am innocent before God!'

Such fierce moments were like the finest brandy to the soul of Sherlock Holmes. All this time, however, he had been watching another man who spoke not a word in the proceedings. Mr Hardinge Giffard was junior counsel for Smethurst, behind his leader Mr Parry. His face was gentle and pale, trimmed by a line of dark whiskers. The future Lord Chancellor Halsbury had yet to make his way at the English bar. Yet Holmes already knew something of him and divined the massive intelligence that would one day fill library shelves with successive volumes of *Halsbury's Laws of England*. As the court rose, Holmes took a card and wrote upon it, 'Your client is plainly innocent. If you will allow me, I believe I can prove it.'

V

It is no disparagement of Mr Hardinge Giffard to say that, for all his forensic skill, he was mystified by the note. Though he was for the defence, he once told me that he thought at first the case against his client was as conclusive as any he had known. Dr Smethurst had seduced Isabella Bankes and bigamously married her. By his own account he had administered all food and medicine to her in her sickness. No other hand than his could have held the arsenic and antimony revealed by the analyst's reports just before the victim's death. Neither substance was present in any medicine prescribed for her. Smethurst had been seen by another physician, experimenting with poison upon the sparrows. He had prevented the woman from being seen by her own sister and by her family doctor. He had obliged her to sign a will, leaving everything to him, a will written in his own hand. When Miss Wheatley came to witness it he pretended to her it was some other legal document to which her name was to be affixed. The attorney, Mr Senior, intervened, telling him it was most improper to let the witness sign the paper thinking it was something else. Everything about Thomas Smethurst stank of fraud, connivance—and murder.

'Your client is plainly innocent. If you will allow me, I believe I can prove it.'

Mr Hardinge Giffard might have dismissed the offer as preposterous. That he did not shows the glimmer of the great Lord Chancellor of our own times in the young and penniless barrister of those days. Next evening, he called upon Sherlock Holmes in his rooms. No appointment had been made and Holmes was at his reading-desk with the gaslight white above him when his visitor was announced.

'Mr Giffard,' he said softly, shaking the young lawyer's hand, 'I had been expecting you.'

He took the visitor's hat and coat, laying them on a table at one end of the sitting-room. Then he gestured him to a chair, beside which on a small table lay a cigar box, a spirit case, and a supply of soda water in a gasoque.

Mr Giffard lowered himself into the chair.

'Mr Holmes, time is very short. The law now holds Dr Smethurst guilty of murder and will proceed to execution at once.'

'Your client's guilt is a proposition which I take the liberty to doubt,' Holmes said smoothly.

'Nevertheless, in a week or two he will die as a felon. You tell me that you believe you can prove his innocence . . .'

'I have not the least doubt that I shall.'

At that moment, Mr Giffard changed tack, as he might have done with a witness under cross-examination.

'Why should you take such interest in his innocence or guilt?'

There was a quick movement of Holmes's face, an impatience which many, who knew him only a little, thought was a smile or humorous quirk.

'I was engaged upon an inquiry into Dr Smethurst's treatment of Isabella Bankes, at the request of her sister. It was too late. The *soi-disante* Mrs Smethurst died before I could properly begin.'

'So I am told.'

Holmes stood up, poured his guest a glass of brandy, preferred the cigar box and left Mr Giffard to judge the gasoque for himself.

'When I began, Mr Giffard, I first established the facts. After all, one does not care to make libellous accusations. I verified the two marriages of Dr Smethurst, one valid and one bigamous. I consulted the copy of the will deposited at Doctors Commons.'

Hardinge Giffard put his glass down.

'Impossible, Mr Holmes. Miss Isabella Bankes's will is not proved yet, let alone registered.'

The same impatience tweaked Holmes's lips.

'Her father's will, Mr Giffard. By that will, Miss Bankes had eighteen hundred pounds, on the interest of which she might live. It was hers to do with as she pleased. She also held a life interest in five thousand pounds, which at her death would pass to other members of her family: a brother and several sisters. The income from it died with her. Curious, is it not, Mr Giffard? A man may be the blackest rascal but will he destroy a woman who is worth four times as much to him alive as she is dead?'

'Perhaps he did not know of her father's will,' Mr Giffard said quietly.

'Perhaps he did not,' Holmes said. 'But if he did not kill her for money, what else? Bigamy? He had only to run off, back to his first wife, if necessary. He had only to avoid marriage to Miss Bankes in the first place by sweet promises. Did he kill her because she was carrying his child? He had only to desert her, as men desert women in such circumstances a thousand times a day. No, Mr Giffard. There is no good nor sufficient reason why Thomas Smethurst should murder Isabella Bankes. No reason whatever why he should run his head into the hangman's noose on that account.'

Holmes paused and a look of dismay darkened his visitor's face.

'And is that all of it, Mr Holmes? If it is, then you will not save him. Supposition will no longer do. There must be irrefutable proof of his innocence.'

Holmes leaned back in his chair, his long legs stretched out, and touched the tips of his fingers together.

'Suppose, Mr Giffard, suppose there was no arsenic in her body, at any time.'

As Holmes relaxed, Hardinge Giffard sat upright.

'There *was* arsenic, Mr Holmes. Professor Taylor found arsenic. Dr Todd tested the substance and confirmed that it was arsenic. Mr Barwell tested it and agreed that it was arsenic. What good will it do to pretend that it was not?'

Holmes shrugged. 'Very well,' he said, as if resigning himself to defeat. 'Let us agree that it was arsenic. I never doubted it for a moment.'

There was a pause while Mr Hardinge Giffard sought words to extricate himself with the least possible discourtesy and find his way to the street outside.

'What more have you discovered, Mr Holmes?'

'Beyond the obvious fact that your client is innocent, very little,' Holmes remarked. 'I can prove it but not without your assistance.'

'What would you have me do?'

'The samples that were taken from Miss Bankes before her death, those in which arsenic was found—I take it that the untested portion of the specimens is still available?'

'No doubt it is.'

'I should like it brought to the chemical laboratory of St Thomas's Hospital. It will be made up into solution, under supervision. I will show you your client's innocence in the presence of anyone who cares to be there. Professor Taylor, if you wish, Dr Todd, the Lord Chief Baron himself.'

'When is this to be?'

'Dear me,' said Holmes. 'On any day before your client is hanged, I suppose.'

VI

Three days later, on an afternoon in late August, a distinguished company had assembled in the Chemical Laboratory of St Thomas's Hospital. Holmes was on familiar territory and was master of the scene. So many of his days had been spent in this lofty riverside room, lined and littered with countless bottles and apparatus. Though he was a hunter all his life, most of his quests so far had been among these broad low tables with their retorts, test-tubes and the blue flames of the little Bunsen lamps.

Like a host greeting his guests, he led the visitors to a table on which apparatus had been set up for the Reinsch Test. A quantity of solution from a sealed bottle, in which the specimens taken from Isabella Bankes had been dissolved, was poured into a glass vessel. The liquid was pale blue in colour.

'Gentlemen,' said Holmes, introducing the apparatus to his onlookers like a stage magician at the Egyptian Hall, 'the Reinsch Test is simplicity itself. Our solution of the specimen is boiled in a vessel which contains copper gauze. If arsenic is present in any quantity, it will collect as a grey substance upon the gauze. If it appears, simple treatment with nitric acid will confirm that it is, indeed, arsenic. That, Dr Taylor, is a fair summary I believe.'

'It is, Mr Holmes,' the professor said. 'In this case, however, you have also considerable quantities of chlorate of potass. This will tend to damage the copper gauze. However, after two or three pieces of copper gauze have been used, the chlorate of potass will have been exhausted. Then you will see whether you have arsenic or not.'

The light blue liquid was heated three times in all, a separate piece of copper gauze being used on each occasion. The first two pieces of copper gauze were corroded by the chlorate and no sign of a dark-grey substance appeared on them. A third time, Holmes took a new piece of gauze and applied the flame of the lamp. In the quiet room above the Thames it was hard to imagine that whether a man was to be strangled by a rope noose in a few days' time depended upon the outcome of such an academic test.

For a few minutes, the pale blue liquid shimmered and then boiled. Holmes drew the flame away. The bubbling ceased and the copper gauze was clearly seen again. It was almost completely coated with a dark-grey sludge. The sense of doom, for Thomas Smethurst, hung heavy in the air. It was Dr Taylor who broke the silence. He spoke courteously but emphatically.

'When you test that substance with nitric acid, Mr Holmes, you will find that it is arsenic. Enough arsenic to kill the poor woman twice over. There can be no doubt.'

'No doubt at all,' Holmes agreed.

'Then there is an end of the matter,' Mr Hardinge Giffard said, astonished at the speed of Holmes's apparent failure. 'There is no more to be done.'

It was an awkward moment, some of those present feeling sorry for Sherlock Holmes in his disappointment, others resentful at having their time wasted by a trick that failed. They seemed about to turn and leave without another word.

'One moment, if you please!' said Holmes and they turned back to him again. He addressed Dr Taylor. 'Did you attempt to establish the presence of arsenic by the Marsh Test?'

Dr Taylor frowned. 'Mr Holmes, there is arsenic on the copper gauze. You may see it for yourself. You acknowledge it is there in quantity enough to commit murder. What need is there of the Marsh Test or any other experiment?'

'There is the greatest of all needs, Dr Taylor. The need of a man who will in a few days be hanged for a murder he did not commit, for a murder that was never committed by anyone.'

Dr Taylor could not quite bring himself to leave. 'Next you will tell us that she died of natural causes,' he said irritably.

'Oh, I think it very likely that I shall, doctor,' Holmes said imperturbably. 'Indeed, I may tell you that now.'

'And that she never consumed arsenic?'

Holmes gave a quick, impatient smile. 'I should wager that Isabella Bankes never consumed arsenic in her life.'

There was a murmur of laughter at the absurdity of his claim. I would have given a good deal to have been in that chemical laboratory during the next few minutes. Holmes had set up the apparatus for the Marsh Test on the next bench in the laboratory. Like the Reinsch process, the Marsh Test is essentially simple. Arsenic is the easiest poison to detect in a body because it vaporises readily. A white fragment may be dried and tested simply by a detective officer. Placed in a sealed tube and heated, it will vaporise and then condense on the inner surface of the tube. In nine times out of ten, when this occurs with a suspect specimen, it will prove to be arsenic.

In the Marsh Test, which Holmes now conducted, the pale blue solution taken from the dead woman's specimens was diluted with a chemical base in a retort and heated until hydrogen was given off. The gas passed into a sealed tube that was warmed—a 'mirror', as it was called. If arsenic was present in the gas, it would collect as a greyish substance on the inner surface of the tube. When all the hydrogen was given off, Holmes turned down the flame of the Bunsen lamp. The 'mirror' tube was still perfectly clean. The same solution which had just before shown enough arsenic to kill Isabella Bankes twice over now showed none at all.

Imagine the consternation at this! Among those who watched Sherlock Holmes at work with his apparatus, there was relief and expectation among the defenders of Thomas Smethurst, dismay among those whose evidence had helped to cast upon him the shadow of the hangman's noose.

How could it be that one time-honoured and infallible test showed no arsenic and the other, equally honoured and infallible, enough poison to hang a man? You may be sure that Dr Taylor and his colleagues hastened to repeat these experiments, only to come to the same conclusion as Holmes. Yet one thing could not be denied. There was arsenic in the Reinsch Test, enough to bring Smethurst to the gallows.

Rumours spread of the strange discovery and, as the world knows, there was agitation for a reprieve. The Home Secretary of the Liberal government, Sir George Cornewall Lewis, found himself caught between the process of law and an opposing clamour of the scientific world. Physicians, lawyers, public men all protested against the hanging of Thomas Smethurst on such evidence as this. There was a petition to the Home Office and another to Her Majesty the Queen for a free pardon. Sir George, caught in this fix, summoned the one man in England who could explain the predicament in which he found himself, Mr Sherlock Holmes.

VII

It was the first time that my friend had ever visited the Home Office but it was by no means the last. The day appointed for the execution of Thomas Smethurst was little more than a weekend away. Indeed, it was very nearly too late to save him. Men were customarily hanged in public on a Monday morning but just then a new law of Sabbath-day observance was being debated. It was objected that the men who erected the gallows on the roof of Horsemonger Lane gaol would have to work on Sunday. The question was whether Thomas Smethurst should be hanged early, on Friday, or late, on Tuesday. They gave him until Tuesday and so saved his neck.

Sir George Lewis was a grave scholarly man, a former editor of the famous *Edinburgh Review* and author of *Observation and Reasoning in Politics.* There was never a Home Secretary more ready to be persuaded by logic and rational argument. On that summer evening he sat with his back to the Venetian window of his office, a view of the colliers and penny steamers on the Thames behind him, facing his visitor across the desk. The conversation had reached that point where Holmes felt confident enough to reveal his secret.

'I have always preferred to shave with Occam's Razor,' he said equably. 'The precept that when you have discarded all impossibilities, whatever is left, however unexpected, must be true. In the case of Thomas Smethurst, I confess I was also troubled by an absence of sufficient motive. He is a rogue, a cheat, a seducer. But, while I have known of men who have killed for gain, I have never known such a man who killed a woman when she was worth several times more to him alive than dead.'

'All that has been accounted for, Mr Holmes. It is only the matter of arsenic which remains at issue.'

'Very well,' Holmes said, 'I listened to the evidence that was given in court. When Dr Taylor tested the solution he looked only for arsenic. He did not need to test for chlorate of potass. He assumed that, if it was there, it had been used to flush out any trace of noxious substance from the poor woman's body. If he had any doubts, of course, they were soon settled. The chlorate of potass attached itself first to the copper gauze, corroding it. By using three pieces of the wire gauze, he was able to exhaust the chlorate. On the third piece, he collected a good deal of arsenic.'

'And this would happen if there was arsenic in the body?' Sir George said sympathetically.

'Indeed,' said Holmes, 'and it would happen even if there was no arsenic in the body.'

The Home Secretary shifted uncomfortably in his leather chair. 'I think you had better explain that.'

'When there is merely arsenic, Sir George, the experiment is infallible. That is the case ninety-nine times out of every hundred. Dr Taylor had never encountered one that was otherwise. This time there was also chlorate of potass. He was right in thinking that the chlorate of potass must be exhausted before arsenic would gather on the copper gauze. It was after this that he made his error.'

'Dr Taylor's reputation stands high, Mr Holmes. He is one of our foremost chemical analysts.'

Holmes inclined his head. 'Dr Taylor is all that you say. However, as students, our paths diverge. He is the scholar, I am merely an inquisitive amateur. For some months I pursued researches into mineralogy with a view to improving the apparatus used in detecting murder by poison. I studied not only the chemicals that were tested but the constituents of the materials used to test them.'

'Do you say, Mr Holmes, that the Reinsch Test is unreliable?'

'Entirely reliable,' Holmes said, 'provided that one tests only for arsenic. Copper gauze, however, is a curious substance. It is copper, to be sure, but it cannot be refined to a state of absolute purity. There is seldom any necessity for it. It contains, among other impurities, quantities of arsenic.'

The colour began to flow from Sir George's face. He thought, no doubt, of men hanged in the past who might have been innocent. Holmes waved away his anxieties.

'This does not invalidate the test, as a rule,' he said quickly. 'Usually there is no corrosion and arsenical impurity is not released from the copper gauze. In this rare case, the chlorate of potass corroded the metal gauze, releasing the arsenical impurity from the metal into the very solution being tested. Dr Taylor is a fine chemical analyst but he is no mineralogist. The Reinsch Test should never be used, where there is chlorate of potass in the solution tested. The Marsh Test would have shown no arsenic in Miss Bankes.'

Sir George Lewis cleared his throat and seemed as if he was trying to gain time for his reply. But there could be no reply save one.

'Then you insist, Mr Holmes, that the arsenic came not from the dead woman but all of it from the copper gauze? It is beyond question?'

'There can be no question,' Holmes said, 'I had already tested a solution that contained only chlorate of potass—no arsenic whatever. Yet the third piece of copper gauze was coated with as much arsenic as Dr Taylor found. It was little enough, but remember that the specimen from Miss Bankes, in solution, was tiny in itself. Had this amount of arsenic come from such a minute sample, when multiplied by the total amount taken from her, it was enough to have killed the poor woman twice over.'

The bombshell that his visitor exploded in this manner was not yet enough to alter the Home Secretary's mind. Sir George Lewis stood up and gazed from his window across the coal wharves and the masts of the collier brigs, the slow barges under rust-coloured sails and the smoke-trails from the tall funnels of the little steamers.

'He put prussic acid on the bread, Mr Holmes, and tested its strength by feeding it to the sparrows.'

'Prussic acid, sir, is a constituent of effervescent medicine given to ease the type of vomiting from which Miss Bankes suffered. It proves nothing.'

The Home Secretary turned round again.

'And he surely gave her the chlorate of potass. What reason for that, unless to flush from her kidneys before death all trace of arsenical poison?'

'It was that, sir, which made the use of arsenic still more plausible. However, I took the liberty of testing for substances which were beyond the purview of Dr Taylor. Though the results were not conclusive, I believe that elaterium and veratrine were both present in the specimens taken from Isabella Bankes. They are not mineral irritants, like arsenic, but vegetable irritants. Their effect is to produce symptoms of vomiting and dysentery, very similar to those shown in this case.'

'Then he killed her, whether by arsenic or not?'

Holmes shook his head.

'Veratrine and elaterium are not the weapons of the poisoner. Their effect would be too uncertain. They are prescriptions of the abortionist. Isabella Bankes was in her second month of pregnancy when she died. Had she borne a child, Thomas Smethurst's bigamy would have been in great danger of discovery and his plans would have been at an end. Miss Bankes suffered from a degree of sickness beyond that found in most pregnancies. Combined with the substances used to bring on an abortion, she was subject to vomiting so severe that she could keep nothing in her stomach. She died of starvation. In her feeble state, the exhaustion of vomiting was enough to kill her. I reaffirm my conviction that Thomas Smethurst valued her more alive than dead. She stood, ultimately, to inherit thirty-five thousand pounds. That is the point where I first began, when I sought out her father's will.'

By the time that Sherlock Holmes stepped into the sunlight of a September evening, Sir George Lewis's private secretary had already drawn up copies of the letter of reprieve for immediate delivery to the High Sheriff of Surrey and the Governor of Horsemonger Lane Gaol. In his own hand, the Home Secretary himself began a more confidential memorandum. 'Sir George Lewis, with his humble duty to Your Majesty . . .' In the course of that memorandum, the name of the young Sherlock Holmes was first brought to the attention of the highest in the land.

VIII

The world knows the conclusion. Smethurst was reprieved from the gallows on the last day. The eminent toxicologist, Sir Benjamin Brodie, was appointed to inquire into the facts. He confirmed the findings of Sherlock Holmes in every particular.

Thomas Smethurst received a pardon, only to be arrested for bigamy and sent to prison for a year. On his release, he sued for compensation in respect of the murder trial. His effrontery failed. However, he then went to the Court of Probate and claimed the estate of Isabella Bankes, bequeathed to him under her dying will and testament. It went against the grain but, since the will was valid, the jury had no alternative than to find a verdict in his favour.

Holmes was later to remark to me, in the case of Grimesby Roylott of Stoke Moran, that, when a doctor does go wrong, he is the worst of criminals. In his determination to destroy the child of the woman he loved, even at the risk of her life, Smethurst had proved himself a standing example of this, whatever the law might determine. History does not record the last years of our bigamist. No doubt he returned to the life of Bayswater boarding-houses and the fluttering hearts of middle-aged spinsters. It was some years afterwards when Holmes first told me the story of the case.

'And the humour of it is, Watson,' he concluded, 'that a scoundrel such as he should owe his life to the laws of Sunday observance.'

'How so?'

'Why, if they had erected the gallows on Sunday, they would have hanged him at eight sharp on Monday morning. By observing the Sabbath, they had to respite him until Tuesday, the first morning when the platform could be ready. But for that, he might have been dead and buried before he could be reprieved.'

Then he lay back in his chair with that look of satisfaction for his youthful skill, which was perhaps the nearest he ever came to smugness.

The Case of the
Crown Jewels

I

It is only now, with the death of the last public man involved in the scandal, that I feel easy enough in my mind to set down the truth of the strange affair of the Irish Crown Jewels. So long as Sir Arthur Vicars remained alive, Sherlock Holmes would permit nothing to be written that might revive the accusations against that unfortunate gentleman. Moreover, the manner of Sir Arthur's death is germane to the story. Since many of my readers will recall nothing of it, I shall give a brief summary of the events accompanying it.

On the morning of 14 April 1921, an early mist veiled the blue Atlantic sky over the hills behind Kilmorna House. Pleasantly situated in the far south-west of Ireland, Kilmorna was a Victorian country house built of brick in the Tudor style. Its tall chimneys and tower rose among well-kept lawns and trees. Latterly, it had been occupied by Sir Arthur Vicars and his wife, Lady Gertrude, who was considerably younger than her husband. Though my friend Sherlock Holmes spoke seldom and briefly of any relatives that he might possess, I have reason to suppose that he was distantly connected with Sir Arthur Vicars.

By the time of the tragedy, Sir Arthur's health was not robust and he made a habit of rising late after being brought his breakfast in bed. On that spring morning, when the maidservant had removed his tray, he lay propped on the pillows, discussing the business of the day with his estate manager. He saw nothing of the trap that now closed upon him.

From the trees that flanked the carriage-drive of Kilmorna, a group of men moved stealthily towards the house. There were about thirty of them, casually dressed, like a line of beaters with a gamekeeper. Some held revolvers and one, whose forehead was bandaged, carried a double-barrelled shotgun. The man with the shotgun smashed a pane of glass, reached through and entered the house by the main door.

At the sound of breaking glass, Sir Arthur got up and pulled on his dressing-gown, just as Lady Vicars ran into his room to tell him that the house was surrounded by armed men. As the couple and their estate manager went down the stairs, they smelled smoke and paraffin or petrol. Kilmorna had been free of the 'troubles' affecting other parts of Ireland and it was surely remarkable that such attacks should begin now. The Government of Ireland Act had been made law at Westminster and in five more days the independent Irish state was to come into being. Yet there was no doubt that the house had been set on fire by the intruders and that the lower panelling was already ablaze. Sir Arthur at once told the estate manager that they must save the most valuable paintings and furniture in the ground-floor rooms by passing them out of the library windows on to the terrace.

There was far too little time for that. In a few minutes more the flames were leaping and dancing on the interior woodwork. It was as much as the Lord of Kilmorna could do to save himself. He came out on to the terrace of the burning house and confronted 'Captain Moonlight', a ruffianly figure in cap and gaiters, the commander of the raiders. Thick clouds of smoke were floating across the lawns. Several men followed Sir Arthur as he turned away across the terrace, half hidden by a curtain of smoke. The estate manager lost sight of him but heard shouts and an argument. Sir Arthur said, 'You may shoot me first, but you won't get the key.' The man in cap and gaiters told him to prepare to meet his God. One of the other bandits began to count, 'One . . . two . . . three . . .' Sir Arthur said firmly, 'All right, fire away.' There was a brief silence and then several revolver shots cracked across the smoke-filled garden.

The servants huddled in fear of their lives at one end of the terrace but there was no further sound. It seemed that the raiders melted away behind the smokescreen, empty-handed. The estate manager went forward alone. He found Sir Arthur Vicars lying dead at the foot of the further terrace steps with bullet wounds in his body. Round his neck was a card bearing the legend: 'spy. informers beware. ira never forgets'.

How absurd it seems! I believe that the card and the legend were far more likely to have been the work of common thieves than of the IRA. Of what use was this death to the republicans when they had already gained the treaty they sought? Sir Arthur was a genealogist and historian, who had once held the office of Ulster King of Arms, presiding over the ceremonial of the Viceroy of Ireland's court at Dublin Castle. But that was fourteen years earlier. He was now an invalid with little interest in the politics of Ireland. In the columns of *The Times*, the senseless murder committed at a time when political differences had been resolved was condemned by the British Prime Minister, Mr David Lloyd George, as a cowardly and brutal crime against a man who had given no cause for offence.

There was, however, another explanation. Only a few of Sir Arthur's friends, including Sherlock Holmes, knew that Kilmorna House boasted a certain 'strong-room' or vault. 'Captain Moonlight' and his men had paid a previous visit, when they tried by brute force to smash their way into this strong-room through the ceiling above. Concrete and steel girders defeated the assault. You may be sure that their object was not Sir Arthur's modest collection of English silver or his library of genealogy. The raiders believed that in the vault at Kilmorna lay a treasure-house of diamonds, rubies, and emeralds, all set in gold, the regalia of St Patrick and the Crown Jewels of Ireland, which the world had not seen for fourteen years.

Such was the prize for which Sir Arthur Vicars died. His murderers were not patriots of any sort, but common robbers.

I could not hear of this outrage without recalling another death in the same family. Seven years earlier, when Sir Arthur's nephew, Peirce Mahony, was shot through the heart in the grounds of his father's house at Grange Con, south of Dublin, Captain Moonlight was nowhere to be found. But like his uncle, the young man had held office in the court of King Edward's Viceroy at Dublin, Lord Aberdeen.

The circumstances of his death were these. On Sunday, 27 July 1914, Peirce Mahony was with a family party at Grange Con. The talk was of the Austro-Hungarian ultimatum to Serbia, the mobilisation of the Austrian army on the Russian frontier, of what France and England would do. After lunch, Mahony took his gun and went out to shoot duck. By dusk he had not returned. A search of the grounds revealed the young man's body lying in the lake. Mahony had been shot twice through the heart by his own gun. There was very little spread of shot. The gun had been fired when the mouths of the barrels were more or less touching his chest, perhaps pressed against it.

Suicide was impossible, since Mahony would have been unable to reach the trigger if the muzzle was pressed above his heart. It was assumed that there had been an accident when he climbed over the wire fence to reach the lake. Perhaps he propped his gun against the fence. Perhaps he unwisely reached over to lift it by its muzzle with the mouths of the barrels pointing at his chest. A strand of wire caught in the trigger-guard and pressed the trigger back. The barrels were discharged simultaneously and he was knocked back into the water by the force of the impact.

Sherlock Holmes was far away from this tragedy but he later examined the trigger-guard of the shotgun with great care. There were no scratches on the metal, such as barbed wire might have made. All the same, why should anyone choose to murder a decent young fellow like Mahony? Holmes guessed that Mahony was a man who had learned some truth about the loss of King Edward's

Crown Jewels and was too honest to keep that truth to himself. My friend was of the opinion that the young man boldly threatened to unmask the thief who had stolen the regalia of St Patrick. If so, the thief had now murdered his accuser. If this version of events was correct then the killer, as Holmes judged him, escaped justice only for one more year before being seized after he had shot a policeman dead in a Hampstead street.

Of the three public figures involved in the 1907 scandal of the Crown Jewels, two had met violent deaths. Only one remained alive. Frank Shackleton. He was known to Mayfair society as the younger brother of the famous Antarctic explorer, Sir Ernest Shackleton. Sherlock Holmes described him to me more bluntly as 'a man of the worst reputation and a disgrace to a fine family'.

The deaths of Peirce Mahony and Sir Arthur Vicars were the last acts of the drama that had begun in the early summer of 1907 and involved Sherlock Holmes and myself in one of our most sensational cases. To that drama, I shall now return.

II

A reader of these sketches of the life of Sherlock Holmes would find it remarkable, perhaps incredible, had my friend's talents not been employed by the authorities in the more dangerous world of the new century. The long reign of Her Majesty had come to an end and she had been succeeded by the Prince of Wales as Edward VII. There was greater affluence and freer style at court. All the same, it was a world where political assassination and terrorist outrage had assumed menacing proportions.

Holmes had by now a reputation that stretched back over some decades. He was known to the mightiest in the land and was on close personal terms with men of influence. Among them, as young men, were two future Lord Chancellors, Halsbury and Birkenhead, as well as the great defender, Sir Edward Marshall Hall, KC. Once or twice in the earlier years of our friendship, when Holmes had rendered some private service or other, he would be absent afterwards to keep an engagement for lunch or tea 'in the neighbourhood of Windsor'. After his success in the matter of the Bruce-Partington plans in 1895, he returned from such a visit with a remarkably fine emerald tie-pin as a token of royal appreciation.

In a few more years, it was in the shadow world of such organisations as the 'Special Branch' of Scotland Yard or the new department of Military Intelligence at Queen Anne's Gate that Holmes was most often consulted. The 'Special Branch' of the CID had been created in 1884, in response to Fenian outrages by gun and bomb. Among the targets attacked by the dynamiters were the Houses of Parliament, the offices of *The Times*, the London railway stations, and Scotland Yard itself. From the first, Chief Inspector Littlechild, Assistant Commissioner Monro, and successive commanders of the Branch consulted Holmes in many of their most important cases.

From my notes, I see that it was in February 1907 when I accompanied my friend on a visit to Scotland Yard. At that time, our friend Lestrade had served more than thirty years in the Metropolitan Police. He had risen to the rank of Superintendent and there was no better commander within the higher echelons of the Special Branch.

He received us with that bluff courtesy which is his hallmark. We sat in leather chairs either side of the fireplace in his room, the curtains closed against a fusillade of rain on the windows that winter evening. Our host was plainly bursting with news of some kind and we did not keep him from it long.

'An announcement of importance will be made in the next few days, gentlemen. His Majesty the King is to pay an official visit to Ireland this summer. This is the year of the Irish National Exhibition in Dublin and it will not do to keep the King away. The world would think that he cannot safely set foot in that part of his dominions. It would never do, Mr Holmes. King Edward himself is determined on the arrangement and his officials are inclined to let him have his way. All the same, it poses a considerable risk.'

The impatient smile-like muscular spasm plucked at Holmes's mouth.

'Well, Lestrade, if the King will have it so, there is little you or I can do to stop him. In any case, His Majesty is quite right. If it seems that he dare not set foot in part of his dominions, there is an end of royal authority. You had better let the thing go ahead, my dear fellow.'

Lestrade looked uncomfortable at this and stroked his moustache.

'The King—or, rather, His Majesty's advisers—hoped that you might consent to play a part in the plans, Mr Holmes.'

This suggestion, made with some timidity, broke the tension in the room. Holmes threw back his head and uttered his dry sardonic laugh.

'My dear Lestrade! I have so many enemies in the world that I should merely draw fire upon the King. With me at his side, His Majesty would be twice as likely to be shot!'

'Not at his side,' Lestrade said quickly. 'You would have no objection to a visit beforehand to view the arrangements for his safety? Or to being there as an observer for the two days of the visit?'

Holmes sighed and stretched out his long thin legs towards the fire. 'I cannot say that I had included Dublin in my summer itinerary.' The superintendent paused and then came out with his trump. 'It was our late Lord Chancellor who suggested to His Majesty that your assistance might be called upon.'

My friend paused and the aquiline features assumed a look of dejection. His bohemian nature had given him a strong aversion to society and ceremonial, 'flummery', as he termed it. However, as soon as Lord Halsbury's name was invoked, I knew that the superintendent had won the day. Holmes looked a little despondent, as it seemed to me.

'You hit below the belt, Lestrade,' he said gloomily. 'Lord Halsbury knows I can refuse him nothing.'

So it was decided. We talked over a few matters and at length got up to leave. Holmes turned back to Lestrade.

'One thing, Lestrade. Where is His Majesty to be lodged in Dublin?'

'The Viceregal Lodge in Phoenix Park, as I understand.'

'Impossible.' Holmes brought his hand down flat and hard on the desk. 'It is the first place that would be made a target. Let him make the crossing on the royal yacht, anchor off Kingstown, and live on board. And let there be a cruiser either side of him. I cannot undertake this business if he multiplies the risks by living ashore.' I confess there had grown about my friend something of the prima donna in such matters. He must have his way. As the world knows, however, King Edward sailed on the *Victoria and Albert*, anchored off Kingstown, and lived aboard. The cruiser *Black Prince* was moored on one side, the *Antrim* on the other.

III

King Edward's visit was to take place on 10 and 11 July but the Irish International Exhibition opened in Herbert Park, Dublin, on 4 May. This was the occasion of our first glimpse. At eleven o'clock that morning, a grand procession set out from Dublin Castle for the official opening.

In the cool spring sunlight, the carriage of Lord Aberdeen, the Viceroy of Ireland, passed out through the triumphal arch of the castle gateway to the salute of sentries on either side. The glossy geldings turned down the short incline of Cork Hill into Dame Street, its cobbles ringing with the hollow hoofbeats of two squadrons of hussars, the upright plumes of their fur shakos stirring a little, their red tunics laced with gold and the sabres bumping against the dark blue thighs of their overalls. Behind the Viceroy and the Countess of Aberdeen came several more carriages, bearing officials of the viceregal household, including Sir Arthur Vicars, Ulster King of Arms. Holmes and I rode in the final carriage as guests of Lord Aberdeen.

Holmes longed to be anywhere but in the middle of such aimless pageantry. The familiar look of ineffable boredom on his sharp features was painful to behold.

'This will be the death of me, Watson,' he said from the corner of his mouth as we rattled along Dame Street, past the coloured glass arcade of the Empire Music Hall and the pillared elegance of the bank. He looked with complete incomprehension upon those who had turned out to clap and cheer the procession, as the Viceroy lifted the cocked hat of his court-dress in acknowledgement. The women waved and the men stood bareheaded, as if at the passing of a funeral.

Where the carriages and escort swung round College Green, the trams had been drawn up to allow the procession past the grey classical façade of Trinity College. There was a glimpse of lawns and chestnut trees. Then, behind the railings, rose a jeering outburst. The uniformed officers of the Dublin Metropolitan Constabulary moved quickly as clenched fists were raised at the King's Viceroy and his lady. Holmes brightened up at the promise of an affray.

Among the long residential avenues of south Dublin lay the exhibition grounds in Herbert Park with newly erected African villages and Canadian settlements, an Indian theatre and children's amusements. The cold May wind whipped and snapped at the flags of the nations on their poles. Each gust blew clouds of sand like stinging hail from the newly laid paths.

Inside the domed hall, as the procession formed up, rose the soaring chords of the *Tannhäuser* overture for organ and full orchestra. The dignitaries moved forward, led by the Knights of St Patrick in richly jewelled collars and the slim figure of Sir Arthur Vicars, Ulster King of Arms, in his herald's tunic bearing the royal lions in gold, like a figure from a Tudor court.

Sherlock Holmes stood in morning coat and trousers, still a picture of misery and boredom. I could not repress the thought that he would probably have been happier planning the assassination of the Viceroy's court than preventing it. Life returned to his dark brooding eyes only at the appearance of the two lesser functionaries, Peirce Mahony and Frank Shackleton, who walked behind the knights. Frank Shackleton, the Dublin Herald of the Viceroy's court, had about him that whiff of dark good looks and criminality which revived Holmes's spirits. He was a young man of no obvious fortune and considerable debts. Yet he contrived to run a household in San Remo, as well as a far more expensive London home in Park Lane. Each establishment had a separate mistress.

Holmes stared at the dark curls which gathered on the back of Shackleton's head as the music drew to its conclusion with Elgar's 'Pomp and Circumstance'. The procession halted. Cool sunlight caught the display of treasure that was borne slowly past us. I swear that my friend's thin and fastidious nostrils twitched, as though the golden horde gave off a fine and subtle perfume.

Glittering like broken flame, the Crown Jewels of the Irish kingdom shone in coloured fire on robes and tunics. The Viceroy's robe bore the Star of St Patrick. It seemed the size of a soup-plate, a shamrock of rubies and emeralds set in solid gold, bordered by Brazilian diamonds that blazed with flashes of white heat in the sun, every stone the size of a walnut. The eight points of the star were encrusted with Indian diamonds of smaller size.

Frank Shackleton bore on a black cushion the great Badge of Viceroyalty. Round its circumference was the motto *Quis separabit?* picked out in rose-tinted diamonds, looted by the British commanders from the Indian tombs of Golconda. With his dark curls and striking profile Shackleton looked every inch the part. Then the Knights of St Patrick walked by, each noble neck encompassed by a collar of finely wrought gold links, set with precious stones.

As the procession paused, emeralds, rubies, and clustered diamonds set in thick gold glowed and sparkled more richly in the shadows than in the sun. I saw Holmes's lips moving silently and mockingly for my benefit in the words that so often accompanied the music of Sir Edward Elgar, which now fairly deafened us.

'Truth and right and freedom, Each a holy gem, Stars of solemn brightness, Weave thy diadem.'

The look of misery was gone as he gazed upon the royal treasure, not for its beauty but for its eternal appeal to human greed and criminality.

'I think, Watson,' he said softly, as the orchestra fell silent, 'I think we must see how all this is managed.'

The safety of such treasures was no part of our business. However, there was no difficulty in arranging that we should accompany the jewels back to Dublin Castle. Our plain black carriage arrived immediately behind the police van containing the jewel cases, as it drew up outside the Bedford Tower, safely within the upper courtyard of the castle.

Apart from Ireland's Crown Jewels, the Bedford Tower contained the Irish Office of Arms with a fine collection of bound volumes and manuscripts on matters of genealogy and heraldry. It was not, strictly speaking, a tower but a classical pavilion with a fine portico of Italianate arches before the main door. An octagonal clock-tower with a cupola dome rose above. It faced the elegant viceregal apartments across the yard with the guard-room of the Dublin garrison next to it and the headquarters of the Dublin Metropolitan Police within a few yards. On the other side of it was the arch of the castle gate, where two sentries and a policeman were on duty day and night. If they could not between them secure such treasures, I was quite sure we should never do so.

'I think, Holmes, we might leave the matter there. Anyone might have read your face like a book just now but, surely, this is the safest place in the country for the regalia. Perhaps safer than the Tower of London itself.'

He chuckled but there was no laughter in his keen eyes.

'All the same,' he said, 'we must not disappoint Sir Arthur. He will die of chagrin unless we allow him to show us how well protected his treasures are.'

We got down into the sunlit courtyard and walked across to the figure of Ulster King of Arms in his Elizabethan tabard and breeches.

It will be as well if I say something of Sir Arthur Vicars, as he appeared to me then. He had held his office for fifteen years and lived much of his life at his Dublin town-house in St James's Terrace. At this time, he was still a bachelor, loyal to the English cause, and a ritualistically inclined member of the Established Church. He had a bland face and wistful air, the locks and whiskers of an

Elizabethan courtier. In his manner, he was apt to be pedantic, fussy and rather old-maidish.

On that afternoon, he appeared to have stepped out of a distant costumed past as he escorted us through the Bedford Tower to his office on the first floor. There were two rooms opening off the ground-floor vestibule. The library was to the right; ahead there was the clerk's cubby-hole office, which contained a steel door, the only way to the strong-room itself. Sir Arthur ushered us into the library, its shelves lined with handsomely bound volumes of genealogy and heraldry. Against the far wall, between two windows, stood a large 'Model A' Ratner safe, four feet wide and five feet tall. Sir Arthur walked across to it and then turned round to us.

'As you may see, gentlemen, we are pretty well provided for here. This is where the smaller items of the regalia are kept. The safe was installed by Ratner's four years ago. It has walls of two-inch steel and double locks of seven levers each. It is proof against any lock-picking or forcing. Nothing short of dynamite would blow it open and the amount required would bring down the entire Bedford Tower. For good measure, the gateway arch is outside. On the other side of this wall, there are two sentries and a policeman on guard day and night.'

'I congratulate you,' said Holmes with only the least trace of irony in his tone. 'How many keys are there and who holds them?'

Sir Arthur smiled. 'Two, Mr Holmes. One is always with me. The other is concealed in a place to which I alone have access and which is known only to me.'

'But would it not be better still to have the safe installed in the strong-room?'

A brief look of irritation disturbed Sir Arthur's self-confidence.

'After the strong-room was constructed, it was found that the safe was too wide to pass through the doorway. I have spoken several times to the Board of Works but nothing has been done.'

Holmes nodded and our heraldically costumed guide led us through the vestibule to the little office, which had just enough space for a chair and a desk.

'Our messenger and general factotum is here during working hours,' Sir Arthur said, 'William Stivey, formerly of the Royal Navy. He has been with us for six years. A conscientious worker of exemplary character.'

'Indeed?' said Holmes politely, but he was staring at the bonded steel of the strong-room door to one side, 'And this, I take it, is the work of Messrs Milner of Finsbury Pavement? The type is unmistakable. Double locked. Harveyed-Krupp steel plate of several inches, about half the thickness of a battleship's hull-armour and able to withstand a direct hit from a hundred-pound nickel-plated shell fired by a six-inch gun at a range of fifty yards.'

'You are admirably informed, Mr Holmes, I must say.' Sir Arthur spoke with the displeasure of a professional who finds himself outpaced by an amateur.

'Ah well,' said Holmes with a touch of insouciance, 'it comes only from inspecting such doors as these after they have been broken open.'

The wind left Sir Arthur's sails at this remark, for Holmes described the very thing our guide dreaded. It seemed as much as Sir Arthur could do to unlock the heavy steel door and draw it back on its smooth hinges. We entered the strong-room. The interior was about twelve feet square, like a library alcove with shelves and cupboards housing the more valuable genealogical volumes. Its window, looking on to the castle yard, was heavily and securely barred. Though most of the jewels were in the library safe, the strong-room contained within its locked cases several of the collars of knighthood, as well as the Irish sword of state, a gilt crown and sceptre, and two silver maces.

Immediately in front of us, as the door was drawn back, was a locked steel grille. I was surprised to see that the key to this interior grille was already in its lock and asked why.

'There is only one key,' Sir Arthur said. 'It would not do for it to be lost. It is as safe in here as anywhere. Therefore, we leave it in the lock at all times.'

Holmes nodded at me, exchanging a significant look.

'Besides,' said Sir Arthur quickly, 'beyond that wall is the head-quarters of the Dublin Metropolitan Police and beyond the other is the guard-room of the military garrison.'

Though Holmes had teased him a little, there was little doubt that Sir Arthur had done his job well. Whatever might happen to King Edward himself, Ireland's Crown Jewels were surely as safe as if they had been in the Bank of England or the Tower of London. The strong-room door was closed and locked. We followed our guide up the spiral staircase to the other floor. There were two rooms at this level, one for Sir Arthur and the second for his secretary.

'And who has keys to the strong-room door?' Holmes inquired.

Sir Arthur stiffened at this renewed questioning.

'I have one,' he said. 'The other is with Stivey while he is on duty. It is returned to me when he leaves. While he is in his office, the strong-room is open so that the books and manuscripts may be consulted by me or my secretary. If he leaves the office, he locks the strong-room door and puts the key in a concealed drawer of his desk. We who are authorised to use it would know where to look, a stranger would not. There is a third key, which is not in use. It is kept in a drawer in the strong-room itself, oiled and wrapped.'

Holmes touched his fingers together. 'How many members of your staff use this building?'

Sir Arthur frowned with an effort of recollection. 'Stivey is one. My secretary George Burtchaell is another. There is Peirce Mahony as well. Stivey has the key to the strong-room while he is on duty. All three have a key to the front door. Detective Officer Kerr patrols the building from time to time when the office is closed. There is a key to the front door, which is kept in the Metropolitan Police office for his use. The only other person to use it is the cleaning woman, Mrs Farrell. She comes early in the morning and reports first to the police office.'

'It amounts to this, then,' Holmes said quietly. 'You, Burtchaell, Mahony, Stivey, Kerr, and Mrs Farrell have a key to the front door. You yourself have a key to the strong-room. Stivey and your staff have the use of one when the office is open. But you alone have a key to the safe in the library.'

'Precisely, Mr Holmes,' Sir Arthur said.

'And what of Mr Shackleton?'

'Mr Shackleton? He has no keys. He is Dublin Herald. Sometimes his letters are sent to him here. But he does not work here any longer. Indeed, he is rarely in Dublin. He has no key of any kind, nor has he need of one.'

'When he comes to Dublin, he is frequently a guest in your house, I believe.'

'Whether he is or not, Mr Holmes, can surely be no concern of yours. I repeat that Mr Shackleton has no access to a key nor any need of one.'

'Your keys to the safe and the strong-room—' Holmes began.

'Neither Mr Shackleton nor any other person, Mr Holmes, knows where they are kept.'

Holmes appeared to be satisfied by this but he walked across to the window above the courtyard only to return to the attack.

'I am a burglar, Sir Arthur. I approach the door of the Bedford Tower. What prevents me?'

'The policeman on duty or the guard commander will ask you your business.'

'And if I satisfy him that I have business?'

'Then you will still find the door locked against you until you ring the bell and Stivey opens it. If you have business, you will be attended every moment you are in here. I promise you, you will not be left alone. After the office has closed, you would be intercepted as soon as you came near it.'

I have several times remarked that Sherlock Holmes worked for love of his art rather than for the acquirement of wealth. So it was on this occasion. The jewels of the Order of St Patrick were nothing to him. So far as he had a duty in Dublin, it was the safety of the King. The contents of the safe and the strong-room in Dublin Castle were worth as many hundreds or thousands of pounds as you might care to name. Holmes would not have given a shilling for them. Yet the cleverness with which they were guarded intrigued him, and the means by which a thief might outwit such precautions occupied him for the rest of the day.

I wearied far more quickly of the topic and said so bluntly as we drank brandy and soda in our rooms that evening.

'I have always suspected that you have no soul, Watson,' he said jovially. 'Can you not imagine the effect of this morning's display of those gems on every dishonest mind in the hall?'

'I saw clearly enough that no one is likely to open those locks and doors except Sir Arthur Vicars himself.'

Holmes shook his head. 'By the time we left the Bedford Tower, I saw quite plainly the three separate methods by which the jewels and regalia might be removed from the safe and the strong-room without their guardians being able to lift a finger to prevent it.'

'Surely that cannot be,' said I.

He smiled. 'Then you did not notice the fatal flaw in Sir Arthur Vicars's self-confidence, while we were in his room?'

'Indeed I did not.'

'Why, my dear fellow, he told us that Shackleton did not know where the keys to the safe were hidden.'

'What of it?'

'A man may be certain of what he himself knows. He cannot tell what another may know or may find out. To think otherwise, my dear Watson, is a capital error when one deals with a first-class rogue. Who can tell what such a scoundrel knows?'

IV

It was more than another two months before the King's visit to Dublin was to begin, on 10 July. Holmes and I returned to England for the intervening period. So did Shackleton, whose visits to Ireland as Dublin Herald were now rare enough and whose business ventures kept him in London. Seven weeks passed. It was on the morning of 29 June, at about eight o'clock, that I woke from a deep sleep to find Holmes standing by my bed. My friend had never been an early riser but now he appeared in a large purple dressing-gown with a blue telegraph form in his hand.

'Wake up, Watson! We must be on our way. Events are moving in Dublin, as I expected. Sir Arthur has lost his key to the door of the Bedford Tower.'

I fear I was a little put out, since our planned departure for Ireland was still two days away.

'The tower? Is that all, Holmes? Half a dozen people have keys to it.'

'I should not knock you up without good reason,' he said a little sharply. 'Now, there is a boat-train from Euston at noon. We shall be in good time for the night boat from Holyhead and be in Dublin first thing tomorrow.'

I fear that I grumbled a good deal at this sudden change in our arrangements. All the same, I agreed to cancel my engagements for the next couple of days and accompany my friend. As the express of the Northwestern Railway carried us beyond Birmingham, I read the *Times* list of social engagements for the previous day. Among the guests at Lady Ormonde's luncheon party in Upper Brook Street was the name of Francis Richard Shackleton of the Royal Irish Fusiliers, the Dublin Herald. I handed the paper to Holmes.

'Whatever may have happened to Sir Arthur's key to the tower, Frank Shackleton cannot have taken it. He is here, in London.'

'I have no doubt of that, Watson. Shackleton has never left London since he returned from the opening of the exhibition in early May.'

'Are you so sure?'

I could almost swear that Holmes looked a little awkward.

'Our friend Lestrade has had officers keeping a watch. I think you may rest assured that Shackleton has scarcely been outside Mayfair, let alone London.'

He closed his eyes and never showed so much as the tremor of a lid until we pulled into Holyhead. I could think only of the inconvenience of having to wait more than a week in Dublin for the King's arrival. My displeasure was not diminished upon our arrival at the North Wall in Dublin early the following morning.

Detective Officer Kerr was on the quayside with a cab to take us to our lodgings.

'I fear, gentlemen,' he said sympathetically, 'that you have been disturbed without necessity. Sir Arthur mislaid his key to the Office of Arms two days ago. He could not find it on his dressing-table that morning. He came to me at once and reported this. I used my own key to let him in. Last night, however, I received a message from him. The key was on his dressing-table after all. It had slipped under the hollow base of a brass candlestick.'

'Hmm,' said Holmes, as the cab turned into the long elegant boulevard of Sackville Street. 'What of the strong-room and the safe?'

'All the keys are accounted for and the contents are secure, sir,' Kerr replied.

I was inclined to agree that the discovery of the missing key was the end of the matter. In any case, even a man who could enter the Bedford Tower was far from being able to open the strong-room or the safe. What more natural than that Sir Arthur had mislaid his copy of the door key?

Four days in Dublin passed without incident. On Wednesday, 3 July, a week before King Edward's arrival, Holmes and I had finished breakfast. We were sitting with the newspapers before us. Outside the handsome houses, there was a sound of children playing among the lawns and trees of the gardens at the centre of St Stephen's Green. I noticed in the *Morning Post* that Frank Shackleton had been at a reception in London the day before with the Duke of Argyll, husband of the Princess Louise and, hence, son-in-law of the late Queen and brother-in-law of King Edward VII. Scoundrel though he might be, Shackleton seemed to have little difficulty in securing social advancement. But he could not both be with the King's brother-in-law in London and making mischief in Dublin.

I had no sooner thought this to myself than there was a knock at the door and our landlady inquired whether it would be convenient for Mr Sherlock Holmes to receive Mrs Mary Farrell. We looked blankly at each other.

'Mrs Farrell from the castle,' the good woman explained.

Our looks changed and Holmes said, 'By all means send her in.' When the landlady had gone out, he added to me, 'No doubt this is some lady of the Viceroy's court. We had best see her.'

Imagine our surprise when there appeared in the doorway a gaunt and venerable figure dressed in black. Her clothes were the 'Sunday best' of the working-class widow-woman, the feather boa, the leg-of-mutton sleeves, the bonnet perched high on the tightly drawn hair, a handsome face hardened by toil and care. I do not think it had occurred to either of us that our visitor would be Mrs Farrell the cleaning-woman of the Bedford Tower. Now that we saw her, it seemed certain that she was the good woman whom Sir Arthur had mentioned in this connection. A look of concern contracted her features slightly and it deepened when she saw that Holmes was not alone. He rose, however, and received her with as much courtesy as if she had been a duchess or a *femme fatale*.

'Good morning, Mrs Farrell. This is an unexpected pleasure. My name is Sherlock Holmes. This is my intimate friend and associate, Dr Watson, before whom you may speak as freely as before myself.'

She looked a little awkwardly from one to the other of us.

'Pray take a seat, Mrs Farrell,' Holmes said gently.

Our visitor sat down, clutching her handbag on her lap.

'I must speak to someone about the tower,' she said in a tense quiet voice. 'I must speak, for I should not want to be thought any way dishonest.'

'Indeed, not,' Holmes said.

She looked at us both again.

'Well, sir, I came to clean as usual this morning, just on seven o'clock. The door of the tower was shut as it always is. When I put the key in the lock, it would not turn. I tried the handle and the door opened. It was unlocked all the time, Mr Holmes. For what I know it was unlocked all night. I cleaned as usual and could not see anything wrong with the building. Still, when I finished, I waited for Mr Stivey and told him I had found the door unlocked.

Mr Stivey told Sir Arthur, as soon as he came in. The strong-room was checked at once and they found everything in order. Nothing more is to be done.'

'Then you have no more to worry about, Mrs Farrell.'

She looked at him intently. 'If anything should be found amiss, sir, I would not have it come back on me. I cannot afford to lose work, Mr Holmes. I thought, if I spoke to you now, you might vouch I have been every way honest.'

Holmes smiled to reassure her. 'You need have no fear of that, Mrs Farrell. You have behaved as honestly as any woman might. Tell me, though, might not the door have been left accidentally unlocked?'

'It might,' she said doubtfully.

'And who would have been the last person to leave the tower before you?'

'Sir Arthur, Mr Holmes. He is always the last of the gentlemen to leave in the evening. But then Mr Kerr, the detective officer, makes his inspection, usually between seven and eight o'clock at night. Sir Arthur, Mr Mahony, Mr Burtchaell, and Mr Stivey all have keys. If any of them had come back later still, they might have left the door unlocked.'

Holmes assured her several times that she had done the proper and honest thing. Appearances may deceive, yet it was impossible to look at Mrs Farrell and think her anything but decent, loyal, and industrious.

'We ourselves will say nothing of this to Sir Arthur and his colleagues,' Holmes said to me, as soon as Mrs Farrell had left us. 'Nor to Detective Officer Kerr. Strictly speaking, the Bedford Tower is none of our concern.'

'And what of the jewels?' I protested, somewhat alarmed by my friend's apparent ease of mind.

'I think we may assume, my dear Watson, that St Patrick's regalia is as safe as it was yesterday—no more and no less.'

With this enigmatic comment he dismissed the topic, nor could he be persuaded to return to it.

V

Three more days passed and we came to the morning of Saturday, 6 July, four days before King Edward's arrival at Kingstown on the *Victoria and Albert*. There was no further explanation of the unlocked door, as Mrs Farrell described it, unless either Sir Arthur or Detective Officer Kerr had left it so. The matter was not mentioned to Holmes or myself by anyone but Mrs Farrell.

Holmes said with a shake of his head, 'By the nature of the thing a man cannot be sure of what he has forgotten. I think it would be safer to assume that the door was left accidentally unlocked and let us watch the consequences.'

What those consequences were to be became clear on Saturday morning. At about eleven o'clock, a boy in brass-buttoned livery arrived at St Stephen's Green with a regally embossed envelope. It was addressed to Sherlock Holmes in confidence by the Viceroy of Ireland, Lord Aberdeen, requesting him to go at once to Dublin Castle. There had been a discovery in the Bedford Tower which gave His Excellency cause for concern and materially affected the King's visit.

It was less than twenty minutes later when we entered the upper courtyard of Dublin Castle through the arched gateway on Cork Hill. Holmes rang the bell at the door of the Bedford Tower and we were admitted by William Stivey, a slightly built man of about fifty whose tanned face and somewhat rolling gait proclaimed his previous occupation.

'If you don't mind, sir,' he said to Holmes, 'you're to come straight to my office. Sir Arthur has a visitor with him just this minute but he'll see you as soon as he can.'

'Really?' said Holmes. Though he did not quite sniff, there was an air of scepticism about him. We followed Stivey to the little office and there found Mrs Farrell sitting in a chair with Detective Officer Kerr standing behind her. Kerr was a fine red-headed giant with the look of a man who has his career to make. Stivey announced Sherlock Holmes. Kerr, straightening up, at once told Mrs Farrell to tell us the story she had first told Stivey.

'It was like the other morning, sir,' the woman said, eyeing Holmes earnestly, 'but this time it was the steel door of the strong-room.'

'You mean it was unlocked?' Holmes asked quickly.

'I mean, sir, that when I came to work at about seven this morning, the door of the strong-room was partly open. I could see the grille inside it, which I never saw before, and there was a key in the lock of the grille. I took that key out and put it on Mr Stivey's desk, knowing he would be the first gentleman to arrive. Then I wrote a note, describing what I had found, and put it with the key. I closed the door to the strong-room but could not lock it, having no key.'

'You did right,' Holmes said. 'And what did Mr Stivey do?'

He swung round on the former naval rating who met his inquiry without flinching.

'As soon as Sir Arthur arrived, Mr Holmes, I went up to his room and told him that the strong-room door had been found unlocked and slightly ajar.'

'And what did Sir Arthur say?'

'He said, "Is that so?"'

Holmes stared at William Stivey.

'Did you not think that a curious thing to say?'

But William Stivey was loyal to his master. 'Sir Arthur had come in with a gentleman from West's the jewellers. He was much occupied, sir. The knight's collar intended for the investiture of Lord Castletown has been altered to bear his name and was returned this morning. Sir Arthur was preoccupied at that moment. I was able to tell him that I had checked the strong-room and that nothing was missing nor out of place. He was reassured by that.'

'Very well,' said Holmes, though he did not sound as if he thought it was very well. 'Then how comes it that the strong-room door was open?'

'It was not open at half-past seven last night,' Kerr said. 'I made my patrol then. As I turn the corner I always swing myself round by the handle of the strong-room door. I should have known at once if it was open or unfastened. If it was open this morning, someone unlocked it during the night. Apart from the key kept in the strong-room itself, there are two copies. Sir Arthur and Mr Stivey have one, though Mr Stivey's is handed to Sir Arthur when he leaves.'

'Do you say that Sir Arthur must have opened the strong-room door?'

Kerr shook his head. 'Sir Arthur was seen to leave at seven o'clock last night. He collected his mail from the Kildare Street Club at half past seven and was home at St James's Terrace when dinner was served at eight. To have returned here and then gone home again would have taken him almost an hour. He was seen constantly by his servants until after eleven o'clock last night. He retired to bed a little before midnight and, by his own account, did not leave the house again until nine o'clock this morning. Had he returned during the night, he would have been recognised at once by the guards on the castle gate.'

'Dear me,' said Holmes, as if to himself, 'how very singular. You are quite sure that you made a thorough patrol of the building last night?'

Detective Officer Kerr flushed a little, as fair-skinned redheads of his type are apt to do when falsely accused.

'So thorough, Mr Holmes, that I went through every room on both floors, even the coal cellars beneath. The one room I did not enter was the strong-room, to which I have never had a key. Only Sir Arthur has the keys to that.'

'The cellars,' said Holmes quickly. 'Do they have a coal-chute which might be used to enter the building?'

Kerr shook his head. 'There is a coal-hole but it is in the castle entrance. The military guard and the duty constable stand within a few feet of it, sometimes on top of it. In any case, it is fitted with a coal-stop, precisely to prevent an intruder getting in that way.'

Holmes nodded, as if he understood. Just then a bell rang on the floor above and Stivey, with a seaman's agility, went up the spiral staircase to answer Sir Arthur's summons. He returned a few minutes later with a leather box and a key.

'Sir Arthur presents his compliments, Mr Holmes, and will be down in a moment. If you will excuse me, I must return Lord Castletown's collar of knighthood to the library safe.'

You may be sure that Holmes and I followed the messenger as he walked into the next room where the Ratner safe stood between two windows. Stivey took the key, which Sir Arthur had just given him and which fitted each of the double locks. When he tried to turn it, the look of worry and irritation on his face told us that neither the key nor the lock would move.

'Turn it the other way, Mr Stivey,' said Holmes coolly.

Stivey did so. We heard the bolts move. He tried the handle but the steel door would not move.

'Ah,' said Holmes, 'now you have locked it. In other words, it seems that the safe as well as the strong-room door was unlocked this morning.'

Stivey backed away from the tall steel safe as if he feared it might explode. He turned to go back up the stairs and inform Sir Arthur Vicars but at that moment Sir Arthur was coming down. He nodded brusquely to us, like a man busy with the details of a royal visit four days in the future.

'Let me have the key,' he said impatiently, taking it from the messenger. Holmes, Stivey and I watched him. In his morning dress, Sir Arthur Vicars was no longer an Elizabethan courtier but every inch a modern official. He slid the key into the first lock, turned it and heard the bolts slide back. He repeated the process with the second lock and then drew open the safe door with something of a flourish.

We stood behind him, looking into the steel maw. There were shelves laid out with leather jewel cases, orderly and neat. As if he was in a hurry to get the matter over with, he drew out the first leather case and opened it. I could not see what it might contain. I heard only the hushed and tragic voice of Ulster King of Arms.

'My God! They are gone! The jewels are gone!'

VI

We stood in the sunlit library while Sir Arthur opened each box in turn and, at every discovery, the word 'Gone!' hung like the motes of dust in the summer air. Apart from two collars of knighthood in the strong-room and a third belonging to Lord Castletown, the entire Crown Jewels of the Irish Kingdom had vanished. Gold, diamonds, emeralds, rubies, sapphires had disappeared from a safe to which only Sir Arthur Vicars had the keys.

Holmes said nothing but watched Ulster King of Arms with sharp eyes, noting every nuance of his behaviour. Sir Arthur swung round on Detective Officer Kerr, as if to hold him to blame.

'Kerr!' he said in bitter panic. 'All the jewels are gone! Some of the smart boys that have been over for the King's visit have made a clean sweep of them!'

And still Holmes said nothing. Sir Arthur, in his misery, turned to him.

'The Board of Works are at fault in this,' he said pathetically, 'I have asked them for a good safe. I have correspondence to prove it. They refused it and did not give it to me. I have no confidence in this safe.'

To listen to him, you would never have thought that anything more was amiss than some trifling clerical error. Not that the entire regalia of Ireland's jewels had vanished into air. The sword of state, the orb and sceptre were still in the strong-room. But all that might most easily be sold for fifty thousand pounds had gone. He turned next to me.

'I would not be a bit surprised if they were returned to my house by parcel post tomorrow morning.'

Had he gone mad? Had the loss turned his mind? That was my first thought. Jewels are not stolen merely to be returned by parcel post next day! Sherlock Holmes said nothing.

'I must fetch Superintendent Lowe,' Kerr said. 'He must be told.'

'Indeed,' said Holmes at last, 'and someone will have to tell the King. I should not care to be that person. I do not suppose that His Majesty will be much amused.'

Then Sir Arthur Vicars was off again. 'My late mother's jewels, you know. I kept them in there for safety. They have gone too.'

There was, to say the least, something a little zany about his behaviour. In my own opinion, however, he betrayed shock rather than guilt. We went with Sir Arthur to his room on the next floor and awaited the arrival of John Lowe of the Dublin CID. Ulster King of Arms sat with his elbows on his desk and his head in his hands, a most abject study in self-pity as he bemoaned the loss. From below us we heard the sounds of a search beginning. Presently Superintendent Lowe arrived from the headquarters of the Dublin Metropolitan Police a few yards away. There were shouted commands. Detective Officer Kerr was given charge of three men who were to turn over every scrap of coal in the cellars.

I managed to get Holmes away from Sir Arthur.

'Are we to do nothing? I daresay the jewels were not our concern but yet—'

He shook his head and put his finger to his lips for silence. Presently he walked to the top of the spiral staircase and, leaning over the rail, called down, 'Mr Lowe! Before you trouble yourself any further in this matter, send for Cornelius Gallagher!'

'Who the devil is Cornelius Gallagher?' I asked.

'A locksmith, Watson. The finest in Dublin. He is employed by Ratner's as their leading man.'

In all my years with Sherlock Holmes, I had never before seen a smith take to pieces the lock of a safe. It recalled to me an experience of watching the most delicate surgical operation in my student days at Bart's. We stood over the bulky and breathless figure of Cornelius Gallagher as he dismantled the lock of the Ratner safe with his tiny screwdrivers, meticulous as a watchmaker. Within the lock were the seven slivers of metal, levers or mirrors as they call them. Each must be lifted by a segment of the key before the lock will open. Mr Gallagher unscrewed them one by one. Then he examined each through a small but powerful glass, turning the metal this way and that.

'Are they marked, Mr Gallagher?' Holmes inquired.

'Quite clean, sir. Not a scratch. They might be new.'

Holmes stood back. 'Then we may say, gentlemen, that this safe has never been opened except by the two keys which were made for it. A duplicate, however skilfully cut, is not perfect. Its tiny irregularities scratch the mirrors sufficiently for the marks to be seen with a jeweller's glass. A pick or a probe would do much worse. Is that not so, Mr Gallagher?'

Cornelius Gallagher twisted his head round.

'It is, Mr Holmes, sir. This safe was never tampered with, only opened in the usual way.'

A look amounting almost to terror seized Sir Arthur Vicars, though it was terror seen in farce rather than melodrama.

'Oh, no, Mr Holmes!' He seemed about to kneel and clutch my friend's legs. 'You cannot say it of me! It is unfair, unjust! You cannot say so, Mr Holmes!'

VII

That evening, after Lowe had left our rooms and we were sitting with brandy and soda, I said to my friend, 'Well, it cannot be Shackleton. He is still in London or still on his way to Dublin, and has not been in this city since the jewels were checked when the door of the Bedford Tower was found unlocked. You have Lestrade's word for it.'

Holmes said only, 'Hmm.'

'And if it was opened with the proper keys, both were in the possession of Sir Arthur Vicars and he alone knew where they were.'

'Does Sir Arthur Vicars look to you, Watson, like a man who would know how to sell the jewels even if he had them?'

'No,' I said, 'but I don't see how it could be Shackleton if he was never in Dublin.'

'Don't you?'

'If he was not here when it happened, which Scotland Yard itself confirms, it amounts to an alibi.'

'Does it?'

Conversation was impossible. Holmes had something in mind but no skill of mine would prise it forth. Next day there was worse news for Sir Arthur Vicars. Cornelius Gallagher examined the locks of the strong-room door, which had also been found open by Mrs

Farrell on that fateful Saturday morning. There was not a scratch nor a blemish on the polished steel mirrors of the lock. It had been opened with one of the proper keys. One of these was locked in the vault itself. The other two were in the possession of Sir Arthur and their whereabouts known only to him.

Of course, it was quite impossible that the scandal could be kept quiet for more than a few hours. The investiture of Lord Castletown was cancelled on the King's orders. How could the Knights of St Patrick parade shorn of all their splendour? It would have appeared ridiculous. By this time His Majesty was on the royal train, travelling to North Wales, where the *Victoria and Albert* lay at Holyhead, ready to carry him across the Irish Sea. His fury over the stupidity of the Viceroy's court for letting itself be robbed in this manner may be better imagined than described. In the meantime, the press burst upon us with headlines that stood inches tall. The value of the missing jewels was put at £50,000 and more. The stones represented the prize of empire in the eighteenth century and had been the gift of King William IV to the Viceroy's court in 1833.

Holmes seemed remarkably unperturbed by the disappearance of the jewels. Knowing his dislike of ceremonial occasions, I believe he took a secret pleasure in the discomfiture of the officials. He was present when Sir Arthur Vicars was questioned in his office by Superintendent Lowe two days after the robbery.

'I believe the jewels were taken by a man you know,' Sir Arthur began, 'a guest in my house. I am obliged to think he spied on me to find the safe key. I am sure that he must have taken impressions of my keys while I was in my bath. He sometimes came to this office on Sundays to collect his letters and he borrowed my key to the main door of the building.'

Superintendent Lowe, a sharp moustachio'd fellow, looked at Ulster King of Arms with pity.

'You forget, sir. The safe and the strong-room were opened with their proper keys. Impressions were not used.'

Poor devil! Sir Arthur was trapped, cornered, and there was an end of it.

'However it was done, it was he!' he cried.

Holmes sighed. 'I believe, Sir Arthur, that the jewels were last checked three weeks before. Frank Shackleton has not left England in the past month. I am informed that for the last two days, including that of the robbery, he has been a guest of Lord Ronald Sutherland-Gower at Penshurst in Kent. His travelling companion was the Duke of Argyll, the King's brother-in-law.'

'Then I do not know,' Sir Arthur said wretchedly. 'It cannot have been he. I have done him a great wrong by suggesting it. But the truth is that the young fellow has caused me a good deal of concern. I guaranteed two bills for him, fifteen hundred pounds owed to Wiltons the moneylenders in Piccadilly. And more for furniture bought from Wolff and Hollander. Wiltons charge steep for a loan, as much as fifty per cent in all. I hope I shan't be called on for it but I can't tell.'

The more one heard about Frank Shackleton's business ventures, the more unsavoury they sounded. Superintendent Lowe cleared his throat and flexed his moustaches. He unwrapped a sheet of paper and drew out two identical keys. They were the keys to the Ratner safe.

'These two keys, sir. This one was at all times worn round your neck? Day and night?'

'It was.'

'And this? As I understand it, this was wrapped and hidden in the spine of a certain volume on your study shelves.'

'It was.'

Holmes intervened. 'And did you check frequently to ensure that it was still there?'

'Every night, Mr Holmes, before I retired.'

'Then it would appear that the safe cannot have been opened by anyone but you,' Holmes said calmly.

Sir Arthur expostulated with an energy so nearly hysterical that I thought my professional assistance might be needed. There was a flaw in his temperament, as I saw it. He had become the most pitiable object. If logic meant anything at all, the innocent Sir Arthur had stolen the jewels and Shackleton the rogue could not have done so. Yet Holmes seemed entirely content to accept impossibilities. Shackleton was the thief and Sir Arthur Vicars his victim.

'It cannot be, Holmes!' I insisted that evening for the twentieth time. 'Vicars alone could have opened the safe and the strong-room. Shackleton could not have done it, even if he had travelled from London to Dublin and back at the speed of a bullet!'

My companion chuckled, lit his pipe from a coal in a pair of tongs, and said nothing.

'If you know the culprit, it is your plain duty to say so. It is the only means by which the jewels may be recovered!'

He looked at me with mild surprise and took the pipe from his mouth.

'My dear Watson,' he said gently. 'Do you not see? That is the means by which they would be irretrievably lost.'

VIII

There was a brief interruption, if it can be called so. King Edward arrived off Kingstown two days later. On Wednesday morning, 10 July, the early summer light revealed the graceful clipper hull and the twin buff funnels of the *Victoria and Albert* anchored off Kingstown Harbour, the royal standard at the mast flickering in a light breeze from the Irish Channel. To either side was anchored the more substantial bulk of a Royal Navy cruiser, *Black Prince* to port and *Antrim* to starboard.

Though the flagged streets of Kingstown were packed with sightseers by 10 A.M., they had to wait almost another two hours before the cruisers boomed out their royal salute and the steam pinnace puffed its way across the harbour to come alongside Victoria Wharf. It was a warm summer morning, the Royal Marine band playing and the welcoming dignitaries gathered expectantly in a closely guarded pavilion, hung with flags and bunting. King Edward and Queen Alexandra stepped ashore to the cheers of the crowd. Lord Aberdeen, minus certain items of the usual regalia, came forward to greet the King. The press assured us that King Edward was 'beaming with smiles and looking in splendid health ... his hat raised in recognition of the kindly reception'. According to Lord Aberdeen, the royal gaze was fixed on the viceregal breast so intently that the King's representative wondered if he might be in some way improperly dressed. 'I was thinking of those jewels,' His Majesty said bleakly.

Another visitor had also landed at Kingstown, down the gangway of the *Black Prince*. He was a dark-suited nondescript figure, muscular and bowler-hatted. John Kane, Chief Inspector of the Special Branch, had been despatched by Lestrade to inquire into the matter of the missing gems. Kane described to us the King's fury at the incompetence of the Viceroy's court.

'And the worst of it is,' the Chief Inspector added, 'that Mr Shackleton was with His Majesty's brother-in-law when the robbery was discovered. And three days before, the young scoundrel was a guest at a luncheon party in Upper Brook Street. The Dublin visit and the jewels were mentioned. And do you know, Mr Holmes, what the young devil did? He smiled and told them that he would not be a bit surprised if the jewels were stolen one day!'

'Really?' Holmes replied with a yawn. 'You don't say.'

Kane became more earnest. 'It must have been Friday night they were stolen, Mr Holmes. Why else would the door of the strong-room have been open next morning?'

'Why else, indeed?'

'And it must have been Sir Arthur who opened the strong-room and the safe. That's what makes the King so mad, Mr Holmes. His Majesty knows as much now as you or I and the thought that a man in such a position of trust should betray it is beyond bearing.'

Holmes sat—or almost lay—in his chair, his eyelids drooping as if he could scarcely stay awake.

'King Edward himself is more likely to be the thief than Sir Arthur Vicars. Sir Arthur is one of the very few men who certainly could not have done it.'

Kane stared at him and Holmes raised his eyelids a little.

'If you know something, Mr Holmes . . .'

Holmes laughed. 'It is my profession to know something, my dear Kane. A week or so ago, there was a curious business of the Bedford Tower main door being found unlocked one morning. For several days before the robbery, I had arranged that a watch should be kept discreetly on Sir Arthur's house in St James's Terrace. Superintendent Lowe obliged me. In addition, when Sir Arthur left his office, I was in the habit of keeping an eye upon him until he was safely home. I followed him on Friday evening. He speaks the truth when he says that he left the Castle with his secretary and then went alone to Nassau Street, to the Kildare Street Club. He was there about ten minutes, perhaps collecting his post. From Nassau Street, he went directly home and was there for dinner at eight o'clock. He did not leave again until just before nine on the following morning, when he went to his office to find the strong-room door open and the safe empty.'

'And that was all?' Kane asked uneasily.

'Almost. A little after 10 P.M., a young woman who might have been a servant was admitted to the house. Her name is Molly Malony, or sometimes Molly Robinson, and she has a certain reputation. By that time, however, the light in the study had gone on and off as it did every night at the same time. In other words, Sir Arthur had checked that his key to the safe was in its hiding-place. The second key and the key to the strong-room were on his person. Even if the young woman could have got them, neither she nor anyone else left the house until the following morning.'

Kane looked at him soberly.

'Then, Mr Holmes, the robbery of the jewels can't have taken place on Friday night after all. Not if all the keys were in the right place. Friday can't have anything to do with it.'

'On the contrary, Mr Kane. It is the only night on which it can possibly have occurred. I'm surprised you don't see it.'

Sherlock Holmes had a greater capacity of infuriating his colleagues by these paradoxes than any other man I have known. He now appeared to lose all interest in the case. It seemed certain that the robbery must have occurred on Friday night. But the keys with which it had undoubtedly been committed could surely not have been used on Friday night. Chief Inspector Kane parted with us, not in the best of spirits. On the following afternoon, Holmes announced to me, 'I think I shall go back to London, my dear fellow. To speak frankly, Dublin has begun to weary me and I feel I shall do no good here.'

It was so contrary to his character to throw up a case like this—and one of such significance—that I wondered if he was quite well. I said as much.

'I was never better, Watson. All the same I shall go back. You must stay here, of course, and do exactly as I tell you without question.'

'But are the jewels lost for ever or not?'

'For all I know they may be,' he said with a casual shrug.

IX

I remained in Dublin alone. The case made little progress and it seemed to me that nothing of the least consequence happened. Whoever Molly Malony might have been, not the slightest interest was shown in her. The thieves had scattered such confusion in their wake that I felt sure we had seen the last of the gems.

Yet what had happened before was nothing to the madness that followed. First there was a message brought to Sir Arthur Vicars at St James's Terrace. A young woman who was a spiritualist medium had seen the missing jewels in a dream. They were hidden in a graveyard not far away. The Dublin police announced that this corresponded with a theory of their own and a search of several old and overgrown burial grounds was begun at Mulhuddart and Clonsilla. How any sane person, let alone a Special Branch officer, could sanction this hocus-pocus was beyond me.

Nothing was found. How could it be? Next, there was a message that the jewels would be found in a house at 9 Hadley Street. Of course, they were not. We had a week of this nonsense and then Sherlock Holmes summoned me back to London.

My first question, as we sat at last in our own rooms, was to ask him what the devil it all meant.

'Oh dear,' he said, 'I have kept you in the dark too long, Watson.'

'Seeing that you know neither how it was done nor by whom, that is hardly surprising.'

He looked at me with concern.

'My dear fellow, I have known from the beginning how it was done. Duplicate keys were used.'

'Why did they not scratch the mirrors of the locks?'

'They were not used on the mirrors of the locks. That is the goose chase which Kane and Lowe have followed.'

'You had better explain that,' I told him.

'Very well,' said Holmes. 'You recall that there was a spare key to the strong-room door locked in the strong-room itself? No one had looked at it for a year. There was also a second key to the safe hidden in Sir Arthur's bookshelves. He checked every night to make sure it was there. But he never used it to open the safe. Why should he, when he had one round his neck all the time? The great point of this crime, Watson, is that the duplicate keys were cut and were used. But they were not used to open the safe or the strong-room. Their task was merely to lie where the original keys had lain. By that means, all suspicion was cast upon Sir Arthur Vicars. He was, of course, entirely innocent, except perhaps of felonious and unlawful carnal knowledge of Molly Malony.'

'And the method?'

'Frank Shackleton, so often a guest of Sir Arthur's, must have discovered the second key to the safe hidden in the bookshelves. Perhaps it was accident, perhaps persistence. No doubt he saw Sir Arthur checking it one night. Shackleton had all day, after Sir Arthur left for Dublin Castle, in which to take that second key from the bookshelf to Sackville Street, have an impression cut, wrap the impression and slip it into the binding, keeping the genuine key for himself. That was probably done months ago. There was not the least danger of discovery. If Sir Arthur had ever examined the key closely and felt suspicious, he need only try it in the lock of the safe. It would have worked. But why should he? Each night, he felt a key wrapped in the binding of the book and was content.'

'So much for the key to the safe. And the strong-room?'

Holmes smiled. 'Shackleton was Dublin Herald. Nothing more natural than that he should visit the Office of Arms when he was staying with Sir Arthur. If Stivey was out of his office, Shackleton knew from experience where the strong-room key was hidden in the messenger's desk. He could open the strong-room and, even if Stivey came back, there would be nothing sinister in the Dublin Herald having gone into the strong-room to consult a volume of genealogy. The other strong-room key that was kept in the room itself had not been used for a year. Probably it was never looked at. Shackleton could safely pocket it, take it to Sackville Street, have a copy made, return the copy to the wrapping in the strong-room drawer and keep the original for himself. He now had the original keys to both strong-room and safe. He needed only a key to the door of the building. But that was a quite ordinary Yale. You recall he borrowed Sir Arthur's key to collect his letters? A copy would have been the easiest thing in the world to obtain. It could have been cut for him in a few minutes while he was on his way to collect his letters from the Bedford Tower.'

'And the door key that Sir Arthur mislaid for several days? And the fact that Mrs Farrell found the door to the Bedford Tower open several days before the theft?'

Holmes shrugged. 'Who knows? Perhaps Sir Arthur genuinely mislaid it. Perhaps it was stolen and copied then. It is of the highest importance in the art of detection to be able to recognise, out of a number of facts, which are incidental and which are vital. The mislaid key and the fact that the door to the tower was found open may be accident or coincidence. I am inclined to regard it as a coincidence but no matter. What signifies most is that our thief now had keys to open the main door, the safe, and the strong-room without leaving a single scratch on the mirrors of either the Ratner or the Milner lock. The most difficult part was no longer the robbery but returning the genuine keys of the safe and the strong-room to their proper places.'

'Yet it was done.'

Holmes gazed through the smoke from his pipe.

'The robbery began early, Watson, not during the night. I feel quite sure that when Detective Officer Kerr made his rounds at seven thirty that Friday evening, the thief was already there, locked in the strong-room. Kerr could not open that door and would not know of the intruder. When Kerr left, the thief let himself out and—if he had not already done so—emptied the safe of its jewels. He locked the safe. Then came the most important moment.'

'The key?'

'The genuine key to the safe must be returned to Sir Arthur's bookcase. The thief had a confederate. Molly Malony, I daresay. Perhaps she was with him in the building; more likely she was waiting outside. She slipped out with the key or, probably, she was already outside the tower. In that case he had only to drop it out through the letter-flap or a window. All you would see is a girl passing by, kneeling a moment to adjust the strap of her boot. A little later the key was in its proper place in the bookshelf at St James's Terrace.'

'What of the strong-room?'

'After the thief had emptied the safe, he waited until it was safely dark. About ten P.M. perhaps. He could then slip out of the door of the Bedford Tower into the shadows of the portico without being noticed. But when he left, there was one thing he could not do. One slight imperfection in a perfect plan. He must leave the genuine key to the strong-room wrapped in a drawer of the strong-room itself. He could not lock the strong-room door unless he used the duplicate key that had been cut. But that would scratch the mirrors of the lock. It would spoil the scheme by which all the evidence points to Sir Arthur. And so he chose to leave the strong-room door unlocked, as Mrs Farrell found it a few hours later on Saturday morning. With his carpet-bag in his hand, he let himself out into the shadows and slipped away. The duplicate keys were destroyed and there is an end of the matter. The original keys are all in their proper places once more and it seems that only Sir Arthur Vicars can have been the thief.'

'One thing remains,' I said quickly. 'It cannot be Shackleton. Who, then, is the thief?'

To my discomfiture, Holmes began to laugh, as if in sheer enjoyment of the tale he was telling.

'I think, Watson,' he said at last, 'it is as well that I have never tried on you my powers as a clairvoyant!'

X

'You?' The whole thing seemed preposterous. 'The message from the clairvoyante about the jewels in a graveyard? It was you who caused that to be sent?'

He was intent for a moment on recharging his pipe with coarse black tobacco.

'It was I, Watson,' he said with a sigh. 'Oh, I never doubted that Shackleton was the rogue but there was not a shred of evidence against him. If he was not in Dublin, he could not have taken the jewels himself. Therefore he had a confederate. But how to find that confederate among so many tens of thousands?' He put down his pipe. 'Imagine yourself in Shackleton's position. You have played your part. You suppose that the jewels are in the hands of your accomplice. But then you hear, or read in the newspapers, that they are to be found discarded in a graveyard. Worse still, you hear that the authorities are directed to Hadley Street, which you know to be the lodging of a young woman who assisted in the crime by seducing Ulster King of Arms. What will you do?'

I looked at Holmes. He lowered his eyelids and regarded me as a cat might study a mouse.

'I should want to know what the blazes was going on,' I said emphatically. 'But I should keep well clear of Dublin. I suppose I should send a letter—or better still a telegram. But if things are as bad as they seem, I should simply tell my confederate to bolt.'

His eyes opened and he beamed at me.

'Excellent, Watson! What a capital fellow you are.'

'I should tell him to bolt and lose no time about it, taking the young woman with him if need be.'

'Of course you would, Watson. I confess that when our friends at Scotland Yard convinced themselves that Shackleton could not be the thief, I took to watching him myself. I decided I would flush the game from cover. So I became the clairvoyante who wrote to say that her daughter, in a dream, had seen the jewels in a graveyard. I became the informer who wrote to direct Kane's attention to Hadley Street. I knew he would not find the jewels. But Shackleton would have been superhuman had he kept silent while such commotions were going on. My *pièce de résistance* was in knowing Sir Patrick Coll, a former law officer of the Crown. He and Shackleton belong to the same club and are known slightly to one another. Sir Patrick obliged me by saying in general conversation with Shackleton present that he had read a report of the jewels being recovered in Dublin.'

He smiled at this and continued.

'On top of the search in Clonsilla graveyard and the visit to Hadley Street, all in a few hours, it was too much for Shackleton to bear. He left Park Lane and walked quickly to the post office in Grosvenor Street. I watched him write his message on the pad of telegraph forms, tear off the page and go to the counter. I pretended to write on the next leaf, tore it off and followed him. He was agitated in the extreme and had therefore pressed hard with the pencil, as I expected he would. Even without dusting over the imprint, his indentation was easy enough to read. It was addressed to Captain Richard Gorges of the Royal Irish Fusiliers at Dublin Castle. It asked him to communicate at once with the sender.'

'Who the devil is Captain Gorges?'

'A greater scoundrel still, Watson, and the thief who worked to Shackleton's orders. My researches tell me that they served in the South African War together in a unit of irregulars. Gorges was a drinker, womaniser, and petty thief. Before the war was over, they drummed him out of the regiment. They did it in the proper style. Every man had a kick at him as he passed.'

'Then how comes he to be in the Royal Irish Fusiliers?'

'By the influence of Frank Shackleton, Dublin Herald. To speak the truth, he is not established in the regiment but serves it as a small-arms instructor. For all his faults, Gorges is a marksman. Who less likely to be stopped by the guard on the gate of Dublin Castle than an officer who passed that way regularly in the course of his duty?'

'Where is he now?'

'Gone, my dear Watson, no doubt with the jewels. Gone before he could receive Shackleton's telegram. Who knows where?'

'And Molly Malony?'

'Our friends in the Sûreté have traced her in Paris. She registered alone at the Hôtel Raspail in the Boulevard Montparnasse, forty-eight hours after the robbery, as Molly Robinson. I imagine she had been paid off.'

'And how is Captain Gorges to be found?'

'By Frank Shackleton,' Holmes said softly. 'Shackleton is in desperate straits. He must soon be revealed as a bankrupt and a man utterly disgraced. I am told that his debt to Cox's Bank in London alone exceeds forty thousand pounds. His business affairs have been gangrened by fraud. Prison is all that awaits him unless he has redeemed his position by robbery. The motive for the theft was as simple as that. Now we must wait. But he will answer, Watson, never fear.'

The fact that Gorges had escaped abroad with the jewels before he could be prevented might have soured Holmes's triumph. He had discovered to the last detail how the jewels were stolen and who had done it. But the evidence was not such as would secure a conviction in a court and the treasure seemed lost for ever. He remained philosophical.

'The jewels were stolen in the first place, Watson, by the British invaders from the tombs of their colonial subjects. At least they have very likely returned to those parts of the world whence they came.'

XI

In order that the story may be concluded, I must look forward a few years after the robbery. In Holmes's scrapbook is a cutting from the *London Mail* for 11 November 1912. It quotes a witness who saw Molly Malony leaving Dublin Castle at the time of the robbery and alleges that Sir Arthur Vicars himself provided the money to put her out of the way in Paris, as the scandal broke. For this last allegation, Sir Arthur recovered libel damages.

What of Frank Shackleton? For a year or two his fortunes improved surprisingly. He maintained a lavish *ménage* in Park Lane between the mansions of the Attorney-General, Sir Rufus Isaacs, and Lady Grosvenor. A few months after the robbery, he acquired a most expensive limousine for the sum of £850. Though he was the embarrassment of his brother, Sir Ernest, and the despair of his father, old Dr Shackleton, the law could not touch him. I did not doubt for one moment that he lived upon money remitted to him by the mysterious Captain Gorges, who was then disposing of the stolen gems in the secret markets of Africa or Asia.

But then the remittance of funds ceased. Shackleton returned to his old ways as a swindler. In desperation, he launched a succession of bogus companies, intending to fleece dupes, who were in many cases his wealthy friends. One after another, enterprises that existed on paper alone came to market. They gathered in the investors' funds, and failed. The Montevideo Public Works Corporation was followed by the North Mexican Land and Timber Company. This undertaking, upon its inevitable bankruptcy, was quickly succeeded by a series of Shackleton's commercial fictions.

As the storm broke about him, Frank Shackleton fled to Portuguese West Africa, beyond the reach of English law. From time to time, Holmes heard reports and complaints of Shackleton's conduct in Africa and Asia, usually in the safety of Portuguese colonies and enclaves. For all their chicanery, neither he nor Captain Gorges had the least aptitude for business or for dealing in gems. They themselves were robbed by more accomplished cheats among local traders and they had no grounds on which they dared to complain.

At length, Frank Shackleton fell foul of the laws of the Portuguese colonies and was held without trial in a festering gaol in Benguela. The conditions of this squalid and disease-ridden African prison were so atrocious that he volunteered to surrender himself to officers from Scotland Yard, if they would only take him back to England. To Inspector Cooper, who was sent to arrest him for fraud, he said, 'I will do anything to get out of this place. If I have to remain here much longer, I am sure I shall be dead.'

By the time that he stood his trial at the Central Criminal Court, Shackleton had no money and no jewels. He went to a long term in prison for fraud, having cheated his dupes of £84,000. Though there was still too little evidence to charge him with complicity in the jewel robbery, justice had him in her clutches. Though it is a platitude, he left prison many years later, a broken and dying man.

Captain Gorges, however, was to have a brief notoriety. As war threatened Europe, he slipped unnoticed into Ireland and then to England. Holmes had not the least doubt that, somewhere, Captain Gorges came face to face with Sir Arthur's nephew, young Peirce Mahony. I daresay by now Mahony had guessed the truth and threatened to unmask the scoundrel. Before he could do so, Mahony was found floating in the lake at Grange Con, his chest blasted open by the barrels of his own gun. That it was murder, rather than accident, was not proved.

Unknown to any of us and under an assumed name, Captain Gorges came to London, where he lodged with a professional boxer, Charles Thoroughgood, at Mount Vernon, Hampstead. Information had reached Special Branch independently that the house was an arsenal for the gunmen of Sinn Fein, for whom Gorges now acted as quartermaster. Two officers entered the house and searched it while it was unoccupied. They found only a revolver and two hundred rounds of ammunition.

That evening, after Gorges had returned to his basement room, the house was surrounded. The wanted man appeared on the area steps with his hands behind him. As the officers closed in and one of them seized him, it was evident that he was holding a gun behind his back. The first man, Sergeant Askew, struggled with him. During the scuffle, the gun went off and by an unhappy fluke shot dead Detective Constable Alfred Young, who was coming down the steps to assist his colleague.

Richard Gorges was taken to Cannon Row police station and charged with manslaughter, for which he later served twelve years' penal servitude. As the charge sheet was filled in, he said pathetically, 'Don't call me "Captain", for the honour of the regiment.'

No more than Shackleton would Gorges say what had become in the end of the Irish Crown Jewels. Those who knew no better assumed that Sir Arthur Vicars, the only man to possess the keys to the safe and the strong-room, had been the thief. He was dismissed from his post, though not for the theft. Later he paid with his life because a party of looters believed, as did others, that he had been the thief and that the treasure must still be in his strong-room at Kilmorna.

What of the stolen jewels? Their story was the strangest of all. There was no doubt that the thieves had sold them on the underworld market as best they could, though being cheated themselves in the process. Then, when the old King died in 1910 and preparations were made for the coronation of the present sovereign George V, a strange report began to circulate among those who would be first to hear such things. The jewels, or as many of them as could be found, had been 'ransomed'. The money had been paid by Baron William James Pirrie, Chairman of Harland and Wolff shipyards in Belfast. The story appeared only once in the press and was instantly denied on all sides. Great persuasion was used upon other editors to prevent its republication.

It was Sherlock Holmes, after all, who solved the mystery. I returned to his rooms in Baker Street one afternoon, not long after the coronation of George V and Queen Mary. Holmes had a picture paper spread on the table with several photographs beside it. It was not usual for him to take much notice of picture papers and more unusual for him to read Mr Bottomley's effusions in *John Bull*.

He had a magnifying-glass in his hand and was studying minutely the photographs of the royal couple and the princes and princesses. The article asserted that the Dublin jewels were once again in the possession of the royal family, having been sought and purchased from those who had them after Shackleton and Gorges lost them. Few men in England could rival Holmes in the particular knowledge of mineralogy required to identify precious stones.

'Even when they are recut, Watson, their shape cannot be entirely altered. A stone may only be cut along certain lines, as a triangle must always have three sides.'

He gazed again through the glass at the photograph of Queen Mary in the magazine and then at the photographic print on the table beside him.

'See here, Watson. If you will look at the stones in the Star of St Patrick, as I have marked them there, and the tiara of our gracious Queen there, I see no room for doubt. The jewellers have worked with the utmost discretion. The stones have been reset in new stars and badges for the new reign. After all, in the present political situation, it is hardly likely that His Majesty will require a set of Crown Jewels in Ireland much longer.'

Though I yield to no one in my estimation of Sherlock Holmes's forensic skills, I could not quite bring myself to believe him. Surely, the recovery of the Irish jewels would have been accompanied by some triumphal announcement. Surely he was mistaken. Surely sovereigns and governments do not deal in the dark like this. How wrong I was!

As I now look at his papers, I see a copy of a Home Office file, with the number 156, 610/16. By the time this account is published, the curious will be able to consult the document for themselves in the record office. It confirms that the Badge of the Order of St Patrick had survived intact, come into the hands of Sir Arthur Vicars, and had been returned to the King. The document was stamped, 'Most Secret'. Whether Lord Pirrie had paid a ransom and returned the jewels through the good offices of Sir Arthur, I cannot say. That some benefactor had done so, albeit anonymously, I could not doubt.

When I first read this secret file, not long after the death of Sherlock Holmes, I wondered why it should have been passed to him by the Home Office. After all, his name appeared nowhere in it. Why should it concern him? But, as I thought the matter over, I knew I had done my friend an injustice.

That afternoon many years before, he stood over the picture papers magnifying-glass in hand. He was so sure that Queen Mary's tiara, made for the coronation celebrations of 1911, contained lost gems of the Order of St Patrick. Could any man, however expert, be so certain of that when he had seen only a newspaper photograph? Perhaps, after all, even skill in mineralogy was not enough. Lord Pirrie may or may not have provided the ransom, that I cannot tell. But who more likely to have been the government's intermediary in those shadowy negotiations for the recovery of the precious stones than Sherlock Holmes himself? Who but government or monarchy would have the wealth to buy such a collection?

Of course Holmes had said nothing of all this. It was his usual habit, when the monarch was concerned in one of the investigations, to maintain a complete silence, even to me. But I swear that Holmes knew that King George and Queen Mary were in possession of the gems again long before he saw Mr Bottomley's picture paper! Alas, by the time I read the Home Office file on the subject, my friend was dead and I could not ask him.

As we sat in the firelight, on that evening long ago, I recall saying, 'So Shackleton and Gorges have escaped justice?'

He flung himself down in his chair and filled his pipe.

'I do not think they would agree with you upon that, Watson. A man who is in prison suffers. What more is there? He may commit two crimes but he cannot suffer twice at the same time. Those men are ruined beyond redemption and that is enough.'

He stared at the fire for a moment.

'All the same,' I protested, 'you seem to take the robbery rather lightly, for such a crime. Indeed, I find that you have never suggested that the theft itself was of great moral consequence.'

Holmes stared at the dancing flames.

'Perhaps I remember that there was another robbery, long before.'

'A theft of the jewels?'

He looked up at me. 'Of course, Watson. These were the holy treasures of the royal tombs at Golconda and elsewhere. Our imperial commanders ransacked those shrines to provide gew-gaws for the Kings and Queens of England. Theft compounded by sacrilege. A far worse crime, my dear fellow, than anything that Shackleton or Gorges could devise. If our sovereign or his subjects choose to buy back these stones from the very countries to whom they first belonged, so be it. I daresay the treasure could not safely go back to Golconda now. But if England took them without giving a single penny on the first occasion, I see no objection to her paying a fair price on the second. I call that true justice, my dear fellow. Don't you?'

The Case of
the Unseen Hand

I

In that series of events which I call 'The Case of the Unseen Hand', everything appeared to turn against us from the outset. Yet, at its conclusion, Sherlock Holmes enjoyed a private success that was seldom matched in any of his other investigations.

Readers of 'The Golden Pince-Nez', a narrative made public in *The Return of Sherlock Holmes*, may recall my reference to the earlier triumph of the great detective in tracking and arresting Huret, the so-called 'Boulevard Assassin' of Paris, in 1894. Holmes was rewarded for his services with a handwritten letter from the President of France and by the Order of the Legion of Honour. The presidential letter was written in January 1895 by Félix Faure, who had just then succeeded to the leadership of his country at a most difficult moment, following the assassination of President Carnot and a few months of unhappy tenure by Casimir-Périer.

Holmes had a natural sympathy for Félix Faure, as a man who had risen from humble circumstances to the highest position in France. It was unfortunate for Monsieur Faure, however, that a month before he assumed office, Captain Alfred Dreyfus, a young probationary officer of the French General Staff, had been condemned by court martial to life imprisonment in the steaming and unbroken heat of Devil's Island for betraying his country's military secrets to Germany. In the aftermath of the trial there were rioting crowds in the streets of Paris, demanding the execution of Dreyfus. The President himself was attacked in public and spat upon for his leniency. The mob threatened death to any man courageous enough to doubt the guilt of 'the traitor'. Dreyfus was first 'degraded' on the parade ground of the École Militaire and then transported to that infamous penal colony off the French Guianan coast of South America. He was confined to a tiny stone hut, day and night, in the breathless heat of Cayenne Île du Diable. Though escape was impossible from such a place, his ankles were locked in double irons attached to a bar across the foot of his cot. His true punishment was not imprisonment for life but death by slow torture. A firing-squad would have been a more humane sentence.

The facts alleged against Alfred Dreyfus were that he had sold his country's secrets to Colonel Max von Schwartzkoppen, Military Attaché at the German Embassy in Paris. The court martial was held *in camera* but the details of the accusations were public knowledge. The paper, which his prosecutors insisted was in the hand of Dreyfus, conveyed to Colonel Schwartzkoppen specifications of the new and highly secret 120 mm gun, its performance and deployment; the reorganisation plan of the French Artillery, and the Field Artillery Firing Manual. Only an officer of the General Staff could have held such information.

Sherlock Holmes, like Émile Zola and a host of impartial men and women, never believed in the guilt of Captain Dreyfus. My friend's skill in graphology convinced him that the handwriting on the letter to Colonel Schwartzkoppen was not that of Alfred Dreyfus but, perhaps, a half-successful attempt at imitation. Like Monsieur Zola, Holmes also deplored the bigotry of the prosecution, the whole manner of the court martial and condemnation. Years later, our *Dreyfusards* were proved right. Colonel Hubert Henry of the Deuxième Bureau and Lemercier-Picard, who had both forged further 'evidence' to deepen the guilt of Dreyfus after his condemnation, committed suicide.

In the years that followed our adventure, the innocence of Dreyfus and the guilt of a certain Major Count Ferdinand Walsin-Esterhazy were to be established. Restored to his command, as a gallant officer of the Great War, Captain Dreyfus was to join Sherlock Holmes as a Chevalier of the Legion of Honour. The manner in which justice was done at last forms the background to my account of our own case.

II

In January 1899, when the presidency of Félix Faure and the imprisonment of Captain Dreyfus had already lasted for four years, Holmes and I travelled to Paris on behalf of the British government. Our confidential mission, which had been warmly supported by our friend Lestrade at Scotland Yard, was to meet the great Bertillon. Alphonse Bertillon was a former professor of anthropology, now head of the Identification Bureau at the Préfecture de Police. The 'Bertillon System' had enabled the French police to identify a man or woman uniquely by measuring certain bony structures of the body, notably those of the head. It was claimed in Paris that these measurements would render all criminal disguises and false identities futile. The objection at Scotland Yard was that such a system was far too complicated for general use. In England, Sherlock Holmes and Sir Francis Galton had been working upon the simpler method of identification by fingerprints, which Bertillon had also pioneered. They had been set upon the task by Mr Asquith, as Home Secretary in 1893. At first their opponents argued that no jury would be persuaded to convict a defendant upon such a whimsical theory. Twelve years later, however, the Stratton brothers were to be hanged for the Deptford Street murder on the evidence of a single thumbprint.

When we set off for Paris in January 1899, it was our mission to persuade Professor Bertillon to join his efforts with ours in championing this simpler method of criminal detection. One of Bertillon's original objections had been that a great many surfaces retain no visible fingerprint. Holmes had answered this when he devised in our Baker Street rooms a system for making these unseen or 'latent' fingerprints visible, by the use of silver nitrate powder or iodine fumes. Bertillon then demanded of him how such evidence was to be displayed in court. In reply, Holmes had painstakingly adapted a small Kodak camera by adding an open box to the front, so that the lens always looked down on the fingerprint from a uniform distance and was therefore permanently in focus. By this means, any number of photographs of a fingerprint might be made for a criminal trial. He had brought his prototype of the camera to display to the great French criminologist. All the same, there was no sign as yet that such advances would persuade Professor Bertillon to change his mind.

On a chill but windless January day, we crossed from Folkestone to Boulogne by the *Lord Warden* steamer. Holmes stood at the ship's rail, his sharp profile framed by his ear-flapped travelling-cap. As soon as we cast off from Folkestone harbour pier, it seemed that his interest in his French adversary underwent a significant change. Fingerprints and skull measurements were discarded from our conversation. He unfolded a sheet of paper and handed it to me.

'The affair of Captain Dreyfus, Watson. Read this. It is a private note from my disgraced friend Colonel Picquart, late of the Information Branch of the Deuxième Bureau. Even in this matter it seems that we cannot escape the shade of Bertillon. Picquart tells me that the professor is immoveable, convinced that the incriminating letter of 1894 is in the hand of Captain Dreyfus. For a man of Bertillon's capability to believe such a thing is quite beyond my comprehension. Unfortunately, however, his reputation as a criminal expert will count for far more in a courtroom than all Monsieur Zola's denunciations of injustice.'

He shook his head and gave a quiet sigh, staring across the Channel. The sea lay calm as wrinkled satin towards the sands of France, pale and chill on the horizon of that winter afternoon.

'Then what will you do?' I asked, handing back to him the sheet of paper.

'I shall pray, Watson. Not for a miracle—merely for an opportunity to demonstrate to Professor Bertillon the error of his methods in graphology and identification alike. There is a battle to be fought and won for Captain Dreyfus but it must be fought at the right time and in the right place.'

During the next few weeks our Baker Street quarters were exchanged for two bedrooms and a sitting-room at the Hôtel Lutétia in the Boulevard Raspail. It was an area of business and bustle, having more in common with the nearby railway terminus of the Gare Montparnasse than with the bohemian society of poets and artists which the name of that district more often suggests. The Hôtel Lutétia rose like the hull of an ocean liner above a quayside in this commercial avenue of tall houses with their grey mansard roofs, their elegant windows and balconies set in pale tide-washed stone. In front of many a grander building, a handsome *porte-cochère* entrance remained. Yet the days of Second Empire quiet had gone. As afternoon drew on, the winter sun threw up a dusty light from the constant traffic.

I was not present at the private discussions between Holmes and Professor Bertillon, which were concluded in a day or two. In truth, there was little to discuss so long as the two men remained immoveable. The silver nitrate, the iodine fumes, the special camera, were mere toys in Bertillon's view. To make matters worse, a further hostility arose in general conversation when the professor repeated his view that the incriminating message of 1894 to the German Military Attaché was written in the hand of Captain Dreyfus. The first day's meeting ended with ill temper on both sides. Next morning Bertillon returned to the debate over scientific detection, insisting that fingerprints might be disfigured or erased, or even prevented by the wearing of gloves. They were no substitute for the measurement of criminal heads, where counterfeiting was an impossibility. With that, he indicated that his exchange of views with his English visitor was at an end. Holmes returned from the Préfecture de Police in a filthy temper, his vanity bruised, and his appetite for battle with the French anthropologist all the keener. I could not help thinking—though I judged it best not to say so at the time—that the sooner we returned to Baker Street, the better.

I had begun to look forward to our return and was already picturing myself among the comforts of home, when I heard my companion in the lobby of the hotel, informing the manager that we should require our rooms for at least another fortnight.

'But why?' I demanded, as soon as we were alone.

'Because, Watson, an innocent man is condemned to suffer the nightmare of Devil's Island until he drops dead from exhaustion or the brutality of the regime. Bertillon, the one expert whose word might yet save him, refuses to say that word. As it happens, he also rejects, unexamined, the only infallible method of criminal identification upon which others have lavished years of toil. I do not greatly care for Alphonse Bertillon. I swear to you that these two issues may yet become a personal matter between us.'

'For God's sake, Holmes! You cannot fight a duel with the head of a French police bureau!'

'In my own way, Watson, that is just what I propose to do.'

After so much bluster, as I thought it, Holmes became inexplicably a pattern of idleness. So much for his threats against Professor Bertillon! Like a man who feels that the best of life is behind him, he began to describe our visit to Paris as a chance that 'might not come again'. Yet I could not believe that it was some premonition of mortality that determined him to spend two or three weeks longer in the city. More probably it was his usual mode of life, in which he alternated between intense periods of obsessional activity—when he would sleep little and eat less—and weeks when he seemed to do little more than stare from his armchair at the sky beyond the window, without a thought in his head.

The indolence that came upon him now was not quite of the usual sort. He tasted something of bohemian café society at the Closerie des Lilas with its trees and its statue of Marshal Ney. He spent an entire day reading the icy tombstones of Montparnasse cemetery, as he was to do next day at Père Lachaise. For the most part, we walked the cold streets and parks as we had never done in any other city.

A frosty morning was our time for the tree-lined vista of the Avenue de la Grande Armée, the lakes and woods of the Bois de Boulogne extending before us in a chill mist. Down the wide thoroughfare, the closed carriages of fashionable society rattled on frozen cobbles. The shrubbery gardens of the adjacent mansions lay silent and crisp beyond the snowcaps of tall wrought-iron railings.

'My dear Holmes,' I said that evening, 'it is surely better that we should go our separate ways for a little. There is no purpose in our remaining longer in Paris. At least, there is no purpose for me. Let me return to London and attend to business there. You may stay here and follow when you think the time is right. There can be no use in both of us remaining.'

'Oh, yes, Watson,' he said quietly, 'there is the greatest use in the world. It will require us both, of that I am sure.'

'May I know what the use is?'

'The question cannot be pressed,' he said vaguely. 'The purpose must mature in its own time.'

It matured at a snail's pace, as it seemed to me, for almost a week. During those days our morning rambles now took us through the red revolutionary *arrondissements* of the north-east. We crossed the little footbridges of the Canal Saint-Martin. Holmes studied the sidings and marshalling-yards of Aubervilliers with the rapt attention that other visitors might give to the *Mona Lisa* in the Louvre. A late sun of the winter morning rose like a red ball through the mist across the heroic distance of the Place de la République, where the statue of Marianne stands like a towering Amazon protecting the booths and shooting galleries. By evening we were in the wide lamplit spaces of the Place de la Concorde, the tall slate roofs of the Quai d'Orsay rising through a thin river mist on the far bank.

Five days passed in this manner, as if Holmes were mapping the city in his head, noting the alleys, culs-de-sac, escape routes, and short cuts. That evening, there were footsteps on the stairs. At the door of our rooms, there appeared briefly and dimly a visitor who brought an envelope of discreet and expensive design with the gold initials 'RF' interwoven. Holmes read the contents but said nothing.

Next morning, he came from his room in a costume more bizarre than any of his disguises as a tramp or a Lascar seaman. He was wearing the black swallow-tailed coat and white tie of court dress. Before I could ask what the devil this meant, there was a discreet tap at the door and our visitor of the previous evening reappeared, now similarly attired in formal dress. I caught a murmured exchange and the newcomer twice used the form of 'Monsieur le Président', when indicating that time pressed. Holmes accompanied him without a word. I turned to the window and saw them enter a closed carriage, its black coachwork immaculately polished but without a single crest or other emblem to indicate its origins. I could only suppose it was for this summons that Holmes had been waiting while we walked the streets of Paris.

III

In the hours that passed before I saw him again, I no longer doubted that the 'purpose' of our visit was working itself out. Holmes had used his influence, the Order of the Legion of Honour, as well as the reputation of a man who had rid Paris of the Boulevard Assassin, to obtain an audience with President Faure. The intention could only be to convince Félix Faure that Captain Dreyfus was no traitor and that the letter sent to Colonel Schwartzkoppen, the Military Attaché, would be shown on scientific examination to be the work of another hand.

It was late in the afternoon when my companion returned. He knew as well as I that there was no need for an explanation of his absence. He stood in the sitting-room of the hotel suite, a familiar figure in the unfamiliarity of his formal costume.

'Your patience may be rewarded, Watson,' he said with the quick movement of his mouth, which was sometimes a smile and sometimes a nervous quirk, 'I have put our case to President Faure.'

'Our case?'

He smiled more easily. 'Very well, then, the case of Alfred Dreyfus. The matter of the handwriting. We have, I believe, a chance to vanquish Professor Bertillon on both fronts. Who knows? If we succeed in this, there may be a path to victory over him in other matters. I have struck a bargain with Félix Faure. The evidence against Dreyfus will be reviewed. Indeed, though he still thinks the man guilty, in all probability, he has not set his face against a retrial.'

'Then you have succeeded?' I asked the question because, to anyone who had known him for a length of time, it was evident that Holmes was holding back some unwelcome detail.

'Not quite,' he said, another nervous movement plucking at his mouth, 'I fear, Watson, you will not like our side of the bargain. We are to remain in Paris for a few more months.'

'Months! What the devil for?'

'That, my dear friend, will be explained to you within the hour by President Faure's confidential secretary. It is not too much to say that the fate of France and the peace of Europe may depend upon the safety of the treasure we are to guard.'

'Treasure!' I exclaimed. 'What treasure?'

But Holmes waved his hand aside, recommending patience. He turned and went to his room, exchanging formal clothes for familiar tweeds and Norfolk jacket. Short of pursuing him and standing over him while he changed, there was little I could do. I walked about the tall corniced sitting-room on the first floor of the Hôtel Lutétia, folding a paper here and tidying a table there, in anticipation of a visit from the confidential secretary of the President of the Republic. Then I paused and stared down into the Boulevard Raspail with its busy traffic from the suburbs and markets. Would Félix Faure's confidential secretary really make a habit of visiting confidants in what was almost a public room? I thought of Sir Henry Ponsonby and Sir Arthur Bigge as Her Majesty's private secretaries, conducting confidential negotiations in the hotels of Bayswater or Pimlico. The idea was plainly absurd.

This was one of the rare occasions when I suspected that Holmes, on unfamiliar territory, was out of his depth. He had just reappeared in his tweed suiting, when there was a knock at the door. It was a hotel pageboy who had brought our visitor from the lobby. The stranger entered the sitting-room. As the page closed the door again, Holmes bowed, took the hand of the President's confidential secretary, and kissed it with instinctive gallantry. This newcomer was not the type of Sir Henry Ponsonby nor Sir Arthur Bigge, but one of the most striking young women upon whom I had ever set eyes.

IV

She might have been eighteen, though the truth was that she was thirty and already had a daughter who was ten years old. Yet there was such a soft round beauty in her face, a depth to her wide eyes, and a lustre in the elegant coiffure of her dark hair that she reminded one irresistibly of a London *débutante* in her first season. To describe her figure as elegant, narrow-waisted, and instinctively graceful in every movement is to resort to the commonplaces of portraiture. Yet Marguerite Steinheil was possessed of all these attributes and was never commonplace.

Such was Félix Faure's confidential secretary. Though I was struck by her beauty, even her modesty of demeanour on this occasion, the thought that preoccupied me was that no English politician's reputation could have withstood such an association with a young woman of so remarkable a presence as hers.

'Watson!' Holmes turned to me with a look of triumph. 'Let me introduce to you Madame Marguerite Steinheil, the emissary of President Faure. Madame, allow me to present my colleague, Dr John Watson, before whom you may speak as freely as to myself.'

Somehow, I scarcely recall how, I mumbled my way through the pleasantries of formal introduction in the next few minutes. If

I had thought before this that Sherlock Holmes had plunged into the Dreyfus affair beyond his depth, I was now utterly convinced of it. Madame Steinheil took her place on the chaise-longue, Holmes and I facing her from two upright gilded chairs. She spoke almost perfect English with an accent so light that it added to the charm of her voice.

'I believe,' she said, 'that I may soon be able to bring you good news of Captain Dreyfus, of whose innocence I have never myself entertained the least doubt. However, I may only help him, or help you, if you will assist me in return.'

'Then you must explain that, madame,' Holmes said quietly. 'I believe it is the President whom we are to serve, is it not?'

She smiled quickly at him and said, 'It is the same thing, Mr Holmes. More than four years ago, I became his friend because of his interest in art. My husband, Adolphe Steinheil, is a portrait painter. Our drawing-room has long been a meeting-place for men and women from literature, art, music, and public life. We have a house and a studio in the Impasse Ronsin, off the Rue de Vaugirard, near the Gare Montparnasse. Félix Faure was a guest at my *salons*, a friend before he became President. After his election, he bought one of Adolphe's paintings for the private rooms in the Élysée Palace. He is the President but he is also the greatest friend in the world to me. I must make this confidence to you. My own father is dead but Félix Faure has been, in his way, a father to me and I, perhaps, like a daughter to him.'

The more I heard of this, the less I liked it. I saw that Holmes's mouth tightened a little.

'Forgive me, Madame Steinheil, but you are not—are you?—a daughter. You are a confidential secretary and you will betray your trust if you seek to be anything more.'

She put her hands together and stared down at them. Then she looked up with the same smile, the same openness of her face and gaze, that would have softened any accusation in the world.

'Mr Holmes,' she said quietly, 'I need not tell you that the Third Republic of France was born from war and revolutionary bloodshed almost thirty years ago. Since then, there has been scandal, riot, and assassination. In England, I think, you have not known such things. Were you to see the secret papers of the past thirty years in our own country, you would be more deeply troubled still and perhaps a good deal more shocked than you have been even by the affair of Captain Dreyfus. These papers of which I speak are known to very few people. Naturally, they have been seen by fewer people still.'

'Of whom you are doubtless one, madame!'

The cold precision of his voice was a harsh contrast to the softer tones of Marguerite Steinheil. Yet she was a match for him.

'Of whom I am one,' she said, inclining her head. 'Since the President came to office, he has suffered abuse in the Chamber of Deputies, he has been physically attacked in public and spat at. Lesser men would have resigned the office, as his predecessor did, and France would go down in civil war. But he will not resign, Mr Holmes. He will fight. In order to fight, he must have a weapon. The pen, as you say, will prove mightier than the sword.'

'If it is used with discretion,' Holmes said gently.

She smiled again and then dropped her voice a little, as if fearing that even now she might be overheard.

'For the past three years, Félix Faure has been engaged upon his secret history of France since the Franco-Prussian War of 1870. It is to be his testament, his justification of steps that he must take, before the end of his *septennat*—his period of office.'

'And you, madame?' Holmes inquired coolly. 'What are you to him in such a crisis?'

There was no smile as she looked at him now.

'What am I in all this? Félix Faure saw in me a friend who would offer an undivided loyalty, a loyalty that is not to be found among the ministers and officials surrounding him. You have not lived in France during the past ten years, Mr Holmes. From your well-ordered life in London, it is hard to imagine the scandal and near-revolution that plagues this city.'

'One may deduce a little, even in London.'

'No,' she said, and shook her head with a whisper of disagreement, 'Félix Faure was called to office among the mortal injuries which France seemed determined to inflict on herself. The Boulangists would overthrow republicanism and restore the monarchy. The Anarchists would plunge us in blood. We had watched the *bourse*—the stock exchange—and the Quai d'Orsay brought to near-ruin by the Panama corruption scandals and the disappearance of two hundred and fifty million francs. We had seen governments created in hope, only to collapse in dishonour after a few months. Six months before my friend was called to the highest office, President Carnot himself was stabbed to death at Lyons by a terrorist. President Casimir-Périer was driven from office by libel and ridicule within a few weeks. During those weeks came the Dreyfus affair.'

Holmes was about to say something but seemed to think better of it.

'I watched that man's epaulettes torn from his tunic,' the young woman continued softly, 'on the parade ground of the École Militaire, his sword broken over the adjutant's knee. Mobs shouted for his death in the riots that followed. France had degenerated into such chaos that government itself seemed impossible. In our relations with the world, we had drifted from our alliance with Russia and were close to war with England over Fashoda and the Sudan. Félix Faure tried without success to persuade his ministers that a *rapprochement* with England and Russia was our sole salvation abroad. He failed to move them. How could he succeed when, as the secret papers confirm, his closest adviser in foreign affairs was a man whose mistress had for years been in the pay of the German Embassy? Four months ago, in October, matters were so grave that Monsieur Faure considered carrying out a military *coup d'état* as President, taking absolute power to impose order on the country by martial law.'

'And you, madame?' Holmes still pressed for an answer to the most important question of all. 'What were you to Félix Faure?'

'I was his eyes and ears throughout all this, as well as his amanuensis. I went privately to sittings of the Chamber of Deputies and the Senate, to certain receptions and parties. He is surrounded by enemies in government and now he knows it, through me. I was better able to identify certain men who might have destroyed him, had they been appointed to office. They are, Mr Holmes, without scruples or principles under their masks of public virtue. They are *arrivistes* ready to sell themselves to achieve their ambitions.'

Sherlock Holmes held her gaze dispassionately.

'As a woman, however, you were surely in greater danger of being compromised in your role of adviser than a man would have been?'

If Marguerite Steinheil blushed a little at the innuendo, I saw no sign of it.

'My sex was my advantage. No man is inscrutable to a woman, Mr Holmes, especially when that woman is devoted to one whom she has decided to help, and when she is supposed to care for nothing more essential than music, flowers, or dress.'

'But you do not play quite the same part now, I take it?'

'No,' she said softly. 'The dangers and the threats became so numerous that there could only be one answer—"The Secret History of France under the Third Republic". It is a weapon so powerful that our adversaries dare not provoke its use. Every afternoon, the President adds several pages to it, on foolscap paper which I buy for him myself. At first these pages were locked in an iron box at the Élysée Palace itself. Then, in the crisis of last October, Fèlix Faure asked me to take home the pages as he wrote them. Until this afternoon, three people in the world knew of this precaution: the President and I, of course, and Monsieur Hamard, Chief of the Sûreté, a man of honour to whom Félix Faure would entrust his very life. Dr Watson and yourself must now be admitted to the secret.'

'Then I trust, madame, you will use such a weapon as a shield, not as a sword.'

The young woman smiled at this. 'A shield is all we ask, Mr Holmes. The President's enemies cannot be sure what revelations drawn from the secret papers these chapters may contain. Yet he has taken good care that those from whom he has most to fear are aware of the consequences. If such pages were to be made public, the reputations of those men would be blasted. It would be impossible for them to hold office and they would be fortunate indeed to escape prosecution as common criminals. Perhaps you think such a threat unchivalrous? No doubt it is. I assure you, however, that there is nothing in those pages except what is the proven truth.'

She paused and Holmes said nothing for a moment. He took his pipe from the pocket of his Norfolk tweeds and then replaced it.

'It is on this account that you wish Dr Watson and myself to remain in Paris?'

'Only for a while,' she said gently. 'In a month—two months at the most—enough of the work will be done. A copy will be made and deposited elsewhere, to make the work safe for posterity. Meanwhile, new pages and documents will be taken back each night to a hiding-place in the Impasse Ronsin. In the past weeks, the President has been warned by Monsieur Hamard that visitors to the Élysée Palace are being watched by those who may be agents of foreign powers but more probably of our enemies within France. Some of our visitors are being followed. It would not do for a single page of the history or a single document to fall into the hands of those who would destroy us.'

Holmes spoke courteously but the scepticism in his eyes, as he regarded her, was inescapable to anyone who knew him.

'You have begun well, madame, by ensuring that the manuscript is removed from the Élysée Palace. You must surely have more enemies in that building than in the rest of the world. In a crisis, that is the first place where those whom you fear would search for it. As for the opinion of Monsieur Hamard, he and I have been acquainted ever since the case of the Boulevard Assassin. I hold him in the highest regard. If he warns you of a danger, you would be well advised to take heed.'

'Indeed,' she said, 'it is on Monsieur Hamard's suggestion that I am here this afternoon. Knowing that you were in Paris to confer with his colleague Professor Bertillon, he believed you might be prepared to assist. He advises that, for the future, any papers which

I take with me to the Impasse Ronsin each evening should be a decoy, documents of no importance. The pages of the manuscript itself will be entrusted to you. At a distance, you and Dr Watson will be my escort and courier. When you are satisfied that no one is watching or following, you may deliver the envelope through the letter-box of the Impasse Ronsin.'

Holmes looked unaccountably gloomy.

'Yes,' he said thoughtfully. 'Well, Madame Steinheil, I have had this put to me in similar terms by the President. It is hard for a humble ratepayer of Baker Street to oppose the will of a head of state. However, I shall ask you a question that I might not ask the President. What purpose is served by Dr Watson and myself remaining in Paris to do something that any well-trained policeman might do? Indeed, you might employ a different officer each evening, so that whoever attempted to shadow you would not recognise him. As for the papers, you scarcely need more than a porter to convey your luggage.'

There, I thought, he had tripped her. Marguerite Steinheil looked her prettiest at him.

'A President is surely entitled to ask for the best?'

'No, no, madame!' said Holmes with a flash of irritation. 'That really will not do for an answer!'

She flinched a little. 'Very well, then. Among the papers from which the narrative is drawn—in the pages of the narrative itself—will be found evidence to prove the innocence of Colonel Dreyfus beyond all argument.'

'Then let that evidence be published now,' Holmes said abruptly.

Again she shook her head. 'The man who might put the case beyond any further argument is in Berlin. He has been forbidden from speaking by the Chief of the German General Staff and by the Kaiser himself. If our plan succeeds, they will find in a month or two that they can command him no longer.'

There was a moment's silence. In that comfortable hotel sitting-room on the Boulevard Raspail, we pictured Dreyfus the innocent, the man of honour, riveted in his irons in the jungle mist of Cayenne Île du Diable, condemned to rot until death released him.

'*Fiat justitia, ruat coelum*', Holmes said at last, still with reluctance. 'Let justice be done, though the heavens fall. Madame, you shall have your way. God knows, it is a small enough price that we pay for the poor fellow's liberty.'

After she had taken her leave, he sat without speaking. Then, as he was apt to do when something of great weight was on his mind, he walked to the window and stared out into the street. It was dark by now and the scene was one that might have been painted by Pissarro or Manet. Each flickering gas-lamp threw out a misty halo, its shivering image reflected in pools of rain. The traffic of cabs and horse-buses dwindled from the brightly lit shops of the Rue de Rennes to the quiet elegance of the Boulevard St Germain. Men and women hurried homeward by the darkened skyline of the Luxembourg Gardens.

'So,' he said, turning at last, 'we are to remain here in order to guard a few sheets of paper every evening, to prevent them from being snatched away in the street! Can you believe a word of it, Watson? It reminds me of nothing so much as that other useless occupation, the Red-Headed League, whose history you were good enough to preserve in your memoirs! A man was paid handsomely for the aimless daily exercise of copying out the whole of the *Encyclopaedia Britannica* by hand. A pretty piece of villainy lay behind that!'

I was a little shocked by his tone.

'You do not call Madame Steinheil a villain?'

'Of course I do not!' he said impatiently. 'Wayward, perhaps. She has, I believe, the reputation of what is delicately called, among the fashionables of Rotten Row, a "Pretty Horse-Breaker".'

The vulgar phrase sounded oddly in his fastidious speech.

'Then you believe she has not told us the truth?'

'Not the whole truth! Of course not!' He looked at me in dismay, unable to see how I had missed the fact. 'It does not require the two of us to prevent an envelope being snatched from her hand or to see whether she is followed. She knows that as well as you or I!'

'What else is there to prevent?'

'After all that we have heard from her of *coups d'état* and treason, you still do not see why our services are preferred to those of the Sûreté or the Deuxième Bureau?'

'I do not see what else she hopes we may prevent,' I said with the least feeling of exasperation. 'What is it?'

Sherlock Holmes gave a fatalistic sigh.

'In all probability,' he said softly, 'the assassination of the President of France.'

V

During the next few days, the prediction seemed so preposterous that I had not the heart to remind him of it, even as a joke. Every afternoon, we took the same cab to the same drab stretch of the Rue de Vaugirard with its hospitals and public buildings. In the Impasse Ronsin, the tall house with its studio windows rose beyond a high street-wall and garden trees. As if at a signal, a second cab turned out on to the main thoroughfare and preceded us by way of the Boulevard des Invalides, the elegant span of the Pont Alexandre III, across the River Seine, and past the glass domes of the exhibition pavilions.

Sometimes, when the winter afternoon was sunny, the young woman would dismiss the cab at the river bridge and walk across the wide spaces of evergreen gardens with their regimented trees and little chairs, at the lower end of the Champs Élysées. This was done to give us a better opportunity of seeing whether she was shadowed. From time to time a man might look sidelong at the narrow-waisted beauty, the collar of her coat trimmed with fur that lay more sensuously against the bloom of her cheek, the coquettish hat with its net veil crowning her elegant coiffure. Many wistful and casual glances came in her direction yet no one followed her.

Quickly and unobtrusively, she was admitted by the little gate in the gold-tipped iron railings of the presidential palace, at the corner of the Champs-Élysées and the Avenue de Marigny. Not a soul took the least notice. Several times, on her return, she got down from the cab among the little streets of the Left Bank that run from the *grands quais* of the Seine, opposite the Louvre. In the early dusk, she paused at the shop-fronts of the Rue des Saints Pères in dark green or terracotta or black with gold. Curios and jewellery shone in the lamplit windows. The shelves of the *bibliothèques* glowed with the rich leather bindings of rare editions. Holmes and I knew from long experience that in such territory the hunter easily becomes the prey. The shadow must dawdle or feign interest or linger in his cab, while his quarry visits one shop after another. If there was such a man on these evenings, the trained eye of Sherlock Holmes failed to see him.

On several afternoons, Holmes and I were admitted by the same little gate to the grounds of the Élysée Palace, by the authority of the President's *chef de cabinet*, Monsieur Le Gall. The President's office was on the ground floor of the left wing of the palace, looking out upon a private garden. Beyond the presidential office and the private study, these quiet apartments ended in an elegant bedroom, used by Fèlix Faure on the frequent nights when he worked into the small hours, so that Madame Faure should not be disturbed by his late arrival.

On our occasional visits to Le Gall, neither Holmes nor I was admitted beyond an outer office, where the *chef de cabinet* guarded the entrance to the presidential suite. It was on 16 February that we were last there. Madame Steinheil was a little later than usual, arriving at about 5.30 P.M. to collect the papers that the President had been writing. We were received by Le Gall in his outer office a half-hour later. To that moment, there was no sign of anyone—man nor woman—shadowing the 'confidential secretary' who had been put under our care.

At the time of our arrival, Madame de Steinheil was already in the office or study of the presidential apartment, no doubt copying pages for the use of her patron. The President himself had just finished a conversation with a visitor who came out of the apartments, escorted by a chamberlain, taking his leave almost as soon as we had begun speaking to Le Gall. Even had I not seen his face in the newspaper photographs of the past few days, I should have guessed by his purple cassock and biretta that he was Cardinal Richard, Archbishop of Paris.

The purpose of the Cardinal's visit to the President was never revealed. As soon as His Eminence had left, however, Le Gall ushered Holmes and me to a waiting-room at one side. The door swung to but failed to catch, leaving us with a narrow aperture into the *chef de cabinet's* office. A tall saturnine man in evening dress with a purple sash and the star of a royal order walked slowly past. On the far side of Le Gall's office, another door opened and closed. There was a murmur of voices. Holmes stretched in his arm-chair, took a pencil from his pocket and wrote something in his notebook.

'The Prince of Monaco,' he said quietly. 'This promises well, Watson. My information is that, for several months, His Serene Highness has been the go-between of the President and the Kaiser in the matter of Captain Dreyfus. Berlin is less threatened by the scandal than Paris but it would suit both parties to have the matter settled.'

Shortly after this, Le Gall or one of his assistants must have noticed that the waiting-room door was a little ajar. It was closed from outside, by whose hand we did not see. Whether the Prince of Monaco had left or the interview with the President continued was hidden from us.

In recollecting what followed, I believe it was about three-quarters of an hour that we had been waiting for our summons to escort Madame Steinheil back to the Impasse Ronsin. I was immersed in a Tauchnitz pocket-book and Holmes was reading the evening paper. Not a word passed between us until, without warning, Holmes threw the newspaper down and sprang to his feet.

'What in God's name was that, Watson?'

His face was drawn into an expression that mingled horror and dismay, a fearful look more intense than any other I can remember in the course of our friendship. The look in his eyes and the angle of his head assured me that Holmes, who had the most acute hearing of any man known to me, had caught something beyond my range.

'Do you not hear it, man? You must hear it!'

In two strides he was at the waiting-room door, which he flung open without ceremony. As he did so, I caught the shrill escalating screams of terror which rang through the private apartments of the President of France. They were a woman's screams.

Of Le Gall, there was no sign, though the fine double doors of white and gold that led to the President's office stood open. After so much talk of traitors and assassination, you may imagine what my thoughts were. The screams stopped for an instant, only to be resumed with greater urgency. They were not cries of pain but shrieks of unbridled fear. Perhaps, then, we should be in time to prevent whatever was threatened.

Holmes strode through the presidential office with the red buttoned leather of its chairs and the walnut veneer of the desk. Beyond that, the single door to the private study swung lightly in the draught. The curtains were still open. Outside, in the private garden, thin snow drifted down through the lamplight on to the lawns and formal paths. There was no one in the study itself but the far door opened into a small book-lined lobby. This lobby framed a further pair of doors—again in white and gold—which guarded the boudoir of the presidential suite. Those doors were closed and Le Gall stood facing them, pushing with his arms out and hands spread wide, as if seeking some means to force his way through. The shrieks, which now redoubled, were coming from the bed-room itself. I thought I heard the word 'Assassin!' with its French emphasis and pronunciation.

Holmes pushed the *chef de cabinet* aside, for had we left it to Le Gall he would never have broken open the locked doors. My friend's right foot rose and he crashed the heel of his boot into the ornamental lock. The double doors shuddered but held. Holmes took a pace back and again smashed the heel of his boot into the fastening. One of the two doors burst open and flew back against the inner wall with a crack. Holmes was first through the opening,

Le Gall after him. I brought up the rear with Holmes already calling out, 'Here, Watson! As quickly as ever you can!'

I stood in the doorway and saw before me such a sight as I hope never to see again.

VI

The tangled bodies in their nakedness were like nothing so much as a detail from some canvas depicting a massacre. Fèlix Faure was a well-built man of the heavily handsome type. Approaching sixty years of age, he had a head that was broad and tall, pale blue eyes, and a long moustache. He lay face down, naked as he was born, the gross bulk of him sprawling and slack in a manner that meant only one thing to me. Under him, trapped by his weight, without a shift or a stitch upon her, lay Marguerite Steinheil. There were spots of blood upon her face and shoulders which had come from his nose or mouth.

It was a horrible and yet, in its way, a commonplace tableau to a medical man. The tragedy of an old lover and a young mistress, cerebral congestion, apoplexy occurring in the excitement of some venereal spasm, is a textbook fact that needs no moral commentary here. I reached Fèlix Faure in time to detect a pulse that faded under my touch. In the moment of his seizure, the dying man had clenched his fingers in the young woman's hair, adding to her terror beyond measure. With some caution, I straightened the fingers one by one. Holmes and I turned the dead President on to his back. Le Gall snatched a dressing-gown from the closet and wrapped Madame Steinheil in it. She stood before us, still crying out hysterically, until there was a crack like a pistol as Holmes slapped her across the face.

Le Gall's hand was on the bell.

'No!' shouted Holmes. 'Wait!' Thereupon he took command of the situation while the *chef de cabinet* did his bidding. 'Get this young woman dressed!'

It was easier said than done. Without going to indelicate lengths of description, I can record that Madame Steinheil had been wearing a corset, which few women could put on again without the assistance of a ladies' maid. So it was that she was helped into her outer clothes, the rest being bundled into a valise.

'Touch nothing, Watson, until I get back! Nothing!'

With that, Holmes led the poor trembling courtesan out by a side entrance into the snow. I watched them cross the lawn to the little gate, with Le Gall following. On the *chef de cabinet*'s authority, the private gate at the Avenue de Marigny was opened and Madame Steinheil was put into the cab, which had been previously ordered to wait for her, with directions to the driver to proceed directly to the Impasse Ronsin.

In my friend's absence, I had found a nightshirt in the armoire. Between us, we managed to draw it over the head of the corpse and impart some decency to the mortal remains of the late Félix Faure.

'Monsieur!' Holmes spun round on Le Gall. 'Have the goodness to find a priest. Any priest! The Madeleine will be your nearest church.'

Le Gall was like a man in a stupor.

'No,' he said. 'There is no purpose. The President is dead and formalities must follow their course.'

'Formalities!' Holmes snapped at him, like a man waking a dreamer. 'Do you not see that there is enough scandal in all this to have a revolution on the streets of Paris before tomorrow night? That is where formalities will get you! Find the first priest that you can and tell him President Faure is dying!'

Badly shaken though he was, the *chef de cabinet* went out. In five minutes Holmes and I had drawn the sheets over the body and Félix Faure lay on his back, his head on the pillow and his eyes closed. Holmes paced the room, looking here and there, as if for some lost clue to explain the tragedy. But the explanation lay only in the medical textbooks.

'Here, I think!' he said presently, picking up a small ochre-coloured bottle from the dressing-table. 'What, my friend, do you make of this?'

As he held it before me, I could read only another parable of human frailty and old men's folly. There was little doubt that Félix Faure had taken a philtre of some kind which he hoped would aid his failing powers where women were concerned and which surely was the precipitating cause of his death. I thought, but did not say so, that he might have taken one of the capsules before the visit of the Prince of Monaco interrupted his intentions and had then taken another following it. For a man in his condition, it had been a most dangerous dose. Holmes took a small bag from his pocket and carefully dropped the bottle into it.

'It will not do, Watson, to leave such a thing where it may be found. The poor fellow is dead; let that be enough.'

Though little more than five minutes had passed, Le Gall was back with a young priest in a cassock, a prison chaplain who had been passing the main entrance of the palace on the Rue du Faubourg St Honoré as the *chef de cabinet* hurried towards the Madeleine. A little overawed by the magnificence of the death-chamber, the young chaplain murmured the phrases of absolution over the President's remains.

'Now,' said Holmes to Le Gall, 'you will have the goodness to send for a doctor and for Madame Faure, as quickly as possible. My colleague and I will take our leave by the gate into the Avenue de Marigny.'

Le Gall, in his confusion and grief, promised that no reward we might ask was too great for having averted a scandal that would surely have led to civil disturbance and bloodshed. Even as matters stood, the Paris newspapers were not long in circulating a rumour that the President had met his death through the murderous cunning of a Judith or a Delilah employed by the fanatics of Captain Dreyfus.

'I will take no fee and no reward,' said Holmes, 'unless it be a trivial souvenir of a great man.'

'Whatever you wish is yours,' Le Gall insisted.

With great delicacy, my friend lifted a little box of pale rose-coloured Sèvres *porcelaine tendre*, an exquisite thing no more than two inches square that might have been a snuff-box.

'Is that all?' the *chef de cabinet* asked, embarrassed by so slight a gift.

'Yes,' said Holmes quietly. 'That is all. And now I think it best that, so far as we are concerned, we should leave Paris and this matter should be at an end.'

VII

So it seemed to be. There were riots by an unthinking mob, encouraged in the right-wing press, who accused the *Dreyfusards* of murdering their President, but there was no revolution. Fèlix Faure was mourned and buried by the better part of his compatriots with a dignity befitting his rank. Dreyfus himself was still condemned to remain worse than a slave for life in the tropical hell of Devil's Island. Marguerite Steinheil and the 'Secret History of the Third Republic' were two subjects which Holmes swore he never wished to hear mentioned again.

We gave our notice to the Hôtel Lutétia next day. As Holmes said several times, we had been made fools of by Madame Steinheil and had wasted valuable words on Professor Bertillon. Worst of all, the death of Félix Faure in the arms of his young mistress had perhaps dashed all hope among those who sought justice for Dreyfus. As our last resort, Holmes swore that nothing would do but he must go to Berlin and confront Colonel Schwartzkoppen. He would have confronted Kaiser Wilhelm himself, in his present mood, had he been granted an audience.

Two days later, on a dull February morning, our train pulled out from the Gare de L'Est, among the departure boards for Vienna and Prague, Munich and Berlin, under the long span of the shabby Rue Lafayette with its workshops and warehouses. Holmes stared out at the open ironwork of bridges that carried the grey streets of La Chapelle and La Villette above the broad expanse of railway tracks. In the grey light of winter we entered a canyon below tall stone houses with peeling shutters and mansard roofs, the darkness of a tunnel enclosed us.

'And this,' said Holmes at last, 'is to be our reward. Let it take a place among our curios, Watson.'

He held lightly between his finger and thumb the little box of Sèvres porcelain. In his other hand lay several capsules, the contents of that box.

'The evil potion,' I said without thinking.

'Not the most evil, however,' Holmes remarked. 'Not evil enough, perhaps, to kill a man. Think how easy even that would be to someone who knew the weakness of Félix Faure and had the opportunity of access to him. Empty capsules may be bought from any pharmacy. They may be filled with anything, from stimulants for an old man's lust to the most deadly and instant poison. Dr Neill Cream, the Lambeth Poisoner seven years ago, was just such a killer.'

'You think she poisoned him?'

He shook his head. 'No, Watson. Not she. But what might not a man with evil in his mind do if he could fill one capsule with an instant poison and slip it among the others? Sooner or later his victim would take it. And when that victim was found dead with his mistress, as Félix Faure was found dead, would not his loyal servants act just as we have done? Who would demand an autopsy upon the body of a dead president in those circumstances? We believed that he had died from a foolish act of his own which would not bear the light of public scrutiny. Suppose it was worse—suppose it was poison. A murderer would scarcely need to cover his tracks, when we were eager to do it for him.'

'Then it truly was his assassination that she feared!'

Holmes shrugged. 'She had better fear for herself. If Félix Faure died by the hands of his enemies, the documents which those enemies feared are now in the hands of Marguerite Steinheil. I do not think, Watson, that I should care greatly to be in that young woman's shoes in the years to come.'

VIII

I thought that it was one of our worst defeats, complete as it was rare. We had lost both battles with Alphonse Bertillon. We had failed to save Félix Faure from destruction or self-destruction, whichever it might be. We had not been the triumphant saviours of Alfred Dreyfus. Even Colonel Schwartzkoppen returned the card of Sherlock Holmes with his pencilled regrets that official duties in Pomerania made a personal meeting impossible. Sometimes, in the months that followed, I wondered what had become of Félix Faure's 'Secret History of France under the Third Republic'. Did it ever exist? What did that matter now? The man to whom it would have been a shield was dead. His enemies might be uneasy at its existence but they would surely hesitate to commit murder as the price of its destruction. Though I read the daily news from Paris, I did not hear that Madame Steinheil had been murdered.

So we returned to London and I indulged Holmes so far as not to mention either Alphonse Bertillon or Marguerite Steinheil unless he did so first, which he did seldom and briefly. Yet the next twelve months saw a remarkable advance in the fortunes of Alfred Dreyfus. His persecutors had overreached themselves by arresting and imprisoning Colonel Picquart, Holmes's friend who was now head of counter-intelligence in the Deuxième Bureau. Picquart's crime had been to question the authorship of the treasonable letter to Colonel Schwartzkoppen.

Of the two men who had fabricated evidence against Captain Dreyfus, Colonel Hubert Henry cut his own throat with a razor on the day after his arrest. Lemercier-Picard anticipated his own arrest by hanging himself in his room. Among such events, the entire French civil judiciary demanded a retrial of Dreyfus, a call that the new President, Émile Loubet, dared not resist. At Rennes, to which he was brought haggard and white-haired from five years on Devil's Island, a military tribunal confirmed the guilt of Dreyfus but set him free. Frail but resolute, he promised to fight them until his innocence was recognised.

Time passed and Alfred Dreyfus won his last battle. His ally, Colonel Picquart, set free and vindicated, was about to become Minister of War in a new government led by Georges Clemenceau as Prime Minister, a man who had also demanded justice for Dreyfus.

'I fear,' said Holmes, laying down his morning *Times*, in which he had just read the news, 'that our friend Picquart will find nothing in the files to incriminate the persecutors of Alfred Dreyfus. The defeated party will have gone through the secret papers at the Élysée Palace and elsewhere with a fine comb to remove and destroy whatever might be used against them. More's the pity.'

Had he really not seen it?

'You forget the secret history,' I said gently. 'That is not in the Élysée Palace but, if it exists, in the Impasse Ronsin.'

He sighed, shook the paper out, and returned to it. The name of 'that young woman' was not mentioned after all.

'Yes,' he said quietly, 'I daresay you are right. Perhaps the Impasse Ronsin is where that strange concoction of fact and imagination had best remain.'

It was a matter of mere days before the wire came from Marguerite Steinheil, imploring the assistance of 'the great detective'. She was in the prison of St Lazare, awaiting trial for her life, on charges of having murdered both her mother and her husband on the night of 30 May. Had this been a fictional romance, I could not have believed such a thing. Next day, however, a brief report by the Paris correspondent of *The Times* assured us of its truth.

I quite expected that Holmes would decline to leave Baker Street. However, he withdrew to his room and I was presently serenaded by the sounds of cupboards and drawers being opened and closed, luggage being thrown about. I went to the door. Without question, he was packing all that he might need for Paris.

'You are going?' I said.

'We are going, Watson. By the night ferry.'

'After the manner in which she made fools of us?'

'She?' He straightened up and looked at me. 'She?'

'Marguerite Steinheil.'

'Madame Steinheil!' Holmes raised his voice loud enough to bring Mrs Hudson quite half-way up the stairs. 'I care nothing for Madame Steinheil! They may guillotine her tomorrow at dawn, so far as that goes!'

'Then why?'

He opened a drawer and took out a shirt, each movement tense with exasperation.

'Why?' he looked at me grimly. 'To seize an opportunity which will in all probability never present itself again. To settle a final account with Professor Alphonse Bertillon. That is why!'

With that he slammed shut the lid of the case and locked it.

IX

After all that, it was sweet as a nut, as the saying goes—one of the neatest of conclusions. Best of all, Holmes won the contest against Bertillon: game, set and match.

The Impasse Ronsin behind the shabby Rue de Vaugirard had changed by scarcely a brick or a pane of glass since we last saw it. The double murder had occurred on the night of 30–31 May. On the following morning, Rémy Couillard, the Steinheils' valet, entered the upper floor, where Marguerite Steinheil, her husband, and her mother—Madame Japy—slept in three separate rooms. The valet found the rooms silent and ransacked. Adolphe Steinheil lay dead in the doorway of his bathroom, kneeling forward as if he had died without a struggle as the cord was tightened round his throat. Madame Japy, the mother, had died upon her bed. The old woman had been gagged with such violence that a broken false tooth was found in the back of her throat. It was certain that she must have suffocated before the noose was drawn round her neck.

Marguerite Steinheil was found tied to her bed, bound and gagged but still alive. She told a confused story of having woken in the night to be confronted by three men and a woman in black ecclesiastical habits of some kind, the woman and one of the men having red hair.

'Where is your family's money?' they demanded. 'Where are your jewels? Tell us or we will kill you and them as well!'

Pleading with them not to harm her or the other members of her family, Madame Steinheil had told them. Until the valet came next morning, she lay on the bed with her wrists tethered above her head in such a way that at every attempt to move her hands the rope drew tighter about her throat. Her ankles were bound to the foot of the bed. Cotton wool had been forced into her mouth to silence her. Though she had heard Madame Japy's cries as the intruders gagged the old woman, she did not know until the morning that her mother and her husband were dead.

Madame Steinheil was not believed by the officers who investigated the crime. Her prosecutors insisted that she had first murdered her husband, then her mother, and had finally ransacked the house and tied herself up to support the story of a burglary. The motive was a wish to be rid of a weak-willed, improvident husband and to marry one of her numerous admirers.

Holmes glanced down the *résumé* of the evidence as we stood in the office of Gustave Hamard, Director of Criminal Investigations, opposite the monumental façade of the Palais de Justice, where Madame Steinheil appeared before her judges.

'The prosecution theory in that form may be disposed of at once,' Holmes said quietly to the French detective. 'I grant that Madame Steinheil might have strangled her husband, though the difference in their build and physical strength makes it unlikely. Why, though, would she first gag her mother, if her intention was to strangle the old lady?'

'Only the prisoner can tell us,' Hamard said sceptically.

Holmes shook his head. 'Consider this. The valet who released Madame Steinheil next morning did not undo the ropes. He cut them. The knots are still to be seen. She had been tied once or twice with a galley-knot. True, she might have tied herself to the bed but a galley-knot would be impossible in such places. It is, in any case, rarely used except among sailors or horse-dealers.'

'It would require a single accomplice,' Hamard said, 'who, in return for a reward, tied up the young woman and disposed of the other two. What better than to tie up Madame Japy and gag her, so that she might later be a witness to seeing a stranger in the house? Her suffocation appears to have been an accident.'

Again Holmes shook his head. 'It will not do, monsieur. If Madame Japy's death was not intended, why was the cord tightened round her throat? The poor old woman could not be permitted to live. It argues that at least one intruder was someone whom she might recognise and identify.'

For a week or two, the Steinheil murder case had threatened to cause almost as much disorder in Paris as the Dreyfus affair. One half of the city swore that Marguerite Steinheil was the victim of robbery, conspiracy, and worse. She had endured a night of terror, at the end of which the bodies of her husband and her mother were found lying in the other rooms. It was certainly true that four ecclesiastical costumes, identical to those in which she described her attackers, had been stolen from the property-room of the Théâtre Eden a few hours before the crime at the Impasse Ronsin. That in itself proved nothing.

The other half of Parisians thought her a notorious harlot who had paid villains as evil as herself to stage a make-believe robbery. The object was to murder her husband—of whom she was weary— so that she might make a better marriage. As for the pearls and other jewels, which Madame Steinheil claimed to have lost, they had never existed.

Holmes cared nothing for the jewels, whether they existed or not. There was another item which the valet and other servants testified to having seen in the house before the fatal night and never again after it. It was a package wrapped in brown paper and sealed. On its top was written the name of Marguerite Steinheil and the instruction, 'Private Papers. To be burnt unopened after my death'. Here and there the brown paper was torn and it was possible to see the corners of envelopes which the wrapping contained. This bundle of envelopes was, to all appearances, the secret history of the Third Republic and lay in a concealed wall-cupboard of Adolphe Steinheil's studio.

Madame Steinheil now swore that these were not the papers that might cause such embarrassment to the enemies of Félix Faure but a 'dummy' package to deceive burglars. The papers from the Élysée Palace were hidden in a secret drawer of her writing-desk.

There was never so inconclusive an investigation for the police. Dr Balthazard, forensic detective of the Sûreté, found nothing that would prove or disprove Madame Steinheil's story. Of the famous history of the Third Republic no more was said. As the judicial examination of Madame Steinheil began, it was widely doubted whether such a history existed—or had ever existed.

Professor Alphonse Bertillon used every means of scientific investigation at his disposal to identify those who had been at the Impasse Ronsin on the night of the crime. Despite his reservations over the technique, his assistants 'fingerprinted' every room and every article of furniture in the house. It was all to no effect. To be sure, there were fingerprints by the dozen in every room, and they were photographed and catalogued. Unfortunately, the system had been so neglected by the Sûreté, that it was impossible to check the identity of such prints without great difficulty.

Holmes was on better terms with Gustave Hamard, whose authority allowed my friend to tread where the great Bertillon had gone before, to examine the interior of the house in the Impasse Ronsin on behalf of his client. He had no wish to consult Madame Steinheil in prison. If ever there was a case to be decided on cold and precise points of evidence—away from the hysteria of the mob and the suspect—it was this. Hamard had shrugged his broad shoulders at the futility of further examination but granted the request.

By the time that Holmes finished his examination, the trial of Marguerite Steinheil on charges of murder had begun at the Palais de Justice. The final leaves of autumn fell from the birch trees of the Île de la Cité, which we had last seen breaking into a green haze of spring across the Boulevard du Palais.

A few days later, Sherlock Holmes and Alphonse Bertillon faced each other across the desk of Gustave Hamard. The duel that Holmes had promised was about to begin, with Hamard and myself as seconds. My companion took from his pocket a photographic card upon which the ridges and whorls of an index finger were plainly seen. He handed it to Bertillon, who shrugged and pulled a face.

'There were hundreds, Mr Holmes,' said the great anthropologist, taking off his glasses, brushing his eyes with the back of his hand, and replacing the spectacles. He took a page of fingerprints which was lying on the desk and ran his eye down it, looking aside from time to time at the image Holmes had given him.

'Try number eighty-four,' Holmes suggested whimsically.

Bertillon picked up another card and glanced down it.

'Indeed, monsieur,' he said affably, 'you are quite correct. The print of this finger was found a number of times, among many many others, in the studio of Adolphe Steinheil. It was not found, I see, in the rooms of the upper floor where the crimes were committed. The studio was entered by so many visitors that it can count for little, I fear.'

'Forgive me, monsieur,' said Holmes quietly, 'but the fingerprint upon the card I have handed you did not come from the studio of Adolphe Steinheil, nor from anywhere else in the Impasse Ronsin.'

'Then where?' asked Bertillon sharply.

The voice of Sherlock Holmes was almost a purr of satisfaction.

'From the presidential apartments of the Élysée Palace on the sixteenth of February 1899, at a time when the late Félix Faure had just received the last rites. You will recall that you and I were at that time exchanging views on the use, or otherwise, of such prints. Having received as a present from Monsieur Faure's family a small pill-box of Sèvres ware—a charming thing—I was boorish enough to subject it to dusting with silver nitrate and exposure to a fixed-range Kodak, a contraption of my own.'

Bertillon went pale. Hamard spoke first. 'Who do you say this print comes from?'

'The Comte de Balincourt,' said Holmes smoothly, 'alias Viscount Montmorency, alias the Margrave of Hesse, sometime assistant chamberlain at the Élysée Palace—under what name I know not, as yet. Dismissed after the passing of President Faure for some trivial dishonesty. A dozen witnesses will tell you that, not a few weeks before his murder, Adolphe Steinheil began a commission to paint in his studio a portrait of the Comte de Balincourt in hunting costume.'

Hamard's eyes narrowed. 'Do you say, Mr Holmes, that Steinheil knew such a man as Balincourt?'

'Not only knew him, Monsieur, but was heard in the studio discussing with him Félix Faure and the secret history of the Third Republic. There is a fingerprint, matching exactly the one I have shown you, on the door of a casually concealed wall-cupboard in the studio, where Balincourt was told that the papers of that secret history were kept. A package of papers remained there until the night of the two murders, inscribed with the name "Marguerite Steinheil" and with instructions that it was to be burned unopened upon her death. On the morning following the crimes, that cupboard was empty. The scratches on the mirror of its lock indicate that it was opened by a little force and a good deal of fraud.'

'Then the trial must be adjourned!' Hamard said. 'My God! What if all this were to come to light and she had already been condemned?'

'And where,' interrupted Bertillon, 'is the Comte de Balincourt?'

Holmes shrugged. 'At the bottom of the Seine, I imagine, or the bed of the River Spree, depending on whether his political masters are in Paris or Berlin. I do not think he will bother us again.'

'The papers!' Hamard said furiously. 'The manuscript! Where is that? Think of what it might do to the politics of France—to the peace of Europe!'

'The history of the Third Republic is quite safe,' Holmes said coolly.

Hamard looked at him with narrowed eyes. 'The cupboard was opened and the manuscript stolen, was it not?'

Holmes shook his head. 'Madame Steinheil trusted no one, least of all the discretion of her weak-willed and garrulous husband. She let it be known in the household that the wall-cupboard contained the manuscript and the secret drawer of her writing-desk held a dummy package. Alfred Steinheil did not know this when he boasted to the President's former chamberlain. In truth, it was the dummy package to which he unwittingly directed the man. After the blackest of crimes, the Comte de Balincourt handed his masters a bundle of old newspapers and blank pages. You may imagine how they will have rewarded him.'

If an Anarchist bomb had gone off in the tree-lined Boulevard du Palais and blown the windows out, Hamard and Bertillon could scarcely have looked more aghast.

'You say Balincourt is a murderer?' Bertillon demanded. 'Yet the same fingerprint was found nowhere upstairs.'

'Not for one moment did I suppose he had committed murder. I think it likely that he entered the upper rooms and that he was accidentally seen by Madame Japy. The poor old woman would have recognised him from his portrait sittings, for which reason she was put to death. Balincourt or his masters had hired men who would not scruple to take that precaution for their own safety as well as his.'

'A little convenient is it not?' said Hamard sceptically.

Holmes took from his pocket three more photographic prints.

'You will not know these fingerprints, for I believe they are unique to my own little collection. However, I shall be surprised if you do not find photographs of the three men in your Office of Judicial Identification. Baptistin is a young and violent criminal. Marius Longon, "The Gypsy", is a skilled and ruthless thief. Monstet de Fontpeyrine is a Cuban, a stage magician and a specialist in hotel robberies. He was seen last autumn, loitering in the Rue de Vaugirard, near the Impasse Ronsin. From there he was followed to the Metro station of Les Couronnes, where he met the other two men, a young woman with red hair, and a third man who is now identified as the Comte de Balincourt.'

'You know where these other men are?'

'In the same deep water as Balincourt, I should imagine,' said Holmes dismissively. 'I scarcely think you will hear from them either.'

'And the papers of the Third Republic?' Hamard persisted.

'Ah,' said Holmes with an air of false regret. 'They are where they will do no harm. I regret, however, that it is not in my power to produce them.'

'You will be ordered to produce them!' Hamard shouted.

Holmes was moved invariably by poverty, misfortune, desperation in others, never by browbeating.

'Those papers, monsieur, are essential to my client's defence. You have my word that, as yet, they have been seen by no other eyes than my own. After she is acquitted, which on the evidence I have produced to you is what justice must demand, I can promise you that these documents will trouble the world no more. If, after all that has been said in this room, she is condemned to execution—worse, if she *goes* to the guillotine—I will stop at nothing to see every word of them published in the leading newspapers of every capital.'

Gustave Hamard strode from the room and we heard his voice raised as he gave instructions to his subordinates. The trial of Madame Steinheil was adjourned early that day on the far side of the Boulevard du Palais. Two days later, its result was to be published across the world. After midnight, in the small hours of 14 November 1909, the jury that had retired to condemn Marguerite Steinheil was summoned into court again. De Valles, the president of the tribunal, imparted certain instructions to the jurors in the lamplit courtroom, his voice fraught with an anxiety that he had failed to show in the earlier stages of the proceedings. They retired and returned again to acquit Madame Steinheil of all the charges against her.

So much is history, as is the change in Professor Alphonse Bertillon's view on the usefulness of fingerprints. During the day or two left to us in Paris, he became almost a friend to Sherlock Holmes. The two men were now disposed to regard their past differences as something of a joke, each assuring the other that he had never really said the things that were reported—or that, if he had said them, he had never really meant them.

We came back to Baker Street by the night ferry to Charing Cross and arrived home in good time for lunch. That evening,

THE SECRET CASES OF SHERLOCK HOLMES

as I watched Holmes arranging some experiment or other upon the familiar stained table, I brought up the subject that had lain between us for the last few days.

'If you are right about Balincourt, Holmes . . .'

'I am seldom wrong in such matters, Watson,' he said gently, without looking up.

'If that man tampered with the box of capsules in the Élysée Palace . . .'

'Quite.' He frowned and took a little brush to dust a surface with white powder.

'Then it was not an old man's lust that destroyed him, though it gave the opportunity.'

'Quite possibly.'

'Balincourt or one of their spies knew that Faure was about to change his policy—that he would turn to the *Dreyfusards!* That he would order a retrial! She had persuaded him.'

'I daresay,' he murmured, as if scarcely hearing me.

'It was not a love philtre but an instant poison, after all, disguised among the other capsules!'

He looked up, the aquiline features contracting in a frown of irritation.

'You will give me credit for something, I hope! My first analysis in Paris was confirmed by a more searching examination here. What was in the remaining capsules was a homoeopathic quantity of canthar. They call such pills "Diavolini". The truth is that their contents would not even stimulate passion in a man, let alone kill him. Their effect, if any, is entirely upon the mind.'

He returned to his studies.

'Then we witnessed it, after all!' I exclaimed.

'Witnessed what, my dear fellow?'

'The assassination of the President of France by those who had most to fear if Dreyfus were found innocent!'

'Oh, yes,' said Holmes, as if it were the most ordinary thing in the world. 'I had never supposed otherwise. However, it would not do for you to give that to the world as yet, Watson, in one of your little romances. Sleep on it a little, my old friend. Speaking of romances, there is one that requires our attention without delay.'

He took a bundle of papers from a Gladstone bag and broke it open. A pile of well-filled foolscap envelopes slithered out randomly across the table.

'I have made my promise to Gustave Hamard,' he said. 'Madame Steinheil has paid me in kind. All debts are now discharged.'

He took the first sheaf of papers, on which I just had time to catch sight of a few names and phrases in a neat plain hand. 'General Georges Boulanger . . . Colonel Max von Schwartzkoppen, König-grätzstrasse, Berlin . . . Pensées sur le suicide du Colonel Hubert Henry . . . Les crimes financières de Panama . . . L'affaire de Fashoda . . . Colonel Picquart et le tribunal . . .' An envelope lay addressed in black ink to Major Count Ferdinand Walsin-Esterhazy, Rue de la Bienfaisance, 27, Paris 8°.

The fire in the grate blazed whiter as the first pages burned. Holmes turned to take another envelope and emptied it. There fluttered down to the floor a note on the stationery of the Italian Embassy in the Rue de Varenne, inviting Colonel Schwartzkoppen to dine with Colonel Panizzardi. He scooped it up and dropped it into the flames. The fire blazed again and a shoal of sparks swept up the chimney. For half an hour, the secret ashes of the Third Republic dissolved in smoke against the frosty starlight above the chimney-pots of Baker Street.

The Case of the Blood Royal

I

The adventure of 'The Final Problem' formed a concluding narrative to *The Memoirs of Sherlock Holmes*. In the following case, its readers may find a prologue to that fateful and famous death-struggle at the Reichenbach Falls. They will also find an epilogue, twenty years later, with which I now begin.

Sherlock Holmes was not present on 1 February 1911 to see justice done. His part in the investigation had ended at the Falls of Reichenbach and it was judged best that he should now remain concealed from public scrutiny. We were assembled in the Lord Chief Justice's Court at the Royal Courts of Justice, a large wainscotted chamber of oak carved in the Gothic fashion with curtains and hangings in dark green, the Royal Arms in bold relief. Even had Holmes wished to observe the trial of Edward Mylius, he might have found himself too busy at that moment with another matter. He was so greatly trusted by Lord Stamfordham and the Royal Household that he was more urgently engaged in an attempt to obtain from Daisy, Countess of Warwick, the love letters of the late King Edward VII, written to her ladyship when that monarch was still Prince of Wales. It was a delicate and expensive negotiation but my friend succeeded in averting another palace scandal.

Upon the judicial bench, in wig and scarlet robe, sat the Lord Chief Justice, Lord Alverstone. Below him the Attorney-General, Sir Rufus Isaacs, was in attendance for the Crown. On the bench behind Sir Rufus was the Home Secretary, Mr Winston Churchill, accompanied by Sir John Simon, then Solicitor-General and our future Lord Chancellor. Mrs Churchill and a number of other ladies sat in the Judge's Gallery. I was one of the few on the public benches, such was the success of the government in preventing advance information about the nature of this hearing. No indictment was laid before a magistrate or presented to a grand jury. The case was brought directly by the Attorney-General, whose office requires no such preliminaries in charges of this sort.

We were gathered almost *in camera* for a Special Jury to determine an issue of the gravest consequence. Whether Our Sovereign Lord, King George the Fifth of Great Britain and Ireland, Defender of the Faith, Emperor of India, had been guilty of the wilful crime of bigamy on the island of Malta in the year 1890, as defined by the Offences Against the Person Act 1861.

Few people who lived during the years from 1890 until 1911 escaped some rumour of this scandal. Until 1892, when his elder brother the Duke of Clarence died suddenly at the age of twenty-eight, Prince George had not been in the most direct line of succession to the British throne. It was still occupied by his grandmother, Queen Victoria. After her, Prince George's father was to succeed as Edward VII. Then it was supposed that the Duke of Clarence would succeed as elder son and after him any children he might have. These last hopes were cruelly ended on 14 January 1892 by the death of the young Duke of Clarence. George, 'The Sailor Prince', who had looked forward only to the life of a naval officer, became heir apparent to his father.

In the following year, 1893, Prince George was betrothed to his dead brother's fiancée, Princess May of Teck, and the couple were married a few weeks later. Yet even before the day of the betrothal passed, on 3 May, the *Star* newspaper reported that the future King had already contracted a morganatic marriage in 1890 or thereabouts with the daughter of a British naval officer. The *Star* was a mere rag of a newspaper which had risen to fame by its salacious reporting of the Whitechapel Murders in 1888 and its invention of the vulgar sobriquet 'Jack the Ripper'. However, its charges against the future King had been made and were not to be ignored by the gossips.

Prince George himself had been twenty-five years old in 1890, if that was the year alleged, and commander of the first-class gunboat HMS *Thrush*, sailing via Gibraltar to the West Indies. The ship was laid up at Gibraltar for more than two weeks, awaiting the torpedo boat that she was to tow across the Atlantic. It can do no harm now to reveal that the unnamed naval officer whose daughter's name was associated with the future king's was Admiral Sir Michael Culme-Seymour, who commanded the Mediterranean Squadron. Sir Michael had also been Naval Aide-de-Camp to Queen Victoria for five years while Prince George was a child. There were two Culme-Seymour daughters, Laura who was to die in 1895, and Mary, who married Captain Trevelyan Napier in 1899.

The story was taken up by the press and aired from time to time in *Reynolds News*, the Brisbane *Telegraph*, and the *Review of Reviews*. Worse still, however, was the allegation arising from the reports that, before Prince George's betrothal to Princess May, two children were born of this former union.

Upon the death of King Edward in 1910 and Prince George's accession to the throne as King George V, it might have been hoped that such gossip would die of repetition. Quite the contrary. The embers were fanned again in the very weeks preceding the opening of the new King George's first parliament and the coronation ceremony itself. Holmes later showed me His Majesty's comment upon the allegation of a morganatic marriage. 'The whole thing is a damnable lie,' King George wrote in his forthright quarter-deck manner, 'and has been in existence now for over twenty years!'

The accused, who was called up to the dock on that winter morning in 1911, was one of many to repeat the story. However, he was surely the most deserving of the law's attention. Edward

Mylius was a thin saturnine man of thirty, dressed in black, who lived in Courtnell Street, Bayswater. He was the English editor of a republican magazine, the *Liberator*, published in the Rue St Dominique, Paris, by Mr Edward Holden James, a cousin of the famous American novelist. Mylius had denounced King George's coronation in an article entitled 'Sanctified Bigamy', which condemned the Church of England for its complicity in having knowingly wed a married man to Princess May and for preparing to crown the bigamist. A copy of the article was sent by its author to every Member of Parliament and the unsavoury matter was even raised in the House of Commons by Mr Keir Hardie and others. Mylius assured his readers that after a few years of his first secret marriage and the birth of two children, Prince George 'foully abandoned his true wife and entered into a sham and shameful marriage with a daughter of the Duke of Teck'.

During the winter of 1910 there had been much discussion among members of the government of Mr Asquith as to the advisability of prosecuting Mylius for a criminal libel on the monarch, this being by far the most scurrilous version of the story to be published. Mr Churchill, as Home Secretary, was most anxious to proceed against the 'buffoon', as he called him. Yet a prosecution for a criminal libel on the sovereign had not been brought since the worst days of King George IV in 1823. The Law Officers of the Crown advised the cabinet on 23 November of the danger that lay in giving courtroom publicity to Mylius and his story. If it were to be done none the less, they said, it had best be done quickly and quietly. He was arrested on 26 December, held to bail for £20,000, which he could not possibly find, and kept in strict confinement, allowing him no opportunity of communicating with the press before his trial.

The first that the public knew of the case was when they read in the newspapers of 2 February that the trial was over. It was stated in court and in the papers that neither King George nor the Culme-Seymour daughters had been in Malta in 1890. Sir Michael, though by now elderly and in poor health, gave evidence of this, as did his surviving daughter.

There was one moment when a chill touched my spine. Sir Rufus Isaacs, like a handsome dark-eyed eagle in wig and gown, was examining Mary Culme-Seymour—as I still call Mrs Napier. In answer to his question, she replied that she had never so much as met Prince George from 1879, when she was eight, until 1898, five years after his marriage to Princess Mary. It was not the truth and there was public proof of that! As Holmes and I had reason to know, not only had she met him but on one occasion she and Prince George had opened the dancing at a grand ball in Portsmouth Town Hall on 21 August 1891. Worse still, the fact had been reported at length in the *Hampshire Telegraph and Sussex Chronicle* at the time, for anyone who cared to read it! Happily for Sir Rufus Isaacs, this was not a newspaper that Mylius had seen. This untruth or slip of memory did not, of course, make Mary Culme-Seymour the wife of Prince George. At the same time, it might have opened the way for the accused man to dismiss her evidence, if only he had known of the error.

Mylius had refused to be represented by counsel. Instead he issued a most impudent subpoena which summoned King George to give evidence and to be cross-examined upon it! This device would have been outrageous, had it not been so foolish. The Attorney-General knew the law of the constitution, if Mylius did not. The sovereign cannot be summoned as witness in a court where he is the source of justice. It is true that Edward VII before coming to the throne gave evidence in the Mordaunt divorce case and in the Tranby Croft libel action, when one of his friends had cheated at baccarat in his presence. He did so as Prince of Wales, however, and not as monarch.

As the cold February evening drew in, Mylius endeavoured to justify the truth of his libel. He could not do so to the satisfaction of the jury, which took against him from the start. All day, Mr Churchill had sat behind Sir Rufus Isaacs, murmuring to him the questions that should be put to witnesses and, more importantly from the view of Holmes and myself, warning him of the answers that were not to be pursued. Mylius, of course, stuck to his story.

Thank God that, in one or two essentials, the scoundrel had got it wrong!

In that marble temple, which forms the lobby of the Central Criminal Court, I afterwards overheard Mr Churchill's comment to Sir Rufus Isaacs. A few minutes earlier, Edward Mylius had been taken down the steps of the Old Bailey dock, after the Lord Chief Justice had sentenced him to a year's imprisonment and a substantial fine. The smile of a portly cherub lit the Home Secretary's face.

'A man of that sort cannot resist the temptation to fight to the last ditch,' he said. 'It was as well for you, my dear Rufus, that the guttersnipe did not plead guilty and say he was only repeating what a dozen other newspapers had written already. Then you might have had to indict 'em all and we should have had the gravest constitutional crisis on our hands for the last fifty years.'

Sir Rufus Isaacs with his dark dignity stared unsmiling at his companion.

'The scoundrel has gone to prison, Winston,' he said suavely. 'That will be the end of him. To the people of this country, a man who goes to prison on a jury's verdict is a liar. He might publish the marriage certificate itself and they would not believe him now.'

'Well,' growled the Home Secretary cheerfully, 'we may all thank God for that!'

As the world knows, there was spite enough to come but the worst damage had been avoided. No incriminating papers of any kind could be produced by Mylius and his gang. The libeller served his year in prison and was released. He made his way to New York and there, beyond the reach of English law, he published his booklet, *The Morganatic Marriage of George V.* In these pages he described, as he had not done in court, how Prince George had been at Gibraltar from 9 June until 25 June 1890, with ample time to reach Malta and return, and how a Miss Culme-Seymour was at Marseilles at the same time.

By then, of course, it was too late. The wretched fellow had been branded as a liar and a criminal. Sir Rufus Isaacs was quite right in predicting that no one would listen to him now, even with the marriage certificate in his hand. I believe that only Holmes and I knew the entire truth of why that certificate could not be produced, even had it existed. Now the whole disagreeable business was to be eclipsed by the splendour of the coronation of King George V and Queen Mary in Westminster Abbey, by the spontaneous affection and loyalty shown all along the route by their subjects. That was answer enough to the libel.

On the February evening of the trial I took a cab back through the damp streets of Holborn and Marylebone to Baker Street. Sherlock Holmes had retired in 1903 to Fulworth, near Cuckmere Haven on the Sussex coast. I never thought it would last. After six months, he had wearied sufficiently of his bee-keeping to spend two or three days of almost every week in our old haunts at 221B Baker Street. Though I had been married for nine years, Mrs Watson's occasional absences from London on family matters, and the discovery of a most efficient *locum*, had led me increasingly to spend a few days at a time in our old diggings. Indeed, I had been a regular visitor ever since the mystery of the Irish Crown Jewels.

There had been little news of the Mylius case in the evening papers, for they were scarcely prepared for it. Holmes had spent the day in tedious negotiation with the representatives of Lady Warwick but he was impatient to hear the outcome of the trial. He stood with his pipe in his hand and nodded at every sentence in my account, looking up only when I described Mary Culme-Seymour's slip in the witness-box. When I revealed how it had all ended with the removal of Mylius to begin his sentence in Wormwood Scrubs, he let out a long sigh.

'It would not do for the truth to come out now, after all this time.'

'The truth of the marriage or the lack of it?'

He drew his pipe from his lips and shook his head.

'No, Watson. The truth of the part which you and I played in that intimate drama. I should not care for that to be known during the lifetime of either of us.'

In that observation, of course, he was quite right.

II

Such was the end of the story, the least sensational part of it. When this scandal of a bigamous marriage first threatened the British throne, we had confronted far worse men than Mylius, including one to whose existence I have only alluded obliquely in the past, under his alias of 'Charles Augustus Milverton'. Our adventure began soon after breakfast on a sunny morning more than twenty years before during one of my residences at Baker Street. All one's instincts were to chuck work for the day and walk under the elms and chestnuts of Regent's Park. For Holmes, of course, that would not do. I do not believe that my friend ever chucked work for a single day of his life.

We had come home late the previous evening from a Joachim recital at the St James's Hall, where Holmes had sat with his eyes closed and a faint smile upon his lips as the great virtuoso filled the concert room with the plaintive melodies of Beethoven's Violin Concerto. As we entered the sitting-room and I turned up the lamp upon the table, the light fell upon a card. It had been left by Sir Arthur Bigge, who had scribbled in pencil on the reverse his intention of returning at 11 A.M. next day. If it was impossible for us to receive him then, we should find him at the Army and Navy Club in St James's Square. The matter was of such urgency that he would not leave London until he had laid the facts of it before Sherlock Holmes. He did not need to be more precise, for all England knew that Sir Arthur Bigge, later Lord Stamfordham, was Assistant Private Secretary to Her Majesty the Queen.

Neither of us had the least idea what had brought the young courtier from Windsor. He was by then in his thirties, a man of good family with a distinguished career as a young subaltern in the Zulu Wars of 1879–80. Slight of build and unassuming in manner, his fair-haired military moustache betraying his former profession, he was to serve loyally as Assistant Private Secretary until 1901, when he became Private Secretary to the late Queen's grandson, first as Prince of Wales and then as King George V. He seemed to me always to have about him an inbred air of anxiety. It was particularly marked on the following morning when we received him in Baker Street. Sir Arthur looked from one to the other of us, as he sat forward in the fireside arm-chair, where we had installed him.

'Gentlemen,' he said quietly, 'what I have to say must be said to you both, though it is repugnant to talk of such things at all. I know something of our antagonists and I am sure that this is not a commission to be undertaken by any one man. Before you ask me why I have not gone to your friend Lestrade at Scotland Yard, let me tell you simply that a prince of the blood is threatened with blackmail—not without reason, if one can use that term for such a loathsome crime. I will also tell you that neither the Prime Minister, the Attorney-General, nor any member of the government has been approached.'

Holmes stood at the window, looking down at the immaculately polished coachwork of the waiting carriage with its two glossy bay geldings. Unlike Sir Arthur, he spoke without the least trace of astonishment that such a crime should now threaten the stability of the British throne.

'I assume you will not object, Sir Arthur, to telling us the name of the blackmailer. Will you also tell us the name of his intended victim? You have our word, of course, that neither will go beyond the walls of this room.'

Sir Arthur shrugged. 'You will have to know both, Mr Holmes. From my presence here, it will not surprise you to know that Her Majesty's grandson, Prince George, is the object of this villainy, though it touches his elder brother, the Duke of Clarence.'

'And your blackmailer?'

'I cannot tell you the name of the plot's contriver, Mr Holmes. I know only of the man who presents himself as the agent of it.'

'The agent?'

'The agent of one who says that he wishes well to Her Majesty. One who has in his—or her—hands stolen papers that would infallibly bring disgrace on the royal house. Letters from two royal sons to women of a certain kind. Part of Prince George's private diary.

The letters were easy to steal from their recipients—the diary easier than it should have been from a ship of the fleet. The client professes to be one who seeks only to ensure that the documents are never disclosed. To this end, he proposes to name a price!'

'A loyal subject!' Holmes exclaimed sardonically. 'Who represents this anonymous patriot?'

'You have perhaps heard of the name of Charles Augustus Howell?'

'Ah!' said Holmes reminiscently. 'I know of him well enough, Sir Arthur. I have yet to meet him privately but his name occurs frequently in my files.'

'What do you know of him, Mr Holmes?' For the first time there was a light of hope in Sir Arthur's eyes.

Holmes assumed a grimace of distaste. 'You might call him an interesting subject, in his way. He has been a diver for pearls and sheikh of a North African tribe. He is Anglo-Portuguese by birth and escaped from criminal vengeance in Portugal after a card-sharping scandal when he was just sixteen years old. Since then he has followed a career of dishonour with dedication. As a young man, he was implicated in Orsini's plot to assassinate the French Emperor. He defrauded Mr Ruskin, as a secretary, and endeavoured to facilitate the great man's meetings with very young girls.'

The lines of Sir Arthur Bigge's face relaxed and he said thankfully, 'Then you know the worst of him, Mr Holmes.'

'Indeed, Sir Arthur. Howell is known in artistic circles, in the pawnbroking trade, and in houses of ill fame, whether they be the stews of Seven Dials or the more genteel mansions of Regent's Park and St John's Wood. He is provider of pleasures to the dissolute, though he does not spare the innocent. Some time ago, he was Mr Rossetti's agent and marketed pictures ascribed to that artist which were rank forgeries. Among poets, he facilitated Mr Swinburne's perverse enjoyments at a house in Circus Road, St John's Wood, and then blackmailed Admiral and Lady Swinburne as the price of his silence. He defrauded Mr Whistler in the matter of a valuable Japanese cabinet, which he "borrowed" and then sold simultaneously to two different dealers, leaving the artist to reimburse them both. I could tell you more, Sir Arthur, but I trust that will suffice to assure you that my files contain a number of facts about Mr Howell that are otherwise known only to the criminal and his victims.'

Though our visitor breathed more freely, a look of concern betrayed his unease at the extent of such depravity.

'And what do you find his methods to be, Mr Holmes?'

Holmes walked from the window, sat in the opposite chair and chuckled.

'His methods are not subtle but they are apt to succeed. Mr Rossetti was unfortunate enough to lose his wife, the beautiful Elizabeth Siddal, from an overdose of chloral. He was so distraught that he buried a notebook—the only copy of his poems—in his dead wife's coffin. After several years, Howell insisted that the gesture was quixotic, a ruinous loss to literature. He persuaded Mr Rossetti to have his wife exhumed from Highgate Cemetery at night and the poems retrieved. It was not the least improper. The Home Secretary signed an exhumation order. Yet, to the grieving husband, it was a necessity at which he shuddered. Within weeks he heard from Mr Howell—'

'Did he?' Sir Arthur sat forward again, his face tight with anger. 'Did he, by any chance, hear that certain sensitive letters and documents had been pasted into Howell's album? Did he hear that his friend Howell had fallen on hard times and been obliged to pawn his possessions—including that album? Did he hear that Howell was unable to redeem the album for lack of funds? Was he told by this blackguard that he would be best advised to go to the pawnbroker and negotiate before the album went to auction? And when he did so, did the pawnbroker demand a king's ransom to prevent these confidential papers being sold at an auction without reserve?'

'It was the case in every detail,' Holmes said quietly. 'Howell works hand in glove with one or two villains in the pawnbroking trade. Mr Rossetti's letters contained nothing dishonourable, yet he would have died rather than see his private feelings about the woman he loved held up to public auction and the curiosity of the multitude. Six hundred pounds was, I believe, the price.'

Sir Arthur looked pale, though he was thinking of Prince George rather than Mr Rossetti.

'Could nothing be done to bring such a criminal to justice?'

Holmes spread out his bony fingers and studied them.

'I beg you will not underestimate him, Sir Arthur. He shows a practised cunning. No law is broken. A man who writes a letter to another makes that other the owner of the letter. The other may not, of course, publish it without the consent of its author. In this case, publication was unnecessary to Howell's scheme. Possession by whomsoever he chose to buy the letters was sufficient threat. Had Howell attempted blackmail, he would have gone to prison for fourteen years. But he might claim that urging his victim to go quickly to the confederate pawnbroker and purchase the letters was a friendly act, designed to forestall embarrassment.'

'Nothing was done?' Sir Arthur inquired fearfully.

'No,' said Holmes abruptly. 'Nor was anything done when the same trick was played upon Admiral and Lady Swinburne. Their son fell into a bohemian set and, among women at such houses as that in Circus Road, indulged passions that belong to the alienist rather than the moral censor. You have perhaps, Sir Arthur, noticed the works of the Baron von Krafft-Ebing in the past three or four years? The treatises on psycho-pathology of Cesare Lombroso or Démétrius Zambaco?'

Sir Arthur Bigge shook his head. It was evident from his expression that he had not the least idea what Holmes was talking about. The most arcane rituals of the Zulu tribes against whom he had fought as a young officer would have meant more to him than the great alienists whose works my friend had at his fingertips.

'No matter,' Holmes said casually. 'Suffice it to say that Admiral and Lady Swinburne paid a considerable sum for the album of letters describing Circus Road pleasures, which their conceited young son had addressed to his friend Howell. Howell pleaded again that poverty had forced him to pawn the correspondence and that he had not the money to redeem it before the sale must take place.'

There was a silence. Sir Arthur could scarcely bring himself to the point. At last he looked up and said, 'It is the same, and yet it is worse.'

'Because it is Prince George?'

Our visitor stared at the carpet and shook his head. 'Because Prince George will one day be King George.'

I interrupted and said, 'But surely his elder brother, the Duke of Clarence, will be king?'

'He would be,' Sir Arthur said quietly, 'if he lived. I shall have to tell you so much that I must add this as well. The Duke of Clarence suffers from a wasting disease. I would give all I possess to be proved wrong, gentlemen. Yet I doubt that the Duke will even outlive his own father. The plot against Prince George is a plot against our future king.'

History was to prove Sir Arthur right, for the Duke of Clarence died not long afterwards, while his grandmother was still queen. I did not dare ask what the wasting disease might be for so often, even in the case of great leaders like Lord Randolph Churchill, it proves to be syphilis contracted through youthful folly.

'I believe, Sir Arthur,' Holmes said gently, 'you must trust us with the nature of the plot.'

The royal secretary nodded. 'It is this, Mr Holmes. Howell claims first to have letters and documents which establish a marriage, contracted upon the island of Malta, between Prince George and the daughter of Admiral Sir Michael Culme-Seymour of the Mediterranean Fleet.'

To my astonishment, Holmes threw back his head and laughed in the heartiest manner that I had heard from him for a long time.

'Oh, he does, does he? I believe I know a little of the British constitution, Sir Arthur. In the first place, the Royal Marriages Act of 1772 would make such a union unlawful. Prince George may not marry without consent of the monarch until he is twenty-five. When he is over twenty-five, he may marry by giving a year's notice to the Privy Council and there being no objection from the Houses of Parliament within that period. Prince George is scarcely of an age to dispense with royal consent for a lawful marriage.'

Sir Arthur was briefly but gravely displeased.

'Had that been all, Mr Holmes, I should not have bothered to come to Baker Street or to trouble you in any way. Of course, Prince George denies that, having met Miss Laura or Miss Mary Culme-Seymour on the island of Malta, he eloped with her. Yet if this story is made public and believed—even half believed—how could he make a royal marriage later in the face of all mankind? If he did so, could he be crowned with the rest of the world believing that he had taken his solemn oath to Miss Culme-Seymour and fathered children by her? It will not do to talk of the Royal Marriages Act! That has no validity to the common sense of the human race. If this story were believed, he could not be crowned. That much is certain. If he were not crowned, under such circumstances, the very foundations of the monarchy and the state must tremble. Do you not see that?'

There was a slight, scarcely perceptible movement of Holmes's eyes and the laughter went out of them.

'You must forgive me, Sir Arthur, if I do not follow you in seeing why those foundations must tremble. Howell claims to have documents which would establish the existence of a morganatic marriage between Prince George and the daughter of Sir Michael Culme-Seymour. Whether there are grounds for believing this to be so is something I will not ask. Whatever the outcome, would you not be wise to call Howell's bluff without delay, to let him do his worst? The nation will forgive a young man who makes a romantic marriage. Let him abdicate his claim to the throne, if necessary. If neither Prince George nor the Duke of Clarence should be king, there are three sisters. Any one of them might be queen in her own right.'

'If it were as simple as that, Mr Holmes, I should not be here.' Again Sir Arthur gazed at the carpet. 'The lie of a secret marriage is but one of the items with which Howell or his client threatens us.

The others are not lies. Forgive me, I do not find this easy. Might I have a glass of water?'

The water was poured and our visitor continued.

'Prince George is at sea a good deal. When he returns to Portsmouth, there has been a young woman to whom he goes. One with whom he lives and one whom he knows, in the biblical sense. Howell's client has her name, the address of the house, the stolen letters, the times of the prince's arrivals and departures.'

'Indeed,' said Holmes thoughtfully. 'Yet Howell is a mere collector of documents, Sir Arthur, not the midnight spy.'

Sir Arthur brushed the objection aside. 'Whatever the prince's dealings with Miss Culme-Seymour may be or may not be, she is a respectable young woman of good family. It is not the case in Portsmouth, where he has chosen for himself and indiscreetly. Howell has the details from his client.'

'I think I should like to meet this client,' Holmes murmured.

'There is worse,' Sir Arthur continued. 'Prince George and the Duke of Clarence are named in another matter. It concerns a girl in St John's Wood whom they share between them. I cannot put it more delicately.'

'One moment, Sir Arthur!' Holmes raised his hand more gently than his voice. 'This sounds such a *canard* that I must break a rule I made for myself just now and ask you whether this is true—and how you know it can be true.'

'Because Prince George himself told me,' our courtier said sadly. 'He called her a clipper or some such name from yachting.'

'And Howell or his client knows all this? That the young woman in St John's Wood is shared by the royal brothers?'

'Yes, Mr Holmes, he knows it. And even if the story of the royal marriage is a *canard*, as you use the word, the other stories are true. If there is a public scandal and those are proved to be accurate, will not the world also believe the marriage story which cannot be so easily proved?'

I sat in my chair and listened to such things said and discussed calmly in the familiar surroundings of the Baker Street rooms. It was as if someone would come in presently and tell me it was all a joke or a misunderstanding. The heir to the throne, who was indeed king twenty years later, had confessed to having a paid woman with whom he slept in Portsmouth—where Miss Culme-Seymour was also to be found!—and to sharing the bed of a girl in St John's Wood with his own brother, which had more than a hint of incest. In all the time I had known Sherlock Holmes and in all the cases of crime and infamy whose details had been paraded before us, I had heard nothing to equal it.

This was far worse, however, because the sin of lust had opened the way to the crime of blackmail.

'There is another matter,' Sir Arthur said sadly, 'which touches the Duke of Clarence, though it does not involve Prince George.'

He sipped his water and seemed scarcely able to continue.

'You had best tell us all, Sir Arthur,' Holmes said kindly.

'Very well, Mr Holmes. You recall that the courts dealt lately with certain cases arising from a house in Cleveland Street, where unnatural vices had been practised. It touched both Lord Arthur Somerset of the royal stables and Lord Euston, though the latter was quite innocently associated with the place.'

'Something was reported by the papers,' Holmes said vaguely.

'It was not reported, Mr Holmes, that the Duke of Clarence was innocently at that place and was seen by witnesses. At the first hint of impropriety he left, as did Lord Euston. Indeed, Euston threatened to knock down the first man who spoke to him.'

'Then Howell knows all this?'

'A number of people know of it, Mr Holmes, but only Howell seeks to make something of it. The scandal that he threatens over the so-called marriage may come to nothing. Yet when he talks of the girl in Portsmouth, another in St John's Wood shared by the royal brothers, the fact that the Duke of Clarence—however innocently—was in that house in Cleveland Street, he talks of what is true.'

Holmes shrugged. 'Then you had better buy from the scoundrel whatever papers he possesses at whatever price he asks.'

Sir Arthur Bigge shook his head. 'It is not so simple, Mr Holmes. He will not sell them. His client's documents are in a bank vault, as he calls it. They will remain there in confidence so long as he is paid on behalf of that client. If the client were to come to any harm, those documents would be published to the world. They are, you might say, his form of life insurance. Set aside the business of the Culme-Seymours and think what the rest of the scandal might do.'

'So you are to pay him—and pay him again whenever he asks—and in exchange for that the papers remain where they are?'

'Unless you can find means to outwit him, Mr Holmes.'

For a moment Holmes said nothing. Then he looked directly at our visitor.

'I have no doubt I shall. However, if you will take my advice, Sir Arthur, you will put Mr Howell from your mind for the present.'

'Ignore him?'

'Ignore him, if you prefer to put it that way. I will tell you, here and now, that none of this is the work of Charles Augustus Howell. Oh yes, he is party to it in a small way. But behind him there is a far stronger and more devious mind. The client. If I am right, the client is a man who might crush Mr Howell—or any one of us—in a single clenching of his hand. If I am right again, this is a man who has not so far demanded money because his true reward would be power beyond price. He holds this threat over you in order that he may be your equal—beyond the law, above the law, perhaps above the Crown itself. That is not Howell, Sir Arthur. That is a man whose shadow falls on his victim with an unearthly chill. I almost seem to know his name.'

'Yet the name is not Howell's?'

Holmes shrugged. 'I am probably wrong in my guess. Yet to blackmail our poets and artists is work for soft hands and men like Howell, whose crimes are those of weakness rather than strength. To attempt such a thing against the greatest power in the realm—the greatest in the world—requires a man with a will of steel and a heart proof against fear. That man is not Howell.'

'Then you will not meet him or negotiate with Mr Howell?'

Holmes sighed. 'I will meet him if you wish, Sir Arthur, since one must begin somewhere. But it will not be for the purpose that Mr Howell supposes.'

III

Such was the unwelcome commission that came our way. There was nothing for it but to arrange a meeting between Holmes and the man whom Sir Arthur Bigge took to be our enemy. It was less easy than I had imagined. Mr Howell was apprehensive, with good reason, of traps that might be set for him. There was not a room in London where he would consent to be alone with Sherlock Holmes. So it was that this most secret of negotiations occurred in the most public of places.

The two men sat side by side in steamer-chairs, hired by the hour along that stretch of Hyde Park that slopes down towards the waters of the Serpentine. They might have been taken for genial companions, but for their looks. The soft lines and shallow honesty of Howell's face was made a contrast to the sharp intelligence of Sherlock Holmes's profile that it was hard to imagine they had anything in common. Far off the riders moved in a light cloud of dust along Rotten Row, beyond the glittering waters of the boating-lake. The trees sighed in a light breeze and on the bandstand the musicians of the Coldstream Guards enlivened the sunny afternoon with the overture to *The Marriage of Figaro*.

Holmes and I had laid our plan. For the moment I sat at a little distance reading the *Morning Post* and was, I believed, unrecognised by Mr Howell. Much of the time, I could not catch the words that passed between the two men. Only at intervals, as the breeze dropped or the band fell silent, did I hear a few isolated exchanges.

'My dear sir,' said Howell, in his whimsical insinuating manner, 'it is a little curious, is it not?'

Holmes gazed at the spring sunlight among the trees of the park but his voice was as cold as the Himalayan snows.

'You must forgive me, sir, but I am not here to discuss curiosities.'

'All the same,' Howell said languidly, 'it remains one. There is such a bother about a marriage which, arrived at unofficially or even by elopement, is an honourable estate among men, as the liturgy has it. Yet much less is said about common whoredom, even where the woman is shared between two brothers.'

'You will do me the courtesy,' Holmes said acidly, 'of confining our conversation to the issue.'

There was almost a lisp in Howell's voice as he said, 'It is necessary, Mr Holmes, that those who have sent you here should understand one thing. I am no republican—indeed, I wish well to Her Majesty—but nor am I a sycophant. When a woman is bought and sold, it is whoredom, whether it be on the Ratcliffe Highway or in St John's Wood, whether the purchaser be a crossing-sweeper or a prince of the blood.'

Holmes said something but I could not catch it. They talked a little longer and I supposed that my friend might be trying to negotiate an outright purchase of the stolen documents, to put an end to the matter. At any rate, what I next heard, several minutes later, was Howell saying more loudly, 'They lie in a bank vault, sir, let that suffice. That they should do so is my insurance against chicanery on your part or on the part of those who instruct you. Times, dates, documents are all there. Even if you could destroy those papers, you could not destroy the knowledge. Instructions have been given to those whom it may concern. If some misfortune should befall me or my client, the contents of those papers will be public knowledge within the week.'

Holmes muttered something else, which I could not quite hear. I caught Howell's answer.

'Quarterly, Mr Holmes, is the suggestion. Each quarter day by banker's draught to an account which I shall open. It will then be forwarded to my client.'

Holmes spoke again and Howell replied.

'My client allows me a little elbow-room,' he said suavely. 'If you wish, you shall see a *résumé* of the contents of the documents—a

149

bill of lading, as it were—which will entirely convince you of the necessity of our coming to an understanding. Better still, I shall bring you, within forty-five minutes, a page of a letter in Prince George's handwriting. You shall have sight of either—or both—if that will settle your doubts.'

'Within forty-five minutes.' That would surely put the repository of the stolen papers within a mile or two of the Serpentine. It was little enough to go on but, as I thought then, it limited somewhat the area of the search.

'I will wait forty-five minutes and not a moment longer,' Holmes answered coldly.

'You would do well not to be so impatient, Mr Holmes,' said Howell with a soft chuckle. 'I cannot make it too plain that, if our little negotiation should fail, there will be no lack of other bidders. Though I may regret it personally, two foreign governments and a number of less reputable organisations have shown a lively interest in the Windsor papers, as I call them. It is provoking to hear fornication, adultery, sodomy, and the like mentioned in the same breath as the illustrious personages against whom the accusations are levelled—often levelled against themselves in their own words.'

Holmes said something which I heard only as a growl and his companion laughed again.

'Mr Holmes, your interests and mine are indivisible. I am, in a most unusual way, your friend. You have every reason to wish me health and prosperity. If, for any reason, misfortune overcame me, you would not be offered the same chance a second time. You would not hear of these Windsor papers again until they shamed publicly those who were indiscreet enough to pen them.'

To those strollers who passed them, these were men of affairs sitting and discussing the terms of the most innocent commercial contract. As they did so, I wondered what darker and more powerful figure stood behind the slippery and evasive presence of Mr Howell. I could see that Sir Arthur Bigge did not believe in such a master criminal. For myself, I doubted whether the blackmailer of Mr Rossetti or Mr Swinburne was a match for the present crime without a more resolute figure behind him.

It was Holmes who later repeated to me Howell's parting remark to him.

'Forty-five minutes will suffice, Mr Holmes. Please do not think of following me or communicating with your friends. You are watched at this moment and I shall know if you have left this place for a single instant during my absence. If that is reported, you will never see me again and your employers know what the consequence will be.'

Even without this warning, it would have been quite impossible for Holmes to follow Howell as the other man left the park. The long paths, even with the trees to either side, are poor cover for the hunter. For that reason, my friend and I had agreed that any tracking of our adversary must be left to me. I did not walk straight after Howell but cut down to Rotten Row, at a right angle from him, and then turned so that our paths would converge near Hyde Park Corner. It was a weakness in their scheme that because they watched Holmes, they could scarcely keep track of me at the same time, or so I thought.

As soon as I was clear of any possible observation, I began to stride out, looking behind me from time to time to make sure that no one matched my pace. Either a pursuer must do so or lose me and I saw no sign of pursuit. As I came out of the park near Apsley House and the start of Piccadilly, Howell was ahead of me on the far side of the busy street that runs by Green Park. It suited me well. Suddenly he turned into a side-street and I dodged between the cabs and twopenny buses to keep him in sight. The side-street turned again and brought me out into the busy thoroughfare of St James's Street, the sunlight golden on the clock-face of the palace at the far end.

By now I felt sure that the destination was one of those old banking families whose premises are ranged along Pall Mall. So it proved to be. Howell looked hastily about him, seemed to scent no danger, and walked swiftly up the steps of Drummonds Bank.

I could hardly believe it would be so easy. In my mind's eye, I saw a police cordon thrown about the bank, Lestrade in his uniform presenting a search-warrant to Henry Drummond, the papers seized and returned to Sir Arthur Bigge at Windsor, where Prince George or the Prince of Wales himself would entertain us to tea as a token of gratitude.

Walking back a little down the broad street, I stood concealed by the ancient brick archway of St James's Palace itself. I kept no count of time but it was surely no more than five minutes later that Howell reappeared with an attaché case in his hand. This time I allowed him to get far ahead of me, for I knew his route.

I kept my distance, pretending to watch the riders on Rotten Row. What I saw of the encounter was Holmes, Howell, and the attaché case on a park bench. A sheet of paper was handed to my friend, presumably for verification. By accident or design, Holmes seemed to let go of it. The light breeze carried it several feet into the air and then let it drift slowly to the grass a yard or two further off. Howell was after it, like a greyhound from a trap. He seized it, came back, and picked up the attaché case to restore the document. Soon after this the meeting ended and the two men went their separate ways. Holmes walked in my direction. I waited at the edge of the riders' avenue, so that he passed behind me. As he did so, there was no slackening of his pace and no movement of recognition. I heard only the crisp tone of his voice.

'Get after him, Watson! See where he goes!'

You may be sure that I did so, as unobtrusively as I could, Holmes striding away in the other direction. I was certain that, if we were spied upon, no one would guess that there had been any communication between us.

I knew quite well what would happen next. Charles Augustus Howell walked back the way he had come, a somewhat overweight figure with his soft face and wavy hair. He carried the attaché case up the steps of Drummonds Bank and I waited for him to reappear. He did so a few minutes later, still carrying the attaché case. Had he deposited the papers in the bank vault already—or was he still carrying them?

What made his reappearance the more curious was that he came down the steps into Pall Mall at almost the same moment as a second man, who carried an identical case. Picture a tall and stooping figure, a gaunt spectre, clean-shaven and pale, his forehead forming a white dome-like curve and his eyes appearing all the more sunken for that. I had no idea who this might be. Yet he and Howell carried attaché cases so alike that it was impossible to say which of them had been taken into the bank a moment before.

This appearance might have been a coincidence but I was sure it was not. At the foot of the steps, the stranger turned right towards Charing Cross and Howell turned left towards St James's Palace. It was impossible to follow them both. If Howell had reappeared without an attaché case, I should now have shadowed the stranger. As it was, I heard in my mind the last instruction of Sherlock Holmes and obeyed it. 'Get after him, Watson! See where he goes!'

He went smartly under the brick archway of the palace towards the Mall. I knew I must not lose him now and so I cared little if he saw me or not. Across the Mall he went, Buckingham Palace quiet in the sunlight at the far end. He dived into St James's Park and began to cut across towards the ducks on the lake, as if he was making for Birdcage Walk. He was hurrying but not sufficiently for me to lose sight of him. Then he paused. I stepped aside behind a chestnut trunk. Howell looked about him, as if to see whether he was alone. Then he thrust the attaché case into a box at the edge of the path, a green wooden receptacle in which the gardeners deposit grass clippings and fallen leaves.

What the purpose of this could be, I had no idea. As he strode off, I made my way as quickly as I could to the box and took out the leather case. It was not even locked. I opened it, expecting a bomb or a bundle of state papers, I know not what. It was empty. I might have followed either of the two men who came out of Drummonds Bank into Pall Mall. I knew now that I had followed the wrong one.

IV

'Let it be a consolation to you, my dear fellow, that they have made fools of us both.'

Holmes was examining the empty attaché case by the morning light that filled the sitting-room windows from above the Baker Street chimney-pots.

'Then who is he?' I asked. 'Which is the other man?'

'The client, I should say.' Holmes frowned and threw down the leather case as yielding no further clue. 'I know you will forgive the deception, friend Watson, but as you followed Howell back to Pall Mall, I followed you. When Howell came out again, I watched you shadow him and I went after the other man. The same trick was played in the Strand. My man went into Grindlays and two men with cases came out. By instinct, I followed the new man. He led me east to Cheapside, to the City and Suburban Bank. Our opponents were playing a game and did not care if I knew it. Two of them came out again into Cheapside but the second one was that same tall stooping man whom I had lost the last time in the Strand. I followed him again and lost him at the Banque Indo Suez in King William Street. That is how they play it and they can play it until doomsday. One man goes in and two come out. It would take Lestrade and fifty of his officers to keep track of them all. They are playing the game because they believe they hold every card in the pack. A dangerous folly.'

At this point, several days had passed since the meeting between Holmes and Howell. If there had been progress, I had seen none.

'Then it is all a wild-goose chase?' I said.

'So it would seem.' Holmes spoke as if he did not greatly care. 'Matters cannot be left as they are, however. I must invite Mr Howell to ask his client to name his terms. Howell may bring them to me tomorrow night. I will communicate them to Sir Arthur Bigge and leave the issue there.'

'Then we are not to get the better of these scoundrels?' I asked incredulously.

Holmes nodded at the empty attaché case. 'As the score stands now, Watson, it seems that we are not.'

This indifference was so unlike him that I wondered if Holmes might be unwell. I decided to test him.

'Then you will not require my further services? If not, I have a practice to attend to and preparations to make for Mrs Watson's return.'

He nodded, as if he quite understood. Then he looked up at me.

'One more thing,' he said, 'I should be grateful for. If Howell comes tomorrow night, I should prefer these rooms to be under observation. If it will not inconvenience your practice and Mrs Watson, perhaps you would keep Lestrade company.'

'Keep Lestrade company? Where?'

He gestured at the window. 'I have taken a room in Camden House across the street. It will give you a good view of these apartments. Should anything untoward take place, my signal for assistance will be the turning down of the gas.'

He was not himself, I now felt sure of it. That the great Sherlock Holmes did not dare be alone in his rooms with a spineless wretch like Howell, unless I and a Scotland Yard man were within call, was quite out of character.

'Has Lestrade agreed?'

'Yes,' said Holmes quietly, 'Lestrade has agreed. He knows only that it is a confidential matter.'

'Then I shall keep him company.'

'Thank you, my dear old friend,' he said in the same quiet voice. 'I never doubted that I could count upon you.'

V

The next evening it was dusk at about seven o'clock. Lestrade and I found ourselves in a first-floor room, which looked directly across to the Baker Street lodgings. Camden House was between 'lets' and this room contained little more than two chairs with a plain table. Holmes had pulled down the cream blinds and put up the gas.

He was sitting in his chair, the shadow of his sharp features and square shoulders thrown upon the blind by the gaslight. Indeed, if Howell or one of his confederates intended some desperate act, Holmes might have made a perfect target from one of the buildings opposite or from the street itself. Presently he got up and moved about the room beyond our vision. A light rain began to fall in the long street, and the people on the busy pavements wore coats and cravats, collars turned up and umbrellas open.

'Tell me,' I said to Lestrade, 'do you find anything unusual in Holmes's behaviour of late?'

Our Scotland Yard man sat in the twilight, puffing at his cigar, his pea-jacket and cravat giving him a somewhat nautical air.

'There's no use denying that, Dr Watson. It's not like him to want protection from me against whatever twopenny-halfpenny scoundrel that calls on him.'

'Indeed it is not!'

'Nor to have these fancy ideas about spoiling the paintwork of the London banks.'

'Oh?'

'Seems to have some bee in his bonnet about a man going round London defacing the paintwork and the fittings of the banks. I've not seen such a thing, sir. Have you?'

I assured him I had not. Before I could say more, the hooves of a cab horse slowed and stopped as a hansom drew up outside 221B Baker Street. Holmes's visitor had arrived. We could see little of him beyond the door opening and closing again as he was admitted. Holmes himself was still upstairs, turning in his fireside chair as he heard the footsteps. The cab moved off, to return again at its appointed time. Someone, Holmes presumably, now drew the curtain part-way across the window.

There was very little more to be seen. From time to time Holmes or his visitor threw a partial shadow on the blind. It was, I suppose, an hour later when the cab returned and the visitor left. As if in salute to the departing guest, there was the faint but unmistakable sound of Holmes striking a little Mendelssohn from his violin.

We waited twenty minutes more and then, as I had expected, the gas was turned down in the opposite room. Lestrade picked up his black canvas bag.

'Well, Dr Watson, I can make neither head nor tail of the business, nor shall I try.'

We crossed the street and Holmes greeted us—or rather met us—at the door. He was subdued and pale as a ghost. Lestrade refused his invitation to brandy and water. I remained for no more than an hour.

'The matter is concluded,' he said, 'so far as Howell is concerned.'

'Concluded?'

'Concluded,' Holmes said and closed his eyes. I thought it best to let it go at that.

VI

I had almost finished my surgery on the following evening. At any rate, I was told that there remained only one patient still waiting to see me. I looked up as he came through the doorway of the consulting room.

'Lestrade? What brings you to Paddington? Surely not a need of medical advice from me, of all people?'

He sat down across the desk from me, an unfamiliar sight among the bottles and sterilising dishes. His face expressed a mingled anxiety and anger.

'What's going on, Dr Watson? That's what I want to know. What the devil's up?'

'Nothing so far as I know. What should there be?'

'Mr Charles Augustus Howell!'

My heart sank at the revelation that Lestrade so much as knew of the man.

'What of him?'

'He wouldn't have been Mr Holmes's visitor last night, would he?'

'I have not the least idea. You must ask Mr Holmes.'

'Oh!' Lestrade's eyebrows shot up, almost humorously. 'I'll be asking Mr Holmes that, all right, the first chance I get. What concerns me just now is whether you and I might not have been used as an alibi.'

'An alibi for what?'

'You haven't heard then? An hour after Mr Holmes's visitor left last night, Charles Augustus Howell was found in the gutter outside the Green Man public house in Chelsea. His throat had been cut and a half-sovereign was wedged between his teeth.'

'The sign of vengeance on a slanderer . . .'

'The sign of something that has to do with Mr Holmes,' Lestrade said fiercely. 'They think a soldier did it, a Colonel Sebastian Moran who wrote letters to a young woman—letters that Howell was trying to sell back to him, for what that matters now. There's a tale from two informants that Mr Holmes put Colonel Moran on Howell's track last night, even that he was there. That's as much murder as if he did it himself! I'll tell you something worse, doctor! They took Howell to St Thomas's Hospital. He was dead by the time he got there, if not before. A murder inquiry was to begin this morning. Then I'm told, Dr Watson, there's to be no inquiry. Not a question to Colonel Moran! Someone very important— friend of Mr Holmes, I daresay—put a stop to a Scotland Yard investigation. I wasn't going to hold for that, so I inquired at the hospital. I asked what was on his death certificate. Do you know what it says? It says he died of pneumonia! Pneumonia! Did you ever hear the like?'

'No,' I said, half to myself. 'No, Lestrade, I don't think I ever did.'

'Pneumonia!' Lestrade said self-pityingly. 'That leaves nothing to investigate. But he didn't have time to die of pneumonia, Dr Watson. I saw him with my own eyes, lying there with his windpipe slit and looking like a real Robin Redbreast, if ever a man did. I'd like to know what's going on, that's all.'

But poor Lestrade was never to learn the half of that.

VII

'But if Howell is dead, we have lost the scent!' I repeated with greater exasperation. What was the matter with him? Could he not see it? Holmes lit his pipe with a spill from the fire of the Baker Street sitting-room. He shook the flame out in a flick of his wrist and puffed smoke over the room.

'I have observed several times of late, Watson, your tendency to over-dramatise the commonplaces of life. Even making allowances for the burdens that fall upon you as a married man, I cannot applaud it.'

I cut him short. 'This is not a common event. The heir to the throne is blackmailed. Howell is the one man who might have led us to the heart of the conspiracy. Howell is dead and so is the scent. Where shall we begin again? There is a good chance now that we shall never know where the documents concerning Prince George and his brother have been secured.'

He looked at me in genuine surprise, unable to believe I could be so dull.

'But, my dear fellow, since the day after I met Howell by the Serpentine I have known where they are. According to my best information, they have not been moved since.'

'But you cannot have known.'

'They are in Walkers Repository, the Cornhill Vaults at 63, Cornhill. I have been occupied with other matters or I should have had them out before now. Your new life has softened—blunted—your detective instinct. Did you suppose that I should go to meet Howell unprepared? Did you truly believe that I might not prove a match for such a petty trickster as he?'

'That does not explain it,' I said with some little asperity.

'Very well,' said Holmes in a more conciliatory manner. 'I will only say that I expected something of what happened. Suppose a man has goods to sell, stolen goods in this case. He must prove that he has them. I did not know whether Howell would bring them or fetch them. I thought he would fetch them in order that he and his friends might see if he was followed. His accomplice spotted you from the start, I fear.'

'I saw no one!'

Holmes waved his hand generously.

'It matters nothing, Watson. They were seduced by their own cleverness. When Howell returned with the paper in the attaché case, you were standing at a little distance. Perhaps you noticed a paper slip from my hand—a *résumé* of the stolen documents? It was carried several yards by the breeze in the park. As I hoped, Howell went after it like a hungry pigeon after a breadcrumb. It was only for a few seconds but his back was, necessarily, turned to me.'

'Of what use was that?'

Holmes stood up, walked to the table and picked up a small and tightly sealed bottle.

'It is a modest preparation of my own, slow-drying, colourless when wet, setting like a semi-luminous coat of white paint. Like many albumens it forms a white layer as it coagulates. Seen through a magnifying glass, it appears speckled with silver and aluminium grey from its other constituents. I do not think I would mistake even the smallest spot of it for any other compound. It was the easiest thing in the world to daub the bottom corners of the attaché case before Howell turned to me again. The back of the seat and my own coat concealed the movement of my hand from any other observation. The white smudges would not show on the leather until it dried hours later. Even if it was remarked, it would seem like some accidental blemish imparted during their use of the case.'

'So that was it!'

'I quite believed Howell when he told me that he and his confederate would keep the stolen documents in a strong-room—and that only he and the other man knew the contents of those documents. When one enters a bank, there is generally a special booth to one side of the counter at which to apply for access to such a vault, partitioned from the other clerks for privacy. It would be the most natural thing in the world for Howell or his confederate to lay an attaché case upon that counter, while his business was attended to. Of course, in those banks where they merely played their little game of one man going in and two men coming out, there would be no trace of my patent compound on the varnished wood. They would not go to the counter in such a place for they had no business there. Sooner or later, however, they would reach their destination. I flattered myself that, as it lay upon that counter, the attaché case would leave a mark that would be visible at once to the trained eye.'

'You could not be certain.'

Holmes sighed philosophically.

'Nothing, Watson, is certain. If it were, I should find it impossible to earn my bread. Let me say I thought it inconceivable that it should not be so. The following day I visited every counter of every bank vault and safe repository in the City of London that I thought at all likely. I was an inquirer after the facilities that they offered. At Walkers Vaults in Cornhill, there was a blemish on the polished wood, as if a brush loaded with white paint had touched it carelessly. Under the pretence of imperfect sight, I was able to examine it through my glass as I glanced at a paper. The characteristic specks of silver and aluminium grey were unmistakable.'

I shook my head.

'It will not do, Holmes. Even if you are right so far, you do not know where, in an entire bank vault, the papers are to be found.'

He did not reply directly.

'Do you recall, Watson, that two men came out of Drummonds Bank, when you followed Howell there a second time?'

'Distinctly.'

'Do you recall the second man, tall and thin, stooping as if from long hours of study, pale and sunken-eyed, a head so heavy with intelligence that it hangs—or lolls—as if it were too heavy for his neck to carry?'

'I should know him again at once.'

'I hope you will, Watson. That is Professor James Moriarty of mathematical celebrity, the man I describe in my notes as the Napoleon of Crime. When I told Sir Arthur Bigge that I felt I almost knew the name of our blackmailer, I already thought it was he. This plot bears the hallmark of his demented genius—for genius he is, in his way. He uses no alias and employs no disguise, believing that the brilliance of his mind alone is proof against all detection or arrest. Scotland Yard might find him at any time, for what good that would do them. His appearance on the steps of Drummonds Bank proves me right. Professor Moriarty is the "client" of the late Charles Augustus Howell, a man who might hold Howell in the palm of his hand and crush him with a clenching of his fingers, as I picturesquely described it to Sir Arthur.'

'But who is he? How can he be a professor of anything?'

'Oh, he is, Watson, or rather he was until proceedings for moral turpitude put an end to his career. The ruin of that poor young woman walks the *pavé* of the Haymarket to this day. Moriarty had won international fame at twenty-one for his paper on the binomial theorem. He is the first man in two centuries to prove Fermat's Last Theorem, the first in a hundred years to demonstrate the truth of the Goldbach Conjecture. He has no scruples, no morals, no pity. He is a genius, Watson, a criminal genius, and without doubt the most dangerous man in all Europe. Nothing would please him better than the prestige of having laid low a great royal house and a great nation. Think what his threats might command after that!'

'How do you connect him so positively with the Cornhill Vaults?'

Holmes smiled rather wanly. 'I did not trust to a smudge of paint alone, my dear fellow. When I made my inquiry as to the possibility of renting a strong-room drawer, I assured them that I could provide whatever references they needed. I offered your name, Watson, and I fear they shook their heads, for they had never heard of you as a healer of the sick in Paddington Green. I then offered the name of Professor James Moriarty and their faces radiated confidence. He is, they tell me, one of their most valued customers.'

'Then you will compromise with him? If you know where the papers are, you surely have him cornered.'

'I would shoot him like a rabid dog before I compromised with him,' Holmes said with some little heat.

'Then what are we to do?'

'This morning is Friday,' Holmes said. 'By Monday, our adversary may have discovered that his agent did not die of pneumonia, after all. Therefore, Watson, you will spend Saturday with a tray round your neck, selling matches for the benefit of a truly charitable cause. What shall we say—what heroes shall we commemorate? I have it! You shall sell matches for a group of old and forgotten soldiers. The Last of the Light Brigade, as Mr Kipling has it in the verses which he kindly read at our recent meeting.'

'And you, Holmes? What of you?'

He took the pipe from his mouth. 'Dear me,' he said. 'I see nothing for it but to turn safe-breaker and visit the Cornhill Vaults.'

VIII

A madcap scheme if ever there was, or so it seemed. However, as readers of our other narratives will recall, Sherlock Holmes had the arts of the cracksman at his fingertips and was not averse to using them when justice required it.

The Cornhill Vaults stood on one of the busiest streets in London, until the traffic dwindled at noon on Saturday and the city lay quiet over the weekend. The premises were equipped with a series of safes, Milner's Quadruple Patent, described as 'Violence, Robbery, and Fraud-Resisting', and steel drawers for documents. These were also fire-resisting chambers, the safe doors of half-inch wrought iron and the bodies quarter-inch. The stacked document drawers and the safes themselves were ranged against the iron-lined walls of the room.

A curiosity of the room was that it was on constant display to the public. Iron shutters were drawn down to the pavement whenever the premises were unoccupied but these shutters were pierced by holes, whereby pedestrians, including policemen on the beat, might look through narrow apertures into the strong-room. The interior was brightly lit by gas, day and night. It was a novel form of security, simple as it was ingenious, and was coupled with a reward of £500 to any member of the public who provided information of an attempt upon the safes. To facilitate this, several mirrors had been arranged in the vaults by which every approach to the safes and the stacks of steel document drawers would be visible through the holes in the iron shutters.

From 2 P.M. on Saturday afternoon, it was my duty to stand by the iron shutter with my tray of matches and wooden collecting box. By then the business of the week was over for the banks and offices of the City of London. Cornhill would lie as empty as a country road until Monday morning. At the approach of a pedestrian, I was to rattle my collecting-box loudly enough for Holmes to hear on the other side of the aperture, also calling out, 'Last of the Light Brigade!' When the pedestrian had passed, I was to rattle the box again but without speaking.

From the start, I feared that it would go wrong. Next to the Cornhill Vaults, at street level, was a tailor's shop. There were other business premises on the upper floors—a watch-maker, an insurance agent, a re-coverer of umbrellas—which were reached by going through a narrow arch to the rear of the building and up the courtyard stairs. All the premises, like the tailor's shop, closed for the weekend at 1 P.M. on Saturday or before. Holmes had reconnoitred the building the previous day by taking an umbrella for repair.

At about noon on Saturday, the elderly woman who kept watch on the door in the little court was surprised by the arrival of the gasman. He was a rather stooping grey-haired figure who had seen his best days, his moustache straggling and his eyes owl-like behind rimless spectacles. Someone had reported a smell of gas. The good woman had not herself noticed it. On being invited out of her cubby-hole, however, she found a distinct smell of gas on the stairs. Holmes the Gasman had prepared a tin of coal-tar, adding to it such ingredients as would enhance the smell of gas, when the lid was surreptitiously removed.

It was almost 1 P.M., while the woman was on the top floor making her final tour of the building, when the gasman found his leak and noisily tightened the joint of a pipe with a spanner, which he took from his leather bag of tools. He shouted up to her and ambled off down the stairs. She heard him close the courtyard door as he went out. Holmes, of course, had closed the door and remained in the building. On his first visit, he had noticed a cupboard under the stairway with a sloping ceiling, where the cleaners deposited brooms and buckets. It had a little bolt on the outside, just sufficient to serve as a catch and held in place by tacks. There was no reason for the female guardian to look in there but, to make assurance doubly sure, my part was to enter the courtyard door with my tray of matches and push the little bolt across. If the good woman glanced at all, she would think it quite impossible that anyone could be in there while it was bolted from the outside. To distract her a little further, I shouted up the stairs from the doorway to inquire whether any of the tradesmen on the floor above might care to support a worthy cause. She replied abruptly that they had all left for the weekend.

Within ten minutes, she had gone, locking Holmes alone in the building, the safe-breaker's tools in his gasman's bag. To force open the cupboard door which concealed him, wrenching out the slot of the little bolt, was the work of a moment. Then, for appearance's sake, he had tacked the metal fitting back into place.

He made his way to the work-room at the back of the tailor's shop, secure in the knowledge that he would scarcely be disturbed before Monday. Freeing the carpet at the rear wall, he folded it back, taking up two short lengths of board. Lowering himself through the gap, he was in the unlit foundations, rubble underfoot and boards above, divided from the Cornhill Vaults by a rough stone wall.

This wall was a crude division rather than a load-bearing support. There was even a ventilation grille between the two premises. In the next hour, Holmes was able to tap out the grille and two stones adjoining, which gave a sufficient space to slither through. By two o'clock, as I took up my sentry-go with the collecting box and the matches, he was in the space that served as foundations for the Cornhill Vaults.

From his previous visit to the Vaults, Holmes told me that he had a good idea of where the attack must be made. To try the strong-room floor above him was out of the question. The floor, like the walls, would surely be reinforced by iron. Behind the strong-room, however, was an office with a carpet at its centre, stretching almost to the walls, where varnished boards formed a surround a few inches broad. It was possible, from underneath, to use the old jack-in-the-box safe-breaker's tool which lay in his gasman's bag. The jack could bring pressure of a quarter of a ton against a safe and as its iron thread extended upwards the nails holding down the floorboards burst from the joists. By half-past two, Holmes was in the rear office of the Cornhill Vaults.

I could picture him as he confronted the strong-room door. His long experience and the sensitivity of his tools would put a locksmith to shame. I had watched him practise his skill on the latest locks, laying them on the table in Baker Street. Once, as his accomplice, I had seen him tackle a safe that was almost identical to the strong-room lock of the Cornhill Vaults. I pictured him now, as then, unrolling his case of instruments and choosing each one with the calm scientific accuracy of a surgeon who performs a delicate operation. He would work with concentrated energy, laying down one tool, picking up another, handling each with the strength and unhurried delicacy of the trained mechanic. You might have exploded a bomb outside and he would not have heard it. Yet he could read in his mind, as if it were the softest music, the tiny whisper of steel touching steel in the mechanism. One after another, he patiently guided five metal probes into the lock, each covered with lamp-black and each designed to show the position of one of the levers as the probe was turned and the lamp-black scraped off by contact with the metal.

Caution, as well as skill, brought him his reward on these occasions. Taking the measurements, Holmes would adjust a skeleton key, until its five teeth met exactly with the five levers in the lock.

After a few minutes, the steel skeleton turned freely and the lock of the door rolled back.

The Cornhill Vaults provided another obstacle. Within the next few paces, Holmes would be revealed to the spy-holes of the iron shutter by the mirrors that covered the approaches to the safes and stacks of steel document drawers. Outside, the street of banks and commercial premises was clear, except for an elderly man and a middle-aged couple strolling on the far pavement. I could not help turning and caught the reflection of the 'gasman' standing by a tall stack of deep metal drawers, each locked by its own key. They were not, of course, identified by the names of the customers but only by their numbers. However, each drawer contained a little frame with a card, which indicated when the drawer had been opened by its tenant, the initials of the visitor verifying this. Holmes first eliminated all those that had not been opened at least twice on the previous Tuesday, once to take the 'specimen document' out and once to return it. There were two drawers remaining. He would have broken open both, had not one card borne the initials 'J. M.'

'The Last of the Light Brigade!'

I shouted the warning even before I rattled the collecting box, which as yet held only the coins I had put in at the start. The policeman on his beat was walking slowly along this side of the street, glancing at doors and windows, sometimes testing the handle of a door. Prudently, I moved a little away down the pavement from the iron shutter of the Cornhill Vaults so that I might not appear to be concealing anything. It seemed an age before he reached the spot where I had been standing. He stooped a little and put his eyes to the holes in the iron shutter. Then he straightened up, saluted as he passed me, and walked slowly on with his rolling gait. I let him get twenty or thirty yards away before I shook the box once more. Holmes, who had moved out of range of the mirrors, stepped back and resumed his task.

To break open a document drawer, as to break open a safe, two implements are used. The first is a metal wedge known as an 'alderman'. It is heavy and will widen the gap between the door and the frame of almost any safe that has ever been built, provided there is time enough and power enough behind the hammer-blows that are struck. It may take six or seven hours where the safe is of the strongest kind but the gap will open in the end. To avoid more damage and more labour than is necessary, several smaller wedges, known as 'citizens', are employed second to force clear the tongue of the lock.

Holmes used the 'alderman' once and with great delicacy. He followed this with three 'citizens' spaced along the top aperture between the drawer and the frame. Twice more I had to interrupt him but at last, doing as little damage as possible, he felt the drawer move. The documents that had threatened so much now lay before him in the depth of the metal drawer. There was a slim journal-volume, two packets of letters in their envelopes, tied with ribbon, and several papers in a folder.

The hardest part, he told me, was to manipulate the lock of the drawer so that it gave some semblance of being fastened again. A bank official or a locksmith would know at once that it was not working properly. So would our adversary but he dared not say so. He would find the drawer empty and would know that he had got the worst of the battle, hoist by his own petard.

For the next few hours, as the afternoon mellowed into sunset and evening came, Holmes retraced his steps. He could not, he told me, leave everything perfectly in order. His aim was to leave such an *appearance* of order that he would cause no alarm nor even curiosity among the guardians of these premises. His greatest concern was for the steel document drawer. Yet if its tenant did not complain that it had been tampered with or that its contents were missing, what reason had the guardians of the vault to suggest it?

The closing of the strong-room door was as meticulously effected as the opening of it. Holmes then wrapped a probe with lint soaked in surgical spirit. Using this, he wiped away as much of the lamp black as was possible. Regaining the office behind the vault, he dropped down through the gap in the floorboards, drew the edge of the carpet into place and slid the two boards into the gap. He could not force the nails of the last board into the joist but trusted to the first man who walked across the carpet to do that for him. At the worst, it would merely be taken for a loose board.

At the rough wall, dividing the foundations from those of the tailor's, he replaced the two stones and the grille. By the time he had finished, it appeared that the mortar holding them might have crumbled but without giving cause for suspicion. Then it was simple enough to pull himself up through the gap and into the work-room behind the tailor's shop, replacing the boards and treading them down. The lamps had scarcely begun to glimmer down the length of Cornhill when he let himself out quietly into the darkness of the courtyard at the back of the building. The skeleton key was adjusted to three simple levers and the door was locked after him.

Next day, Sherlock Holmes begged an appointment with Sir Arthur Bigge at Windsor. He reported that the plot consisted of Howell and his 'client', the professor. There had been other men hired by them to carry attaché cases here and there—but without knowing why. Yet Holmes was sure that only those two conspirators had known the secrets of the stolen papers. Howell had met a sudden death. Professor Moriarty, in the next few days, discovered that the documents by which he set such store were no longer in his possession. He did not complain of this, for he dared not. If our information was correct, our adversary paid his final bill for rent at the Cornhill Vaults and fled.

IX

Our adversary had fled! Would that he had! Months passed and then a dreadful ordeal, what I have called elsewhere 'The Final Problem', was upon us. One meeting of Holmes and his adversary was described in that narrative as a mere report. In truth, I witnessed it but could scarcely bear to think so.

A week or so after the visit to the Cornhill Vaults, I was with Holmes in the Baker Street sitting-room when a cab stopped outside. My friend stood up.

'That voice!' he said, as the passenger dismissed the cab. 'It is he, Watson. You had better leave. No! You had better stay. Go into the bedroom and wait. He will not, I think, try violence here but it is as well to be prepared.'

I did as he said. Holmes had been lounging at ease in his dressing-gown and now made no attempt to change for there was scarcely time. As I went into the next room, I heard him call out to Mrs Hudson to show the visitor up. Then I heard him open a drawer and there was the bump of metal against wood. This guest, then, was the professor of reptilian face, as Holmes described him, who had won his youthful laurels by a commentary upon the binomial theorem. I heard the new arrival say, 'It is a dangerous habit, Mr Holmes, to finger loaded firearms in the pocket of one's dressing-gown.'

There was a sound of the pistol being laid on a table.

'Pray take a seat,' said Holmes coldly. 'I can spare you five minutes, if you have anything to say.'

'All that I have to say has already crossed your mind,' the visitor remarked.

'Then possibly my answer has crossed yours,' Holmes replied equably.

'You stand fast?'

'Absolutely.'

Through the crack in the door I saw that the other man, whom I first set eyes upon walking down the steps of Drummonds Bank with Howell, had clapped his hand into his pocket and Holmes raised the pistol from the table. But his guest merely drew out a memorandum-book in which he had scribbled some dates.

'You crossed my path on the fourth of January, Mr Holmes. On the twenty-third of January you incommoded me. By the middle of February I was seriously inconvenienced by you. At the end of March I was absolutely hampered in my plans. Now I find myself placed in such a position through your continual persecution that I am in danger of losing my liberty. You must drop it, Mr Holmes, you really must, you know.'

Holmes said something which I did not quite catch.

'It is necessary that you should withdraw,' the other insisted. 'It has been an intellectual treat to me to see the way in which you have grappled with this affair of Prince George's marriage—for I am assured he really was married, you know—and it would be a grief to me to take any extreme measure. I anticipated that you must surely be the one man to whom Sir Arthur Bigge would turn. It was my hope that such a design as mine would draw you out and that we should meet at last—that we should meet upon equal terms and perhaps become partners in some great enterprise. My mistake, I confess, was in allowing Mr Howell to impose himself upon me.'

'A mistake on his part too,' Holmes said drily, 'though certainly a far greater mistake on yours. There is a world of mathematics where you might enjoy such fame and such respect as you never will among common criminals.'

'I had hoped,' the professor said, 'that our recent test of skills might bring us into harmony. Come, now, do not play the outraged subject of the Queen! You care no more for flummery and majesty than I do! Confess it!'

'I care nothing for flummery,' Holmes said, his fingers never more than a few inches from the pistol, 'nothing at all. I care, however, a good deal for honour and, in general, for truth.'

'But evidently not for the truth which I have revealed!'

'No, sir.'

'I did not do it for money,' Professor Moriarty insisted, his eyes staring and his large head rolling a little. 'I have more than I need. I hoped you and I, in sympathy, might forge a revolution that would change the world. There will be such a revolution, you may be sure. Why should it not be ours, the work of men who stand above the vulgar herd, the hero whom Nietzsche promises?'

'If you know the least thing about me,' Holmes said brusquely, 'you will be aware that such a suggestion can hold no charms for me.'

The stranger sighed with a regret that seemed entirely genuine.

'Then I must tell you that you will stand in the way not merely of an individual, Mr Holmes, but of a mighty organisation. Within it, you might have untold influence. If that is not for you, however, you must stand clear or be trodden underfoot.'

Holmes stood up and spoke with the coldest insolence he could muster. 'I regret, Professor Moriarty, that in the pleasure of this conversation I am neglecting business of importance which awaits me elsewhere.'

Moriarty now stood as well.

'It has been a duel between us, Mr Holmes, this matter of the royal papers. As yet, however, we have exchanged but the first shots. You hope to place me in the dock. I tell you I will never stand in the dock. If you are clever enough to bring destruction upon me, rest assured that I shall do as much to you.'

How those words were to echo, after the two men met on that dreadful day at the Reichenbach Falls. All ended well, I suppose, though the missing years of Sherlock Holmes were like missing years in my own life too. When, three weeks after that day on which I last saw him, an invitation to Sandringham arrived in the hand of Sir Arthur Bigge, my own state was such that I was obliged to present my humble duty to His Royal Highness and decline, on a card that was edged with black. Three years were to pass before death gave back my friend and Holmes was able to collect his diamond tie-pin after all. His return to London was final confirmation that Professor Moriarty, the second man who sought to blemish the reputation of our royal house, was dead. What secrets there might be were now safe for as long as it should matter.

In those three years of separation, when I believed my friend dead, not a day passed without my thinking that he had gone willingly to his death to ensure the simultaneous destruction and silence of Professor Moriarty. The secrets of the stolen papers could not be safe again until both men who had known them were dust. The documents might be recovered but the knowledge was stolen for ever. Did Holmes take a secret vow that both Moriarty and Howell must die—so that the knowledge should die with them—even at the cost of his own life?

I thought that was why he had gone without protest to his fate at the Falls of Reichenbach. But what of Charles Augustus Howell?

Was Lestrade right, after all in his suspicion that he and I had been tricked to provide an alibi for Sherlock Holmes? It would be hard to imagine a better witness than a Scotland Yarder!

Night after night I lay awake and thought. Could Holmes have left the rooms at 221B Baker Street, while Lestrade and I watched them? Could he have been absent for an hour while we thought him there, so that he might track down Howell in Chelsea as a matter of cold necessity, cut the man's throat, wedge the half-sovereign between his teeth, and return home? I would get up from my bed, light the lamp, and examine for the hundredth time how such a trick might be performed. We had seen Holmes's outline against the blind. But my friend had once shown me that perfect bust made of him by Oscar Meunier of Grenoble, a masterpiece of reality if ever there was. And then we had heard the snatch of Holmes playing Mendelssohn upon the fiddle at a time when he must have been several miles away slitting Howell's windpipe, if he were the murderer. But Holmes was an enthusiast of the American phonograph and had acquired a machine as early as 1889. I later watched as he recorded Joachim's music for *Hamlet* by playing into the mouth of the great horn on to the cylinder of wax. What had we heard? The music of Holmes or his ghost?

Sitting in my chair on such sleepless nights, I pictured to myself a scene in which Mycroft Holmes was the muffled figure who arrived by cab, responding to his brother's most pressing request. While Mycroft Holmes from time to time adjusted the shadow of the bust against the blind, adjusted the wax cylinder upon its spindle and wound the phonograph, his brother slipped out by the back door of Baker Street, met the cab by appointment, kept the fatal rendezvous and returned. Was it an absurd midnight imagining or the truth? After so much of his cleverness with locks and strong-rooms, was not the simple truth that two men knew the secrets of royal scandal in all their facts and all their truth—and that those two men must die to ensure silence? Colonel Sebastian Moran, a bad enough man indeed, was merely a name thrown in to confuse Lestrade. If all this was true, Holmes had gone to the Reichenbach Falls to meet destiny in the only way that would put an end to the case, as a soldier will sacrifice himself in battle to save his comrades.

He would never discuss it after his return, or rather he laughed it off. Meantime, the removal of Professor Moriarty had happier consequences than that of Howell. Even before Sherlock Holmes's triumphant reappearance, Prince George was betrothed to Princess May of Teck. Two months later, the future King and Queen were married in the Chapel Royal of St James's Palace. Charles Augustus Howell lies in Brompton Cemetery, a victim of 'pneumonia'. I did not hear that the body of Professor James Moriarty was ever recovered.

The Case of the Camden Town Murder

I

In the course of his professional career, Sherlock Holmes seldom worked in collaboration with the great legal names of his day. Yet on the few occasions when his advice was sought, he owed the recommendation to a famous barrister whom he once helped as a young man and never met again.

The encounter took place late one evening, in the very last months of the nineteenth century. I was about to wish Holmes goodnight and turn in when there was a clang of the bell at the street door of our rooms. It was repeated almost at once with a note of greater urgency. In a few moments, the housekeeper, who had been roused from bed herself, announced that a young gentleman of the most respectable appearance insisted upon seeing Mr Sherlock Holmes at once and would take no refusal. I quite expected my friend to make some protest at the lateness of the hour, but he said only, 'Dear me, Mrs Hudson. Then, if he is so very insistent and respectable, I suppose we must grant him an audience.'

The good lady showed up a tall and thin-faced young man, a saturnine and somewhat satanic-looking figure in a Norfolk jacket and knickerbockers. A handsome dark-haired young devil he looked, with eyes that were black in an intensity of natural passion. He appeared, Holmes afterwards remarked, as if immaculately shaved and barbered not an hour before. Only when the housekeeper had withdrawn and the door was closed did he tell us that he was Mr Frederick Edwin Smith, a junior barrister on the Northern Circuit, and that he had killed a man in Liverpool the night before.

Holmes seemed little surprised but insisted that Mr Smith should tell us his story carefully and calmly from an armchair with a glass of brandy and soda in his hand.

For fifteen minutes my friend and I listened without interrupting to the man whom the world later knew in succession as F. E. Smith, Member of Parliament, Attorney-General, Earl of Birkenhead and Lord Chancellor of England in the government of Mr Lloyd George. His tale that evening was dramatic and yet curiously commonplace. This young man, not long called to the Bar at Gray's Inn, had been on a municipal tram-car in Liverpool late the previous night. A ruffianly fellow had attempted to get on at a stop near the centre of the city, just as a young lady was getting off. He had thrust her aside so hard that she stumbled. Mr Smith's chivalry brought him to his feet and he struck the ruffian hard on the jaw. To his dismay, he saw the man fall backwards from the boarding platform of the tram. The poor devil dropped heavily into the street and hit the back of his head with terrible force on the stone kerb of the pavement.

Our visitor knew at once that the man was dead, as the next day's newspapers confirmed. At the time of the accident, with instinctive panic or great presence of mind, our young client had leapt from the tram and had run as fast as his legs would carry him from the scene. In a torment of indecision, which was quite out of character, he had come from Liverpool to London to consult Sherlock Holmes, the one man in England whose discretion and resource he trusted. Money was no object and, as to his immediate course of action, he put himself entirely in our hands. Holmes showed not the least hesitation.

'I have no doubt, Mr Smith, as to what you must do. First, tell no one else of this event. I make it a habit to read a little of the *Law Quarterly Review* from time to time and have seen some excellent pieces of yours on Maritime Law. It is a sphere of commerce in which you seem admirably informed. I assume from this that you have certain business connections thereabouts. Go to a friend whom you can trust implicitly, preferably a man in the shipping trade. Arrange to travel as secretly as you can and as far as you can—and stay away for as long as you can. I should say that six months would probably be sufficient. I concede that you are more expert in law than I, but I believe I may claim an advantage in knowledge of the police and their methods. If nothing is discovered in six months about this mishap—for one can scarcely call it a crime—the Liverpool police will have lost interest in the investigation. I think you may return then without risk of being called to account for it.'

The young Frederick Smith did as Holmes advised and found his confidence in my friend well placed. In the years that followed, several cases of greater interest came our way, most of them I believe on the recommendation of the famous barrister to whom Holmes was a good friend and counsellor on that evening in his youth.

These occasional investigations were usually in cases over which Sherlock Holmes was approached by solicitors whose clients faced the gallows or long prison sentences. Among the most famous defenders of innocent and guilty alike, he had known very few. It was not until 1907 that he first met the great Sir Edward Marshall Hall, though the two men had been equally celebrated in their respective fields for almost twenty years by that time.

Holmes and Sir Edward shared that curious balance of a passionate temperament and a cold dedication to forensic analysis. Both were expert in the mysteries of firearms and medical curiosities. Yet there was a deeper sympathy between them. Holmes was one of the few men to know the details of the great private tragedy that had made Sir Edward Marshall Hall turn his back upon hopes of domestic happiness for many years and throw all his energies into a public career. As a young barrister, Sir Edward had married a beautiful wife, a match that was the envy of the world of London society. Within hours of the wedding ceremony, his young bride told him that she never had and never could care for him. She would be his wife in name only. Why she should have married him at all was a mystery that only a physician might resolve.

On their honeymoon in Paris, the poor deranged young woman disappeared for days or nights at a time. She sought in the habits of the street-walker some solace for her dark cravings. After a few years of unutterable misery for them both, she died at the hands of an abortionist and in the presence of a young lover whose child she feared to bear. To those who knew him professionally, Holmes had a mind that was cold and precise to the point of seeming pitiless. Yet I had seen him moved to tears by human tragedy, never more profoundly so than in the secret agony of Sir Edward Marshall Hall.

Their first meeting was the result of a few paragraphs in the morning papers on 13 September 1907. Like the death of the ruffian who had fallen from the Liverpool tram, the story was dramatic but commonplace in the twilit world where it had occurred.

A young London prostitute, Emily Dimmock, who went by the name of Phyllis Shaw, had been found with her throat cut in shabby lodgings, in the little streets of Camden Town. The wound was so deep that her head was almost severed from her body. The police surgeon's examination suggested that she had been murdered in the small hours of the morning of 12 September. Her body was not found until her common-law husband returned a little before noon from his overnight duty as Midland Railway cook on the express between King's Cross and Sheffield. He, at any rate, was innocent of her death. The poor girl's naked body lay face-down on the bed. In the other room were several empty beer bottles and the remains of a meal set for two, the sole evidence that she had had a companion with her that previous night.

Several days passed and little was added to the reports of the crime. There were no arrests, despite the appeals of the police and the offer of a £500 reward. It was three weeks later when Holmes folded his morning paper and leaned back in his chair. This was the hour after breakfast when he was accustomed to deliver his opinions on the news of the day. He handed me the paper.

'From the point of view of the criminal investigator, Watson, the Camden Town murder promises a most interesting suspect. They have charged an artist, a *protégé* of the late Mr William Morris, with cutting the throat of that unfortunate young woman.'

'An artist?'

He leaned forward and tapped the newspaper report with the stem of his pipe.

'Mr Robert Wood, twenty-eight years old. A painter of designs on glass for the Sand and Blast Manufacturing Company of Gray's Inn Road. A young man whose talent was praised by no less a patron than the last of the great Pre-Raphaelites. You see? When an artist turns to murder, Watson, it augurs well for the student of unusual psychiatric syndromes. You should read again De Quincey's "On Murder Considered One of the Fine Arts", if you have not done so of late.'

I thought my friend's view of the sordid crime in Camden Town a little grandiose and absurd. Yet Holmes was wont to pass frivolous comments on the blackest of crimes, for the fun of seeing if I would rise to the bait. I had grown accustomed to letting such sallies pass without comment.

Unfortunately, it was plain that my friend was not prepared to let the matter drop. We returned from our ramble that afternoon, during which it had taken all my persuasion to prevent him from setting out across the autumn lawns of Regent's Park to examine the back-street of Camden Town, where the murder had been committed. After tea he took a glowing cinder with the fire-tongs and lit the long cherrywood pipe, which he preferred to a clay pipe when he was in an argumentative mood. It was a relief to me, just then, to hear the jangle of the doorbell and the housekeeper's steps on the stairs before he could begin. Mrs Hudson entered with a card on a tray. Holmes took it up.

'Mr Arthur Newton,' he read out, 'Attorney of Lincoln's Inn. By all means, Mrs Hudson. Show Mr Newton up!'

He looked happier than I had seen him all week. Our visitor was a dapper man of forty with an old-fashioned collar, a round and rather sallow face, dark hair that was a little curly, and the general air of an Italian baritone. He made his apologies for intruding, was reassured by Holmes, and then came to the point as we seated him by the fireplace.

'I daresay, gentleman, you will have read by now something of the death of a young woman in St Paul's Road—'

Holmes shot forward to the edge of his chair.

'The Camden Town Murder!'

'No murder has been proved, Mr Holmes. Nor do I intend that it shall be. Not against Mr Wood, at least.'

I intervened at this point. 'All the same, Mr Newton, a coroner's jury has found murder and Mr Wood is named by them as the perpetrator.'

I thought, as the saying goes, that my reply took a little of the starch out of Mr Newton. He seemed ready to make peace.

'Very well, gentlemen. I believe in his innocence but I must concede that matters look black for Mr Wood. For that reason it is the more imperative, even before we brief counsel, that we should endeavour to build a secure defence. There we have a great difficulty. Because of it, and because I fear an innocent man may go to the gallows, I have asked leave to retain your services in the matter of gathering evidence.'

'Quite so.' Holmes sat back and studied the end of his pipe. 'And what, pray, is your great difficulty, Mr Newton?'

'Mr Robert Wood himself. He is a young man of respectable family who, unknown to his father, has for some time kept company with those prostitutes frequenting the public houses of Camden Town and the Euston Road. He was with Miss Emily Dimmock on the three nights preceding her murder. Indeed, at the police station after his arrest, he was pointed out on the identification parade as the last person to be seen with her. It was a few hours before her throat was cut, gentlemen. Worst of all, he was picked out by a witness as the man seen leaving the house in St Paul's Road where the dead woman was found. It was a few minutes before five o'clock in the morning, at just the time she met her death, on the evidence of *rigor mortis* and the digestion of her last meal. He has also been identified, by the peculiarity of his gait, as a man seen walking away from the house at the same time. This last suspect was seen to hold the left arm bent awkwardly as he swung it and the right shoulder forward. The Crown has a witness or two who will swear that Robert Wood used to walk in that manner, even if he can prevent himself from ever doing so again.'

Holmes got up and went across to the window. He stood between the parted blinds, gazing down into the dull neutral-tinted London street as the October afternoon thickened into twilight.

'A strong case in circumstantial evidence, Mr Newton. Apart from the fact that your client was identified as the man seen leaving the house in the early morning, it might be plainly answered. Even with that identification, I hardly think a jury will convict on the uncorroborated statement of a single witness who has never seen Mr Wood on any other occasion. There is little in such evidence which might not be countered by his apparent lack of motive for the murder and the good character of the accused. Your client is a *protégé* of Mr William Morris, is he not? That may stand him in good stead.'

Mr Newton turned in his chair to face Holmes.

'There is more to it, Mr Holmes. A postcard to Miss Dimmock, signed "Alice" but in my client's handwriting, was found in the dead woman's room. In the fireplace were fragments of a burnt letter, the unburnt pieces in his handwriting.'

'Hmmm!' said Holmes. 'Not so good.'

'Furthermore, Mr Holmes, my client behaved unfortunately after the murder.'

'In what manner?'

'He asked a friend, a young bookseller in the Charing Cross Road by the name of Joseph Lambert, to keep secret the fact of seeing him with Dimmock in the bar of the Eagle public house opposite Camden Town station at ten thirty on the night of her death. Worse still, he persuaded his own mistress, an artist's model known as Ruby Young, to concoct an alibi with him for the whole evening.

Both Lambert and Miss Young have informed the police of these collusions, for fear of being charged as accessories to the murder.'

'Is that all?' Holmes inquired.

'No, Mr Holmes. The worst of it, as I say, is Wood himself. He is vain as a peacock and sure of his own cleverness. He makes the worst possible witness.'

'Then you must not call him,' I said, intervening again.

Mr Newton looked at me sadly.

'Until the Criminal Evidence Act became law in 1898, Dr Watson, the accused was not permitted to give evidence in a murder trial. Now that he is permitted, it is also expected. The worst conclusions are drawn if the defendant in a murder trial fails to tell his story and be examined upon it. True, prosecuting counsel is forbidden from commenting on a refusal to give evidence. The judge, however, may say what he pleases to the jury—and usually does.'

Holmes turned to me.

'Mr Newton is correct, Watson. If Wood refuses to appear in the witness-box, he will hang as high as Haman.'

Our visitor spread out his hands. 'So you see, gentlemen, our one hope is to ensure that the case can be won upon the facts, despite all that young Mr Wood may do to destroy himself.'

'Just so,' said Holmes thoughtfully, puffing at his pipe and gazing down into the fire. 'If you have so difficult a client as this young man, the facts are the only things that may save him—if they do not hang him first.'

Half an hour later, Mr Arthur Newton took his leave. In the middle of that night as it seemed, I was woken by Holmes shaking me briskly by the shoulder. He was holding a lantern and its light showed him to be fully dressed.

'We must hurry, Watson. It is very nearly four o'clock and it will not do to be in St Paul's Road later than a quarter to five.'

Holmes was habitually a late riser and, until that moment, I had no idea that we were to visit the scene of the murder at the same hour as the crime was committed. With some grumbling to this effect, I dressed and was ready a little before twenty past four. Dawn remained a good way off and the weather seemed the worst that autumn. In the tempestuous October morning, the wind screamed and rattled against our windows as we drank black coffee which Holmes had prepared. Presently we battled our way to the all-night cab-stand in the Euston Road, where the drivers lounged against the counter of the stall with its steaming urns.

Ten minutes later, in the lamplight, our cab turned into the Hampstead Road and then into the huddled streets of Camden Town. It is that area where the great railway lines run north in cuttings or on arches from Euston and King's Cross, the night air torn by the scream of engine-whistles and the rush of steam. St Paul's Road was a vista of houses in soot-crusted yellow brick, behind them on one side a blank railway wall. Below that wall, the engines of the London and North-Eastern snorted, goods wagons shunted and clattered, the red eyes of the signal gantries glowed in the dark as the night express rattled and hooted its way across the steel points of the tracks to Edinburgh and the north.

The house where the young woman had met her death stood tall and shabby at the end of a terrace. A long flight of stone steps led up to the front door. A man leaving these premises would be on full view to passers-by while he closed the front door and came down the steps to the street. Had it been any other house in the row, he might have been less plainly visible. However, number 29 was illuminated from both sides by street-lamps, as plainly as a spot-lit stage. As if to prove this point, the witness MacCowan had picked out Robert Wood at once from the men lined up in the police station yard.

Holmes said nothing. We stood with the collars of our coats turned up, the wind too strong to allow an umbrella. Five o'clock came. Half past five followed it. There was no sign of a man on his way to work with his left arm bent and his right shoulder hunched forward. It seemed a fruitless vigil. We walked back to Camden Town station and took another cab to Baker Street. Holmes sat silent in his chair, the morning papers unread. The plain truth was that Robert Wood had behaved with every sign of guilt in asking two friends to lie on his behalf. He had been picked out as the man who stood in the lamplight, and as he who walked in the unusual manner. He was the last person to be seen with Emily Dimmock. Mr Wood, it now seemed to me, was likely to become our first client to be hanged.

II

I quite expected Holmes to be anxious or subdued by this confirmation of Mr Newton's fears. Instead, he appeared to behave in a most frivolous and unaccountable manner. In the evenings of the following week, he was seldom at home. Nor, indeed, did he return until the small hours of the morning. He had not been near Camden Town. Most of his time was spent at the Café Royal or, more often, at Romano's with its famous upstairs bar and tables, its oysters and champagne, its fish-tank in the bright first-floor window that blazed across the Strand.

I had not the least idea, nor would he say, what purpose there could be in so much time spent with sporting swells like 'Flash Fred' Valere or 'Little Jack' Shepherd, with rowdy guardsmen and Gaiety girls. Robert Wood was certainly no part of their world. When it was not the Café Royal or Romano's, Holmes's steps took him to the Criterion Bar, always among much the same company. In my anxiety, I lay awake and listened for his return. I would hear his footsteps on the stairs, then Holmes moving about the sitting-room, murmuring to himself the tune of the latest ditty from his new companions.

> O, Jemima! O, Jemima! Your poor old mother's heard
> All about our little games—she has upon my word . . .

He no longer read The Times after breakfast, preferring the tinted racing columns of the Sporting Times or the Pink 'Un, whose editor John Corlett was one of his new friends. I bit my tongue and kept silent.

Then he was gone for two entire days and nights. Mr Newton called, anxious for news of our progress in the inquiry. I could tell him nothing and feared the lawyer's apprehension might soon turn to anger at the lackadaisical manner in which Holmes seemed to be treating the investigation.

This anxiety was nothing compared with the callers at our street door. There were quite a dozen in the course of those two days and more to follow. They were an evil and violent-looking procession of ruffians, some with 'cauliflower' ears, a picturesque variety of broken noses, burly and crop-haired for the most part, a few of them smaller in build but all the more malicious in their attitude.

By the time that those two days were at an end, I had confronted a goodly number of such visitors, many of whose photographs no doubt adorned the rogues gallery at Scotland Yard. One and all of them had called to see Captain O'Malley. They had been told that, if the gallant officer was not at home, they were to leave an address at which they might be contacted. I was used to receiving such inquiries for 'Captain O'Malley' or 'Captain Basil' when Holmes was away on business. I took their messages but nothing would have persuaded me to allow a single one of these savage-looking fellows across the threshold.

There was one who left no address. Though he looked less of a villain than the others, his manner was more threatening.

'Cap'n O'Malley live 'ere, does 'e?'

'I regret that Captain O'Malley is not at home.'

'Well, p'raps that's jist as well for 'im. You tell him, with my com-pliments, I ain't no bloody liar and 'f he says again that I am, I'll be round to smash his face for him. All right? Understood?'

I had had more than enough of this 'prank' but it was not quite over. The last to arrive was somewhat different in appearance but I cannot say that I liked the look of him much better. He was a rakish young workman with a goatee beard and a self-confident swagger.

'Cap'n O'Malley?' he said, as if I might be he. Before I could reply, he struck a match on the sole of his boot and lit a clay pipe with a gesture of insolence. Then, with an audacity beyond belief, he blew a cloud of foul-smelling tobacco-smoke in my direction and began to elbow his way past me into the hall.

'What the devil—'

Before I could go further, the apparition threw back its head and laughed.

'Excellent, my dear Watson! My thespian labours are rewarded indeed!'

I fear I was abrupt with him as we reached our rooms.

'There are a dozen messages left for you by the most lawless ruffians to whom I have ever opened our door. Happily, I was able to keep watch and reach them before Mrs Hudson.'

'Good!' he said enthusiastically. 'Capital!'

'Another of them says that you have told lies about him.'

'So I have, Watson. One after another.'

'Then you had better know that he proposes to call here again to smash your face.'

Holmes turned and, despite his disguise, his features were a study in triumph as he put down the scraps of paper left for him and heard of the threat that had been made.

'Splendid, Watson!' he said. 'That will be Mr MacCowan, I expect. A most estimable man. To smash my face? That shows true feeling. And these slips of paper too! I had scarcely dared to hope for so many replies and such complete success.'

As he stood beaming at the scraps of paper in his hand, I had not the least idea what his outburst meant.

'Do you mean, Holmes, that young Mr Wood is no longer in danger of being hanged?'

He looked at me with an air of surprise. 'I should say, Watson, that he is in very great danger of being hanged. But that will be because he plays the conceited young ass in the witness-box and the jury takes against him. I think I can promise you that he will no longer be hanged on the evidence. He will have to do the job for himself.'

With that he turned to his bedroom to remove the goatee beard and the rest of his impersonation. Before leaving the room, however, he took a large sheet of paper which had been folded in his pocket. He threw it on the table and said, 'Here, Watson. See what you can make of that.'

I saw columns of figures with dates beside them and the name 'ELSIE' scrawled in pencil at the top. By now I was in something of an ill temper and decided that I would let Holmes explain the matter himself.

On his return, he rang for Mrs Hudson and warned her that we should receive a number of visitors in the next few days. The good lady was not to be alarmed if they included a desperate-looking man, who was in truth as amiable as an old family dog. There might also be a man who wished to smash the face of one or other of us, but he was really a most respectable fellow. There might also be a young lady of great presence and poise but with a certain past to live down. All were to be admitted at any hour.

III

For the first day we heard nothing. On the second, in response to a letter which Holmes or 'Captain O'Malley' had written, there arrived at noon one of the ruffians whom I had encountered on our doorstep. He now strode into our presence with a great air of self-confidence. Holmes treated him like a Crown Prince.

'Mr William Westcott? My name is Sherlock Holmes. May I introduce my colleague, the medical examiner Dr Watson? We are here on behalf of Captain O'Malley, who is abroad at this moment, as I explained in my card to you. What is your occupation, Mr Westcott?'

Our visitor lowered himself into a chair and the wooden frame of it creaked a little ominously under his bulk.

'I'm a ticket-collector, Mr Holmes. Midland Railway at King's Cross.'

'And the fact that you received my card and came here presumably means that you still live at 25 St Paul's Road? Is that not very close to where the Camden Town Murder happened?'

Our visitor was only too glad to share his moment of fame with us.

'That's right, Mr Holmes. I must have left that morning about the same time as the murderer was seen leaving the house two doors down, being on the early turn that week.'

'The early turn, Mr Westcott?'

'At half past five. I always allow thirty minutes for the walk and five minutes for clocking in. It means I leave home at five to five on the dot.'

'Just as well that you avoided the murderer,' said Holmes with a pleasant laugh, 'though they say there was a policeman standing opposite the house.'

Mr Westcott's pouched and rubbery face creased in a grimace of indifference.

'No policeman that I could see. And certainly no one leaving 29 just then. There was a cove coming down the road from the far end, same way as me. He walked after me but he wasn't a bit like the chap they arrested for cutting her throat.'

Holmes laughed again. 'So you suffer no nightmares from the memory of the man who was following you.'

Mr Westcott's grin revealed gums that lacked most of the usual set of teeth.

'I can look after myself, Mr Holmes. It'd take a mighty fine murderer to give Bill Westcott nightmares.'

There was laughter all round.

'No,' said Holmes pleasantly. 'And Mr Westcott didn't get a broken nose and a cauliflower ear from being a ticket-collector.'

Westcott joined in the laughter again.

'Well now, Mr Westcott,' said Holmes more earnestly, 'before we go further, perhaps you wouldn't mind just walking up and down the room a few times so that Dr Watson can make a note of your mobility.'

The chair creaked again as our visitor heaved himself up and began to pace between the fireplace and the door. He moved as if gathering energy for some great effort. The big man walked with his left arm swinging and crooked a little, his right shoulder hunched forward as if to protect his jaw. No one who saw him could sensibly doubt that this was the fellow whom one witness had seen, going about his innocent business in St Paul's Road at the time of the murder.

We had a pleasant discussion of the prospects of Mr Westcott, ticket-collector and amateur boxer. Holmes was as good as his word. 'Captain O'Malley' had spoken to several of his new friends at Romano's, from whom he had obtained the names of likely contenders for an amateur knock-out contest at the National Sporting Club in Regent Street. Before the eyes of wealthy connoisseurs of the noble art, Bill Westcott became the Camden Conqueror before the year was out.

'How the devil did you find him?' I asked, when Holmes and I were alone again.

'My dear fellow,' he said quietly, 'that you of all people should ask that! When Mr Newton described the gait of the man whom the witness had seen, it could only be a boxer. You recall the shoulder hunched forward, the left arm crooked?'

'Then MacCowan saw Mr Westcott come down the steps from 25 and not Wood from 29!'

Holmes shook his head.

'We may even doubt that Mr MacCowan saw Mr Westcott or anyone else on the morning of the murder. He says there was a policeman standing on the far side of the road and Mr Westcott tells us there was not. Perhaps Mr MacCowan remembers the wrong morning. That is something we cannot prove. Yet I was sure that one witness had described a boxer. I judged it imperative to discover where that boxer had come from and who he might be.'

'Romano's and the *Pink 'un*!'

'Precisely, Watson. I spent several agreeable evenings among sporting entrepreneurs who live on the art of such men as Mr Westcott. As Captain O'Malley, I passed as one of them. I advertised by word of mouth and in the *Sporting Times* for men to compete at the National Sporting Club. My informants had told me of such a contest yet to be announced, so I deceived no one. He could only have been a boxer, Watson. I am still amazed you did not see it from the start. Young Mr Robert Wood may have his genteel talents, but he would not last two minutes in the ring with Mr Westcott.'

For the rest of that day, Holmes divided his time between lounging in his chair, staring at papers which I swear he did not read, and pacing before the window.

'Damn it, Watson!' he said several times. 'Where is the fellow?'

'You mean MacCowan?'

'Of course I mean MacCowan. He is a witness in the case and I may not approach him. That would be contempt of court. I must make him come to me. If he does not, Mr Wood may still be lost.'

Despite Holmes's anxiety, the doorbell on the following morning announced the arrival of this second visitor. Mr Robert MacCowan was not, in truth, the type to go about smashing faces. When the door was opened to him by the redoubtable Mrs Hudson, the wind quite left his sails and he murmured no more than a wish to see Mr Sherlock Holmes, for 'Captain O'Malley' had been kept exclusively for practitioners of the noble art.

Indeed, when Mr MacCowan was shown up, he proved to be a tall and rather thin fellow with a shock of fair hair and a face haggard beyond his years. I placed his voice as that of a Norfolk man, though Holmes afterwards assured me it was Suffolk.

'Mr Holmes?' he said plaintively. 'I have a bone to pick with you.'

'Indeed?' said Holmes. 'I understand that my face was to be smashed.'

'So it ought to be,' said MacCowan. 'So it should be for what you have done. You were in the Eagle at Camden Town station. You were in the Rising Sun in the Euston Road. Where else you might have been I can't say. But everywhere that you were, you put about the story that I had lied as a witness to the police, and to the justices, and to the coroner's jury. I'm a man that hasn't had regular work the last eight months and if such stories are told about me I may never work again.'

Holmes motioned the tall, sad man to a chair.

'Come, Mr MacCowan, please sit down. If it is in my power, as I believe it is, to procure employment for you, rest assured that I shall do so. I have never called you a liar. I have simply offered a harmless wager or two that events referred to in your witness statements did not take place.'

MacCowan, who had half sat down, stood up again and was not yet mollified.

'That's as good as to call me a liar.'

Holmes stood as well.

'We may all of us be mistaken or confused in our recollections, Mr MacCowan. It does not make us liars, I hope.'

'You had no business, Mr Holmes. None whatever to say such things in a public place.'

The amiability went from Holmes's eyes and there was the faintest suggestion of a hiss in his breath. His hand, half-way to his pipe with a spill from the fire, froze in mid-gesture.

'I have business indeed, Mr MacCowan. I have such business when an innocent young man stands in the shadow of the gallows, that I will stop at nothing to see that business completed.'

He lit his pipe, tossed the spill into the grate, and continued.

'Moreover, Mr MacCowan, I do you a service if I save you from making a fool of yourself in the witness-box.'

'I don't need saving, Mr Holmes. I know what I saw. I saw that man!'

'If you will not sit down, Mr MacCowan, I shall. Which man was that?'

'Which man? The man I picked out in the police station yard. The man I saw standing on those steps of the house with two lights shining down on him. Robert Wood.'

'And what about the second man, Mr MacCowan? The one who was standing opposite the house when you passed at five minutes to five on the morning of the twelfth of September?'

MacCowan's shoulders moved in a pretence at laughter. 'The policeman? You don't think he cut her throat!'

Holmes put his pipe down. 'I am quite sure that he did not. How was this policeman dressed?'

MacCowan scowled at him. 'Same as they all are. And he'd got his cape on, it being a wet morning.'

Only those who knew Sherlock Holmes well would have noticed the slight dropping away of tension in his body as he felt the prey within his grasp.

'And yet, Mr MacCowan, on this wet morning as you call it, from midnight until the next midnight, the reports tell us that not a single drop of rain fell upon the whole of London.'

MacCowan was first disconcerted, then scornful.

'I never said it was raining, Mr Holmes. It was damp, murky.'

'Ah,' said Holmes, taking up his pipe again. 'Quite so. Murky and misty. Poor visibility. Without the lights, you might scarcely see across the road.'

He stood up and handed his visitor the sheet of paper headed 'ELSIE' with its columns of dates and figures.

'What's this?' MacCowan asked. 'Who's Elsie?'

'The goddess of light,' said Holmes quietly, 'EL . . . C . . . The Electric Company. Those, my dear sir, are the times at which street lights all over London were turned off automatically on the morning of the twelfth of September when Emily Dimmock met her death. If you will look just down here, you will see that the lamps in St Paul's Road, Camden Town, were turned off at five thirty-nine A.M., sixteen minutes before you claim that two of them shone brightly enough to identify Mr Robert Wood, despite the distance and the murk of the morning.'

MacCowan blinked, like a man hit hard but still on his feet.

'Then I was earlier than I thought. I was at the Bread Company in Brewery Road to look for work at five o'clock. I must have passed down St Paul's Road earlier. I come from home, Hawley Road in Chalk Farm.'

'Indeed,' said Holmes coldly. 'It is noted by the gatekeeper that you arrived at the V. V. Bread Company in time to be one of the first group of workers taken on that morning at five o'clock precisely. I have checked that for myself. You may also care to know that the distance from Hawley Road to Brewery Road is half a mile—29 St Paul's Road is at the mid-point. I grant that a man may take a little longer than he first thinks to walk such a distance. I am a little puzzled, however, as to how a man in possession of full health and who says he was not delayed in any manner could take almost twenty minutes to walk a quarter of a mile—half the distance from Hawley Road to Brewery Road.'

MacCowan sat in silence, looking at his hands.

'Come,' said Holmes a little more kindly. 'Either you passed the house at five minutes to the hour, when you cannot have seen the man who left because there was no light to see him by. Or else you passed no later than twenty minutes to the hour, when the lights were on and when you cannot have seen him because, according to this evidence, he did not come out for another fifteen minutes.'

MacCowan caught at a straw. 'There were other lights, Mr Holmes, that's what you'd know, if you weren't so bloomin' clever. Lights from the railway that runs by the street. I didn't just exactly notice at the time where the light was from. There's lights all along that railway and they keep 'em on.'

Holmes nodded. 'So they do, Mr MacCowan, and those lights may have been on at five minutes to five. If you were to measure, however, you would find that the railway line on to which the lights shine is forty feet below the level of the road. Moreover, there is an unbroken line of houses opposite the one we are discussing, shielding it from any reflection. There cannot possibly have been any light of any kind shining upon 29 St Paul's Road by which you could identify any man leaving the house.'

Robert MacCowan left our rooms still blustering yet with a dreadful light of fear in his eyes. He had nailed his colours to the mast before the coroner's jury and the magistrates. Nothing could save him, in a few weeks' time, from a public martyrdom at the hands of Edward Marshall Hall in the witness-box of the Central Criminal Court. Yet Sherlock Holmes was as good as his word. Captain O'Malley retained sufficient influence among his sporting friends to obtain for Mr MacCowan a place as table-waiter at Romano's, through whose famous window we once or twice glimpsed him in the years that followed.

We had one other visitor, the saddest of all. She was a dark-haired young woman of delicate beauty and moral frailty, the artist's model, Ruby Young, who had been Robert Wood's mistress. She came because, in her fear, she believed that she had now betrayed her lover to the gallows. As soon as the murder was reported in the press, Wood had asked her to swear a false alibi that they were together the night of Emily Dimmock's death and had not parted until 10.30 near Brompton Oratory.

Uncertain what to do, dreading that the false alibi she had given might make her an accomplice in murder, she had confessed to the police. With tears, she now pleaded with Holmes to assure her that she had not done a terrible wrong.

'Not in the least,' Holmes said airily. 'You have done Mr Wood a great service.'

She looked up at him. 'But it was I who asked him to meet me and led the police to him!'

'Madam,' said Holmes, 'consider this. Emily Dimmock was seen alive at ten thirty P.M. by Joseph Lambert the bookseller, and by others in the bar of the Eagle, in the company of Mr Wood. She ate a meal soon afterwards and met her death three hours after consuming it, to judge by the state of digestion of the food found in her stomach. She cannot have died before 2 A.M. at the earliest. The degree of *rigor mortis* in her body when it was first examined suggests that she more probably died at about 5 A.M.'

'I did not know,' she said simply.

'Nor could Robert Wood have known anything about the medical evidence when he asked you for an alibi,' said Holmes firmly. 'It was not public knowledge until the coroner's inquest. Consider his dilemma beforehand. He was a young man who knew that questions would be asked by the police of all those who had been seen with Emily Dimmock on the last evening of her life. He was also a young man who dreaded that his family, with whom he still lived, would hear that he kept the company of prostitutes in the public houses of Camden Town and the Euston Road. That was the reason why he wanted an alibi for Wednesday evening. Not murder! Do you not see it, Miss Young? The alibi for which he asked you, covering the evening until half past ten, was useless to him as a defence against a charge of murdering Miss Dimmock in the small hours of the morning. But only the murderer himself would have known that at the time when you were asked for a false alibi. Therefore, the murderer was not Robert Wood.'

The world knows the conclusion of the story. The case against Robert Wood was not dropped, despite Mr Arthur Newton's best efforts. Our young artist went on trial at the Central Criminal Court in December 1907, where the great defender, Edward Marshall Hall, cut up the witnesses for the Crown into very thin slices, as the saying goes. Robert Wood was acquitted and left the court to the cheers of the crowds outside. The unfortunate Ruby Young was jeered and chased down the street for her betrayal of her lover, as the London mob believed.

The name of Sherlock Holmes was not mentioned directly at the trial. Yet his shadow fell upon it in consequence of the visits we had received from the belligerent Mr MacCowan and the tearful Miss Ruby Young. Those who care to read the proceedings in the Notable British Trials volume that contains the case of Robert Wood will find a comment by Mr Justice Grantham at page 149, with reference to a complaint by MacCowan.

> I learn now that MacCowan was a witness before the magistrates. If the persons who are guilty of causing the annoyance are brought before me, they will not forget it in a hurry—that is all I can say. It is intolerable that witnesses should be subjected to attack and abuse for giving evidence, and if the person responsible is brought into this Court, it will be some time probably before he goes free.

Holmes insisted that he had not interfered with the witnesses in the case. One and all had come to him of their own free will, even

MacCowan. He had not obliged them to seek him out. Perhaps my friend was a little disingenuous. They walked into a trap, which he had baited with great care. So far as the courts of law acknowledged his existence, Mr Justice Grantham's comments on my friend's investigation of the murder of Emily Dimmock was as close to the wind as Sherlock Holmes ever sailed.

IV

After the acquittal of Robert Wood, no other person was brought to trial for the Camden Town murder. Detective Inspector Arthur Neil and his assistant, Sergeant Page, had gathered all the evidence available to them. If it did not point to Wood, it seemed to point to no one. Yet there was a curious epilogue, if one may use the word for so bizarre a conclusion.

In the attic of our Baker Street diggings, the first lumber-room alone remained orderly enough to have been a work-room. Holmes had a horror of destroying documents, especially those connected with his past cases. Yet it was only once in every year or two that he would muster energy to docket and arrange them. From time to time one or other of us had occasion to go up to this first room. On the wall hung a painting, which was curtained in red velvet, as if to protect it from the light. I had once seen what lay beneath and had no wish to repeat the experience.

Thereafter, Holmes was the only person who ever drew that curtain back. It veiled a painting by a friend of Robert Wood and was the only token of thanks that Holmes ever received from the young man. The artist was the impressionist painter Walter Sickert, more famous in later years than he was at the time for his studies of low life. This canvas was a horror. It showed Emily Dimmock as she was found with her throat cut on 12 September 1912. Other studies from Sickert's *Camden Town Murder* series have long received public display and general interest. Holmes judged that this item had best remain curtained from innocent eyes. On his visits to that lumber-room, he once told me, he would stand with the curtain drawn back, smoking his pipe as he gazed at the image on the canvas and pondered what manner of man was, in truth, the Camden Town murderer.

Several years after the case was concluded, Holmes met Walter Sickert for the first time during an artists' dinner of some kind at the Café Royal. There was a good deal of boastful talk, which led Sickert to assert that 'a painter cannot paint something of which he has no experience'.

My friend was struck by this remark. A few weeks later, he secured an invitation to the artist's studio in Camden Town. It was there that he saw a portfolio of drawings on the same subject and purchased one inscribed *Persuasion*, in which a man sits on a bed, a woman lying across his lap and his hands obscurely round her throat, either in a caress or an act of strangulation. The painter afterwards became sensitive to questions about his 'Camden Town murders' and changed the title of the series to 'What Shall we Do for the Rent?'

Holmes sought occasion over some other matter to invite Inspector Neil to our rooms. In the course of the visit, he displayed a few souvenirs including the snuffbox of Sèvres porcelain which had belonged to President Faure and the diamond tie-pin which he had brought home with him after a visit to Windsor in 1890. Then the two men went up to the lumber-room.

I did not accompany them but noticed that Inspector Neil came down a good deal paler than he went up. Guessing the cause of this, I poured him a glass of brandy and soda, setting it on the little table by his chair.

'A nasty daub, that painting,' I said reassuringly, 'and all the worse for being in a blotchy impressionist style. If it were mine, I should burn it.'

Sherlock Holmes intervened. 'Robert Wood, after he was released, acted as the model,' he said.

Neil looked up at him. 'That's not it. I saw Wood's likeness clear enough. That's not it.'

'What is it, then?' I asked.

'That room of hers, where she died!' he said. 'It's as we found it, in every detail! I'm no artist, Dr Watson, and I know little enough about the ways of art. But he has got that room and the girl herself as plain as if it were a photograph!'

'Do you say,' asked Holmes innocently, 'that a painter cannot paint something of which he has no experience?'

Neil stared into his glass.

'I can't say that, Mr Holmes. You might, if you understand art. I know little enough of such things—and where's the evidence now? Wood never denied he'd been to her room on earlier nights—and he might have described it to anyone. But Dr Watson is right. If that thing were mine, I should take it off its hook and burn it before I looked at it again.'

Holmes made a sympathetic sound but, from his eyes, I could see that for him Walter Sickert's daub now took on the quality of a true work of art.

The Case of the
Missing Rifleman

I

In order that the reader may understand more readily the investigation that follows, it may be as well if I say something of the origin of the inquiry. It was the second case in which the path of Sherlock Holmes crossed that of Sir Edward Marshall Hall, thirteen years after the trial of Robert Wood for the Camden Town Murder. On this later occasion, however, there was to be a certain bruising of vanity in both parties.

The mystery dated from the summer of 1919, the first after the Great War, a time when a good number of young men and their officers were returning to civilian life from the army and the trenches of the Western Front.

A few miles to the east of the town of Leicester lie a number of little villages connected by a network of small country roads or lanes. Once these were farming communities—now they supply labour to the factories and industries of Leicester itself. Annie Bella Wright was a respectable young woman of twenty-one who worked in a rubber factory and was engaged to a naval stoker. On 5 July 1919, she came off the night shift and cycled home the few miles to the little village of Stoughton, where she lived with her parents. She went to bed and, after several hours' sleep, got up to finish writing some letters. She posted these at about 4 P.M.

At 6.30 that evening, she took her bicycle and set off for the hamlet of Gaulby, three miles away, to visit her uncle, Mr Measures, and his son-in-law, Mr Evans. By the time that she arrived at their cottage in the centre of Gaulby, Bella Wright had a companion, a young man riding a green BSA bicycle. Safely inside the cottage, she assured her uncle that this young man was a perfect stranger, who had overtaken her as she was cycling from Stoughton and had engaged her in conversation on the remainder of the short journey. Mr Measures clearly remembered that his niece had said to him, 'Perhaps if I wait a while he will be gone.'

When Bella Wright left her uncle's house, however, the young man had returned, as if he had been waiting for her. 'Bella, you *have* been a long time,' he said pleasantly. 'I thought you had gone the other way.' The two of them rode off together, the time being about a quarter to nine and the summer evening still light. Half an hour later, Bella Wright was found lying dead less than two miles away in the Gartree Road, which was not her direct route home. Her head had been badly injured and the first doctor who was called thought she had died as a result of a bad fall from her bicycle. Next day, a policeman who searched the narrow country road at the point of the incident found a spent .455 cartridge on the ground, seventeen feet from where her body had been lying. A post-mortem revealed the entry wound of a bullet in her left cheek, just below the eye, and a larger exit wound at the top of her head.

A curiosity near the scene of the crime was the discovery of a carrion crow, lying dead in the adjoining field, about sixty feet away. It was described at first as being gorged with blood, which was presumed to have come from the dead girl's wound. The amount that the bird had consumed was said to have caused a surfeit from which it had died. There was a field gate on to the road a few yards from where the girl's body lay. Between the white-painted gate and the body were what appeared to be twelve bloody claw-tracks, six in each direction, as if the bird had moved to and fro between the gate and the corpse.

A description of the man on the green bicycle and of the machine itself was issued by the police. A reward was offered for information.

Many months passed and nothing more was heard, except from two girls of twelve and fourteen, who had been cycling in the lanes nearby. They agreed that, earlier on 5 July, a man riding a bicycle came towards them, smiled and spoke to them as he passed. Having gone by, he stopped, turned his bicycle and began to follow them. The girls, feeling uneasy at his interest in them, reversed their own direction and rode home towards Leicester.

It was little enough to go on. The summer ended. Winter came and went. The investigation got nowhere and the Leicestershire county police were not helped by a complete lack of any apparent motive for the killing. Bella Wright had been neither robbed nor assaulted in any way. Why should any individual, the rider of the green bicycle or not, shoot dead a blameless and industrious young woman?

Holmes had followed the scanty newspaper reports with a vague interest but, in truth, there seemed little that even he could have done with such disjointed scraps of evidence. His attention was caught at last when he read, in March 1920, that a man had been arrested and charged with the murder of Bella Wright. The accused was an assistant master at a school in Cheltenham, a former engineer who had been an officer of the Honourable Artillery Company, invalided out of the service with shell shock at the end of the late war. Until his appointment to the school two months earlier, he had lived with his widowed mother in Leicester. Yet even this information was nothing to the expectation that glinted in Holmes's eyes when he saw that the young man, Ronald Light, was to be defended by Sir Edward Marshall Hall.

Neither Holmes nor I supposed at the outset that there was anything likely to involve us in the investigation. Since the acquittal of Robert Wood in the Camden Town murder case, thirteen years had passed during which both Sherlock Holmes and I had admired the skill of Sir Edward from a distance. The newspapers of those days were filled with the triumphs of his advocacy and, no less, with reports of sensational trials in which even he had not been able to save his client's neck. Dr Crippen, George Joseph Smith of the 'Brides in the Bath' murders, and Seddon the poisoner were among his clients who had gone to the gallows. In the most famous of his cases, Holmes was of the opinion that Sir Edward could have saved Dr Crippen, had not the defendant's chivalry forbidden the calling of any evidence that might implicate his young mistress, Ethel Le Neve.

It was the more surprising that, within a few days of Ronald Light's arrest, my friend should have received a wire from Sir Edward's clerk, Mr Archibald Bowker, asking us as a matter of urgency to attend a conference at his chambers in Temple Gardens on the following Monday. Sir Edward was at that moment conducting the defence of Eric Holt at Manchester Assizes, where this other young officer of the late war was accused of having shot his mistress. Holmes had shown himself increasingly reluctant to act as Mahomet summoned to the mountain by his clients, but even he could scarcely decline an invitation from a man of such public reputation.

To enter the presence of Sir Edward Marshall Hall in his middle years was a little like sharing the company of a great actor. It was well said that he had a head of Roman nobility on shoulders of Saxon power. By now his hair was silver and his profile a little sharper. Yet his voice retained a characteristic resonance and range, a depth of passion that would have been the envy of Henry Irving or Beerbohm Tree. The effect of his performance upon a jury was such as to make him the despair of even the most eminent of prosecuting counsel. Add to this the acuity of his mind, the speed and drama of his response, a knowledge of forensic science unparalleled at the English bar, and you will have some idea of the power of the great defender, as he was called. He could no longer enter a courtroom without every head turning in his direction, with a stir of excitement and a murmur running from floor to gallery.

Sir Edward stood in the window of his room at 3, Temple Gardens, as we entered. To either side, the break-front walnut bookcases housed maroon leather volumes of case reports, their green labels stamped in gold. Behind him, the lawns and trees fell away to the glitter of the Thames below Westminster Bridge, the smoke of steamers and the sails of barges along the Surrey shore. He shook our hands with a powerful grip, rang for tea and cakes, then motioned us to leather chairs. His desk was piled with briefs tied in pink tape and marked for his attention. I could not help noticing that one of these was inscribed 'Rex v. Light' and endorsed with the words 'Special 50 Guineas'. Sir Edward was not a member of the Midland Circuit and the etiquette of the Bar required that he could not appear there unless he was briefed 'special' in addition to his usual fee and daily refreshers. He looked at us a little forlornly, as it seemed to me.

'Gentlemen, I regret that I have had to bring you here but I must be at Manchester again tomorrow and had not the time to come even as far as Baker Street on this visit. Let me get to the point at once. It will not surprise you, I daresay, to know that the matter at issue is what is called the Green Bicycle case. You have no doubt read something of it.'

'A little,' said Holmes cautiously. 'Enough, at any rate, to follow the story as far as your client's arrest. May I ask how it was that he became a suspect, after so many months?'

Sir Edward's mouth tightened.

'Nemesis, Mr Holmes. There is no other word for it. Last month, on the twenty-third of February to be precise, a boatman was taking a load of coal into Leicester by the canal. Close to the town gasworks, the tow-rope from the horse ran slack and dipped under the surface. When it tightened and came up, it lifted from the water the frame of a bicycle. The man was able to see it for a moment before it slipped from the rope and fell back into the water. He returned next day, no doubt remembering the rewards that had been offered in the case of Bella Wright. A canal dredger dragged the water until the bicycle was found again. It was the frame of a green bicycle, a BSA De Luxe model, without the rear wheel. The individual number of the bicycle had been filed away. However, the owner evidently did not know that the De Luxe models have a further number-stamp on the handlebar pillar. From this it was established that the machine was made in 1910, ordered by a wholesaler in Derby, and sold to Ronald Light. Mr Light has also been paraded by the police and identified by Mr Measures and Mr Evans as the last person seen with Miss Wright before her death.'

I could not restrain my feelings after this last revelation. 'Well, sir, this looks even blacker than the Camden Town murder did for Mr Robert Wood!'

'Blacker yet,' Sir Edward said. 'Valeria Craven and Muriel Nunney, the two schoolgirls who were followed by a man on a bicycle, also identify Ronald Light as that man. Bella Wright's uncle and another member of the family who was in the cottage at Gaulby identify him by his appearance and by his voice as the man who waited outside for Miss Wright, while she remained indoors and hoped he would go away. They are quite sure that it was his voice which said, "Bella, you *have* been a long time," when she left them.'

'Curious,' said Holmes to himself, but the advocate held up his hand, entreating a further explanation.

'There is worse, Mr Holmes. When the police dragged that same stretch of the canal a few days ago to see what else might be found, they retrieved the holster of a Webley Scott .455 service revolver, such as Mr Light was issued with during the war. It was filled with .455 ammunition, identical to the bullet which killed Miss Wright.'

'And the revolver?' Holmes inquired.

Sir Edward shook his splendid head. 'It was not found.'

Holmes gave a sceptical sniff. 'He throws away the holster and the ammunition but not the gun, the very article that might hang him!'

'Perhaps it is there but not found, Mr Holmes. I scarcely want to encourage a further search.'

'Would it not be found in a canal, Sir Edward? It is little more than dragging a pond. Smaller items like a holster or cartridges are found but the revolver is not? Singular, to be sure. And does your client offer any explanation for his extraordinary conduct?'

Sir Edward looked grim but resolute.

'He insists that he met Bella Wright for the first time that evening as she was riding to her uncle's cottage. She was standing by the side of the road. The front wheel of her bicycle was loose in the fork and she asked him if he had a spanner to tighten the nuts. He had not. They rode carefully to her uncle's cottage. Ronald Light claims that he had a slow puncture in his front tyre and could not ride for very long at a time without stopping to pump up the tyre. He met her again as she left her uncle's cottage and kept company with her for about ten minutes until their routes parted. With his slow puncture, the short distance took some time. He then rode on back to Leicester. That was the last he knew of her.'

'He has told you all this himself?' Holmes asked quickly.

'No, Mr Holmes. I have not met Light and I shall not do so until the day of the trial. To speak frankly, his character was not of the best during his military service. Moreover, when he was arrested he first intimated that he had an alibi for the evening on which Bella Wright met her death. Then he threw that defence away, admitted his ownership of the bicycle and his meeting with her, but insisted that she was alive and well when he last saw her at about five minutes before nine P.M. Twenty minutes later she was dead.'

'And will you not probe him further?'

'Mr Holmes, I fear that if I were to discuss the case with Light, he would either blurt out some half-confession of guilt or solicit my advice as to the best story he might invent. I should have to withdraw from the case, if anything of the sort were to happen. There are clients whom it is best to represent at a distance. We must put Mr Light aside and concentrate upon the evidence, the facts in the case. If you are prepared to assist in the matter, I should consider it an honour to retain your services and those of your colleague, Dr Watson.'

There was no delay in agreeing this, since Holmes was intrigued beyond measure by the mystery of the case. Before we left, however, he returned to two points which seemed to Sir Edward of little significance, by comparison with the evidence of firearms and bullets.

'Strange, is it not?' Holmes said. 'They have only known one another for fifteen or twenty minutes at the most, according to what the poor girl said to her uncle. Yet as she left the cottage, Light called her "Bella". The exact words were, "Bella, you *have* been a long time." Hardly a familiarity that a stranger would use. Is it not more likely that he said "Hello"? "Hello, you *have* been a long time"? It would be easy enough to mistake the two words. "Hello" might sound like "Bella" if spoken rather softly or heard at some distance.'

'Mr Measures insists that the man with the bicycle called her "Bella".'

Holmes sighed. 'Well, Sir Edward, that is as nothing compared to the difficulty of the bird, the carrion crow, as the newspapers describe it. I assume its cadaver has not been preserved as evidence?'

'There was no apparent reason to do so, Mr Holmes. It was dissected but nothing was found. No shot and no bullet.'

'With the greatest respect, Sir Edward, there was every reason to preserve evidence in this matter. Take, for example, the matter of the tracks.'

'Which tracks, Mr Holmes?'

'The twelve little tracks of blood that we are told ran to and fro between the gate of the field and the body of the unfortunate young woman,' Holmes said thoughtfully. 'The police recorded those tracks with their usual meticulous care. We are invited to believe that this evil bird sat upon the gate. I have no doubt that it did. We are further invited to believe that it then flew to and fro, gathering blood from its victim and returning to the gate to consume it.'

'Well, Mr Holmes?' It was impossible not to see that Sir Edward Marshall Hall's expression had darkened a little with displeasure. He had staked everything on firearms or ballistics and was in no mood for a lecture on ornithology.

'Well, Sir Edward, if you observe a carrion crow or any other bird of its sort, you will see that it does not fly to and fro. Unless it is disturbed, it stands over its loathsome feast and continues to feed there until it has finished. But, of course, there is a far greater objection to the tracks of blood.'

'Indeed?' said Sir Edward coolly.

'There are twelve!' Holmes said. 'I am surprised that even the local constabulary did not notice the absurdity of it. Twelve! I ask you, Sir Edward!'

He sat back with a flourish of his hand as if in despair at all human intelligence.

'You think them too many?'

'Not the least,' said Holmes reassuringly. 'Thirteen, if you like. Or twenty-three, or thirty-three. But not twelve or fourteen or sixteen or eighteen or any other even number. If the bird went to and fro from the gate, be it flying or hopping, it would not have had blood upon it when it first made towards the body. Therefore the number of tracks surely cannot be twelve or any other even number, if we are to believe the story we have been told. You had not noticed that, Sir Edward?'

It seemed that Sir Edward had not, nor was he best pleased by having it drawn to his attention in this casual manner. However, we got through the remainder of the interview without further damage to vanity on either side. A few days later, in the sunlight of an early spring morning, Holmes and I took the London and North-Eastern Railway from St Pancras to Leicester.

II

Holmes spent the greater part of the journey reading again those statements of evidence which Sir Edward Marshall Hall had had copied for him. I had read them the previous evening but could add little to my friend's remarks at our meeting in Temple Gardens. At the same time Ronald Light, like Robert Wood in the Camden Town case, had made the task of defending him infinitely more difficult by his foolish or guilty conduct. Instead of coming forward at the time of Bella Wright's death to tell the police what he knew, Ronald Light—like Robert Wood—had behaved as a murderer might have done. In Light's case, he had got rid of his green bicycle in the canal, throwing his revolver-pouch and ammunition after it. Had these items never been discovered, he might have lived undisturbed for the rest of his life as a teacher of mathematics in Cheltenham. Yet the boatman's tow-rope on the Leicester canal might now prove to be the very rope that hanged him.

We were almost at Northampton before Holmes put the papers down and lit his pipe.

'The story will not do, Watson,' he said. 'It will not do at all. I do not care for this case in the least. Sir Edward's brief is to fight for his client at all costs and win whatever it may take. As a dispassionate investigator, I find that uncongenial.'

'You think Ronald Light guilty?'

He stared at the flat fields in which the winter rain still lay like a lake.

'I think him very foolish. At the moment, I think no more.'

I gave a laugh and said, 'Then you must be the only man in England who thinks no more than that. Even Sir Edward will not go near him, for fear of being compromised.'

Holmes thought for a moment.

'I do not say a jury will find him guilty, Watson. Sir Edward will find a good deal to say in his defence. Consider this. We are to believe that Light went out on his bicycle to meet, or seduce, or rape, girls or young women. There is no evidence that he had ever done so in the past but set that aside. We are also to believe that he took with him a Webley Scott service revolver for the purpose. He is a professional man of some intelligence and must have known that he dared not use the gun without the probability of being hanged, as the last man seen with the poor girl. There again, the sound of a shot carries a good distance on a quiet summer evening in the country and would surely be heard. Even to threaten a young woman with a gun in broad daylight on a public road would be his downfall. Surely it would be reported. If it is true that he behaved in such a manner none the less, Watson, it falls in the area of mania. That subject belongs to your profession rather than to mine.'

'Yet he may have had such a purpose, gun or no gun, since two girls were followed by him on the same day.'

'Were they?' asked Holmes laconically. 'They did not make statements to the police about it until some months later. One of them picked out Light on an identity parade but only after first seeing his description. Moreover, they were not asked by the police on which day the incident happened but whether it happened on the fifth of July! A leading question, if ever there was! I fancy Sir Edward will make short work of all that in court.'

And, on that last point, Holmes was to be proved right.

'It leaves us with the gun, then,' I said.

'And the bird, Watson. We must not forget the bird.'

It seemed that the bird was to prove more important in this case than anyone had imagined.

III

For several days we rode from Leicester round the five or ten miles of country lanes with their undulating fields showing the first green shoots of spring. We passed through villages that were hardly more than clusters of cottages and handsome churches. Flat hunting land stretched as far as the eye could see from every crest of the road.

Seldom had the time and place of a murder been so precisely defined. Bella Wright was alive at quarter to nine in the evening when she rode from Gaulby in company with Ronald Light. It would have taken her some fifteen minutes to cycle to the spot where her body was found by Farmer Cowell. She had died at that spot between nine o'clock and quarter past, to take the period at its longest. Though she cannot long have been dead, Farmer Cowell heard no shot, except perhaps the pop of a rook rifle, and saw no one. Perhaps, then, Miss Wright was shot at nine or a few minutes afterwards—not with a rook rifle.

Holmes and I stood at the scene. The hedgerows of the narrow road were already high and would grow to almost eight feet by midsummer, the season of Bella Wright's death. They would screen the narrow road and the fields from one another. To one side was the white-painted field gate on which the crow had sat and beyond it was the field in which the bird's body had been found. There was the stretch of road rising towards a junction and the spot where Farmer Cowell had found her. Seventeen feet beyond that the spent bullet had been discovered next day by Constable Hall. The bullet had been greatly deformed, as it was thought, by being trodden under a horse's hoof.

'Watson,' said my companion presently, standing astride the saddle of his bicycle. 'Be good enough to imagine that you have a gun in your hand. You are to shoot me from at least five feet. We are told the old wives' tale that the distance was not less, since the victim showed no burned powder on her skin. Let that stand for a moment. The bullet is to enter below my left eye and exit from the crown of my head. I am standing here and we are arguing.'

I flatter myself that I handle a service revolver pretty well and know a good deal about the wounds inflicted by one. I tried to imagine the line that Holmes described and could do so only by going down on one knee immediately in front of him. It was not a position from which Sir Edward's client would have been likely to threaten or murder Bella Wright.

'Now,' said Holmes, 'try again, as if I were riding along with my head a little down as I pedal harder and approach the crest of the rise.'

I did my best and then gave up.

'It is quite impossible, Holmes,' I said at last. 'I should almost have to lie under the wheels of the bicycle.'

'Interesting, is it not?'

He took some measurements and presently I said, 'You would never hold your head back far enough while you were cycling for that wound to be made. Suppose, however, that she did not fall from the bicycle as a result of being shot, but was shot when she was already lying on her back in the road. That would perfectly explain the angle of the wound.'

'My dear Watson, I do not understand why he would shoot her when she was lying in the road, if he had not done so when she was upright. You are quite correct, however. It is a possible line. Unfortunately, there was no sign of injury before death to suggest such a fall. An accident, however, would be a quite different matter. Imagine a young fool playing about with a gun—perhaps to threaten her. The barrel is pointing down but the gun goes off. The bullet hits the road and comes up at a ricochet. Bella Wright falls dead and Ronald Light flees in panic. Let us look further.'

He propped his bicycle against the white-painted gate and entered the field. After about thirty feet, we came to a stone sheep-trough.

'Hmmm,' he said to himself, 'it is rather as I supposed. Convenient, if mundane.'

Without further explanation, he took his magnifying glass and examined the stonework of the trough along its upper edges, touching the masonry here and there where it seemed a little brighter from some abrasion or other.

'Someone has used this often as a firing-post,' he said presently. 'We had best go and present our findings to Sir Edward.'

'It seems to me, Holmes, that we have found very little of use to him.'

'Precisely,' he said cryptically. 'In that case we had better go and tell him so. I feel, however, we may assure him on the matter of the unfortunate crow.'

'The crow?'

'Yes, Watson. I confess that the crow has been the biggest impediment to this investigation. There have been only two exhibits of significance in this case so far: the blood of the crow and the bullet that was found flattened on the roadway the day after the girl's death. It is most unsatisfactory.'

On the evening of our return to London, Holmes withdrew after dinner to the cellar that we had leased as part of our premises, and which extended a little under the pavement of Baker Street, where there was a coal-chute. Soon after our arrival as tenants, Holmes had filled one end of the underground tunnel with rubble and masked it with iron plating, so that it was even possible to test heavy-calibre big-game rifles without danger. For some time he had been investigating the possibility, yet to be demonstrated at that time, that he might be able to identify the individual gun from which a particular bullet had been fired, as well as the type of weapon. To retrieve the bullet, he fired into a row of fifteen twelve-bore cartridge boxes stuffed tight with cotton wool. A Webley Scott service revolver would penetrate six and a Mauser twice that number. His method was so precise that he knew without fail in which box a spent bullet might be found. Once it had been retrieved, he would go to work with his comparison microscope.

On that spring night of our return from Leicester, homeward-bound pedestrians might have been a little puzzled by a series of powerful but muffled thuds from below the paving stones. Until long after midnight, the cellar was brightly lit.

On the following afternoon, we took a cab to Temple Gardens to report the extent of our progress. It was not the happiest of occasions as we sat once again in the bay-fronted room overlooking the quiet lawns and trees. Our findings were meagre enough. There was also an air of rivalry, for Sir Edward Marshall Hall, no less than Sherlock Holmes, regarded himself as an expert in the matter of firearms and ballistics, which Sir Edward was eager to discuss. Holmes preferred the dead carrion crow.

'I believe, Sir Edward, that we may now be certain the bird was shot either as it sat upon the top bar of the gate or, more likely, a moment after it had taken off.'

Sir Edward passed a hand over his noble jaw. 'We are told that it died because it was gorged with the girl's blood.'

'Such a thing would be quite impossible,' said Holmes. 'Look at the proposition for one moment. We are invited to believe that it died of apoplexy, the result of consuming a surfeit of blood. The annals of ornithology will show that birds do not die in such circumstances, or very rarely so. If there is a surfeit, they regurgitate. In this case, the interval between her death and the finding of the body was a matter of minutes. It scarcely allows time for our bird to gorge itself. Then we have the bloody tracks between the gate and the young woman's body, the impossible number upon which the theory of surfeit relies. It is surely plain that the bird was shot, and that its blood sprayed or splashed from it in the direction of Bella Wright's body. That gives the direction of the bullet. It was shot by someone in the field, not far from the gate.'

'Yet the body of the bird was found fifty or sixty feet away from the gate.'

'Precisely,' said Holmes, 'Forgive me, Sir Edward, but I have made a little study of how birds and other creatures die when they are shot. A bird that is shot while in the air, assuming that our crow had just taken off, will "tower" upwards immediately after the impact, rather than dropping straight down. It gains height for a moment and then falls dead. Yet it still does not fall in a straight line. The consequence is that it will very probably hit the ground at a little distance away. Sixty feet would be nothing.'

'At what range do you say was it shot?'

'Twenty-two feet,' Holmes said without hesitation.

The lawyer's eyes narrowed. 'You can be so precise?'

'I can, Sir Edward. There is a stone sheep-trough in the field, twenty-two feet from the gate. A man or boy hunting crows or other vermin might kneel behind it for cover, no doubt waiting for his prey to show itself. A shot fired at the gate from such cover would travel upwards at an angle of about twenty degrees. It would pass through the body of the bird, which the splashes of blood suggest, and continue upwards with its force somewhat reduced.'

There was no mistaking the excitement in Sir Edward's eyes. He got up and walked to and fro across the window, illustrating by his movements what he believed to have happened to the dead girl.

'Just so, Mr Holmes. Bella Wright is cycling on the near side of the road. Her attention is caught by the bird or the presence of the man. She turns her face in that direction, however briefly. This happens in the interval of her passing the gap in the tall hedge, where the gate stands. The unlucky shot is fired by the man, who has tightened his finger on the trigger before seeing her. The bullet passes through the bird and by the most dreadful chance continues upwards, entering Miss Wright's left cheek just under the eye. Still travelling upwards, it makes its exit wound at the crown of her head. She falls dead from the bicycle. The second impact robs the bullet of most of its force and it strikes the ground seventeen feet away, where it was found next day. There we have it, Mr Holmes.'

He sat down again.

'Not quite,' said Holmes coolly. 'There are two items of evidence missing in your defence, Sir Edward. There is the identity of the man who fired such a shot and there is the gun that might have been used. Moreover, as the Attorney-General will point out to you, your client is the last person to be seen with the dead girl. He concealed evidence from the police. He lied to them when arrested, and he threw his bicycle into the canal. Worst of all, he possessed cartridges identical to that found on the road and which he threw away immediately after the murder. We have only his word for it that he no longer possessed the Webley Scott service revolver for which ammunition of that calibre was designed.'

Sir Edward stood up, reached across the wide desk for a folder and opened it.

'You would agree, Mr Holmes, that if Light shot this young woman, he must have done so at close range and that, presumably, he would have used the Webley Scott revolver?'

'I think it probable.'

Sir Edward displayed a gruesome post-mortem photograph.

'Mr Holmes, have you never seen someone shot in the head at close range by such a weapon? Look for yourself. The bullet not only makes an entry wound and an exit wound. It is hardly too much to say that the victim's head is almost blown apart by the velocity of the bullet. Moreover at such close range, the skin would be marked by the discharge of powder from the barrel.'

'Indeed,' said Holmes sceptically. 'Indeed, Sir Edward, what you say of the head being blown apart might be true if the ammunition were in good condition. Where, however, cartridges have been kept as souvenirs and are of indeterminate age, the results are quite different. A bullet will go off rather like a damp squib. It would have power enough to pass through the victim's head at close range. Yet the powder blast would be relatively slight and the force of the bullet insufficient to do more than make the wounds of entry and exit. It would not be remarkable that it should drop to earth seventeen feet further on. As to the scorching of the skin, I have myself tried experiments with portions of a cadaver. Small-calibre ammunition does not scorch the skin greatly. Even when it is of larger calibre, as in this case, the powder may be washed away by something as simple as a flow of blood.'

Sir Edward Marshall Hall sat back in his chair and met his adversary's gaze with a long stare. It was impossible not to see that he was thanking whatever gods might be that the services of Sherlock Holmes had been retained on behalf of his client and had not been put at the disposal of the Crown.

'Then what, Mr Holmes, are we to think? The bullet that was found has been misshapen by some such impact as a horse's hoof while it lay unnoticed in the road. However, you will not deny that it has been fired by a rifled barrel and that such rifling indicates a rifle.'

'It may indicate that,' said Holmes smoothly, 'but it does not prove it. I must warn you, Sir Edward, that if you ask such a question in cross-examination, you will be told that a Webley Scott revolver has a rifled barrel, though it is not a rifle, and that it leaves seven narrow rifling grooves on any bullet fired from it.'

For the first time in our dealings with him, a shadow of alarm crossed the great lawyer's handsome countenance.

'Do you say, Mr Holmes, that this bullet could not have been fired from a rifle?'

Holmes shook his head. 'No one can say for certain that it was not fired by a rifle. However, a .455 cartridge would suggest a rifle of unusual power. An elephant rifle, perhaps.'

Sir Edward sat upright. 'An elephant rifle?'

'Quite so,' said Holmes, 'and you will no doubt be asked how many of the good folk in these charming villages go out in the evenings to shoot crows with an elephant rifle.'

'This will not do, Mr Holmes!'

'Very well,' said Holmes, 'I will give you an argument, though it is not one I should care to use myself. Let us take a military rifle made by thousands and used by cadets or volunteer companies. The Martini-Henry is frequently of .452 bore, some were rebarrelled to various bores when the Lee-Enfield was brought in. It would be hard to prove that a Martini-Henry or any other particular gun had not fired a bullet as badly deformed as this one. The fact that the rifling is so defaced by a horse's hoof in this instance might suggest a badly worn Martini-Henry. Since the war, a Martini-Henry is the most common rifle to be found, as .455 is the most common calibre of ammunition.'

It was all the comfort that Sir Edward seemed likely to get. He walked with us to the door and Sherlock Holmes turned to him with fastidious courtesy.

'I hope you will not think me precipitate, Sir Edward, if I tell you that I have now done almost everything that I can on behalf of your client and that I positively must withdraw from the case. I shall, of course, accept no fee.'

There was no doubt from his face that Sir Edward felt a dread that his defence of Ronald Light would prove to be built upon sand.

'Withdraw, Mr Holmes? For God's sake why?'

'It will be better if I keep my reasons to myself,' Holmes said quietly. 'However, if I may offer a last piece of advice it is this. Mr Robert Churchill, the gunsmith of Agar Street in the Strand, has given evidence in many cases of this kind. His knowledge and skill are unparalleled. I must urge you to retain his services at once, unless you wish your client to be hanged.'

For all his forensic brilliance, Sir Edward Marshall Hall was baffled—and exasperated.

'What can Mr Robert Churchill tell me that you cannot?'

'I will only repeat,' said Holmes quietly, 'that unless you retain his services at once, you are likely to see Mr Light hanged.'

At that moment, I thought I saw a glimmer of comprehension in the grey eyes of Sir Edward Marshall Hall. Whatever it was that he comprehended was quite beyond me.

As we stood outside in the sunlight of Temple Gardens, I was almost dumbfounded. Never, in all our acquaintanceship, had Sherlock Holmes ever behaved in such a manner towards a client.

'You have abandoned him!' I said incredulously. 'Indeed, you have abandoned them both, Sir Edward and Ronald Light!'

He looked at me without expression. 'On the contrary, Watson. I believe I may just have saved Mr Light from the gallows and Sir Edward from a terrible defeat.'

IV

As was too often the case when Holmes appeared to play the prima donna, he refused positively to discuss the matter with me. All the same, we attended the days of drama in the courtroom of Leicester Castle when Ronald Light stood trial for his life, charged with the murder of Annie Bella Wright.

Sir Edward Marshall Hall played a desperate game but he never played one with greater skill. The two young girls who claimed that Light had followed them were dismissed from the case. In their stupidity, the police had not asked them when they were followed but *whether* it had been on 5 July. That leading question was an end of their evidence. Worse still, the two girls had picked out Light from the men at the police station only after having first been given his description.

When it was known by the prosecution that Mr Robert Churchill was for the defence in the matter of the guns, it was supposed that Sir Edward had an ace up his sleeve. The Crown was content to call a local gunsmith of Leicester, Mr Henry Clarke. He was no match for the forensic power of Sir Edward Marshall Hall. In cross-examination, he agreed that the .455 bullet had been standard ammunition for at least thirty years past and had been made in thousands of millions. He agreed that the rifling marks on the bullet that killed Bella Wright were consistent with its having been fired either from a revolver or a rifle. He still maintained that it might have been fired from close range, passed through the young woman's head, hit the road, then risen and landed further on. He was not, however, able to find the mark on the bullet that would have been caused by the first of two such impacts with the road.

Having got so far in the matter of the gun, Sir Edward Marshall Hall did not call evidence for the defence on this point from Mr Robert Churchill or anyone else. Nor was this surprising. Ronald Light had escaped the gallows by a whisker. Later, Holmes handed me a summary of the report that Mr Churchill had made to Sir Edward, a document that the lawyer passed to my friend with a brief note of gratitude for his advice in retaining the famous gunsmith.

In Robert Churchill's opinion, the bullet that killed Bella Wright had been fired from a Webley Scott service revolver and no other weapon. Not only had the victim been shot by a revolver of the type for which Ronald Light possessed holster and ammunition, she had been shot from such close range that the bullet had scarcely begun to gather speed. No hunter shooting crows with a rifle had killed her. If Mr Churchill had given such evidence in court for the Crown, Ronald Light would surely have been hanged.

'My dear Watson,' said Holmes equably, the night after Light's acquittal on the grounds that the lingering effects of shell shock had unnerved him from going to the police when first suspected, 'I quite thought you had grasped my reasons at once.'

'Your reasons for what?'

'I withdrew from the case in order that Sir Edward might retain the services of Mr Robert Churchill. It is a simple matter of legal procedure. Mr Churchill is perhaps the greatest expert on firearms this country has ever known. If the defence retained him, the Director of Public Prosecutions could not. Sir Edward was good enough to suggest that my expertise might equal Mr Churchill's and it would be ungracious to argue over that. By my withdrawal, he was able to ensure that neither of us gave evidence for the Crown. He dared not put Mr Churchill in the witness-box once he had read his report. Yet he had deprived the other side of that advantage.'

'For God's sake, Holmes! You have saved the girl's murderer from the gallows?'

He stretched out his legs and laughed.

'There is no murderer, Watson! Why do all of you fail to grasp that essential point? Somewhere in the Leicester canal or a similar hiding-place lies the Webley Scott revolver once issued to Lieutenant Ronald Light. It is not the weapon of a murderer, though it killed Bella Wright. He was, I imagine, playing the fool with it to impress or amuse her. To his horror, it went off, the bullet hitting the stone-work of the road, glancing upwards and passing through her head. It is the only angle consistent with the wound and therefore the only likely explanation. Light knew that his record in the army had not been of the best. His conduct with young women was much the same. It was a dreadful accident, not a murder, but who would believe him now?'

'And the carrion crow?' I asked sardonically. 'Did he shoot that before he killed Bella Wright—or afterwards?'

Holmes smiled to himself.

'Not far away, under those same muddy waters that hide the revolver, there lies a rifle. Not an elephant-gun to be sure. Not even a gun of .455 calibre. Perhaps an old Martini-Henry used by lads or even their fathers to take pot-shots at crows and the like. Far more likely a rook rifle. It belonged to some other young man who fled from the scene of the tragedy in terror. Imagine him concealed behind the sheep-trough as the crow lands on the gate. He sights the bird and shoots it. Then he gets up and continues on his way to the gate itself. Looking over, he sees the most dreadful sight, the poor girl dead upon the ground, the bicycle beside her.'

'And where is Ronald Light?'

'There is no one to be seen, Watson. For this young woman was shot at about nine o'clock and it is now ten minutes later. The fellow with the gun thinks what Sir Edward made the jury think. The bullet from his rifle passed through the crow, hit the road and glanced up, passed through the girl's head and came to rest. A .455 bullet! It would have blown a crow to pieces.'

'It is what Sir Edward himself thinks, as well as the jury,' I said firmly.

'Then he really is quite mistaken, Watson. The lad—for rook-shooting is a game for lads—saw what he had done. Or, rather, what he thought he had done. He did not stop but took to his heels in terror with the phantom of the hangman at his back. For how was he to prove that it was an accident and no murder?'

'Two shots at once? Something of a coincidence, surely?'

'Two shots, Watson, at an interval of ten or fifteen minutes. Not so much of a coincidence in such splendid hunting country on a fine summer evening.'

In what was to become known as 'The Green Bicycle Case', the explanation that Holmes expounded was the only one to explain the features of the case. For five or ten minutes we sat either side of the fireplace, smoking and thinking.

'Then what do you think of Ronald Light in the end, Holmes? What judgment will you pass on your former client?'

'I only think, Watson, that he is one of the luckiest young men alive. Lucky to be alive and not hanged by the neck in Leicester gaol.'

He added a little brandy to his soda. Half an hour later, he yawned and stretched.

'I believe you have found our little adventure in Leicestershire one too many for you, Watson. Just now you thought I had protected a murderer. I assure you, I have done no more than to save a fool. If you should ever include the case in those romantic fictions of yours, you will find it easier to compose if you first hit upon a good title. I will give you one. You will not talk of bicycles, nor revolvers and cartridges, nor the habits of the carrion crow. You will call it simply, "The Case of the Missing Rifleman". That will explain it completely.'

He puffed at his pipe and said no more. The rest of the world speculated on whether the single bullet that killed Bella Wright passed first through the body of the carrion crow. To Holmes, it was far simpler. There were two bullets. The coincidence of two guns being fired in hunting country within fifteen minutes on a summer evening was trivial compared with the coincidence of a single bullet passing through such a remarkable trajectory. The perversity of his opponents in the debate produced only a shrug from Holmes at the hopelessness of arguing with frailer intellects, who were driven to suggest that the deed must have been done by a lad shooting rooks with an elephant gun! As for Sir Edward Marshall Hall, it seemed a certain awkwardness had been generated between us by this disagreement, for he never communicated with either Holmes or myself again.

The Case of the
Yokohama Club

I

Looking back on the career of Sherlock Holmes, it is plain that the years from 1894 to 1901 were those during which his services were in the most constant demand. Each new case of public importance or private investigation came close on the heels of the last. Gone were the easy-going days of the eighties, when he would lean back in his chair after breakfast, unfold his morning paper at leisure, and fold it again ten minutes later with a lament that it presented few possibilities to the mind of the criminal expert.

Our rooms in Baker Street now received visits from the great and the humble alike. One week our inquirer might be an emissary from Windsor, Downing Street, or one of the chancelleries of Europe. Next week it would be a poor widow-woman or an old soldier with nowhere else to turn. Holmes worked, as he said often, for the love of his art. Yet his instincts and his sympathies were with the weak rather than the mighty. Distress was never turned away from his door.

During these busy years, the manner of his life was everything that a healthy man's should not be. The needle and the cocaine, his chosen implements of self-poisoning, lay conveniently to hand in their drawer. He would spend such hours of recreation as his engagements allowed shut away from sunshine and fresh air, breathing the fumes of some chemical experiment or playing his favourite Haydn and Mendelssohn on the violin. That was all the solace he knew, apart from his pipe. So great was the burden of work that even his rivals in the detective profession were concerned for him.

'Mr Holmes will run himself into the ground, if he keeps up this rate,' said our Scotland Yard friend Lestrade to me after one of our shared adventures. From observation, I was bound to agree. Yet I knew from experience that nothing was more useless than to offer advice to Holmes in medical matters.

With such calls upon his energies, it might seem remarkable to those who knew him only by reputation that he should have given so many weeks of his time in 1897 to an investigation that took him to the other side of the world. Perhaps he was moved by the plight of a young woman—little more than a schoolgirl—facing death at the hands of an arcane and unjust law. Perhaps he also saw from the first how easily a private wrong of this sort might become a scandal and a public disgrace to the British Crown, if her execution were to take place. Whatever the reason, his interest in the story began, as so many of our inquiries did, in the familiar surroundings of Baker Street. For convenience, I have gathered the disparate events that followed under the title of 'The Case of the Yokohama Club'.

Those who remember the London autumn of 1896 may recall that it rained as if it never meant to stop. It did not wash away the city fog but reduced it to an oppressive mist. As the days shortened, the lowering skies in the west seemed to bring perpetual twilight and it was dusk by three in the afternoon.

On such an afternoon towards the end of the year, as the sunset faded before tea-time, Holmes was sitting at the table with a large folio pharmacopoeia open before him and a test-tube of malodorous green liquid in the rack to one side. His long thin back was curved and his head was sunk upon his breast in the attitude that had always suggested to my mind a large and gloomy bird of grey plumage with a black top-knot. I was about to break in upon his thoughts when the sudden clang of the doorbell forestalled me.

Holmes appeared not to hear it as he turned another page of his folio and settled morosely upon the next paragraph. Standing by the window, I moved the curtain a little and looked down into the street. An empty cab was just moving off with the driver's 'Yah-yah-poop!' to the horse and a flick of the reins. From what I could see, the man who stood awaiting an answer to his summons was a stranger to us. The gas had already been lit in the house, so that the fanlight of the door beat full upon the gleaming shoulders of his waterproof, which ran with steady rain. There came an exchange of voices in the hall and the light knock of Mrs Hudson at our door.

'A gentleman, Mr Holmes,' the good lady said unnecessarily. 'Mr Jacob has no appointment but begs you will see him on a matter of the greatest urgency.'

How many times had I heard these words, or their like? Holmes looked up from his calculations and his face seemed brighter.

'Very well, Mrs Hudson. If Mr Jacob takes no more than half an hour of my time, I will listen to what ails him.'

Our housekeeper closed the door and presently, after our visitor had been relieved of his waterproof in the hall, we heard a heavy tread upon the stairs. A broad-shouldered fair-haired man of thirty or so entered the room, well built but with a wan, sensitive, clear-cut face. His blue eyes seemed the brighter for the dark shadows round them.

Holmes watched him cross the room and then stood up to take the visitor's hand.

'Please,' he said, indicating the vacant chair by the fireplace. 'Please take a seat, Dr Jacob, and tell me how I may be of service to you.'

Our visitor went, if that were possible, a little paler on being addressed as 'Doctor'.

'You know me, Mr Holmes?'

'I had never heard of you until a few minutes ago,' Holmes said reassuringly. 'That you are a doctor is, I fear, betrayed by the double deformation which the side pocket of a jacket acquires from carrying the two metal tubes of a stethoscope with the ear-pieces overlapping the edge of the cloth. This is my colleague, Dr Watson, before whom you may speak freely. I have had ample opportunity of observing the ill effects of that medical instrument upon his tailoring.'

Dr Jacob seemed relieved by this simple explanation. He sat down.

'All the same, Mr Holmes, it is disconcerting to be seen through so easily.'

Holmes stood before the fireplace with legs astride, arms folded, one elbow cupped in the other hand.

'Come now, Dr Jacob. I mean you no harm. It is a matter of inference only. I cannot be sure of everything. I am very probably wrong. I should say, however, that you had not long moved to the house in which you live and that it is conveniently near to the railway station. You travel up to Victoria or, possibly, Waterloo. Victoria, I think, is more likely. I am already persuaded that the matter on which you have come to see me is indeed of great urgency. It evidently involves someone dear to you who is far away. The worst news of her reached you yesterday, somewhen following lunch. After a night that was passed in waking rather than sleeping, you decided this morning that you must come here in person and ask me to undertake a long journey on behalf of this lady. I regret that I cannot promise I shall be able to oblige you.'

It would scarcely be too much to use the cliché and say that our visitor's mouth fell open with astonishment and the poor devil's eyes started.

'You cannot know, Mr Holmes! Someone has surely been here before me. One of the Carews!'

Holmes sat down on the sofa and crossed his long legs comfortably, as if this would reassure Dr Jacob.

'No one, I promise you,' he said kindly. 'I know nothing of any Carews. I observe only that you came by cab to our door, so that your shoes are scarcely wet. Yet they show that you have walked a little in the rain earlier today. They have dried since then, so it cannot be in the last fifteen or twenty minutes. If you went on foot from your own house to the station, the condition of your shoes suggests that the distance cannot have been great. However, the wet has caused particles of stone or shingle to adhere to the uppers as they dried. Some are little more than husks. I have experience of those and I recognise them as sea-dredged aggregates. They are used very commonly on roads of new houses in Surrey and Sussex, conveniently close to the channel dredging. One finds them on byways not yet adopted by the local council and not yet treated with tarmac. Therefore, I assume you cannot have lived long in your present home, and that it is in Surrey or Sussex, near the station.'

'That at least is correct,' Dr Jacob said. He seemed relieved to discover that scientific deduction, rather than witchcraft, had revealed so much of him.

'Furthermore,' Holmes said quietly, 'you came here by cab. The square of pasteboard shaped by the cloth of your waistcoat pocket is, I believe, a railway ticket, but not a metropolitan one. It is in any case merely a return half. The underground railway line from Waterloo to Baker Street is very convenient and generally faster than a cab. Not so from Victoria. I am inclined to think you came from Victoria Station. As for your purpose, I suppose it merely by the weight and size of the notecase in your inner breast pocket, which appears—once again by the deformation of the suiting—to be more than amply filled. I beg you will take care, Dr Jacob. It is an invitation to thieves and footpads to carry so much money with so little concealment. I observe from your face that you slept badly last night and that, though perfectly clean-shaven yesterday, the hand that held your razor has been less certain today. I infer that whatever ill news you received reached you yesterday, too late to bring you here at once.'

Dr Jacob stared at him bright-eyed but said nothing. He seemed mesmerised, or perhaps a little fearful, at the performance which Holmes was giving for his benefit.

'I do not wish to be presumptuous,' Holmes concluded, 'but I should be surprised if you had not come here today in the expectation of paying in advance a large sum in cash. That a cheque will not suffice and that the sum is so large suggests to me both that the matter is urgent and the expenses far greater than would be justified unless the investigation involved foreign travel of some kind. Put all these things together and I infer that only some person dear to you and now in great peril would explain them in their entirety. That the person is a lady is, I confess, mere conjecture. Yet nine times out of ten, in such circumstances as these, it is so. She is not your wife, I think. Either you would be with her or you would be on your way to her before now. A daughter, at your time of life, would be too young. A sister, shall we say? Or perhaps a cousin? A sister, I think, is the more probable.'

For the hundredth time, as it seemed to me, I saw emotions of astonishment and relief cross the face of a client, like clouds driven in succession over a windy sky. For a moment, Dr Jacob seemed too overwrought to speak. At last he said, 'It is my sister, Mr Holmes. She is the youngest of us, as I am the eldest. You are correct in every detail of your account. In the last few minutes you have convinced me that everything said about you is true. You alone can save her, if any man may.'

'And where is your sister, Dr Jacob?'

'She is in Yokohama, where she is very likely to be hanged.'

The name of Yokohama fell like a thunderbolt into the room. In my mind I had thought of Paris, Berlin, perhaps even Rome or New York, as the probable scene of the drama. But Yokohama! It was impossible, surely, that Holmes would contemplate such a commission?

My friend got up and walked to the window, the curtains still open, and stared out into the street.

'Yokohama!' he said at last, very softly but with an excitement that was unmistakable. He gazed out into the dismal London night, deeper in thought than I had seen him for a long time. 'And very likely to be hanged!'

It was raining more heavily now and the gaslight of the room shone dimly out through the streaked and dripping glass, falling upon the pavements and the black ribbon of the wet street. Holmes kept his thoughts to himself a moment longer. In the silence, the air was full of the sounds of rain, the thin swish of its fall, the heavier drip from the eaves, and the swirl and gurgle down the steep gutters and through the sewer grating. At last he turned round.

'Dr Jacob, before we go further, I should be very glad if you would tell us slowly and quietly of your sister's difficulty and how it is that you think we might help her. I must tell you, however, that I am a criminal investigator and not a worker of miracles.'

So we heard the story of Mary Esther Jacob and the late Walter Raymond Hallowell Carew. In brief, Carew was a married man and Miss Jacob was thought to have been his mistress, one of many in the course of his colonial career. The man had led a rackety sort of life in the Malay Straits Settlement, Hong Kong, and last of all in the English colony at Yokohama. For some time before his death in October 1896, he had been Secretary and Manager of the Yokohama United Club, where English and American officers and businessmen were wont to gather. Seven years ago, he had married Edith Mary Porch in England and taken her to the Straits Settlement. There he spent several years as a Treasurer in the Colonial Service. Brandy and soda had very nearly killed him in such a climate. Then both he and his bride had fallen ill with malarial fever and, after a spell in Australia, they had come to Yokohama. Neither was ever in perfect health and medication was regularly prescribed for them.

There was no disputing Carew's vices. He had begotten children by a number of women before his marriage. One was even supported afterwards out of his wife's money. The couple also had two children of their own and Miss Mary Jacob, previously living with her brother, had gone out to Yokohama as nursery governess. Another infection from which Carew suffered was of the venereal type, a case of gonorrhoea known only privately until the report of the inquest upon him at the Royal Naval Hospital at Yokohama in October last.

Mrs Carew was little better than her husband, he playing the part *of mari complaisant*, so long as his own pleasures were not interfered with. Edith Carew had found lovers easily in the foreign settlement area of Yokohama. Her husband shrugged at this. The couple even gave such men the nicknames of 'The Ferret' or 'The Organ Grinder'. The latest young man prepared to give his life for her was Harry Vansittart Dickinson, a clerk at the Yokohama branch of the Hong Kong and Shanghai Banking Corporation. Letters of a compromising kind had passed between Dickinson and Mrs Carew for several months, in which the young man urged the errant wife to seek a divorce and become his own bride.

The story of Mary Jacob in such a flashy and sickly household was one of the oldest in the world. It was not long before the inexperienced young governess believed herself in love and became Carew's mistress. This adulterous *ménage* was broken up several months later by the death of the man himself. He had been ailing for several years, since the venereal infection had occasioned a stricture. Far worse, his drinking had brought on symptoms of an incipient cirrhosis of the liver. He could no more resist brandy and soda than he could ignore a pretty servant. With the easy credit and bonhomie of the Yokohama Club, those who sent him on colonial service to cure his drinking had better have sent him to Hades as an escape from summer heat. The state of his liver grew worse and the doctors in Yokohama threatened him with acute jaundice. Carew ignored them. He preferred to put his faith in self-prescribed 'tonics' containing a homoeopathic dose of arsenic as well as sugar of lead.

After his death, Miss Jacob fled the house, as if on suspicion of poisoning a lover who had spurned her. It was certain that during the last weeks of her residence Carew's health grew rapidly worse and he lapsed into delirium. He had died on 22 October, having been taken to the British Naval Hospital at Yokohama a few hours previously. His final illness had lasted for about a fortnight but he had grown suddenly worse in the last twenty-four hours.

The inquest found that Carew had died from arsenical poisoning. What motive was there for murder? Mrs Carew enjoyed freedom in her married life to do as she pleased and had little reason to murder her husband. However, Mary Jacob had far greater cause for vengeance when she discovered that the lover who had cast her off might also have infected her with a dreadful disease.

The suspicions of Carew's doctors had been roused very late. In the last two days they forbad any member of the household to be alone with the invalid. They appointed nurses of high character, one of whom was always in attendance. Yet as late as the last night, when the nurse was away from the room for a few minutes, two servants had seen Mary Jacob standing before the medicine cabinet in the sick man's room. The bedroom door had been locked to prevent this very thing. Miss Jacob must surely have kept or copied a key given her by her lover in happier days. Next day he was dead from a final and fatal dose of arsenic, the equivalent of a one-ounce bottle of Fowler's Solution of Arsenic. Three such bottles were found almost empty in the house. Miss Jacob alone, it seemed, had found the opportunity and motive to do away with him.

'It is most unfortunate, Mr Holmes,' Dr Jacob added, 'that after Carew died, my sister went to the chemist to ask for the return of the order-form for the last bottle of Fowler's Solution. It was written in her own hand, you see. She swears that Carew ordered it and that she merely wrote his instructions.'

Unfortunate! If anything further were needed to put the noose round young Miss Jacob's neck, she had surely provided it by going to beg back this paper written in her own hand! Holmes seemed unperturbed, however, and asked about the behaviour of Carew himself during these last weeks, so far as Dr Jacob knew of it. The dead man's final words offered little comfort to our client.

'I have taken a whole chemist's shop today,' the witnesses heard Carew gasp as he waved away the glass, despite the pain that consumed his entrails. 'I do not want more medicine. I want a brandy and soda.'

That brandy and soda was the last the poor fellow ever drank for by some means the murderer had evidently added the entire bottle of Fowler's Solution to it. By the next morning, the last of his life, he was in such agony and sickness that it was necessary to give him a morphine injection, as well as tablets of cocaine. Carew was in a pitiful state, swearing in his delirium that he could feel worms crawling under his skin and driving him to madness. He also murmured of Mary Jacob and her secret visit to him on that final night. He blessed her as the angel who had poured brandy and soda and held it to his lips in his fever. Had she not been seen by the servants, that might be thought mere delusion. He was in such a state that, in the darkened room that last night, he would believe anyone to be his sweetheart who said she was.

'There is no question, Mr Holmes, that my sister bought Fowler's Solution of Arsenic from the chemist,' said Dr Jacob with a sigh. 'But she swears that she did so on Carew's orders. It was poured into the brandy and soda or into the tonic he took against the state of his liver. Now he is dead and cannot speak for her. It is said that she made evil use of the tonic, for one single-ounce bottle of Fowler's Solution contains twice the fatal dose. The other witnesses, one and all, agree that in those last days there hung about her a scent of lavender. It does not grow in Yokohama, Mr Holmes.'

Holmes's features contracted in a frown.

'Indeed not,' he said softly.

'But all the world knows that Fowler's Solution of Arsenic is strongly scented with lavender to make it more palatable. Dr Watson will bear me out.'

I was about to do so, but Holmes intervened before I could agree. 'I can bear you out, Dr Jacob. I have made a little study of such matters.'

There was worse news that came to our visitor. It was discovered that Mary Jacob had been in the habit of going through the waste-paper baskets to find fragments of letters sent to her employers, especially to Mrs Carew. She took these to a friend, another nursery governess in Yokohama by the name of Elsa Christoffel, who pasted and stitched them together. Mary Jacob was later seen by a witness practising Mrs Carew's signature on a sheet of paper, also marked by the initials 'A. L.' Indeed, Miss Jacob had shown this to the witness as proof of her skill in forgery or imitation.

The foolish young woman seemed determined to wear the rope and spring the trap. Before and after Carew's death there were letters from 'A. L.' and 'Annie Luke', suspected of being written by Mary Jacob. 'Annie Luke' had been Carew's mistress, according to her claims in these letters. In the last one, written to Mrs Carew's lawyer, Mr John Frederick Lowder, the writer confessed in every detail her wicked murder of Carew. Though the letters were signed by Annie Luke, the hand was still said to be that of Mary Jacob.

Dr Jacob's sister now faced trial for murder on the far side of the world by a British consular court, whose like would never have been permitted in our own country. Any jury chosen from the few hundred members of the British community at Yokohama must already know of Miss Jacob and the Carews. They would very likely hold her guilty before the case was opened. She would be held in the British Naval Prison at Yokohama and hanged there by a military executioner, if the verdict went against her, as it now seemed that it must.

'Mr Holmes,' said Dr Jacob softly, 'it is a nightmare. She is beyond help, condemned by a system that I do not begin to understand. Can it be justice?'

Holmes put down his pipe.

'It is the law,' he said quietly, 'whether or not it be justice. Law is what concerns us, Dr Jacob. Law and evidence. The system dates from the treaty with Japan in 1858. Great Britain may exercise consular jurisdiction over her citizens in the five Treaty Ports. They live in foreign settlements within these ports. In return, they are forbidden from travelling more than a few miles from the settlements. In such cases as this, they are tried before the consul's court and acquitted or convicted there. In a conviction for murder, the trial and the execution are to be carried out by British officials in Japan.'

'But that is not justice!' he exclaimed. 'Can she not be brought to England?'

'The law does not provide for that,' said Holmes in the same quiet voice. 'It deals with such a crime in the place where it was perpetrated.'

'How can it be dealt with?' the poor fellow asked in despair. 'How can there be an impartial jury chosen from the few British residents in a port like Yokohama, where all know one another? They will all have taken sides by now. I fear they will listen to the doctors and the other witnesses that the Carew family will put forward, rather than to a seduced and vengeful nursery governess. Forgive me, Mr Holmes, but that is what she will be called!'

'Then we must see to it, Dr Jacob, that, if your sister is innocent, she is acquitted on the evidence, rather than convicted on prejudice.'

'Acquitted, Mr Holmes? I beg you will not mock her.'

Holmes stood up.

'I was never more serious in my life, Dr Jacob. If the facts are as you have described them, I begin to have hopes.'

But I looked at Dr Jacob and, for a moment, I thought the poor fellow might break down in tears. There was such agitation in his face as he thought of the helplessness of this poor girl—for his sister was quite ten years his junior—facing her doom alone on the far side of the world. By the fastest route, Yokohama was almost four weeks away from London. Events there were moving with a terrible speed, while he was trapped so far away. He seemed like a sleeper in a fearful dream, the course of which he could neither alter nor even influence. If Holmes could see a way through the case against the girl, I could not.

'Someone must go to her, Mr Holmes!' Dr Jacob began again. 'She has no family there, no friends that I can call upon. She must have help!'

Holmes stared at the stem of his pipe, his mind further away than Yokohama. A moment later he was the cold and practical thinker once more.

'From what you tell me, Dr Jacob, there would seem little to persuade a jury that your sister is innocent. Fortunately for you, I am not that jury. I find one or two points in the evidence a little curious. I daresay they are nothing but I should like to probe them further. One, at least, has a certain air of fabrication. While

Carew was dying, your sister was seen in his room alone with him. Standing before the medicine cabinet. How many witnesses are there to that?'

'Two. Both are servants of good character. They are girls from the Tokyo Mission School, employed by the Carews.'

'At this time, no other person, not even Mrs Carew, was permitted to be with him unsupervised?'

'No. And I cannot tell you, Mr Holmes, how my sister came to be with him in the few minutes the nurse was absent. The windows of the room were inaccessible. The door was locked and two witnesses on guard outside it. She could neither get in nor out, unless she had a key given her by Carew when he was her lover—or she had stolen one. My sister is no magician, Mr Holmes.'

Holmes stared at him, long and steadily. At last he said, 'I daresay she is not. However, it is not your sister who concerns me, Dr Jacob. I should like to know how these two estimable young witnesses from the Mission School saw your sister standing before the medicine cabinet, if she was alone.'

Dr Jacob shook his head. 'There was a sound in the room, as if someone had banged the window to. They looked through the keyhole of the locked door and saw her. She was standing before the medicine cabinet on which was a triple table-mirror for dressing.'

The faintest smile of triumph touched my friend's fastidious mouth.

'Were I intent upon being locked in with my victim, Dr Jacob, I should take care to leave the key in the lock after I fastened the door behind me. It is convenient if one needs to leave quickly and it prevents any intrusion. It also blocks the view. No one, however morally estimable, even from a Mission School, would see me through the keyhole with the key in the lock. A little curious is it not? Pray, continue.'

Just then, for the first time, I knew that Holmes was set upon Yokohama. It was a madcap adventure but he had never resisted an adventure of any sort.

'The smell of lavender,' Holmes said quietly, 'how was that noticed?'

Dr Jacob shook his head, as if to clear it. 'In the days before the man's death, Mr Holmes, there was a scent of lavender that seemed to cling to my sister's clothes, to her hair. The very same smell was noticed in the sick room.'

'Lavender water is a common enough perfume, Dr Jacob. What matter if your sister chose it—or if someone gave her a present of it to use?'

Dr Jacob looked at Holmes with the faintest suggestion of disappointment in my friend's abilities.

'You are well informed in the pharmacopeia, Mr Holmes, as I infer from the copy at present on your table. You know, perhaps better than I, the extent to which Fowler's Solution of Arsenic is perfumed with spirits of lavender to make it more palatable.'

'Hmmm,' said Holmes drily. 'From where did your sister buy the Fowler's Solution that she was sent to get?'

'Maruya's Pharmacy in the town. She went there rather than Schedel's European Pharmacy because it also sold books and stationery.'

'Mrs Carew was a customer of Schedel, I take it?'

'I daresay she was,' Dr Jacob looked up a little sharply. 'But spirits of lavender are a characteristic ingredient of Fowler's Solution of Arsenic.'

'In England,' Holmes said, as if finishing the sentence for him.

'But Fowler's Solution is universal, Mr Holmes.'

'Indeed, it is, Dr Jacob but the British Pharmacopeia is not.'

He stood up, pulled a pamphlet from the shelf, and handed it to our visitor.

'You would perhaps care to consult this most interesting monograph by Professor Edwin Divers of the Chemistry Department of the Imperial University of Tokyo—late of the Medical School of Middlesex Hospital. Dr Divers, being expert in the toxicology of tropical medicine, is something of an inspector-general of pharmacies in the Far East. His analysis establishes beyond question that neither spirits of lavender nor sandalwood tincture are used in Japanese Fowler's Solution, such as Maruya's would sell. You will find the comment on page eighteen at the end of the second paragraph.'

He handed the open pamphlet to our guest. Dr Jacob looked up.

'I had no idea, Mr Holmes, that Fowler's Solution from a Japanese pharmacy would be differently constituted, nor would most of my profession.'

'No,' said Holmes languidly. 'Nor did the person who sought to incriminate your sister by so foolish a trick. That alone does not acquit her nor incriminate Mrs Carew. From what you tell me, much of the evidence and motivation is still against Miss Jacob. Yet this point has a certain interest, does it not?'

Dr Jacob drew a handkerchief from his pocket and blew his nose bravely.

'Then you cannot promise anything, Mr Holmes?' he asked, standing up like a man of courage to face his executioners. Holmes remained seated.

'I did not say that, Dr Jacob. I said that much of the evidence and the motivation appears to be against your sister. Appearances, however, invite investigation. I must urge you not to entertain false hopes but, if you wish, I will see what can be done for Miss Jacob.'

'You will go to Yokohama?' It was plain that Dr Jacob could not credit this. Nor could I. Holmes, however, inclined his head.

'If that is what you wish.'

'To Yokohama, Holmes?' I could not restrain my interruption. 'To Japan?'

'I understand that it is where the port of Yokohama is to be found.'

Dr Jacob still stared at him, as if he thought my friend would qualify such a promise. Then he saw the truth.

'Mr Holmes, I did not dare to believe that you would—or could! That you would do this for a stranger, whom you never saw until today!'

Holmes laid down his pipe. 'I ask no thanks, Dr Jacob, and I make no promises. I would not go at all if it were only to please you. I confess, however, that the case against your sister intrigues me. It is so strong—almost too strong—and yet the matter of the keyhole and the impeccable Mission School witnesses, like the perfume of lavender and the irreproachable nurse, possesses a certain undeniable attraction.'

The continuation of the analysis was lost upon our visitor, weary with grief and bewildered as he was. He reached into his pocket and drew out the amply filled note-case. Holmes held up a hand.

'If you please, Dr Jacob, we will have no payment and no discussion of fees as yet. When I bring your sister safely home, you may repay me. If I do not, then I fear I should be unable to accept anything for my services.'

II

'What the devil is this, Holmes?' It was ten minutes later and we had parted with our visitor until the next day. 'We are to set out for Yokohama, with all that remains to be done here? We are to chase after a foolish girl, who from everything we are told is probably guilty of the crime with which she is charged? We are to do all this without any certainty of having so much as our expenses paid?'

'We are to do all that, Watson, just as you say.'

'But why?'

'My dear Watson,' he said smiling, 'have you learned nothing of the criminal mind in all these years of our acquaintance? In this case, all my instincts are one way and almost all the facts are the other. Yet there are one or two curiosities. Did you ever hear of a devious poisoner, who calculates dosages and times with such care, but deliberately takes the key from inside the door so that she may be broken in upon at the moment that will reveal her guilt?'

'That means nothing, Holmes. It may happen all too easily in the stress of the moment, when the crime is so monstrous and the criminal lacks experience or thought.'

'Does it not strike you, Watson, as a little too convenient?'

'I can't say that it does,' I answered in some little pique.

'Very well, then. Did you ever hear of a murderer who writes a confession of the crime, disguising her name as another but writing in a hand obviously or even probably known as her own to all involved in the investigation?'

'She may be a lunatic.'

'She may be indeed,' he said philosophically. 'She may be mad—or bad—or both—or neither.'

'And for that we are to go to Yokohama? To the far side of the planet?'

Holmes sat down and closed his eyes.

'It is more than enough, Watson. Who knows when such a chance will come again? Never, perhaps! Neither of us is immortal, my dear fellow. Think of Yokohama and the Orient! You have no soul, Watson! No, that is too harsh. You have a soul without an ounce of romance, if you cannot see that we must go. We are meant to go. And there may be a glorious victory in store.'

It was impossible to argue with him in this mood. I could not help feeling, however, that he might find the reality of Yokohama and the Orient something less alluring than his pipe-dream.

III

A man cannot decide to go to the other side of the world one evening and set off next morning. Days passed before our departure from Euston Station for Liverpool and the liner *Parisian*, the pride of the Allan Line, that would take us to Montreal. On our last two days, Holmes disappeared from breakfast until late afternoon, ferreting in the registers of Somerset House. When I asked why, he shrugged and said, 'My dear Watson, we are about to travel to the far side of the Pacific on the assumption that Mary Jacob has a brother and that the brother was our visitor. A little confirmation from records of births, marriages and deaths is in order before we commit ourselves further.'

I could not dispute the wisdom of the precaution. Then, that last evening, he announced that we should take our ease at the Egyptian Hall, London's temple of magic, which looks as if it had been lifted by a genie from Abu Simbel and set down among the mansions of Piccadilly.

'Have you entirely forgotten, Holmes, that we leave for Japan tomorrow morning?'

'Just so, Watson. Then let us make our farewells to Egypt tonight.'

Mad though it seemed to me, we sat through the entire programme of Maskelyne and Cooke, Hercules carrying a pyramid of seven burly men round the stage on his shoulders, Mazeppa in tights and spangles locked in the Indian Basket to be run through with pitiless swords, only for the opened basket to be empty and the houri to enter with a smile from the far side of the stage, the disembodied head of Socrates answering the magician's questions. Holmes chuckled and applauded like a schoolboy. When it was over, he slipped backstage for a moment to congratulate the performers.

'One forgets, Watson,' he remarked as the cab bore us homewards, 'that no theatrical feat can equal the perfection of well-practised illusion. Not Shakespeare, not the opera nor the ballet can ever have quite that absolute success—for absolute success or failure it must be. The least hitch means utter disaster, as it never would for Miss Ellen Terry or Sir Henry Irving. Magnificent, was it not?'

I agreed that I supposed it was, in its way. Next day our journey began and Dr Jacob was at Euston to see us on our way. He brought little presents and messages for his sister but it was the sight of his anxious face, so drawn and newly marked by distress, even since our first meeting, that made it impossible to begrudge the journey after all.

The first part of our voyage was familiar to us from previous expeditions. A few days later we anchored in the mouth of the St Lawrence River. The waterway was crowded with tiny brown rocks and great islands, the majestic Laurentian mountain range beyond and French-Canadian villages on the shore. By the next night we were at Montreal, whence the long and heavily laden train of the Canadian Pacific Railway would take us to Vancouver in a few days. Our travelling companions, who were American, Chinese, and Japanese, as well as Canadian and English, broke their journeys for a day at the modern cities of Winnipeg or Banff. Holmes, however, would not delay longer than necessary. For three hours, our powerful engine climbed slowly up the great backbone of the American continent until the train reached the Kicking-Horse Pass, where streams flow down one slope to the Atlantic and down the other side to the Pacific. Before us lay flimsy-looking trestle bridges and miles of snow-sheds. High above, domes and spires of ice towered to the sky over the hard sheen of glaciers. Deep gorges lay below, with foaming streams and great cataracts.

Two days later we joined the liner *Empress of India* at Vancouver, a fine new city entirely lit by electricity and served by electric tramcars, the wharves of its harbour lined by ships from China and Japan, Australia and the South Seas. Our Pacific crossing was long and lonely, the horizon broken only once by a sail and once by a view of the bleak and barren rocks that are the Aleutian Islands. The long sea voyage was not to Holmes's taste and he seemed to care little for either the scenery or the miracles of nature. More than once he invoked the comment of Dr Johnson to Boswell on the Giant's Causeway. 'Worth seeing, but not worth going to see,' as Holmes phrased it.

My great concern had been that we might not reach Yokohama before the trial of Mary Jacob opened in the British Consul's Court. Holmes had wired Miss Jacob's counsel, Mr Scidmore, to this effect. An adjournment was sought. As our white-painted liner with its three buff funnels entered Tokyo Bay, we had several days to spare.

Yokohama was the end of the liner's voyage, just short of the Japanese capital but in the same picturesque bay, with little fishing villages, shrines and pagodas along its shores. At anchor off the harbour were warships and merchantmen, sampans that might have been mistaken for gondolas crowding round our hull. The entrance to the fairway is marked by a lightship and a pair of buoys. Our white liner came in close to shore and let go her anchor. Holmes at last shrugged off the *ennui* of the voyage and his eyes were keen with excitement at the sights and scenes around us. Half an hour later we were ferried ashore to the granite breakwater within the harbour light. A further half-hour was enough to bring us through the Customs House, where we were met by Mary Jacob's attorney, Mr Scidmore.

Mr Scidmore was a man of impressive appearance, well suited to that of counsel in court or an opera singer on the stage. He was about fifty, tall and portly, with imposing features and an air of command. He scorned the white ducks and tropical uniform of his compatriots. His taste ran to a sombre and rich style, black frock-coat, shining hat, neat brown gaiters and well-cut pearly-grey trousers.

His first concern was not with the case but with which hotel should accommodate us.

'You might stay at Wright's,' he said cautiously, 'but Lowder the prosecutor has put up there, so that would never do. You will find the Grand Hotel and the Club Hotel facing the Bund, as they call the sea wall. Mr Dickinson, a prosecution witness, is at the Grand so that would scarcely be advisable. There is the Oriental at the back of the Grand on Main Street, near the Consulate. Mrs Carew has connections with both so you had best not stay there. Perhaps, after all, it would be best if you were to stay at the Yokohama United Club. A man may keep himself much more easily to himself there than in any of the hotels.'

The Yokohama United Club, like the English villas and bunga-lows, stands on what is called The Bluff, looking out across Tokyo Bay. This is the English compound. Like the other four Treaty Ports, Yokohama has its area of 'Foreign Settlement' where the national laws of the inhabitants are applied.

The road from the port to The Bluff is steep and like all journeys within the town is accomplished by a 'ricksha', something like a bath-chair with shafts, pulled by a runner. Among the public buildings at this upper level we passed the Club Germania, a Masonic Temple, and a public hall for plays and other entertainments. Just then, an exhibition of wonders was advertised, including the performance of the Indian Rope Trick. The English villas were newly built and had the handsome four-square look of Bournemouth or Cheltenham. Some of the English shops were on the quiet Bluff and many more lay below in the streets of the busy town. The Yokohama Club itself was a recent building that might not have seemed out of place in St James's Street or Pall Mall.

Until one lives a week or two in one of these enclaves, it is impossible to imagine the power that lies in the hands of Her Britannic Majesty's Consul. James Troupe, whom we met next day, was Consul, Magistrate, Governor of the Prison, Superintendent of the Hospital, Judge of the Criminal Court and, in all but the literal sense, Executioner. Dr Jacob had never seen the place but his worst fears of injustice in his sister's case seemed well founded.

Holmes was not one who cared greatly for gentlemen's clubs. Indeed, he loathed fashionable society with his whole bohemian mind. The Yokohama United Club was imposing in appearance but less so in its ambience. Holmes found himself among strangers who knew one another but to whom he was a man of no great significance. He did not want their company but it would have pleased him had they sought his. Such was the egotism which I more than once observed to be a strong factor in my friend's singular character.

A change for the worse came over him as he looked about him at the well-appointed club house. The loud talk and fatuous laughter, the guzzling and swilling, the shallow pleasantries of his compatriots, were contemptible to his fastidious sensibility. Far from being the exotic adventure he had pictured, the case of Miss Mary Jacob seemed, on that first evening, one that he was anxious to have done with, so that he might book the next passage home.

'From such people as this,' he hissed to me, 'they will choose twelve men to decide whether that unfortunate girl shall live or die! It is intolerable!'

Matters were not improved by our being hailed on our way into dinner by Mr Rentiers of the British Consulate. He was an arrogant young buck in his white mess-jacket but the story he had to tell improved neither Mary Jacob's chances nor the temper of Sherlock Holmes. He had been put 'in charge' of us by Mr Troupe, the Consul, as if to see that we came to no harm. There was no easy or courteous way of getting rid of this young flunkey. He sat us down in the spacious dining-room under the slow ceiling-fan, the portrait of Her Majesty looking down at us from the far end of the room. Mr Rentiers ordered largely and confidently from the Chinese waiter who came in answer to his snapped fingers.

'We don't think a lot of the old-fashioned ways out here,' he said airily. 'I daresay Carew wasn't a saint, but then most aren't.'

Holmes broke off a small piece of bread. 'Really?' The tone of his voice encouraged the conceited young ass to continue.

'Waste of time, you know, it really is,' Rentiers said dispassionately. 'What is?'

'Trying to stir up mud about the Carews. Granted he'd had the pox but that was bad luck. Walter Carew took the bad luck for most men of his age out here alone. As for his liver, you can't drink in the Malay Straits or Yokohama as freely as you can at home. Most find that out too late. So did he.'

Holmes stared at Rentiers as if considering him for dissection. 'And Mrs Carew?'

The thin lip under the wispy moustache lifted a little in a smile of appreciation.

'Edith Carew's a sport. A real old sport. Race Course, Regatta Day, tennis, cricket, everything. Part of it all.'

'And Mary Jacob?'

Rentiers tasted the wine and pulled a face.

'A thieving nursery governess, she and her little friend Elsa Christoffel. Two of the same. Blackmailers the pair of 'em. If Mary

Jacob wasn't to be tried for murder, she might get fourteen years for blackmail anyway. So might her conniving little friend. The evidence is laid before the Consul already. Two other servants saw Jacob fetching scraps of torn-up letters from the wastepaper baskets in the Carews' villa. Christoffel sewed the scraps together. Mostly letters from Harry Dickinson to Edith Carew. Letters of a compromising kind. What do you suppose the two little sluts were going to do with them unless it was blackmail?'

'I have not the least idea,' said Holmes expressionlessly.

'What's more, the servants saw Jacob practising Edith Carew's handwriting. Forging it, in other words. Even before Carew died there were letters coming to him and his wife from Annie Luke, a woman he'd had before he married. A woman in a black veil called at the house when he was out. Harry Dickinson saw her crying on the street corner by the Water Street entrance of the club on the day of Carew's funeral. Almost the last time that Carew left his house, he went round Yokohama trying to find her. We've got witnesses to that.'

'And was Annie Luke here, in Yokohama?' Holmes asked gently.

Rentiers leaned back and laughed at him. 'Not she! It was a stunt by Christoffel and Jacob. Like the other letters.'

'What other letters?' asked Holmes casually.

'They both wrote other anonymous letters to men in Yokohama. Christoffel admits in her witness statement that she did it. Jacob denies it but she was the one who wrote the "Annie Luke" letters. A pound to a penny. Christoffel was Edith Carew's rival for Harry Dickinson. She admits she wrote anonymous letters, begging him to leave Edith Carew for her, talked about humiliating herself in front of him. She admitted it, when they examined her at the committal proceedings. The little bitch actually laughed about it in the witness-box! Laughed in our faces!'

Holmes reached for the pepper. 'Indeed? And Miss Jacob?'

Rentiers grinned. 'That's the best bit. She must have thought the tricks with the letters would never be found out. In the last one, Annie Luke confessed to the murder of Carew. But Annie Luke isn't in Yokohama. Never was. So if Mary Jacob wrote those letters from so-called Annie Luke, as will be proved, then Mary Jacob has already confessed to the murder of Carew. There's a naval prison here and that's where Miss Jacob is now. There's a naval hangman too—petty officer with two ratings to assist. So if this goes wrong for Miss Jacob, she'll be six foot under by the prison wall in a few weeks' time. And good riddance.'

Rentiers opened his mouth in a large silent grin of appreciation at his own cleverness. How Holmes kept his composure in the face of this insolent young scapegrace, I did not know. Rentiers took another spoonful of soup. Then he said, 'Anything else you wanted to know?'

'Yes,' said Holmes courteously, 'Why did Mr and Mrs Carew refer to you in their conversations and letters as "The Organ Grinder"?'

It was a pistol-shot through a bullseye. Rentiers put his spoon down. From his shaven neck to the roots of his hair, his young face went the shade of ripe raspberries. He said not a word but rose from his chair, and walked from the dining-room without a glance to either side. We never saw him again.

'Holmes! How the devil did you know?'

Holmes stared after him.

'I have not the least idea, Watson. No more than an instinctive sense of human frailty. But you, of all people, my dear fellow, will acknowledge that in such matters I am very seldom wrong. Now, at least, we may finish our meal unmolested by the chatter of that young jackanapes.'

In that, he was right. No one but the Chinese waiter came near us for the rest of the evening. After Holmes's casual insult to a consular official, we had advertised ourselves as lepers.

IV

The name of Sherlock Holmes meant little to the English colony of Yokohama, an isolated and inward-looking community of adventurers and younger sons who had been despatched to the East so that they should not incur scandal or expense at home. The Consul and his officers presided over them for all the world like schoolmasters trying to manage unruly boys.

It suited Holmes that he and I should be regarded as nothing but two more 'griffins', as new arrivals are contemptuously called. He would not have given two-pence for the entire English settlement. When he drew my attention, it was to admire the natural beauty of the Japanese girls with the blue-black *bandeaux* of their *coiffure* immaculately dressed so that not a single hair was out of place, the piled tresses revealing the prettiness of each face and the ivory perfection of the nape and ears. Or else he would be struck by the reality of Japanese life and how perfectly its scenes resembled the decorations on fan, ornamental tray, or screen. He watched the jugglers in the street, many of them children, and the skill with which a spinning top seemed to move as if by wizardry.

Our first encounter with the members of the Carew household was when Holmes interviewed Rachel Greer, a Eurasian girl who had assisted Mary Jacob in the nursery, and Hanauye Asa. They were brought to the secretary's office in the club and left with us. These were the two who had been Mission School pupils before entering service and neither of them faltered in her story. Their honesty was so palpable that I confess my heart sank a little for Mary Jacob. Rachel Greer spoke for both of them, interpreting many of Hanauye Asa's replies. Yet even to judge by her expression and manner, Hanauye Asa spoke the entire truth of what she had seen.

'Be kind enough to explain,' said Holmes gently to Rachel Greer who stood before the desk like a naughty child, 'how it was that you saw Mary Jacob in Mr Carew's room the evening before his death. I am correct, I believe, in saying that the only door to the room was locked at that moment during the few minutes the nurse was away and that the nurse had posted the two of you to see that no one came near, while she was absent?'

'Yes,' said the girl earnestly. 'No one passed.'

246

'No one?' asked Holmes gently. 'But Mary Jacob passed, did she not?'

Rachel Greer shook her head. 'Not while we were there. We heard a sound, while the nurse was out of the room. The window banged. We knew it could not be Mr Carew, for he was too ill to get out of bed. We looked through the keyhole and saw Mary Jacob standing in front of the mirror.'

'Which mirror?'

'The triple-mirror on top of the cabinet, where the medicines were kept.'

'Just standing there?'

Rachel Greer nodded. 'She stood for a moment, looking at it. Then she looked down at something in her hands. Then I think she moved away and we could not see her.'

'What else happened?'

'Someone in the opposite room downstairs, on the far side of the courtyard, shone a bright light to see what had made the noise. It was Mrs Carew who shone the light from the nursery window opposite when she heard the window bang. But she swore she saw nothing in the garden or the house. Almost at once, we heard the nurse coming back and Mrs Carew calling us down. She asked what the noise was but we could not tell her. We told her that Miss Jacob was in the room.'

'And what did Mrs Carew say?'

'She said it was impossible for Mary Jacob to be in the room unless she had passed us. Just after that, Mary Jacob was in the nursery.'

Not by a single facial movement did Holmes suggest that Rachel Greer might not be telling the truth. Yet if she was, then Mary Jacob was the last person to be alone with Carew on the final night of his life except his nurse. Rachel Greer and Hanauye Asa stood guard outside the door all night, on Mrs Carew's insistence, so that even when the nurse was absent for a few minutes no one could enter. From the time that the two servants had looked through the keyhole until the moment of Carew's death, no one but Mary Jacob or the nurse could have administered the three grains of arsenic that had killed him. The nurse had already been acquitted of all suspicion.

'Had you ever seen Mary Jacob in Mr Carew's bedroom at any other time?' Holmes asked. The girl stared at her hands with an air of modesty.

'Before he was ill, yes.'

'Did she take the children in there to see their father?'

Something rather like a smirk of embarrassment touched Rachel Greer's lips.

'She went to him alone. When Mrs Carew was out, playing cards or riding.'

The point was so hopeless that Holmes seemed to give it up.

'And what of the letters belonging to Mrs Carew that Mary Jacob took?'

'Mrs Carew used to tear up letters after she read them and throw the pieces in the basket. Miss Jacob would take the pieces and put them together. She and Miss Christoffel. She showed them to me. I saw her take them from the basket.'

'Why did she take them?'

Rachel Greer shrugged. 'To find out what Mrs Carew was doing. Things that she should not do. Some of the letters were from a gentleman.'

'And what else did you see?'

The girl looked up at him, direct and sincere in her emphasis.

'She used to copy Mrs Carew's writing. Her signature. I saw a paper where she had written Mrs Carew's signature. She copied other writing as well. She copied Annie Luke.'

There seemed no more to be done. Holmes thanked the two girls and then paused.

'One moment,' he said quietly. 'Mr Carew's bedroom faced the nursery, did it not? Across the little lawn?'

'Yes,' said Rachel Greer simply.

'How many other rooms were there to either side of his?'

'None on one side. On the other side there was Mrs Carew's room.'

'So they slept in the two adjoining rooms on that last night. Was there a door from one to the other?'

'There was a door but it was locked. On Mr Carew's side, it was bolted at the top and bottom by the nurse who was with him.'

'Did you see Mrs Carew go into her own room that last night?'

'Yes. She went in at eleven o'clock and she did not come out until the morning. It was just before they sent for the doctor and the ambulance to take Mr Carew to the hospital. But it was impossible for Mrs Carew to go through the other door between the rooms. She must come out on to the landing.'

'No one was with Mr Carew when the nurse was away for a few minutes during the night?'

Rachel Greer shook her head again. 'Mr Carew was alone then. No one could go to him. We stayed outside the door all the time, on the landing. Mrs Carew did not come out of her room and she could not get through the other door. The Consul's men examined that door between the rooms to see if it had been tried.'

Later that evening I could not forbear saying to Holmes that our client had cooked her own goose. She was Carew's lover, either spurned by him or infected by his dreadful disease. She had ordered and bought 'plenty poison', as the chemist called it, for Carew's tonic. The three bottles of Fowler's Solution of Arsenic had been found in the house after the man's death. All three were nearly empty. A lethal dose of it had found its way into him. Much as Edith Carew might have hated her husband in secret, it was impossible to see how she could have got near him during the night when the fatal dose was administered. Short of believing that the doctors or nurses had poisoned the poor devil, Mary Jacob was the only suspect. If she had been in the room alone with him the evening before his death, she had only to empty an entire ounce of Fowler's Solution into his brandy and soda. By then he was delirious and calling for his drink. Fowler's Solution in Japanese pharmacies contains no lavender. It is intended to be tasteless and would certainly be so in a stiff brandy of the kind Carew drank. Who but Mary Jacob could have done it?

Holmes sat in his chair, eyes closed and fingertips pressed together under his chin, as I listed the evidence that would hang Mary Jacob. Then he said lightly, 'You have something still to learn about circumstantial evidence, Watson. It is never more suspect than when there is too much of it. There is too much of it in this case. Far too much. If the wind should shift to another quarter, the accusation will lie in quite a different direction.'

Next morning we were taken by appointment to interview Miss Mary Jacob at the British Naval Prison. It was a beautiful winter morning on The Bluff, milder by far than anything in England, the elegant villas and bungalows commanding a fine view of Tokyo Bay. At the prison, they had made a cell for her from a room in the commandant's quarters. It was bare enough with its bed, chairs, a table under its barred window, a smaller one by the bed. Whatever passion Walter Carew may have felt for her, Mary Jacob was not a beauty but more of a simple village lass. Small wonder if her elder brother took her under his wing. Her dark hair was rather scragged back just then and the strong lines of her face reminded me a little of Kate Webster, who had gone to the gallows twenty years earlier for killing her mistress with an axe. Mary Jacob's face had an air of resentment, even towards those who had come to help her. There was resolve in the line of her chin and a natural anger burned at the corners of her wide cheekbones. When she turned her brown eyes upon us, there was the look of fear and hate that one sees in a cornered animal.

She sat at the table, Holmes sat opposite her, and I at the end.

'Miss Jacob,' said Holmes after we had introduced ourselves, 'I do not conceal from you that your case is one of the most difficult that has lately come my way.'

She scowled at him and said belligerently, 'They are all against me. Because of him.' The sullen accusation would do little to help her.

'That may be so,' Holmes said persistently, never once raising his voice. 'What concerns me more than the people you say are against you is the amount of evidence which is undoubtedly against you. It is more than enough to hang you, unless you pull yourself together. Now, if you please, we will have truthful answers to questions.'

She looked up in astonishment, as if her defender had just slapped her face, when he dealt with her in this manner.

'First,' said Holmes, 'you bought enough arsenic from Maruya's Pharmacy in Yokohama to kill Mr Carew several times over.'

'Because they told me to. He asked me to get it.'

'At Maruya's?'

'No, not at any place in particular, only to get it.'

'Miss Jacob,' he said quietly, 'there is incontrovertible evidence that you bought that poison. There is no evidence whatever, apart from your own assertion, that you were ever asked to get it.'

'I didn't even know what it was!'

'Come!' said Holmes gently. 'The order was in your own handwriting.'

'Fowler's Solution? I didn't know what Fowler's Solution was! Only a tonic. I wrote down what he told me.'

'But when he died, you went to the chemist and asked for that writing back, did you not? Is that the action of an innocent person?'

'I was frightened!' At last there was something that sounded like a cry.

'So you might well be,' said Holmes in the same quiet voice, 'but more frightened, perhaps, if you were guilty than if you were innocent. The truth might protect innocence but never guilt.'

From time to time, I could not help reflecting upon the worldly success that might have awaited Holmes in a career of cross-examination at the Criminal Bar. Yet I was more than a little anxious at the tone of scepticism that he continued to employ upon Mary Jacob. With the weariness of an unbeliever, he turned to the next topic.

'You were seen by two independent witnesses taking the torn fragments of Mrs Carew's letters from the wastepaper basket. Why?'

'I thought they were mine!'

'How could Mrs Carew's letters be yours?'

The tears began to sparkle as the poor young nursery governess spoke of her home and her family.

'She kept my letters from home and never let me have them. I never received my mother's letters to me all the time I was in that house. Never an answer to mine. Perhaps she stopped my letters as well. Only she wrote to my home and told them how happy I was and how well treated. Well treated, Mr Holmes? She used me like a slave! I thought perhaps they were my letters from home torn up and thrown in the basket, so that I should not see nor answer them.'

'Perhaps your mother had not written to you.'

'I'm not a fool.' The anger burned again at the points of her cheekbones. 'Even Mrs Carew's brother, when he came out from England, said I'd been written to.'

Holmes looked her in the eye.

'I think you had better explain why Mrs Carew should stop your mother's letters.'

The tears had dried and there was a look of triumph on the girl's face.

'They never told you? Mrs Carew lived in Somerset, near Glastonbury, before she married. My people were at Langport in those days, a little way off. She didn't know where I came from until after I arrived out here because I wrote from my brother's in Surrey. I was a doctor's sister, that's all she knew. Now she's frightened that I'll hear about her from home, how she's never been any better than she should be. I might have told Mr Carew. I might have told all her precious friends on The Bluff and at the Club, as well as the ones at the Race Course and the tennis courts. Oh yes, I was her servant right enough. But I had a mother who knew who my father was, which hers never did!'

'Quite,' said Holmes coolly, 'but why stick the fragments of the torn letters together?'

'To show to Mr Carew, if Mrs Carew went on treating me as she did. Perhaps then he would love me and not her. Let him see what a fool she and Mr Dickinson were making of him. He'd turned a blind eye before, but this time he was ready to divorce her.'

'Really?' said Holmes, with the least flicker of interest. 'Why, then, did you practise writing Mrs Carew's hand and her signature? And the writing of Annie Luke?'

'Annie Luke was just a name I heard from Mr Carew. A young lady from Devonshire that he knew once in the days before he was married.'

'And Mrs Carew's writing?'

'I was going to pay her out,' the girl said miserably. 'He was never going to love me, after all, was he? And then I found out about the disease he had and how I'd been deceived by him. I was going to pay them both out. I thought I could write to Mr Dickinson, pretending to be Mrs Carew. I should tell him that I couldn't see him again because I knew about the disease Mr Carew had. Let them show their faces on The Bluff after that!'

Holmes sat back and stared at her for a moment. Then he said, 'I much fear, Miss Jacob, that you have just supplied almost all the motivation necessary for the Crown to establish a case of murder against you.'

There was horror in her eyes as the trap seemed to open under her. 'You won't tell them? Oh, God, you won't!'

'I am not retained, Miss Jacob, to supply the deficiencies of the Consul's investigators. I shall not repeat so foolish a story as the one you have just told me. However, it is now plain that our only hope is to attack the circumstantial evidence. I have but one question to ask you.' She watched him, half doubting and half hoping. 'Were you in Mr Carew's room at about eight thirty on the last evening of his life?' Holmes demanded simply. 'Think carefully before you answer. Two reputable and independent witnesses swear that they saw you standing before the medicine cabinet.'

'No!' It was a shout rather than a cry. 'I was in the garden.'

'Alone, no doubt?'

'I was reading a book!'

'Reading a book in the dark?'

'No. I was sitting on the verandah seat, under Mr Carew's window, where the seat and the lantern is. I liked to sit there alone and read.'

Holmes stood up and walked across to the window-ledge as the girl watched him. He picked up two novels. *The Play Actress* and *A Romance of Two Worlds* by Marie Corelli.

'A book like these?'

Mary Jacob seemed puzzled. 'No,' she said. 'Those were left here for me, from the Club library.'

Holmes rippled the pages, sniffed, and put them down.

'What happened while you were sitting there, reading your book, at about eight thirty?'

'I was asked that,' she said. 'There was a bang from up above, in Mr Carew's room, like someone pulling the window shut. Something fell on the grass. A piece of wood or stone, even loose paint perhaps. It was too dark to tell.'

'What did you do?'

'I just looked up, I suppose.'

'And what else?'

'Mrs Carew must have heard the bang as well. She opened the curtain facing across the little lawn from the nursery side and shone the big lantern to see what was happening. Then I heard her call Rachel and the other girl.'

'You know that Mrs Carew has deposed that when she shone the light out, you were not sitting on that seat, nor were you anywhere else to be seen until five or ten minutes later when you were in the nursery?'

'But I was there!' the girl cried, the tied length of dark hair swishing on the back of her dress as she looked from one to the other of us.

'And you know that Rachel and her companion both swear that they heard the window bang and saw you in Mr Carew's room at the very same moment?'

'They're lying!' she cried again. 'Mrs Carew gave him poison in the night!'

Holmes looked at her coolly.

'You also know that one or other of the nurses was with Mr Carew the last two days before he was taken to hospital, except for occasional intervals of a few minutes each? Mrs Carew could not have come out on to the landing to go into his room without being seen by the two servants. The other door in the wall between the two rooms was locked and bolted on Mr Carew's side. No attempt was made to force it. The only arsenic in the house was in his room, in the medicine cabinet. You were the only person seen there, apart from the nurses.'

Mary Jacob sat before us, abject and exhausted.

'I was never in that room,' the poor girl said helplessly, 'not that night, not that day, not the night nor the day before that!'

'I fear that will not answer in the court,' Holmes said, though his voice was not unkindly. 'We must see what better can be done.'

'And the nursery amah and the other girl who say that they saw me? What of them?'

'Well,' said Holmes drily, 'I imagine they are very likely to be believed.'

At this she bowed her head over the table and began to weep, arms hanging down in dejection, not attempting even to cover her face.

'I beg you will not cry,' said Holmes irritably. 'Listen to me! I shall return this evening. It will be quite late. Until then, you are to leave every article in this room where it is at the moment. Do you understand?'

The poor girl looked up, not understanding in the slightest, but she nodded.

'Do as I say,' he said more gently. 'The next hours are of great importance.'

I was used to the insouciance of my friend on such occasions but as the cell door closed behind us on the picture of fear and dejection that Mary Jacob presented, I could curb my feelings no longer.

'Is that all?' I asked him, as we walked away towards The Bluff.

'Naturally,' he said, with a shrug of his thin shoulders. 'What else can there be? If Miss Jacob was not in the room on that last night, she could scarcely have put three grains of arsenic in Carew's brandy and soda. If she was in the room, then she was quite certainly the person who did so. I imagine the case hinges on that.'

'For God's sake, Holmes! How could you? You might as well have told the poor child that she was going to the gallows and have done with it!'

He was not the least put out. 'Left to your detective skills at present, Watson, that is precisely where she would be going.'

'Stop a minute,' I said with malign satisfaction. 'While you were busy browbeating that poor girl, you quite missed the most important clue in her defence.'

'I daresay,' he murmured, walking on, but I stood still and made him stop, turn and listen to me.

'When the window banged and something fell, Mrs Carew drew back the curtain of the opposite room in a second or two and shone the big lantern out. Even the servants agree.'

'Well?' he asked quietly. 'And what if she did?'

'Don't you see it, Holmes? For that to have happened in a second or two, the lantern must have been already lit. No woman sitting in a nursery or in any such room keeps a big outdoor lantern lit. It would take fifteen or twenty seconds at least for her to prepare it, light it and shine it out, not two or three. Surely she must have known beforehand that the window of the upper room would bang at that moment. But how could she know? What would be the purpose in knowing?'

He looked at me kindly. 'My dear Watson, I owe you a most profound apology. I had quite begun to think that the enervating air of Yokohama had sapped your powers of observation and deduction. And now, if you please, we will try the luncheon at Wright's Hotel in the town. I am a little weary of the Club and Her Britannic Majesty's Consular Kingdom. The prospect of meeting counsel for the prosecution would be more agreeable than another encounter with Mr Rentiers. Indeed, though Mr Lowder is the prosecutor, he has agreed with Mr Scidmore that we may inspect the scene of the crime this evening. I think it probable that your questions about Mrs Carew's curious conduct will then be answered.'

'Would it not be better to go in full daylight?'

'I think not,' said Holmes firmly. 'This was a crime of darkness and had better be examined under such conditions.'

V

That afternoon saw Holmes in one of the queer humours that overtook him unpredictably from time to time. He seemed to lose all interest in the investigation, quite indifferent to the fate of Mary Jacob, and took himself off to the library of the Yokohama Club. He sat in the depths of a green leather chair, absorbed in the trashier type of fiction that graces such colonial outposts as this one. He flipped through volumes of games and sports which, under normal circumstances, would not have lightened his most jaded mood. Even the bound volumes of the *Japan Gazette*, as the English paper is called, occupied him for some time.

After all this, I found him in a better mood than at any time since our arrival. He had spent a pleasant hour interrogating the librarian on the excellence of George Meredith's fiction, the fine intellectual cruelties of the great novelist. It was evident that the club librarian had never read *The Ordeal of Richard Feverel* or any other of the author's works but he committed the unwise sin of pride in pretending at first that he had done so. Holmes found him out at once but never revealed the discovery to his victim, enjoying fine sport at the poor fellow's expense. Before long, the guardian of literature was only too happy to discuss any other topic under the sun than the works of Holmes's favourite novelist. I left my friend to his amusements until the time when we were to collect the keys that Mr Lowder had left for us. We made our way on foot to 160 The Bluff, part-way down the hill.

Since the death of her husband, Mrs Carew had taken rooms at the Continental Hotel, as if the memories of the final ghastly days at the villa were too much for her. The Carew villa was a modest house in a garden of trees and lawn, befitting the Secretary and Manager of the Yokohama United Club. It was built on three sides round a narrow lawn. Carew's room was on the second level, at the end of one of these narrowly separated 'wings'. It looked across to the rooms of the other wing, one of which was the nursery.

In the past few years, there had been minor structural alterations to the building. The two adjoining bedrooms of Carew and his wife had once been a large single room but a substantial partition wall with a communicating door had been inserted. The verandah of each bedroom had been glassed in to form a dressing-room area, though at ground level the verandahs of the lower rooms had been retained. The metal-framed windows of the dressing-rooms above could not be opened, except for a fanlight at the top, some two feet square. Under Carew's room was the wooden seat where Mary Jacob claimed she had sat when the window banged and when his wife had shone her light across the strip of garden to see what the noise might be. She had not seen Mary Jacob sitting there, nor had the other witnesses.

Holmes and I stood on the narrow lawn between the two wings of the house, looking at the wooden seat and at Carew's window on the floor above.

'However else our client entered Carew's bedroom, she did not pass through the door from the landing while it was guarded by the two angels of truth from the Mission School.'

'Could she have reached it from the garden?'

'I think we may say, Watson, that for Mary Jacob to have entered the room from the garden, she must have had a ladder or, at least, a rope. Picture her climbing up and finding no way in but by the fanlight of the dressing-room window. I daresay she could get through an opening of that size, though she must have fallen to the floor. Perhaps, as she did so, the fanlight banged after her. The sound was heard. A light was shone. But where was the ladder or the rope? And how can she be one moment half-way through the fanlight with nothing to aid her descent into the room, and within a split second—as long as it takes to crouch and look through a keyhole—she has fallen or dived silently from the opening, tumbled on to the floor without making a further sound, picked herself up, rearranged her dress, and is standing before the medicine cabinet without a hair out of place.'

He betrayed his feelings no more than by a certain twitch of the mouth.

'It could not be done,' I said with a little irritation. 'If there was a rope she must also draw that up or kick away a ladder. Far more likely that she got into the room earlier and hid there, waiting her chance until the nurse was away for a few minutes. She might take her bottle of poison and pour it into his drink or his water-bottle then.'

'Admirable, Watson,' he said, leading the way into the house as dusk deepened in the garden, 'and how did our cunning murderess get out of the room again? A bright light was shining on its exterior. Mrs Carew and the other servants were hurrying up the stairs by this time. The nurse was coming back, for Rachel Greer and her companion heard her as they were going down the stairs in answer to Mrs Carew's summons. Yet Mary Jacob must have got out, for she was seen in the nursery a few minutes later. Could she have scrambled up five feet of window-glass unaided, gone feet-first through the fanlight, got down eighteen feet to the garden in the glare of the light, unseen and without making a sound? She was not seen doing so, and no sound was heard by any of the witnesses, therefore she was invisible and inaudible.'

The answer came to me at once, as I thought.

'She had a key, not to the landing door but for the communicating door directly into Mrs Carew's room. If the nurse saw her coming out of Mrs Carew's room, she would suspect nothing.'

Holmes paused on the staircase.

'Unfortunately, Watson, she would be suspected at once. She might unbolt and unlock the party-door to the other bedroom and she might lock it after her. But there is no means known to criminal science by which she might fasten the bolts on the far side of the door. No means, either, by which she could have got out of Mrs Carew's room unseen in order to be in the nursery a few minutes later. It will not do, my dear fellow. Perhaps we shall have better luck if we examine the scene.'

It was a chill sensation to enter the bedroom where Carew had endured the agony and delirium of his last days. There was the bed, as if it had scarcely been re-made. There was the table beside it and the dressing-room area made out of what had once been the verandah. There was the fatal medicine cabinet with its mirror on top. To see the wall of glass, which the window formed, with its fanlight at the very top, was to see the impossibility that Mary Jacob could ever have come or gone by that route. A professional burglar would not have given it a second glance.

Holmes spent a little while examining the window and the medicine cabinet with its wooden-framed triple-mirror on top, his fingers delicately turning and adjusting the glass as he did so. I gave my attention to the communicating door in the partition wall between the two bedrooms. It remained locked and bolted. Door and frame had been painted long before Carew's death and there was no sign of any chip or blemish that indicated an attempt to tamper with the fastenings.

Holmes seemed content with all that he had found.

'Be so good, Watson, as to stand on the landing with the bed-room door locked and the key in your pocket. When you hear the window bang, look through the keyhole and see what you may see. Do not, on any account, unlock the door.'

'And you, Holmes? What of you?'

'I shall go down to the garden and smoke a pipe.'

'What if the window should not bang?'

'As to that,' he said with a smile to himself, 'I think I may promise you that it will.'

Before I could register a further protest, he had made his way down the stairs and vanished. The house was silent and in almost complete darkness as all light faded from the garden. I waited for what seemed an interminable time but was perhaps no more than five minutes. I was about to give up and go down to the garden when there was the unmistakable rattle or bang of the bedroom window, so unexpected by now that it made me jump. If I hesitated, it was no more than two or three seconds before I was down on one knee and peering through the keyhole of Carew's room. There, standing before the mirror of the medicine cabinet and smoking his pipe was the figure of Sherlock Holmes.

VI

I twisted my head and tried to see through the tiny aperture how the devil he could have done it. Then he moved from my field of vision, for the keyhole gave a very imperfect prospect of the room as a whole. Then he came back, and then he went for good. I waited several minutes like this, kneeling and trying to see where he might be, until my heart jumped as a voice behind me said, 'My apologies for startling you, Watson. I can scarcely believe, though, that this is your first encounter with Professor Pepper's ghost. I flatter myself that they would hardly have done it better at the Egyptian Hall.'

Holmes, whom I had just seen through the keyhole of the locked door, was now standing behind me. I struggled to my feet and turned upon him.

'Who the blazes is Professor Pepper?'

Ignoring my question, he took the key from me, unlocked the door, and laughed.

'To tell the truth, I half suspected something of the sort when Dr Jacob first told the story in Baker Street. Then I thought perhaps they lacked the expertise. It was the window banging and something being thrown out that convinced me.'

We stood in Carew's room once more and now Holmes lit the lamps.

'Picture yourself, Watson, sitting on that garden bench. Above you, the window bangs and something is thrown out. What is your natural reaction?'

'To wonder what the devil is going on.'

'Be more precise.'

'Well,' I said, half suspecting a trick, 'I should look up to see who it was and what had happened. Then I might look for what had fallen, if I could find it.'

'Excellent!' Holmes said, rubbing his hands. 'It is what any sensible person would do. How long would you look up?'

'A minute or two, until I could see what the matter was.'

'And if you saw nothing—or nothing that signified?'

'I should go on with what I had been doing, if all I had heard was a window banging.'

'Just as Mary Jacob did. Suppose now that you are guarding a room with the door locked. Inside is a man alone, lying asleep, between life and death, his very existence in peril from assassins. The nurse is absent. Inside the room the window bangs. What would you do?'

'I should try at once to see what was going on in there.'

'But how? You cannot open the door and you have no means of seeing through the window itself.'

'The keyhole, of course.'

'Precisely.'

'But what if I were to run for help without bothering to look?'

'You might, Watson. But if there were two of you, the chances that one at least would look through that keyhole are doubled. It is well-nigh inconceivable that one of you would not do so before running for assistance. Is it not the instinctive thing to do, just as Mary Jacob's instinct would have been to look upwards?'

This was all very fine but I was getting a little weary of the joke and I knew nothing of Professor Pepper or his ghost. Holmes took from his capacious pocket a copy of a book which he had purloined, apparently, from the library of the Yokohama Club. *Secrets of Stage Conjuring* by J. E. Robert-Houdin, published by George Routledge at London in 1881. He pointed to a page which appeared full of geometrical figures and a tribute to Professor Pepper of the London Polytechnic.

The principle of the stage illusion was simple enough. A figure stood below the stage at the level of the orchestra pit, concealed from the audience and looking upwards. Also at that level, hidden from the audience, a bright light shone directly upon the figure's face. The face looked up at a sheet of glass, angled as a fanlight might be. The result, in the darkness of the surroundings, was to produce a perfect replica of the face. The darker the surroundings, the more vivid the image.

'The principle is simple, Watson, but the art is making the image perfect. It is as you see your own ghost outside the window of a railway carriage when you travel at night.'

He opened Robert-Houdin's book again. In its pages was a slip of paper, which recorded that the volume had been borrowed from the club library on 8 September last by Edith Mary Hallowell Carew.

'I am a little surprised that she should have needed it,' said Holmes quietly, 'for Edith Mary Hallowell Porch, as she was then, was a devotee of the magic arts. A witness at her wedding was Miss Julia Ferret of the Recreations Japonaises, as that performance of wizardry is known in England. She assisted at a famous performance in Yokohama by Josef Vanek, the Professor of Physics at Budapest, who forsook his laboratory for the stage.'

Holmes had constructed his own geometrical plan of the trap laid for Mary Jacob. He had drawn it up with the precision of Euclid or Pythagoras. The pebble, stone, or other object, had hit the window quite gently above Mary Jacob's head, and fallen on the ground. The sound, as the glass and frame vibrated, had caused the girl to look up, where the fanlight was open at an angle. What more natural than that Edith Carew might draw the curtain back at the noise and a stream of electric brightness be directed across the narrow lawn?

As Mary Jacob tried to discern what had happened in the room of the man who had once been her lover, her face was reflected in the square of fanlight glass, clear as day in the darkness. From the glass it was caught in one side of the triple mirror and caught again in that other side, which had been carefully angled so that it filled the view from the keyhole of the door. That Mrs Carew should 'put the mirror straight' when she visited her husband would cause the nurse no unease whatever.

'Stop a minute, Holmes,' I said insistently. 'I grant you Professor Pepper's illusion works well enough, for I have seen it myself just now. I daresay Edith Carew had the skill to attempt it. But this is not a theatre. She could not be sure that Mary Jacob would sit on that bench at that time or that she would look up at the sound. She could not know that the nurse would leave the room or that the two servant girls would look through the keyhole.'

I thought that my friend looked at me in a little disappointment.

'My dear Watson, you have not grasped it, after all. The solution to this mystery depends very little on Professor Pepper's ghost and almost entirely on the operation of the criminal mind. Edith Carew is a cold-blooded poisoner. I have thought so from the first. The arsenic was obtained well in advance, through Mary Jacob as an innocent messenger. This was no crime of passion but a calculated act of cruelty. What if the ghost illusion had failed? It was probably one of a dozen stratagems. Perhaps some had already been tried and had failed. If this one had not succeeded, there would have been others. Sooner or later, by whatever means, she would rid herself of the husband who stood between her and a guilty liaison with a younger man—Henry Vansittart Dickinson. A husband, Watson, who had not only possessed himself of her money for his own pleasures and his vices but also threatened her with a vile and incurable disease.'

So far I could follow him. The rest was sheer impossibility.

'What you say, Holmes, may acquit Mary Jacob. It cannot convict Edith Carew. When she knew that she had trapped Miss Jacob, she must have acted at once to commit murder. Yet it is impossible that she could ever have got near Carew again. That last night she went into her own room. The nurse was alone with Carew, absent once or twice for only a few minutes. Edith Carew could not come out on to the landing because Rachel Greer and Hanauye Asa would have seen her. She could not have gone through the communicating door between the two rooms because it was locked and bolted on Carew's side. How, then, could she have put three grains of arsenic into Carew's brandy and soda or anything else he drank?'

'I should say, Watson, that she put three grains into each vessel, so that whether it was his brandy and soda, his drinking water or his medicine, he was done for. She had ample time to wash out the glasses and bottles next day, after they had removed him to hospital but before arsenic was suspected.'

'But how could she do it, if there was neither door nor window by which she could enter the room?'

Holmes stared at the partition wall. 'By doing what Professor Vanek used to do every night in front of several hundred people,' he said. 'In a house as casually constructed as this, a child might almost do it.'

VII

In my mind's eye, I can still see the wall with its communicating door as it had been built between those two rooms. The rooms had a common floor of planking, which ran lengthwise, parallel with the windows. Where it formed the floor of the dressing-room area it ran over the verandah at ground level. To install the partition wall, they had first laid a strip of stout rubberised felt across the boards of the dressing-rooms to insulate the carpets from the winter damp or cold of the verandah beneath. Then they had laid a heavy beam across the boards, wall to window, and constructed a lath and plaster wall upon this. It might not be the way of building in London but it was solid enough in such a climate as this.

It was impossible that Edith Carew or an accomplice could have passed through that wall or the communicating door while the nurse was absent. Nor could there have been a way over the wall without breaking through the ceiling. There was a tiny gap between the supporting beam and the floorboards with their insulating felt which it traversed. That gap was not half an inch. It would have been possible, of course, to have taken up the floorboards, climbed down to the verandah and climbed up into the other room through a gap on the far side. To reach the floorboards, however, would have required cutting through the felt, which ran in a single length across both dressing-room floors under the beam.

'If it was done,' I said a little morosely, 'I'll be hanged if I can see how. Edith Carew or her accomplice could not have gone through that wall, over it, or under it without leaving traces of the damage they caused. And there are none.'

'But then, my dear fellow,' said Holmes gently, 'you are no physicist—and Professor Vanek was. Once Mary Jacob was compromised, Edith Carew knew that she must strike her blow that night.'

'How?'

He beckoned me from the room and we went down the stairs. Holmes took a lantern from the hall and lit it. We stood in the verandah that ran along the narrow lawn, just under the dressing areas of the bedrooms. The ceiling of the verandah, if one can call it that, consisted of what were now the floorboards of those dressing-rooms, nailed down on several joists. The lower surface of the boards, like the rest of the verandah, had been painted white.

Holmes stood on the bench where Mary Jacob had sat. He stretched his thin arms upwards and the boards under the partition wall of the two rooms shifted a little.

'I thought as much,' he said, screwing his face up and looking at them more closely. 'Edith Carew could not risk being seen to tamper with them afterwards or even asking someone else to do so. The floorboards at the centre have been prised up from the joists. There are no nails holding them down.'

He moved one a little and there was a fall of tiny debris. Wood scraped on wood as he drew one end of the first board down at an angle.

'Hold the lantern up, Watson, there's a good fellow.'

It was, I suppose, a four-foot length of board, several inches wide, that came clear. He handed it down. Five more of the same size followed until, as we looked up, only the waterproof felt separated us from the room above and the beam supporting the new partition wall.

'She could not have done it from here, of course,' he said. 'That felt is complete and uncut from one end of the two rooms to the other. We had best go back up.'

Back in the dressing area of Mrs Carew's bedroom was evidence enough to indict her, if not to convict her. It was as if, under the heavy waterproof felt, a stage trap-door had been opened. Though strong and thick in itself, the material sagged all the more for being at the centre of the flooring. The gap of half an inch under the supporting beam of the partition wall was now half a foot. By moving one or two pieces of furniture from the dressing area to the main bedroom, it was possible to make the felt sag further as the weight holding it in place was lessened.

'I had supposed,' Holmes said, 'that she must have had an accomplice. Her lover Harry Dickinson, for example. Yet she might have done it for herself. There is a gap under the partition beam that even I might get through.'

He took off his jacket, folded it, and eased himself under the beam, head-first and on his back. The bony knuckles whitened as the strong fingers gripped the beam from underneath as a support. Then his long legs were drawn after him and Holmes stood in the other room on the far side of the partition wall.

'There was surely an accomplice,' I said, as we prepared to leave the house half an hour later. 'Someone to see Edith Carew's signal that the nurse had gone, to draw the boards clear from underneath and to replace them when a second signal was given.'

'Perhaps,' he said thoughtfully. 'Yet it needed only the edge of a carpet on the other side to conceal the way in which the felt was sagging. In that case, she could have drawn the boards out much earlier, before she came up to her room for the night. I daresay we shall never know.'

'Could a woman undertake so much?' I asked.

He chuckled in the darkness of the driveway as we made for the lights of The Bluff.

'My dear fellow, your incredulity as to the resolve of the fair sex on these occasions never ceases to amaze me! Mrs Edith Carew was about to prepare a fatal dose of arsenic for her husband and chance the gallows for it. It was that night or never, if she was to let Mary Jacob hang in her place. Compared to such a gamble, I do not suppose that removing a few boards from the verandah or turning back a carpet and wriggling under a beam caused her the least hesitation.'

I had no doubt that he was, as always, correct.

We went at once to the British Naval Prison, where Holmes demanded—rather than asked—to see Mary Jacob. The poor little soul was, if anything, paler than before. I swear she was more frightened of Holmes than of those who would hang her.

'Very well,' he said, as we sat at the bare table. 'I see you have done as I asked and left everything in this room as it was. Before we go further, be so good as to fetch me the birthday present Mrs Carew gave you in September.'

Mary Jacob looked astonished.

'How could you know that my birthday was in September or that she gave me a present?'

'Never mind that,' he said gently. 'Fetch it and show it to me.'

Mary Jacob got up and went to the little table by her bedside.

'For God's sake, Holmes!' I said under my breath. 'How do you know there was a birthday present?'

'Because, my dear Watson, Edith Carew loathed her far too much to risk giving her a present on any other occasion. Even she could hardly ignore the girl's birthday. It fell, most conveniently, in September. The records of Somerset House confirm her date of birth. You must give me credit for sometimes following the strait and narrow path of the obvious.'

Miss Jacob returned and set down before us the bottle of Yardley's Lavender Water. Holmes unscrewed the top and sniffed at it, then he held it up to the light.

'They have made it almost too easy for me,' he said wistfully to himself, then turned to his client again. 'If I may say so, Miss Jacob, you have used a good deal of spirits of lavender in the few weeks since your birthday.'

She looked a little abashed.

'There was an accident. It was upset on the dressing-table when the Chinese boy, Ah Kwong, was cleaning the room.'

'Poor boy! No doubt the perfume seeped into all the drawers and among their contents,' Holmes said sympathetically. 'And were you there when this unfortunate accident happened in the first week or so of October, Miss Jacob?'

'No,' she said, seeming surprised. 'Mrs Carew told me when I came back from running her errands down the town.'

'And even before you returned, poor Ah Kwong was dismissed for an act of clumsiness that was by no means his first.'

'Yes,' she said earnestly. 'But how could you possibly know that it was not the poor boy's first clumsiness or that it happened in the first week of October, unless someone else has told you?'

Holmes laughed, this time to reassure her.

'You give me too much credit, Miss Jacob. I do not know such things: I merely guess them. Very often I am wrong. I hope, however, that you will keep the empty lavender-water bottle in a place where you may always see it, to remind you of a very narrow squeak.'

He got up and left the little room. Through the open door I heard him demanding—rather than requesting—the immediate release of his innocent client.

VIII

'You knew from the first, Holmes!' I said as we left the building. 'This whole business might have been cleared up without our having to leave Baker Street!'

'Not quite,' he said with a sigh. 'I was pretty sure from the second day after Dr Jacob visited us. The date of Mary Jacob's birthday, of course, I got from Somerset House. Then I went to pay a call on brother Mycroft at the Diogenes Club. Remarkable place for the recherché, Watson. I suppose you would scarcely credit that their reading room takes the *Japan Gazette*. The latest issues are a little delayed but they had the report in full of the inquest on Walter Carew. I had to be sure that Dr Jacob's information was correct—and so it was. Mrs Carew gave evidence that she had once bought

Fowler's Solution from Schedel's European Pharmacy on The Bluff. Mary Jacob, as we have seen for ourselves, had a penchant for the more sensational type of fiction. Naturally she went to Maruya's in the town, a bookshop as well as a pharmacy. If only Mrs Carew had known that, when Fowler's Solution is prepared in Japanese pharmacies, spirits of lavender are not added, I doubt if I should ever have left Baker Street at all.'

The true financial cost of the investigation would have taken all the money from Dr Jacob's note-case and a good deal more. Holmes preferred to regard his expedition to Japan as a voyage of experience. He positively refused to take a fee of any kind from our client. His last meeting with Mary Jacob, however, was no more comfortable than the others.

'You would do well to remember, Miss Jacob,' he said dispassionately, 'that taking letters addressed to others and practising their signatures is a game in children and a crime in adults. I hope that you have learned that lesson thoroughly.'

The world knows the conclusion of the story. The case against Mary Jacob collapsed and the prosecution in Her Britannic Majesty's Consular Court at Yokohama was withdrawn. In that same court, Mrs Edith Carew was afterwards convicted of the murder of her husband. On a day of winter rain driving in from the Pacific Ocean, Mr Justice Mowat, who had sat beside Consul Troupe throughout the trial, placed the black cap upon his head and pronounced a sentence of such unusual jurisdiction that Holmes positively would not leave Yokohama until he had heard it.

'The sentence is that you Edith Mary Hallowell Carew, be forthwith taken from the place where you now stand and be taken to the British Consular Gaol in Yokohama, and therein interned. And that on a day appointed by the proper authority, you be taken to the place of execution, and there be hanged by the neck until you are dead . . .'

The sentence of death on Edith Carew, to be carried out at the British Naval Prison in the presence of the Consul, was forwarded to the Ambassador in Tokyo for confirmation. The Ambassador recalled, however, that on the day before her conviction, the Japanese Emperor had proclaimed a remission to all his subjects who were under sentence that day. It was accordingly ordered that Mrs Carew should be reprieved and sent to penal servitude with hard labour for life. She was brought home to Aylesbury prison to serve her sentence, from which she was released fourteen years later.

In the sunshine of what seemed like a spring afternoon, Holmes stared across the sparkling water of the natural harbour.

'You see, Watson? It is just as I told you. The true mystery after all was not Professor Pepper's ghost nor the tensile strength and elasticity of materials as Professor Vanek of Budapest and other physicists had studied them. Our interest must be the mind that can purchase and measure death by spoonfuls day after day with a kindly smile and without the least remorse for the martyrdom of pain. Not death by a single blow, my dear friend, but by slow and deliberate torture. I confess that I find the new science of psychopathology deficient in its study of this most interesting of all states of the human mind. Our experience here ought not to pass without some commemoration of it. I wonder whether I might not spend the leisure of our homeward journey in writing a short monograph on so deserving a topic.'

Author's Note

The stories in this volume are based upon historical events, over which the shadow of the Great Detective is allowed to pass. Apart from Sherlock Holmes and John Watson, almost all the other figures in the stories played the parts ascribed to them here, except where minor characters have been invented to give continuity to the narratives.

'The Ghost in the Machine' alters little except for the introduction of Sherlock Holmes, as the scientific detective who saved Dr Smethurst from the gallows. The near-fatal error of the forensic investigators occurred in fact, as it does here in fiction.

In 'The Case of the Crown Jewels', the explanation of the robbery is based upon the characters and activities of two gentlemen-crooks of the Edwardian period, Frank Shackleton and Richard Gorges. Gorges survived his imprisonment for shooting a policeman and died as a pauper in an institution in the 1950s. Sir Arthur Vicars and Peirce Mahony died in the circumstances described here. The Crown Jewels of Ireland have never been found.

'The Case of the Unseen Hand' is based upon events in the history of the Third Republic, between 1894 and 1909. The main story is taken from Marguerite Steinheil, *My Memoirs*, Eveleigh Nash, 1912, which describes President Faure's 'Secret History'. The account of the President's death, in bed with Madame Steinheil, was given by President Casimir-Périer to the French Ambassador to St Petersburg, Maurice Georges Paléologue. It was suppressed until the publication of Paléologue's *Journal de l'Affaire Dreyfus*, Librairie Plon, 1955. Gustave Hamard and Alphonse Bertillon were prominent figures in their respective branches of the Súreté. The criminal activities of the Comte de Balincourt and his three associates are described in Marguerite Steinheil's memoirs. There exists a heroic painting, *The Deathbed of President Faure*, in which the great statesman expires decorously with his ministers, family, and priests standing round. Madame Steinheil triumphed over the scandal and the double-murder prosecution. She was to die in England, at the seaside town of Hove in 1954, as the sixth Baroness Abinger.

Rumours of a morganatic marriage between the future George V and the daughter of Admiral Sir Michael Culme-Seymour at Malta in 1890 circulated in the press until the specific allegations by Edward Mylius brought the case to court in 1911. The allegations referred to in 'The Case of the Blood Royal' are in the Public Record Office at PRO KB28/704/1. The manuscript of the Prince's diary for 1888, cited in Kenneth Rose, *King George V*, Weidenfeld & Nicolson, 1983, and James Lees-Milne, *Harold Nicolson: A Biography 1930–1968*, Chatto & Windus, 1981, refers to the unnamed girl with whom he used to sleep at Portsmouth and another in St John's Wood, whom he shared with his elder brother, the Duke of Clarence. 'She is a ripper,' he added. The death of the blackmailer Charles Augustus Howell—whom Conan Doyle presented as 'Charles Augustus Milverton'—was reported by Oscar Wilde and by Thomas James Wise in *A Bibliography of the Writings of Algernon Charles Swinburne*, 1919–20. His death certificate more tactfully describes the victim as dying of 'pneumonia'.

The defence of Robert Wood and the Green Bicycle Case were among the greatest triumphs of Sir Edward Marshall Hall as a defence lawyer. 'The Case of the Camden Town Murder' and 'The Case of the Missing Rifleman' make Sherlock Holmes the colleague of the great defender. Each criminal investigation took the form and had the outcome described in the two stories. The Camden

Town killer was never caught. However, Walter Sickert's obsession with painting and drawing the subject led to suggestions of his involvement. Sickert (1860–1942) was a friend of the young artist, Robert Wood, who stood trial for the murder, and helped to raise money for Wood's defence. In Stephen Knight, *Jack the Ripper: The Final Solution*, Harrap, 1976, it is suggested that Sickert's dedication to the Camden Town Murder extended to an involvement in the Whitechapel murders of 1888.

The murderer of Bella Wright was never brought to justice. Marshall Hall's attitude to Ronald Light, before and after the trial, suggests that he believed Light had killed the girl, probably by accident. As counsel, he appears never to have discussed the case directly with his client except for a few minutes after Light had already entered the dock. A short story in the *Strand* magazine described how a single bullet from a hunter's rifle, intended to shoot the crow on the gate, might pass through the bird and kill Bella Wright. The story did not explain why the hunter would shoot crows with ammunition of .455 calibre or what weapon could be used for this.

'The Case of the Yokohama Club' involved criminal proceedings little reported in England but carried verbatim in the *Japan Gazette* in 1896–7. Mary Esther Jacob was prosecuted at the instigation of Edith Carew before the Court of the British Consul at Yokohama, on a charge of having murdered her employer, Walter Carew. The evidence against her was such as the story describes. The case collapsed suddenly when further evidence was uncovered against Mrs Carew. Edith Carew was tried and sentenced to death by the same court in Yokohama but reprieved as a result of the intervention of the British Ambassador in Tokyo. She was brought back to England and was released from life imprisonment in Aylesbury gaol in 1911. The stage-magicians described in the story were well-known figures of Victorian entertainment. The ghost illusion is described at length in Chapter 6 of J. E. Robert-Houdin's *Secrets of Stage Conjuring* (1881).

Some further light is shed on the lives of Holmes and Watson. It has long been known that Holmes retired in 1903 to a life of bee-keeping on the southern slopes of the Sussex Downs, near the coast at Cuckmere Haven, taking with him Mrs Hudson as housekeeper. It is not surprising that, after a while, he should have missed his old acquaintances and the stimulus of criminal investigation. His services to the nation also required his presence in London. As several of these stories indicate, he took on the Baker Street rooms again when they fell vacant, alternating professional work in London and retirement in Sussex until after the First World War.

Dr Watson's first two marriages interrupted his residence in Baker Street, which ended at last with his third marriage in 1902. He was, however, the guest of Sherlock Holmes during weeks when the third Mrs Watson was absent from London 'on family business' and when the two men were engaged in such matters of national importance as the disappearance of the Irish Crown Jewels.

II

Sherlock Holmes and the Voice from the Crypt

For Linda
Ilia quae libros amat, a libris quoque amatur
Fragment De Popina Candelarum

Contents

The Two 'Failures' of Sherlock Holmes

A Fragment of Biography by John H. Watson MD

It is an acknowledged truth that Sherlock Holmes loathed with his whole bohemian soul the reputation of being a 'schoolbook hero'. This thought must have occupied me unconsciously one evening, while I was thinking of how I should introduce the cases which follow. Nothing seemed to suit my purpose. Then, as I sat there, I heard in my mind that familiar voice.

'Watson! If you are an honest man, you will record this also and set it against my successes!'

Well, I am no believer in ghosts! Still, this set me wondering where I had heard those words before. A moment later, I had it. More than thirty years had passed since Sherlock Holmes stood by the sunlit windows of Regent Street, shaking his head and uttering these very thoughts. We had been left, like a pair of fools, watching our quarry vanish from sight in a hansom cab with no means of pursuit. It was the first skirmish in a dark narrative of family misfortune, given to the world as *The Hound of the Baskervilles*.

In the next few weeks, as the world knows, we faced the beast with the blazing fangs in the lee of the rainswept Dartmoor rocks. We tracked John Stapleton of Merripit House to his slow death in the foul ooze of the Grimpen Mire. Yet that sunny moment in Regent Street was recalled by Holmes when he knew better than any man how close the end of his own life must be.

'If you are an honest man, Watson, you will set these records against my successes!'

He was sitting on the plain wooden stairs that led up to the Baker Street lumber-room, holding out to me several folded legal documents and a notebook. On the cover of the book, in ink now tarnished by damp, he had written simply, 'A Tabular Analysis of Hyoscin as a Homicidal Poison.'

Long before this, he had tried retirement and soon wearied of it. The simple life of bee-keeping on the Sussex downs was not for him. Having protested so much that he longed for rural solitude, he returned to Baker Street and took on his old rooms again. The excitement of life as a 'consulting detective' was as necessary to him as the vice of cocaine and a good deal less injurious. When his hands were idle, the drug mania laid claim to him. I never knew him to have the least need of narcotics when his mind was occupied.

The records of many unpublished adventures lay in the lumber-room, to which he would retire each day after lunch and remain until the winter afternoon darkened. The tin box, which formerly reposed among the bric-à-brac of his bedroom, had been carried up to this attic level on the orders of Mrs Clatworthy, his resident nurse. This good woman vowed repeatedly that she would not be 'answerable' if her patient's bedroom were not put into better order.

But where the box went, Holmes followed at every opportunity. It contained a mass of papers, most tied in bundles with red ribbon and each representing a case long concluded. Some dated from a time before I had first met him. Others dealt with matters 'for which the world is not yet ready', to use the familiar phrase by which he forbad publication. Two or three recorded his 'failures'.

One afternoon, he had retired to make a survey of these records. I went up at five o'clock to help him down to the sitting-room again, as the October light faded. He was sitting on the stairs, which declining strength obliged him to use as both chair and desk. His head was bowed over a black-letter legal parchment from one of the bundles, on which he had written in his own hand, 'The Case of the Naked Bicyclists.' He handed it to me without a word, so that I might replace it in the box and turn the key. While I did so, he made his way slowly but unaided down to our rooms.

I took the document he had handed me and gathered up a number of other papers whose red tapes he had not even bothered to tie again. Here and there I noticed some familiar copperplate script. It was usually the hand of a legal clerk, more often than not Mr Bowker, from the chambers of Sir Edward Marshall Hall. That 'Great Defender' had performed almost as many wonders in the court-room as Holmes the 'Great Detective' accomplished outside it, many of them when the two men worked in harness.

Among the writing on the briefs, I caught sight of *R v. Crippen and Le Neve*, then *Oscar Fingal O'Flahertie Wills Wilde, Esq. v. John Sholto Douglas, Marquess of Queensberry, and R v. Oscar Slater*. More perfunctorily, in Holmes's own writing upon the back of a legal brief, was 'The Yarmouth Beach Murder.'

Some of these names recalled his most difficult clients. Yet no other man would have regarded his efforts as a failure. I recall the summer of 1910 when, on the recommendation of Edward Marshall Hall, Dr Crippen's attorney called upon Holmes in the preparation of that famous murder defence.

All the world knew that Hawley Harvey Crippen had poisoned his faithless and violent wife, burying her dismembered body under the cellar floor of their house at 39 Hilldrop Crescent, Kentish Town. 'Belle Elmore', as Cora Crippen called herself on the music-hall stage, might have been a bullying slattern, but the little doctor surely put the rope round his own neck by his conduct after her death. He fled to America on the cargo liner SS *Montrose*, taking his demure young mistress Ethel Le Neve, whom he disguised to little effect by dressing her as a boy. Even before their arrival in Quebec, the Hilldrop Crescent cellar had revealed its macabre secret to Scotland Yard. The fugitives were pursued by wireless telegraph and fast passenger liner. Inspector Dew came aboard the *Montrose* off Quebec, disguised as the pilot, and arrested the two fugitives before they could leave the ship.

The drama of the chase turned the trial into the most celebrated criminal case for fifty years past. Mention the words 'cold-blooded murderer' and the world thinks at once of 'Dr Crippen'. How different was the truth!

Holmes was retained as the greatest 'criminal expert' on the rarer and more recent types of poison. He begged that Crippen would confess the truth, by admitting that Ethel Le Neve was present in the house and, indeed, in his bed, when the hyoscin was administered to Cora Crippen. The properties of this hypnotic drug, which derived from the deadly nightshade plant, were then not commonly known. However, it was used by physicians in a small dose as a sleeping draught or to treat delirium tremens.

In pursuit of the truth, Holmes shut himself away in the chemical laboratory of St Bartholomew's Hospital. While the rest of the world took its August holidays, he worked among shelves of bottles, benches and retorts, test-tubes and Bunsen burners. By several gruesome and malodorous experiments, he first proved that some of the hyoscin in Mrs Crippen's body was of animal origin and had been produced naturally by the decomposition of her corpse. Then he established beyond any question that a fatal dose in a woman of her size and weight would be between .25 and .5 of a grain. The amount found in Mrs Crippen's body was .29 of a grain. It was a very narrow margin of suspicion. Take away the amount produced naturally by the decomposition of her body, and there was no sufficient proof that Dr Crippen had administered even the minimum fatal dose to a woman so well-built, let alone that he had intended to kill her. The case against him was reduced from proof to mere speculation.

I truly thought that Holmes had saved Dr Crippen. If only the doctor would admit the fact that he had smuggled Ethel Le Neve into the house on that fateful night, his life was as good as saved. Hyoscin, in its anaesthetic dose, abolishes the memory of events, so that one who is rendered unconscious by it comes round with no memory of having been unconscious. Was this not the weapon of the adulterer rather than the murderer? Strychnine or aconitine were a killer's weapons. Was it not plain, Holmes argued, that Crippen merely intended to use a non-fatal dose of hyoscin to render his wife unconscious while Ethel Le Neve was on the premises and in his bed? In the event, the dose had proved lethal by a very narrow margin of miscalculation. Surely a man who hoped to kill his victim would have administered a far larger dose to make sure of the result.

The work that Holmes had done in the chemical laboratory certainly appeared to disprove any motive or intent to murder. Logic, too, seemed to rebut the case for the Crown. One look at Miss Le Neve was enough to convince those who saw her that she was too timid to be Lady Macbeth or Queen Clytemnestra. Poisoning is a planned murder, not one committed in the heat of the moment. If Dr Crippen were the cold precise killer that the prosecution alleged, would he risk his neck while there was a witness like Miss Le Neve in the house, when he might as easily have done the deed in secret? He would certainly have been far better without his young mistress as an accomplice, for Ethel Le Neve could not have held out for two minutes under a police interrogation.

Holmes insisted to Dr Crippen's attorney that a first-rate defender like Marshall Hall would persuade a jury to find the accused man guilty only of manslaughter. Indeed, it might be no worse than a conviction and a short prison sentence for the lesser offence of administering poison so as to endanger life.

Would that it had been so! What peals of victory would have rung through the halls of the Central Criminal Court and the pages of the morning papers! Sherlock Holmes, the Great Detective, would be trumpeted as the saviour of Dr Crippen, the most notorious defendant in a trial for murder! Yet the fruit of triumph turned to ashes of 'failure' almost at once.

I could scarcely believe my ears when I heard that Dr Crippen would have none of it! Why the devil not? The answer was simple. He loved Ethel Le Neve more than his own soul. Nothing would persuade him to admit that she was anywhere near the house at the time of Cora Crippen's death. When he heard of the suggestion that her presence was to be put in evidence, he refused to let his solicitor brief Marshall Hall to defend him.

That solicitor, Arthur Newton, and Sherlock Holmes argued with Dr Crippen in vain. They assured him that the door of his prison cell would open to set him free, if only he would admit that Ethel Le Neve was in the house on the night of his wife's death. The stubborn fellow shook his head. Suppose, for reasons that even Marshall Hall could not foresee and despite all that the great advocate could do, the jury took against him? The defence would fail. The verdict would be murder and, far worse, his young mistress would be an accomplice. Ethel Le Neve would be hanged as surely as he.

There was never such a 'disappointment' for Sherlock Holmes. Crippen loved this young woman so tenderly that he was determined to shield her to the last with his own life. He would have nothing said in his own defence that might imperil her. A lesser defender than Marshall Hall was found for him and the services of Sherlock Holmes were dispensed with.

Dr Crippen went to the gallows and Miss Le Neve was saved. Among the Crippen papers in the tin box is a letter to Holmes, the prison ink darkened and the paper a little yellowed. It was written by the condemned man on the night before his execution. 'In this farewell letter, written as I face eternity, I say that Ethel Le Neve has loved me as few women love men, and that her innocence of any crime, save that of yielding to the dictates of the heart, is absolute . . .'

Holmes could never read that letter without a moistening of the eye and a certain gruffness in the throat. Not Eloisa and Abelard, nor Tristan and Yseult, let alone a mere Romeo and Juliet, could hold a candle to Hawley Harvey Crippen and Ethel Le Neve. To my friend, Dr Crippen was ever afterwards 'a gallant little gentleman'. Holmes insisted on making the terrible journey to Pentonville to see the condemned man, late on the last night. He told me that the only time the poor fellow's courage failed was when they brought him a final telegram from the young woman. His request, that two of her letters and her photograph should be buried with him by the prison wall, was granted. He died declaring his innocence of any intention to murder his wife, something which Holmes never doubted. Wrongly hanged he may have been, but he had his reward when Ethel Le Neve was acquitted of any part in the crime.

Few people ever knew how closely Holmes was involved in some of the most sensational cases of the day. He was triumphant again and again but success did not always come his way. He worked with Marshall Hall on the so-called 'Yarmouth Beach Murder' of 1900, when Herbert Bennett was convicted and hanged for the murder of his wife, despite the solid evidence of an alibi witness. When I asked my friend, on his return from court, as to the outcome of the case, he said dryly, 'I fear, Watson, that British juries have not yet attained that pitch of intelligence when they will give preference to my theories over Inspector Lestrade's evidence.'

How hard it was in some cases to distinguish success from failure! In the ordeal of Oscar Slater, who was first condemned to death and then reprieved to life imprisonment, Sherlock Holmes thought he had failed where, in truth, he succeeded. Upon the evidence he gathered, showing that Slater could not be the murderer of Miss Gilchrist in a shabby Glasgow tenement, a campaign was built which set the innocent man free after eighteen years in prison. It is much to be regretted that the intransigence of the authorities delayed this act of justice until it was too late for Holmes to savour the victory.

All the same, those cases in which he was unable to secure a verdict for his client were few indeed. More often than not, as in the tragedy of Dr Crippen, they were investigations where the client turned away from the advice that had been offered. There was never a more memorable and obdurate example of this than the late Mr Oscar Wilde, who visited our Baker Street rooms on a windy afternoon in February 1895.

It must be said that the self-admiring paradoxes and the egregious vanity of the playwright were anathema to Sherlock Holmes. They were two men, each accustomed to being the centre of attention, and therefore ill-suited to one another's company. I do not think, however, that the pathological inclinations of Mr Wilde much perturbed my friend. Holmes had been well-acquainted with the work of Professor Krafft-Ebing since its first appearance in German nine years earlier. Indeed, he was to contribute three cases to later studies by Dr Havelock Ellis, as well as making available to him findings based on his own privately published monograph, 'The Mechanism of Emotional Deviation'. In the first weeks of 1895, Oscar Wilde was enjoying a theatrical fame that can scarcely have been equalled in modern times. *The Importance of Being Earnest* opened at the St James's Theatre to enthusiastic audiences and universal praise. *An Ideal Husband* was still running at the Haymarket Theatre a little distance away. I had, myself, been to the opening night of the earlier play and had returned full of its praises. Holmes was engaged in calculating the errant weights of base coinage at his 'chemical table' in the corner of the room. He made no response until I said, in the hope of interesting him, that I had never experienced such a torrent of epigrams as in the first act of the *Ideal Husband*.

He did not look up from his nicely-balanced miniature scales, but said quietly, 'A torrent of epigrams, indeed! I daresay you would do well to remember, Watson, that everything which shares the properties of a torrent necessarily has in common with it that it is shallow at the source and wide at the mouth.'

Argument, like discussion, was futile on such occasions. However, when the second play opened, the subject of Mr Wilde came up between us again. It was plain that Holmes's antipathy towards the author was as sharp as ever. In this case, the unfortunate truth was that both Holmes and a younger contemporary, the historian Sir George Young, recognized the origins of many of the witticisms and paradoxes in the famous plays. They were not Oscar Wilde's own, but had been purloined by him from the clever sayings of the author's fellow undergraduates at Oxford a decade before.

I was thunderstruck by this. However, everyone had heard that an entire act had been cut from *The Importance of Being Earnest* to match the more usual length of a West End theatrical performance. Holmes was informed by his brother Mycroft that this superfluous act was full of these stolen gems. Among them was a deathbed pleasantry by Dr Benjamin Jowett, the great Master of Balliol, who had been a controversial debater in theological wars of faith and doubt many years before. To a young female friend, who questioned him on his present belief, the old man replied with a kindly smile, 'Ah! You must always believe in God, my dear. No matter *what* the clergy tell you!' When Mycroft Holmes and his fellow members of the Diogenes Club heard of this proposed larceny in the mouth of the stage-character of Dr Chasuble, they threatened to fill the first night of Mr Wilde's play and cry 'Cheat!' every time a stolen paradox was uttered. For whatever reason, the superfluous act was cut from the performance and the immediate cause of offence removed.

The borrowing of other men's epigrams was not the worst scandal attending Mr Wilde. Among the glitter of theatrical success, only a few people had yet heard of a certain friendship contracted by the playwright with the Marquess of Queensberry's son, Lord Alfred Douglas, while the young man was an Oxford undergraduate. The father's resentment at this infatuation grew beyond all restraint. Mr Wilde's world of aesthetes and green carnations filled him with honest disgust and made him suspect something far worse.

Even I had heard nothing of this until Holmes himself was approached by the greatest criminal solicitor of the day, Sir George Lewis. Mr Wilde had gone to him, alleging defamation by Lord Queensberry, whom the world still knew best for his formulation of the Queensberry Rules in boxing. However, Sir George found himself in a fix, being both a friend of Mr Wilde's and yet already retained as legal adviser to the marquess. He resolved this conflict by withdrawing from the case completely but he could not act, in good faith, as an informal adviser to Mr Wilde. He urged the playwright, before taking any other course of action, to consult Sherlock Holmes.

Before Mr Wilde's visit, we had received from Sir George Lewis an outline of the events in the case. Lord Queensberry had left his misspelt and often misquoted card with the porter at the Albemarle Club, to which Mr Wilde belonged. He had written five words upon the back of it. 'To Oscar Wilde, posing somdomite.' If Mr Wilde was to be believed, this was by no means the first insult of its kind he had received from Lord Queensberry but the public nature of it made it by far the most serious. Having been unable to retain Sir George Lewis, the author had gone to another and more pugnacious lawyer, Mr Charles Humphreys. Humphreys at once recommended prosecuting the marquess for a criminal libel.

As we awaited our client, Holmes showed little of his usual relish for the fight. It was not, I think, that he found the nature of the case distasteful, given his unconcealed fascination with human waywardness. It was rather the prospect of Mr Wilde's habitual self-appreciation that grated upon Sherlock Holmes.

When our visitor came through the sitting-room doorway, he gave the impression of a clumsy and ponderous man, with something of the gait of an agricultural labourer, despite his verbal adroitness. There was heaviness in his body, his head, and in the features of his face. Surprisingly, he exuded an air of weariness in his conversation. To meet the famous aesthete in the flesh, however, was still to catch something of the pose of the photographic studio. The whole world had seen photographs of Mr Wilde, at theatres and in booksellers' windows, taken in the years of his fame. He stood before us now with that familiar expression, jaded and unsmiling, indeed with the mouth pressed tighter than seemed natural.

He ignored the chair that Holmes had indicated and sat awkwardly in another, directly facing the great detective with the late winter sky at his back.

'I throw myself upon your mercy, Mr Holmes,' he said with a half-wave of his hand, 'Sir George Lewis is unable to take me on. To hear a lawyer turn away one's money undermines one's confidence in the entire natural order of the universe.'

Holmes accepted this pleasantry without a movement. His features might have been carved in ivory.

'I am acquainted with the circumstances, sir,' he said coolly. 'Pray continue.'

Mr Wilde was more than a little shaken by such unaccustomed abruptness. His face seemed a little more tired and flabby.

'Very well, Mr Holmes. I must decide by tomorrow whether I am to bring an action against Lord Queensberry for a criminal libel. Mr Humphreys is for proceeding with it. Sir George Lewis, I think, would not.'

'I daresay Sir George is the wiser,' Holmes said quietly. 'Do go on.'

'Eddie Carson . . .' the unfortunate author began, 'I am told that Sir Edward Carson QC is to be briefed in any defence.'

'A foeman worthy of your steel, Mr Wilde. I take it that you are prepared to face cross-examination by him over this matter?'

'I am sure you know, Mr Holmes, that we were undergraduates together at Trinity College, Dublin. He will no doubt carry out his duty with all the added bitterness of an old friend who has since been neglected.'

Holmes received this witticism in arctic silence, then he said, 'That was not precisely what I asked, sir. Play games like that with Sir Edward Carson and he will cut you in pieces.'

Mr Wilde was brought up short. He stumbled on—there is no other phrase for it. However, he still talked in his other-worldly terms.

'Games? An artist, Mr Holmes, is one who plays sublime games with immortal words. I cannot deny that an artist in the eyes of artisans appears, therefore, as a figure of affectation. Lord Queensberry's crime is to confuse the affectation of genius with a perversion of the soul's beauty.'

Holmes touched his fingertips together before his chin. His words, when they came, were so softly-spoken that I scarcely heard them but they struck with the speed and accuracy of a whiplash.

'I beg, Mr Wilde, that you will make no such error! By the law of the land, Lord Queensberry's crime is either a criminal libel—or there is no crime. As to the rest, whether a man appears affected may be a question of opinion. Whether he is perverted in his actions is a matter of fact. In this, the burden of proof will lie upon you as the prosecutor. If that burden is too great . . .'

Our visitor had recovered himself sufficiently to interrupt.

'My reputation, Mr Holmes, has been trampled in the gutter! That is indisputable. Does any other fact matter, beside the damage done publicly to my reputation by these foul accusations?'

'For the purposes of this case, Mr Wilde, you may take it from me that it matters.'

'Very well,' said our visitor sulkily, 'let us suppose that the distinction between the affected and the perverse may be in issue. Yet the difference lies only in the eye of the beholder.'

'You would do well to remember, sir,' said Holmes brutally, 'that under the Criminal Law Amendment Act of 1885, the difference between affectation and perversion is the thickness of a prison wall.'

I was never so uncomfortable in my life as during the next thirty minutes of these exchanges. At last Mr Wilde could bear it no longer.

'Mr Holmes, I have listened to your sermonizing for the past half-hour and I have to say I am none the wiser.'

'I daresay not,' Holmes muttered, 'but much better informed, I trust.'

'And that is all you can do for me?'

It was almost like a child's cry.

'Not quite,' said Holmes. 'You say you are an innocent man. Then I will give you my advice without charge. Take that absurd visiting card of Lord Queensberry's and tear it into fragments. Then, if you are an innocent man, continue to behave innocently and you will have nothing to fear. It is as simple as that, Mr Wilde. The action you propose to bring against Lord Queensberry will publish this libel across the world, whether you are innocent or not. Whatever the outcome, the wise world will think that there is no smoke without fire.'

'This is abominable! I would stop at nothing to make my protest!'

'Methinks . . .' said Holmes. And through all our minds ran the rest of that famous line from *Hamlet. The lady doth protest too much, methinks.* The colour rose from the base of Mr Wilde's soft neck until he blushed the colour of a beetroot.

'I will take no more of your time.' In anger or embarrassment, he stumbled over the words again.

'Tear up that card!' said Holmes, rising from his chair.

'I shall be the judge, Mr Holmes, of what is to be done in this case!'

'I doubt that you will,' Holmes said grimly, 'I doubt that very much.'

On this note of mutual antipathy, they parted. Little as I sympathized with Oscar Wilde the man, I was shocked by my friend's dealing with him.

'How could you, Holmes?' I said angrily when the street door had closed. 'You gave the poor fellow no chance!'

He was standing at the window now, staring down into the street as he watched the waiting hansom drive away with a light rattle of harness.

'Because I would save him from destruction, little as I care for him.'

'He will be destroyed if the message on that card is the gossip of London and he takes no action!'

Holmes shook his head.

'No. Gossip may merely harm him. He will be destroyed only if he goes into court.'

'How?'

'The evidence will destroy him.'

'How can you say that? Neither of us has seen the evidence on either side!'

'We have both seen the evidence in this case. I was the only one to realize it.'

This shook me, for I did not understand how it could be so.

'You have seen it?'

'And so have you, if you had cared to observe it! Did you not take note, Watson, how he ignored my invitation and sat in another chair?'

'What the devil has sitting in a chair to do with it? Perhaps he was more comfortable.'

'Did you not notice that he was careful to sit with his back to the light, so that we should not see his face so clearly?'

'What has that to do with the case? We had seen his face already when he came through the door. The tone of his voice would have told us the rest.'

'He dare not go into court and confront a jury. No matter what the cause of the offence.'

'I cannot see it, Holmes.'

'He did not intend that you should. But the jury will see it. The judge will see it. Sir Edward Carson will see it. My dear Watson, if that man goes to court he is doomed. As soon as he opens his mouth, his case is lost. Small wonder that his lips are so tight in all his photographs!' His voice became softer.

'Perhaps, my dear fellow, you were not at an angle to see his teeth.'

'His teeth? He is not being libelled for his teeth!'

'He might as well be. Those teeth, Watson, are all in place and healthy in appearance, somewhat protuberant—but uniformly black! Did you not notice, when he stood in the doorway, the habit of putting a hand near his mouth when he spoke?'

I stared at him, for it was something I now recollected but had thought nothing of at the time.

'Does that mean nothing to you, Watson, as a medical man?'

'Mercury? That he has been treated for syphilis?'

'Precisely,' Holmes turned back from the window. 'A man is treated by mercury in that manner for one reason and one alone. Mercury and blackened teeth, the subject of cruel jokes and private gossip. At the trial, he must stand in the witness-box of the Central Criminal Court with the light full upon him. When he opens his mouth to give evidence, he will advertise to every man on the jury that he, the champion against slander and indecency, is in the grip of a most loathsome disease, contracted in a very familiar manner. If he hung a card about his neck, he could make it no plainer to the world. What chance will he have of a verdict then?'

It was many months later that I was to hear from Sir George Lewis how the famous playwright had contracted this disease from a woman of the streets, as the result of undergraduate folly while at Magdalen. I now guessed why, when the Prince of Wales and the leaders of society applauded and called for the author at the end of the first night of *An Ideal Husband*, Mr Wilde had prudently absented himself.

'He must not do it,' Holmes persisted, 'but nothing I could say would stop him. Little as I care for Mr Wilde, I should not like to be in court when Sir Edward Carson begins to cross-examine a fellow so vain and, worse still, when he begins to interrogate those young gentlemen who dote upon their master. Believe me, I would not wish on any man the destruction that our client is hell-bent to bring upon himself.'

I was still more astonished by this.

'Then he is still our client?'

Holmes shrugged.

'The matter is at his discretion.'

But we never heard from Mr Wilde again.

I shall let the words of that afternoon's encounter fade from my mind. I fold the stiff law-stationery of *Oscar Fingal O'Flahertie Wills Wilde, Esq. v. John Sholto Douglas, Marquess of Queensberry*, and lay it in the tin trunk.

As I sit in my chair and recall that familiar room in Baker Street, I see the chemical corner with its acid-stained, deal-topped table. There upon a shelf stands the formidable row of scrap-books and volumes of reference, which so many of our adversaries would have been glad to burn. The diagrams, the violin-case, and the pipe-rack, the Persian slipper which contained his tobacco—all these take shape in the imagination. As for Sherlock Holmes, I imagine him most often at the breakfast table, having risen late as was his custom. The silver-plated coffee-pot stands before him. *The Times* or *Morning Post* lies beside his plate. Sometimes his profile is like a bird of prey as he scans the columns and says sourly, without looking up, 'If the press is to be believed, Watson, London has singularly little of interest to offer the criminal expert at the present time. I wonder whether our friends in the underworld have become a good deal less active of late—or a good deal more clever.'

This impatience was usually short-lived. Sometimes, even before the remains of his mid-morning breakfast had been cleared away, a clang of the bell or a stentorian knocking on the well-hammered Baker Street door would be followed by the appearance of Mrs Hudson with a card upon her salver. Or else Holmes would lean back in his chair at the end of his meal and hand me the newspaper, where his finger had dented a paragraph, saying simply, 'Read that.'

On such occasions, as the newspaper was put down or the visitor's tread was heard upon the stairs, he would chuckle and say quietly, 'I believe, after all, that this morning may present us with infinite possibilities.' How familiar these memories are and how often were we confronted by infinite possibilities! Yet the earliest bundle of papers that comes to my hand dates from several years before my friendship with Sherlock Holmes began. Looking at it now, who would think that it threatened to rock the state and government of Great Britain, to bring down law and order in utter ruin? It is inscribed with the laconic title that Holmes himself gave it: 'The Case of the Racing Certainty'.

The Case of the
Racing Certainty

I

This remarkable case in the career of Sherlock Holmes was concluded four years before the summer day when I first met him in
the chemical laboratory of Barts. From time to time during the
period of our friendship, as we sat over the fire in Baker Street on
a winter evening, he would lug from his room the familiar tin box
and hand me a bundle of documents, tied in red tape. In one of
these I first encountered the case of the *Gloria Scott*, in another the
mystery of the Musgrave Ritual, published long ago in *The Memoirs
of Sherlock Holmes*.

One evening, I learnt of a bizarre adventure, dated several years
before our first meeting in 1881. We were talking of Inspector Lestrade and I remarked that I had never been quite clear how he and
Holmes became acquainted. My friend withdrew and brought me
one of the familiar bundles. With an eye to life's absurdities, he had
inscribed upon it, 'The Case of the Racing Certainty'.

By the time of our first meeting, Holmes had been 'a consulting
detective' for some years. He was trusted in matters of great delicacy
and had been called upon by Scotland Yard, notably by Lestrade, when
that officer had 'got himself into a fog over a forgery case'. Odd though
it now seems, I had never yet heard the details of this investigation.

When Holmes handed me two papers from the bundle, chuckling as he did so, I saw at first no connection with Lestrade. My friend had untied a mass of documents, including counsel's brief for the Crown, marked *Regina v. Benson and Kurr 1877*. How that prosecution affected our colleague at Scotland Yard, the reader will presently see. Meantime, as a storyteller's narrative is preferable to a mere report, I tell the tale as I heard it from Holmes that night but with no apology for interpreting the nuances of the drama. The first sheet which he had given me was a page from a newspaper devoted to horse-racing. It was *The Sport*, dated 31 August 1876. Still chuckling, he watched me read an article devoted to the misfortunes of Major Hugh Montgomery, evidently a man of honour, and a hero to whom the nation owed debts of gratitude upon many a field of battle, from Inkerman to the Abyssinian campaign.

Major Montgomery was that legend among racing men, a gambler who has never lost a bet—or nearly so. *The Sport* outlined his career, naming many winners he had backed. I am no racing man, but even I had heard of most. Alas, this gallant officer had now fallen victim to a conspiracy among the bookmakers of England, who had ganged together to refuse his bets.

The editor of *The Sport* rounded upon these 'vultures', as he called them, whose sole object was to take a man's money when he lost and to refuse payment when he won. Knowing little of the turf, I should not have realized the extent of Major Montgomery's tragedy but for the newspaper's account. My first thought was that he could surely continue his success by giving the name of each horse to a friend who would place the money for him. Alas, this proved to be impossible. As *The Sport* reminded its readers, betting must take place on the race-course, where the Jockey Club is supreme. By its rules, no person may bet for another. This had become a necessary regulation, after the Gaming Act of 1845 had made gambling losses irrecoverable at law. The article ended with another blast on the major's behalf against the 'vultures' of the profession.

The second sheet was a still more curious production. It was a letter from 'The Society for Insuring Against Losses on the Turf'.

It was written in French and this particular copy had been sent by Major Montgomery, the apparent founder of the philanthropic body, to the Comtesse de Goncourt living near Paris, at St Cloud. He drew her attention to the article in *The Sport* and explained that neither the Jockey Club nor the Gaming Act could prevent bets being placed for him by those living beyond the jurisdiction of the English courts. However, the Act required that money from abroad must be placed only with a 'sworn bookmaker' in England. I had heard of 'sworn brokers' on the Stock Exchange and supposed these others were something of the same kind.

Major Montgomery's letter went on to explain how he had at first demurred at trusting large sums of his money to strangers. However, he had approached the Franco–English Society of Publicity to ask if they could recommend men and women of proven integrity in France who might assist him. The name of the Comtesse de Goncourt had received the society's warmest endorsement.

The fact that Holmes found the business so amusing made me uneasy. Yet I could not see how those who assisted Major Montgomery could be losers. At regular intervals, he would send them a cheque, drawn on the Royal Bank of London in the Strand, and the name of the horse to be backed. They would forward the cheque and the horse's name to the 'sworn bookmaker' in England. If the horse won, as it always seemed to do, Major Montgomery would send his new friend ten per cent of the proceeds. If the animal failed, the major would bear the cost. The Comtesse de Goncourt felt, as I had done, that she could not lose. On the contrary, she stood to gain a substantial sum for very little effort. Holmes assured me that Major Montgomery sent his first cheque, the bet was placed, and Madame de Goncourt received news that the horse had won. A cheque for her share of the winnings followed. So did another cheque to be 'invested' and the name of a horse for the next race.

At that time, Sherlock Holmes still had 'consulting rooms' a little to the south of Westminster Bridge. They were convenient for the laboratory of St Thomas's Hospital, to which he had grace-and-favour access. I have written of his origins among the English squirearchy. The indulgence shown him by the hospital governors stemmed from a bequest made by one of these kinsmen. To the handsome but decayed terraces and tree-lined vistas of this neighbourhood Holmes returned each evening from his labours among test-tubes and Bunsen burners.

He came home on a fine but windy autumn evening in 1876 to find that a visitor had been waiting for half an hour in his landlady's ground-floor parlour. Holmes described his guest as a welldressed 'pocket Hercules', dark haired, and with a face to which nature had given the pugnacious lines of a fairground bruiser. As soon as Mr William Abrahams opened his mouth, however, he was no show-ground boxer. In a voice that was gentle yet inflexible he apologized, as they entered the upstairs sitting-room, for calling upon the 'consulting detective' without notice. Holmes waved the courtesy aside.

'It is I, Mr Abrahams, who should apologize for keeping you so long. I confess I have been a little pressed today. However, had your problem not been so confidential as to require my anonymity, I should willingly have come over to your Temple chambers and saved you a crossing on the penny steamer. Now, I fear, you have missed your train home and it may be well past dinner time before you arrive in Chelsea. Ladies are sometimes impatient on these occasions, so I daresay it as well that you are not a married man.'

Mr Abrahams stared at him, the lined face more deeply incised with suspicion.

'Surely we are perfect strangers, Mr Holmes? How can you, to whom I had not spoken until this minute, talk of my chambers in the Temple, or my travelling habits, or my house in Chelsea, or the fact that I am not married?'

Holmes smiled and motioned his guest to a chair.

'Pray sit down, Mr Abrahams. It has been a dry day and yet there are fresh water-marks upon your shoes. Though you carry a hat, your hair, if I may say so, is a little ruffled. Where does a man ruffle his hair most easily on a blustery day? Why, on the river, crossing by steamer from the far bank. Where does water lie to wet the

shoes so conveniently as on the decking of the piers at the ebb—
and notoriously upon the Temple Stairs? That you are a lawyer is
suggested by your manner. It is confirmed for me by a small blot
of sealing-wax on your right cuff and the seal upon your waistcoat-
chain. A man who seals documents for himself is something more
confidential than a mere trader. You might be a banker, of course.
Yet the banks have already been closed for some hours. The courts
frequently rise later, so that the time of your arrival suggests to me
a busy lawyer.'

Mr Abrahams relaxed, smiled, and nodded his head in
acknowledgement.

'As for your mode of travel,' Holmes went on, 'like many men
of affairs, you have a habit of concealing the return half of your
ticket in the lining of your hatband, causing a slight deformity
of the silk which is visible to the trained eye. The Temple station
would take you as far as Chelsea. You might, of course, travel a
shorter distance on that line but a man whose time is as valuable
as yours would more probably take a cab for a short journey. As
for being a bachelor, I observe that you wear a gold signet ring and
one other. I have found, when a man wears rings and is married,
a gold wedding-band appears on the fourth finger of his left hand.
In your case it does not. I daresay, however, that I am quite wrong
in every particular.'

Mr Abrahams laughed, like a child delighted by a Christmas
conjurer.

'You are correct in every detail, Mr Holmes. What you have said
persuades me that you are the man whose help I need. Expense is no
object, sir, for there is a good deal of money at stake. You might call
it a fortune. I represent the interests of the Comtesse de Goncourt
in England and would like your opinion on these documents.'

So saying, he handed my friend the two sheets of paper which
I was to read so many years later. While Holmes perused them,
the lawyer walked over to the bookshelves and learnt from their
contents something of the man whose advice he sought. No one
boasted so oddly-assorted a library as Sherlock Holmes. You

would look in vain for volumes that were in half the families of England. But if you sought industries peculiar to a small town in Bohemia, or unique chemical constituents of Sumatran or Virginian tobacco leaf, or the alienist's account of morbid psychology, or the methods by which a Ming is to be distinguished from a skilful imitation, you had only to reach out a hand for the answer. In far more cases, however, Sherlock Holmes carried all those answers in his head.

'Dear me,' he said presently, laying down the papers. 'How far, Mr Abrahams, has this merry little swindle progressed?'

The lawyer swung round from his study of the bookcase.

'You are sure it is a swindle?'

Holmes gave him the glance of the cold practical thinker.

'Major Montgomery boasts that he is able to insure against losses on the turf, a proposition which I take the liberty of doubting. Of course, the terms of his offer suggest no more than a tawdry racecourse deceit. Yet I am much mistaken if this does not disguise a plot of quite remarkable scope and ingenuity.'

Mr Abrahams sat down again.

'I had hoped you would tell me that you had heard of Major Hugh Montgomery.'

'I have not,' said Holmes coolly, 'nor I imagine has anyone else, for the very good reason that Major Hugh Montgomery does not exist. I ask, again, how far this lamentable matter has proceeded.'

William Abrahams drew out another sheet of paper, which he consulted but did not hand over.

'I knew nothing of it, Mr Holmes, until a communication from Madame de Goncourt today. I went to call on the major at once. There was no news of him at the accommodation address he gives in City Road. Several weeks ago, however, Madame de Goncourt replied to him and offered to place his bets. She received by express a cheque, the names of three horses, and the address of a sworn bookmaker, Archer & Co., in Northumberland Street, Charing Cross. She forwarded these papers and in due course received a wire from Major Montgomery informing her that all three horses had won. Some days later came a cheque for herself and another to back two more horses.'

'But you have not gone to the police? Nor has the lady?'

'So far, Mr Holmes, we have no evidence that this man—swindler though he be—has swindled anyone. Must we wait until that happens? Impossible!'

'But, Mr Abrahams, if that is all, why come to me? Madame de Goncourt places the money and the major continues to pay her when his horses win. What more is there?'

The lines of Mr Abrahams's face tightened, as if with embarrassment. He was silent for a moment while cabs and carriages rattled through the autumn dusk from Westminster Bridge to St George's Circus.

'Madame has been much taken with the major's obvious skill and evident honesty. Why else should *The Sport* have come to his aid? In short, she has begged him to let her add a wager of her own.'

'Ah,' said Holmes. 'This grows warmer! And so soon! What then?'

'The major wired her and swore he could not take the responsibility, if he were to fail her. She wired him back and insisted. He relented at last but begged her to bet only upon those horses of which he could be absolutely certain—while urging her to place whatever she could raise upon those.'

'And she has done so?'

Mr Abrahams looked at him mournfully.

'It is worse, Mr Holmes. She did it twice last week and won both times. A cheque came to her for her winnings. Then Major Montgomery wired her in great haste. He advised her to back two sure things, as he called them, Saucebox and Minerva at Brighton, with all the money she could raise or borrow. He swore they were the surest racing certainties of his career. He had confided this only to his most loyal friends, for fear of shortening the odds. Such a chance, he added, comes only once in a lifetime. She has done as he advised and waits the result. I have had only an hour or two to act upon my information. As you say, there is nothing as yet for the police. By the time there is, we shall be too late. So I have come to you. I confess my first instinct was to go straight to the sworn bookmaker and see if the money might be retrieved.'

'On no account must you do that,' said Holmes sharply. 'If this is the plot that I suspect, you would alert the conspirators before it matures.'

He stared at the lawyer for a moment longer and then said, 'It is better that Madame de Goncourt should learn wisdom late than never. Her money is probably lost already, from what you tell me, but you may rely upon my doing all I can.'

Mr Abrahams looked very straight at him. 'And what will you do, Mr Sherlock Holmes? I should like to know.'

Holmes stood up, plainly indicating to him that the time had come to leave.

'It is better that you should know nothing, sir. It is also better that you should say nothing. Indeed, it is better that your visit here should be regarded for the next few hours as something that has never taken place.'

His visitor also stood—and looked decidedly uneasy.

'I do not understand, Mr Holmes.'

'I did not intend that you should. You, Mr Abrahams, are a professional man. You are not only amenable to the criminal law but to the Law Society, who may discipline or expel you for something much less than a crime. I, on the other hand, am answerable only to myself. Have no fear, I shall communicate with you at the earliest opportunity. Let us pray that we may yet save this lady from her most ruinous folly.'

II

An hour of the windy evening passed, while Mr Abrahams distanced himself from what was to come. Sherlock Holmes charged his pipe with strong black tobacco, lay back in the comfortable old-fashioned chair, which was his parents' sole legacy to him, and stretched his long thin legs towards the fire. From time to time, he began a slow chuckle at the preposterous 'Society For Insuring Against Losses on the Turf' and the gullibility of its victims. Firmly in his mind, however, was the address of Archer & Co., Sworn Bookmakers, of 8 Northumberland Street, Charing Cross.

At half-past seven precisely, he buttoned himself into a long grey travelling cloak and close-fitting cloth cap. Turning towards Lambeth, he strode into a clout of icy air, then north into a razoring wind, where the river slapped against the steamboat pier and the wharves. The bell was ringing as he hurried through the toll-gate, paid his penny, and jumped aboard the paddle-boat a second before the plank was withdrawn. The pilot stood at the helm, the cable was cast off, and the paddle wash frothed against wooden piles. A few minutes later he was at Hungerford Stairs.

The broad boulevard of Northumberland Avenue lay lamplit but deserted. To one side, the dark lane of Northumberland Street led to the Strand, many of its old and shabby houses used for still darker purposes. The narrow front of number eight consisted of a house door with an uncurtained sash-window to one side. Of 'Archer & Co., Sworn Bookmakers', there was no sign.

Yet, as Holmes had intimated to Mr Abrahams, the address to which money was sent must be the hub of the conspiracy. There was enough street-light to see through the sash-window that the office was a mere shell of an unfurnished slum house, a narrow stairway at the rear leading to the upper levels. A number of envelopes strewn on the floor behind the door was evidence of uncollected post. Yet since so many cheques might still be in transit, it seemed probable that the birds of prey had not yet flown.

At one end of the street, cabs and buses flashed by in the lamp-light of the Strand. Along Northumberland Street, every window was dark and the narrow thoroughfare appeared deserted. Holmes required only a means of entry, for the lock on the house-door was one that would open easily from inside to let him out again. He touched his hand to the peak of his immaculate travelling cap, as if to straighten it, and drew a slim file from the lining of its brim. A casual inspection would detect only a wire frame that kept the cap-brim rigid. Now, however, this fine steel entered the division between two halves of a sash-window in an unlit side-lane and eased back the catch. In a moment more, he had crossed the sill, dropped down in the darkened room, and locked the window behind him. With the natural caution of the professional burglar, he put the house-door on the latch to ensure an immediate means of escape.

In the room lit by reflection of the street-lamps, he picked up from the door-mat eight letters addressed to 'Archer & Co'. Seven had been through the post. Two of the stamps were French. The last envelope was addressed in pencil and delivered by hand. A trained observer would notice the slight movement of Holmes's fastidious nostrils. He breathed the air of each envelope in turn, as if searching for the boudoir fragrance of a billet-doux. He placed seven on the window sill and retained the eighth, with its pencilled address.

Slipping a hand into his cloak he drew out a small enamelled pocket-knife, chose a tiny blade and, with the delicacy of a surgeon excising a growth, eased open the envelope down an inch of its side, so that the top would remain intact. He drew from it a single folded sheet of paper. This he held to the light, and saw an advertisement. It displayed a tin of cleaning-powder and a row of sparkling dinner-ware on a sideboard, proclaiming the brilliance of Oakley's Silver Polish. It was Holmes's habit not to finish with any specimen of paper until he had looked for a watermark. He therefore examined the envelope and slipped the advertisement into his pocket.

The office of Archer & Co. had been almost stripped, like premises at the end of a lease or upon a bankruptcy. In one rear corner there remained a cheap plywood desk, on which he saw only a dried-out ink-bottle and a cardboard blotter. The drawers yielded nothing but a small quantity of envelopes and a few sheets of paper with the firm's letter-heading. Like the envelope he had opened, those in the desk bore an identical 'Windsor Superfine' mark.

He tore one sheet of headed paper in half and inserted the blank lower half in the opened envelope. Then he returned to the desk, stooping over it with his long aquiline profile in silhouette. His fingers ran over the cardboard blotter with as much sensitivity as they ever touched the strings of his beloved violin.

Presently he took a twist of paper from his cigarette-case and struck a match. Holding the match to one side, he sprinkled a little graphite powder from the twist of paper and smoothed it on the blotter at one end. Shaking out the spent match, he struck another and saw, pale in the dark graphite, 'Archer & Co., Most Immediate and Confidential'. Crossing back to the window, he picked up the pencilled envelope, and returned to the desk. Seeing that the hand-writing on the envelope was identical to the imprint on the blotter, he slid the envelope out of sight beneath the cardboard square.

A second or two later, a chill at the nape of his neck caused the skin to contract and the hair to rise minutely. Only then did he hear a creak of the floorboards in the room behind him. In Sherlock Holmes, that uncanny sense which knows a sigh of timber or the movement of a rat in the wainscot from a human footfall, was super-naturally developed. He looked up at the door to the street and saw a shadow blocking the crack of light at its base. With his hypersensitive sense of danger and his acute perception, he could have sworn that no one had seen him as he entered the building. In any case, they would surely have made their move against him at once. Therefore, the alarm had been given by those who chanced to see the flare of a match in a darkened building—or perhaps heard his movements through the adjoining wall—and had now trapped him.

He afterwards claimed that in the few seconds of liberty remaining, he was struck by a lightning-bolt of inspiration, beside which the finest moments of the great poets appeared mundane. With scarcely time to reason, he took his pencil from his pocket and wrote by instinct in block capitals upon the blotting paper. MOST URGENT. MEET ME UNDER THE ARCHES CHARING CROSS STATION OPPOSITE THE KING WILLIAM IN VILLIERS STREET TOMORROW—TUESDAY 3 PM SHARP.

Then two of his assailants were through the unlatched doorway from the street. The older man with mutton-chop whiskers and a drinker's face was followed by a wiry bulldog of a young fellow with a lean body and grim features.

As he drew himself up to meet them, a third man ran into him from behind, knocking him against the desk. Holmes, though no lover of sport or exercise for itself, had been trained in his youth as boxer, swordsman and single-stick player. In a movement that a circus artist might have envied, he went forward in a tight roll across the desk, with such force that the man on his back was thrown over his head and landed sprawling on the bare boards. Holmes followed in a gymnast's fall and sprang up to face his two remaining antagonists. As he did so, he wondered if murder lay behind the humorists of the Society for Insuring Against Losses on the Turf. These men had the look of race-course roughs and he quite thought, as he said afterwards, that such desperadoes meant to have him at the bottom of the river in a few minutes more.

In that bare room, by reflected lamplight from the street, the confused and brutal struggle could have only one outcome. He was seized from behind again by his first attacker. The two men in front closed on him. Had they been the ruffians he imagined, Sherlock Holmes would have fought his last fight.

To his astonishment, his arms were wrenched behind his back and his wrists were circled by steel. He heard a click of handcuffs. A freckled giant with ginger hair said in a Scots brogue, 'So y'would, would you, my dandy?'

A bullseye lantern illuminated the scene as the shutter was drawn back and the older man in the loose-fitting flannel suit said, 'I am Inspector Clarke, Metropolitan Police. Now, my fine fellow, we'll have some account of who you are and why you might be on these premises.'

Holmes contrived to be unruffled.

'I am here to inquire after Major Montgomery, on behalf of the Comtesse de Goncourt, not to be set upon like this by footpads. You can see for yourself that the door is unlocked. Montgomery had presumably gone out for a few minutes, so I came in to wait for him. He owes me money.'

As he spoke, he knew that he staked everything on his belief that they had not seen him come in but had been attracted by the intermittent light of the matches. His explanation that Major Montgomery owed him money must do for the present.

As they studied him by the lantern and heard him speak, they became a little less sure of themselves. Sherlock Holmes was more dangerous to civil order than a regiment of Fagins or Artful Dodgers, but he did not look it. Clarke stepped up and stared him hard in the face.

'Your name, if you please.'

'By all means,' said Holmes equably, 'William Sherlock Scott Holmes, of Westminster Road, South-East.'

The contempt of a police functionary for the born gentleman was plain in Clarke's face.

'Very well, Mr William Sherlock Scott Holmes, I think it best if Sergeant Lestrade and I were to escort you a little way down the street to the rear gate of Scotland Yard. We shall have a talk about this story of yours. See if you feel quite as frisky then! What have you to say to that? Eh?'

'I think it an entirely admirable suggestion,' said Holmes politely, as they still scrutinized him by the light of the bullseye lamp. 'Indeed, I should have insisted upon that, had you not proposed it yourself.'

Inspector Clarke was unmoved by this suavity. He gave a light snort of contempt.

'I daresay you may find it less admirable when you are charged as being found on enclosed premises with intent.'

Sergeant Meiklejohn was left to secure the premises. As Holmes walked in handcuffs the short distance towards the river, between Clarke and Lestrade, he said cheerfully, 'With intent to commit a felony, to give the phrase its full value, Mr Clarke.'

'As a burglar,' Clarke said indifferently.

'Oh, I think not a burglar. Not when the night is still so young. I have always understood that the crime of burglary begins at one minute past nine, when house-breaking ends. Not before.'

'Housebreaking, then,' said Clarke abruptly.

'But I think it cannot be housebreaking where nothing is broken. Can it? You found the door on the latch, why should not I? A civil action might lie for trespass, of course, if Major Montgomery can be found. I expect he was just called away for a moment.'

This continuing chaff rattled Inspector Clarke, as Holmes intended it should. They came to a halt in the street and the inspector turned upon his captive.

'In a moment, while we are among ourselves, I may teach you to learn better than to come the letter of the law with me, Mr William whatever-it-was Holmes.'

'William Sherlock Scott,' said Holmes pleasantly. 'But it is not I who will come the letter of the law with you, Mr Clarke. The law itself will do that. Upon the bookstalls you will find, newly-published, Mr Justice Stephen's admirable compendium, *A Digest of the English Criminal Law*. You would find it a rewarding and, if I may say so without offence, an instructive volume.'

Clarke aimed a vigorous clout of his open hand at the side of Holmes's face. But where the face had been half a second before, there was only space. Disconcerted by the speed of his victim's response, the inspector swore at him, and walked on.

Lestrade later confessed that he was appalled by the incident. Though George Clarke boasted of giving many a felon a 'fat lip' for less insolence than this, he had seldom exhibited such an abrupt loss of self-control. Lestrade dreaded being a witness to an assault on a man of Holmes's calibre. He must either deny the truth or live as a traitor to his colleagues for having told it. Perhaps Holmes sensed this, for he kept silent. However, as they approached the rear of Scotland Yard, he said, 'When we arrive, Mr Clarke, perhaps you would present my compliments to Superintendent Williamson of the Detective Police. Pray inform him that I should like an interview at his earliest convenience. He will know who I am.'

Clarke's fists tightened as he walked but he said nothing more. The two detectives brought their prisoner to the charge-room and stood him before the desk-sergeant, among the drunkards and pickpockets called to answer before the night-court of the Westminster magistrates. Clarke withdrew to confer with the night-inspector. When his name was called, Holmes stepped up with a quick nervous smile to hear the decision in his case. The sergeant looked at his sheet.

'Police bail of ten guineas in your own recognizances to appear here three days from today.'

'I shall appear,' said Holmes quietly, 'you need have no fear of that.'

Then he dangled his handcuffs for the sergeant's attention.

'Perhaps you would care to have these back. I trust I shall have no further use for them.'

'Who took those off?'

'I did,' said Holmes amiably. 'There is no trick to it, I assure you. Merely art.'

III

Sherlock Holmes was not in general an admirer of the press, whose practitioners he was apt to describe in the good old phrase as 'lice upon the locks of literature'. He was fond of remarking that newspapers exist 'to promote the interests of those of whom one has never heard before and of whom, in all probability, one will never hear again. Of whom, I may add, one is vexed to have heard at all.'

In this condemnation of the daily press, however, he made an exception of the criminal news and the agony column. 'The latter is particularly instructive.'

He had just finished this column next morning at the end of a leisurely breakfast, following his late return the night before, when there was a knock at his door. His landlady announced Mr Abrahams. Holmes had already set aside thoughts of the chemical laboratory that day and admitted to a lifting of the spirits at the sound of the lawyer's name. William Abrahams came bustling upstairs in the landlady's wake, his face drawn in lines of vindictive satisfaction. Without ceremony, he threw down his hat and burst out, 'Well, sir, she has done it! Such utter stupidity never was! By God, Mr Holmes, I have had a fool or two as a client but this beats them all!'

Holmes raised his eyebrows inquiringly and gestured his visitor to a chair.

'May I take it that Madame de Goncourt has had another little flutter?'

Mr Abrahams looked a shade grimmer.

'Give or take a few centimes, she has placed the equivalent of five thousand pounds with Archer & Co., upon those two horses of Major Montgomery's. God knows how many other idiots have done the same!'

Holmes pushed the silver cigarette-box towards his guest.

'I take it that these unfortunate animals lost their races—or not?'

It seemed to the lawyer that his detective quite failed to understand him.

'They neither won nor lost, sir. They did not exist. I cannot find that Saucebox or Minerva ever ran at Brighton. Nor did the races take place in which they were said to be entered. As for the cheques, it appears, there never was a Royal Bank of London, whose spurious notes were used to pay the victims their first winnings. Then, as I ascertained this morning, there has never been anything known to English jurisprudence as a sworn bookmaker. It was a swindle, start to finish, as anyone less foolish and rapacious than my client would have seen.'

In his agitation, he crossed to the window and stared over the cold wastes of the Westminster Road. Then he turned round.

'Mr Holmes! These criminals not only forged cheques for a non-existent bank, they fabricated a page from a well-known racing newspaper. Therefore they have a printing press. A press that may even print bank stationery! This is larceny on the grand scale. What might they do next?'

Holmes brushed a fleck of cigarette ash from his waistcoat.

'As to that, Mr Abrahams, I believe I know precisely what they will do next. I know when and I know where. Almost to the minute.'

This quite took the wind out of the lawyer's sails.

'How can you possibly know that?'

Holmes tried to calm him.

'Let us return for the moment, if you please, to Archer & Co.'

In his agitation to deliver the news from Paris, William Abrahams had so far given Holmes no chance to describe the events of the previous night. When he heard them, the lawyer turned quite pale.

'Arrested for housebreaking? You might go to prison for fourteen years!'

Holmes tossed his cigarette into the fire.

'I think not,' he looked up at Mr Abrahams. 'I am not charged with any offence so far but released on bail for lack of motivation or a witness. I am a little curious as to the speed with which Mr Clarke and the night inspector sent me on my way, but we may return to that matter in a while. As for the evidence against me, I should imagine the police will find witnesses of Major Montgomery's calibre remarkably shy. I went to the firm's premises in a legitimate response to his advertisement as a tipster. I found my way open, I broke nothing. The police can hardly prosecute if Major Montgomery declines to appear. As Madame de Goncourt now knows, the major is only a name, a ghost. While I am disposed to allow that spectres may sometimes trouble our sleep, I recall none materializing in the witness-box of the Central Criminal Court.'

He took Oakley's 'Silver Polish' advertisement from the table.

'When I was brought to the charge-room last night, my pockets were turned out and a most shoddy search carried out. My little pocket-knife was remarked upon but it was so clean and slight that it could not be evidence against me. This advertisement, quite the most important clue in the case, was ignored. Such, I fear, is the blinkered mentality of Scotland Yard.'

Mr Abrahams looked up at him.

'Oakley's! Why the devil should they concern themselves with an advertisement for silver polish?' A tic of ill-temper teased the lawyer's mouth as he handed the paper back. Holmes smiled.

'It lay with the post, just inside the door, where it would attract no particular attention. It was addressed in pencil and appeared to be delivered by hand.'

'Is that so unusual with tradesmen's circulars?'

'I observed the blotter on Messrs Archer's desk,' Holmes said evenly. 'The softness of blotting paper takes a remarkably good impression. The mere fingertips of a criminal expert may trace the more forcible indentations. A skilful application of graphite will highlight anything of that kind. Of course, my practice excludes the matrimonial tragedies of the divorce court. However, I can assure you that pencil impressions have dissolved many a happy marriage.'

'And what are we to conclude?' Mr Abrahams sat stiff-necked and sceptical.

'That someone came with an urgent and secret message to Northumberland Street. The person to whom he wished to speak was not there. I daresay no one was there. However, the visitor had been able to enter the office—believe me, it is not difficult. The circular in his pocket was already prepared for such a situation. But it must reach the right person. What then? He put it in an envelope and addressed it in pencil. He slipped it among the letters on the floor. It would attract no notice from anyone, except the man who expected it. Even a policeman would drop it in the dustbin.'

'I daresay,' Mr Abrahams began impatiently but Holmes held up his hand.

'The visitor was plainly agitated, however. His pencil indentation went through both sides of the envelope, through the folded sheet of the circular, and deep into the blotting-paper. Haste is also evident to the trained eye. I noted the breaking of a pencil point on the first down-stroke of "Northumberland".'

'All for a silver-polish advertisement?'

Holmes chuckled. 'For the message it may carry. A prearranged code depending on certain letters from Messrs Oakley's well-known slogans is too fanciful. No, sir. As I picked up the letters, I sensed an odour from this envelope. There are certain chemical and aromatic scents which the criminal expert should be able to identify. Household bleach or ammonia is among the most common. It is also one of the most significant, being the most easily perfected form of invisible writing.'

'Then you have read a secret message?'

Holmes shook his head.

'I was tempted. However, I require a witness to testify as to what I do.'

'As a policeman might have done last night.'

'Not a policeman, I think. If you will draw closer, I will hold this paper before the fire. As the vulgar saying has it, if some phantom script does not manifest itself in a minute or two, I shall be quite prepared to eat my hat.'

The two men watched. For a moment they saw only the glow of flames playing behind the printed pattern of silver vessels. Then a brownish edge appeared on the blank margin at the foot of the paper, as though it might scorch and burn. Pale marks on the tawny patches began to take the form of letters. In a moment more they ran round the margins of the circular like figures on a frieze.

Dear Bill,—Important news. Tell the young ones to keep them-selves quiet and be ready to scamper. I must see you as early as possible. Bring this note with you under any circumstances. I fancy the brief is out for some of you. If not, it soon will be. So you must keep a sharp look-out.

'There you have it,' said Holmes softly.

In that moment, Mr Abrahams's attitude towards him underwent a total conversion. He saw that Sherlock Holmes was the one man in the world who might even now save his client. Yet he still nagged at the difficulties.

'If their man opens the envelope you have left and finds blank paper, will he not expect trouble?'

Holmes frowned a little.

'The reverse, I think. If the man who sent this message opens the envelope, he may assume that my blank paper means his message has been received. He will be reassured. The other man will perhaps suppose it to be a signal or warning. There will be confusion for a while, rather than suspicion, which I confess suits my purpose admirably.'

Though better-disposed towards Holmes, the lines of anxiety in the lawyer's drawn face remained deeply incised.

'At the best, Mr Holmes, I fear this may be a goose-chase that will take months to conclude. It may lead us all over Europe.'

Holmes affected genuine astonishment.

'I should be sorry if that were so, Mr Abrahams. I had proposed to bring the entire investigation to its conclusion by the end of the week—or next week at the very latest. As for distance, I shall be surprised if our inquiry takes us more than five miles from where we are now sitting. However, there is no time to lose. It is imperative that I should immediately interview the commander of the Scotland Yard detective police, Superintendent Williamson. It must be done this morning.'

Mr Abrahams looked at him in dismay. 'Impossible! You would be fortunate to see him a week from now. If you follow the political news . . .'

'I do not,' said Holmes hastily.

'If you did, you would see that he is appearing morning and afternoon just now before a parliamentary select committee on criminal law reform.'

'Is he indeed?' Holmes walked across the room and took his cape from its cupboard. 'That is where my elder brother Mycroft will prove of the greatest assistance to us. He is the government's interdepartmental adviser and was instrumental in setting up that very committee, to which he told me the other evening that he now acts as secretary. I do not generally take a great interest in such bodies but where criminal law is concerned I allow an exception. Mycroft Holmes, as you perhaps know, is also a founder of the Diogenes Club in Pall Mall. Almost all its members belong to that little circle of government in Whitehall. Brother Mycroft knows everyone who is anyone in that celebrated thoroughfare. Prime Ministers may come and go but he goes on for ever. By a happy chance, he was the seconder when Frederick Adolphus Williamson—who, by the way, is known as "Dolly" to his friends—was proposed for membership of the Diogenes.'

'You astonish me,' said Mr Abrahams, smiling for the first time that morning.

Holmes finished the last button of his cape and looked up.

'I had not intended to surprise you. However, I believe you will find that Lord Llandaff, as chairman of the select committee, will find it inconvenient to sit between eleven o'clock and lunch today. He does not yet know that, but I promise you it will be so after I have communicated with Mycroft. As for Mr Williamson, he will find himself a captive with time upon his hands in the Palace of Westminster. The company of a fellow member of the Diogenes Club will be some consolation to him. I daresay, he will quite welcome a little chat.'

IV

A few moments before noon, Sherlock Holmes followed the footsteps of a uniformed flunky down a corridor that was tiled in blue, yellow and brown diamonds. Officials in red livery with buckle-shoes hurried by, playing-card figures overtaken by time. The gothic doors, embellished by fretwork or gilding, were labelled as 'Motions' or 'Questions', 'Court Postmaster' or 'Table Office'. Fan vaulting spread high above him. In bright murals, King James threw the Great Seal in the Thames, and King William found it again.

The flunky opened a door and stood back, as Holmes entered a long room looking upon the river. Foundries, glass-houses, and printing-works on the Surrey shore poured their feathery smoke into a cold sky. An oak table ran the length of the room, set with upright chairs carved in Tudor style and padded with red leather. By a grey marble fireplace stood two men, one of whom was recognizable as the brother of Sherlock Holmes, despite differences of size and shape.

Mycroft Holmes was the elder by seven years, a big lethargic man, his heavy face lined by the same incisive lines as his younger brother's. His unwieldy frame supported a massive intelligence in the great brow and in penetrating steel-grey eyes. He extended a large flat hand, which those meeting him for the first time were apt to think of as the flipper of a seal. He turned to his companion, a stocky nervous figure, a dwarf beside Mycroft.

Frederick Adolphus Williamson was a broad-faced man with mutton-chop whiskers and a gentle manner. The son of a Hammersmith constable, he had risen by self-education and diligence to exercise an uneasy command over the Detective Police of Scotland Yard. The three men sat down at one end of the long table, still littered with papers from the joint select committee.

'Archer & Co.,' said Mycroft to his brother, 'Northumberland Street. We are ahead of you there, Sherlock. Would you not say so, Dolly?'

'An international affair,' Williamson replied with a quick smile of apology, 'Scotland Yard and the French police at the Sûreté.'

The keen profile of Sherlock Holmes showed the least suggestion of hostility.

'You speak of forged newspapers and fraudulent investments?'

'Just so,' said Williamson, sweetness itself.

'I should guess, Sherlock,' mused Mycroft Holmes, 'that, grateful as we are to you for noticing the matter on our behalf, we shall soon have the City of Paris Loan swindle well in hand.'

'Guessing is a shocking habit!' Sherlock Holmes said sharply. 'It is destructive to the logical faculty . . .'

Mycroft broke in with a mocking apology.

'You see, Dolly? My brother could keep a red-hot coal in his mouth more easily than a clever remark. The City of Paris . . .'

'I am not here about the City of Paris,' said Sherlock Holmes quietly. 'My concern is with a Society for Insuring Against Losses on the Turf, and its creator, Major Hugh Montgomery.'

Mycroft and the superintendent looked at one another. It was plain that they had never heard of Major Montgomery.

'Not the City of Paris Loan?' Mycroft inquired. 'Perhaps, Sherlock, we must take you into our confidence a little.' He raised his eyebrows at Superintendent Williamson who looked down at his hands, then gave a quick nod.

'The City of Paris Loan,' Mycroft went on slowly, 'is advertised as a means to finance the rebuilding of ancient sewers in that city. It promises to eliminate death by cholera and similar contagions. It is said to be backed by guarantees from the French government, who will pay fifteen per cent a year to stockholders with return of capital in full after five years. English and French private investors have been solicited and are almost begging the promoters to take their money. As well as the company's brochures, these investors have received copies of the most enthusiastic pages from the French papers. *Figaro*, *Le Monde*, and the Paris financial press describe it as the investment of a lifetime. Small wonder that there has been such a race among English clients to invest while the loan-stock remains on sale.'

He glanced at the superintendent who sat, as Sherlock Holmes later described it to me, like a man hunched under the knell of doom.

'May I tell my brother the rest?' asked Mycroft Holmes.

Williamson hesitated, then nodded but without looking up.

'I think it may be necessary.' Mycroft Holmes turned to Sherlock again. 'What I tell you must not be repeated outside this room. I must have your most solemn word that you will not disclose the matter to another soul until it has been brought into public view.'

Sherlock Holmes assented by a certain petulant quirk of the mouth at the thought that his brother should have stooped to demand his solemn word in such a manner. Then Mycroft Holmes continued.

'The City of Paris Loan and the turf fraud of which you speak, but of which I had never heard until just now, are only the latest of their kind. A series of these crimes has occurred during the past three or four years, though they have been kept from the public and the press. Presently you will understand why. Sometimes the villains are Gardner & Co. in Edinburgh, then they are the Paris Discretionary, next we have Colletso and the Egyptian Loan, then comes George Washington Morton and the New York Discretionary Investment Society. They grow like summer flowers, are cut down, and appear again next day. There is no end to them.'

'And the perpetrators?' Sherlock Holmes inquired sceptically. 'Are they so fleet of foot?'

'In every case so far, it seems they have been trapped, only for the arresting officers to find the premises empty and the criminals gone.'

'It is often the case,' said Sherlock Holmes with a philosophical yawn. 'Can it really be for no more than this that I am sworn to secrecy?'

Mycroft shook his head.

'You are sworn to secrecy for this.'

He drew out an envelope containing a photographic print. Sherlock Holmes took it, fingered a magnifying-glass from his breast pocket and studied it. The print showed three fragments of half-burnt paper, photographed when they were almost too brittle to touch and in the moment before they would crumble to ash. There was little to be seen except the words 'Gardner & . . .' on one fragment, '19 January' on another, and 'wanted in connection . . .' on the third.

'And this,' said Mycroft Holmes, as he handed his brother a second print.

Sherlock Holmes wasted little time on the second specimen. There was a crest of the City of Edinburgh Constabulary, a day and a month. The words 'drawn on the Clydesdale Bank', appeared faintly and 'to be detained for questioning' very plainly.

'Dear me,' he said quietly to Mycroft, 'this is rather as I had supposed. Will you tell me where these interesting scraps were found?'

'They are all that remains of several sheets of paper, which the man—or men—who disposed of them thought had been entirely destroyed. The fragments were found on separate days, so we may never know how many more acts of this kind were not even suspected. Each of these fragments was picked out from the back of an office dog-grate, which stands clear of the wall a little. In both cases, someone had overpitched the grate by placing so much coal on the papers that it preserved them in part rather than destroying them completely. These scraps were found unburnt at the rear of the ash-cans. For that we must be grateful to someone whom I will merely call an honest servant.'

'Indeed,' said Sherlock Holmes casually. 'And am I to be told where this grate—or grates—may be located?'

Mycroft glanced at the superintendent but received no response. He turned to his brother again, watching the face of Sherlock Holmes with the calculation of a falcon.

'In the offices of the Detective Police at Scotland Yard. One in the Sergeants' Office and one in the Inspectors' Room. The date of the discovery in both cases is that upon the messages. Their receipt was not entered in the office day-book and they must have been destroyed soon after their arrival by whoever opened them. Therefore, it seems a moral certainty that these most urgent messages from another police force, requesting the immediate detention of suspects or known criminals by the Metropolitan Police, were being systematically burnt upon the office fires by men of the Detective Division. The fact that one was found in the Sergeants' Office and the other in the Inspectors' Room indicates the extent of the conspiracy.'

While Mycroft Holmes made this careful explanation, Superintendent Williamson appeared to be suffering death by a thousand cuts.

'A matter of some gravity,' said Sherlock Holmes, calmly indifferent to moral considerations. 'If my advice is sought, I would first of all observe that a common mistake on these occasions is to search high and low for the traitors within. On the contrary, one should begin by deciding which men among them all may be shown to be honest beyond doubt.'

Williamson looked up at him.

'You will be relieved to know, Mr Holmes, that we have proceeded on those very lines. Of twenty officers in the Detective Division, I believe without hesitation that a great majority are innocent. Inspector Tobias Gregson, for all his faults, is no traitor. I would stake my life on that. Sergeant Lestrade is most certainly innocent.

Apart from his moral qualities, he was not in the division at the time of these felonies and so had no possible connection with any conspiracy.'

'Indeed,' said Holmes airily, 'I have met Sergeant Lestrade and may say from personal knowledge that what you believe of him seems to me true.'

The superintendent was startled but also gratified.

'Tell me, Mr Williamson,' said Holmes presently, 'would you lend Mr Lestrade to me for a few days? A week perhaps?'

'Lend him to you?' Mycroft Holmes burst in like thunder. 'In heaven's name why, Sherlock? To what end?'

'The reason,' said his brother in the same off-hand manner, 'is that I have only one pair of hands and cannot be in two places at once. The end? So that the conspiracy which threatens my client through the action of a gang of swindlers, and that other conspiracy which threatens to bring down Scotland Yard in ruins, and then the Paris swindle, may all be a thing of the past by this time next week.'

The suggestion roused the superintendent.

'I do not see what purpose it would serve. Besides, it would be materially irregular, Mr Holmes! Entirely without precedent!'

But, on reflection, Mycroft Holmes now moved to the side of his brother.

'Hardly more irregular or without precedent, Dolly, than to have Scotland Yard in ruins and to see anarchy upon our streets. If Lestrade's leave of absence for a week or so may avert that, I believe I can settle any questions that the Home Secretary or the Prime Minister may care to put to me.'

The two brothers were seldom so united in their views and purposes. When they were, I truly believe that no power on earth could stand against them.

V

Sergeant Lestrade's secondment was to begin that evening. Meantime, Holmes went alone to Villiers Street in the afternoon, lightly disguised by snow-white hair and whiskers, shoulders stooped like an older man, so that his posture and movements took two or three inches off his height. When he told me the story of the Racing Certainty, he chuckled over that message, written in block capitals the night before on the blotter of Archer & Co., a moment before he was seized. It seemed to him one of the neatest things he had ever done. MOST URGENT. MEET ME UNDER THE ARCHES CHARING CROSS STATION OPPOSITE THE KING WILLIAM IN VILLIERS STREET TOMORROW— TUESDAY—3PM SHARP.

Who would read it? And who would the reader believe the author to be? It was ten minutes to three when he took a table in the window of the saloon bar of the King William, from where he might survey that narrow street running down to the river. On the far side, station arches supported the booking-hall and the platforms, where the South-Eastern Railway runs out across Hungerford Bridge. Below the station, Villiers Street with its little shops was like a busy canyon in perpetual shadow.

The crowds that flowed between the Strand and the Embankment would have daunted any man who lacked the trained eye of Sherlock Holmes. He had practised his art until, if you had filled Trafalgar Square with as many people as it would hold, he could pick out a single face in an eagle's sweep.

A few minutes before the hour, a man appeared at the top of the street. This was a burly fellow dressed in a dog's-tooth check suit that belonged to the enclosure at Epsom or Newmarket, a sporting fashion-plate from the *Winning Post* or the *Pink 'Un*. Holmes did not suppose for one moment that this uncouth figure was the likeness of Major Montgomery. The tout waited for a moment, looking down the street, and then said something over his shoulder to another man who was still out of view round the corner. Then his companion appeared, a dapper dark-haired man of slight build in a frock-coat, grey trousers, spats, and lemon-yellow waistcoat. This ill-assorted pair began to walk slowly down Villiers Street towards the arches. The racing-man had a rolling gait, like a sailor ashore, the other walked with the precise steps of a dancing-master. Sherlock

Holmes uttered to himself that quiet chuckle which usually boded ill to someone. He recognized his quarry.

The two strollers were looking at a man who was walking carefully towards them from the Embankment. Holmes watched this tall figure with ginger hair and pale freckled face. He heard in his mind the words spoken behind him the previous evening, as he was seized in the offices of 'Archer & Co'.

'So y'would, would you, my fine dandy!'

Sergeant Meiklejohn walked slowly towards the other two men. He came to a halt before them. The dapper dancing-master engaged him in conversation, while the heavily-built tout scanned the street as if to see whether they were observed. At this distance, watching them through the interstices of the moving crowd, it would be impossible to gather much of their exchanges. Yet Holmes saw all that he needed from the expressions on their faces. He knew that Meiklejohn and the natty dresser were each asking whether the other had left a message in pencil on the blotter, an urgent appeal which brought them together now. And now each was shaking his head to deny it. Presently they were asking one another how it came to be there. They were looking about them as they spoke, trying to do so unobtrusively, waking too late to the trap that had been laid for them. Then something else was being discussed. Holmes guessed that it was the blank half-sheet of paper found by one man in the envelope where the other man had left a different message.

They were taking leave of one another now, carefully but quickly. Holmes stood up behind the barroom window, watching through the crowds, intending to follow the dapper little man and the racecourse tout. Meiklejohn was nothing to him now. As he stepped into the street, however, he glanced down towards the river and saw a fourth man, Inspector George Clarke. Whether Clarke had been in company with Meiklejohn it was impossible to say. He was nowhere near Meiklejohn, as he handed a copper to the newsboy, took his paper, and walked slowly down to the Embankment and Scotland Yard.

The two men whom Holmes had in sight used every familiar tactic to shake off an unseen pursuer. They stopped, walked back, then turned and walked on again, to see if this would make their shadow reveal himself. Holmes outflanked them, watching from the eminence of the stairs to the railway platforms. They could not be sure there was anyone on their trail at that moment but, for safety's sake, they now split up and went in opposite directions. Holmes had expected this and had decided long before that the dapper fellow was the one he would track. By now, however, Holmes bore less resemblance to the man who had tracked his quarry from the King William. His coat was reversed to show the shabbiest gabardine waterproof and his natty cap had undergone a transformation into a working-man's 'cheese-cutter'. He wore heavy spectacles whose lenses had the thickness of a counting-house clerk's with failing sight. Most of all, however, it was the metamorphosis of the upright carriage of Sherlock Holmes into a pathetic round-shouldered drudge which concealed him most effectively.

At first, the game was played out in Charing Cross Station. For twenty minutes, there was a curious hide-and-seek as the dancing-master performed a pattern of turns and diversions to shake off any possible pursuer, leading the way round the busy platforms, over the footbridge, down to the washroom, through the booking-hall where he purchased a ticket and walked at once past the barrier on to a platform. Holmes watched, sure that a man who intended catching a train would not have bothered to lead him such a dance beforehand. He was proved wrong as the quarry opened a carriage door of the first train to pull in.

Now it was the turn of Sherlock Holmes to stride across the booking-hall and take a ticket for Dover. With a moment to spare, he passed the ticket-barrier and entered the last carriage. The train rumbled slowly across the iron span of the long river bridge and pulled in at Waterloo. There was a slamming of doors and then a pause. By use of a pocket-mirror, Holmes surveyed the length of the train without showing his head outside the carriage. The whistle blew. At the last moment, a door at the far end flew open and the dapper man sprang out. Holmes leapt for the concealment of a laden luggage-trolley before the other could finish closing the carriage door and turn to look at him.

Cat and mouse began their game again, the cat never quite seen by the mouse but scented none the less. For a moment, Holmes lost his man yet knew the way he must have gone. Striding up the covered stairs of the footbridge, two at a time, he reached the top and to his surprise found the crossway empty above the tracks below. There had surely been time only for his prey to reach the first stairs down to the next platform. Holmes sprinted and then descended cautiously, alarmed to find the platform also empty. On the far side of the next railway track, however, a train was pulling out on the return to Waterloo. The dapper man was waving to him from behind the window of the first carriage.

Another hunter might have lost the game in that half-hour. For Holmes, so much had been won. His quarry had striven with ill-concealed desperation to shake off his tracker. Most important to him was the determination of the quarry to return to Charing Cross. Why such resolve? What bound him to that railway station? Was there a train to be caught to another destination in London— or England? No, for every train that leaves Charing Cross goes to Waterloo. Was there a confederate to be met? No, because the half hour when that might have happened was now gone. What else? Why must he return, as if to his home? Because it was his home! What place could be more useful to a man who links the City of Paris Loan and insures against losses on the English turf in Northumberland Street? Where was closer to the phantom Royal Bank of London in the Strand—even to Scotland Yard?

Like a grand excrescence in the mind of Sherlock Holmes blossomed the Parisian opera-house splendour of the Charing Cross Hotel.

Twenty minutes later, his appearance restored to dignity and with a newspaper in his hand, Sherlock Holmes was reflected by a gilt-columned mirror between pillars of raspberry-coloured marble. In a moment more the reflection was gone and he sat patiently near the door of the writing-room, behind the wide concealing pages of the *Morning Post*. Yet his eyes never left the mirrors. Almost an hour passed, before he caught a momentary reflection of a man tipping his hat to an elderly woman in black velvet, as she walked forward with the aid of a stick. There was no mistaking the trim, chivalrous figure in his suit of cream linen, the moustache neat and the eyebrows trim. If he had been holding a cane just then, he might have swung it with the air of a boulevardier.

From behind a pillar, Holmes caught the murmurs at the reception-desk.

'The Marquis Montmorency . . .'

' "Poodle" Benson, as I live and breathe,' said Holmes softly, for his own benefit.

VI

'They tell me, Lestrade, that you are an honest man.'

'I hope that I may prove so, Mr Holmes,' said the Scotland Yard officer without a flicker of resentment.

'Quite. To prove the truth of that hope is the reason for your presence. You are also said to be an intelligent and resourceful detective officer. Too many of your colleagues are apt to give the alarm everywhere and discover nothing.'

'That must be for others to judge, sir,' Lestrade said guardedly.

'You may depend upon it that they will.'

Such were the first words spoken directly between Holmes and the future Inspector Lestrade of the Special Branch and the Criminal Investigation Department, as the two men occupied a cab in the forecourt of the Charing Cross Hotel that evening. It was dark and a light drizzle was falling through the mist. Wet cobbles caught the lamplight in wavering pools. Through this gloom, the profile of Lestrade's face appeared still leaner and grimmer. Holmes was wearing his cloak and ear-flapped travelling-cap, a leather bag beside him, labelled for the night-ferry via Folkestone and Boulogne.

He turned a little in his seat to look directly at the policeman.

'Your orders for the next few days are quite clear in your mind?'

'What Mr Williamson and Mr Mycroft Holmes told me at the Home Office is plain, sir. I am to carry out your instructions, provided they are not manifestly illegal. If I have doubts in the matter, I am to communicate with Mr Williamson through Mr Mycroft Holmes at the Home Office department.'

'I could almost wish,' said Holmes piously, 'that it had been possible to leave my brother out of this business. I suppose, however, that would not have done.'

'As to that,' Lestrade said enigmatically, 'it would not be for me to say.'

'Very well, then these are your orders and the reasons for them. For as long as I am allowed to give you instructions, you will be employed at the reception-desk of the Charing Cross Hotel, or in whatever other employment is most prudent.'

'As a clerk, sir?' There was no mistaking Lestrade's alarm. 'I know not the first thing about hotel clerking, Mr Holmes!'

'You are supposed to be there on approval in whatever capacity is necessary. You will not be required to work alone and there is only one person, in a very senior position and entirely trustworthy, who knows your true identity.'

'And that is all I am to do, sir?'

Holmes made an effort at infinite patience.

'You will earn your wages, Lestrade. At this moment, a most dangerous criminal conspiracy embraces both Paris and London. Therefore, one of us must be here and the other in Paris. I shall go to Paris tonight, being familiar with the language, the city, and the officials whose assistance may be necessary to us. I shall probably be away for a few days. What needs to be done here is merely work-a-day but it must be done none the less.'

In the reflected oil-light, Lestrade looked apprehensive.

'Done by me?'

'Of course. The Charing Cross Hotel, estimable in many ways, is convenient for international criminals, standing as it does at the heart of London yet so close to the route to Paris and the Channel ports. I have just spent two hours at the Home Office. My brother has information of a new conspiracy against James Lester Valence, a most powerful man in Australian commerce. That is all we know at present. He is by no means the first victim of these scoundrels but stands head and shoulders above the rest. Valence made and lost a fortune in the gold-fields, then made another from building railroads in New South Wales and Queensland. He was in London six weeks ago, staying at this very hotel to which he is about to return. I cannot protect him for the moment, therefore you must. You will report every day to the Home Department and will receive your instructions there. Do not attempt to communicate with me in any other way. Do not go anywhere near Scotland Yard. As for Valence, he has been touring in Europe, and is due here in a day or two. I understand he is soon to be married. Whatever villainy is plotted against him, the Charing Cross Hotel appears to be the scene of it. Such is the extent of my information.'

'Does that information include a photograph of him?' Lestrade asked hopefully.

'I have not seen one. However, you could scarcely mistake him. The description I have from my brother is of a man taller than you or I, as well as a good deal more bulky. He wears a black and some-what bristling beard. His face, such as one may see of it, is marked by the outdoor life of sun and wind. When going out, he carries as a matter of habit a black ebony stick with a silver band, embossed with a small griffin and the initials "J. L. V." '

'And his voice?' the detective asked quietly. 'Appearance is one thing, Mr Holmes, but the voice gives a man away.'

Holmes looked at him, as if he had not thought of this but approved of Lestrade's quick-wittedness.

'As to his voice, I fear we know nothing. None of us has ever heard it.'

The Scotland Yard man was not to be beaten to the post by his temporary employer. He reached for his bag.

'Then I shall bid you good evening and a pleasant journey, Mr Holmes. There may be much to be done in the next few days and

I should like to make a start. I am to go to the desk and ask for the manager, I presume?'

'Just so,' said Holmes, staring acutely through the gloom at his new accomplice. 'You will hear from me, through my brother, either tomorrow or the day after.'

The policeman opened the door and stepped out into the drizzle. In such circumstances, Lestrade set out upon his first adventure in partnership with Sherlock Holmes.

VII

Two mornings later, from behind the polished mahogany of the reception-desk, Lestrade first set eyes upon James Lester Valence, crossing the hall between pillars of raspberry marble. It was impossible not to recognize the unkempt giant whose outlines had been described by Mycroft Holmes to Lestrade.

Sherlock Holmes had also been correct in his description of Valence as a burly bearded figure who had lived much of his life in the roughest terrain. He seemed more like the habitué of a farmers' inn than of a grand hotel. Yet beneath this exterior there was evident gentleness and simplicity. The hard-handed gold-prospector and railroad-builder behaved like a mere child among the ways and wonders of European cities.

Two things in particular drew Lestrade's attention to this new arrival. In the first place, Valence was an inveterate smoker of strong cigarettes. So far as he occupied the public rooms of the hotel, he was always to be found in the genial, tobacco-stained dimness of the smoking-room, with its darkened oil-portraits of famous sportsmen, its subdued lighting, brass lamps and table-furniture, card-tables and red plush. A second matter of interest was the arrival by every morning and evening post of a lightly perfumed envelope on pink stationery, addressed to Valence in a neat female hand. A small and discreet coronet was printed in blue on the flap of the envelope. From this Lestrade concluded that whatever trap was laid for the Australian, a woman might be the bait.

Two other pieces of correspondence, identifiable by a printed sender's address on their envelopes, appeared to be grateful acknowledgements to Valence by the Distressed Gentlefolks Aid Society. When he reported all this information to Mycroft Holmes, Lestrade was greeted by an outstretched telegram. He caught the words 'Holmes, Hotel Crillon, Place de la Concorde', and then the message. KINDLY TELEGRAPH ALL PECULIARITIES OF ANTIPODEAN SUBJECT'S LEFT THUMB AND ANY APPARENT CHANGE OF SAME AT MORNING OR EVENING.

Lestrade confessed to me, years later, that nothing in his dealings with Holmes had ever baffled him so much. How could Valence's left thumb have any relevance to the case? What changes could occur in its abnormalities during the course of the day?

Happily for the detective officer, the manager was able to leave him pretty much at liberty. There was no means by which he could answer Holmes's query, except by closely observing Valence throughout the day. The Australian's attachment to the smoking-room and the card-table made this easier than it might have been. Lestrade became a supernumerary smoking-room attendant.

However diffident Valence had been in the outer world of London society, he came into his own among the familiarities of the card-table, which was occupied by hardier souls day and night. To one bluff racing-man and that linen-suited aristocrat, the Marquis Montmorency, who seemed to be his habitual neighbours, Valence remarked that poker was his game but that during his travels he had improved his hand at baccarat.

The conviviality of the game, rather than the hock and seltzer which accompanied it, loosened the tongue of this diffident giant. He spoke of a sweetheart in England. Indeed, he went so far as to draw out his notecase and produce a photograph of a young woman whose every feature confirmed her breeding. Compliments and polite congratulations were breathed in his direction from all corners of the table.

So far, the vigilance of the Scotland Yard man revealed no immediate sign of abnormality in Valence's left thumb, nor any change as the hours passed. However, on the second evening, as he was emptying and polishing the glass bowls that had contained cigarette and cigar ash, he heard Valence speak of marriage and the diamond necklace which was to be his gift to his beloved upon their betrothal. He had ordered it from a Bond Street jeweller before departing on his tour of Europe. Now he had returned to collect and present the finished article. The racing-man inquired politely where the necklace was being made.

'Regniers in Bond Street,' said the Australian modestly.

The Marquis Montmorency looked astonished.

'I am delighted to know it, sir, for Henri Regnier himself is related to me by marriage, through my cousin, Antoine Mellerio of the rue de la Paix. A small world, to be sure! I congratulate you on your choice of craftsman. You know, I imagine, that it is possible in the trade to arrange a little discount for oneself or one's friends. Perhaps you have already done so.'

The bearded giant looked abashed.

'A discount? No, Marquis. It never crossed my mind to suggest such a thing.'

Montmorency looked down at the cards in his hand and shook his head.

'That is much to be regretted. The reduction is not so great, of course. Ten per cent. Perhaps less. But on so large a sum . . .'

He left the rest unsaid. Lestrade was now obliged to move out of earshot. He saw only that, during the rest of the evening, Valence pulled ahead of the others and at the end of the game was almost thirty pounds to the good. A little after midnight, as they pushed their chairs back and rose to go their separate ways, the dapper marquis twinkled at his companion.

'I would not for the world, sir, presume upon so short an acquaintance. However, if you would permit me to put in a word, I will see if my cousin might not arrange a discount, even at this late stage of the purchase. Between ourselves, you understand. If you will trust me with the details, I will see what can be done tomorrow. It is usual to agree these things at the beginning of a transaction but a man in your situation, who would be so valued a customer for the future, surely deserves a degree of *ex post facto* consideration.'

Valence plainly had no idea what the term meant and appeared troubled by embarrassment at such unexpected kindness. Yet he could scarcely refuse so generous an offer, made out of pure friendship.

The next morning brought another of the perfumed envelopes, which Lestrade was certain must come to Valence from the intended recipient of the diamond necklace. The Australian spent most of that day in his room. In the mild warmth of late afternoon, however, he went out alone with nothing to indicate where his destination might be. Almost as soon as Valence had entered a cab, Lestrade noticed the racing-man and the Marquis Montmorency going up the stairs together in something of a hurry. To the mind of a detective, they appeared an ill-matched pair. Following at a distance, Lestrade saw the two men take separate directions at the first landing. The racing-man retired to his room, his companion followed the corridor where Valence slept.

Lestrade was clear as to what was about to happen. Montmorency had by now had ample opportunity to acquire a copy of the key to Valence's room. The means might be easy enough in a hotel of this size. He or his racing friend had only to ask for Valence's room number, take the key, then return it a few minutes later, apologizing or complaining that it was the wrong one and did not fit his door. Such errors, in all honesty, were not frequent but nor were they uncommon. In this case, a wax impression of the key would soon be taken.

By the time that Lestrade turned the corner of the landing, the corridor ahead of him was empty. There had been no time for Montmorency to reach the far end, unless he had done it at a sprint. Therefore, he was in one of the rooms. The detective reached Valence's door, knelt down, and squinted through the keyhole. He saw only a segment of the sitting-room but it was enough to show him the marquis patiently going through the contents of Valence's ash-bowl, examining the cigarette-butts, holding them up and considering each in turn. Presently he put the ash-bowl down and swung round to the door. Lestrade moved quickly but without a sound. There was just time to reach the end of the corridor and disappear from view.

However, from where he stood, the Scotland Yard man was able to hear the door of Valence's room opening very slowly, as if the dapper little aristocrat looked cautiously in either direction, slipped out, and closed the door very softly behind him.

To enter Valence's room for no other reason than to inspect the remains of the cigarettes he had smoked, ignoring money and valuables, was surely the maddest thing in a mad business. Or so it seemed to Lestrade.

VIII

A further day passed and Lestrade had yet been unable to observe the essential peculiarities of Valence's left thumb. It was a thumb that pressed upon the pasteboard cards with as firm a hold as any man's round the card-table, nor did it appear to change as the day progressed. Perhaps the change was a certain twitching that sometimes occurred as the evening wore on. Lestrade felt that he certainly noticed something of the sort. Upon his next visit to the Home Department, Mycroft Holmes silently handed him another telegram.

MATTERS IN FRANCE COMING TO A HEAD STOP. KINDLY ATTEND TO PREVIOUS INSTRUCTIONS IN MINUTEST DETAIL STOP. ESSENTIAL YOU CONTINUE TO DO SO STOP. HOLMES HOTEL CRILLON.

In the course of his smoking-room duties that evening, the Scotland Yard man caught another scrap of conversation. Montmorency, the smiling gamester, said to Valence, as they drew their chairs in round the table, 'I must tell you that it is all arranged, my dear fellow. Twelve per cent is to be the discount on your purchase. I tried for fifteen on your behalf, but twelve was the best I could manage. Still, it is preferable to nothing, is it not?'

The black-bearded giant, in his good-natured simplicity, seemed so overcome by such a selfless action that for a moment he appeared tongue-tied.

'Twelve!' he said at last. 'But that is far more than I had expected! Five, I had thought, perhaps ten at the extreme. What can I have done to merit such consideration from you? It is more than I can guess.'

'In that case, my dear Valence, you need only guess that you are a good sportsman and a most agreeable companion,' beamed the dapper little lord. 'Besides, these jewellers always stick the price on at first, thinking they will be beaten down in negotiation. In that case, old fellow, it is only justice to knock 'em down a bit. They quite expect it, you know. And then, what is this world, if we cannot do one another a good turn from time to time?'

'What, indeed, sir?'

'However, if you will permit me,' the dapper nobleman went on, 'I believe it would be best if I were to collect the necklace myself and bring it to you. Though the matter is arranged with my cousin, I shall be better acquainted with the shopman than you would be. If I deal with him, you may be sure that your discount will not wash off, as they say!'

At this there was something, less than suspicion but more than doubt, which flickered briefly in the Australian's eyes.

'Then you would wish me to give you the cash or a cheque, so that you might take it to Regnier's?'

He did not so much as hint at a natural misgiving that this man he had known only as a card-player might run off with his money, though the suspicion ran through the minds of everyone else present. As if to confound them by sheer good-nature, the slightly-built Montmorency lay back in his chair and fairly rolled about with laughter, like a pleased child, at such a suggestion.

'I should not dream of it!' he giggled at last. 'No, my dear Valence. I will pay for the necklace with my cheque, it is better that way and will absolutely secure the reduction in price. My cousin would not go back on his word to me, of all people! When I return to the hotel with the necklace, you may reimuburse me for a sum twelve per cent less than you thought the cost would be. Is that fair?'

The bulky Australian was in a confusion of gratitude and remorse for having suspected the other man's good faith.

'It is more than fair, sir. It is generosity on a grand scale. May I ask how you would like the money to be repaid?'

The marquis looked a little sheepish.

'As it is most convenient to you. I confess, however, that having written a cheque for such an amount, I should not at all object to being reimbursed in cash. Specie may be paid into the bank so much more easily and quickly. After all this, I should not care to hear that the cheque I had written had been returned by my bank for lack of funds!'

There was general laughter round the table at the absurdity of such a proposition.

'All the same,' Valence said, as if now eager to make amends for his suspicion, 'why should I not give you a cheque or money in the first place to take to Regnier's?'

The Marquis Montmorency beamed and spread out his hands.

'You shall not pay a cent, sir, until the necklace is in your hands. I insist upon that. Besides, suppose I should be waylaid by footpads between here and Bond Street?'

There was great hilarity at the notion of such an old-fashioned robbery in the streets of the modern West End.

'I do not know,' said Valence softy, 'I never dreamed when I came to Europe that I would receive so much friendship on all sides.'

Despite the strictest instructions in the latest telegram from Holmes, Lestrade abandoned his surveillance that afternoon, as Valence withdrew to his room. Instead, the Scotland Yard man shadowed the Marquis Montmorency. In his fawn hat, cream linen suit and lemon waistcoat, patent-leather shoes and spats, a rose in his buttonhole, the slim figure of the nobleman was not hard to track. He did not take a cab but walked quickly past the clubs of Pall Mall, up the broad elegance of St James's Street, across Piccadilly, and so into Bond Street.

Outside Regnier's, with its old-fashioned shopfront and gilt mouldings, Montmorency paused to watch a man taking the jewels on their velvet display-cushions from the window, in preparation for the shop to close. Before the metal grille was put across the window, however, the marquis had slipped inside. Lestrade could see him talking to the frock-coated shopman. After a few minutes, the customer came out and made his way back to Charing Cross.

Whatever suspicions Lestrade might have had about the purchase were put to rest by Montmorency's insistence that he would take no money until he handed over the necklace. Nor could it be doubted that he behaved with perfect openness and honesty to Valence in reporting the afternoon's visit. That evening, as they sat down to cards in the dark-walled smoking-room, Lestrade heard him say to the Australian, 'I paid a call on Regnier this afternoon. There will be no difficulty at all in the transaction. If you choose, of course, you may just write a little note, authorizing me to collect and pay for the item on your behalf. As for your discount, however, it is as safe as if it were in your pocket at this moment.'

Perhaps this was as well. They played baccarat that evening and, by the end of it, Valence was quite twenty pounds down. However, he had won as much on other occasions and could scarcely begrudge such a sum to his benefactors. Lestrade could not, in all conscience, see any trickery in the game. He was familiar with the most common ruse at baccarat whereby, under cover of his sleeve, a man might slip an extra counter over the line, or not, to adjust his stake according to the fall of the cards. There was not the least sign of that.

Indeed, Lestrade thought, he would have believed entirely in the good faith of the Marquis Montmorency, had it not been for the curious business of the nobleman entering his friend's room to inspect the stubs of his cigarettes in so furtive a manner.

On the following day, Mycroft Holmes, behind his wide desk, the green spaces of St James's Park filling the window behind him, showed a magisterial indifference to Lestrade's report.

'One is apt to think that men who play cards for greed and are fleeced deserve it,' he observed at one moment. 'As for the matter of the necklace, I opine that it is a service being performed so that Mr Valence will feel obliged to remain at the card-table in a game where the others take money off him. After all, they have him as a companion now whether he likes it or no, do they not? I daresay my brother would take a different view of the matter. For a third time, by the way, he asks after Mr Valence's left thumb.'

'It is a thumb,' Lestrade said bluntly, 'that is all it is.'

Mycroft Holmes heaved his untidy bulk from the chair and shook his large head, like a dog coming from water.

'No, it is not all. If my brother occupies himself about it to this extent, you may be sure that it is not all. However, I can make no more of it. Nor can I answer your question about the ends of the cigarettes. There is a war breaking out between the Khedive of Egypt and Abyssinia, into which we may all be drawn. Turkey threatens to make trouble between ourselves, the Russians, and the German Empire by carrying out massacres in Bulgaria. It would be expedient if you and my brother should realize that I have more to occupy myself with than left thumbs and cigarette ends. Good day to you.'

However, the suspicion that Valence was being held at the card-table and fleeced by a specious promise of discount on a necklace was wired to Sherlock Holmes. The reply came almost at once.

REQUIRE FACTS NOT CONJECTURES STOP. CEASE OBSERVATION OF LEFT THUMB OF VALENCE STOP. HOLMES HOTEL CRILLON.

IX

Valence's losses were little enough at the card-table on the next day. Indeed, for much of the game he was ahead. The day following that, he lost moderately. If he took this disappointment philosophically, it was because his friend Montmorency was able to inform him that the diamond necklace would be ready next day and might be collected in the afternoon. Valence assured the amiable nobleman that he would make arrangements to reimburse him for the cost immediately.

Lestrade gathered enough of these exchanges to know that the purchase was almost complete. Next day, towards the end of the afternoon, Valence retired as usual to his room and the card-table was deserted. Montmorency approached the polished mahogany sweep of the reception-desk in the hotel's marble foyer. Lestrade heard him ask that his bill should be made up in readiness for his departure on the following morning. Then the dapper marquis walked out into the Strand and called a cab from the station rank.

Try as he might, Lestrade could still see nothing worse than a hint of sharp practice at the card-table. Even this was more than balanced by Montmorency's act of generosity. As for the racing-man in the dog's-tooth check, he was scarcely a proper companion for a marquis. However, as Lestrade remarked to me years afterwards, the association seemed no more questionable than that of the celebrated Marquess of Queensberry and his kind with the riff-raff of the sporting world and the smoking-room. The detective officer had half made up his mind to follow this benevolent marquis, out of curiosity, when a bell on the panel rang and he was summoned by name to Mr Valence's room.

According to the account given in the papers of Sherlock Holmes, events now followed with great rapidity. The Marquis Montmorency kept his promise to the last detail. He ordered the cab to wait for him in Bond Street, outside Regnier's shop, while he went in and greeted the jeweller with unfeigned geniality. He then wrote his cheque, took the necklace, and returned to the Charing Cross Hotel. There, in company with his friend the racing-man, he asked at the reception-desk whether it might be convenient to call upon Mr Valence, who was expecting him. The clerk inquired and replied that it would be most convenient but that Mr Valence would be grateful for a delay of ten minutes while he finished dressing for dinner.

When this interval was over, the two men were shown up to Mr Valence's room by a page-boy. The lad knocked and was summoned by a voice from within. The Marquis Montmorency and his friend entered, surprised to find that Valence was not alone. Beside him stood the wiry grim-faced figure of the smoking-room attendant, whom the card-players had laughed at behind his back as the hotel's drunken butler. Most disconcertingly, for the marquis and his friend, James Lester Valence, gold prospector and railroad-builder, had lost his Australian voice. He had acquired a more precise and rather clipped English accent.

'Lock the door, if you please, Lestrade,' he said crisply.

The cadaverous butler obeyed, stepping round the other two men to do so.

'One cannot be too careful in dealings of such value, after all,' Valence observed for the benefit of Montmorency and his friend.

This seemed to reassure them a little.

'You have the necklace?' Valence asked, raising his eyebrows at Montmorency.

The dapper little nobleman drew a leather case from his pocket and handed it to the Australian.

'Eighteen hundred pounds, sir.'

Valence nodded as he opened the case and drew up from its velvet a ripple of glass fire that hung and swayed from his fingers.

'Admirable,' he said softly, 'wholly admirable. Shall we say—not eighteen hundred pounds, of course—perhaps eighteen pounds?'

The racing-man seemed about to start forward at Valence but Montmorency laid a hand on his friend's arm and smiled at the Australian's pleasantry.

'I can promise you, Mr Valence, that I have a receipt from Messrs Regnier in my pocket for eighteen hundred pounds.'

'I do not doubt it,' said Valence politely. 'Nor do I doubt that somewhere else you have a receipt for eighteen pounds—or whatever the price may be—for a set of imitation glass, made up as a replica of the true necklace. True diamonds do not sparkle in the light as these do, they glow in twilight and obscurity.'

Montmorency stared at him.

'Then I have been as much deceived as you, sir.'

'I do not doubt it, though not deceived in quite the way that you imagine.'

'I should like a word with that fellow Regnier!'

'You shall have one, never fear. Mr Regnier, if you please!'

The door leading to the bathroom opened and the jeweller appeared.

'I regret that you were kept waiting downstairs, sir,' said Holmes to Montmorency, 'but it was necessary that Mr Regnier should be one of our company. Be so kind, Mr Regnier, to repeat to these two gentlemen what you have already told Lestrade and myself.'

The jeweller cleared his throat and began.

'A little while ago I was visited by you, Mr Holmes . . .'

'Holmes?'

The Australian, with a slight wince of discomfort, peeled aside the bristling black beard to reveal that familiar aquiline profile.

'Though I have had some little theatrical success in my youth, even playing the role of Horatio on the London stage with the Sasanoff Company,' he remarked wryly, 'I have never mastered the art of drawing off a beard without pain.'

Next he raised from his head the unkempt pate of dark hair and laid it aside.

'Now, Mr Benson,' he said, 'forgive me but I cannot continue to call you the Marquis Montmorency without some feeling of mirth. Nor would Major Montgomery serve you as a title any longer. Let us resume the narrative. I beg your pardon, Mr Regnier.'

The jeweller began again.

'I was visited by Mr Holmes who informed me that a plot by professional swindlers was in preparation against himself, masquerading as a wealthy Australian gentleman. With the knowledge of the authorities, I gave my consent to assist in frustrating this. A few days later, I was visited by a man who gave his name as the Marquis Montmorency and who I now know to be Mr Harry Benson. He explained that he wished to buy a very fine diamond necklace which I then had in stock. Mr Holmes had already spoken to me of this article. Mr Benson, as the Marquis Montmorency, said he would pay for this necklace with a cheque. However, he would leave both the necklace and the cheque with me until such time as the latter had been cleared and the funds were in my account. How could I have any objection to that arrangement?'

'How, indeed?' Holmes murmured.

'However, gentlemen, the Marquis Montmorency also wished to have a good imitation set made, so that his wife might generally keep the original necklace at her bank and have the imitation at home for less formal occasions. It is not an uncommon request and the imitation, being mere glass and paste, was easily done. This afternoon, as agreed, the Marquis Montmorency came with his cheque. He left the diamond necklace as a pledge for the cheque's clearance and took away the imitation. Naturally I wrote him two receipts, one for each article.'

There was a moment of total silence.

'And so,' said Holmes at last, 'Mr Benson brings us the imitation necklace with a receipt for the genuine one. In respect of this, Mr Valence, as he believed me to be, would pay him eighteen hundred pounds in cash. A vast sum of money for an imitation that is worth next to nothing. In due course, Mr Regnier would discover that the cheque had not the value of the paper it was written on. However, he would still have his diamond necklace and would not be much worse off. It was Mr Valence who was the target of the conspirators.'

The dapper little man's eyes flashed with anger.

'No, sir! It is I who am the victim and you who are the conspirator! You are a prime mover of the plot!'

'I baited the trap,' said Holmes modestly, 'and the bait was taken.'

But Harry Benson had now recovered his self-command.

'I do not think, Mr Holmes, that such a case of trickery or entrapment would stand a moment's examination in court, once your chicanery was revealed. You might very well find yourself in prison.'

Holmes wiped the Australian climate from his cheeks with a handkerchief.

'You may well be right,' he said cheerfully. 'Indeed, I have always rather suspected that I should find myself in prison one day. Yet I think in this case that the forgery—the cheque signed to Mr Regnier as the Marquis Montmorency—would be more than enough evidence to put the boot on the other foot, as the saying has it. As it happens, I am little concerned for that. My client is the Comtesse de Goncourt, or to be more accurate Mr William Abrahams. My object has been to flush out those who sought to cheat that lady of many thousands of pounds. When you stand your trial, Mr Benson, it will not be for the necklace swindle but for a grander design represented by Archer & Co. of Northumberland Street and the City of Paris Loan, perpetrated from the rue Réamur. In the world of the racing certainty, a single forged cheque passed to Mr Regnier will come in a very poor third.'

Billy Kurr, the racing-man, had so far watched these proceedings with a dumb incredulity. Now he reached into his pocket and drew from it a small but efficient-looking revolver. Benson swung round to Lestrade.

'Give me the key to this door!'

Lestrade's features were set more like a bulldog than ever.

'Put that gun down!' he snapped at Kurr.

'Give Mr Benson the key, Lestrade,' Holmes said calmly.

'I shall do no such thing.'

'By the authority of Superintendent Williamson, you are under my orders until this matter is concluded. The lives of all those in this room are in my keeping. Now, give him the key!'

There was such rage in the face of the Scotland Yard man that Holmes thought he would still refuse, or else make some move to wrest the revolver from Kurr's grip. However, the fight seemed to go out of Lestrade and he tamely handed the key to Benson. The 'Marquis Montmorency' unlocked the door, ushered his companion through it, then locked it securely on the outside.

Lestrade rattled the handle of the door unavailingly.

'I owe you an apology,' Holmes said equably. 'However, it was necessary that you should think me in Paris. Brother Mycroft connived in getting the telegrams relayed. Had you known of my Australian masquerade, I feared your behaviour might have betrayed it.'

'And the thumb?' Lestrade asked gruffly.

'Ah, yes, the thumb. I am glad you paid such attention. By keeping your eye upon it, I could be sure that you were seldom too far off to miss the conversation of Benson and his companions. Had I merely asked you to eavesdrop, I fear you might once again have given the game away.'

Lestrade made no reply to this but returned to his rattling of the door-handle.

'Something must be done, Mr Holmes! They're getting away!'

Holmes had stepped out of the specially-built shoes which had increased his height by two full inches and was now divesting himself of the padding which had given such bulk to James Lester Valence. In the course of this transformation, he spared the Scotland Yard man a glance.

'Of course they are getting away! Have you grasped nothing, sergeant? In captivity, Benson and Kurr would be of no use to us. The diamond necklace is no more than a necessary bauble in my scheme. Even the Turf swindle and the Paris Loan are little enough. Let us allow Harry Benson a little freedom and he will lead us to the heart of the conspiracy.'

X

As they walked out of the hotel entrance, Sherlock Holmes tightened his collar against a cold street-wind that had come with the darkness of the spring day.

'Poor Regnier,' he said wistfully, 'I believe he thought we should never have been released from our room. And now, if you please, Lestrade, we must look lively and take a cab to Canonbury. From there we shall send a telegram to Scotland Yard, while there is still time.'

Lestrade stopped and turned to him.

'But we could walk to Scotland Yard from here, Mr Holmes, quicker than any telegram might get there. Five minutes would be more than enough.'

'So it would, Lestrade, and that is precisely why we shall not do it. A telegram describing the day's developments, sent to the duty-officer of the Detective Division from Canonbury, will serve the purpose far better. I have taken the precaution of obtaining a copy of the duty roster from Mr Williamson, so that I may know who the recipient will be.'

As the wind fluttered the gas-lamps, the two men were driven from the elegance of the Strand, through the streets of Clerkenwell, past the smoky brickwork of St Pancras and out to the more spacious suburb of Canonbury. Lestrade's apprehension appeared to deepen as they passed Holloway and Highbury.

'You know,' said Holmes conversationally, 'I am a little surprised that someone as sharp as Benson did not sniff me out. I thought from time to time that he half-suspected something.'

'He was in your room yesterday afternoon, sir, going through the cigarette-ends. That I can tell you.'

'Was he, by Jove?' said Holmes approvingly. 'I should certainly have done the same in his place. With such a beard as I was sporting, a man who smoked a cigarette down to the very end would singe his whiskers, if not set fire to himself. He knew that I did not try to do so in company. Had he found that the butts in my room were smoked to the limit, he would have known for a certainty that the beard was false. You see? It was as well that I allowed for that.'

Sherlock Holmes was unknown to the Canonbury police-station in 'N' Division. However, one or two of the officers were acquainted with Lestrade and this paved the way for the request that Holmes was about to make. When he heard that request, as Lestrade told me long afterwards, he came closer than ever to a 'turn-up' with Holmes. 'For two pins, Dr Watson, I should have refused point-blank to have anything more to do with this madcap business.' The detective officer had lost almost all confidence in his temporary employer. Even the unmasking of Harry Benson had led only to the trickster's escape.

At length, on Holmes's insistence, Lestrade asked for a telegraph message to be wired urgently to Scotland Yard. When the form was provided, Holmes wrote upon it in bold pencilled capitals.

HENRY BENSON, ALIAS MONTGOMERY, ALIAS THE MARQUIS MONT-MORENCY, NOW IN CUSTODY HERE STOP. AWAITING INSTRUCTIONS STOP.

Then he addressed it carefully to the duty-officer of the Detective Division, and marked it 'Most Immediate'.

Lestrade stared at the message. In a shadowy corner of the Islington police-station charge-room, there was a muttered exchange.

'But he's not in custody, Mr Holmes! You know he isn't!'

'Nor ever will be, Lestrade, so long as you continue to obstruct my investigation.'

'But what's the use?'

'It has many uses,' said Holmes, in the same muttering tone, 'one of them being to save your career and possibly to keep you out of prison.'

At this point, Lestrade concluded that his mentor had gone off his head or that, in any case, argument was useless. The wire was sent. Twenty minutes later, the reply rattled out. Holmes read it and showed it to his companion.

FIND THAT BENSON IS NOT THE MAN WE WANT STOP. RELEASE FROM CUSTODY STOP = CARTER, INSPECTOR, SCOTLAND YARD.

Lestrade looked up with a terrible realization dawning in his dark eyes.

'Carter? I have never heard of any Inspector Carter!'

'No,' said Holmes grimly, 'nor has anyone else. However, I would scarcely expect our correspondent to put his own name to this. I had intended to leave the arrest of Benson and Kurr until tomorrow but you may be sure that before this wire was sent to us another was despatched to them, advising them to get out of the country at once.'

'You know where they are?'

Holmes paused, then he said, 'They are not unfamiliar to me. Unless I am greatly mistaken, they are in a house owned by Kurr at Canonbury, packing their traps. To say that there is not a moment to lose is generally an exaggeration. On the present occasion it is correct. Gather all the men you can from this division and we shall do this thing by dark. They cannot expect us yet.'

Twenty minutes later a dozen helmeted officers followed Holmes and Lestrade through the darkened avenues of Canonbury.

'How could you know where to find him?' Lestrade asked uneasily.

'Benson has a villa on the Isle of Wight. They would scarcely have gone there at this time of night. Billy Kurr is a bookmaker and the owner of two racehorses. The names of the animals and their proprietor are to be found in the breeders guide. Ah, yes! The Laurels, if I am not mistaken.'

They were standing at the gateway of a house set back at the end of a long drive. Through the fir trees and the laurel shrubberies, Holmes could make out a long veranda with two doors and several windows opening on to it. There were lights on behind two of the three windows, though the curtains were drawn. With Lestrade and two of the senior men from Canonbury, he went on ahead. They walked on the wet grass to one side of the drive to silence their footsteps. It was not difficult to keep the thick laurel bushes between themselves and the windows. Yet the wind was so strong that evening and its gusts moved the branches so erratically that it was hard to tell whether anyone was concealed ahead of them.

Where the drive curved to the left, towards the portico of the house, Lestrade was suddenly blinded by a magnesium brilliance. He could hear his antagonist but it was impossible to see him through the glare. Holmes had stopped, his hand shielding his eyes.

The flare illuminated him like a stage spotlight. At that moment there was a crash that made his ears ring. The bullet made a sharp crack as it chipped a stone wall.

Lestrade and the two men from 'N' Division threw themselves flat. Holmes remained upright, without the least movement, like a predator about to spring. Lestrade assured me that he could swear our friend's pulse did not change nor did that steely resolve falter as a second bullet flew past him.

Holmes, however, paid no less a tribute to the Scotland Yard man. Lestrade was on his feet again. He scarcely raised his voice, yet his words rapped across that damp shrubbery as plain and ominous as the bullets.

'Don't be a fool, Billy Kurr! This means murder!'

There was no sound nor movement.

'You haven't got enough bullets in that gun for us all, Billy! One of us will catch you if the others don't. And if it comes to that, you'll hang long and hard!'

There was a long minute of silence. Lestrade spoke again, as if someone had just given him news.

'Give it up, Billy! The others have taken Benson! You can't do it on your own!'

A man walked towards them slowly from the light. Billy Kurr stopped and looked at Lestrade. Then he looked at Sherlock Holmes, who said not a word, and then at the other men barring the driveway. Lestrade, lean and grim, was the hero of the hour.

'It's no good, Billy. The game's over.'

Kurr, in the same dog's-tooth check and gripping the revolver that he had held on them in the hotel-room, stretched out his hand and surrendered the weapon to Lestrade.

The other men came into the glare of the lamp.

'You haven't got Benson,' said Kurr sadly. 'You couldn't have. He's still in the house.'

Sherlock Holmes nodded to Lestrade. He walked forward with long easy strides, pushing open a veranda door to claim the fugitive.

XI

The scandal that broke in the wake of these arrests filled every newspaper in October 1877, when a third of the Detective Division of Scotland Yard stood in the dock of the Central Criminal Court. Both Sergeant Meiklejohn and Inspector Clarke, the second-in-command of the division, were among them.

Benson and Kurr had already gone to prison for a string of frauds so long that there is scarcely room to recite them here. As Mycroft Holmes had told his brother, the Society for Insuring Against Losses on the Turf and the City of Paris Loan were only the two latest in a series stretching back for many years. No sooner were the criminals in custody, however, than Harry Benson offered the authorities what he called 'Flower Show Information'.

Believing that his Scotland Yard officers, whom he had bribed and entertained so lavishly over the years, had deserted and deceived him, Benson gave his gaolers the full story of systematic corruption within the Detective Division. In Edinburgh and other cities he had practised the boldest and most widespread swindles, knowing that he had only to run back to London to be safe. From police forces throughout the land, even from the Continent, had come letters and wires to Scotland Yard, naming Harry Benson and Billy Kurr as the wanted men. One after another these messages were destroyed by officers so steeped in corruption that to turn back was more perilous than to continue. Detectives and criminals alike stood in fear of their crimes being brought to justice.

Holmes took little pleasure in witnessing the tragedy of such men as Clarke and Meiklejohn. Yet the consequence was that he now established himself as a confidant of Superintendent Williamson and the senior echelons of the Metropolitan Police. Inspector Lestrade, in his new rank, was vindicated as an honest and able officer, despite the occasional strictures passed upon him by Sherlock Holmes. Indeed, though the old structure of the Detective Police was abolished and a new Criminal Investigation Department set up, Lestrade was first to be a senior inspector in the newly-created

Special Branch, whose activities were naturally of great interest to Sherlock Holmes.

I have always thought that the arrest of Benson and Kurr, as well as the cleansing of 'Williamson's Augean Stables', to use Holmes's term for it, was the culmination of my friend's early career. Within a fortnight of being called upon, his skill had put an end to the most dangerous series of frauds and rooted out corruption at the heart of Scotland Yard. In dealing with the swindlers, his keen mind had seen where the weakest point of his antagonists lay. He knew that a sharper like Benson would never be able to resist a 'mug' like James Lester Valence. Taking the jeweller Regnier into his confidence, Holmes had laid his snare with a skill that few confidence men could have rivalled. He assured me he knew, before he started, that 'Poodle' Benson had performed a similar trick on a wealthy American in Paris. The chance to repeat it in London would therefore be irresistible. My friend would tell his story, chuckle, and then say, 'I don't mind confessing to you, Watson, I have always had an idea that I would have made a highly efficient criminal.'

For that reason alone, he was a match for Harry Benson and Billy Kurr. Perhaps, in describing his triumph over them at the Charing Cross Hotel, he might better have called his adventure, 'The Case of the Biter Bit'.

The Case of the
Naked Bicyclists

I

It was very seldom that I felt a sense of oppression during the tenancy of our Baker Street rooms. However, the visit of Mr William Coote, Solicitor to the National Vigilance Association, scarcely promised to be a light-hearted affair.

Holmes and I had met Mr Coote several years previously in the matter of a forged will. During that transaction, the lawyer elicited that Holmes had been a friend and admirer of the late Sir Richard Burton, renowned as an explorer, anthropologist and translator of *The Arabian Nights*. Mr Coote had heard that Lady Burton intended to dispose of a manuscript of her husband's, Sir Richard's translation of *The Perfumed Garden*, a somewhat racy classic of Arabian love-literature. Mr Coote expressed great interest in purchasing this rarity.

We assumed that Coote intended to publish this work in a learned edition or perhaps to offer the autograph to the British Museum. What was our horror on hearing that the relic had been bought so that he and his confounded vigilance association might commit it to the flames! The burning of any book, let alone this monument to a friend's labours, was an abomination to Sherlock Holmes.

It had therefore taken some persuasion before my friend would consent to receive Mr Coote in his consulting-rooms. Had it not been for the inertia of the criminal classes in the warm summer weather, and the tedium consequent upon this, Holmes would scarcely have bothered to listen to Coote's submission. As it was, he promised 'to hear what the wretched fellow has to say'. I quite expected him to grant Coote an audience merely for the pleasure of telling him to go to the devil. Indeed, I believe that had been his intention. As for Miss Pierce, the client who accompanied her legal adviser to Baker Street, she was described as the tenant of a grim, remotely-situated house near Saffron Walden, and a warm supporter of the Vigilance Association.

It is seldom that two people look so absurd, side by side, as this couple appeared. Mr Coote, with his ample watch-chained waistcoat, large head, mournful moustache, and a soulful superiority in his brown eyes, brought to my mind Mr Chadband in *Bleak House*: 'A large, greasy, self-satisfied man, of no particular denomination'. Whether the lawyer's baritone voice sounded unctuous or melodious must be a matter of taste.

Miss Pierce was a starveling sparrow paired with a glossy crow. She was a lady of middle years, slight and frail, the type who is destined to outlive us all. She wore a grey old-fashioned bonnet, trimmed with mauve and white silk flowers, a specimen of headgear whose very fit was tight and mean. Her features were strict and almost motionless. Such movement as there was came principally from the glint of her spectacle-lenses in gold-wire frames.

After Holmes had waved them to their chairs, Mr Coote presented his client's complaint. Miss Pierce said little, except that she had a curious habit of echoing softly what she considered the most important word in the lawyer's previous sentence, lest Holmes should miss it. Sometimes she gave sound to the word. Where the utterance was repugnant, her pursed lips formed the syllables with significant emphasis but no voice. Mr Coote cleared his throat deeply and significantly, as if to launch into an aria beside a piano and a fern.

'Miss Pierce, as I indicated in my letter Mr Holmes, has been much troubled in past weeks—months I might say—by the indelicate conduct of her neighbour.'

'Indelicate,' mouthed Miss Pierce in her slight, bird-like tone, 'yes.'

'My client is a maiden lady, living alone, but for the company of a single servant-woman.'

'Servant,' Miss Pierce murmured, with an eye to the niceties of social class.

'My client's residence lies in a remote part of Essex, separated by a field and a rivulet from the adjoining property of Coldhams Farm. It is six-and-a-half miles from Saffron Walden, eight-and-a-half from Bishop's Stortford. From the railway at Audley End, it is four miles, twelve hundred and twenty-seven yards.'

I guessed that these meticulous measurements would prove a useful means for Mr Coote to run up a tidy little bill at Miss Pierce's expense.

'I find it curious,' said Holmes quietly, 'that such care has been taken over these distances and none at all as to that between your client and the house at Coldhams Farm.'

Mr Coote gave a faint but satisfied smile.

'Mr Holmes, we should require permission to go upon Captain Dougal's land. My client would rather not make such a request.'

'Rather not,' echoed Miss Pierce nervously.

'Very well,' Holmes shrugged, as if it did not much matter, since he might give Coote his marching orders at any minute. 'Pray continue if you wish to.'

'Captain Dougal,' said the lawyer, frowning at such levity, 'is the proprietor of Coldhams Farm, scarcely more than a small-holding. The offence alleged is one of the most blatant indecency.'

'Blatant!' Miss Pierce mouthed the word silently but with a significant nod.

'I venture to think,' said Coote in a silkier Chadband voice, 'that it may in all probability be a case of devil-worship.'

At this point, Holmes ceased lounging and sat up.

'Pray do continue, Mr Coote.'

'Dougal is a man of bad character and evil reputation with young women. In the three years he has lived at the farm, no less than four paternity summonses have been served upon him on behalf of young women of the labouring class.'

'Summonses!' Miss Pierce gave a satisfied nod at the memory of seeing justice done.

'Female servants have come and gone. Respectable girls are soon fetched away by their families. Those of no character remain until they depart to childbed. It is common knowledge that while there were two sisters in his employ, he had his way with one of them in the very presence of the other.'

Miss Pierce looked quickly at the three of us, finding no word that could be decently echoed.

'Forgive me,' said Holmes with the faintest hint of malice, 'I take it that your client does not seek a post as servant in Captain Dougal's household. Nor is she of the labouring class. I daresay that Captain Dougal is as you paint him. However, there is surely nothing in law that even such a man as he may not live on land adjoining Miss Pierce's.'

'It is a matter of the bicyclists in the field, Mr Holmes, if it is not indeed something worse,' Mr Coote said abruptly.

Miss Pierce looked at us significantly. Holmes stared at Mr Coote.

'I see—or, rather I do not see. What bicyclists in which field?'

The solicitor assumed the expression of a man weighted with grief.

'This scoundrel, Dougal, leads a life of unrepentant viciousness and unexampled impiety. In such a remote part of the county, it is not difficult for a rascal of a little wealth and plausible manner to entice the ruder and more rustic young women into his repellent practices. I concede that what he does in his own house is something difficult to control. What he does in the open air, in the public view, is quite another matter. I speak of Captain Dougal and a dozen of the village girls, as they perform their lewd ceremonies in the field adjacent to Miss Pierce's land.'

Miss Pierce gave us a flash of her spectacles.

'Like Satan at a witches' coven,' Mr Coote continued, 'this man spends his nights training these female clodhoppers as a team of naked bicyclists!'

'Naked!' Miss Pierce's lips formed the word soundlessly but with great vigour.

Holmes and I avoided one another's eyes, though I confess I was reduced to the expedient of vigorous nose-blowing.

'Dear me,' said Holmes at length, addressing Mr Coote and avoiding Miss Pierce, as seemed to be her wish. 'Then you already have the remedy at hand, my dear sir. The rural constabulary, though slow in acting upon information received, may generally be relied upon in the long run. There are laws of public nuisance, are there not? There are statutes to punish indecent display.'

'Exactly!'

'Then surely, my dear sir, you have your answer.'

Mr Coote shook his head.

'No, Mr Holmes. You misunderstand me. If Miss Pierce were to lay an information in that way, she must be drawn into the centre of the scandal, for these particular activities in the field affect only her. Publicity could scarcely be avoided. Suppose that it should be, as I suppose, some form of diabolism! Greatly though I sympathize with my client . . .'

Miss Pierce nodded emphatically.

'. . . it would scarcely do for the name of a legal adviser to the National Vigilance Association to be quoted in such a context. There are not wanting those who would mock, Mr Holmes!'

There was a silence while Miss Pierce looked round at us all and waited.

'Am I to take it,' said Holmes slowly, 'that you propose my name as the centrepiece of this bicycling scandal?'

Mr Coote had the grace to look a little embarrassed.

'You are known as a detective, Mr Holmes. Your name has been associated with murder, robbery, blackmail, adultery, espionage. It would do you no harm and, I say without doubt, you would put a stop to these insults easily enough.'

'Indeed!'

'Chivalry will remind you, Mr Holmes, how much a lady of gentle ways like Miss Pierce would suffer. The local esteem in which she is held would be compromised by association with such proceedings. Of course, if you will not take the case, you will not. I urge it as a matter of respect for gentility, sir.'

Miss Pierce performed a brief cat-like and confidential closing of the eyes.

Sherlock Holmes reached for his pipe. Miss Pierce uttered a quick cough-like sound of alarm. He withdrew his hand.

'Tell me, Mr Coote. What precisely takes place in the field at night?'

'As I understand it, Mr Holmes, these women are entirely naked. They disport themselves in gross rituals, forming a circle about the evil one, if I may so term him. Captain Dougal stands at the centre and commands their depravities.'

'I do not quite follow you. How does he command them?'

'I believe he shouts at them,' said Mr Coote self-consciously. 'He tells them what to do.'

'And what do they do?'

'I understand that they perform lewd acrobatic postures upon bicycles,' said Mr Coote, a little angry at this continued cross-questioning.

'Postures,' Miss Pierce confirmed.

'Dear me,' Holmes said, as if the outrage were beyond anything he had supposed, 'and what costume does Captain Dougal wear?'

'None,' said Mr Coote snappishly. 'He stands there quite naked!'

'Quite!' said Miss Pierce, sharp in her turn.

'In a state of gross and rude excitement,' added Coote portentously.

After twenty minutes more of this sort of thing, Mr Coote and Miss Pierce took their departure. Sherlock Holmes had yet to commit himself but assured them that he would give their request, that he should make an immediate visit to the neighbourhood of

Coldhams Farm, his most careful consideration. As soon as they had gone, I turned to my friend in some indignation.

'I call that the most infernal cheek! To come with such a story, when they had only to go to the police-station at Saffron Walden! Do they suppose we have nothing better to do with our time than follow a goose-chase of this kind?'

Holmes was lounging in the old-fashioned chair, filling his pipe in earnest.

'You are quite right, my dear fellow. It is absurd, is it not? That is half its attraction. It verges upon the pathological. Indeed, there is an item in the works of the great German baron upon *equus eroticus*. Unless I am much mistaken, Watson, there lurks in that bleak fen-land a criminality of which Mr Coote and Miss Pierce have never dreamt. I doubt if there could be better use of our time than a visit to this bucolic Lothario and his bumpkins.'

I feared there would be something like this, as soon as I heard a suggestion of devil-worship.

'I don't see it,' I said impatiently.

He chuckled.

'I daresay not, my dear old Watson. We will reflect, and then discuss it again this evening. For the moment, let us just take the precaution of consulting Bradshaw upon the trains between Liverpool Street and Bishop's Stortford. In this instance, I believe the Cambridge line will prove the most convenient.'

II

After so much scoffing at the absurdity of Miss Pierce's complaint, I do not think that in all my life I was so occupied as in the next few weeks. Two days later, Holmes and I stepped from the train at Bishop's Stortford to be met by Henry Pilgrim's pony and trap, commandeered as a cab in this flat desolate country. We drove through summer fenland for several miles, the hedges white with hawthorn blossom, at first following the railway line where it ran northwards to Cambridge. Then our driver veered briskly into a lane, which soon forked into a smaller lane, then into a track that was scarcely a lane at all.

Ahead of us I glimpsed, through a screen of trees, the outline of a modest farmhouse with a steep dark roof, diamond-patterned by tiles of a lighter red. There was a yard in front of the door. A narrow water-filled moat appeared to surround the property, with a screen of dark firs and stunted apple-trees that made a gloomy enclosure even on a sunny afternoon. I supposed that this must be Miss Pierce's residence but our driver pointed his whip as we clattered past and said confidentially, 'Captain Dougal, Coldhams Farm.'

I suppose a further half-mile passed before we turned into a by-way of trim hedges and clipped verges, ending at our client's porch.

'It seems a good distance between the properties for her to see from one to the other, with the light failing,' I said to Holmes sceptically.

He glanced round.

'I daresay it does. If you will observe the lie of the land, however, the field surrounding Coldhams Farm comes out almost as far as this.'

So much for our arrival. As I feared, the grim outer landscape of fens and drainage ditches was a pinprick compared to the comfortless domestic economy of Miss Pierce. Supper was a spartan celebration of boiled cod and hard peas, which I should prefer to forget and could not eat. When I murmured a complaint to Holmes, he merely said, 'Since the mental faculties become refined and sharpened by starvation, I suppose one should not object to such a bill of fare. It has often crossed my mind, Watson, to remind you that what the digestion gains from the blood supply is lost to the brain.'

It was then almost ten o'clock and we were led by Miss Pierce and Mr Coote to a room at the attic level. From this vantage, we were to keep observation that evening, and all night if need be.

'Forgive me,' said Holmes, as he passed to a round-arched landing window at the level of the main bedrooms, 'surely one's view of

Captain Dougal's field is blocked at this height by the lime tree and the beech?'

Mr Coote looked as if he were dealing with a simpleton.

'Of course it is, Mr Holmes. It is from the top floor that one sees the performances of Captain Dougal and his harlots.'

Holmes and I glanced at one another but made no reply. We followed our guides up a narrower set of bare wooden stairs to a box-room at the level of the attics. A single camp-bed with three army 'biscuits' as a mattress was the sole concession to sleep. At this level, it was true, a window looked directly across the field to the little moat and the dark stifling fir trees of Coldhams Farm, almost half a mile away. In the foreground a waning half-moon glimmered on reedy pools and patches of mud in the intervening pasture. Black trees stood low on a vast horizon and the dim figures of cattle were visible here and there.

I do not know how long we waited, with the intense silence of that landscape weighing upon us. I thought of Baker Street and how we should now be taking a glass of something warm in the company of Inspector Lestrade and hearing news of Scotland Yard. At length Mr Coote said, 'See for yourself!'

I looked at the field before me but saw only the grey outlines of cattle. Even Holmes, as he narrowed his keen eyes, looked puzzled.

'I see nothing,' I said gruffly.

'Of course you do not!' said Miss Pierce angrily. 'Not here! Over there! Take these! And stand up there!'

With that she handed me a pair of binoculars whose variable lenses included a pair for night vision. They were such glasses as would only be used by a serving officer on campaign—or a troublesome crone determined to spy on the world after dark. She also indicated a stout wooden shoe-box, necessary to increase her own diminutive height as observer but scarcely for us.

What Holmes and I saw—through a glass most darkly—was a foggy impression of Dougal and his rustic wenches two or three hundred yards away. There was an occasional call or cry and a fleeting drift of laughter. What I saw might have been libidinous, had it not been so absurd and indistinct. Half a dozen clod-hopping young females were riding bicycles with a little difficulty over the fenland turf.

At this distance, it seemed that each young equestrienne had been chosen for her ample or muscular form, each pair of haunches more than overlapping the saddle while strapping legs strove to drive the pedals. From time to time, one or other of these rustic valkyries would attempt to perform some mildly acrobatic feat in response to the command of her ringmaster, and several fell off. Since the turf was soft, I suppose it was little hardship.

At the centre of this ensemble stood a tall and portly man with dark hair and an abundant beard. He was completely naked and, unless my eyes deceived me in such obscurity, both his face and his loins suggested a state of priapic frenzy.

Though I am conscious that I may already have described too fully a scene which would better remain veiled, some account of it is necessary to an understanding of what followed. Our hosts retired, leaving Holmes and me to perform the rest of this ridiculous sentry-go. From our observation, it was supposed that we were to present a complaint against Dougal—in our own names, so that the modest cheeks of Miss Pierce or Mr Coote should not be brought to the blush. What fools they were making of us!

As soon as we were alone together I swore to Holmes that I should return to London the next morning. If necessary, I would go alone. My friend was convulsed with laughter, struggling not to allow his eruptions of mirth to be heard all over the house.

'That woman cannot see so far as her own end of the field but by climbing up a window in the attic,' I said furiously. 'Even then she can make nothing out except with military binoculars. Do not tell me, Holmes, that her maiden modesty is insulted! She has done everything to ensure that she may not miss a single lewdness! I daresay the whisper of her conduct has got round the neighbourhood, so we are now brought in to save her reputation.'

For reasons which I could not have anticipated, however, we did not go back to London the next day. At breakfast, while the servant was replenishing the coffee-pot, I remarked to Holmes that the case against Dougal was a fuss about nothing. I did this in the hope that Miss Pierce, who was in the adjoining parlour with Mr Coote, might hear me—or that if she did not hear herself, the honest servant would repeat my words to her. The servant, a round-faced aproned body, put down the pot and said, 'Never mind those young trollops on the bicycles, sir. You ask him where that poor gentle soul Miss Holland went to. She's gone a year or two now and never been seen nor heard from since.'

The change in Sherlock Holmes was characteristic. His back straightened, his features were as still as carved ivory while he listened to her. Then he said softly, 'Tell me about Miss Holland, if you will.'

The woman looked towards the parlour, where lurked Miss Pierce and the lawyer.

'I can't tell you more, sir. All I say is that such a refined and gentle lady as she was, she went unaccountably away without a word and never came back. Not a word of warning. As if she'd been swept off the face of the earth.'

'Will you not, at least, tell me who she was?'

Now there was no mistaking a mixture of triumph and contempt in the servant's face.

'Mrs Dougal, she liked to call herself, until the real Mrs Dougal come and put a stop to it all.'

'Then it is scarcely surprising that she should vanish, is it?' I suggested.

But the woman would say no more, beyond murmuring significantly that she knew the value of her place and the cost of an action for slander with which Captain Dougal had threatened others. Miss Pierce, when asked about Miss Holland, professed to know nothing about the dealings of the captain with any of his women.

'Such creatures come and go at Coldhams week by week! How should anybody know which is which? Mrs Dougal? They'd all be

Mrs Dougals, if they had their way. As it is, there's half a dozen that must have borne his children but don't bear his name.'

Breakfast had been little more than bread and gruel, accompanied by coffee whose odour was chiefly of dandelions and chicory. Nothing would persuade me to spend another day under Miss Pierce's roof. I had gone to pack my overnight things. Holmes announced his intention of taking his morning pipe out of doors, smoking being forbidden on Miss Pierce's premises.

I finished my preparations and waited. A full hour passed as I stood at the window of that uncarpeted and unpainted box-room, staring morosely across the fenland that glimmered in the morning sun. The dark trees screened Captain Dougal's property and his rustic harem from the world. There are those who, in the smoking-rooms of their clubs, might chaff one another about the captain's midnight romps with country lasses. To such vulgar souls, the promiscuous intercourse of Dougal and his bicyclists seems no more shocking than the couplings of bull and cow. Perhaps it was my mood that morning, or perhaps it was the flat and unfrequented countryside before me, that made Coldhams Farm appear at that moment one of the darkest and most sinister retreats upon this earth.

It was quite an hour and half before I heard Holmes climbing the attic stairs. He threw open the door, looking extraordinarily pleased with himself.

'I think we shall move on,' he said cheerfully.

'Do you mean to return to London?'

He sat down on the only chair, an abandoned relic of the dining-room, and began to refill his tobacco-pouch.

'Not quite, Watson. However, I have found a far more agreeable lodging from which we may continue our observation.'

'Why continue it? Have we not seen everything there is to see?'

He frowned and put away the pouch.

'I should have thought so until this morning. Yet something in my bones forbids me to abandon this investigation just yet.'

'Miss Holland?'

'Precisely.'

'But what have we to do with Miss Holland?'

'Possibly nothing, Watson. Ladies may vanish and never be heard of again in the place where they were. That is quite true. The naked cyclists are exciting only to a sterile soul like Miss Pierce and a pompous buffoon like Mr Coote. Put it all together, however, add the gloomy spirit of Coldhams Farm, and I should never rest quite easily if I returned to London today.'

'Then you feel it?' I asked eagerly. 'The sinister air that the place has, so remote, so enclosed, like something out of . . .'

'A gothic romance?' he suggested with a laugh.

'But where shall we find rooms? We must be miles from anywhere.'

'It is arranged. Moat Farm takes in paying guests. I am to be Professor Holmes, holder of a chair of entomology at Cambridge, here for a few days' holiday, and you—well, naturally, my dear fellow—you are Dr Watson.'

'Where is Moat Farm?'

'Very close. We passed it yesterday.'

For a moment I was puzzled and then a doubt clouded my mind.

'You don't mean . . .'

'Moat Farm,' said Holmes simply, 'is the name that Captain Dougal gave to Coldhams when he purchased it.'

III

'Impossible!'

'Hear what I have to say,' Holmes suggested soothingly. 'Dougal is not the particular villain that Coote and Miss Pierce have painted, though he seems to have arrogated the rank of captain to himself. In many respects, he is thought to have led a blameless, even estimable, life. He is spoken of at Quendon, in the Hare and Hounds, as a very decent fellow.'

'He did not seem so last night!'

'You have never seen the man. Can you swear that the creature was Dougal? Perhaps, if it was he, there is still a better side to the man. Even you, Watson, can scarcely believe that those bicycling antics amount to devil worship! That is all Coote's nonsense.'

'A better side to him?'

Holmes stood up and crossed to the window.

'What would you say as an army man, Watson, to a fellow who had served for twenty-two years in the Royal Engineers, earned a pension for it, and was described on his discharge sheet as being of excellent character?'

'How have you seen his discharge sheet? Or how do you know what is said about him in a public house?'

'I spoke to the landlord, with whom I fell in during my stroll. As for the discharge sheet, Dougal himself showed it to me.' Holmes turned from the window. 'He takes in paying guests, has rooms vacant, and produces his army record to seal the bargain.'

Despite my misgivings over Coldhams Farm, I relented a little towards its owner.

'I have still half a mind to go back to London this morning.'

Holmes sighed.

'One more thing, before you do. On my little walk, I spoke to two other folk who happened to pass me. They do not seem to like Captain Dougal much. For that matter, nor are they much smitten with Miss Pierce. One of them, however, also recalled Miss Holland and the abrupt manner of her departure from Dougal's household. If my informant is correct, there was talk of foul play at the time and the matter was investigated by the local police. They were convinced that there was nothing sinister in Miss Holland's departure.'

I moved towards my leather bag.

'Then it is high time we were on our way.'

Holmes touched his finger to his lips.

'One moment, friend Watson. Do I assume that you now regard a rustic police force as the last word upon a lady's disappearance?'

'Unless there is evidence to the contrary in this case.'

'There is a further puzzle in this, more suited to the alienist than to a police officer. I am told that Miss Camille Holland was a genteel spinster, quite fifty, older than Captain Dougal. In religion, she adhered to the quaint London sect of the Catholic Apostolic Church in Gordon Square. A devout lady of some means, her family consisting of two nephews with whom she rarely communicated.'

'Scarcely surprising, then, that no one knows where she went.'

'One moment more. There was, it seems, another side to Miss Holland. She was quite fifty. Yet her hair was coloured and styled, her face was improved, in such a way that she looked some ten years younger. She strove also, they say, to wear the trousers. Our fading spinster relished equally the roles of vamp and martinet. Aphrodite and a dash of Juno.'

'My dear Holmes, this is nothing. A woman of some maturity may surely try to make herself look less than her age. As for the martinet, women who are uncertain with men, or lack experience, sometimes take refuge in a maternal authority. Miss Holland's type is not at all uncommon. I see no puzzle.'

'The puzzle,' said he, 'is what such a ladylike, refined, devout creature was doing in the arms of a reprobate like Dougal.'

'Perhaps she was not in his arms.'

'Why, then, did she bother to present herself as Mrs Dougal to everyone in the neighbourhood?'

I shrugged and gave it up.

'Unfortunately, Holmes, you and I have reason to know that refined, ladylike creatures are not infrequently drawn to reprobates and ruffians rather than to men of their own kind. I can tell you no more than that.'

He stared from the window at the wide sky and the vast fenland horizon.

'It is true,' he conceded, 'that the most abandoned female lusts often thrive more vigorously in the school-house or the rectory than in any den of thieves. How curious, however, if she should be buried somewhere out there.'

'If it is so, and if we stay under that fellow's roof, we may soon be buried out there ourselves. We have already missed the best morning train from Bishop's Stortford. At this rate, we shall miss the 1.30 from Cambridge to Liverpool Street as well.'

But even as I spoke, I knew that Holmes would not leave matters as they were. I knew also that I could not return to London without him.

IV

Closer acquaintance with Dougal and Coldhams Farm did not reconcile me to either. He was a large man with an abundant head of hair, a brown pointed beard somewhat streaked with grey, brows high and slanting. His eyes were almost Mongolian in shape and had a cruelly humorous look. I fear he laughed at the world rather than with it. Despite Holmes's suggestion, he was at once identifiable as the figure standing among naked bicyclists the previous night.

No doubt this owner of the farm, with a little money in hand, would be thought a good fellow in the public house where he stood drinks to the locals. At home, two lumbering young servants, Sally and Agnes, attended the captain and his guests. I cannot say that I witnessed improprieties between the young women and their employer, yet the glances between them were more eloquent than spoken assignations or invitations. The nocturnal orgy in the field was not repeated during our stay. Even Dougal was not blatant enough to amuse himself a few yards from the windows of his guests. I supposed that he took his bicycling troupe elsewhere for the duration of our visit.

I concede at once that the food and accommodation proved in every way superior to Miss Pierce's joyless fare. Captain Dougal ate separately but our table was plentifully supplied with well-cooked dishes and local ale.

'Professor' Holmes of Cambridge was also masquerading as an amateur lepidopterist. Therefore, next morning, we set out for

Bishop's Stortford to procure a butterfly-net, a chloroform bottle, and a specimen case. Holmes then took the precaution of despatching a telegram to Lestrade at Scotland Yard. I caught only the last line. REPLY CARE OF MARDEN, ESSEX CONSTABULARY, SAFFRON WALDEN STOP. LETTER FOLLOWS STOP.

That afternoon, Holmes went off, conspicuously alone, in tweed-suit and gaiters, deer-stalker, magnifying-glass in hand, butterfly net upon his shoulder. His satchel contained the killing-bottle and specimen case. The hedges were bright with white flowers in May sun, the little rivers well-watered.

I made a survey of our quarters. Moat Farm, as Dougal called it, was surrounded by twenty feet of lawn. Beyond that, the entire plot was cut off by the moat, several feet wide and well-filled. A single footbridge crossed the water to the farm-yard, with its cowshed and an annexe for the pony-trap. Beyond a screen of trees lay a pond and barn, then the open stretches of flat pasture stretched to the very horizon.

Next morning, with sandwiches and a flask, we started together in our search for Purple Emperors and Marbled Whites. Once out of sight of the farm, Holmes took a field-path that led to the village of Quendon. A few minutes more and we had negotiated the hire of a horse and trap. By eleven, we faced Inspector Marden at the table of the interview room in Saffron Walden police-station. Marden was a tall cadaverous man with a look of gloom that might have graced a professional pall-bearer. Yet he was a decent enough fellow, who spoke quietly and made his arguments with care. Before he had finished, I was sure we must pack our bags and go home, for all the good we should do here.

'I don't see it, Mr Holmes,' he said cautiously, 'Miss Holland left Captain Dougal, as all his ladies seem to do sooner or later. There was talk at the time, there always is. Inquiries were made and they proved entirely to our satisfaction. We made them discreetly, of course. I don't suppose he or she knew of them.'

'But not so discreetly made as ours may be,' Holmes said quickly, 'for we are under the man's roof.'

'So you may be, sir. A police force, however, is not to engage upon espionage. Nor, if you take my advice, will you.'

'Where did she go?'

'I understand she left Captain Dougal to travel abroad with another man. She was to join him on a yacht, I was told. Just before she left, Miss Holland bought new clothes accordingly. The captain had no reason to get rid of her, for as long as she was with him, her money was there.'

'Did he have much need of it?'

Marden pulled a face.

'I can't see he did, Mr Holmes. He owns the farm outright, or did when we made inquiries. Since then, he always seems well-breeched, as they say.'

'And what of her money now?'

'She does not draw directly at the bank, but then she never did. The last we heard, Miss Holland was drawing by cheque so that it went to wherever she might be or to whomever had to be paid. When necessary, she would write for a new cheque-book. Her family bankers are the National Provincial in Piccadilly. Her stock-brokers are Messrs Hart of Old Broad Street in the City of London. She dealt with them both long after she left here. Mr Hensler, her broker, and Mr Ashwin, the senior accountant of the National Pro-vincial, both swore that the signatures on her cheques and letters match the specimen signature she gave at the bank a little before she left here. We asked advice from our handwriting experts. They confirm it.'

'These signatures . . .'

'Ah, yes, Mr Holmes. Your reputation goes before you.'

Marden managed a dry smile as he opened a drawer and shook several photographs from an envelope. They were exact confidential copies, taken from the files for our benefit. I could see plainly the specimen in the book and the signatures on the cheques. 'Camille C. Holland'. There was a further photograph of a demure woman, slightly-built and pretty, her fine hair elegantly-coiffeured.

'Golden-haired,' I said at a guess, feeling sure it was so.

'So she was, Dr Watson, and may be still.'

Holmes studied the prints through his glass for several minutes. Then he looked up.

'It pains me to say so, Mr Marden, but there can be no doubt that the hand which wrote the signatures upon the cheques is also that which provided the specimen in the book.'

'There you have it, sir,' said the inspector philosophically. 'If that is her signature, then she was certainly still alive a little while ago, two years and more after the rumours began.'

Holmes nodded. He put away his glass and picked up his hat.

'You are a busy man, inspector, and we will take up no more of your time. I shall communicate with Lestrade directly.'

As Marden led us to the police-station entrance I felt a mixture of regret for my friend's disappointment and relief that we might see our comfortable quarters in Baker Street that evening. As we stood with the inspector upon the steps, Holmes said casually, 'Tell me, did your informants recall any other event about the time Miss Holland attended the bank to sign the specimen book?'

Marden looked blank for a moment, then he nodded.

'There was one matter, though of little relevance. Just before this, her younger nephew's little girl had died. Miss Holland was much affected by the child's death and wrote very kindly to her nephew. However, Mr Holland recalled that his aunt did not attend the funeral. Perhaps she feared questions about her removal to Quendon, or suspicions that she had taken a lover. I fear that will not help you much, Mr Holmes.'

'I daresay not,' he remarked cheerfully. On walking back to the waiting horse and trap, I noticed with misgiving that his step was far jauntier than upon our arrival. When we were out of earshot of Inspector Marden, he turned to me.

'She is out there, Watson!' he said softly, 'I thought so once—and now I know it!'

V

How he could know anything of the sort from Inspector Marden's answers was quite beyond me. Holmes, as usual, preserved an infuriating silence upon the matter, which was usually the prelude to some startling discovery. That afternoon, he set off alone again with his net and satchel. As he passed the wicket gate of the bridge across the little moat and strode towards the sunlight of the pale green fens, he had altered nothing in his dress or physical appearance. Yet, suddenly, he was every inch the professor from Cambridge, as if he could never have been anything else.

He returned half an hour before dinner. There was not a butterfly to be seen in his killing-bottle, for he abominated the destruction of such beautiful creatures. Instead, there reposed the remains of a most unpromising insect which appeared to be a cross between a daddy-longlegs and a dark brown moth. I am no expert on the vast insect population of the English fields and had not, so far as I was aware, ever noticed this one in my travels. Holmes said nothing further and I was not disposed to inquire. When I went to rouse him from his room, as the gong sounded downstairs, I found him with the creature lying on a square of white paper, his pipe in his mouth and his magnifying-glass closely applied to the remains. From time to time, he would jot a note and then resume his scrutiny.

Jaded by the collapse of our adventure, I retired after dinner with a copy of the *Lancet* and an article upon Richet's discovery of abnormal sensitivities to the anti-diphtheria serum, a matter of possible interest in my own practice. A little after ten o'clock, I was aware of voices below me, a burst of dull-witted laughter, a gate closing, and then silence. Absorbed in my journal, I paid no attention. A moment later there was a thundering on my door. Before I could reply, Holmes had thrown it open.

'Get up, Watson! Quickly, man! We must make the most of every minute.'

'To what end?'

'To search the house, of course! We are alone here for the moment, unless Miss Holland—or rather some other woman of his—should be a prisoner or a corpse within these walls. He has gone out with those two young women, his servants. I swear that they and the others are up to their games again, no doubt at a more discreet distance during our tenancy. I believe we may count on an hour at least before his return.'

With the greatest reluctance I heaved myself out of bed and followed him. It seemed a further waste of our time. Each room was just what it appeared to be. The dining-room, the parlour, the kitchen, the master's bedroom, the servants' attics, even the cellar. Not a door was locked or bolted to prevent our progress. This was scarcely the lair of a secretive and hunted man. To be sure, we did not know what furniture had belonged in the first place to Dougal, Miss Holland, or any of his other mistresses. The same was true of women's clothes which hung in one of the wardrobes of the spare room. Though some were of a size to fit the petite figure of Camille Holland, as she had been described to us, others would have done justice to the ample forms of his servant-girls.

'The clothes will tell us little,' Holmes said impatiently, 'but there is something here that will hang him more surely. I know there is.'

As he spoke he was opening, inspecting, closing again, a series of round hat-boxes at an upper level of the mahogany tall-boy.

'We shall have to give up presently,' I said anxiously, 'he will be back.'

Just then he gave a cry of triumph. In his hand was a bottle of liquid, which might have been the very colour of Miss Dougal's artificially-golden hair.

'What of it?' I said furiously. 'If she left that behind it still proves nothing.'

He looked at me pityingly and produced from the hat-box a pad of golden hair, a tortoise-shell comb and a wire hair-frame upon which the hair and comb would have been worn. He placed the pad upon the frame, added the comb and we saw again the back of

Camille Holland's head as it had appeared in Inspector Marden's photograph.

'She left them behind,' I said hopefully. 'What can it signify? She had no need of them. To whom else would they be of any use?'

He paused and said, 'To the woman who visited the National Provincial Bank in Piccadilly, when the form with a specimen of her hand was signed in Miss Holland's name.'

'They had seen her before. They would recognize an imposture. Ashwin at the bank knew who she was. A pad of hair would be no disguise.'

Holmes sat down on the bed.

'I was certain of it, as soon as Marden described the death of her nephew's child.'

'What the devil has that to do with it?'

'If I did not know you better, my dear fellow, I should believe that the country air had addled your brains. Think, man! What does a woman do when there is a bereavement in her family?'

'She attends the funeral and makes herself useful, but Miss Holland did neither.'

'Quite so. What else?'

'She goes into mourning.'

'In what form?'

'I daresay black crape, weeds anyhow, mourning jewellery, a veil. . .'

As soon as I said it, the whole thing was clear.

'Exactly!' He sprang from the bed and paced about the room. 'Miss Holland in mourning garb attended the bank that she and her family have used for a generation, though she seldom visited it. Her little niece was dead, a fact which the very newspapers might confirm and Mr Edmund Holland would, in any case, be obliged to refer to at some point. Mr Ashwin knew this lady by her dainty form, the golden hair-pad supported by the wire frame and the familiar comb. The veil was not too heavy to prevent her features being dimly discerned but enough to make them somewhat indistinct. Her voice was quiet in her grief and a little thickened, perhaps, by tears. With a proper sense of delicacy, Ashwin left her to sign the form in her own time.'

'If it was so.'

'If it was? My dear fellow, you heard Marden say that the child's death was the only other event remembered at the time of the visit to the bank! I am concerned at what may not be remembered. Was this other Camille Holland able to write in a passable imitation of the true signature? It would not have to be of the finest quality. Convinced of her identity and seeing her shaken by grief, even Mr Ashwin was convinced. Or was there a sympathetic female companion or male escort who formed the actual signature? Was Dougal himself somewhere at hand? Whatever the answer, when the work was done the form was inserted in the file of papers for her account and became her signature so far as the bank was concerned.'

He stared at the open hat-box, closed it, and replaced it on its shelf in the tall-boy. Then he turned to me again.

'That child's death was a gift from the gods for him—or rather from the devil. The only true part that the devil has had to play in all his schemes! How easy it must have been! At any other time, the imposture would have been plain. But the bank's knowledge of the child's death and the evidence of their own eyes that showed them the woman in mourning was a perfect coincidence.'

'If she was murdered by him . . .'

'She is out there, Watson, lying in this dark night, somewhere beneath the dank fenland, while Dougal and his naked trollops caper upon their bicycles above her.'

'I was about to ask whether you had concluded that she was murdered before or after the visit to the bank.'

'As to that, my friend, I have an open mind. After the visit, I expect.'

I was relieved to find him a little less dogmatic and this made me bolder.

'More to the point,' I said, 'if she is out there as you say, how are you to find her body in mile upon mile of fenland stretching from here to Cambridge, supposing that by this time there is anything left to find?'

He smiled.

'I should not allow that to disturb your rest, Watson. I have an extremely clear idea of how this investigation will end. I believe I know where she is.'

Then we had a day of Holmes at his worst. He would do nothing but lounge in a basket chair in Captain Dougal's conservatory, reading the papers and then purloining my copy of the *Lancet*, which I had scarcely begun. This continued all day. Next morning, while we were at breakfast, a boy in a blue uniform came running over the bridge and handed an envelope to Captain Dougal. Dougal brought the telegram to Holmes at the breakfast table. He made no pretence of courtesy, standing by the table as my friend read it. Holmes put it in his pocket.

'Dear me,' he said in a tone of mild apology, 'I believe I shall have to start back in a day or two. I had quite forgotten that there is a common-room meeting on Tuesday, at which we must elect a new Senior Tutor.'

Captain Dougal gave a smile that revealed, rather than hid, his contempt for such a milksop as this.

VI

As soon as Dougal was out of the room, the academic gentleness dropped like a mask from the face of Sherlock Holmes.

'We must make our move, Watson, before that fellow twigs what we are up to.'

'Why should he?'

'If I knew the answer to that, old fellow, it would not concern me. Wait here.'

I saw him go out, across the bridge and into the first field. He stood by the hedge at a point where a rabbit had made its burrow, or more sinisterly, where an animal of some sort had dug. After a careful inspection, he came back.

'I think that we must abandon the niceties of butterfly-hunting, go straight to Saffron Walden, wire Lestrade, and summon the assistance of the local police force. No, my friend, let us postpone explanations until we have Marden in our company. Once is enough.'

It was not Inspector Marden but his colleague Eli Bower who confronted us, a man who plainly loathed Holmes and his kind as much as Holmes distrusted him. Ten years later, Bower was to secure the conviction and execution of John Williams in the Hooded Man murder, which my friend always swore was a grave miscarriage of justice. We confronted this squat burly figure across the table where we had first met Marden.

'For a start, Mr Holmes,' said Bower sternly, 'I don't need your assistance in this matter. I have men enough to carry out any investigation and . . .'

'Yet you have failed to do so!'

The inspector's colour deepened.

'Who says I have not done so?'

'This little fellow says so.' Holmes took the jar from his satchel, spread a sheet of notepaper on the table, and shook on to it the remains of the insect he had been studying.

'What the devil might that be?'

'The species is a phorid fly,' said Holmes deliberately, as if addressing a backward student. 'The identification is confirmed by this telegram from Dr Cardew of the Natural History Museum, the leading man on the subject.'

'I have a police-station to run, Mr Holmes! What should I care for flies or museums?'

'Very little I should say, and very little about running a police-station either, it seems. Perhaps it will assist you if I add that the insect is more commonly known as the coffin-fly. This fragment to one side is the pupae sheath of a second specimen. In other words they are still breeding at the site.'

The mention of coffins brought Bower up short. He looked at the remains on the notepaper with a twist of revulsion in his mouth but also with a new respect.

'Where did it come from?'

'Coldhams Farm,' said Holmes casually. 'Please listen, Bower, to what I have to say. The coffin-fly begins its disagreeable work at the time of burial. Some three years are required for it, or rather its maggots, to devour a corpse. When that is done, the colony dies in its turn. Whoever or whatever is buried at Coldhams Farm cannot, therefore, have been dead more than three years. Dougal has been in residence some four years. Death and burial therefore took place within the time of his occupancy. Do I make myself plain?'

Bower, so confident a few minutes earlier, was now like a trapped animal.

'How did you get that thing?'

'It came to me,' said Holmes equably. 'A fox, a dog perhaps, had been digging by the shed in the farmyard. I confess I had been looking for such activity in and around the property. I noted a dozen sites, for the most part in the surrounding pasture, where the earth had been disturbed, had settled a little, and had then been subject to feral digging. A phorid fly would only get above ground if the excavation had been shallow with a means of egress. Whatever—or whoever—lies there, is not far down. Do I continue to make it clear to you?'

Inspector Bower did not growl his defiance, but looked as if he would like to.

'I understand, Mr Holmes, that Inspector Marden has already explained to you that there is ample evidence of Miss Holland being alive and unharmed.'

Holmes looked at him coldly. Then he looked at his watch and said, 'Miss Holland is dead. As dead as you and I will one day be.'

Before Bower could reply, there was a knock and a constable handed the inspector a telegram. I contrived to see at its foot the words, LESTRADE, SCOTLAND YARD. The capitulation of Eli Bower was now complete and unconditional, though scarcely graceful. He sighed.

'Very well. What would you have me do?'

'Gather every man you can and whatever equipment is available to you. Begin to search at once, starting under the shed where the pony-trap is kept.'

'That cannot be done without a warrant!'

'Then I suggest you lose as little time as possible in getting one.'

Before the afternoon was over, a justice's warrant had been obtained. Two serge-clad constables in gum-boots, assisted by a labourer, had cleared a shallow trench along one side of the shed. While Bower watched, his sergeant stood guard at the wicket gate of the bridge. A little after six, the digging stopped. A constable lifted an object, from which clay fell in scattered lumps. Despite the coating of earth, there was not the least doubt that this was a human skull.

The four diggers, the sergeant, Holmes and I gathered round.

'Fetch Dougal!' said Bower to his sergeant. The proprietor of Coldhams Farm was 'Captain' no longer. The sergeant and one of the constables crossed the little bridge and entered the house. There was a pause, during which I had a dreadful suspicion that Dougal might have taken his own life, that he might even now be dangling from a rafter in anticipation of the hangman's work. Then the face of the sergeant appeared at a bedroom window.

'He must have got a plank over the moat on the far side, sir,' he called to Brewer. 'He's done a bunk!'

Brewer's face went dark as thunder. Holmes turned to him.

'I congratulate you, inspector. I confess I had underestimated your reading of the man.'

'What?'

'You are too modest,' Holmes said, his face as straight as a poker. 'You might have put him under guard and got nothing from him. But you knew that a guilty man, given the chance, would bolt from such a terrifying revelation as this. You let him go, confident in your own ability to find him again easily enough. There are few officers, in my experience, who might play the game with such subtlety.'

Bower stared at him, uncertain whether Holmes was skinning him in fine strips or paying him a true compliment. He made no reply but shouted at the men to resume work, for there were more than two hours of daylight left. But those two hours revealed nothing more, nor did the whole of the next day. The site by the shed was exhausted without any further discovery. Worse still, I was obliged to tell Bower that this skull was too large to belong to a petite woman, five feet and two inches in height. Worse than that, for the inquiry he was pursuing, it was the skull of a man. Worst of all, I was more confident than not that its owner had died many years before Dougal's arrival at the farm.

'Which scarcely matters,' said Holmes indifferently, 'for if Miss Holland were not here somewhere, Dougal would surely not have bolted as he did.'

VII

Next day, Dougal's description was wired to every police force in the land, while Bower and his men searched what was now called Moat Farm. Every inch of the house was tapped and measured without result. Holmes and I found quarters ten miles away in Cambridge, at the University Arms. At Quendon, the diggers had taken over the farm-house, cooking and even sleeping there. The lawn was soon a trench fortification with Bower's constables working up to their waist in fenland slime. At the end of three days they had found nothing.

The moat seemed, to our earth-bound inspector, too good a chance to miss. In his mind he created a story of an argument or fight between Dougal and the little woman, as he called her. The brute killed her, by a blow of his fist or the thrust of his thumbs on her windpipe, and flung her body into this narrow moat.

'Very good,' said Holmes coolly. 'A little strange, however, that the body never came to the surface during decomposition.'

We watched them drain the moat and saw the constables digging away the filthy black mud of its bed. Bower was standing beside us as Holmes took a heavy stone with a sharp edge. Shouting to the diggers to stand clear, he tossed it down and heard it land with a thud in the bottom of the moat. It splashed the mud a little but remained in full view.

'If a stone of that weight will not sink below the bottom of the moat,' he said reflectively, 'you may be sure a human body did not. What remained of the skeleton, now that your digging has removed the sludge, would be lying in our view at this moment. It is not. Therefore, I suggest, Miss Holland was not thrown into the moat, either alive or dead.'

Bower glared at him. I think the word is not too strong.

'And do you care to suggest, Mr Holmes, where we should look instead?'

Holmes affected not to notice the anger. In his most friendly manner he said, 'I observe a line of young trees on the far side of the yard. You see? They run from the moat to the pond. I should guess they were planted two or three years ago. The level of the earth along that line stands somewhat higher than the yard. That is often the case when digging, or rather filling-in, has occurred. Something lay along that line. It was dug up, or at least filled in, about three years ago and trees were planted. You may find that of interest.'

There was a steely triumph in Bower's narrow eyes.

'We found it of such interest, Mr Holmes, that we inquired about it two days ago. There was a drainage ditch from the farm-yard to the pond. Dougal had it filled in and trees planted upon it. It was done at a time when Miss Holland was still alive and they were living amicably together here for weeks afterwards.'

'Dear me,' said Holmes, unruffled by the disappointment. 'Then it would hardly seem to warrant digging.'

'My very thought, Mr Holmes.'

Holmes turned to the inspector with eyes that seemed to look straight through him.

'And perhaps it was Captain Dougal's very thought, as he chose the place to dispose of the body of the woman whom he had just foully murdered.'

Bower was a little rattled by this but not defeated.

'Now,' said Holmes politely, 'we will take ourselves off. We shall return by train to Cambridge for the night and be with you again tomorrow.'

Bower did not look best pleased at this promise of our return. However, we had made ourselves comfortable at the University Arms and turned out on that fine evening to stroll along King's Parade in the late May sunshine. As we did so, a tradesman of some kind passed us, tipped his hat and said, 'A very good evening to you, Professor Holmes, sir.'

I scarcely liked the sound of this, but my companion gave a slight self-conscious smile and would say nothing.

We returned next morning to watch the progress of the digging by the line of trees. At one end, where the topsoil was removed, the drainage ditch had been filled in by blackthorn cuttings. This loose-packed layer was cleared by two men with pitch-forks, the surrounding earth being sodden with sewage and liquid manure from the yard. Then there came a shout from one of the diggers. He held up his fork, from one of whose prongs dangled a piece of old cloth.

We gathered round that spot, knowing yet dreading what might be underneath the blackthorn. I heard the fork strike something solid. The labourer stooped and drew out a small boot from the muddy soil. From where I stood, I saw inside the boot the delicate bones of a human foot. The work went on more cautiously. Soon we were looking down at a shape, little more than the half-clad skeleton of a woman, face-downwards with her head turned slightly to one side. On one side, where the body rested against the mud, almost everything had been destroyed. On the nearer side, the corpse had been sheltered from the mud by the cuttings of the bushes, its state of preservation much better. By the end of the afternoon, the poor woman's remains lay upon a trestle-table in the greenhouse. A wire hair-frame was found in the muddy grave, the twin of that found by Holmes in the hat-box. From that moment, 'Captain' Dougal's number was up.

We returned to Baker Street the next day. That evening, we received our usual visit from Lestrade. After the horrors of Moat Farm, as Coldhams was now universally called, it was a relief to be among homely surroundings and friendly faces. Lestrade settled himself, took a long pull at his glass, and said, 'Well, gentlemen, I suppose you have had something of an adventure. But how you persuaded that cuss Eli Bower to start digging, when his face was set against it, I do not know. He is the most stubborn and dogged fellow, as a rule.'

'I was able to show him where he might find a skull,' said Holmes innocently. 'After that, the rest followed.'

'So that was it! Well, you may put that skull from your mind. It has been examined by the pathologist and is far too old to have anything to do with Dougal. Dr Watson was right about that.'

'And what of Dougal?'

Lestrade's face assumed an expression of humorous self-importance.

'That is my news. This afternoon, Detective-Inspector Henry Cox of the City of London police was duty officer at the Bank of England. He was called discreetly to the office of the bank secretary at the request of the clerk. It seems that Mr Sydney Domville, of Upper Terrace, Bournemouth, had presented fourteen ten-pound notes to be changed for gold sovereigns. There were irregularities in nine of these notes, for they could not be traced as issued to Mr Domville. They had, however, been issued through the Birkbeck Bank account of Samuel Dougal.'

'Ah,' said Holmes, closing his eyes in contemplation, 'so that was it.'

'On being challenged, the suspect Domville admitted he was Dougal. Mr Cox then escorted him to the detective office at the bank. At the door, Dougal suddenly turned and ran, clear of the bank, and fled towards Cheapside. Cox caught him at Frederick's Place and they fell to the ground together. Padghorn, a uniformed constable, saw them. He recognized Mr Cox and handcuffed Dougal. You may be thankful, gentlemen, that you have not been briefed to defend Dougal, for there was never a clearer case against any man.'

'I do not defend the guilty,' said Holmes gently, 'merely the innocent.'

When Lestrade had gone, there still was one piece of unfinished business.

'Tell me, Holmes. What is all this mystery about Professor Holmes of Cambridge? Why did that fellow call out to you on King's Parade?'

Holmes drew at his pipe and said, 'I daresay he was mistaken.'

'I think he was not! He called you Professor Holmes! After our talk with Marden, you were not to be seen for several hours after lunch. There was ample time to take the Cambridge train from Audley End and return with what you called a coffin-fly. It was more likely a common hedge-moth. It is the only time when you were out of my sight long enough to go to Cambridge alone.'

'Your deduction is entirely admirable,' said he.

'Why did you go? What for?'

'Hold hard a moment, Watson,' he said with a laugh, 'I do not say I was there!'

'It was for something that would fit into your satchel. My God, it was that skull! You went to the university anatomy suppliers, as medical students do to buy a skeleton. You bought that skull! You buried it by the cart-shed, so that Marden or Bower must dig! You knew they would find it and would dig up the entire place! That coffin-fly was a harmless insect, vouched for by a telegram sent to yourself from Cambridge the next morning! There is no Dr Cardew!'

'Such a welter of deductions, my dear chap . . .' His eyes shone with laughter.

'Suppose Miss Holland had still been alive—had driven into the farm-yard in the middle of Bower's digging?'

'She could drive nowhere, Watson. She was lying dead at the bottom of the drainage ditch, if you recall.'

'But you could not have known—so you fabricated evidence to make them dig!'

'Forgive me, my dear fellow, I have known she was dead since the moment that Marden mentioned the tragedy of her nephew's child.'

'Yet the rest of what I say is true?'

He laughed again.

'My old friend, you really must allow justice to the accused, which accords to every man the right to silence.'

'You mean that what I do not know, I cannot tell!'

'That is certainly true, in any event.'

For a moment we were silent. Then I put my last question.

'There is one flaw in your hypothesis. Where is the woman whom you claim impersonated Camille Holland at the National Provincial Bank?'

He shrugged.

'That is no flaw. I simply do not know. Alive—or dead. Perhaps not far away. Search your mind, Watson, for a demure petite of Miss Holland's type.'

'I cannot say we have cast eyes on one.'

'Oh, come,' he said, 'surely we have done that, even if it be not she.'

I did not follow this at first. Then it dawned upon me what he meant.

'Miss Pierce? The very idea of her and Dougal is outlandish.'

'So was that of Miss Holland. The conquest of devout spinsters, no longer young, seems to have been something of a profession with Captain Dougal.'

'She would hardly ask us to take action against him, if that were the case.'

'As I recall, it was to avoid publicity that she came to us and not to the police.'

'Absurd,' I said, thinking as I did so that perhaps it was nothing of the kind.

Holmes sighed and knocked out his pipe.

'Hell hath no fury like a woman scorned, Watson,' he said, standing up and yawning. 'Especially if she who has forfeited her virtue for love be a subscriber to the National Vigilance Association.'

The Case of the
Sporting Major

I

The intuitive faculty of Sherlock Holmes was generally beyond my power to comprehend, let alone to emulate. From time to time, however, I matched him in his anticipation of regular events. One of these was the impending arrival of a certain eminent guest, whose visits had long been familiar to us. On such occasions, Mrs Hudson's nervous housemaid would open the door to make her announcement with the air of a twittering cage-bird. Or Billy the page-boy would appear with eyes bright at the excitement of an adventure to come. Even our impassive and long-suffering landlady would utter the six resonant syllables in a tone of superior awe.

'Sir Edward Marshall Hall!'

Before us stood that splendid figure, an athlete and philosopher of noble brow with a fine sweep of hair. Small wonder if Lord Birkenhead remarked that no man could possibly have been as wonderful as Marshall Hall appeared. His presence and voice were such as Sir Henry Irving and the great actors of the day would have given a fortune to possess.

Yet Marshall Hall had a nobler fame. He was the Great Defender in the criminal courts, equipped with sharp intelligence and eloquent address. Times without number, he saved from the gallows those whom public opinion had already condemned. He opened the gates of life for a score of men and women, in defending the humble prostitute Marie Hermann, Edward Lawrence the brewer, Robert Wood the Camden Town artist, Thomas Greenwood reviled as a poisoner, and then among his greater triumphs came the Green Bicycle case, the Derham shooting, and the acquittal of Madame Fahmy who had killed her unnatural husband.

One fine September morning in the last years of the late Queen's reign, Marshall Hall sat upon the sofa of our Baker Street lodgings, his eyes bright, his fingers drumming upon the padded arm of the furniture. That whole being was alive with a characteristic energy which wants to be up and doing—a perfect mirror of Sherlock Holmes! It might seem at first that their only common pleasure was in chaff and banter. Beneath this, however, lay an adamantine resolve to see justice done and innocence set free.

On this particular morning, Marshall Hall wore the black velvet jacket of those more casual days when he was not engaged to appear in court or chambers.

'Whatever your business, Sir Edward,' said Holmes airily, 'I am pleased that you first had leisure to sit and listen to your wife playing the Chopin Polonaise in A Flat Major, upon a Schiedmayer concert grand-piano. I regret that the tone of the instrument was not all that it might have been. I should recommend you to consult Messrs Chappell in New Bond Street, should you require advice in the matter.'

Another visitor might be dumbfounded that Holmes should know the very piece of music that Sir Edward had heard half an hour before, who had played it to him, the precise make of the instrument, and what had been discussed. Sir Edward merely threw back his head and laughed at his friend's cleverness.

'My dear Holmes, you will plainly not be content until you have explained your brilliance. Put us poor mortals out of our misery!'

Holmes shrugged, disclaiming any gift except common sense.

'I observe your jacket. Nature has designed velvet fabric as a means of collecting evidence. Upon your right sleeve, a little above the cuff, you have picked up a fleck of cream-coloured felt, some-what worn. If one looks closely, the cream has a red inlay of a different texture along its edge. I grant the red is scarcely perceptible, but it is there. Such a combination of fabrics comes from one source only in my experience. It has been acquired from a damper of the string on a grand-piano. The precise key is close to the middle C. That particular red inlay is characteristic of the instruments made by Schiedmayer of Stuttgart, which I have several times tried in Augener's showroom. It occurs solely on the damper, where the felt is softer than the hammer and more inclined to fray. The great use made by so accomplished a pianist as Lady Hall must require the re-felting of hammers and dampers alike. The more commonly-used the key, the greater the wear, hence in the region of middle C. How easy it would have been for your sleeve to brush the mechanism as you were closing the piano-lid for Lady Hall. The fact that the lid was closed so early in the day hints—does it not?—at some dissatisfaction with the state of the instrument. Hence your discussion.'

'Is that all?' asked Marshall Hall tauntingly.

'Not quite. That discussion was plainly interrupted, in turn, by the arrival of a message which brought you here at once. A letter, I believe. I should say your advice has been sought urgently in a case to come before the Scottish courts. The north of England would be possible but, on the whole, I think Scotland. It would have been too early in the day for so complex a telegram as the facts of such a case require. Therefore I plump for a letter by the second post. Yesterday's post from Manchester, York, or the English counties would be delivered first thing. So we must look further afield. I observe that the Scottish courts are already sitting, the English assizes are not. It remains to decide what matter might have been referred to your particular accomplishments. I have seen in the *Morning Post* some reference to the dramatic arrest in Glasgow of a certain Major Alfred Monson in connection with the shooting dead of a fellow officer during a hunting-party. That has a ring of probability to it. I daresay I am quite wrong.'

Sir Edward laughed again.

'You are quite right Holmes, and you know it, otherwise you would not have dared the deduction. And, indeed, Lady Hall's practice-piece this morning was the Chopin Polonaise.'

'I thought as much,' Holmes said reassuringly. 'Its rhythm is exceptionally well-defined. When a man fingers his impatience on the arm of a sofa, he is very likely to imitate unawares the last melody he has heard. But enough of these games. Precisely what has occurred in this case to bring you here at a time when you might otherwise have been in chambers?'

The laughter went from the fine eyes of Marshall Hall.

'The evidence against Major Monson, gentlemen, is indeed of murder and the case is as black as it could be. My friend Mr Comrie Thomson holds a watching brief. It was impossible that I should do so. I have other commitments and am neither a member of the Scottish bar nor sufficiently conversant with Scottish criminal law. To speak frankly, on the evidence available to me, the major's situation appears hopeless.'

'Excellent!' said Holmes with relish. 'Do, pray, continue.'

'Alfred Monson is a middle-aged, down-at-heel retired major who tutors young officers to pass War Office examinations and so advance their careers. The pupils that he chooses are men with quite a little money. They live with Monson, his wife, children, and nursemaid. They are coached for these War Office tests and in every case appear to have been systematically plundered. His latest dupe was one Lieutenant Cecil Hamborough. Hamborough's father soon guessed the major's intentions. He resented the influence of the Monsons and sought to end the association. Unfortunately, young Hamborough would not see sense. He appeared blind to reason, even though he was bled white by Monson and a criminal scoundrel known variously as Edward Scott, Edward Davis, and Edward Sweeney.'

'The disgraced bookmaker from Pimlico, who two years ago lost his licence for fraud!' cried Holmes, as if recognizing an old friend.

'Precisely. Monson and Scott worked hand-in-glove with a so-called money-lender, Captain Beresford Tottenham, lately and briefly of the 10th Prince of Wales Hussars. Hamborough's money was obtained by IOUs combined with an extortionate rate of interest. The last of his funds was used to rent Ardlamont House near the Kyles of Bute, where he, the Monsons, and Scott would spend the summer and the August shooting season. After they had drained the poor young devil, I daresay they meant to be rid of him one way or another.'

'What a story to put to a jury!' Holmes said thoughtfully.

'That is by no means the worst of it.' Marshall Hall inspected and removed the fluff on his velvet sleeve. 'Some time after their arrival at Ardlamont there was a boating accident in which young Hamborough was nearly drowned. Next morning he was shot dead, apparently by accident, while out hunting rabbits with Monson and Scott, *alias* Davis, *alias* Sweeney.'

Holmes reached for a pencil and made two or three notes on his shirt-cuff as Marshall Hall continued.

'Both men swore that Lieutenant Hamborough was walking alone and must have stumbled in the woods, jarring his short-barrelled 20-bore, which had gone off and shot him through the head. The local doctor, never having seen such a thing before, accepted the story and signed a death certificate. Scott then left Ardlamont, that same afternoon, and has not been seen since. It appears, however, that he cannot have fired the shot. Perhaps he feared that the publicity surrounding Hamborough's death would result in prosecution for certain past offences of fraud and embezzlement, if he waited for the police. Young Hamborough was interred a few days later in the family vault on the Isle of Wight. Now I must tell you what the world does not yet know.'

'Pray do so.' Holmes reached a spill to the fire to light his pipe.

'On the day of Hamborough's funeral, two life insurance companies alerted the Procurator Fiscal to a demand by Major Monson for £30,000. Cecil Hamborough's life had been insured in this sum, which he had assigned and made payable to the Monsons in the event of his death. A third company had declined a further proposal for £50,000. Monson had been the intermediary on each occasion, attempting to secure an interest of £80,000 all told, in the event of the young man's death.'

'Making Hamborough worth a good deal more dead than alive,' said Holmes softly.

'Quite. The day after the policies for £30,000 came into effect was the one upon which Monson took Hamborough out into Ardlamont Bay in a rowing-boat, from which the bung had been secretly removed. Nothing was seen amiss at first but water poured in under the boards from the moment the boat was pushed into the sea. The young fellow was nearly drowned. The very next morning he was shot dead in Ardlamont woods, while the three men were hunting rabbits.'

'I fear,' said Holmes, waving aside a cloud of tobacco smoke, 'that no one could accuse Mr Thomson's client of subtlety.'

Marshall Hall shook his head.

'As a result of the reports from the insurance offices, the body was exhumed. There was no blackening round the head-wound, just behind the right ear. Therefore the shot could not have come from less than three feet. By the spread of shot, it was probably thirty feet away. We know from other witnesses that only Monson was that far away at the time. Since the investigation was renewed and the major arrested, Scott has fled and will no doubt be outlawed when Monson is charged.'

Holmes was now jotting a few scattered notes on a sheet of paper.

'After the boating-accident, Hamborough made no accusation?'

'None. However, Monson is arrested on suspicion, for that incident as well as the shooting.'

'And what would you have me do?'

'Prove the major's innocence,' said Marshall Hall simply, 'for that is what it will mean, no matter what the law says about a presumption in favour of the defendant. The facts are deadly and the prejudice at his fraudulent way of life will go deep in any panel of jurors.'

'His position does seem quite hopeless, from all that you have been told?'

'As much so as any I have ever known.'

'Good,' said Holmes briskly. 'Then I shall certainly take the case. I confess that Watson and I had made no plans to go to Scotland just now. However, such a very incriminating set of circumstances really is too good to overlook.'

'Could you go at once?'

My friend looked a little doubtful.

'There is Kreisler at the Wigmore Hall this evening and I must have time to put matters in order for our absence. The criminal fraternity is apt to become over-excited when I am out of town, and Scotland Yard feels lonely. Will you give me a day's grace and allow us to take the North-Western Railway tomorrow?'

There was no mistaking the relief in the lawyer's face.

'That would be splendid. Monson is certain to be formally charged with murder and brought before the sheriff's court. The Procurator Fiscal works more slowly and thoroughly than the English police. Charges will be brought soon but hardly before Wednesday.'

'Capital,' said Holmes quietly, making a final note. 'Then we shall take the North-Western Railway express from Euston, tomorrow morning at ten.'

II

Our first visit in Glasgow on the Wednesday morning was not to Ardlamont House but to the sheriff's court, in whose basement lay a concrete and white-tiled corridor of police-cells. We had been met by Mr Comrie Thomson at the Central Station on the previous evening with the news that Major Monson was now formally charged with the attempted murder of Cecil Hamborough in respect of the boating incident on 9 August and with actual murder for the Ardlamont shooting on 10 August. Of Scott, *alias* Davis, *alias* Sweeney, there was still no sign.

On that Wednesday morning, we met Mr Thomson in front of the grim pillared façade of the High Court Buildings. From there it was a very little distance to the court where Monson was to appear at a formal committal hearing. As we made our way, Mr Thomson said mournfully, 'I cannot say that it looks hopeful, gentlemen. There are now two more witnesses who were in the schoolhouse on the edge of the Ardlamont wood and another who was working on the road to one side. They saw the three men enter the wood, well apart, Monson on the right, Hamborough in the middle, Scott on the left. They all agree that only two shots were fired after that. Unfortunately none of the guns was examined at the time, Dr Macmillan having certified death from accidental shooting. However, the first shot came from the direction of Major Monson, who was behind Hamborough and Scott and to their right. The second was either the accidental discharge of Hamborough's gun, a second shot by Monson, or a shot by Scott. We cannot be sure.'

'What of the ranges?'

Mr Thomson shook his head.

'The spread of the pellet-holes in the trees where the body lay, and the width of the wound behind the young man's ear, suggest that only Monson can have been far enough away to have fired the fatal shot. Had Scott been as far as thirty feet to the rear, he would have been seen from the road that passes the schoolhouse where one of the witnesses was working. He was not seen. I am informed privately on the best authority that if Hamborough had shot himself at a range of even three feet, it would have blown his head clean off.'

'Then we must pay a little more attention to Edward Scott,' said Holmes thoughtfully.

Thomson shook his head.

'Scott was not only too close to fire the fatal shot, Mr Holmes, he was on the wrong side of Hamborough. Hamborough was hit in the right side of the head, where only Major Monson fired.'

'Well, well,' said Holmes philosophically, 'then it does not look good for Major Monson.'

'It looks bad, Mr Holmes. And then there is the insurance on the young man's life . . .'

'So there is,' Holmes said brightly. 'Let us see what our client has to say for himself when the case comes on.'

During these preliminary proceedings, we had what proved to be our first and last view of Major Monson as he stood in the dock of the panelled court-room. When the accused was 'put up', he appeared above the rail of the dock as a stout, unprepossessing man in his late thirties with a clipped ginger moustache and hair to match. His watery eyes and stocky build made him appear somewhat older than he was. I had seen his type often during my army service, the adjutant who passes his life at the depot, shuffling papers, then takes his pension at forty and lives the rest of his life at Cheltenham or Harrogate as the gallant swordsman of a middle-aged spinster's dream. From time to time, during the interval before the proceedings began, a nervous ferret-like smile broke cover from Monson's ginger moustache as he recognized someone he knew.

Before the matter went further, there was some discussion between the sheriff and Mr John Blair who was Monson's agent, or solicitor as he would have been in England. This revealed the unsurprising fact that the major was an undischarged bankrupt and must rely upon a poor prisoner's defence to pay his costs, which had already begun to mount up. This financing of the case occupied several minutes of discussion.

'I understand, Major Monson, that you have been an undischarged bankrupt for the past two years?' inquired the sheriff.

'That is so,' said the rheumy-eyed trickster.

'You and your wife employed a maid, a nanny for your children, and were able to afford a summer at Ardlamont House. How was that?'

'It was all Mrs Monson's money, sir.' The major's eyes watered harder, as if he might weep for pity.

There followed a recital by the prosecution of the preliminary case against the accused. Such evidence was damning enough in itself but Monson made it a good deal worse by his frightened interjections. The sheriff, either wanting to be fair to him or perhaps to let him damn himself, allowed him too much latitude. When Mr Cowan, for the Solicitor-General, remarked that the major had insured Cecil Hamborough's life for £30,000, the watery eyes cleared a little as if there was still some fight in him.

'There is no law against that, sir! The boy had broken with his father. This was the only means by which Lieutenant Hamborough could repay board, lodging and tuition, if he should not live to get his military position, don't you see?'

'Board and lodging at £30,000?' Mr Cowan asked the question of everyone who heard it. 'And, indeed, he did not live to get his position, did he?'

Mr Thomson looked down at the floor and Sherlock Holmes at the ceiling. The major's face was a grimace of pure terror, as if Mr Cowan had been the hangman entering his cell on the last fateful morning.

Presently, in his recital of the evidence for the sheriff's benefit, Mr Cowan came to the events in the woods and the firing of the shot that killed Cecil Hamborough. Monson, unable to endure the allegations of his guilt, blurted out, 'It was a pure accident, sir! The boy stumbled and shot himself, knocking the gun so that it went off.'

He laid himself open to Mr Cowan's retort, directed to the sheriff.

'Forgive me, your honour, but I do not recall any man managing to shoot himself from a distance of three feet—let alone thirty! Even at three feet, your honour, the wound would have been scorched and the skin impregnated with burnt powder.'

'Not with smokeless amberite cartridges, d'you see, your honour?' cried the major hopefully. 'Cecil Hamborough was carrying the 12-bore shotgun with the amberite cartridges. I was the one who had the short-barrelled 20-bore with gunpowder.'

Mr Cowan glanced at his notes.

'Your honour, Major Monson has told the police that he was carrying the 12-bore with the amberite.'

'They have it wrong!' What a cry of pain it was from the doomed man! 'To be sure I was carrying the 12-bore when we set out. As we were about to enter the wood, Hamborough asked to borrow it. We exchanged guns. I said so when they first questioned me at Ardlamont.'

Mr Cowan paused and consulted a uniformed inspector sitting at the bench behind him. Then he turned to the sheriff again.

'Your honour, this evidence about the exchange of guns has been heard for the first time in this court-room at this moment. Nothing was said to the police by Major Monson about it, either at Ardlamont or in custody. Nor is it mentioned in the written witness-statement by the accused man.'

'I thought they had put it in! I did not write the statement myself, only signed it!'

The sight of such a wretch as this, a congenital liar and trickster, struggling forlornly like a summer-fly in the web of evidence which his prosecutors spun about him, was terrifying. It did not end there but the damage that Monson had already done to his own case seemed mortal.

Outside, with Mr Comrie Thomson, I said, 'The poor devil has put the noose round his own neck!'

The barrister, in his quiet Scots voice, added, 'I had hoped, Mr Holmes, that your arrival would give some hope. As it is, I fear your journey may have been to no purpose.'

'Mr Thomson, I have promised Sir Edward Marshall Hall that I will take the case. I have not the slightest intention of abandoning it in the light of what we have heard this morning. All the same, if you have no objection, I shall not interview the client. It would irritate me to be lied to by such a novice in deceit as Major Monson. Indeed, I am bound to say that it would irritate me to be in the same room with Major Monson.'

'Then you will continue with the investigation? You think there is a chance in a million that he might be innocent?'

'Innocent? Dear me!' Holmes looked about him as if he feared that he had caused offence unawares. 'Major Monson is a reprobate and a liar, to be sure. Facts, however, are not liars. If the facts of the case are as I believe them to be, I have little doubt that I shall prove him to be innocent. Indeed, I had almost made up my mind to that effect before leaving Baker Street.'

Comrie Thomson reddened a little at this.

'I do not think I understand you, Mr Holmes.'

'Perhaps not,' said Holmes suavely, 'but in the morning Watson and I are to become seekers after truth at Ardlamont. Thanks to your good offices we shall have the company of Mr David Stewart of the Procurator Fiscal's office. In the meantime, Mr Thomson, I should be obliged if you could find it convenient not to go to your chambers tomorrow.'

The attorney stared at him.

'But there is work to be done, Mr Holmes! Now, of all times!'

'Even so, you would oblige me by doing it elsewhere. Let that be settled. And now let us return to the comforts of the Argyle Hotel, where we may forget our client and his misfortunes over an agreeable glass or two. Malt whisky with water from the Highland springs, I think, followed by lunch.'

III

Next morning we set out by the paddle-steamer *Duchess of Montrose* for Ardlamont Bay. After two hours, we cleared the river and turned north in a freshening breeze towards the Kyles of Bute. With the tide racing against the bow and the wind in our faces, we stood on deck and watched the tree-lined bay approach. Ardlamont House is accessible only by water, unless one makes a considerable detour from Kames. It stands in a wooded bay, where we were met at the little pier by David Stewart, the Deputy Fiscal at Inveraray. Mr Stewart's reputation went before him, a quietly-spoken and courteous man, who had proved deadly to Major Monson in his interrogation.

Ardlamont is a tall white house of recent design, built for solid comforts. Around it lies a considerable estate of pasture and woodland, including a disused school building let to holidaymakers in the season. We paid a brief visit to the house, where the gun-cases and leather chairs in the hall, the shooting-jackets and waterproofs hanging by the hat-stand, the doors to the billiard-room and smoking-room, left little doubt as to its clientele. Since the 'tragedy' a few weeks before, however, not a shot had been fired on the surrounding estate. In point of law, Major Monson had paid the rent, albeit with Hamborough's money, and was still the tenant.

With Mr Stewart, we then walked back towards the main gates, so that we might follow the route taken by Cecil Hamborough and his two companions on the morning of the young man's death. The carriage-drive at the gates is only a short distance from the tideline of the bay. After a hundred yards or so, we passed the stone and brick building which had once housed the village school. The main woodland lay ahead of us, bordering the carriage-drive.

'From the windows of the schoolhouse back there,' said Stewart softly, 'two witnesses saw Major Monson, Lieutenant Hamborough, and Mr Scott. The men had told the butler at the house that they were going rabbit-shooting. It was too early in the month for game birds and, in any case, you can see that the terrain is quite unsuited to that. The three men were carrying shotguns when they reached this point, though the witnesses at the window of the schoolhouse cannot identify which guns were carried by which men. The three of them walked down the main driveway for some distance. A hundred yards or so from where we stand, they found the easiest place to straddle the fence and enter the woodland. They walked at a diagonal into the woods, Lieutenant Hamborough still in the middle, Major Monson to the right, Scott to the left. They walked at this angle and Scott was therefore most easily seen by the witnesses through a thinner screen of trees. The men were spaced out, of course, but the most important evidence from the two witnesses in the schoolhouse shows that Scott and Hamborough were ahead, with Major Monson lagging somewhat in the rear on the right flank. If you please, we will take that way.'

We followed Mr Stewart into this unkempt woodland, among beeches, limes, and rowan, where high birch trees along the paths formed a vaulting that almost obscured the sky. The white house of Ardlamont with its tall sash windows and terrace was now completely hidden. There had been a contested legacy and a protracted sale of the estate, I believe, during which the copses and spinneys had been left to run riot. All the same, these shadowy bridle-paths and alleys, with their carpeting of dark leaf mould which silenced one's footsteps, were a paradise to the hunter with dog or gun. The way was dry underfoot. Though it had rained before the day of the tragedy, it had not done so since and the ground was firm enough now.

The path was so overgrown in some places that it was scarcely any path at all. Tall bracken brushed the legs of our trousers at either side. At length we came out into what might be called a clearing. Across a further expanse of bracken the trees dwindled to a thinner screen of branches. To one side was a 'sunken fence', where the land fell to a lower wood on our left. This fence took the form of a stone retaining-wall at the level of our feet, holding back the earth from the lower woodland, so that we seemed to walk through the bracken upon a terrace. A hundred feet or so beyond this, the trees opened out on our right and there was a view of the house again. Such was the scene of the 'Ardlamont Tragedy', as the newspapers had called it.

Stewart approached the further screen of trees. I noticed that a beech, a rowan, and a lime tree bore circular yellow dye-marks on their trunks, some no more than three feet from the ground and others as high as eight feet. Our guide turned to us.

'Lieutenant Hamborough's body was found just here. Edward Scott told Monson and the doctor that he had seen the young man lying at the foot of the sunken wall and had lifted him up to the higher ground. It may be so, or it may not. There is no independent witness. When the body was seen by others, it was lying at the higher level on its back, the head six feet from the rowan tree and thirteen feet from the beech. The yellow dye-marks painted by our officers on the beech and rowan trunks show clearly the spread of shot as it hit the trees. There had been no shooting in this plantation for two or three weeks before Lieutenant Hamborough was killed. Therefore, where an earlier shot had hit the trees, the pellet-wounds had already healed over. The pellet holes you see marked were new, from the shot that killed Mr Hamborough.'

'And what is the spread?' Holmes asked casually.

'The spread of the shot is about five feet, as you may see from the trunk of the beech. Its trajectory can be traced back. It is a matter of geometrical calculation. By that calculation, the gun was most probably fired some thirty feet behind him and about five feet above the ground. A man who fires five feet above the ground is not shooting at rabbits, Mr Holmes! Nor does one sportsman fire a shotgun thirty feet immediately behind another without knowing that death or grievous injury is likely to result. A defence of accident at thirty feet can scarcely be sustained. Major Monson would surely have heard Lieutenant Hamborough's movements, even if he could not see him. And yet he fired, as the witnesses heard. In Scottish law as in English, Mr Holmes, a man is presumed to intend the natural and probable consequences of his acts.'

'I understand that the major maintains that he did not fire in any such a direction or at such a height,' Holmes said firmly.

Mr Stewart looked at him and shrugged.

'Unfortunately for Major Monson, Scott was seen on the far side of the wood by the third witness, too close to Hamborough to have fired a shot which spread as far as this. He was also on the wrong side of the deceased to have inflicted a wound to the right of the head.'

Holmes seemed not to be listening to him. The keen grey eyes were scanning the trunk of the beech tree, at a higher level.

'Allow me one moment, Mr Stewart.'

He took off his jacket and handed it to me. Then he gave a short jump upwards. His bony hands gripped a lower bough of the beech like a steel clamp. He swung his feet up and caught the branch between them. A moment more and he was astride it, examining the pale grey trunk at a height of ten or twelve feet above the ground. Out came his trusty pocket-knife from his trousers pocket and he attacked a tiny scab on the bark. Presently he called down.

'I fear, Mr Stewart, that your men overlooked a most interesting piece of evidence. I daresay when they found pellets as high as eight feet above the ground, they felt that they had done enough to show that only Monson could have fired the shot. That was remiss of them. I notice that there are three holes at quite twelve feet, not yet healed over, and that a shotgun pellet is still embedded in one of them. You shall see it for yourself in a moment.'

Stewart stared up, as Holmes swung himself down and dropped to the ground.

'Surely, Mr Holmes, all you have done is to turn suspicion against your client into certainty!'

'I have turned it into a matter of evidence, Mr Stewart! The spread of shot is plainly greater than you had measured. It was a capital error that once your men had gone high enough to establish that Hamborough could not have shot himself, they stopped. Given the true spread, the gun that fired the pellets would be quite sixty feet away, would it not? You may calculate it for yourself in due course but you may take it from me that the calibration is correct. Now, sir! What man, seeking to kill another, would choose a range of sixty feet with a shotgun? Would he not be far more likely to wound than to kill?'

The Deputy Fiscal was courteous but unmoved.

'Theories will not alter facts, Mr Holmes.'

'So my friend Lestrade is always telling me. However, I myself deal in facts and only then do I offer theories.'

Before the argument could continue, I was aware of a threshing in the undergrowth and saw the face of the Ardlamont butler, crimson with exertion.

'Mr Stewart, sir. There is a boy at the house with an express telegram, requiring an immediate reply. I should be obliged if you would come at once.'

There was time for only the briefest apology from the Deputy Fiscal before he hurried off in the wake of the butler. Holmes watched him go with an air of satisfaction, tempered by concern.

'A very decent young fellow, Watson. I regret that I had to deceive him.'

'Over the spread of shot?'

He looked at me in despair.

'Of course not! In the matter of the telegram, however, it was a simple matter to send a wire from the purser's office of the railway company's steamer. They undertook to despatch it by way of the piermaster at the next port of call. There are no such facilities at Ardlamont Bay, of course. However, I verified that it would go from Kames Pier half an hour later.'

'You sent Stewart a telegram to be delivered here?'

He looked still more concerned at my obtuseness.

'I sent a wire in the name of Mr Comrie Thomson, requesting an immediate comment on the information that Major Monson is to be released today for lack of evidence against him. I do not think our young friend will ignore that.'

'One day, Holmes,' I said feebly, 'you will go too far!'

'I have always thought that very likely. Meantime, I imagine that poor Mr Stewart is at this moment endeavouring to communicate an incomprehensible message to Inveraray and to get an equally incomprehensible reply in answer from Mr Thomson who, unfortunately, is away from his chambers today at my request. I think we may count on having the woods of Ardlamont to ourselves for at least the next forty-five minutes.'

IV

Holmes put his pocket-knife away and pulled on his jacket.

'Let us go back to first principles. If Hamborough had shot himself with the short-barrelled 20-bore loaded with plain gunpowder, the wound would have been blackened. It was not. If he had shot himself by dropping the 12-bore loaded with amberite, he would have blown his head off. He did not. He was therefore shot by either Monson or Scott. But we are told that Scott was too close for his gun to have spread the shot as widely as the pellet-marks upon the beech tree indicate.'

'I cannot believe that Marshall Hall will thank you, Holmes,' I said curtly. 'As Stewart remarked just now, all you have done is to prove that our client did indeed shoot Hamborough, though perhaps at a range of sixty feet. It is the only conclusion to which your precious facts point.'

Holmes turned to me, his eyebrows raised in surprise.

'They do nothing of the kind!'

'I understood you to demonstrate that the spread of shot was consistent only with a range of sixty feet.'

His aquiline features assumed a weariness born of long patience as he sighed and looked about him.

'My dear Watson, I have demonstrated that the spread of shot so high up the tree-trunks was inconsistent with a range of thirty feet! So it is. But no one could have fired that shot from sixty feet. Consider the situation. Imagine how the pellets would fan out and lose velocity over sixty feet. The spread of shot might cover an area of ten by ten—say a hundred square feet. There might be no more than four or five individual pellets in the area of the victim's head. No murderer could be certain of accomplishing his object in such circumstances.'

'Then Monson shot Hamborough accidentally at a distance of sixty feet.'

'Quite impossible,' said Holmes sharply. 'As a medical man, even as an intelligent observer, one thing must strike you above all. If Hamborough had been killed with a shotgun at sixty feet, the shot would have spread so wide that his head would have been pockmarked by individual pellets. In the report of the post-mortem, there was a single central wound and no pock-marking whatever. You may therefore be quite sure that he was not shot at sixty feet . . .'

'Nor at thirty?'

'Correct. Let us waste no more time on the impetuous theorizing of the Deputy Fiscal. Come, now. There are two paths running back to the carriage-drive. Monson must have approached the scene of the tragedy along one of them. We will search both, as well as the areas immediately to their right and left. I should think fifty feet back along each path would be sufficient.'

'Sufficient for what?'

'To look for a message left by Major Monson at the time of the shooting. To find a few torn scraps of paper.'

Why should the suspect write a message, before or after he fired? Had I not been accustomed to his unpredictable methods, I should have thought Holmes had taken leave of his senses.

'If Monson left a message, why would he—or someone else—then tear it up?'

Holmes ignored this.

'The fragments may be crumpled up very small and possibly singed but, let us hope, not all of them will have been entirely destroyed.'

If my friend was to be believed, Monson had composed a message in the middle of a shooting-party, then torn it up and burnt it. There was no time to argue over this, when the Deputy Fiscal might return at any moment. For ten minutes or so we searched without success for scraps of paper. There was none of any kind. With Holmes on my right, we again followed the two western footpaths, by one of which Monson must surely have made his way through the tangled briars and bracken of the wood.

'All the witnesses agree that it had been raining and that the major was wearing tweeds, not waterproofs,' Holmes said impatiently. 'Monson would therefore have followed the paths rather than stood up to his waist in wet heather.'

'In which case the ink would long ago have run on the paper and any message become indecipherable.'

'I think not. If it is here, and I have no doubt that it is, the message will remain perfectly clear.'

We extended our search further back until we were almost in sight of the fence and the carriage-drive again. Then we turned and made our way towards the scene of the shooting once more, heads down, seeking. We had patrolled up and down a dozen times and were about forty feet from the pellet-marked rowan and beech when I saw, at the edge of his path, what might have been a small white flower head. Before I could direct his attention to it, Sherlock Holmes's long arm reached down and snatched it up. With an unaccustomed carelessness, it seemed to me, he opened the scrap out, crumpled it again, and dropped it into his pocket. I was close enough to see that it was blank on both sides, though a little stained by wet.

A moment later, he darted down again and retrieved two more fragments, neither of them larger when opened than a *carte-de-visite*. If he had found a fragment of a message, my friend certainly kept it to himself. So far as I could see, however, this paper was also unmarked.

'Capital!' he said to himself, so quietly that I could scarcely hear him. Then he turned. 'Now let us walk back to where Hamborough's body was lying when Major Monson first saw it.'

As we reached the place, he took a twig and planted it into the earth to mark a spot that was both six feet from the rowan tree and thirteen feet from the beech.

'Here is where his head lay. The post-mortem gives his height as five feet eleven inches. Here, then, were his feet. The impact of such compacted shot as the post-mortem wound suggests would knock him down almost where he stood. We may allow a little distance but not much.'

'A fatally wounded man may stagger some distance before he falls.'

He sighed.

'A hunter will gallop several yards with a broken back before dropping dead, Watson, but not with such a discharge of shot in its equine brain! Moreover, the rain had stopped, the ground was examined at once and no blood was found except where the head lay.'

'But surely he fell over the sunken wall when he was hit. Scott found him lying down there and lifted him up to this level, out of the bracken. It was the most natural thing to do.'

'Cast your mind back to your military service at the battle of Maiwand,' Holmes said gently. 'Recall how much blood would flow from a wound like this in the man's dying moments, flowing on to the clothes of the injured man and thus on to those of anyone who tried to lift him. The evidence is that Edward Scott vanished from Ardlamont that afternoon in the very tweeds that he was wearing in the morning. No drop of blood appeared on them.'

'If he took the very greatest care . . .'

Holmes inclined his head.

'In that case let us admit that the weight of a man like Hamborough falling upon the bracken below would break it down hard where he landed, for several feet in each direction. I will give you five pounds, Watson, for every broken stalk of bracken that you can find at the foot of this wall. See for yourself.'

He jumped down and I followed him. A man who had fallen from the upper level would certainly have landed within six feet of the sunken wall. At no point below the spot where Scott claimed to have lifted the body was the bracken disturbed. It had plainly grown for months as we saw it now.

'Why should Scott murder him?' I asked.

'For the same reason as Monson might have done. They had squeezed the poor young fellow of everything that they could get while he was alive. There remained only his far greater value to them when he was dead.'

'They planned the murder together?'

'That is possible but I do not think it likely. Neither would trust the other that far.'

While we talked, Holmes was examining a rough footpath, below the sunken wall, trodden through the lower bracken during the spring and summer months. It was no more than ten inches wide on bare soil. Towards the wall, there were a dozen prints of walking-shoes, preserved in compacted earth by the dry weather. They had therefore been made during or just after the last rainfall.

'The very morning of the hunting-party!' Holmes said softly. 'But look! Along here there is the full print of the man's shoes as he walks towards the sunken wall. Then, where the last half-dozen impressions end at this bramble bush, the print is only of the soles of the shoes with no sign of the heels.'

'It was Scott!' I said at once. 'Running the last few paces when he saw the body fall.'

Holmes uttered a dry, humourless laugh.

'No doubt it was Scott! Look at this. One may calculate a man's approximate height by the length of his stride. In this instance, I should judge from the footprints that our sportsman was of less than medium height, say five feet eight inches, the figure given for Scott in the police records. However, when a man runs, his stride lengthens, which is not at all the case here. The stride remains identical, though only the soles of the shoes are imprinted. Be so good as to stand on the higher ground, on the spot where we assume that Lieutenant Hamborough's feet might be once he lay dead.'

I scrambled up to the higher level and did as he asked. Holmes raised his walking-stick as if it were a gun, aiming over the top of the bramble bush towards my head.

'Though it will prove nothing in itself, Watson, my line of sight from here, at a range of fifteen feet or so, runs squarely to the level of your eyebrows. A little high, I grant you. The post-mortem on Hamborough confirms him as being one inch taller than you. Scott is quite four inches less than I am. Those last few prints are not of a man running but of a man standing on his toes, in order to raise his aim at a target situated where your head is at present. Were I to fire from here, I assure you the line would continue beyond your head to the beech tree, to the very centre of the pellet holes in the vertical spread of shot.'

'Stewart could not have missed such evidence!'

'Stewart missed it because his mind was overcome by the theory that the gun had been fired thirty feet behind. His minions found a sufficient spread of shot to make Monson the only suspect. Then they looked no higher. It seems that the incompetence of the Procurator Fiscal's office is quite a match for Scotland Yard. The yellow dye-marks are proof of that. Unfortunately, they could not test the true range by measuring also the horizontal spread, for there are no trees within five feet on either side to catch the pellets. Nor, it seems, had they any conception of a shot that was fired upwards, rather than on the level.'

It was clear that he was right, as he always seemed to be. However, one objection remained.

'The fatal wound was behind the right ear, whereas you or Scott would have been on the young man's left.'

He chuckled, as if moving a chess-piece to checkmate.

'As to that, Watson, you will see the answer written on the lime tree behind you.'

Instinctively, I turned to look. Before I had finished the movement, I knew that Holmes had just shot me through the right side of the head at no more than fifteen feet. He was correct. The vertical spread of the rising shot against the beech tree would make it seem a far greater range, as if fired from a spot where only Major Monson had been standing.

'Then your case is proved!'

He shook his head.

'I wish it were. Unfortunately, it is very far from proved. We have evidence that may convince the firearms experts but the pathologists will hold out against us. So long as the fatal wound is consistent only with a range of thirty feet, no amount of speculation with your head and my walking-stick will save Major Monson's neck.'

V

Our sitting-room window in the Argyle Hotel looked out towards the length of the Trongate. Tall shops with sash windows on their upper floors stretched away like cliffs beyond the signs advertising the waxwork display and Percy's Boot Bargains. It was Saturday evening, when the courts and alleys behind the streets poured out their population into the commercial arteries of the city. The pavements with their ornate lamps were too narrow to contain the crowds, who spread out into the streets among brewers' drays and open-topped horse-buses.

To and fro across this view passed the tall spare figure of Sherlock Holmes, pacing the room with controlled energy, his hands clasped behind his back. As he measured the carpet to and fro, he listened to the case against Major Monson outlined by David Stewart from the sofa, where the Deputy Fiscal sat with Dr Henry Littlejohn.

This Edinburgh police surgeon was principal medical adviser to the prosecution. At length, Holmes stopped and straightened up, taller and gaunter than ever.

'I compliment you, Mr Stewart, on the care and diligence which you and Dr Littlejohn have lavished upon the investigation. However, I have invited you both here this evening to suggest that you should waste no further time upon it.'

'You are beyond me, Mr Holmes,' said Stewart quietly.

'I should not be surprised. For the moment, however, I tender my advice that you should drop the prosecution of Major Monson forthwith. You have not the slightest chance of winning a verdict in court.'

Mr Stewart opened his mouth and then closed it again. Dr Littlejohn looked like a man who has accidentally swallowed a peppermint humbug whole. The Deputy Fiscal recovered his wits.

'With great respect, Mr Holmes, there have been few cases in my experience where the chance of a conviction was greater. Certainly there have been none in which the accused has lied so consistently and so ineptly as Major Monson.'

'Just so,' said Holmes quickly. 'Then you would hang him for being a liar?'

Mr Stewart hesitated.

'He will hang himself, Mr Holmes. Sir, you have a reputation for ingenuity, far beyond London or Glasgow. However, since your request to me yesterday morning, your theory that Lieutenant Hamborough was shot from below the sunken wall by Scott has been examined and rejected.'

Holmes seemed not the least put out.

'May I ask why?'

Dr Littlejohn intervened.

'Such a wide wound, Mr Holmes, some three inches by two at its extreme dimensions, could not have been inflicted on the deceased at so short a range as fifteen feet, for one thing.'

'And for another?'

'Two shots only were heard by the witnesses. They are all in agreement. Major Monson admits firing the first shot. It is quite possible that he fired both of them. However, if Scott fired the second shot, we come back once again to the fact that he did so from too close a range to kill Lieutenant Hamborough by that wound.'

'Moreover,' added Stewart, 'had Scott fired at a range of thirty feet or more to cause such a wound, he must have been much further back down the path. He would have been visible to the witnesses when he fired.'

Holmes paused. Then he swept all this aside.

'I see. May we take it as common ground that Major Monson was lying when he changed his story about the guns to suit the absence of blackening on the skin?'

'Indeed we may!' Mr Stewart was astonished and a little wary at the zeal with which Holmes tightened the noose round his client.

'Good. First he tells us he was carrying the 12-bore loaded with smokeless amberite cartridges. We believe him. Later, when he discovers that this is the only ammunition with which Hamborough could have accidentally shot himself, the major changes guns—or rather stories—and is carrying the short-barrelled 20-bore with gunpowder? We think that is a lie?'

'Correct.'

'Excellent. You see? We are in agreement already! Very well, then Monson was carrying the 12-bore with amberite cartridges, as he said at first.'

'Certainly. Lieutenant Hamborough had the 20-bore whose powder would have blackened his skin at such a range. It did not. Therefore he did not shoot himself by accident.'

'Precisely!'

A great weight seemed to be lifted from Holmes by this general consent that his client was an unprincipled liar. His next observation did little to reassure me.

'I think, Mr Stewart, that we are very near to the end of this case.'

Neither David Stewart nor Dr Littlejohn looked as if he thought so.

'One thing, however,' Holmes swung round to the Deputy Fiscal, a long forefinger raised. 'As adviser to Mr Comrie Thomson, I have requested sight of the packet of amberite cartridges from which we agree that Major Monson was loading his gun on that fatal morning. I should like to see them.'

The packet which Mr Stewart now took from his attaché case was almost empty, containing no more than three or four shotgun cartridges. They were of the most ordinary kind. He handed the packet to Sherlock Holmes, who studied the contents with narrowed eyes.

'Have these cartridges been examined?'

Stewart's answer was abrupt, as if he suspected Holmes of playing some game with him. Had he known Holmes better, the Deputy Fiscal would have had no doubt of his earnestness.

'You may see for yourself, Mr Holmes, that there is nothing to examine. The unused cartridges have been seen and noted for the court as exhibit 241, item 9, in the list of evidence appended to the charge of murder. They scarcely warrant further examination. They were never used, not even loaded in the gun, and played no part in the crime.'

'How very remiss,' said Holmes coolly, sitting down at a small walnut table in the window and taking out his magnifying-glass. 'I fear I must tell you that they played the decisive part in this crime. By such blunders as yours, sir, are innocent men and women hanged.'

Mr Stewart and Dr Littlejohn looked at one another. Holmes put down his magnifying-glass. His eyes flashed and he turned upon his two visitors.

'As I suspected!'

Before anyone could stop him tampering with the evidence, he had opened his neat ivory-handled pocket-knife and was deftly slitting the hardened cardboard of a cartridge case down its length.

'Mr Holmes! I must beg you will desist!'

The Deputy Fiscal was on his feet, crossing the room to rescue this 'exhibit' from the depredations of the sharp little blade. Holmes waved him away. In any event, the damage was now done.

Dr Littlejohn and I got up and joined them. Holmes had spread open the cartridge case like a frog on a dissecting board. There was the percussion cap at the base to detonate the powder when the hammer of the gun struck the pin. The lower half of the cardboard casing was filled with yellow amberite powder. Above that, the interior of the cartridge was divided by a felt wad.

Between this division and a second wad at the top of the cartridge was a space which should have been filled with several hundred lead pellets. Instead, this upper cavity was packed by tightly compressed pellets of paper. Confined as they were by the cardboard tube, they appeared smaller and harder than the paper 'flower heads' which we had found in the woodland at Ardlamont. Yet a single glance at the paper and the fragments was enough to confirm that they were of the same origin. Before Mr Stewart recovered his presence of mind, Holmes had slit open a second cartridge with the same result.

'What is the commonest way of rendering a cartridge blank and harmless?' he said, as if speaking to himself. 'To slit its upper half open neatly and substitute some innocuous substance for the lead pellets. Paper pellets are an excellent replacement. Almost all of them are burnt up in the discharge of the gun. A few are merely dispersed, though many of those are touched by flame.'

As he spoke, he took from his pocket the two scraps of paper picked up at Ardlamont. To be sure they were blank. However, in opening them out he showed that one was singed a light brown down its edge. Such was the 'message' which Major Monson had unwittingly left.

'Monson fired nothing more lethal than paper,' Holmes said quietly to Stewart, 'Scott saw to that. As Monson said at first, he took the 12-bore and the cartridges on entering the woods. To be sure, had he opened a further packet of cartridges he would have fired live ammunition. What remained in the first packet was intended to suffice him until after the death of Lieutenant Hamborough.

During that time, provided he used no more than five cartridges, he was no danger to man nor beast. We know from the witnesses that he cannot have fired more than twice.'

'Then he cannot have killed Hamborough?'

'He cannot,' said Holmes gently, 'but the poor perjured wretch thinks he did, for he believed that he was firing live ammunition and that he alone had the range to cause a dreadful accident! Worse still, after the boating accident and the insurance of Hamborough's life for his own advantage, he thought quite reasonably that not a single juryman in the country would believe in his innocence! As for Scott, his trick would never have been discovered. Monson fired—but did not guess what he fired! If Hamborough's death had continued to be accepted as an accident, as it was by Dr Macmillan, the remaining few cartridges in the packet would have been used up by some other sportsman and Scott's secret would have been safe for ever.'

'But Scott cannot have inflicted such a wound at so short a range,' said the Deputy Fiscal, sitting down again. 'There is no altering that.'

Holmes turned to Dr Littlejohn.

'On what day was Hamborough killed?'

'I understand it was 10 August.'

'The day upon which Dr Macmillan certified accidental death? The poor boy was then taken to Ventnor on the Isle of Wight. He was buried there on 17 August, a week to the day after his death. Correct?'

Dr Littlejohn nodded but said nothing.

'After which,' Holmes continued, 'his body lay in the family vault. For how long?'

'The exhumation was carried out on 4 September and the post-mortem followed.'

'Did it indeed?' Holmes turned to the window and glanced down at the crowds in the Trongate. Then he looked round. 'In your experience as a police surgeon, Dr Littlejohn, how many of the bodies examined by you in cases of suspicious death have been exhumed?'

The bald bespectacled surgeon stared back at him.

413

'Not many as a percentage but quite a few in total.'

'From what causes?'

'Almost always where there is a suspicion of poison. Also I have known two or three who have died from violent blows and where there has been a question raised later of *mens rea*, deliberate harm.'

'I see.' Holmes turned to the window again. 'What is your experience of cases where the deceased has died of gunshot wounds?'

Dr Littlejohn shrugged.

'I have known two cases of homicidal shooting and quite a number of accidental shootings in the hunting season.'

'In how many of those cases was the deceased interred and exhumed before post-mortem examination?'

Dr Littlejohn stared at him, this time without speaking.

'There was not one,' said Holmes at last, 'was there, doctor?'

David Stewart had been fidgeting upon the sofa.

'What can that matter, Mr Holmes? Dr Littlejohn is expert and vastly experienced in the examination of gunshot wounds.'

Holmes bowed his head a little, as if to acknowledge this.

'Indeed he is. Perhaps he is less experienced, however, in the effects upon gunshot wounds of decomposition, a warm summer month later and after a few weeks of interment.'

'There was no decomposition to speak of!' said Littlejohn indignantly.

'Permit me,' Holmes turned to the table, from which he took a sheet of paper. 'Your post-mortem report, Dr Littlejohn. May I read you a word or two? *"The features were swollen . . . Decomposition was making progress . . . The hair, owing to advancing decomposition, was easily detached . . ."* '

'There is nothing in that!' said the Deputy Fiscal, now plainly rattled.

'Is there not, Mr Stewart? Are you familiar with the work of Professor Matthew Hay, who acts as police-surgeon for the City of Aberdeen?'

'I have met him several times.'

'Are you familiar, specifically, with his work on gunshot injuries?'

'His work?'

'His published work.'

'I cannot say that I am.'

'Would it surprise you to know that three weeks after death the progress of decomposition would make any measurement of the surface extent of an original shotgun wound almost impossible?'

The gaze of Sherlock Holmes now pinned his young victim like a moth to a specimen board. He went on without respite.

'The post-mortem report by Dr Littlejohn gives the maximum extent of the wound as varying from two to three inches, which in itself is consistent with a shot fired at a range of fifteen feet. Now, gentlemen, either there was decomposition or there was not. If there was, no accurate measurement of the wound can be given. If there was not, then the measurement is accurate and Hamborough was shot from fifteen feet. He was certainly not shot by Major Monson with paper pellets! In either event, I fear that your case against the defendant is blown to smithereens.'

Stewart stared at him with that mixture of exasperation and incomprehension characteristic of so many adversaries of Sherlock Holmes. The young man seemed to be listening to the door of a trap as it closed behind him. He then made the same mistake as so many of his predecessors, seeing a promise of salvation and leaping at it.

'Why should Scott do Monson's work for him? It was Monson who would benefit directly from the insurance, not Scott.'

Holmes walked across and laid a hand sympathetically on the young man's shoulder.

'He did it for the money, Mr Stewart. He meant to be rich for life. There was no way to do that so long as Hamborough lived, once his funds were exhausted. Scott and Monson were partners in fleecing the poor fellow but until he was dead, they had nothing more. Fortunately for Scott, Dr Macmillan knew little of gunshot wounds and gave the young man a death certificate. Scott then withdrew from the scene to attend to his own affairs. His undoubted intention was that Monson should believe that he himself had killed Hamborough accidentally. If the coast had remained clear, Scott could have returned to claim from Monson the "debts" his young friend Hamborough owed him. I do not doubt that Hamborough's signature, forged where necessary, would appear on far more IOUs than he ever wrote to Mr Beresford Tottenham, the moneylender. Such claims on the young man's estate, on the insurance money of £30,000, were more than enough to make Scott's fortune. The shooting would remain an accident, as Dr Macmillan thought it was. Naturally, when Scott read the reports of Monson's arrest, he preferred not to show his face.'

'Monson would surely refuse to pay him,' said Mr Stewart hopefully.

Holmes shook his head.

'Scott, *alias* Davis, *alias* Sweeney is no stranger to blackmail. Least of all when he might threaten to fabricate evidence of murder against his partner. Monson, the poor swindling booby, already believes that he shot Hamborough by accident. It would only need Scott to whisper in his ear a promise of going to the authorities with a story of having seen Monson creep up on the young man and take deliberate aim. For good measure, he might swear to having seen Monson take the bung out of the rowing-boat the night before. Scott himself, of course, was the perpetrator of that curtain-raiser.'

There was an uncomfortable silence, until Holmes added quietly, 'You, Mr Stewart, would have hanged Monson even on the evidence you have now! Think how much easier your task would have been had Scott offered you such evidence as I have just suggested. Do you still doubt that Monson would give Scott half of the £30,000 to shut his mouth? I promise you he would give him all to save his neck from the rope!'

The Deputy Fiscal got slowly to his feet.

'I will report what you have told me.'

'Please do so,' said Holmes graciously, 'and when you do, pray inform the Procurator with my compliments that Professor Matthew Hay, Police-Surgeon of Aberdeen, has already agreed to give evidence for the defence in any trial of Major Monson.'

It is a matter of history that Professor Hay did so and that the charges against Alfred John Monson were found 'not proven' by the jury at the High Court of Justiciary in Edinburgh. Holmes and I heard no more of the major, except that he sued Madame Tussaud's Waxworks for placing an effigy of him in the Chamber of Horrors. Edward Scott, or Edward Sweeney as he was born, remained at large. I was putting together the papers in the case, so that they might be deposited in the tin trunk, when something struck me in one of the depositions.

'Is it not curious, Holmes, that having hired a place like Ardlamont for the summer, Scott absented himself so much at night? He seems to have risen late, gone to Glasgow by the afternoon steamer and returned late, except on Sundays when he dined with the Monsons at Ardlamont. On Wednesday and Saturday, he went still earlier, to be in the city by two in the afternoon. It is all here in the butler's statement. I suppose the fellow was probably taking street-girls to some low-class hotel.'

Holmes listened with eyes closed and fingertips pressed tight together. Then he opened his eyes and said, 'But scarcely on Wednesday and Saturday afternoons with such regularity.'

He closed his eyes again and appeared to have gone to sleep. Then he sat up abruptly.

'It is his profession! Of course! Not an admirable one but, such as it is, I suppose it is his *métier*. What professional man is occupied every evening but Sunday—and upon Wednesday and Saturday afternoons?'

'I have no idea at this moment.'

'Dear me,' he said with a yawn, 'did you never, in your wild youth, Watson, attend a music-hall? It is available every evening with matinées on Wednesday and Saturday. I daresay you might have found Mr Scott on the stage of the Glasgow Empire.'

'That is quite absurd!'

'So it is. However, if I had a guinea for every occasion on which what is absurd has proved to be true, I should be a good deal richer than I am.'

We did not discuss the matter further. A long time later, a letter came to Holmes from David Stewart, the Deputy Fiscal. Edward Scott had been seen briefly, working as the assistant to a music-hall magician. Then he had vanished for good. In the course of the stage performance, there was some 'trick-shooting', when the blindfold magician shot the segments from an orange on his assistant's head—or something of the kind. The trick is one of the oldest in the world. The fruit, or whatever the target be, is carefully dismembered beforehand. The pieces are plucked from it by a concealed thread in the moment when the audience blinks at the firing of the shot and the scene is veiled by smoke. One of the chores of the brave but humble assistant is to ensure that the cartridges in the pistol of the magician have been rendered blank.

'I assure you,' said Holmes, stretching out his long legs towards the winter fire, 'Scott is probably quite safe, even if he should be found again. To prosecute him now would be difficult in any event. Moreover, if they could not get a verdict against Monson, they will hardly get one against Scott. Mr Stewart and his colleagues must admit publicly the falsity of all their evidence in the previous case and the fact that I was right in every particular. I do not somehow think that they will swallow so bitter a pill.'

It is a matter of history that they never did.

The Case of the Hygienic Husband

On a rainy morning of early autumn, in the last days of peace before the Great War, Sherlock Holmes leant back in his chair, the remains of his breakfast still littering the table. He began to open his correspondence. As I took up the *Times* report on the Serbian crisis, there was an exclamation from my friend. I put aside the paper and saw his face writhing with inward merriment, his eyes shining, as if he was restraining a convulsive attack of laughter.

He read out to me from a sheet of notepaper in his hand.

> *'Sir—In answer to your question regarding my parentage, etc. My mother was a bus-horse, my father a cab-driver, my sister a rough-rider over the arctic regions. My brothers were all gallant sailors on a steam-roller. This is the only information I can give to those who are not entitled to ask such questions—contained in the letter I received on the 15th inst. Your despised son-in-law G. Smith.'*

'Who the devil, Holmes, is G. Smith and to whom is this nonsense addressed?'

He looked at two more sheets of paper and shook his head.

'I have no notion, my dear fellow. At least, it can scarcely be addressed to us. Curiously, however, there seems to be no covering letter. I have no doubt that we shall discover something more before the day is over. One moment. Here is a second from the author of the first!'

He held up this sheet of paper and read it out.

> 'Sir—I do not know your next move, but take my advice and be careful. Yours etc., G. Smith. Now that, Watson, sounds more businesslike. And here is a third, dated like the others within the past ten days. Sir—I have all the copies of the letters, &c., my wife and self has sent to you and yours, also all letters &c., we have received relating to same and family affairs which I intend to keep for the purpose of justice. G. Smith. Whoever Mr Smith may be he shows, does he not, an engaging innocence of the conventions of grammar and syntax?'

'But why have these things been sent to us with no explanation?'

'I believe we shall have an answer to that soon enough.'

Without another word, he knocked out his pipe and stretched upon the sofa with his violin and a score of Scriabin's tone poem *Prometheus*. Holmes had lately conceived an unfortunate enthusiasm for the 'new music' of Stravinsky and Scriabin. Such cacophony may do well enough in a concert hall, but in one's domestic quarters it is insupportable. The score of *Prometheus* he professed to find interesting because the composer claimed that he had allowed religion, occultism, and even the properties of light to dictate the unmelodious music. A better reason for destroying such tosh would be hard to find!

As Holmes predicted, however, there was a happy interruption half an hour later from the clang of the bell at the street-door. Mrs Hudson came upstairs alone.

'A gentleman,' she said, rather archly as I thought. 'He has no appointment but believes Mr Holmes may be in possession of some papers belonging to him. The gentleman is here to collect them.'

Holmes seemed not the least put out as he laid down his violin and bow.

'By all means show him up, Mrs Hudson. He shall have our undivided attention.'

While we awaited this visitor, Holmes recited phrases from the letters as if they had been a schoolboy's lesson.

'My mother was a bus-horse, my father a cab-driver, my sister a rough-rider across the arctic regions. This promises rather well, Watson. I am inclined to think . . .'

What he was inclined to think remained unspoken. At that moment, the door of the sitting-room opened. We confronted a tall pleasant-looking man, a little more than fifty years old. His face was high-nosed and pale, his clothes of a dark clerical cut with a pearl-grey cravat.

'Pray come in, sir, and be seated,' Holmes said genially, 'I am Sherlock Holmes and this is my associate Dr Watson. I imagine, however, that you already know that.'

The tall pale man made a little bow in each direction and said awkwardly, 'The truth is, Mr Holmes, I had heard of neither of you until two days ago. My wife and I lead a quiet and, until recently, a contented life. Even the newspapers have little claim on my attention.'

'No matter,' said Holmes, guiding him to a chair, 'I fear I did not have the pleasure of gathering your name from the letters you kindly forwarded.'

Our visitor looked at him quickly, as if he did not expect Holmes to connect him so easily with the curious correspondence.

'It was not my intention to deceive you,' he said guardedly as we sat down.

Holmes gave him another quick but reassuring smile.

'My dear sir, there was no deceit. What is a name at this stage? It is enough for me that you are plainly a devout man held in high regard. A Methodist local preacher, I fancy, living in Buckinghamshire. Your daughter has made an injudicious marriage to Mr Smith, a scoundrel. On Tuesday afternoon, two days ago, I rather think you went to Oxford to consult Mr Henry Howes, of Howes and Woodhall, solicitors in St Michael Street. On his advice, you sent me copies of three letters from Mr Smith, demanding sums unpaid by you from a promissory note given him a month or two ago. This was understood to be payment for removing himself and leaving your daughter alone. Unfortunately nothing was put in writing to that effect. The result is that he has married your daughter since then and now proposes to enforce payment of the money. This morning, on the advice of Mr Howes, you came up by train and have just walked here from Marylebone station.'

Like so many clients, our visitor stared as if he suspected witchcraft.

'I could almost believe, sir, that you have spied upon me!'

Holmes set him at his ease.

'I have done nothing but exercise a little common sense. The cut and clerical pattern of your suit, like the label in your overcoat, comes from Harris and Rogerson of Victoria Street, close to the Methodist Central Hall, well-known as tailors to the clergy of that denomination. You do not wear a clerical collar but you have the manner and address of a public speaker. This leads me to suppose you are a local preacher in your circuit. You did not come by cab, for we should have heard it draw up, therefore you have walked a relatively short distance or your shoes and trouser-cuffs would be wetter. Marylebone is our closest terminus. Your coat and umbrella have kept you dry for the most part. I merely note that your lower right trouser-leg is marked by rain, while the left is not. After many years of residence, I recognize that as the sign of a man who has walked from Marylebone station in the prevailing wind rather than from the Metropolitan line at Baker Street. The time of your arrival suggests you have come by the line that runs to Buckinghamshire. So early in the day, you could scarcely have come from a greater distance.'

Our visitor shifted uneasily.

'Then Mr Howes has not betrayed my confidence?'

Holmes shook his head.

'I observe that the postage stamp on your envelope was cancelled in Oxford at 6 A.M. yesterday. You yourself would hardly be in Oxford at such an early hour, of course. At least, you would not go all the way to the sorting office to post a letter at that time, when you might just as well have sent it from any post-box during the rest of the day. The envelope was, therefore, placed in the box on Tuesday night, after the day's final collection, at about 10 P.M. If you were in Oxford prior to posting these most important documents, then it is reasonable to suppose that you went to seek advice and that you spent some hours considering whether to follow it.'

'That is the case precisely,' said our visitor, somewhat relieved.

'Indeed,' said Holmes comfortingly. 'As for the recommendation, I am acquainted with Warden Spooner of New College, Strachan Davidson the Master of Balliol, and several senior members of the School of Natural Science at the University. However, they are not men to be approached in such a matter as this. On the other hand, I was once able to render a small service to Mr Howes. He is the most likely person in that city to have mentioned my name to you. The fact that he did not forward the papers himself also suggests to me that you spent some hours pondering the matter. At length, you decided to post them without a covering letter, so that you still did not commit yourself by name. You then returned home by the last train. Aylesbury or Tring on the 10.45 from Oxford, I should guess. I daresay I am quite wrong.'

'Tring was the station, but my home is not there,' said our visitor quietly. 'You are wrong only in that, Mr Holmes, for I live at Aston Clinton, several miles away. I could not have believed in such powers of deduction if I had not witnessed them for myself.'

'I assure you,' Holmes said gently, 'it is not difficult to construct a series of inferences, each dependent upon its predecessor and simple in itself. If one merely knocks out the central inferences and presents only a starting-point and conclusion, it has a startling effect. But it is simple enough, for all that.'

'My name,' said the tall pale man, 'is William Maxse. My daughter Constance is a handsome young woman with a little money. She trained as a nurse for three years at Southsea and has held some excellent positions.'

'Until she met Mr Smith?'

'Precisely,' Mr Maxse's colour rose. 'Unfortunately there is more to it than that. I have a dear friend and colleague at our chapel, Charles Burnham, whose daughter Alice trained with mine. Both girls came from Wesleyan families in the same town. When they went away to Portsmouth, the chapel at Southsea, as well as the hospital, became a centre of their lives. The scoundrel of whom I speak attended the Southsea chapel.'

'Allow me,' said Holmes, who was taking a few notes. 'How long ago did this matter begin?'

'Two years ago, Smith courted and married Alice Burnham, to her parents' great distress. No sooner was the wedding over than he began to demand what he called the money due as a marriage settlement. He did so in the most abusive terms, almost word for word such as you have seen in his address to me.'

'And was the money paid?'

'It was paid, Mr Holmes, for poor Burnham feared that any legal action would destroy his child's reputation.'

'How most unfortunate. Pray continue with your narrative.'

'It almost makes me weep to do so,' said Mr Maxse quietly. 'After Smith and Miss Burnham had been married a little while, Alice Burnham died in a swimming accident of some kind at Black-pool, where they were on holiday. Smith returned to Southsea and appeared once again in the chapel, distraught at his loss. He swore that he could no longer bear the memories which the town evoked and so he went to live elsewhere. I heard this much from Charles Burnham himself and supposed we had heard the last of the wretch.'

'One seldom hears the last of such men,' said Holmes thoughtfully. 'When was it that Smith reappeared?'

'Two years later he returned to Southsea. I think it is not too much to say that he laid siege to my Constance's heart when they met again in chapel. He corrupted my girl's affections, Mr Holmes.

I warned her in vain against him. She wrote back swearing that he was the most loving and Christian-like man.'

Holmes muttered something which I did not catch. Mr Maxse continued.

'The result of my warnings was to turn poor Connie against me. I heard nothing for a week or two and prayed that this meant a separation between them. Alas, it did not. I swear it was Smith who persuaded my girl that it was best to marry him first and tell her mother and me afterwards. So it happened. I knew nothing of their register-office wedding until a week later, when the demands for money began. No bride-cake, no photograph, no loving words from my darling. I ask you, sir, if I may legitimately refuse payment to him and if you can bring my Constance back to me?'

Holmes let his chin rest on his chest, showing his bird-of-prey profile.

'Unless there is money already settled on her in the event of her marriage, he has no such claim on you. As to her return, it is she who must will it.'

'Then let the money go, Mr Holmes! How may I bring my child back and—God forgive me—see this devil destroyed?'

Holmes crossed to the window, and in a characteristic pause looked down into the street for a moment before replying. Then he turned round.

'You may depend upon me to do whatever I can. But you must understand that the law will support your son-in-law as a husband in almost every respect.'

'I care nothing for money!' cried the poor man in his despair.

'Just so. Mr Smith counts on that. I must repeat, however, as to bringing a daughter home, there is little a father can do that will not drive a bride deeper into the arms of such a . . .'

'Such a reptile! I saw it in him the first and last time our paths crossed.'

'Quite. Now your daughter must see it, for herself. When she does so, your time will come. Until then, right remains on your side. The law, unfortunately, is on his.'

Mr Maxse had twisted in his chair to face Holmes squarely, his face flushed with anger.

'Then you can do nothing for me?'

Holmes walked back and sat down just opposite him.

'I did not say so, Mr Maxse. The law can do nothing, as matters stand. I, however, am not the law.'

I never saw such gratitude sparkle in the eyes of a client. Before Mr Maxse left us, Holmes was no less to him than a knight in arms. When we were alone, my friend lit his pipe in silence and sat lost in thought until I interrupted him at last.

'They have been married two weeks already. It is presumably too late for an annulment and certainly too early for a divorce. How is such a case to be won?'

He put down his pipe.

'It astonishes me, Watson, that you have gathered so little. As a medical man, you surely see that Smith is no common scoundrel. He steps full-grown from Dr Albert Moll's admirable treatise on criminal psychopathology.'

I saw nothing of the kind but it seemed neither the time nor place to say so.

'The wedding-photograph,' Holmes said thoughtfully. 'Why was the newly-married Mrs Smith forbidden to send a copy to her parents? Was it not the most natural thing for her to do?'

'Perhaps no photograph was taken.'

'Where there is a wedding,' he said sourly, 'there is a photograph, usually of questionable artistry.'

'You think Smith did not want his wife's parents to see a likeness of him?'

'Come, Watson! They had seen him in the flesh. No. Friend Smith is concerned that no one else should see his wedding picture. What crime might that photograph reveal to a person who saw it by chance and identified him?'

'Bigamy? A wedding under other circumstances can scarcely constitute a crime where the bride is of age.'

He looked at me, as if I might be his despair.

'This illiterate boor exercises such power over two intelligent and capable young women that they, at his command, cast off their parents and all their love for them. Who, short of a hypnotist or Dr Mesmer in person, could accomplish such a feat twice with two such loving daughters—and who knows with how many more? If Mr Smith proves to be a mere bigamist, Watson, I shall regard him as a sad disappointment.'

II

For several days, following Mr Maxse's visit, Holmes abandoned Monsieur Scriabin's tone-poem. Nothing would do but he must lounge about the sitting-room with his violin, singing the phrases of Mr Smith's absurd letters to tunes that took his fancy. I recall, painfully, 'The Keel-Row', tortured on the fiddle-strings until it fitted, 'My mother was a bus-horse, my father a cab-driver, my sister a rough-rider across the arctic regions.'

So far as his case was concerned, he appeared to have forgotten it.

It was several mornings later when I chanced to see an official envelope among the letters awaiting his attention. As he lifted the one above it, the form of address on the lower one was revealed: 'Miss Phoebe Golightly, 221b Baker Street, London W.' I stared at him as he read its predecessor, until at last he looked up, as if suddenly aware of my attention. I pointed at the envelope.

'What the devil is that, Holmes?'

He glanced at it with complete unconcern, then stared back at me.

'It is I, Watson. I am Miss Phoebe Golightly, by courtesy of the typewriter, which is impartial in matters of handwriting and sex. I am a youthful spinster who attended a wedding on Saturday week at the Portsmouth Register Office. Indeed, I was a bridesmaid to my cousin. In the excitement which, for reasons that baffle me, follows these ceremonies, I gave a shawl to be held by the photographer's assistant while the pictures were taken. The jollity of the occasion was such that I was half-way to the reception before realizing that

I had left the garment behind. I feel sure that some register official would know the firms of Portsmouth photographers likely to be present that afternoon.'

I watched him open the letter and scowl at it. Then his face brightened.

'And here we are. Mr Collins of Wellington Street, Southsea, or, perhaps the larger business of Whitfield and Buller of Stanhope Road, Portsmouth. You will observe from the letters sent to Mr Maxse that the Smiths are lodging at an address in Kimberley Road, East Southsea. The probability must be that Mr Collins of Wellington Street was their man.'

'If a photograph was taken.'

'If it was not, Watson, we must pursue another course. I think, however, Mr Smith would not be so foolish as show his true meanness so early to his bride.'

That afternoon, a further fabrication devised by Holmes in the name of Mr Maxse, solicited a copy of his daughter's wedding-photograph. Before the week was out, a stout envelope brought back this full-plate print. The photograph showed too plainly the meanness of the occasion, whose ceremony had been attended only by the bride and groom. The witnesses, who stood either side of the couple, were plainly a pair of register officials. Constance Maxse appeared a well-built and rather plump young woman with dark hair and an air of resolve. She did not seem in the least like a wayward daughter but a figure of somewhat matronly decorum.

Far more interesting to Holmes was the image of the bridegroom. His was a strong broad-boned face in which the nose and chin were sharp rather than regular. He had a full dark moustache, which an Italian waiter might have affected, but wore it as if to conceal a line of cruelty in his mouth. The eyes looked hard and straight under low and frowning brows. They shone with a dreadful clarity and a merciless sanity. His brown hair was worn short and neat, so that the high points of the ears appeared prominently. There was no flabbiness in the face, the skin being tight over the bones and still shining from the razor, yet the neck was one of the thickest in proportion that I have ever seen.

'Ah!' said Holmes at once. 'What would the great Lombroso not have given for the skull of such an hereditary degenerate! Look at the features, Watson! The eyes stare down at you, just as a man regards a beetle in the moment before he crushes it with his boot! The power of those cheek-bones! The strength of that neck! Mr Maxse told us he knew the man for what he was. I doubt if the poor fellow guessed the half of it!'

We studied the portrait in silence for several minutes. Then Holmes said coolly, 'I do believe the strength of that neck may cause some little inconvenience to Messrs Pierpoint and Ellis in the exercise of their gruesome trade. For, Watson, if ever I saw a man born to be hanged, this is he.'

Sherlock Holmes had, to a remarkable degree, the power of detaching his mind at will. He was also exceedingly reluctant on occasions to communicate his plans or his thoughts to any other person. During the next few days I once again concluded that he had given up any active interest in the case for the time being and was now waiting for the sinister bridegroom to make his first mistake. This impression became all the stronger when he told me that his second cousin, Lieutenant-Commander Holmes-Derringer of the admiral's staff at Scapa Flow, had invited him to attend the live-firing tests of the new Whitehead torpedo in the vicinity of that remote island anchorage. For three days at least he would be absent from London. I hoped most fervently that I should not be the subject of Mr Maxse's reproaches during this period.

I was about to say as much, shortly before he left, when I saw that I was already too late. I had been out and had just come back as far as Mrs Hudson's open street door, about to go upstairs, when a neatly-rigged and capped naval officer, his light-brown hair and beard well-trimmed, came cantering down with a brown binocular-case in his hand. He called out to Holmes who was evidently already in the cab that waited in the street, 'Sit tight, old boy! I've got them for you!' Then, as if noticing me for the first time in the shadows, he snapped, 'Morning to you!'

The sharp air of command was such that I very nearly saluted him. So much for Lieutenant-Commander Holmes-Derringer. As I watched, he tossed the overlooked binoculars into the hansom, swung himself aboard as if it might be a battle-cruiser's whaler, and the cab clattered north towards the Euston Road.

In order not to incur the reproaches of Mr Maxse, I decided that I would withdraw to my club for the greater part of the next day or two, leaving Baker Street after breakfast. I should then come home when I judged that the last train from Marylebone to the counties had left.

It was on the second day that I entered the sitting-room, at 11 P.M. or thereabouts, and found a wire waiting for me.

IMPERATIVE YOU SEEK SMITH IN WESTON-SUPER-MARE AT ONCE STOP.
WILL JOIN YOU ON RETURN FROM SCOTLAND STOP. FURTHER INSTRUCTIONS AWAIT YOU TELE-GRAPH OFFICE, TEMPLE MEADS STATION, BRISTOL STOP. = HOLMES, C/O ADMIRALTY INTELLIGENCE STOP.

I put down the scrap of paper with the feeling of a man com-manded to make bricks without straw. With no further information than this, how was I to find Smith, or anyone else, among the resi-dent population and teeming summer holidaymakers of a seaside town that was utterly unfamiliar to me? What further instructions of any value could Holmes possibly send me from his present isola-tion in the Orkney Islands? I certainly had no means of contacting him. I could scarcely wire a message to him through Lieutenant-Commander Holmes-Derringer in the middle of the night and, in any case, I had no time to wait for a reply next day.

I slept uneasily with the phrases of that telegraph running and twisting like railway tracks, crossing and parting, in my brain.

Once I woke sharply from a dream with the face of Mr Smith in his wedding-photograph shimmering like a gargoyle in the darkness. By next morning I decided that there was nothing for it but to do as I was told.

III

By the evening of the next day, the express that had brought me from Paddington was pulling into the long curve of the railway platform at Bristol, the hills of the city rising high above the river on either side. At the telegraph office, to my dismay, there was no wire from Holmes. Perhaps by now he was on the high seas in a cruiser or a destroyer and was forbidden such communication, for German intelligence was keenly aware of our development of submarine warfare. However, on further investigation there was a telephone message for me, which the clerk had scribbled down without bothering to put the name of the sender. I stared at the pencilled letters.

> *Dr Watson to proceed to Grand Atlantic Hotel, Weston, and await instructions.*

As evening sunlight mellowed over the flat coastal fields of north Somerset, I accomplished the last part of my journey and found myself in a fine modern hotel like a French château. There was a view of sands and donkey-carriages, two islands in the foreground, the hills of Wales beyond, and a wide expanse of grey sea stretching to the Atlantic. I had ample time to stare at this prospect from my window, for neither the usual telegraph service nor the next morning's post brought me any instructions. It was a Saturday and the town full of trippers. That afternoon, weary of my confinement, I took my stick and crossed the beach lawns with the object of taking a stroll along the broad two-mile stretch of promenade above the sands, where the sea breeze brought a healthy tingle to the cheeks.

Unfortunately, this broad paving had lately been given over to the American plague of roller-skating. Men and even women of the lower orders rumbled or sped past one, weaving in and out among the respectable pedestrians, endangering the lives and limbs of their betters. The audacity of these pests to society was beyond belief. There was one jaunty fellow, in a tweed jacket, gaiters, and cap, who fancied himself something of a virtuoso. He wove among the walkers, deliberately caught the rear of my hat-brim with his hand and tipped it forward over my eyes. This was an insolent devil with a bushy moustache that failed to conceal the high-coloured cheeks and broken capillaries of the inveterate beer-drinker. I shouted after him but he took not the least notice.

Somehow, though I did not see him do it, he must have circled back. The next thing I knew was a sharp tap behind me and my brim settled over my eyes once more. As I pulled up the hat, he had the damnable effrontery to turn and laugh at me, idling on his skates just beyond the reach of my stick.

'Do that once more,' I shouted, 'I will summon a policeman and give you in charge!'

'Oh dear!' he chuckled merrily. 'I beg you will do no such thing, Watson! I have just established a most cordial working relationship with Inspector Gerrish of the Somerset Constabulary, who is no less than Lestrade's cousin. I cannot but feel that my arrest might cast a cloud upon it.'

To say that this knocked the breath from me would be an understatement. Of course I asked him what the devil he was doing here, when all the world thought he was at Scapa Flow. Indeed, I demanded an explanation as to what all this nonsense about Weston-super-Mare signified.

'My poor Watson,' he said jovially, as he sat on a bench, unlacing his skates before we returned to the hotel, 'I did not dare let you into the secret earlier, for fear you might give the game away. It was imperative that I should be thought to be well out of circulation by Mr Maxse, his daughter, her husband and the whole world. It is true, of course, that I was not at Scapa Flow, but Portsmouth is no less famous in our naval history.'

'Portsmouth!' In the room he had taken at the hotel, which was only a few doors from my own, I watched him peel off the moustache and rub the rouge and gum from his cheeks with surgical spirit. 'You have been down there after this fellow Smith?'

'It was not difficult,' he said more seriously. 'It is clear that he thinks himself quite safe from all but Mr Maxse. However, I confess that even I had not imagined the extent of his depravity. I followed him between Portsmouth and Southsea for a day and a half, to little avail. But then, to my surprise, he suddenly made for the harbour station with a Gladstone bag in his hand. He took the train as far as Bristol, decamped, and boarded the tram to Clifton. Thence he returned with a young woman whose name I gathered from a question or two to an errand boy is Miss Pegler, though known sometimes as Mrs Smith. They are here at the moment, staying as man and wife. What story he has told to his poor bride of a fortnight ago, heaven only knows.'

'There may be enough for a divorce petition when the time comes,' I said darkly.

'Oh, no, Watson. I should be greatly disappointed if this led merely to divorce. Besides, this practice of ours does not stoop to concern itself with what the papers call matrimonial cases. On that, I am inflexible.'

'Where is he now?'

Holmes shrugged.

'I have lost him,' he said, as if it were not of the least consequence.

'Then what are we to do?'

Lights were beginning to twinkle like strings of pearls in the mauve dusk, strung between the lamp-standards along the shore-line. Above the rush of the returning tide, the music of a band drifted inland from the theatre pavilion of the Grand Pier.

'We shall take a walk,' he said jauntily. 'Just so far as the sea-front photographer's kiosk. Mr Jackson, of Jackson's Faces, has become quite a holiday friend of mine.'

Any visitor to the seaside is aware of that other promenade pes-
tilence, the man who pushes his camera at your face, 'snaps' you,
hands you a ticket, and enjoys the privilege of sticking your likeness
on his billboard until you pay to have it removed. Jackson's Faces
possessed a kiosk by the causeway of the muddy harbour, flanked
by those boards on which prints of the photographs taken in the
last day or two were pinned.

'Allow me to present Mr Smith,' said Holmes quietly.

My companion was indicating the somewhat wrinkled photographs pinned on the board. He did not need to tell me which he
had in mind, for it was a most extraordinary picture. It showed an
incongruous couple walking arm-in-arm along the very stretch
of promenade where we now stood, the lights glinting in the harbour tide. The woman wore her hair loose with an expression of
simpering stupidity. The man was absurdly-dressed for a seaside
visit in a top hat, stiff wing-collar and bow-tie, a frock-coat and
waistcoat with gold chain. Such was the holiday masquerade of a
would-be 'man of property'. To anyone who had seen the recent
wedding-photograph, however, there was no mistaking the bold
stride and the contemptuous eyes above the abundant moustache,
a frightening moral indifference to pain or distress.

Such were Mr Smith and Miss Pegler.

'I rather fancy, Watson, that there is enough in that photograph
to send our man to penal servitude for seven years to begin with,
under section 57 of the Offences Against the Person Act.'

'I have no idea . . .'

'Bigamy. Do you not see the ring on the fourth finger of the lady's
left hand?'

'That means nothing. It is for show.'

'I think not,' he said softly, 'I think he may be married to this
lady, validly or not. If validly, then the marriage to Miss Maxse
is bigamous. He wants that young lady's money, or her family's
money, and mere seduction will not do. Whatever else Mr Smith
may lack, he seems accomplished as a professional swindler of the
female sex. One moment.'

He turned into the entrance of the kiosk, from which came the harsh chemical odours of bleach and ammonia. The bald proprietor in his neat suit stood behind the counter.

'Mr Jackson, allow me to introduce my colleague, Dr Watson. Pray tell him what you told me this afternoon about the man in that photograph.'

Mr Jackson's eyes brightened behind his wire-framed spectacles.

'I can't say, gentlemen, that I remember every name that goes with every face. We get too many. But I have a natural recollection of many. That's how I was first called "Faces." '

'Most interesting,' said Holmes impatiently, 'and this one?'

'I'd good reason to remember him, though it was a year or two ago. I took his likeness then, just here by Knightstone harbour, and put it on the board. He never wanted it. However, we keep them there a few days. Just before it was to be took down, a lady came in. Mrs Tuckett that has a boarding house in Upper Church Road above Glentworth Cove. "That man," she says, "him in the photograph. He left the day before yesterday and bilked me of three weeks money." '

'Had she been to the police?'

'Where's the use?' Mr Jackson became philosophical. 'Police won't do nothing. They'll tell you it's a civil matter and you can sue him if you like. If you can find him, they mean!'

'And his name?'

'Williams,' Mr Jackson emphasized the name as if to impress on us the reliability of his memory. 'Him and his wife.'

'And you remembered him and his name all this time?' I asked, I fear with a touch of scepticism.

Mr Jackson looked at me as if I were an imbecile.

'He came back,' he explained slowly. 'That's how I remembered him. His wife came back first, going to stay with Mrs Tuckett again, paying the arrears and offering apologies, saying how her husband had deserted her the year before. She had some money of her own now from her father's estate, he having been a bank manager, and so she paid the debt. A week or two later, as Mrs Tuckett told me, Mrs Williams went out to buy her some flowers. She came back quite shocked, but pleased, saying that she'd just met Mr Williams her husband, that she hadn't seen for a year. There he was, standing by the bandstand near Glentworth Cove, alone and looking out to sea.'

'A curious coincidence,' said Holmes blandly.

'Coincidence?' Mr Jackson tightened his mouth. 'Cold-blooded and deliberate, if you ask me. According to Mrs Tuckett, they were reconciled. First thing Williams did then was to take his wife down to Mr Littlington, of Bakers the Solicitors, in Waterloo Street, and make her sign everything of her father's over to him.'

'Ah, yes,' said Holmes, as if approving of such prudence on the part of Smith, *alias* Williams. 'That is just as it should be.'

Mr Jackson looked at him sharply but my companion smiled and bowed himself out of the kiosk.

'I fear, Watson, that Constance Maxse is by no means Mr Smith's first bigamous bride. I should give a good deal to know how many there are altogether.'

As we walked past the pier and heard the music of the band drifting in towards the shore, I said, 'What can it matter? He will go to penal servitude for seven years, if he goes for a day.'

Holmes frowned at me.

'I should like something better than that for Mr Smith. He is an artist to whom a mere seven years would be an insult. A true artist in crime, Watson, plays the game with nothing less than his feet on two boards, the pit beneath him and the noose round his neck. *Qualis artifex pereo*, as the Emperor Nero remarked wisely at the last. The execution shed is a far nobler exit for such men than a mere convict cell.'

IV

Our return to Baker Street from the coast of the Bristol Channel coincided with another of those periods of lethargy that overtook Holmes without apparent warning. Since the beginning of the investigation I feared that he might be suffering from a psychic ailment of some kind. He seemed, from time to time, to lose interest in a case that was far from concluded. Much of the day he leaned back in his chair, in gloomy speculation. When Lestrade came to see us of an evening to impart the criminal news of London, he now found Holmes leaning languidly against the mantelpiece, scarcely endeavouring to conceal his yawns.

This lasted for about five days after our return, during which he said not a word to our Scotland Yard friend of the inquiry which we had in hand. It was the morning post on the sixth day that put an end to his indolence. I was aware that from time to time an envelope embossed with the crest of Somerset House appeared among my friend's correspondence. He had been indebted on several occasions to Dr L'Estrange, the archivist of that estimable institution where all births, marriages, and deaths are recorded. On this occasion, Holmes appeared from his bedroom well after ten o'clock and, showing none of his usual disdain for correspondence before breakfast, snatched at the Somerset House envelope. In a single cut, he slit it open with the silver and ruby-handled paperknife that had been a token of gratitude from a prime minister of France, Georges Clemenceau, following the resolution of the Dreyfus espionage scandal and the vindication of an innocent man.

He read the enclosed letter with a chuckle.

'Dear me, Watson! We have underestimated Mr Smith!'

I could see that there was a second sheet of paper attached to the letter. He looked up, his eyes shining with merriment.

'This, my dear fellow, is the marriage certificate of George Joseph Smith!'

'To Miss Burnham—or possibly to Miss Constance Maxse?'

He shook his head.

'Better than any of those. This records his marriage, under his own name in 1908, at Bristol, to Edith Mabel Pegler. We should have done that lady a grave injustice in assuming an irregular relationship between them. She is described here as a housekeeper, no doubt to her bridegroom. George Joseph Smith appears as thirty-three years old, a bachelor and general dealer, son of George Smith deceased, described as a figure artist.'

'Then the man is a bigamist! Thank God, there is an end of the matter.'

He looked at me and shook his head.

'My dear Watson, your capacity for bourgeois moral calculation never ceases to amaze me. If Smith is a mere bigamist, then Miss Maxse may be set free and our interest ends. I venture to think that will not be so. However, let us count up. Our general dealer marries Miss Pegler in 1908. Two years later, he marries a woman, yet unknown to us, as Henry Williams. A year later he marries Alice Burnham, now deceased. A few weeks ago, he becomes a bridegroom for the fourth time that we know of. How many times he may have walked down the aisle with other brides is yet to be revealed.'

With that, he began to open the rest of his correspondence, glancing briefly at each letter and tossing it aside.

'Can it be for money?' I asked sceptically. 'How many of these women had much to give him?'

'In the case of Alice Burnham and Constance Maxse, I have no doubt that their families might be blackmailed or bullied into parting with a handsome sum in exchange for Smith allowing himself to be divorced at the first possible moment. Better still, think what he might demand by revealing that a union was yet unconsummated and that a complete annulment might be possible. You see? We can be sure of something like that in two cases. What the financial position of the *soi-disante* Mrs Williams may have been, we have yet to discover. It is certain, from the details already sent me by the Clerk of Probate, Admiralty and Divorce, that no divorce action between Smith and the former Miss Pegler was listed before 1910 or even 1912. As you acutely observe, that makes him guilty of bigamy, a subject we will now put to rest.'

'Put to rest?' I got up from my chair and watched him dismember a kipper. 'But, for God's sake, Holmes, we have a duty to free our client's daughter from the clutches of the man!'

He put down his fork and looked at me.

'Our first duty, Watson, is to use our best efforts to ensure that our client sees his daughter alive again. As matters stand, I should not count upon it.'

I stared at him, not understanding, until he retrieved and handed me a second letter. This was from Mr Maxse. He had endeavoured to contact his daughter, only to be told by the Southsea landlady that Mr Smith had been away for a week—as our visit to Weston-super-Mare already informed us. On his return, the couple had moved from Southsea and were now thought to be somewhere in the Midlands.

'He is on the loose with that poor girl!' I said in dismay, as I put down Mr Maxse's letter. 'Surely, then, the time has come to alert Lestrade? A warrant may be put out for the man, if only for bigamy.'

Holmes stared ahead of him, at the August sky framed by the window.

'I think not, Watson. We will not yet involve Lestrade, if you please. Once our suspicions reach Scotland Yard, they become public property. There is no discretion in that organization. They could not keep a secret if their lives depended on it. Moreover, bigamy is not a crime actively pursued by our police force. They prefer the comfortable method of waiting for the criminal to make an error. In any case, if my suspicions are correct, I fear that any bigamy warrant for Smith might also prove to be the death-warrant of Constance Maxse.'

With this flourish of Hoxton melodrama he dropped the subject and would not be provoked into taking it up again. Nothing was said of it to Lestrade on his visit that evening. Next morning, a further embossed envelope arrived from Somerset House. It contained a copy of the marriage certificate of Henry Williams and Bessie Mundy, dated at Weymouth on 26 August 1910. This was accompanied by a further certificate, recording that Bessie Williams, *née* Mundy, had died of 'misadventure' at Herne Bay on 13 July 1912 and that an inquest had been held.

'A coroner's jury,' I said cheerfully. 'Well, I must say, that rather puts Mr Smith in the clear, so far as everything but bigamy may be concerned.'

Holmes fixed me with an expressionless stare that was far worse, in its way, than any glowering or glaring.

'I doubt that,' he snapped, 'I doubt that very much indeed.'

So it was that on the following afternoon we landed by a steamer that had brought us from Tower Pier to Herne Bay, and were taken by cab to our rooms at the Royal Hotel.

V

Next morning, in a shabby brick-and-tile police office, we sat opposite the rubicund and self-confident figure of Constable John Kitchingham, Coroner's Officer in the case of Miss Bessie Mundy, as the bigamously-married wife of 'Henry Williams' was still known in law. Constable Kitchingham showed an ill-placed self-confidence.

'I'm afraid we aren't Scotland Yard, Mr Holmes, not down here. Nor we aren't Baker Street neither, with respect, and don't need to be.' As he talked, he shuffled through a few papers, looking at them and not at us. 'We know what people are round here, all the same, and that's a good deal. This town, Mr Holmes, has a good name, and we depend upon that for the summer trade.'

Had this bumpkin been looking at us he might have seen the beginnings of cold anger in Sherlock Holmes, usually evident only to those who knew him well, and avoided the consequences before it was too late. Kitchingham opened another folder and read resonantly from a paper.

'Mr Henry Williams took a yearly tenancy of a house at 80 High Street, Herne Bay, on 20 May 1912. He lived there with his wife, Bessie, on affectionate terms for some weeks. On 8 July, he says, they made mutual wills.' Seeing the suspicion in Holmes's eyes, Kitchingham added hastily, 'That had to be done. A new marriage or divorce invalidates an existing will.'

'A fact of which I am aware,' Holmes said bleakly. 'Pray continue.'

Constable Kitchingham continued.

'The premises were shabby and had been derelict for long periods. It seems Mr Williams was vexed there was no bath for his wife. On the day after the making of the wills, an enamelled bath was ordered from Mr Hill, ironmonger of the same street. 'Owever, the rooms had never been brought "up to date", so there was no means of plumbing the bath. It was delivered without taps or pipes, standing by the bathroom window to be filled and emptied by hand. This was done by carrying up hot water in a bucket from a copper in the downstairs kitchen.'

A horse and trap rattled over the cobbles outside the window.

'I don't think you could say, gentlemen,' Kitchingham said proudly, 'that Mr Williams showed himself lacking in duty to a wife that was never a well person. The day after that bath was delivered, he was with her at Dr French's. Epileptic seizures, she having had a bad one the day before, with him there to see it.'

'Forgive me,' said Holmes quietly, 'the inquest report contains no evidence that this lady had bitten her tongue or showed any sign of having had such a fit.'

'Which was remarked, Mr Holmes, but which isn't invariable, it seems.'

'That, at least, is true,' I said reluctantly.

Constable Kitchingham took courage from my approval.

'Dr French thought it advisable to administer a mild sedative of potassium bromide, which would do no harm in any case.'

'Nor much good,' I said. Kitchingham looked at me with the reproach of a man betrayed. Then he resumed.

'However that may be, Mr Holmes, the doctor was fetched two nights later at 1.30 A.M., when the lady had had another seizure. He found her flushed and clammy. Heart and pulse were normal, but she complained of a headache.'

'The files of the *Herne Bay Press*, which I had the pleasure of consulting in the public library yesterday afternoon, tell us that,' Holmes said dryly. 'On another page the paper also records the July temperature for that week as varying between 78 and 82 degrees and remarks on the humidity of the season. I should imagine the entire population of Herne Bay might have been flushed and clammy on such a night. Nor do I see how Dr French could say much about an epileptic seizure which must have been over before he got there. Unless she had bitten her tongue or something of the sort, which once again was not the case.'

Kitchingham shrugged. His tone now assumed a melodramatic self-importance, with which he had no doubt told the story to a good many people before us.

'Two days later, according to Mr Williams, they rose as the town hall clock sounded the half-hour at 7.30. He went out to buy some fish. He didn't fill the bath, so his wife must have done it herself. On his return, about a half hour later, he called out to her, received no reply, and then went into the bathroom. She was lying on her back in the bath, which was three-quarters filled. Her head was under water, her trunk on the bottom, legs sloping up, feet just clear of the surface. He pulled her up, so that she lay against the slope of the bath, her head clear of the water. Then he sent a message to Dr French. "Can you come at once? I am afraid my wife is dead." '

'What does French have to say about it?'

'He came about fifteen minutes later and found her on her back, her head having slipped beneath the water again. There was no pulse, but neither body nor water was cold. She was clutching a piece of Castille Soap in her right hand. They lifted her out and laid her on the floor. Dr French removed her false teeth and tried artificial respiration for ten minutes, while Mr Williams assisted by holding his wife's tongue. But she'd gone. Clean gone, sir.'

'That I do not doubt. When did you first see her body?'

'About two hours later, as coroner's officer sent to take their statements.'

'Where was it?'

'Lying on the boards of the bathroom floor. Being quite a small room it was behind the door as you opened it.'

'What was it covered with?'

'It wasn't, Mr Holmes.'

'Do you mean to tell me that this man left his dead wife naked on the floor behind the door for two hours, while policemen and coroner's officers, landlord and undertakers, the world and his wife, tramped in and out?'

'If you put it like that.'

'If you can think of another way of putting the matter, Mr Kitchingham, I should be obliged to hear of it. Now, the report in the paper says nothing of evidence at the inquest as to the height of the lady and dimensions of the bath.'

Kitchingham gave a fatuous and self-satisfied snigger.

'There was none of that sort of thing given, sir. Where there's no call for it, we don't go in for your kind of clever arithmetic down here, Mr Holmes.'

'Indeed not,' said Holmes with an icy fury that suggested Mr Kitchingham had now caught a tiger by the tail. 'What you go in for, down here, appears to verge upon criminal negligence. When did Williams leave the premises?'

'Almost at once,' said Kitchingham, whose face had reddened gratifyingly. 'Mrs Williams died on Saturday, the inquest was on Monday . . .'

'Before her relatives could hear of it, let alone attend it, I daresay!'

'Couldn't say, sir. Then she was buried on Tuesday, next day.'

'Large funeral was it? Something elaborate?'

'Very small, in the circumstances. Decent but not expensive, as Mr Williams said. Common grave. Still, what could that matter to her, as he remarked?'

'What, indeed?'

'Never saw a man so struck down,' said Kitchingham, warm in justification of the widower. 'Before the burial he saw the agents' clerk, Miss Rapley. Ended his tenancy. Sobbing his heart out on her desk, poor gentleman. Only once he brightened and said, "Wasn't it a jolly good thing I got her to make a will?" Fair play, it was. You don't want grief aggravated by intestacy at a time like that.'

We freed ourselves from the morbid enthusiasms of Constable Kitchingham and strolled back to the Royal Hotel.

'Some mute inglorious Borgia here may rest!' Holmes gestured furiously at the sea-front of Herne Bay. 'For all that the local constabulary know or care!'

'They cannot work without evidence . . .'

'Evidence!' His cry was loud enough to cause an elderly couple ahead of us to turn and stare in some alarm. 'Does no one observe the psychopathic delight of a man in exposing his dead wife to strangers, naked on the boards of the bathroom floor for more than two hours? Does it mean nothing when he asks on the day of her burial in a common grave whether it wasn't a jolly good thing that he got her to make a will? Constable Kitchingham takes it as mere proof of what a splendid fellow he was!'

'Holmes,' I said gently, 'much as you may deplore the inquest, the verdict was never in doubt on the evidence. Bessie Mundy died in an epileptic seizure, which caused her to fall back with her head beneath the water, so that she drowned. The jurors made the only reasonable finding, death by misadventure.'

'I have as little faith in coroners' officers and inquest juries as I have in policemen, Watson. I know only that Miss Constance Maxse is in mortal peril, God knows where. Policemen and jurors will do nothing for her. Truth and facts will save her. Great is truth and shall prevail. Even in Herne Bay.'

In our sitting-room after dinner, at the end of our first day, he stared morosely beyond the lace curtains, where a late sun glimmered warmly on the placid waters of the North Sea and on the rusty sails of barges steering for the Essex shore. Then, without a word, he took from his pocket a telegram and handed it to me. It was a simple reply from Inspector Lestrade concerning the death of that other Mrs Smith, Alice Burnham, lost at Blackpool. THE POLICE HAVE NO SUSPICION OF FOUL PLAY.

The case against George Joseph Smith as anything more than a bigamist and trickster depended solely on the fate of Bessie Mundy at the hands of her devoted and hygienic husband.

VI

In such unpromising circumstances, I never knew by what means Sherlock Holmes was able to command the attendance next morning of Mr Rutley Mowll, the East Kent Coroner, Mr Alfred

Hogbin, undertaker, Dr Frank Austin French, Miss Lily O'Sullivan of the Herne Bay Aquatic Belles, and the unfortunate Constable Kitchingham. The venue was the bathroom of 80 High Street, which was in one of its periods of vacancy. Whether the unseen hand of Lestrade, or of Mycroft Holmes, had contrived this ensemble I have no idea. One thing, however, was certain. Holmes was in the mood of a sergeant-major addressing a defaulters' parade.

An exception to his displeasure was the prettily costumed Miss O'Sullivan, whose swimming dress of frilly blue pantaloons and bodice would have graced the most sophisticated lido. For the rest, Holmes was in a mood to brook no contradictions or evasions and I had never seen any group of people look so thoroughly petrified in his presence.

'We will, if you please, begin with filling the bath!' The words rapped out in that bare, hard room with the grey light of the High Street filtering through its mean windows. 'Constable Kitchingham! Take the two gallon bucket to the kitchen downstairs. Fill it from the copper, which is now brimming. Carry it up here and pour it into the bath. Continue until the bath is half full, then three quarters full, as both you and Dr French found it. Do not interrupt us otherwise.'

He was plainly enjoying his revenge upon them all for what he still called their 'criminal negligence'. He pointed to the cast-iron enamelled bath with its four lions' feet. It stood with its head just under the street-window, as it had done at the death of Bessie Mundy. Then his finger stabbed at the lugubrious black-clad figure of Mr Hogbin, the undertaker of High Street, Herne Bay.

'Now, sir! Take that useful implement of your trade, the tape-measure! Read off the length of the bath!'

Mr Hogbin nervously did as he was told.

'The upper length is just five feet, Mr Holmes. The length at the base is three feet eight inches.'

'And since it is too narrow for her to move much to either side, it is the length which is crucial. You also measured her for her coffin?'

'I did, sir.' He stood with the tape round his neck and shoulders drooping, like a mournful carrion crow.

'How tall was Mrs Williams?'

'Five feet nine inches, sir. Tall for a lady.'

'Such a pity the inquest did not hear that,' said Holmes savagely. 'Nine inches longer than the bath at the top! More than two feet longer than the bath at the bottom!'

'She was found lying flat along it, Mr Holmes,' said Coroner Mowll quickly, 'flat along the bottom but with legs sloping upwards and feet out of the water.'

'I am aware of how she was found, sir! My interest is in how she got where she was found!'

'If you have read the report of the inquest, you will know that it was the result of an epileptic seizure, which caused her to fall backwards under the water.'

'I am informed, Mr Mowll, that you hold your position as East Kent Coroner by virtue of being a solicitor. I wonder if you have the slightest knowledge of the sequence of events in an epileptic seizure.'

'I believe I have some little experience in the matter.'

'Who heard the scream?'

'The scream?'

'An epileptic seizure, unlike *petit mal*, is almost always preceded by a scream of such intensity that those who hear it seldom forget it. There is a street not more than a dozen feet below these windows, which are open in summer no doubt. There are rooms on either side of these flimsy lath and plaster walls. Curiously, when Mr Williams claimed to recite the symptoms of his wife's first fits, several days before, he also made no mention of such a scream.'

'No one heard a scream.'

There was a pause while Constable Kitchingham carried a laden bucket across the bare floorboards of the room and splashed it into the bath.

'A primary characteristic of such a seizure is rigidity,' said Holmes with great deliberation. 'The woman's feet would be jammed against the far end of the bath and her trunk bolt upright. It would be as nearly impossible for her to get her head under water in a bath sixteen inches deep as one can imagine.'

Mr Mowll's eagerness to protect the reputation of Herne Bay led him to ingratiate with Holmes, as one who should pat a hungry lion.

'She was on her back, sir, with her legs sloping up and feet out of the water.'

'Which a single pair of strong hands would accomplish in a moment.'

'Mr Holmes,' said the coroner firmly, 'your reputation goes before you. You are known for your skill in the most difficult cases. However, no man can be expert in every field . . .'

'I trust you may be able to produce authority for that insinuation!' my friend snapped back at him.

'I merely point out, Mr Holmes, that you are plainly not *au fait* with events as they occurred. Nor is your expertise in medicine sufficient to tilt the scales in doubtful questions, where medical men themselves take varying views . . .'

'Forgive me, Mr Mowll, but I decline to undertake responsibility for the vacillations and mutual hostilities of the medical profession.'

That brought silence for a moment until Mr Mowll tried again.

'There is no case of murder by drowning known to English jurisprudence, Mr Holmes, in which a victim who is conscious has not offered the most desperate and violent resistance, sufficient to cause bruising and abrasions to both assailant and assailed. Neither husband nor wife in this case displayed a single bruise or scratch. Nor did Dr French find a drop of water spilt on the floor from a bath three quarters full.'

'As to the last observation,' said Holmes coolly, 'absorption by untreated wood and evaporation on a summer day with the temperature in the eighties would in any case reduce the time that water would be visible on the floor. However, we shall now put the entire question to the proof, with your permission. The bath is only half full, but that is enough for my purposes.'

'If you wish.' Coroner Mowll stood back wearily, with folded arms.

'Miss O'Sullivan, if you please,' said Holmes courteously.

Our bathing belle in her water-costume skipped forward, as if making her bow at a pierrot show.

'One moment,' murmured Holmes, 'allow Constable Kitchingham to add this last bucket of water.'

The final bucket was emptied into the bath with a sound like a gently breaking wave. Miss O'Sullivan raised a dainty foot and stepped into water that came half way to her knees. She adjusted the laces of her cap and lowered herself gently into the wider end of the bath. She gave us all a quick smile and a flutter of her lashes.

'Now, my dear young lady,' said Holmes, more affably than he had said anything to anyone that morning, 'I apologize for the coolness of the water but happily you are accustomed to that in your profession. This will not take long. Let us suppose that you are sitting upright in the bath. Sponging your arms, shall we say. You have no idea that anything is amiss. Of course you have in reality, but let us pretend. You have not a care in the world.'

She sat there, wiping her arms with her wet hands in dumb-show as Holmes removed his jacket and rolled up his sleeves. She smiled at him, a little nervously as I thought. Holmes gave her a quick smile and approached. We were watching to see him place his hand upon her head. He stooped a little at the bath, slipped his left forearm under her knees, his right arm round her shoulders, for all the world like a loving groom about to lift his bride and carry her to bed. It was so naturally done that she began to put her left arm about his shoulders to complete the embrace.

Then, without a word of warning, his left arm that was under her knees lifted them high. The right arm was withdrawn and Miss O'Sullivan went down on her back with her legs drawn high. The shelving depth of the bath was so narrow where she lay that her arms seemed imprisoned, though she managed several futile swimming motions with them. Her neck and shoulders jerked spasmodically and in vain to get her face above the water.

'If seeing is believing,' Holmes said grimly to the rest of us, 'you now know how Mrs Bessie Williams, *née* Bessie Mundy, met her death.'

I thought that no one who saw this dreadful experiment being carried out could have the least doubt of that.

'Mr Holmes!' Coroner Mowll's cry was one of shrill alarm.

'As little as thirty seconds might suffice!' Miss O'Sullivan's struggles seemed feebler as Holmes muttered these words. 'As long as two minutes and more might be necessary!'

'Holmes! For God's sake!'

The girl's face was horribly evident under the slight turbulence of the water as her arms went limp. Her eyes were staring up at us, her cheeks bulging, and a thin stream of bubbles reached the surface. He seemed not to hear me.

'Holmes!'

It is not too much to say that I threw myself upon him from behind. For a second or two longer I could not break his grip. Then the brawny Mr Hogbin joined me and between us we drew him off. Miss O'Sullivan floated to the surface. Her eyes, which had been wide open, fluttered and closed. Letting go of my friend, I drew from my pocket the silver medicinal flask, which my father had given me when I left to join my regiment in India. I unscrewed it and touched it to her lips. The warming whisky made her retch a little and then brought her round.

'So much for epileptic seizures,' said Holmes imperiously to the onlookers.

They stared at him, shocked and terrified, for they could all have sworn he meant to drown the girl as a demonstration. Holmes was completely unperturbed.

'And then there is the matter of the piece of soap, said to be clutched in the right hand. It is also said by Dr French in his evidence that the hand was limp.'

'And so it was,' said French nervously.

'A limp hand cannot clutch a piece of soap or anything else. Perhaps I may refer you to the work of Dr Alfred Swaine Taylor on the matter. Only a quarter of those who drown die of asphyxia. When they do so, the hand would be limp. Had there been death in an epileptic seizure, which there was not, you would have had to prize the hand open. According to your evidence, the hand opened of its own accord and the soap fell out.'

Though Holmes had rattled their self-confidence, he had not changed the mind of the coroner. Mr Mowll was angry now, as well as frightened.

'All that you have done, sir, is to tell us what we knew already. There are two possible explanations in this case for almost every aspect of it. The jury at the inquest heard them all and found its verdict of misadventure. You have stated the alternative hypotheses but you will not change that verdict.'

Holmes looked at him with a mixture of simulated surprise and undisguised contempt.

'I do not deal in hypotheses, sir, but in facts. This man was a brute in his dealings with women and a thief in respect of their money.'

'He was known here only for his loving affection to his wife.'

Holmes took from his pocket several papers.

'With the assistance of the records office, I have spent my leisure hours in town before coming to Herne Bay by following up one or two of the bigamous wives, for there have been several beside the ones so far mentioned. You may have their statements. Miss Pegler of Bristol. *"The power was in his eyes. They were little eyes that seemed to rob you of your will!"* Here is another, cited in her divorce petition ten years ago by one of those whom he flogged into silence when he could be secure in no other way. *"Often he used to brag to me about his numerous women acquaintances. Once I met one of his victims and warned her to her face about him. She was greatly shocked. That night he came home and thrashed me till I was nearly dead."* There, sir, is the true character of the man whom your jury acquitted of all blame.'

'It does not prove the present case!'

Holmes seemed to look through Mr Mowll to a world beyond.

'In the past three-quarters of an hour, in this room, the case against Henry Williams, *alias* George Joseph Smith, has been established beyond the least doubt.'

'You have not done so!'

'Perhaps, sir, I have not. But Constable Kitchingham certainly has.'

They stared back at him and Holmes continued.

'To fill the bath three-quarters full, which Dr French and others observed to be the level, has taken Constable Kitchingham fifty minutes. It is unlikely that Bessie Mundy could do it faster—and her husband swore that he did not do it at all. Suppose Williams, *alias* Smith, has told the truth in his statement to the inquest. Then the couple rose at 7.30. The water was warm when Dr French tested it, therefore the bath could not have been filled earlier or it would have been stone cold. Let us allow that the husband went out, as he said, and returned at eight. We know it was not later, for at eight he sent his message to Dr French that he feared his wife was dead, and that Dr French received the message a little before 8.30.'

'Oh, God!' said Coroner Mowll suddenly.

'Precisely. The filling of the bath would have taken from 7.30 to 8.20 or thereabouts. Let us be generous to the husband and say it was only half filled. I have observed Constable Kitchingham and may tell you that it took him thirty-five minutes to reach the half-way point. If that is the case, even so the filling could not have been completed—let alone Mrs Williams undressed and in the bath—until five minutes after the message to Dr French saying she was dead. Not only was she was still alive when George Joseph Smith returned from the fishmonger, she had probably not even got into the bath when he sent for Dr French, saying that he feared she was dead!'

As so often, the chilling logic of Sherlock Holmes left his audience speechless.

'Smith, *alias* Williams, is not a mere lady-killer,' said Holmes quietly, 'but one of the most cold-blooded assassins that ever walked the face of this earth. You have much to answer for, Mr Mowll.'

'I have nothing . . .'

'Indeed you have. Miss Alice Burnham . . .'

'I have heard of that, thanks to you, sir. There is a vast difference between a domestic tragedy and a swimming or bathing accident upon a public beach, as her father describes it.'

'You may yet find them identical. Far worse, at the moment this bigamist, embezzler, and murderer is in possession of a young woman, Constance Maxse, who knows nothing of her danger . . .'

'I did not swear it was epilepsy,' Dr French interrupted hastily, as Herne Bay began to break ranks, 'only that I could not swear otherwise. There was only what I was told by the man and the woman. I had qualified only two years.'

'His demeanour after his wife's death,' said Mr Hogbin, 'his treatment of the poor dead body. Upon reflection it was callous and hateful in the extreme.'

'I shall return to my office,' said Mr Mowll, 'and seek advice.'

'When you get there,' said Holmes equably, 'you will find Inspector Lestrade of Scotland Yard, waiting to give you a good deal of it.'

Before we left, I gave my professional counsel to Miss Lily O'Sullivan.

'My dear young lady, if I may advise you, we must take you home at once by cab or carriage. It is essential that you should sustain no further exertion and that you should rest, preferably in bed, for the next day or two.'

She gave the shortest laugh I had ever heard.

'Ha! Much chance of that! I should miss two performances tonight.'

'But to take part in them is unthinkable, in your present state of distress.'

Her eyes sparkled.

'Oh,' she said, as if understanding at last. 'You mean this?'

I saw again the gargoyle of the drowning maiden, the dreadful bulging eyes, the swelling cheeks, the blood stagnating in her face.

'You never knew? Mr Holmes never told you?' She grinned at me, but it was not a smile. 'That's part of my act, that is. I can stay under for two minutes or more, if I have to. Only Mr Holmes thought it might look better the way he and I did it. Pleased to meet you. Ta-ta.'

I was so overcome, as she flounced off to change her dripping costume, that I almost said 'Ta-ta' in return. I managed my half-bow only just in time.

We remained in the Royal Hotel to see what Lestrade might accomplish. By 4 P.M. a warrant had been issued, in respect of bigamy, larceny, and murder, for the arrest of George Joseph Smith, *alias* George Baker, *alias* George Oliver Love, *alias* Henry Williams, *alias* Charles Oliver James, *alias* John Lloyd, described as a gymnasium instructor and general dealer. Lestrade had discovered from the criminal records that the wanted man served two years in the Northamptonshire Regiment, teaching gymnastics. Small wonder that poor Bessie Mundy was no match for those powerful hands.

That evening after dinner we looked out from our room across the darkening sea and waited in the hope that Lestrade might have time to pay us a visit before his return to town on the late train.

'He can only be tried for one murder at a time,' I said thoughtfully. 'The evidence in the case of Bessie Mundy is strong but not conclusive. There is almost nothing, except perhaps the filling of the bath, that might not be overturned. Even there, to hang a man because he has the time wrong by twenty minutes . . . It is a cruel thing to say of the poor girl, but if only Alice Burnham had died at home, rather than swimming . . .'

He shook his head in despair.

'Watson! Watson! Of course she died at home, not on the high seas! It is one of my greatest blunders that I did not go to her father at once. However, he could not even bring himself to attend the funeral of that one person in the world whom he loved. So I had hoped, knowing that he could not bear to hear of the tragedy nor to speak of it since it was first reported to him, that I could spare him in this investigation. It was not to be.'

He spread out on the table by the window two telegram forms, one the copy of a message he had sent to Mr Maxse, and one which he had received in reply that afternoon.

TELEGRAPH AT ONCE TEXT OF NOTIFICATION TO YOUR FRIEND CHARLES BURNHAM BY HIS SON-IN-LAW OF THE DEATH OF ALICE BURNHAM STOP. REPLY PAID TO HOLMES, ROYAL HOTEL, HERNE BAY.

How had the scoundrel broken to the father the news of his beloved daughter's death?

ALICE DIED YESTERDAY BATHING NORTH SHORE STOP. SMITH CON-NAUGHT STREET BLACKPOOL.

Reduced to the form of a telegraph message there was also the report of the inquest cut from a few lines at the foot of a column in the local press.

NORTH SHORE TRAGEDY: INQUEST VERDICT: A VERDICT OF ACCI-DENTAL DEATH WAS RETURNED AT THE INQUEST ON ALICE BURNHAM (25) OF CONNAUGHT STREET, NORTH SHORE, WHO WAS DROWNED LAST TUESDAY WHILE BATHING.

'Unfortunately, the word "bathing" has two meanings and two pronunciations,' said Holmes quietly. 'Such was the deceit practised on the unhappy father. The head of the inquest report was snipped out and the rest withheld, so that Smith might persuade him his daughter had died in a swimming accident, when the truth was he had drowned her in her bath. Remember, the murder of Bessie Mundy was already to his credit by then. Therefore, the fewer questions the better.'

'Those telegrams will do no good,' I said, 'if he can only be tried for one murder and the jury know nothing of the other wives.'

Holmes sat down and lit his pipe.

'From my brief and hardly satisfactory experience of student law, Watson, I recall something known as system. It is true that a man may only be tried for one murder. However, where he is charged with others but not tried for them, they may be brought into the case to show evidence of "system".'

'System?'

'Yes. The other cases may not be used to suggest that he committed the murder for which he is tried. But they may be used to show that, if he did commit it, he did not do so accidentally.'

'To stop a verdict of manslaughter?'

He chuckled in a manner that would chill the blood of the greatest optimist.

'In this case, Watson, to ensure that the jury knows every abomination in the career of this reptile. Leave those telegrams on the table a moment. The boards outside our door creak in a manner that betrays a constabulary boot. Come in, my dear Lestrade! We have something here that may interest you.'

As the world knows, George Joseph Smith was tried at the Old Bailey in the first summer of the Great War for the murder of Bessie Mundy. By a choice irony, our friend Sir Edward Marshall Hall was briefed for this hopeless defence. Despite Sir Edward's best efforts and arguments, evidence of system was admitted. With that, his client was doomed. The jurors listened with visible horror to the stories of young women, living and dead, three of them at least drowned as 'Brides in the Bath'.

On a warm August morning, in an early stillness when the rumble of guns on the Western Front could be heard dimly in Hyde Park, George Joseph Smith was led to the execution shed in the yard of Chelmsford Gaol, attended by the chaplain, governor, warders, and the two silent figures of Pierpoint and Ellis. So faltering was his progress that the drop was two minutes late in falling open under him.

That evening, as he took his old-fashioned chair in Baker Street, rum and water in his glass, Holmes sighed and said, 'We have saved Miss Maxse from an early death, Watson, though not, I fear, from a fate worse than death. Be so good as to pass me the *Morning Post*. There is a curious series of incidents in which live rats and rabbits have been deliberately introduced into the plumbing of some of the most elegant addresses in Mayfair and St James's. Such a diversion is, I suspect, the tactic of a master-criminal bent on the greatest robbery of the age. As such, it deserves our attention.'

The Voice from the Crypt:
The Case of the
Talking Corpse

I

Of all the problems submitted to Sherlock Holmes in the years of our friendship, there were few indeed where I was the means of introducing the case to his notice. There was certainly no other experience of mine to compare with a series of grotesque murders which afflicted Lambeth and the shabby areas of the Waterloo Road in the final decade of the last century.

Holmes was wont to argue that the eccentricity or singularity of a criminal is always a clue. Conversely, 'The more featureless and commonplace a crime is, the more difficult it is to bring it home.' There was no lack of eccentricity or singularity in the present investigation. The apparent lunacy of the murderer led him to correspond cheerfully with Scotland Yard, offering to solve the mysteries for money, if the police themselves could not do so.

Our antagonist also appeared to possess a gang of assistants, all as mad as he—and women were among his accomplices. It even seemed we might be wrong in supposing the actual killer and tormentor of the fair sex to be a man! May not a woman have a grudge against the poor creatures of the street? With so much singularity, if Holmes was right in his hypothesis, such maniacs should have been easy enough to catch. Unfortunately, a long passage of time was to prove otherwise.

Let me begin at the beginning. One fateful Saturday evening, I had arrived at Waterloo Station after an informal reunion of several old friends. We had served together in the 5th Northumberland Fusiliers, during the Afghan campaign a dozen years before. Fowler, Osborne, Scott, and I had been subalterns in the draught that was sent up from the depot at Peshawur to the forward encampment of Khandahar. My own military career was short and inglorious. I was detached to the Berkshire regiment for the coming battle of Maiwand, where a Jezail bullet shattered the bone of my shoulder and grazed the subclavial artery. Nor was that the worst. At the base hospital of Peshawur, I was first a convalescent from my wound and then, more dangerously, a victim of enteric fever. How I came home an invalid and made my first acquaintance with Sherlock Holmes is described in my account of the Brixton Road murder, made public under the somewhat sensational title of *A Study in Scarlet*.

More than ten years later, in the mess at Aldershot, the four of us talked much of these things. As I returned from that convivial luncheon, it was as if the gullies and bare mountain ridges of Afghanistan rather than the tenements and warehouses of Nine Elms and the Waterloo Road rose before my eyes. The sound of the well-lit trains thundering into the great terminus under fiery pillars of steam might have been distant salvoes of our artillery covering the withdrawal to Jellalabad.

I walked out of the great railway terminus into a drizzling October evening, the gaslights of the busy street flickering and shining on the wet cobbles. It was a scene of market-stalls and flower-sellers, beggars and ragged children. Thinking of the welcoming fire in our Baker Street rooms, I turned towards the rank of two-wheeled hansom cabs and four-wheeled growlers.

Then I heard a scream, as sharp as any Jezail's knife at Maiwand.

'Help me! Oh, God, help me!'

I cannot do justice to the intensity of it. How common and plain her words appear set down in print! Sometimes I hear that shriek again, in the quiet of the night. The terror of it, in a shabby thoroughfare of market-stalls and four-ale bars, returns as shrill as ever. It was a cry of agony, but more of panic. A physician who has witnessed the worst deaths might recognize it as heralding the cruellest ending of a life. Nothing in the butchery of men and beasts in battle lives with me as clearly as that sound.

The street from Waterloo Bridge to St George's Circus was so crowded at that hour on a Saturday night that, at first, I could not make out where the cry had come from. It was somewhere on the further side of the busy thoroughfare, not far from the double bar-room doors of the York Hotel. The pavement was lit through the windows by chandelier-light, clouded with tobacco smoke. I thought I heard a softer following cry. That was soon lost in the rumble and crash of barrels on a tarpaulined dray, turning out from the railway goods yard.

Then there came only the bursts of laughter and a snatch of music from the hotel's public bar, as the doors swung open and closed again. But that scream was not the cry of a young woman playing the fool. Crossing between the cabs and twopenny buses, I paused as I saw an unkempt girl staggering against the wall of the hotel, her arms clamped across her midriff. She was twisting and lurching as a drunkard might. Her voice was quieter now but with a terrible and sober appeal.

'Help me! Oh, someone, help me!'

Before I could reach her, she had slithered down the wall and was sitting on the stained wet paving, a plump young woman with a frizzy mane of fair hair gathered roughly in a tail and worn down her back. I cannot say that she began to vomit, rather that she strove to do so without effect. By the time I reached her, the screams had stopped. She lay curled on the paving, still groaning more in fear than in pain.

In such a place and with such an appearance as hers, her profession was not in doubt. The street was crowded at that time of night and, even before I had reached her, several people were standing by and looking down at the poor creature. I pushed my way through.

'Let me come to her. I am a doctor.'

This produced a murmur of interest among the spectators, as if the spectacle might be better worth watching. The poor girl's face was ghost-white with pain and her hair was plastered on her forehead by a sweat of agony. I tried to question her as gently as I could but she seemed not to hear me. Her eyes were motionless, staring in an uncomprehending horror. Then, through clenched teeth, there issued a series of shorter, rising hisses as the spasm came again. Her face was set hard in a rictus of convulsive frenzy. It was like that terrible death mask which is sometimes called the 'Hippocrates Smile'. I could get nothing from her. It was as if she could not hear me. Having guessed her way of life and her occupation, I supposed that she was in a last stage of delirium tremens.

Kneeling down, I felt a pulse that was rapid and fluttering, which confirmed my supposition. The torment of alcoholism that she endured had brought on an acute cardiac distress. Her breath was still uneven and she was glistening with perspiration. I asked her what she had been eating or drinking, though the sweet spirituous odour of gin was strong upon her and on her clothes. Her reply was incoherent at first but then I made out that she had been drinking in the York Hotel with a man called Fred. She had drunk gin with 'something white' in it.

'Fred Linnell,' said one of the women in the crowd. 'She's one of his girls. Lor' look at her! She's had her whack all right!'

The dying girl shook her head, struggling to deny the words. There was another scream, feebler this time. Her head went back and her knees came up abruptly into her stomach, as the shrillness fell to an inhuman grunting and jabbering. It was the first of several tetanic convulsions that I was to witness and I knew she would die on the pavement unless treatment was given at once.

Just then a market trader in cap and apron pushed though the crowd carrying a board from a trestle table. Two of his assistants were with him.

'Get her home on this,' he said to them, ignoring me. 'Number eight, Duke Street, off of Westminster Bridge Road. She's Nellie Donworth. Lodges with old Mrs Avens.'

I nodded to his two assistants, for the girl could not be left where she was. I also took out my card and handed it to Jimmy Styles, as the stall-holder's name proved to be, first writing on it 'delirium tremens', 'syncope', and '8 Duke Street'.

'Go as fast as you can to St Thomas's Hospital. Give this to Dr Kelloch, the house physician, or whichever assistant may be on duty. I shall need help at Duke Street. Ask them to send a four-wheeler, to get her to hospital. She lodges close, so we shall have her home before they arrive.'

I had written 'syncope' to emphasize the urgency of the message, for it was now apparent that the poor heart must fail very soon under the distress of such extreme convulsions as were seizing her with greater frequency.

Styles went at a run between the traffic, past the railway terminus, towards the embankment of the dark river, where the hospital stood. His two men took up the board with the girl lying upon it, her body alternately limp and then drawn into a spasm. By the wine vaults on the corner, we turned into Duke Street, a squalid ill-lit alley behind the coal wharves. She was carried to her room on the first floor of a tenement and laid gently on an old brass bedstead covered by linen that was worn to rags.

There was little that I could do until Kelloch or his assistant came. I noticed a dark bottle on the stained wash-stand, labelled as bromide of potassium. Though it is a standard prescription for alcoholism, I dared not give it to her until I knew how much gin she had drunk, for fear I should do more harm than good. Instead, I sent down to the landlady for carbonate of sodium as a palliative.

I had hardly expected that Dr Kelloch would be able to come in person but fifteen minutes later a four-wheeler turned the corner and rattled into Duke Street, bringing his assistant, Mr Johnson of the South London Medical Institute. We had a hasty and murmured consultation outside the bedroom door, the purport of which, on my part, was that the unfortunate young woman should be conveyed to hospital without delay. Though Mr Johnson agreed, I could see that it was already too late.

So passed this young woman of the town, she who had depended for her bread upon prostitution in the streets of a great and cruel city, one of that legion of the lost whom we see about us every day. Like so many of her kind, she had sought oblivion in drink from her brutal way of life and from the squalid lodging houses that were the only home she knew. Like so many victims of drink's false comfort, she had paid the last terrible penalty that the body exacts for such brutish indulgence.

With these sombre thoughts, so different to the memories of military comradeship that had been woken earlier that day, I walked back to Waterloo and called a cab to Baker Street. The case now belonged to Dr Kelloch and Mr Johnson. I had no reason to suppose that I should ever hear of it again, except perhaps as a matter of courtesy. The bottle on the wash-stand, with its familiar 'Bromide of Potassium' label, was evidence that Ellen Donworth was already 'under the doctor' for alcoholism. The coroner seldom sees any reason for calling an inquest, when the cause of death is so plain.

I mentioned the young street-walker's tragedy to Holmes, as an explanation for my late return. However, he seemed disinclined to interest himself in the fate of this 'unfortunate'. Somewhen during that night, in the darkest hours when the city had fallen silent, I woke with the memory of that terrible scream rising from the recesses of my mind. Unnerved by this, I vowed that I must put poor Nellie Donworth from my thoughts.

On the following morning, the bells of Marylebone Church pealed through a thin autumn sunlight. The streets and squares rustled with fallen leaves. Just before noon I received a wire from Dr Kelloch. He thanked me for my attention to the unfortunate girl but regretted to inform me that Ellen Donworth had suffered a final delirium tremens in the cab. In consequence of this, her heart had failed and she was dead upon arrival at St Thomas's Hospital.

So, it seemed, a too-familiar Waterloo Road tragedy had come to its conclusion.

I did not mention her death to Holmes just then. What purpose would that have served?

II

Sherlock Holmes was the most precise and meticulous of men in word and thought, but the most careless and untidy being who ever plagued a fellow lodger. The tray which held his abandoned supper would lie casually on his work-table among piles of papers, or next to some unsavoury chemical experiment, designed to raise finger-prints upon a glass or to separate the contents of a poison-bottle into their constituents. An important clue in a case of homicide or adultery was apt to lie concealed, for safety, in the butter dish.

So it was with some surprise, while the October light turned to dusk under plum-coloured rain-clouds, that I returned from a consultation at the fever ward of the military hospital to discover Holmes putting our Baker Street sitting-room into unaccustomed order. A full three days had passed since the tragedy of Nellie Donworth and I had heard nothing further from Dr Kelloch or Mr Johnson.

As I entered the room, I noticed that the work-table was unusually regimented. Indeed, Holmes had so far forgotten himself as to arrange the cushions in the arm-chairs. A window had been opened at the top to air the fumes of black tobacco. He glanced up as I came in.

'Be so good as to turn the settee to the fire a little. Look lively, my dear fellow! We are to have a visitor.'

'Oh, indeed,' I had heard nothing of a visitor that morning. 'And cannot Mrs Hudson . . .'

'If you will recall, Watson, the week has reached Wednesday afternoon. On that feast of Woden, Mrs Hudson is accustomed to take tea with her married sister in Clapham. Be so kind as to pass me that other antimacassar.'

'What visitor? And why so suddenly?'

'A wire from Lady Russell,' he said firmly, adjusting the angle of a chair to the hearth. 'She comes suddenly because the matter is urgent. Why else?'

My consultation at the military hospital had been long and difficult. I was not best pleased to find a quiet evening disturbed in this manner.

'A good many of the English aristocracy bear the name of Russell,' I said rather shortly. 'Which is this? The law lord's baroness? Surely not the prime minister's widow?'

He looked up at me, as he carried a laden waste-paper basket to conceal it quickly in a far corner of the room.

'Neither of them. Our visitor is Mabel Edith, Countess Russell. I daresay that even you must have heard of her.'

'I wish I had not. She is one young lady with whom our practice could well dispense.'

'Balderdash,' he said, brushing his hands together smartly, to indicate that his domestic chores were complete.

'You may call it balderdash, Holmes. I am told, on the best authority, that her mother Lady Scott was divorced by Sir Claude for reasons one does not usually discuss. Reardon, at the club, assures me that her ladyship's sister works to this day as a masseuse in Cranbourn Street. Walk past and you will see the building at the corner. The ground floor is occupied by that rogue Arthur Carrez, selling certain French books and Malthusian devices, which have several times drawn the attention of the Metropolitan Police upon him.'

Holmes straightened up and looked round him, as if he had not heard a word that I had spoken. He seemed satisfied that the room was fit to receive his young visitor. Then he said, 'It is neither her mother, nor her aunt, who seeks our help, Watson. This young woman herself is in trouble. She asks our advice.'

'That does not surprise me in the least. Advice about what, may I inquire?'

He shrugged in his off-hand manner. 'Oh, a little blackmail. Money demanded with menaces. And murder, of course. We could hardly do without that could we? We have been too idle of late. I confess that even the most insignificant problem would have been welcome in these stagnant autumn days. This one may prove far from insignificant.'

I still feared the worst. The newspaper public had lately been treated to stories of the scandal attending this young woman and her husband, Earl Russell. Frank Russell, as he preferred to be known, was in his early twenties. He had been brought up by his grandfather, the great prime minister, after the death of his parents. His career at Oxford had been brief. He was dismissed in a few months by the master of his college for what was politely described as 'disgusting conduct'. Then, while his brother Bertrand absorbed symbolic logic at Cambridge, Frank Russell threw himself into the pleasures of a certain type of London society.

In no time, that notorious harpy Lady Selina Scott had her claws into this weak young man. Rumour insisted that, at twice his age, she wanted him for herself! The idea was so preposterous that she thought it better to have the young fool enticed into marriage by her daughter, Mabel Edith. Within the year, a splendid wedding in Eaton Place was followed by unedifying court action. The young bride alleged depraved conduct by her lord. She demanded, and got, her separation with a handsome settlement. Since then, she had kept a prudent distance from respectable society, occupying a suite at the Savoy Hotel.

I was still pondering this half an hour later when Holmes crossed to the window.

'Holloa! Holloa! Here we are, Watson!'

From the street below came a familiar stamping of hooves and the long grind of a cab wheel as its metal rim rasped against the kerb. The door bell sounded and the housemaid, whom Mrs Hudson had lately taken into her service, burst in upon us, twittering with excitement like a beribboned sparrow.

Presently, there came a frou-frou of a woman's skirts on the stairs. Then, in the full glare of the light, a slim, dark-haired figure stood before us, a veil over her face, a mantle drawn round her chin. Her breath came quickly, as if the stairs had been an exertion. Every inch of her lithe figure seemed to quiver with strong emotion. When she put up the veil, her young face was clear-cut with a straight nose, dark brows, glittering eyes, and a thin mouth that seemed as if it might form a dangerous smile. The neatness of her face and the skill with which it was painted gave her the air of an expensive doll.

My friend crossed the room to greet her.

'Mr Holmes?' she inquired, her voice low yet richly modulated, 'Mr Sherlock Holmes?'

'Ma'am,' said Holmes punctiliously. He did not bow to this daughter of the aristocracy, for that would have bruised his Bohemian soul, but there was a slight inclination of the dark head and aquiline profile.

Her lips parted in a promise of hopeful innocence, as she took his hand. Still holding the hand, she looked long and directly into his eyes. Holmes stared at her, as if mesmerized. Then he said, as if in an afterthought, 'This is my associate, Dr Watson, before whom you may speak as freely as before myself.'

As I took that cool, delicate hand and looked into the frank blue eyes of our client, I thought that she was the type of young woman who would make you all the world to her for that moment, and dispense with you the next.

'Pray be seated, *ma'am*,' Holmes said gently, 'and tell us how we may be of service.' He allowed her to choose her place on the settee, watched her sit down, then took his own place in a chair diagonally across the carpet.

'Mr Holmes,' she said quickly, as she arranged her skirts, 'I will come straight to the point. You will know that I have been separated from my husband for some months. There is no communication between us, except through our lawyers. However, I am told that there is evidence in the hands of a certain person which would convict him of murder. Of two murders, indeed.'

'Lord Russell?'

She nodded, stood up again, crossed to the small occasional table where she had left her reticule and took a miniature silver box from it. She lit a cigarette and chose a fresh arm-chair, for all the world like a modern matinee heroine at Her Majesty's Theatre or the Haymarket.

'I believe my husband capable of many moral crimes, Mr Holmes, but scarcely of the murders of young women who are strangers to him.'

The slim fingers of one hand curled tightly over the end of the chair-arm, her gaze cool and direct. I saw why Holmes had responded to her appeal for help. A series of young women murdered? Lord Russell? The grandson of England's greatest prime minister in the past fifty years? If there were a word of truth, it was surely the sensation of the century.

'I cannot say whether the charge of murder is true or false, Mr Holmes. I mean to know, however, for a threat of blackmail is made to me.'

Holmes nodded, as if he approved of her determination.

'Whom is it said that he murdered?'

Only the denting of the white cigarette by her fine nails betrayed her anxiety.

'Two names are mentioned in a letter, from Mr Bayne, a barrister. He claims that since our separation Lord Russell has frequented houses in Lambeth and Southwark. The allegation is that Lord Russell derives his pleasure by making poor fallen creatures swallow noxious draughts to cause them torment. A fortnight ago, by accident or intent, he caused the deaths of two young women.'

Holmes looked askance.

'Lady Russell,' he said presently, 'such pathological pleasures are happily rare. They were indulged by certain Byzantine emperors and Renaissance princes, to be sure, and by the Comte de Sade at Marseille in 1772. In my own practice I have met not a single example. May I see the letter?'

She blushed very slightly, unfolding the sheet of paper and giving it to him. Holmes read it, looked at me and raised his eyebrows.

Without asking her leave, he handed me the paper to read.

To the Countess Russell,
Savoy Hotel,
London

Madam,

I am writing to inform you that, since your parting, your husband Lord Francis, Earl Russell, has been a regular patron of many houses of ill-fame in Lambeth and Southwark. He has killed several girls. A week or two ago he gave enough strychnine to Matilda Clover and Lou Harvey to kill a horse. Only it killed them. Two letters incriminating him were found among the effects of Clover after her death. Think of the shame and disgrace it will bring upon you and your family if Lord Russell is arrested and put in prison for this crime.

My object in writing this letter to you is to ask if you will retain me at once as your counsellor and legal adviser for a fee of two thousand pounds. If you employ me at once to act for you in this matter, I will save you from all exposure and shame. If you wait until your husband is arrested, then I cannot act for you, as no lawyer can save you after the authorities get hold of Clover's papers. If you wish to retain me, just put an advertisement in the personal column of the *Morning Post*, saying *Lady R. wishes to see Mr Bayne the Barrister* and I will drop in and have a private interview with you. I can save you and your husband if you retain me in time, but not otherwise.

Yours truly,
H. Bayne, Barrister

As I put the letter down, I confess that my heart had quickened with relief. Whoever Matilda Clover and Lou Harvey might be, they were neither of them the young woman whom I had found dying on Saturday evening.

'How was the letter delivered?' Holmes asked quietly.

'By mail this morning, sent by yesterday's post, the final collection last night.'

Holmes nodded.

'Tell me, who is your solicitor?'

'Sir George Lewis, of Lewis and Lewis.'

He nodded again and brought the matter to an end, as it seemed.

'Then you have no need of my services, Lady Russell. There is no better man than Sir George. Take the letter to him. Request him to bring it to the notice of the Commissioner of the Metropolitan Police. That will put a stop to blackmail. The police may ask you to insert the notice in the *Morning Post*, as a trap to catch the criminal. I doubt if you will hear from your blackmailer again. There is spite in this letter, rather than blackmail. However, if Mr Bayne, or whatever his name may be, attempts to contact you, the police will have him. They will do as much for you as I could.'

Her eyes showed a glimmer of petulance.

'And the young women my husband is said to have murdered a fortnight ago?'

Holmes smiled at her.

'Lady Russell, one murder—let alone two—would have been reported, however briefly, in the press. I assure you there has been no such report. Scotland Yard, in the person of Inspector Lestrade, is also kind enough to take me into its counsels. I believe I can say that neither I nor Mr Lestrade has so much as heard of Matilda Clover or Lou Harvey. Either they do not exist, which is most likely, or they are names of girls alive and well, put there for spite against them.'

'Perhaps the murders have not been discovered?'

'In that case,' Holmes said gently, 'if the murders were secret, there would be no point to the blackmail. Would there?'

She did not answer. I could swear she was almost disappointed to find there was no evidence against her husband. Her fingertips rattled on the chair-arm.

'I will also speak to Sir George Lewis,' Holmes continued, as if trying to mollify her. 'If there is any way in which I may assist you further, he need only say so.'

'Speak to whom you please!' She was standing up now and so were we. 'You may hang Lord Russell at Newgate a dozen times for the murder of Matilda Clover or Lou Harvey before I will pay a farthing to Mr Bayne!'

'Admirable,' Holmes said with every appearance of sincerity.

Lady Russell took her leave with a further assurance that Holmes would be at her beck and call, if Sir George said the word. Then my friend sat down with his legs out straight, the tips of the fingers touched together, his eyes closed.

'Let Sir George Lewis puzzle out the letter,' I said cheerfully, trying to console him. 'That is the end of the matter so far as we are concerned.'

He spoke without opening his eyes.

'My dear Watson, the significance of this case eludes you. What blackmailer would propose a scheme that is bound to put the hand-cuffs on him as soon as he approaches his victim? You saw, did you not, the script? Sharp and yet curiously florid in its decoration of open letters. The initial B of Bayne and the R of Russell were obvious examples. Such a hand is strongly indicative of inherent mania. I think, my dear fellow, that this is not the end of anything at all. I fancy, however, that it may be a most promising beginning.'

Two hours later the street-door bell emitted a single vigorous clang.

Holmes glanced at me, uneasily as I thought. The housemaid's steps rattled up the stairs and she burst in upon us, ribbons fluttering.

'Mr Fred Smith!' she gasped. 'Most urgent Mr Smith is, to see Mr Holmes!'

Holmes looked at me with an ironical despair.

'Then let Mr Fred Smith be shown up,' he said languidly. 'I should not like to think, Watson, that our evening was to be entirely without further diversion.'

III

A sense of farce, as if one actor crossed the stage in pursuit of another, now began to threaten a case which was to prove one of the grimmest. While the maid went downstairs, I stole a glimpse of the windy street from behind the curtains. There stood a dark carriage, its coachman dressed in black, with a crape hat-band and arm-band, a black crape bow on his whip. At this hour on a stormy night, he seemed like a messenger of death come to bear Don Juan down to hell.

A moment later his master was before us in a fur-collared coat, the length of a black silk weeper trailing from the hat he handed to the maid. Now that 'Fred' Smith stood before us, we recognized a man of great influence in England's political and commercial life. His face had lately graced the weekly magazines as the son and heir of a famous bookseller and Leader of the House of Commons, the Right Honourable W. H. Smith, who had died a fortnight since. With his square-set face and quick eyes, the Honourable Frederick Smith, himself a Member of Parliament, appeared as a paragon of action and integrity.

Holmes crossed the room, his hand extended.

'You need not introduce yourself, sir, for Dr Watson and I had the pleasure of meeting you last summer. It was at the Stationers Company, the occasion of a most informative address by Mr Walter de Grey Birch of the British Museum. The chemical effects produced upon logwood ink by the introduction of wood pulp in paper milling.'

Mr Smith faltered.

'You are quite right, Mr Holmes. I had overlooked that.'

'And now,' said Holmes in a graver tone and with a slight inclination of the head, 'permit me to offer you my condolences upon the death of your father.'

Frederick Smith looked as if he hardly knew how to go on. Then he said quickly, 'It is in that connection that I have come to you, Mr Holmes, rather than to the police. I fear that my family's grief is to be compounded by a painful scandal.'

Holmes looked at him a little more keenly.

'I should be sorry for that, Mr Smith. Pray be seated.'

Our visitor sat down, though first he handed my friend an envelope.

'This letter and enclosure came this morning. It is preposterous, of course, and cruel in its persecution of a bereaved family. I hope I may look to you to ensure that we are not taunted in this way. I cannot believe I am obliged to take this nonsense to the police. I should rather trust you to keep a watching brief. You know already, I daresay, of the murders in Lambeth. The death of an unfortunate young woman, Ellen Donworth . . .'

The sound of that name was as if a prize-fighter's fist had knocked the wind from my solar plexus. Holmes gave me a quick look which counselled silence but Mr Smith must have seen something for he repeated carefully, 'Ellen Donworth, and . . .'

'Matilda Clover?' Holmes suggested brightly.

Frederick Smith shook his head.

'Louisa Harvey—or Lou Harvey as he calls her.'

Holmes caught my eye again and looked quickly away.

'Indeed? May I read this curious letter?'

'By all means.'

Holmes glanced at the paper and began to read out loud for my benefit.

'To Mr Frederick Smith, 186 Strand. On Saturday night, Ellen Donworth, sometimes calling herself Ellen Linnell, 8 Duke Street, Westminster Bridge Road, was poisoned with strychnine. Among her effects were found two letters also incriminating you in the murder of Lou Harvey. If they ever become public property they will surely convict you of both crimes. I enclose a copy of a letter Miss Donworth received the day she died.'

Holmes glanced at the second letter but then continued to read the first.

'Judge for yourself what hope you have of escape if the law officers ever get hold of those letters . . .'

My friend skimmed down the page a little, humming to himself.

'My object in writing to you is to ask if you will retain me at once as your counsellor and legal adviser. If you employ me to act for you in this matter, I will save you from all exposure and shame. If you wait till you are arrested before retaining me, I cannot act for you. No lawyer can save you after the authorities get hold of those two letters.'

He sat for a moment with his brows drawn down, staring at the sheet of paper.

'Read the end of it,' Mr Smith said curtly.

'If you wish to retain me, just write a few lines on paper, saying, "Mr Fred Smith wishes to see Mr Bayne, the barrister, at once." Paste this on one of your windows at 186 Strand next Tuesday morning. I will drop in and have a private interview with you. I can save you if you retain me in time, but not otherwise. Yours truly, H. M. Bayne, Barrister.'

Holmes looked up from the paper again and there was a moment of silence, save for the wind from the street rattling the windows.

'It may comfort you to know, Mr Smith, that you are not the only person to be persecuted by the malicious letters of this madman. It is, I assure you, malice rather than blackmail. As a criminal expert, it is my habit to keep track of such murders as may occur in this city. Indeed, I am fortunate enough to be admitted every day or two to the counsels of Inspector Lestrade of Scotland Yard. I may tell you that, to my certain knowledge, no young person by the name of Lou or Louisa Harvey has been found murdered or reported murdered. As to Miss Ellen Donworth—or Linnell—it seems that she was taken

ill with a terminal attack of delirium tremens on Saturday evening
and that she died on the way to St Thomas's Hospital. My colleague Dr
Watson was in the Waterloo Road at the time and was able to render
some comfort to the poor soul until the arrival of the hospital assistant. I think you may confidently put aside all thought of accusation
or scandal. I recognize your correspondent only too well.'

Frederick Smith sat upright in his chair.

'You know his name?'

Holmes shook his head.

'At present, I merely recognize his type. One of my student textbooks, long since, was Henry Maudsley's *On Criminal Responsibility*.
Your antagonist is the hardest type of the criminally insane to deal
with. Such a personality is moved by impulses and attracted to
beliefs at which you and I could scarcely guess. Worse still he is,
like Iago, a man who will smile and smile, and be a villain. May we
turn to the second letter which is said to have been found among
the unfortunate Miss Donworth's possessions?'

He scowled at it and began to read.

> '*Miss Ellen Linnell, I wrote and warned you once before that*
> *Frederick Smith of W. H. Smith & Son was going to poison you.*
> *If you take any of the medicine he gave you, you will die. I saw*
> *Fred Smith prepare the medicine he gave you, and I saw him*
> *put enough strychnine in it to kill a horse. Signed H.M.B.'*

Frederick Smith leant forward in his chair.

'There is no H. M. Bayne in the lists of the Inns of Court. That
has been checked. I infer that the medicine he describes was a
preparation to procure an abortion.'

'Put blackmail from your mind, sir.'

Holmes handed me the letters. Their copper-plate was a script
taught to every child at school. It seemed as impersonal as scraps
cut from a newspaper.

'You are entirely right, Mr Holmes,' Frederick Smith said
simply. 'Of course it is quite mad. Whoever heard of a blackmailer

demanding that his victim should employ him as an attorney? He would be arrested the minute he showed himself. I shall burn this poisonous nonsense and forget the matter.'

Sherlock Holmes looked truly alarmed.

'On no account can you do that, Mr Smith. This villain must be caught. You will greatly oblige me by putting the message in your window as he commands. Meantime, I beg you to take these letters at once to Inspector Lestrade at Scotland Yard. The blackmail threats are too absurd to be carried out and our man must know that. What then is his true object? Perhaps to divert suspicion from some crime of his own that he intends. He shows all the characteristics of a psychopath, and he is at large. There is no time to be lost in the matter. As for his absurd and malicious accusations, I may promise you that no publicity will attend them.'

I should like to say that Frederick Smith looked reassured but that was not so. He stood up and, with a look of reluctance, prepared to make his way to Scotland Yard. As our guest took his hat, Holmes called him back.

'One moment, Mr Smith. A question had best be asked now, since it will be asked sooner or later. Where were you on Saturday evening when this unfortunate girl, Ellen Donworth, died?'

A brief resentment glimmered in the eyes of our visitor but it was soon gone.

'You are quite right, Mr Holmes. That question must be asked and answered. From seven o'clock until half-past ten, I was with the platform party at the Christian Guild meeting in Exeter Hall. I dined at home before that. The Bishop of London was my guest. If you want from me what I suppose you would call an alibi, I was in company from four in the afternoon until a little after eleven.'

'I think we may say that disposes of the matter,' Holmes said smoothly.

'Does it? Am I not accused of preparing a mixture for this poor woman which might destroy her whenever she took it, days or weeks later?'

I was happy to intervene and put his mind at rest.

'You need not concern yourself with that, sir. Miss Donworth showed the classic symptoms of alcoholic poisoning while I was with her. Indeed, there was bromide of potassium on her washstand which had evidently been prescribed by a physician to treat this condition.'

After Frederick Smith had gone, we sat for more than an hour with our glasses of warm whisky and lemon. Holmes was unaccountably silent.

'I should rather like to be a fly on the wall of Scotland Yard,' I said, as if to cheer him up. 'I imagine that Sir George Lewis would despatch Lady Russell's letter to Lestrade at once. Just as the poor devil is packing up for the day. Then, no sooner will he have read it and written his report than he will have two more letters brought by Mr Frederick Smith. It would be worth a sovereign to see his face!'

Holmes looked at the door.

'I believe it would be a wasted journey, my dear fellow. Unless I am greatly mistaken, when Lestrade has read those letters, you will see his face here soon enough.'

I suppose it was a little after nine o'clock when the door-bell sounded below us.

IV

It was no secret that Sherlock Holmes regarded Inspector Lestrade privately as what he called 'the pick of a bad lot' among the senior detective police of Scotland Yard. However, the inspector's defects of reasoning and intuition were redeemed by a gruff tenacity, when once he got his teeth into a case. Moreover, his habit of looking in upon us of an evening kept us in touch with all that was happening at police headquarters.

Mrs Hudson had returned from her sister in time to take our visitor's waterproof before she showed him up to our quarters. He appeared in the doorway, a small wiry bulldog of a man, his pea-jacket and cravat giving him a decidedly nautical appearance.

With a short greeting, he put down the attaché case he had been carrying, seated himself, and lit the cigar that Holmes had given him. Soon he was relaxed before the fire, warming his left hand round a glass of warm toddy. The tone of his visit to us was less amiable than usual. He had the look of a man who has triumphed and is bursting to show it.

'I hear, gentlemen, you have had visitors this evening. Out of the top drawer, as you might say. Lady Russell and the Honourable Mr Frederick Smith.'

'Quite,' said Holmes punctiliously, leaning forward with the poker and stirring the fire to new life.

Lestrade shot a fierce look at my companion.

'Well, we shall have a word about those folk presently, Mr Holmes. In the matter of Ellen Donworth, however, I think you will find that I have been a little in front of you this time!'

The mention of the girl's name knocked the wind from me again. Holmes laid down the poker and looked up.

'Really, Lestrade? You don't say?'

'But I do say, Mr Holmes! I fear that I must have given Mr Frederick Smith something of a knock.'

'I see.'

'I don't think you do, sir! I don't think you do at all. There were you and the good doctor, promising him that the poor young creature had died of alcoholic poisoning. And there was I, sitting across my desk from Mr Smith, with a post-mortem note on Home Office stationery in my hand. From Dr Stevenson this afternoon. Alcoholic poisoning? Ellen Donworth had enough strychnine in her to kill half of Lambeth! What about that, Mr Holmes? Eh?'

Again, I felt the dull blow of dismay. Holmes gazed into the fire.

'Were you a medical man, Lestrade, you would know that tetanic convulsions, accompanied by violent vomiting, are symptomatic both of delirium tremens and of acute poisoning by certain vegetable alkaloids. Dr Watson was present and merely rendered what immediate assistance he could. He is not a walking laboratory. I suppose that it took a Home Office autopsy before the combined intelligences of Scotland Yard so much as thought of poison.'

I tried to recall any evidence of poison on that Saturday evening. There was none that could have been obtained, short of laboratory samples from the victim. That Ellen Donworth was under treatment for alcoholism had further compounded the difficulty.

'She said that she had been given a glass of gin by a man called Fred,' I ventured, 'a glass that had something white in it.'

Lestrade swung round in his chair with a look of pure satisfaction.

'So one of the other witnesses heard her say. Jimmy Styles, the market-trader. Quite took the colour out of the Honourable Mr Smith, though, when I told him the man we wanted was called Fred, the same as him.'

Holmes yawned, the inspector's triumph becoming insufferable to him. But there was no quenching the light of satisfaction in Lestrade's dark eyes. His tongue was moving humorously behind his teeth.

'One word to you,' said Holmes, 'Mr Smith was in company from six until eleven on Saturday evening. I advise you to tread lightly in these matters.'

The inspector grinned.

'I know that, Mr Holmes. But you should have seen him all the same.' He fell silent, puffing at his cigar, then added, 'Mr Smith had no part in this, nor Lord Russell. Whoever the brute was, we deduce he was in the shadows of the Waterloo Road, gloating over his handiwork as she lay there.'

'Forgive me,' Holmes said quietly, 'that assumption has the sound of a fine theory and a questionable fact.'

Lestrade shook his head firmly.

'Oh, no, sir. When Dr Stevenson performed his postmortem this morning, he found the strychnine had been mixed with morphia. Now why should a man do that, if he only meant to kill her, as he knew strychnine must? The only reason, Dr Stevenson says, was to make sure the poor soul should not die too quickly. Without morphia, it would have been over in a few minutes perhaps. This devil wanted to see and hear her lying there, as Mr Styles did, trying to press her stomach on the pavement to ease the agony, pleading with them not to lift her.'

Holmes took a glowing cinder with the tongs and lit his cherrywood pipe. For a moment he said nothing, then he leant back in his chair.

'Perhaps you should arrest Mr Styles. Or Dr Watson. Or anyone who happened to be outside the York Hotel.' He paused and drew at his pipe. 'Forgive me, pray continue with your narrative.'

'The matter of these letters,' the inspector said shortly, 'I don't know what we shall make of them. The one accusing Mr Smith of murdering Nellie Donworth was written a full day before the poison was found in her by Dr Stevenson. Who could know the truth but the murderer himself?'

Holmes waved his pipe.

'True. Or very nearly so.'

'But the letter enclosed with it, and the one to Lady Russell! No one by the name of Matilda Clover or Louisa Harvey is dead, so far as we know, let alone murdered. Wires have gone out to every police district in London and the cities throughout the country. All with the same result. Nothing known for either name.'

'Will you not include the names of Clover and Harvey in your investigation?'

Lestrade looked at him, as if my friend should have known better.

'And a pretty dance our man might lead us! Every time he gives us a name we must send men on a murder hunt! He might give us a new name by every post!'

'And that is the best advice you can offer?'

'No,' said the inspector, 'by no means. There is another side to this, though it won't disturb you here in the quiet of Baker Street. Since this morning, rumours have been flying about as to how Ellen Donworth died. We think they came from an attendant at Westminster mortuary, after the post-mortem. You don't need me to tell you that the mention of strychnine has caused a panic among certain classes in Lambeth. So nothing is to be said about Harvey and Clover. It won't do to have the public mind agitated further by rumours of young women murdered who never have been. You know as well as I, gentlemen, that tragedies of this kind are too often an opportunity for sick minds to vent their frustrations.'

'Indeed,' said Holmes languidly. 'In this case, however, you tell me that the date of posting proves conclusively that this sick mind knew of the strychnine when the rest of the world still called it alcoholic poisoning.'

'Which is just what I thought you would say, Mr Holmes. So, as to Clover and Harvey, I left orders that Sergeant Macintyre is to visit Somerset House tomorrow morning and go through the registers of deaths for Clovers and Harveys, from all causes, for two years past. If our man tries us with any other names, we shall do exactly the same. You'll see we can manage these things quite well enough for ourselves, when we have to, Mr Sherlock Holmes.'

V

Somewhat to my surprise, I came down to breakfast on the following morning to find that Sherlock Holmes had already finished his meal. He was sitting in the large old-fashioned chair, eyes gleaming from a haggard face. Beside him on the floor lay the dismembered relics of the morning papers. He looked like a man who has not been to bed all night, rather than one who has risen early.

'Make the best of it, Watson,' he said, gesturing at the remaining place laid for me, 'I fancy we shall have another visitor before long.'

'Not Mr Bayne the Barrister, I trust!'

'Lestrade, my dear fellow. I have frequently observed that his boast of being able to manage well enough on his own is usually followed by a request that I should supply the deficiencies of the detective police.'

'I doubt that we shall see him, Holmes. After his mood last night, I doubt it very much.'

I had scarcely finished my last slice of toast when the doorbell rang. Presently the familiar wiry bulldog figure appeared, as Holmes had predicted. The inspector seemed a little subdued this morning but by no means defeated.

'Do sit down,' said Holmes, as genially as if the two men had not met for several months, 'and tell us more news of the Lambeth murders.'

Lestrade looked a little uneasy as he said, 'There is only one, Mr Holmes. Ellen Donworth, that is all. Sergeant Macintyre reported to Somerset House at eight this morning and went through the entries for two years past. It was a simple enough matter. There is no entry of the death of Matilda Clover, nor of Lou or Louisa Harvey.'

'Good,' said Holmes, pouring coffee for the inspector. 'Let us be glad of that at least. However, your investigation has plainly run into difficulties or you would not be here. Will you not tell us what they are?'

Lestrade sipped his coffee and stared at Holmes over the rim of the cup.

'We are not in difficulties, Mr Holmes. Indeed, we have more evidence.'

'Oh?' said Holmes sceptically. 'Then let us be glad of that too.'

'A further letter was received this morning by Mr Wyatt, the Surrey coroner. As a matter of courtesy, I thought you should be informed.'

'Ah!' said Holmes triumphantly. 'Our man has set a puzzle of some kind for you?'

Lestrade handed him a single sheet of paper and my friend read it out for my benefit.

'Sir,
I am writing to say that if you and your satellites fail to bring the murderer of Ellen Donworth, alias Ellen Linnell, late of 8 Duke Street, Westminster Bridge Road, to justice, then I am

*willing to give you such assistance, as will bring the murderer
to justice provided your Government is willing to pay me
£300,000 for my services. No pay if not successful.*

A O'Brien, Detective.'

Lestrade looked at us and asked quietly.

'Well, gentlemen. What do you make of that?'

'I think you might throw it in the fire,' I said at once. 'I know, of course, you cannot do that but at least commit it to your files. There is nothing here but a wild goose-chase. Follow the evidence in the case.' Holmes shrugged.

'Three hundred thousand pounds! I do not think I should ever be able to command a fee so large. If Mr O'Brien can obtain three hundred thousand pounds for a single case, he is a far better man than I. Perhaps, Lestrade, you should accept his offer.'

'I call it an outrage,' I persisted, irritated by such facetiousness, 'that the members of a bereaved family like Mr Smith's should be made sport of in this manner and the police put to such trouble by one criminal lunatic!'

'Or two,' Holmes said quietly.

'Or two?' Lestrade was half out of his chair.

'Of course there are two.' Holmes contrived to look astonished and alarmed that the inspector should have missed this. 'I feel sure, Lestrade, that you have not come without the letters to Lady Russell, to Mr Smith from Bayne the Barrister, and the enclosure to Ellen Donworth from H. M. B. Kindly look at them and tell me what you see!'

Self-consciously, Lestrade took the three sheets of paper from his case and made a pretence of reading them. Holmes poured ample salt upon the poor fellow's tail.

'Great heavens, man! Did you truly not see the difference? Come, of course you did! You are merely teasing us! The letter to Frederick Smith and that purporting to be written to Ellen Donworth are in quite different hands. Copperplate can never quite disguise those slight temperamental flourishes!'

'I see nothing,' Lestrade said uneasily.

Holmes sighed.

'Very well. I daresay you do not. To the trained eye, however, it is evident that the epistle to Mr Smith was written by a right-handed scribe, the enclosure by one who is naturally left-handed. No right-handed man could compose that second epistle with such assurance while using his left hand. The acute angle of the backward slope has the character of one who is uniquely left-handed.'

The unfortunate inspector began to struggle a little.

'Then why did you keep silent last night, Mr Holmes?'

Holmes shrugged.

'I suspected that we should soon hear from our correspondent again, as has proved to be the case this morning. It is not in the nature of such compulsives to keep silent. I daresay I would have said something last night. Indeed I was about to do so when you informed me that you would be quite able to sift the problem for yourself.'

An uncomfortable silence followed this piece of temperament on my friend's part. Presently Holmes said, 'I wonder why there are four?'

'Why should there not be four letters as well as any other number?' I asked.

He shook his head.

'No, Watson, you misunderstand. Why should the four letters have been written by four different people? The common experience of the criminal expert is that poisoning, whether for pleasure or expediency, proves to be a solitary occupation. At the most there is one accomplice. Here we have four people. Four letter-writers. Two of them must be known to one another, since their communications came in the same envelope. Indeed, all four *appear* to be united in a common enterprise.'

Lestrade's unease had grown to consternation but Sherlock Holmes was prepared to salt him a little more.

'Very well, Lestrade. We find that the four letters are in different hands, despite an attempt at similarity of style. However, you may not have had leisure to examine this morning's epistle closely enough to see that it comes from a woman.'

'A woman!' Lestrade's dark eyes suddenly appeared the size of marbles.

'Oh, yes,' said Holmes, surprised that the inspector and I could have missed anything so obvious. 'The script appears to be a woman's and, though this is sometimes simulated, I believe in this case it is genuine. A man who was imitating female script might copy well enough the usual rotundity of individual letters, even of complete words. Here however, even with my magnifying glass, I can detect none of those necessary breaks in a word or a letter which always occur sooner or later when another scribe merely imitates an unfamiliar hand. No, my dear fellow, this is too flowing—too much of a piece—to be anything but a female hand.'

'You cannot say that!' Lestrade snapped.

'I can and I do,' Holmes remarked jauntily. 'I also say that while I was reading out the contents of the note just now, for Watson's benefit, I was able to make a close inspection of the watermark. It is Mayfair Superfine, much favoured by ladies for casual correspondence. That in itself is nothing, of course. A man might use it for disguise. However, as I held the paper I was conscious of the faintest air of white jessamine, imparted by the writer's wrist or sleeve. As I have remarked before, there are seventy-five perfumes which it is very necessary that the criminal expert should be able to distinguish from each other, of which this is one. I do not believe you will find that any man who murdered Miss Donworth would affect such a perfume as white jessamine upon his sleeve.'

'Then we have a criminal gang of three men and a woman?' I exclaimed. 'A gang of blackmailers? A gang of poisoners?'

'Out of the question!' Lestrade said abruptly. 'In the findings of Dr Stevenson, we have evidence of a single criminal degenerate. Crimes of this sort are committed by a maniac working alone. He knows, if he is caught, he will be hanged. He would not dare trust his neck to others, even by using them as his scribes. What you say, Mr Holmes, suggests strongly to me that the letters are from a group of mischief-makers. They are not the murderers but are merely exploiting a lust-murder committed by someone utterly unknown to them.'

Holmes shrugged and sighed.

'Then you must explain to me, Lestrade, why two of the letters, in different hands, claim that Ellen Donworth was the victim of strychnine. Except for an unbelievable degree of coincidence, that fact could have been known only to her murderer at the time the letters were posted.'

'Very well,' said the inspector desperately, 'let us take it as a coincidence. I would remind you, Mr Holmes, how often you have said that when all the impossible explanations are discarded, whatever is left, however improbable, must be the answer.'

'I think not,' said Holmes quietly. 'When stated correctly, that is a principle known as Occam's Razor. However, I do not believe that old William of Occam would have thanked you for shaving with it in such a manner.'

This produced silence until Holmes spoke more gently, for the inspector's benefit.

'Perhaps it would be better, Lestrade, if you were to recall how often in the past I have remarked that it is a capital error in our profession to reason in defiance of the facts, however little one may care for them.'

This quiet reprimand induced a silence that no one seemed inclined to break.

VI

With that, the case was at an end—or so it seemed. In the following weeks, the tenuous thread that had connected Inspector Lestrade with the ghostly murderers was to grow more slender, until it seemed to vanish altogether. No more letters were received from murderers or blackmailers. No further clues were gleaned from those which had already arrived. The criminal gang appeared to have shut up shop, as Holmes remarked with a rare absence of concern.

Somerset House was visited by a more senior officer and its records more meticulously checked. No one with the name of Matilda Clover was found in the register of deaths for twenty years past. No entry existed for Lou or Louisa Harvey. The Lambeth murder ceased to be of interest to the press. Even Sherlock Holmes appeared to turn his attention elsewhere.

Once, the inspector thought he had his man in the person of Mr Slater of Wych Street, Holborn. Slater's ways were odd to say the least. He was wont to cross Waterloo Bridge from lodgings near the Strand and make a nuisance of himself in Lambeth, urging repellent suggestions on street-women there. Two of them resented him more than most. Eliza Masters and Elizabeth May swore that this man who molested them was the very person they had seen with Ellen Donworth, not an hour before I had found her dying outside the York Hotel.

Holmes and I were invited to attend the identification parade at Bow Street police station, an event which promised to end the Lambeth mystery once and for all. The two young women walked down the line of men drawn up in the corridor. Each picked out the shabby figure of Mr Slater, a little too easily as it seemed to me. They were thanked and sent on their way.

Lestrade cautioned Slater that he would now be questioned in the matter of the death of Ellen Donworth. He did not look in the least apprehensive, merely surprised. He shrugged his shoulders and said, 'All right then, if you like.'

When asked to account for himself on that fateful Saturday evening in October, Slater reminded Lestrade that he had been detained by a police officer that morning on a complaint by a respectable young woman in Lower Marsh, twelve hours before Miss Donworth's death. Lestrade had been told nothing of this by the Lambeth division and so suspected a trick. However, Slater coolly recalled that there was no magistrates court to deal with him on a Saturday, so that he had been detained in a Lambeth police cell until Monday morning, then bound over to keep the peace. It was quite impossible that he could have had any connection with the young woman's death. This, as Holmes privately observed, was a fact which Lestrade and 'A' Division of the Metropolitan Police at Scotland Yard could have established to begin with, had they cared to communicate with 'L' Division, a few hundred yards away on the other side of Westminster Bridge.

Holmes was both furious and yet triumphant in the face of such official incompetence. For several days, he referred bitterly to 'A' Division as 'Lestrade's Gendarmerie', giving the words a comic opera pronunciation. Then he turned his attention again to other things, declining as he said to supply the deficiencies of Scotland Yard.

It seemed that we faced, as Samuel Johnson once said, a conclusion in which nothing was concluded, until the events of a fine cold morning a month or two later. It was, I suppose, a little before noon when the bell rang below us. I glanced down from the window and saw the uniform cap of a Post Office boy with a telegram. A moment later, Mrs Hudson was before us with the blue envelope on her salver. Holmes opened it, read it, and handed it to me.

HOLMES, 221B BAKER STREET, W.

PREPARE TO COME AT ONCE STOP.

LAMBETH MURDERER THREATENS MASS POISON STOP.

POLICE OFFICER ON WAY TO FETCH YOU STOP.

LESTRADE, SCOTLAND YARD.

'You may tell the boy there is no reply,' Holmes said smoothly to our anxious housekeeper.

By the time we were at the door, a cab was drawing into the pavement with a helmeted constable inside. A few moments later we were bowling down Baker Street towards Regent Street and Trafalgar Square. The matter was plainly of great secrecy. We did not speak to the constable, nor he to us.

From Trafalgar Square we turned at great speed into Northumberland Avenue, past the imperial fronts of grand hotels or offices, and under chestnut boughs. Our hansom rattled towards the glitter of the Thames, almost as far as the rear entrance of Scotland Yard. But then the constable tapped sharply on the roof of the cab and it drew up outside the fine entrance and marble steps of the Metropole Hotel. Why we had been brought to such a place as this, I had not the least idea.

'What are we doing here?' I asked, a little put out.

Before our escort could reply, Lestrade opened the door of the cab and we stepped out into a scene of confusion, like the rout of a great army. The broad pavement of the avenue outside the hotel was stacked with portmanteaus, cabin trunks, hat-boxes, luggage of every description. We could scarcely have reached the back entrance of Scotland Yard for hansoms and growlers ahead of us, each loaded with the possessions of those scrimmaging to escape. There was such shouting of directions, such arguments and questions bawled out, that the place was perfect bedlam. Inside the grand foyer I saw luggage strewn round the gilt-columned mirrors and across the thick carpets, while porters and page-boys endeavoured to make order out of chaos.

'And which of all these very expensive people is our Lambeth murderer going to slaughter?' Holmes inquired amiably of Lestrade. 'Surely not all of them?'

The inspector was bristling with indignation.

'Each one of them, Mr Holmes, each and every one of them has received one of these.'

For a moment I expected him to produce a phial of strychnine but it was a plain printed card. I had never seen such insanity in my life as in what I read just then.

ELLEN DONWORTH'S DEATH
To the Guests of the Metropole Hotel.

Ladies and Gentlemen,
I hereby notify you that the person who poisoned Ellen Donworth on the 13th last October is to-day in the employ

of the kitchens of the Metropole Hotel and that your lives
are in danger as long as you remain in this hotel.
      Yours respectfully,
      W. H. Murray

Sherlock Holmes was not a man much given to outbursts of
laughter. They began deep in his throat, as a rising growl. Then, if
the occasion warranted, he threw back his head and shouted aloud
at the richness of the humour. To Lestrade's dismay, he did so now.
His Olympian merriment echoed through the panic and over the
luggage on the pavement, across the lavishly decorated foyer, where
the hotel manager in his frock coat and striped trousers stood
wringing his hands at the centre of the tumult.

Holmes laughed so long that, in the end, he was obliged to wipe
his eyes before he could turn to the scowling inspector, 'Well, my
dear Lestrade, I can certainly tell you one thing. You may be sure
that our man did this in order that he should be here to see the
fun. I swear he is here now. Which do you suppose it can be? That
horsy fellow over there in the tweed suit, the neat moustache and
the barbered eyebrows? The little old lady in black velvet with
her ivory-knobbed stick? That tall colonial with the brick-red face
who looks as if he might be scanning new horizons in Australia or
Brazil? Any of them or all of them!'

Lestrade's colour rose at the thought that the murderer might be
within a few yards of him and that there was nothing he could do.
He looked about him furiously.

'Since you are always so much to the forward, Mr Sherlock Holmes,
perhaps *you* would like to choose which of them it shall be!'

Holmes laughed again, more gently.

'You had far better give it up, old fellow. Mr Bayne the Barrister,
Mr O'Brien the Detective, Mr Murray from the hotel—whether they
be three or one—may be stood next to you this moment, or in the
foyer, and you would not know.'

I had never seen Lestrade's face so thunderous. The Lambeth
poisoning had vanished from the papers but now it would be back,

a story of how the hunted man had made fools of Scotland Yard. At the manager's request, Lestrade had summoned Holmes by telegram to investigate the hotel kitchens but the inspector was now so furious that he could not bring himself to ask the favour.

When we came home that afternoon, Holmes was still chuckling at the discomfiture of Lestrade, the Metropole Hotel, and its luckless guests.

'You believe the man who sent that note was there this morning?' I asked, as we took off our overcoats and rang for tea.

'I was never more sure of anything in my life.'

I do not know why I said it, but the next moment I blurted out:

'It was you! It was you, Holmes! By God, you sent that circular! No wonder you were so sure that the man was there! It was you!'

He looked quickly at me with bewildered innocence. Not quickly enough, as I thought.

'What purpose would that serve, Watson? What purpose in the world?'

'To start the case moving again. To flush the criminal or criminals from cover,' I said doggedly, but he would discuss the accusation no further.

VII

The evening newspapers got wind of the 'Metropole Sensation', and so it was blown about all over London. Though he would not admit it, I swore this was a subversive attempt by Holmes to 'start the ball rolling' again by means of a clandestinely-printed circular. If the murderer of Ellen Donworth resembled the egomaniac of our fancy, he would be unable to resist a riposte. However, I never expected the ball to roll with such sudden speed or in the direction that it did. Holmes spent a day or two, lounging as languidly and jadedly as ever. A good deal of his time was passed in the old-fashioned chair, a musical score before him, easing his tedium by the mellow tone of his faithful violin.

After lunch two or three days later, he was drawing a mournful beauty from the slow movement of the Violin Concerto of Ludwig van Beethoven. His bow moved effortlessly, his eyes were mere slits, and he seemed almost to sleep. I sat in an opposite chair, listening but letting my thoughts drift over other matters.

The music stopped abruptly, in mid-phrase. The bow and fiddle rattled down on the table as he seized the score that lay open on its stand.

'By God!' he cried. 'What fools we have been! What blind, unutterable fools!'

He was not looking at me but at the score of the concerto, dismayed as if he had seen a ghost there. Then he glared at it and threw it down. I wondered whether the strain of the investigation was leading to some cerebral episode.

'Do you not see?' he cried. 'We have been looking for Matilda Clover . . .'

'I daresay,' I said, rousing myself.

'. . . when all the time we should have been looking for Matilda Clover!'

If I thought his reason tottered the moment before, I was even more inclined to believe it now. He looked at the score again and said, 'Let us pray that dear old Beethoven has succeeded where Lestrade and his minions have failed.'

Then he began bustling about for his ulster, his cap, his gloves, and his stick.

'I must go,' he said sharply, 'I shall not be more than an hour or two.'

'Shall I not come with you?'

'No!' he said severely. 'I can manage this perfectly well on my own. If I am wrong, which I entirely doubt, I shall bear the blame of error alone.'

Then he was gone, to call a cab off the rank. Holmes was often secretive and vexing, but I had never known him behave quite so outlandishly. I picked up the score. It was from Augener's in Great Marlborough Street, a German 'Edition Peters' published at Leipzig. I saw only what I would expect to see, in gothic type upon the cover, 'L. van Beethoven, Konzert Opus 61 D dur'.

How this could have anything to do with the Lambeth mystery was beyond me. I sat and waited for his return, so perplexed that I could neither read nor attend to any other business. More than two hours passed before I heard the cabman's voice and my friend's key in the lock of our Baker Street door. I knew that he bore success and not failure by the way his long legs measured the stairs two at a time—and by the way he came in, flung down his ulster and looked at me.

'Matilda Clover, Watson, died in October of delirium tremens, in Lambeth.'

I could only stare and ask, 'How the devil did you find that?'

'By looking in the very place where Lestrade and his incompetents have been looking for a month past. Somerset House. The registers of deaths.'

'How did you find it, when Lestrade could not?'

He picked up the musical score.

'What a fool I have been! Look, my dear fellow! Konzert—not Concerto! How many times have I seen that word these past weeks and not recognized the truth! Of what use is a consulting detective who never considered that Klover—rather than Clover—is a not uncommon patronymic of Westphalia and Upper Saxony! Such a possibility would never, of course, have crossed the mind of Lestrade.'

'She was German?'

'I very much doubt that,' he said impatiently, putting away the violin in its case. 'Her father or grandfather may have been a sailor who came ashore at the docks. Or perhaps one of the German medical students at the hospital made out her death certificate and gave her the wrong initial letter. Who can say? But at last we have her, Watson, and she brings us very interesting news.'

'How can that be?'

He sat down and looked at me with a mad laughter in his eyes.

'Matilda Clover, as we will continue to pronounce her, died on 20 October.'

'Impossible!'

'In other words, Watson, when Lady Russell came to us complaining that her husband was accused of murdering Matilda Clover—Matilda Clover was still alive. Allow that the note took two or three days to reach Lady Russell, then the death of Matilda Clover was foretold by at least a week.'

A man who writes that his head began to spin is usually guilty of exaggeration. In my own case, at this moment, I swear that the Lambeth case spun my brain like a child's top. I could not see that even Sherlock Holmes would make sense of it. When I looked up at him, he was chuckling like a schoolboy.

'We must inform Lestrade at once!' I said sternly.

He shook his head, still chuckling.

'Oh no, Watson. Miss Clover is to be ours alone for the next day or two. Finders keepers, as the saying is.'

VIII

Despite my misgivings, perhaps it was as well for our investigation that we gave ourselves a few days of grace. On the following afternoon, Holmes had gone to examine a skull, to be purchased in his pursuit of criminal phrenology. It was said to be that of the famous highwayman and informer, Jonathan Wild, hanged at Tyburn in 1725. A little before three o'clock there was a scampering on the stairs, a hurried knock at our door, and the entry of Master Billy. There was generally a 'Master Billy', employed by Mrs Hudson as what she liked to call a 'page boy' but whose duties were merely to fetch and carry. They were all known as 'Billy' and the present holder of the office had proved himself a useful source of information on two or three occasions.

'Medical gentleman to see you, Dr Watson, sir,' he gasped, catching his breath, 'most immediate.'

The young imp handed out a card on his salver. I took it and read 'Dr Thomas Neill, M.B., B.Ch., Faculty of Medicine, McGill University.' I did not know the name but, naturally enough, I assumed that this was a matter concerning one of my own consultations. I told

Billy to show the gentleman up. As he did so, I turned the card over and saw two words pencilled on the back: MATILDA CLOVER.

It seemed indeed that my heart missed a beat. At that moment the door of the room opened to admit a pale, rather scholarly figure, wearing a cape and holding a silk hat in his hand. He had the myopic look of an earnest student and wore a pair of pince-nez with strong lenses.

'Dr Watson?' he said, in a voice that was low and deferential. 'It is a pleasure to meet you, sir, and so good on your part to receive me without an engagement.'

I shook his hand, which had a lean and sinewy grip, then ushered him to a chair.

'If you wish to discuss the matter of Matilda Clover,' I said hastily, 'it is my colleague Sherlock Holmes whom you should see.'

He looked up at me with a nervous smile.

'To meet Mr Holmes would be a great privilege,' he said earnestly, 'and one that I greatly look forward to. However, to speak frankly, I am not sorry to have an opportunity to speak first as one medical man to another. For some reason I cannot pretend to understand, I seem to be the victim of a plot—or hoax—involving the death of a young woman whose name you may already know but I do not. It is rumoured among members of the Christian Guild that Mr Frederick Smith himself was similarly insulted and that he came to you for advice. Indeed, his name is now linked with scandal in the very streets and lodging houses round the hospital. Hence my concern for my own reputation. If you were able to assist Mr Smith, perhaps you can advise me.'

'You are pursuing your studies at St Thomas's?'

He inclined his head.

'I have that honour, sir. However, I am mostly in the country, reading and taking notes. I have rooms near Lambeth Palace, when I am in town.'

Without further ado, he handed me a letter in an envelope. The postmark was two days old. Though I read it with some dismay, its contents now saved us the trouble of searching for the last dwelling-place of Matilda Clover.

Dr Thomas Neill

Sir,

    Miss Clover, who until a short time ago lived at 27 Lambeth Road, S.E., died at the above address on the 20th October through being poisoned by strychnine. After her death a search of her effects was made, and evidence was found which showed that you not only gave her the medicine which caused her death but that you had been hired for the purpose of poisoning her. This evidence is in the hands of one of our detectives, who will give the papers either to you or to the police authorities for the sum of £1,000.

    Now, sir, if you want all the evidence for £1,000 just put a personal in the Daily Chronicle, saying you will pay Malone £1,000 for his services, and I will send a party to settle this matter. If you do not want the evidence, of course, it will be turned over to the police and published, and your ruin will surely follow. Think well before you decide on this matter. It is just this—£1,000 sterling on the one hand, and ruin, shame, and disgrace on the other. Answer by personal on the first page of the Daily Chronicle any time next week. I am not humbugging you, I have evidence enough to ruin you forever.

    M. Malone

Regardless of the different handwriting, this effusion surely came from the minds of 'Mr Bayne the Barrister', 'A. O'Brien, Detective' and the rest of the incognitos. Beside me, Dr Neill's face was a study in quiet despair.

'Tell me, Dr Watson,' the poor scholar asked plaintively, 'what am I to do? I have never heard of Miss Clover. I have only twice in my life been in England and I was not here on 20 October!'

'You should take this beastly letter to the police,' I said firmly, wondering as I spoke why the malicious devils had picked on this other-worldly soul.

'Then to the police I suppose I must go.' There was no doubting the sincerity of his thanks. 'I dread doing so, however.'

'I do not see why you should.'

'Because, sir,' said the mild-mannered American, 'though there is not a word of truth in the accusations, I fear a public inquiry might be ruinous to a medical man. This scoundrel already thinks that he can frighten me into paying him because I know the damage that mere rumour and innuendo can do in our profession. The world, here and in my own country, will say that there is no smoke without fire.'

'I believe you may rely upon the discretion of the English authorities in such matters.'

'I am glad to hear you say so.' There was no mistaking the poor fellow's eagerness to believe me. 'There is, however, something else I should like to share with you.'

'Pray do.'

He looked more wretched than ever.

'My practice has been in Ontario and Chicago. I am here for study leave, a week or two more, to pursue my research into the treatment of nervous disorders. Very few people in England know me. I am not Mr Frederick Smith nor Mr Sherlock Holmes, after all! This fact drives me most reluctantly to the conclusion that my blackmailer—if he be such—my persecutor anyway, is someone to whom I am personally known and who is known to me. Someone very close. Can it be otherwise?'

How often had I seen the keen eyes of Sherlock Holmes narrow as he probed such a confession further! I could only ask lamely, 'Do you have any suspicion who it might be?'

He shook his head, then paused.

'I hope—I believe—it could not be one or two men whose names have crossed my mind. Your advice that I should take this letter to the police is good and right, Dr Watson. My fear is that they would ask me the question you have put. That I might be persuaded to give them the name of a young man who might very likely prove innocent. That would not lie easily on my conscience, sir.'

If the blackmailer—or blackmailers—should be close to Dr Neill and known by him, we were surely very close to the answer of the Lambeth mystery. As cautiously as if I was on tiptoe behind an escaped cage-bird, I said, 'Will you tell such a name to me?'

He hesitated.

'Can you trust me in this matter, Dr Watson?'

I could scarcely say I would not trust him! I nodded.

'Very well. I had hoped this afternoon to hear you say that you knew all about this business and had tracked the criminal down—or very nearly so. Well, that cannot be. Very good. Then allow me a little space to pursue my own inquiry. If my suspicions are correct, I will do all that you say. If they are not—then the police may have the letter for what good it will do. I confess I would rather be mistaken in my suspicions and return to America the week after next with matters as they stand. I will be guided by the event—and by you.'

There was little more to the interview than this. I had hoped Sherlock Holmes might return before its conclusion. However, my visitor stood up to take his leave. At the door, he turned and asked the question I had been dreading.

'Tell me, Dr Watson, is it true that the crime of murder was perpetrated against this unfortunate young woman?'

As yet, only Holmes and I knew that she had lived and died. I did not relish sharing the information with any third person in the absence of my friend. My reply was true but less than candid.

'The police know nothing of any such crime or any such person.'

There was no mistaking the relief on his face.

'Then you persuade me that this is not blackmail, sir, but a jealous hoax! I have half a mind to tear up this foul letter and forget the matter.'

I stood there like a fool, not knowing how much to say.

'Perhaps you should preserve the letter, Dr Neill, until the truth of the matter is known and in case you may receive another of these wicked communications.'

But that was as far as I could go.

IX

Holmes returned half an hour later, glowering. He pronounced the so-called skull of Jonathan Wild a fake. Taking up Dr Neill's card, he glanced at the writing on the back, and remarked sardonically that at least the American scholar had not written any of the blackmail letters himself. But at the mention of an address for Matilda Clover, he summoned Billy at once to whistle a hansom to our door.

Before the sun set that afternoon, the cab bore us across Westminster Bridge, the river so crowded by coal-barges at high water that you might almost have walked from bank to bank. On Holmes's instructions, we turned into the Lambeth Road, where the Waterloo trains shook a low plate-iron bridge overhead and the blue sky was veiled by sulphurous vapour from the engine-stacks. We drew up at the corner of Hercules Road, by a grim mock-Venetian tenement of Orient Buildings. The character of the area was spoken for by the manner in which several shabbily-dressed but feather-boa'd young creatures paraded outside its entrance.

Ahead of us, on the Lambeth Road, stood a row of plain-fronted terraced houses, crusted and blackened by railway soot, with the Masons Arms public house beyond them. Holmes led the way to a door, with the number '27' painted upon it, and rapped the tarnished knocker. As he did so, I noticed that his ulster was unbuttoned at the neck. Either his own collar was oddly disarranged or he now wore the clerical collar of a clergyman. The effect was the same, either way.

The door was opened by a woman of about sixty, wearing a white apron with shoulder-straps over a plain beige dress. Her ginger hair, grown thin from constant colouring and artificial curling, was fluffed out so that one saw a ghostly vision of her pale head through it. She looked at us, attempted a smile, then seemed to think better of it.

'Good morning, madam,' said Holmes punctiliously, though the fastidious nostrils flared just perceptibly. 'My name is William

Holmes of the South London Mission. This is my colleague, Dr Watson.'

I had never heard him use his other baptismal name as a *nom-de-guerre* before.

'I believe,' he said to the grim-faced housewife, 'that Miss Matilda Clover lived here at the time of her death?'

'Perhaps she did,' said the woman suspiciously.

Holmes became uncharacteristically deferential.

'May I take it that you are the lady of the house, Mrs . . .?'

'Phillips. Mrs Emma Phillips.' She still looked less than pleased by his missionary appeal.

Undeterred by her surliness, Holmes drew out a small black notebook and smiled at her.

'Mrs Phillips. Quite so. Miss Clover was under our care, so far as we were able to help her. She came from a respectable family in Kent, much afflicted by her way of life and the manner of her death.'

'I never knew!' said Mrs Phillips, plainly astonished.

'You may take it from me that it was so. Her people are most anxious that those, like your good self, who were friends to her in her last days should not be left out of pocket in respect of any little debts or contractual obligations incurred by Miss Clover . . .'

Until he began to talk of money, the woman's expression had generally remained that of a feral creature defending its burrow. Now her face and voice softened.

'Is it insurance, then? Friendly society?'

Holmes appeared to consult a notebook, whose pages I could see were blank.

'One might say that it comes to the same thing. Tell me, it was in this house that Miss Clover died on 20 October last?'

'Oh, yes! Definitely this house.' I could almost hear in her voice a fear that perhaps she might be disqualified from whatever good things were about to be offered. 'She died here all right! In the top bedroom that she rented a few weeks before. Back in October. To be precise, very early on 21 October. DTs and heart failure. Drunk an entire bottle of brandy the night before, not to say what else. Took very bad about three in the morning, died just after eight. And if you'd known her, you'd only be surprised it hadn't happened before!'

'Indeed!'

'The doctor's assistant was here most of the time. Foreign-sounding young gentleman but quite agreeable. You could ask him. He made a report to Dr Macarthy and they gave her a certificate. Would it be much, the money? See, she had two rooms at the top of the house, in the attic, and there's still rent not paid for her last five weeks, let alone the time since, for which notice was never given.'

'I shall certainly make a note of that,' Holmes said enthusiastically, pencilling something on the blank page of the notebook.

'And the clearing up of the room! Not very nice, at all! Sick? I should say she was sick! By the bucketful! This money, would it be cash? See, unless it was in cash, you'd have to pay me as Mrs Emma Vowles—not Phillips.'

Holmes repeated the name and wrote 'Emma Vowles' and 'not Phillips' in the little book.

'Five weeks' rent, you say?'

'Just that, except there being no notice given, of course. And the room not fit to use.'

'Shall we say six weeks? I see no reason why we should not advance cash today. I wonder if there are any other outstanding liabilities that her friends might know of. Did she have a particular friend who might have helped her out?'

Emma Vowles, *soi-disante* Phillips, pulled a face. Then she shook her head.

'One, p'raps, lodging in this house as well. You can see her now, if you like. She moved into the attic rooms herself, after Mattie Clover was gone.'

'If you would not mind,' Holmes said courteously.

We followed the woman up the stairs with their smell of damp plaster and rotting carpet until we came to a door in the low-ceilinged attic level. Mrs Vowles tapped on it and went in without waiting. We heard her say,

'There's two missionary gentlemen, anxious to see all poor Mattie's debts are settled. I suppose you'd know.'

We heard a murmur from the occupant of the room. Mrs Vowles stepped back, opened the door wider for us, let us pass and said, 'Here you are then . . .'

'Lucy Rose,' said the girl's voice. She stood up from the trestle bed on which she had been sitting, a faded Pre-Raphaelite dove, the face plain and scrubbed, the hair in two braids, a look of weariness in her eyes, as if our presence made no difference to her one way or the other. The last fading of a bruise might just be seen on her right cheekbone. The room itself was all too familiar, its frayed carpet, plain washstand with jug and basin, a single chest of drawers, low windows cob-webbed and stuck fast by old paint.

The Reverend William Holmes took her hand gently.

'Lucy Rose? You were a friend to poor Mattie Clover.'

'We were friends,' she said guardedly, drawing her hand away, 'not close, though.'

'Well,' said Holmes, smiling at her, 'I hope we are all her friends. There is a little money put by which her family would like her friends to have.'

He counted three sovereigns from one hand to another and then gave them to her. She took them without a word of thanks or comment. Holmes looked about him.

'How long have you lived like this?'

'Three years,' she said with a shrug. 'I'm a distressed milliner, ain't I?'

'I see. And how old are you, my child,' inquired Holmes the Missioner.

'Twenty.'

He nodded, as if he believed her. Then he said, as though struck by a pleasant thought, 'And when is your birthday?'

'My birthday? What do you want to know that for?'

He smiled again, as if at her foolishness, 'You were kind and good to Mattie. I believe her mother would like to be kind to you. Next year, Lucy, will be your twenty-first birthday, a very special one. How nice it would be for her mother if she could send you something to commemorate it. If it does not offend you, that is.'

'It doesn't offend me,' she said, staring up at him, 'I just can't see why anyone'd want to do that.'

'Because they are good and kind Christian folk,' said Holmes.

She shrugged.

'Well, fourth day of April it is, if that matters.'

'Tell me,' Holmes said with an air of quiet concern, 'what happened on the night that she died? Were you with her?'

I feared the girl might refuse to discuss this but Holmes had pitched the question with great skill, suggesting that he only wanted the information to comfort someone else.

'She came back with a man,' said Lucy Rose indifferently. 'She was always bringing men back. I saw him in the hall, so did Mrs Phillips and her sister, but they turn a blind eye to that sort of thing in a place like this.'

'What did the man look like?'

'Well, he had his back to the light but he was quite stout-built with a brown moustache. A bit red-faced like a navvy. He was wearing a top-coat and bowler hat. They went up to the room, then she comes down and goes out for some beer. I went to bed, but I heard them go down about an hour later. She opened the door, he said "Good night," and she said "Good night, dear." That's all.'

'I see,' said Holmes, in the tone of a disappointed man returning a bribe to his pocket.

'Until about three in the morning,' she said hastily, 'then I woke up and heard screaming. She'd wedged herself over the end of the bed, pressing her stomach down to get ease from the pain. First thing she said was someone must have poisoned her with some pills she took, not wanting to get in the family way.'

'Do you think she was poisoned?'

502

'Course not!' said Lucy Rose scornfully. 'Unless she poisoned herself with drink. The doctors didn't think she'd been poisoned, did they? Old Mattie used to booze enough for a couple of draymen together. How she screamed, though. Then she'd go into fits and twitch all over. Her eyes rolled about something terrible. It's only drink does that. The DTs.'

'Did she say anything else?'

'She said she was going to die. Well, she was right about that, wasn't she?'

The notion that this hard-faced little dollymop would be a friend to anyone was quite beyond me. However, Holmes played his part and slipped her two more sovereigns. She grinned at him.

'You?' she said scornfully. 'You're not a missioner! No more than I am.'

'I assure you . . .'

'You paid twice! Missioners is too bloody mean to pay twice! What you are . . .'

It pained me to see Holmes worsted by this little slattern.

'What you are,' said Lucy Rose triumphantly, 'is a newspaper man! A reporter! Ain't that it? They're the ones that pays for what they want to hear. Five sovs? Well, I hope it was worth it to you! What d'you want to know about it for?'

'Dear me, young woman,' said Holmes amiably, 'you have the makings of a true detective.'

'You bet,' said Lucy Rose.

As we returned in the cab to Baker Street, I remarked that we should get nowhere in the face of such impertinence.

Holmes spoke quietly, looking out at the evening crowds who pressed homewards across Regent Circus.

'Then how fortunate it was to have a medical man present. We might otherwise have been in danger of confusing an impertinent little minx with a vexed and frightened child. Might we not?'

I looked at him sharply. However, I got nothing more, except his comment that we must give a little help to our friend Lestrade, who seemed to have lost heart over the case.

X

My American visitor, Dr Neill, need not have worried. He was only one among several medical men to get a copy of the mad blackmailer's letter, which he had shown me. By the next morning's post I heard from Dr William Broadbent of Seymour Street, once a fellow student at Barts and now a successful oculist. Broadbent had received a similar communication. In this case, Mr Malone and his operatives had demanded £2,500 for suppressing their 'evidence'. It was quite mad, of course. How should an oculist be in a position to administer strychnine? It was plain to me that whoever was behind this campaign of blackmail had very little knowledge of medicine.

Holmes seemed weary of the letters and more intent on pursuing the case of Matilda Clover. As for Dr Neill and Dr Broadbent, he referred to them with a certain heavy facetiousness as 'your clients' or 'these clients of yours', as if he was washing his hands of any responsibility for their complaints.

After three days, he was prepared to share his recent discoveries with Inspector Lestrade. But when we saw the Scotland Yard man again, it was under circumstances of such horror as I shall never forget. Two nights after our visit to the Lambeth Road, I felt that I had scarcely fallen asleep when I was awakened by a tugging at my shoulder. It was Holmes, standing over me fully dressed. I opened my eyes rather painfully against the light of the candle in his hand. The flame shone upon his eager stooping face and his expression left me in no doubt that something was badly wrong.

'Get up, Watson! Lestrade is in the sitting-room and we must go with him at once. Bring your medical bag, you will certainly have need of it.'

I felt no sense of adventure, only a cold and certain dread. His words must mean Mr Bayne and his friends had taken another life. In my career, I had grown used to nocturnal alarms but had never answered one with such sick foreboding at what awaited me. I pulled on my clothes, picked up my bag, and went into the sitting-room. Holmes was already buttoned into his ulster with a cravat about his throat, fastening his travelling-cap with its ear-flaps, for this was a bitter night.

'Stamford Street,' Lestrade said, as soon as I entered the sitting-room, 'I doubt if much can be done for them but . . .'

'Them?' I was aghast that there should be more than one.

'Yes, sir. There are two young persons this time, doctor, both of the unfortunate class. We shall have to make haste before they are too far gone to tell us what has happened.'

The streets were clear and Lestrade's cab went full pelt through the lamplit city to the Strand, Waterloo Bridge, and Lambeth. Stamford Street ran behind riverside wharves and warehouses, from Waterloo Road to Blackfriars. Its broken and discoloured slum-terraces, whose doors opened on the pavement, were another Duke Street.

The narrow road ran for a considerable distance. Long before we came to the house with '118' painted roughly in white on its door, we saw a little crowd outside. A uniformed constable in a tall helmet and carrying a bulls-eye lantern stood guard at the door. There was a four-wheeler waiting, ready to set off for the hospital, but with no sign of a doctor or an assistant. Small wonder that Lestrade had wanted my company, I thought. From the sounds of disorder that reached us you might have thought a mad party was going on in the house. A man was shouting and women were screaming but the shrillness was of pain rather than merriment.

As we got down from the hansom and went into the narrow house, two policemen with their helmets off appeared to be struggling with a pair of disorderly harpies, as if to get them into the waiting four-wheeler. But the sight of the pair suggested figures in some landscape of the damned, their faces plastered with the sweat of agony and their hair in disarray. Alice Marsh, as I later knew her to be, was covered by her night-clothes, kneeling on all fours over a chair in the hallway, clinging tighter at every attempt to move her. In the front room, Emma Shrivell lay prone on the sofa, where the second uniformed constable had just administered an emetic

of warm water and salt, which now caused her to vomit spasmodically. Like her companion, she was wearing her night-clothes, as if
she had woken suddenly from sleep.

Though it was hard to question the two policemen in the shrillness and shouting, I heard the first man, Cumley, say to Lestrade
that he and Eversfield had been trying for the past ten minutes to
get the two girls to the four-wheeler for St Thomas's Hospital. They
had brought them with difficulty to the foot of the stairs, where
both victims had resisted being moved further as they clutched the
chair and sofa to themselves with the strength of pure terror.

If ever there was a vision of hell, it was in that house on that
night. Alice Marsh seemed not even to understand what was said
to her. Emma Shrivell, perhaps as a result of the emetic, was able
to answer a little. For several minutes, until the rising cramp of
another spasm robbed her of normal speech, she muttered her
answers to my questions. She had eaten tinned salmon and drunk
bottled beer with Alice Marsh and a man they had brought back to
the house. He had offered them each a long slim capsule, promising
that these would heighten their pleasure in the perversities that
he proposed for the three of them. Later he had gone away. Soon
afterwards the first plucking of their final agony began.

Alice Marsh was too far gone to identify her assailant. Emma
Shrivell could only describe a man with dark hair and a moustache.
Eversfield had first thought that the girls might be suffering pto-
maine poisoning as a result of contamination in the tinned salmon.
Believe that who may!

How little prepared is a retired army doctor to confront such
a crisis in civil life! To stand in that cramped house, deafened by
the noise and sickened by such sights, was a horror in itself for any
humane person. Far worse, was the situation of a medical man. If
this were another strychnine poisoning, nothing would save them.
I could have given them morphia, but that would ease their agony
very little and would prolong it for several hours. Indeed, as it later
appeared, whoever had chosen these victims had once again mixed
morphia with the poison. Strychnine alone would have killed

them by now. To wish the two poor creatures out of this world so speedily will seem inhuman only to those who did not see their terrified grimaces or hear the sounds that filled the slum terrace on a winter's night. Was the devil who had devised this drama now haunting the shadows of the alleys and streets outside, listening with a mad delight to the result?

There was nothing more I could do. I insisted to Lestrade that the two young women must by any means be got to hospital where their final hours might be made more comfortable. By taking them to the four-wheeler one at a time, the two constables and I managed to get first Alice Marsh and then Emma Shrivell into the cab. They struggled and shuddered, shouting uncomprehended protests in our ears.

There is little more to add. I went with them as the four-wheeler rattled into the Waterloo Road, turned into Westminster Bridge Road and drew up at the hospital. Just as we came in sight of the river, Alice Marsh uttered a rising cry and fell into a fit. The next moment, the breath came from her in a long groan that emptied her lungs as she fell back against the cushions and died. Emma Shrivell was carried into the hospital entrance on a stretcher. I later heard that she had lived until eight o'clock that morning without adding another word to the evidence she had already given.

In all the investigations which Sherlock Holmes and I had undertaken, I confess I had never felt so badly shaken as by this double homicide. There had been murders enough but none as malicious and brutal as these two. Many criminals of our acquaintance had killed out of passion or for gain, sometimes for jealousy or avarice, but never with such hideous and cruel triumph.

Holmes, when he looked back on the events of this case, was more intrigued than repelled by the criminal mind behind them. He would quote the Renaissance tyrants or 'Philippe the Poisoner' as the Regent of France for Louis XV had been called. These men had poisoned their victims to clear the way to the seats of power. The Comte de Sade's depravities of this sort at Marseille had been mere aphrodisiac experiments. Other young sparks of the *ancien régime* had been content to persuade the Marquise Gacé that she had drunk an incurable poison which they had concealed in her glass. For several hours, they relished her terrors and despair until she realized that it was a mere trick. This time, however, we confronted what Holmes laconically described as 'a great original'.

'I regret, Watson, that the demands on my time do not permit of a little monograph upon the subject of "The Poisoner as Artist". I think, however, I shall write a few lines to the good Professor Krafft-Ebing. I must put him on the trail of that rare mental type whose pleasure lies in obtaining by poison a complete possession of the victim's body and all its functions, controlling every nuance of thought and feeling. It is a significant lacuna in the great professor's otherwise admirable systematization of psychopathology.'

We were at breakfast several days after the deaths of the two poor girls when Holmes delivered himself of this deplorable observation. I drew open my copy of *The Times* newspaper as a refuge from such conversation and merely said, 'It is quite enough, Holmes, that we must deal with such a scoundrel. You had far better leave it there.'

He sighed, as if I should be his despair.

'I have thought for some time, Watson, that you have no appreciation of this case. Without it, you will never arrive at the truth. Among poisoners, I am bound to say that even the great Dr William Palmer of Rugeley or the curious Catherine Wilson, whose last moments I witnessed at a time when executions were still a public spectacle, came woefully short of our present antagonist.'

To me, this was utterly heartless. I was about to say, in no uncertain terms, that I had done my best for two dying girls, while Holmes had airily discussed the finer points of the crime with Lestrade. To talk of the degenerate beast who had killed them—as an artist!—was beyond endurance. Perhaps it was well that we were interrupted by Mrs Hudson with Lestrade at her heels. Before our housekeeper could say a word, the inspector was in the room and holding a sheet of paper towards us.

'As you'll both be witnesses at the inquest on the two young women, Mr Holmes, you'd both of you best see this first. It came for

Mr Wyatt, the Southwark coroner, through the post first thing this morning. It's our man, or one of them, from first to last. Perhaps this time he's gone too far. Perhaps there might be something in it that will give him away.'

I hardly knew whether to feel hope or despair at the sight of it. Holmes read the letter. He looked up, raised his eyebrows, and handed it to me, saying, 'If there is a word of truth in this, Watson, perhaps one of those clients of yours might prove a useful source of information.'

> 'Dear Sir,
>
>   I beg to inform you that one of my operators has positive proof that a certain medical student of St Thomas's Hospital is responsible for the deaths of Alice Marsh and Emma Shrivell, he having poisoned those girls with strychnine. The proof you can have on paying my bill for services to George Clarke, detective, 20 Cockspur Street, Charing Cross, to whom I will give the proof on his paying my bill.
>
>   Yours respectfully,
>   Wm. H. Murray

I noticed that 'Murray' had been copied from the Metropole Hotel circular.

'Tell me, Lestrade,' said Holmes thoughtfully, as I handed the letter back, 'you and I remember something of George Clarke, do we not?'

Lestrade's face tightened.

'What I remember is Clarke left the Metropolitan Police under a cloud, fifteen years ago, as a senior man. Went to be landlord of a public house in Westminster. Still, we can be sure he has nothing to do with this Murray.'

'May we? And why is that, pray?'

There was no mistaking the satisfaction on the inspector's face.

'George Clarke, Mr Holmes, was gathered to his fathers three months ago. Dead. Gone to his long, last home, wherever that may be.'

Unworthy though it might be, I confess I was glad to hear the intellectual fog of Professor Ebing and poisoners as artists dispelled by the cold radiance of fact.

XI

Even before the Stamford Street inquest began, the death certificate of Matilda Clover had been examined and her place of burial was established as Lambeth Municipal Cemetery. Though it took its title from Lambeth, the burial ground was out at Tooting, under the new public health measures introduced by the Burial Act of 1852. On a raw morning, as the frost was dissolving into dew, Miss Clover's mortal remains were to be exhumed upon the orders of the Home Secretary. Holmes and I travelled by the South-West Railway from Victoria to Tooting, where Lestrade would be waiting to take us the short distance to the cemetery gates.

It had scarcely been necessary for the inspector to insist to the recipients of the blackmail threats that no public reference should be made to the anonymous letters. Lady Russell or Mr Frederick Smith, MP were the last people to wish their names tarnished even by innocent association with such crimes. The notes to the coroner might be shown to the jurors, if that seemed necessary, but no reference was to be made to them in the hearing of the press.

As our train pulled out of Victoria station, Holmes, with his sharp eager face framed in his ear-flapped travelling-cap, opened the *Morning Post* and finished his reading of the day's agony column. The early hour of our start had deprived him of a leisurely survey of the day's press. At length he folded the paper, thrust it under his seat, and offered me his cigar-case as we passed through the damp leafless suburbs.

'It is reassuring, Watson, is it not, to find so much continuity in this case?'

I wondered what he had in mind.

'Continuity? I have seldom known a case more plagued by chaos, rumour, and inconsistency.'

He thought for a moment and said at length, 'Take the letters, however. The composition of those sent to the coroner is plainly the work of the same author as the letter to Dr Broadbent. Yet the handwriting is not the same. However, the copperplate of the latest epistle is in an identical hand to that written to Mr Frederick Smith. The threads of this correspondence cross and cross again, do they not? It shows what I would call continuity.'

'It only goes to prove,' I replied abruptly, 'that these blackmailers are known to one another. They must be.'

'Must they? Are they all known to one another—or is there one master to whom each individual servant is separately known?'

'They share the same knowledge and the same style, as well as an identical method of extorting money.'

'You are entirely right about that,' he said at once, 'I could not have put it better.'

The answer seemed too plain to be held back.

'We shall never progress, Holmes, until we accept that the letters are quite distinct from the murders. A maniac is poisoning these poor girls. A gang of blackmailers is exploiting the crimes. They know their victims did not kill any of the young women. Yet they know by experience that innocent people may be weak or foolish enough to pay for their good names. Most will not pay but what does that matter? One or two successes will make the attempts worthwhile.'

'Your friend and client Dr Broadbent will pay, perhaps, or Dr Neill?'

I had expected this.

'Both know they are innocent. Yet if, for example, it is rumoured that Broadbent went to court over such matters, the world would say there is no smoke without fire. In his position, reputation is everything. A scandal might destroy him, innocent or guilty. Being a figure of honour and principle that will not deter him. The extortionists picked the wrong man, of course, but they may be luckier next time.'

Holmes lay back in his corner seat.

'And the fact that they accused Lord Russell of murdering Miss Clover almost a fortnight before she died? That, I suppose, was just a happy chance for them.'

'No,' I had a good part of the answer now, 'she was known to be dying of drink, but not dead. But if a man will pay to have his good name preserved, it scarcely mattered if she was alive or dead. How could he tell? He would implicate himself as much by asking questions. Indeed, why should Miss Clover not have been part of the conspiracy? Prostitution is a trade that runs easily to blackmail!'

Holmes drew the pipe from his mouth.

'And when they told Mr Smith that Ellen Donworth had been poisoned, while the world still thought she died of drink, was that a happy chance for them?'

'Anyone who was outside the York Hotel heard her say that she had been given gin with some white stuff in it by Fred. A rumour of poison would run round a neighbourhood like that. Blackmailers are not dealers in fact. They intimidate those who will pay and who ask few questions. They are not murderers.'

'Well,' he said thoughtfully, 'if they are not, someone else certainly is.'

'I believe,' I said boldly, 'that I may have your blackmailers before long. At least their ringleader. Dr Neill may be a rich American but he is naturally known to only a handful of people in England. He believes the threat comes from someone close to him. It must be so. Let that be our way forward.'

'My dear fellow!' he said in gentle admiration. 'You will have this case concluded before we know where we are.'

But now I could face him on his own ground.

'The last letter, addressed to the inquest on Marsh and Shrivell, says that the two girls in Stamford Street were murdered by a medical student.'

'Very well.'

'You agree that it was written by our blackmailers?'

'As it would seem.'

'In the hope of it being read out at the inquest so that rumours may begin?'

'Quite possibly.'

'Then I will make a wager with you. After the inquest, there will be another letter. It will be sent either to a wealthy medical student, or perhaps to his family. It will accuse him of the murders, for which the writer has proof, and demand a large sum of money for his safety. Will you believe me then?'

He stared at me as if something had distressed him.

'My dear friend, I should never disbelieve you. To disagree is another matter. However, after your success with your clients, I daresay you are closer to the truth of this terrible business than anyone could imagine.'

'They are not my clients,' I said shortly. 'They are our clients.'

He laughed and shook his head.

'Oh no, Watson! I have never met them! How can they be my clients? It is only right that you should have clients of your own. You have long experience and ability. You deserve them, if I may say so, as much as they deserve you.'

A few minutes later, with a grinding of steel on iron, the train rounded a curve and drew into Tooting station. Lestrade, in formal black, was waiting with a cab. The cemetery, behind its plain railings adjoined a main road. Within the gates were the private family plots with crosses and obelisks, weeping Niobes and marble angels. Further off lay the burial ground of the poor, the common graves whose occupants were dug up after twelve years and their scant relics burnt on cemetery fires at night. Green canvas screens had been erected on the frosted grass round one of these graves. The diggers were already at work. As we entered the gates, a crowd of happy urchins ran beside the cab and saluted us with cries of 'Body-snatchers! Burke-and-Hare! Burke-and-Hare! . . .'

'Encouraging, is it not,' Holmes remarked, 'to see how ignorance and illiteracy may be redeemed by a knowledge of the criminal heroes of our past?'

Such was the jumbled burying of the poor that a number of coffins were raised and opened before that of Matilda Clover was found. Holmes and Lestrade watched the gravediggers from a distance as the damp morning turned to a cold drizzle and the piles of yellow London clay grew taller at each new excavation. The railings along the edge of the cemetery were now lined by idle children and their elders. Lestrade glowered at them, then turned to Holmes.

'And what is to be done about Louisa Harvey, Mr Holmes? Whom no one could find, dead or alive?'

'I really do not know,' said Holmes indifferently. He gestured across the expanse of the cemetery. 'I daresay I could find her, if I was obliged to.'

There was no mistaking that this gesture irritated Lestrade.

'One thing we are quite sure of, Mr Sherlock Holmes, is that she is not here. That has been investigated through and through, since Miss Clover was run to earth.'

'Oh, she is here,' said Holmes in a far-away wistful tone, 'I have no doubt of that. She is certainly here.'

'In this cemetery?'

'Where else?'

'I don't see how you can say that, Mr Holmes!'

'I can, Lestrade. I begin to think, you see, that Louisa Harvey and I are quite old friends.'

'Old enough for her to be in the cemetery!' Lestrade said angrily. He stamped off to take a pull at his flask against the raw cold and to shout at a pair of his subordinates who were idling by the canvas screens.

I tried to recall the heroines of our past adventures and could not match a single one to the mysterious Louisa Harvey. I endeavoured to press Holmes about his assertions but it was useless. He watched patiently in the growing mist until a call and a signal from the diggers marked the discovery of Miss Clover.

The body was removed to a shed near the chapel, which became an improvised mortuary. Here Dr Stevenson, on behalf of the Home Office, waited for it with an enthusiasm bordering on the unseemly. The coffin was opened and the well-preserved body of a prematurely-aged young woman was revealed to us.

Until the afternoon, Stevenson was busy in the shed with scalpel, saw, and specimen jars. For all my medical experience, I can never quite accommodate myself to the post-mortem sounds, the cutting of flesh that imitates a rending of tent canvas and the sawing of skull or bones that is crude carpentry. When it was over, Dr Stevenson had filled an array of jars labelled 'Brain of Matilda Clover', 'Intestines of Matilda Clover' and 'Stomach of Matilda Clover'.

Sherlock Holmes, as might be expected, witnessed all this with the curiosity and relish of a true investigator. At the end, he looked at Stevenson who caught his glance, shook his head, and said, 'No doubt of it.'

He took a glass slide, touched a rod to it, and held it out to Holmes.

'Taste that!'

Holmes extended a forefinger. I could not watch, but turned my head away. When I looked again, the lips of Sherlock Holmes were moving like a man savouring the rarest nectar. He stopped and stared at Dr Stevenson.

'Strychnine!' he said, like a happy child.

XII

For all the good it did, we might as well not have found Matilda Clover. So far as I could see, the discovery of strychnine offered not a single clue as to the identity of her murderer. Lucy Rose's description of the thickset visitor with a moustache and a bowler hat might fit a hundred thousand men in London.

Holmes lapsed into another of those irritating moods that enveloped him during certain investigations. He took to his violin and the Beethoven concerto again. He smoked, massively. He attempted to goad me repeatedly by referring to the Lambeth murders facetiously as 'This investigation of yours . . .' or 'This case, which you have so nearly brought to a successful conclusion . . .' and to our visitors as 'These clients of yours . . .' He had surely washed his hands of the whole business. Such work as he did was at his chemical table, where he continued his experiments into base coinage. His attempts at electro-plating gave our sitting-room the sour and acid smell of a battery-charger.

'Do you,' I had asked abruptly next evening, 'still maintain that Louisa Harvey is in Lambeth Cemetery?'

'No,' he said quietly, not looking up from his weighing of tiny metal.

'So, yesterday . . .'

'*Varium et mutabile semper femina*, Watson. The adorable change and variety of womankind.'

'You mean she has dug herself out and walked off?'

'Something of the sort,' he said, touching the scales gently with his little finger.

There was no point in discussing the matter further. I became silent and more morose. I could not conceal my chagrin when we received a report next morning that twice the lethal dose of strychnine had been found in Matilda Clover's body. I still wanted to hold to my belief that we faced two distinct sets of criminals. Yet how could the blackmailers know a fortnight in advance that Matilda Clover would die of strychnine poisoning, unless they murdered her?

The alternative, which Sherlock Holmes apparently embraced, seemed to me equally absurd. We must believe that a gang of men and women, the authors of the various blackmail notes, had perpetrated these four murders and others beside. According to their threats, there was at least one other body, though Louisa Harvey was not to be found in the register of deaths at Somerset House under any spelling of her name. Under what sobriquet, then, had she been buried in Lambeth cemetery?

For three days this state of affairs persisted. Then, on the third evening, we heard the measured tread of Lestrade's boots upon the stairs and the familiar bulldog figure in the pea-jacket and cravat appeared in our doorway.

'Lestrade!' said Holmes, in gentle admiration. 'Do come in and take a chair, my dear fellow. We have missed your visits of late, have we not, Watson? I daresay that the matter of Matilda Clover and Louisa Harvey is keeping you busy just now.'

The inspector sat down scowling and ignored the offer of the cigar case.

'I don't come to talk about those persons, Mr Holmes. We have another letter and I think we may have our blackmailer.'

'Dear me,' said Holmes softly, 'you have quite stolen a march upon us all this time. Pray, do explain.'

'Read this!' Lestrade said sharply. Each in turn we read the curious letter, addressed to Dr Joseph Harper of Barnstaple.

> *Dear Sir,*
>
> *I am writing to inform you that one of my operators has indisputable evidence that your son, W. J. Harper, a medical student at St Thomas's Hospital, poisoned two girls named Alice Marsh and Emma Shrivell on the 12th inst., and that I am willing to give you the said evidence (so that you can suppress it) for the sum of £1,500 sterling, or sell it to the police for the same amount . . .*

Even before I read the rest I knew that there would be the threat to 'ruin you and your family forever', and a command in this case to answer the letter through the columns of the *Daily Chronicle*, with the message 'W. H. M.—*Will pay you for your services.—Dr H.*' The conclusion of the letter revealed a familiar name, the blackmailer of Dr Neill and the Metropole Hotel.

> *If you do not answer at once, I am going to give the evidence to the Coroner.*
> *Yours respectfully,*
> *W.H. Murray*

Holmes offered the cigar case again. This time, the inspector helped himself to a corona.

'You say you have your blackmailer, Lestrade? Under lock and key?'

The colour rose a little in our visitor's cheek.

'Not as such, Mr Holmes. I believe we know who he is, though. An arrest at this moment might be imprudent.'

'Ah,' said Holmes, as if this explained it all, 'and who might it be?'

Lestrade looked like a man on the verge of some grand pronouncement.

'The son of the man to whom this letter is addressed, gentlemen. Mr Walter Harper, the medical student.'

Holmes affected simple bewilderment.

'Then young Walter Harper accuses himself of the murder of these two girls?'

'Only to his father, Mr Holmes. We can't see he is the murderer. He may be or he may be not. However, we believe he knew both girls and that he got one of them into trouble, or nearly so, while she was at Mutton's down in Brighton.'

'But why accuse himself?'

'Because he believed that his father, knowing something of the rumours about his son, would never take this letter to the police. He would pay, rather than see his son disgraced by scandal and his career ended before it had begun. Our information is that young Harper never wanted to be a medical student but was compelled by his father's wishes. If the young rogue is half what we think, his allowance was spent long ago. He is in debt to the money-lenders, and he must have seen one way to clear himself. By blackmailing the only person that would never give him away, having first tried to blackmail a good many others.'

'And the murders?' asked Holmes hopefully.

'As to that, Mr Holmes, how was it the blackmailer and his gang knew so soon that Ellen Donworth had been poisoned? How did they know Matilda Clover would be poisoned before it happened? Take all that together with the accusations in this letter and Mr Walter Harper may have to face something stronger than blackmail before he's finished.'

When the time came for the inspector to leave, Holmes stood up and shook his hand.

'Well, my dear Lestrade, I congratulate you. You have proved yourself the best man in this case and the best man has won. I can only apologize if my own humble efforts, such as they have been, have in any way interfered with your investigations.'

Lestrade glowed a little with satisfaction.

'Very noble of you to take it like that, Mr Holmes. Very generous, I'm sure.'

'One thing, if I may ask. How tall is Mr Harper?'

Lestrade stared at him.

'Tall?'

'High, if you prefer.'

'What has that . . .'

'Believe me it has.'

'Very well, then. About five feet and nine inches, I should guess.'

'Build?'

'He played scrum-half for the hospital rugby, I'm told.'

'Clean shaven? How barbered?'

'Medium brown hair. Short military moustache.'

'Does he wear a bowler hat?'

'He was indoors!' Lestrade said impatiently. 'What might all this amount to?'

'A portrait of your murderer,' Holmes said amiably. 'Mere idle curiosity on my part.'

Idle curiosity or not, I could not help feeling that the inspector was a good deal more uneasy when he left us than when he had arrived.

As soon as the door was closed, I said to Holmes *sotto voce*, 'Did you not see the address of young Harper's lodgings in the letter?'

'Of course I saw it! It is the house where your client Dr Neill lodges on his visits to London.'

'No wonder that Neill thought the blackmailer was someone close to him.'

'No wonder at all,' he said.

'And was not the scrum-half with the brown hair and moustache the man that Mrs Phillips saw at the door with Matilda Clover the night she died?'

'To be sure.'

He leant forward and stirred the dying fire with the poker.

'Then Lestrade has got his man!' I exclaimed.

He looked up at me.

'I never doubted that, my dear fellow. He has got his man. Have we got ours?'

He was back to his old mood again. I gave him a few minutes of brooding over the embers, then asked casually, 'I suppose, Holmes, that you may find it convenient in the next day or two to pay me the money you owe.'

He looked startled.

'Money? What money?'

'The wager,' I said quietly. 'On our way to Lambeth Cemetery the other day, I wagered you that after the letter to the coroner, accusing an unnamed medical student of the Stamford Street murders, the next letter would be an attempt to blackmail a wealthy student or his family. So it has proved to be.'

'By Jove!' he said softly. 'So you did—and so it has. However, just help me with one thing first, there's a good fellow.'

'What sort of thing?'

'With your assistance, Watson, I should like to see the inside of Walter Harper's rooms. I do not much mind whether he is acquitted or hanged but I think it desirable that one or other of these events should take place before much longer. Then we will settle the wager.'

XIII

Two days later, poison in Lambeth threatened the entire borough. Maisie, maid-of-all-work to Mrs Emily Sleaper, answered the knocker in Lambeth Palace Road. The door stood in a respectable set of houses. The day was Monday, the time 9.30 A.M. The wide length of the road lay empty, the trees down either pavement were bare in the approach of spring. On Mrs Sleaper's doorstep stood a stout man of medium height in a bowler hat and moustache, a watch-chain looped ponderously across the waistcoat of his well-worn suit.

'Jeavons,' he said with the least tilt of the bowler, 'Area Inspector, South London Gas Company. Mrs Sleaper home?'

'No, sir,' said Maisie, blushing a little under her white mob-cap.

'Who might be in charge, then?'

In deference to his air of authority, Maisie almost performed a half-curtsey.

'There's only me, sir.'

He glanced at her and his mouth tightened.

'Any smell of gas in the house?'

'No, sir. Don't think so, sir.'

'Don't think so, sir? Meaning what, precisely?'

'Meaning I haven't been through every room yet,' she said petulantly, 'and Mrs Sleaper's gentlemen are all gone out this time of day, so I can't ask them.'

'Any naked lights or flame?'

'Kitchen fire, I suppose.'

'Put it out immediately.'

'I can't do that! She'd skin me!'

His brows tightened.

'Young woman, you have heard of the Lambeth poisoner, I daresay.'

'Oh, yes.' There was a slight but delicious shiver. 'I heard of him, all right.'

'What you haven't heard of is his letter to the gas company yesterday, promising to poison all occupants of houses in this area with household gas, by over-pressurizing the main. In other words, even with taps turned off, the gas leaks at loose pipe-joints, too soft for you to hear. Day or night. You don't smell it and you get drowsy. You fall deeper into your last long sleep. All done in ten minutes.'

'Oh, God!'

'Act sensible,' Inspector Jeavons advised, 'Mr Crabbe, my mechanic, will be here any minute, working his way down the road. Your joints need tightening, miss, that's all. If you smell anything peculiar meantime, come straight out.'

He closed the door, leaving the terrified maid to douse the kitchen fire. In the stillness of the road, a baker's barrow passed, pulled by the roundsman between its shafts. A milk-cart stopped. The man called 'Milk down below!' and whipped up his horse. Then the front door of Mrs Sleaper's house flew open and Maisie almost tumbled down the steps.

'Gas! Gas! Mr Jeavons! There's gas in the house!'

His self-assurance calmed her a little, as he shouted to his mechanic.

'Mr Crabbe, attend to these joints next, if you please.'

Mr Crabbe resembled a turtle more closely than his marine namesake. A large man with fine chest and paunch, bandy-legged from weight, rheumy eyes behind thick glasses, a hopelessly drooping black moustache, and a tattered cap. He had the stoop of one whose life since boyhood has been spent down manholes and in conduits. His tools hung in a greasy satchel over the shoulder of his overalls. His voice had the slight but chronic hoarseness of the inveterate whisky drinker.

'Have the goodness to show me, dear,' he said to Maisie, who scowled at his familiarity. 'Just point out the whereabouts of the pipes.'

She led the way to the front door, taking care to enter only a few feet.

'Don't strike a light, and you'll be all right,' he said roguishly, making to pull loose one of the ribbons behind her apron, as she twisted away from him. He undid his satchel and selected an adjustable wrench, humming to himself, 'I can't get away to marry you today . . . My wife won't let me.'

'Don't you smell it?' she insisted.

'I smell it, my sweetheart. Just wait here.'

A black rubber mask from his satchel covered his nose and mouth, making him a grotesque and frightening clown from Venetian carnival. He went round the ground floor rooms and she heard the grip of the wrench on the piping.

Now he was on the stairs, climbing lightly. Two rooms opened off each upper level, the tenant identified by a printed *carte de visite* slotted into a small brass holder on each door. These apartments were duplicated indefinitely in this neighbourhood of the great hospitals. Entering the first, after a respectful tap on the door, Mr Crabbe found it unoccupied. A well-worn carpet lay before a black-leaded grate, gas-mantels at either side. A mirror hung over the greater width of the mantelpiece. The furniture was spartan and black-varnished.

A wardrobe stood in the adjoining bedroom and two tiers of desk-drawers in the sitting-room. Mr Crabbe drew open the desk-drawers one by one. With a hoarse cough and a sniff he unmasked and rummaged. Then, whistling to himself, 'Here's the very note ... and this is what he wrote ...' he drew out a pad of ivory-cream writing paper. Holding it firmly, he tore off the top sheet and burst into full-throated chorus, 'There was I, waiting at the church ...' He stopped and listened. A black marble Parthenon clock on the mantel ticked away the silence. He sang a little more, as he checked the other rooms. The spanner was heard tightening joints, then he came cantering down the stairs.

'Safe enough now, miss,' he said cheerfully. The pinch that he aimed was rather half-hearted, giving her ample time to turn her back to the wall.

'You sure it's safe?'

'Tight as Noah's Ark. He can turn up the pressure as much as he likes. The joints in this house won't give, gas won't leak in here. Sound as a pound.'

But what if this man was the Lambeth murderer and had loosened the joints instead? She dodged him once more.

'You're not a gentleman!' she shouted after him angrily, 'I've a good mind ...'

Mr Crabbe swung rakishly down the road. His voice carried back to her.

'You be thankful, my girl, that you ain't a-singing "Too-ra-li-too-ra-li-too-ra-lay-ay!" with the 'eavenly choir!'

He turned into Lambeth Road and paused in the dark under a low bridge, its iron ringing at the thunder of Waterloo trains. With no one in sight, he opened his satchel and slipped his cap in. Unhitching the shoulder-bands of his overalls, he stepped out, folded them small and added them to the cap. Glasses and moustache followed. At the Waterloo cab rank, Mr Jeavons was waiting, his foot on the running-board to detain a hansom.

'Though I say it myself, Watson,' the Gas Man chuckled, 'that was one of the neatest and quite the jolliest of all my impersonations to date. You have the bag of peeled garlic and tar that I lodged within the kitchen door?'

I assured him I had. As for what he might have found in Walter Harper's rooms, he would only insist that I must wait and see what I would see on our arrival in Baker Street.

Holmes took the blank sheet of cream paper straight to his work-table. With infinite care, a delicate sprinkling of graphite revealed the indentations of a message written on the sheet above. Rather, it revealed some of them.

I am writing to inform . . . operators . . . indisputable evidence
. . . son, W. J. Harp . . . St Thomas's Hospital . . .

'The young devil!' I exclaimed. 'Then he *was* trying to extort money from his own father!'

Holmes stared at the paper and stroked his chin.

'So it would seem.'

'But he dared not use his own writing, which his father would recognize. So there are at least two of them in this. Surely this is our blackmail gang!'

He drew from his pocket an envelope, addressed to 'Dr Thomas Neill, 103 Lambeth Palace Road SE.' I stared at it.

'Holmes! You have searched my client's room! You have removed his papers!'

He leant back and laughed.

'I have emptied his waste-paper basket left outside his door, my dear fellow, as the maid would have done in any case. It is as well I did, for the writing on this is identical to the letter received by Frederick Smith. My life upon it, Watson!'

'That woman who wrote to Mr Smith also wrote a blackmail letter to Dr Neill? Why did Neill not mention it when he showed me the other?'

'With that very question in mind, I searched the drawers of his desk. The reason he did not mention this envelope to you is that the woman did not write him a blackmail letter. The letter which matches this envelope, and which I took the precaution to scribble down, is a love letter.'

At that point I lost the thread completely. In Holmes's scrawl I could make out that the letter began 'My dearest', referred to the provisions made for the lady in Dr Neill's will, and ended, 'Your loving Laura.' The sender's address was merely 'Chapel Street'. Perhaps the postmark on the envelope, if there was one, would reveal the rest. After this revelation, however, there could only be one answer to the Lambeth riddle.

'Walter Harper and Laura, whoever she may be, must be in this together,' I said, 'They are the blackmailers, perhaps with several others. The man blackmails Dr Neill, the woman seduces him into leaving everything to her in his will, and tries to blackmail Frederick Smith into the bargain! One way or another, they would strip Dr Neill as they mean to strip Dr Harper of Barnstable!'

'Well,' said Holmes thoughtfully, 'Dr Neill is your client.'

'Our client!'

'Your client, if you please. I have never set eyes upon him.'

'Then I must tell him everything.'

'You can scarcely do that without accusing me of housebreaking.'

'That is true. Then what are we to do?'

Holmes chose a pipe from the rack and made a great show of lighting it.

'To speak frankly,' he said at length, 'I should like another corpse.'

'I should have thought there had been enough corpses in this case!'

'I have in mind a special kind of corpse, however. One that will answer when I speak to it. What I need, my dear fellow, is a talking corpse. I believe I could find one, if I had to.'

I gave it up. Next morning, the papers carried stern condemnations of a prank by medical students who had terrified respectable householders into believing that the Lambeth poisoner was about to kill half the neighbourhood with household gas. 'Such humour in our physicians of the future,' wrote *The Times*, 'is highly to be deprecated.'

XIV

All too soon, I was to learn why Holmes insisted upon the distinction between those clients who were mine and those which were his, and why he had referred facetiously to the Lambeth mystery as 'this case of yours, which you stumbled upon one night in the Waterloo Road'. I woke on the second morning after our incognito excursion to read in the paper of the arrest of a suspect in Berkhamstead, on suspicion of extortion. Holmes himself had not yet risen. Indeed his place at the breakfast table remained undisturbed for a further half-hour. Nor was there any sign of him when the telegram arrived.

To wake Sherlock Holmes, when he was determined upon sleep, was next to a physical impossibility. Having been informed by Billy that an immediate acknowledgement of the wire was demanded, I tore open the blue envelope.

HOLMES WATSON BAKER STREET STOP. YOUR ENVELOPE AND
TRANSCRIPTION RECEIVED STOP. ESSENTIAL YOU ATTEND HERE

IMMEDIATELY TO SUBSTANTIATE EVIDENCE STOP. CONFIRM BY
RETURN STOP. LESTRADE SCOTLAND YARD.

I had not known that Holmes had already forwarded to Lestrade the purloined envelope and the scribbled copy of the letter
to Dr Neill. However, I now answered the message in two words.
PROCEEDING FORTHWITH.

Though this was less than accurate, it spurred Holmes into a more
rapid consumption of breakfast and a foregoing of the newspapers.
By eleven o'clock, our cab turned from the Embankment, where
the trees were just coming into bud, and through the gateway of
Scotland Yard. I confess that I looked forward with a certain vin-
dictiveness to confronting the blackmailer of my client.

Those who have passed along the Embankment by the headquarters of the Metropolitan Police will know something of that curious
structure, its towers and turrets of red brick banded with white, like
a storybook castle of legend. Lestrade's quarters, though plainly
furnished, had the size and spaciousness of a drawing-room, with
a bay window overlooking the river.

He greeted us a little more gruffly than usual, as he bade us take
our chairs before his desk.

'We are indebted to you, Mr Holmes, for the envelope and the
transcription. How you came by these is not a matter for my consideration at this moment.'

'The carelessness with which dustbins are emptied in certain
quarters of London leads to many such scraps of paper blowing
in the wind.' Holmes spoke with sufficient insouciance to indicate
that he did not care twopence for Lestrade's 'consideration' of his
methods.

The inspector favoured him with a glance.

'Very well, sir. Let us just say that it is thanks to your quickness
of thought and action that the woman, Miss Laura Sabbatini, is in
custody and that Mr Harper is watched by one of our officers.'

Holmes sighed and sat back in his chair with something of a
small-boy's sulkiness.

'I wish, Lestrade, that you had made better use of my poor offerings.'

Our host was mystified by this.

'Play fair, Holmes,' I said, 'Lestrade has compared and identified the hand on the envelope as being that of Mr Smith's blackmailer and the other paper as having come from Harper's own stationery. He has ensured that Harper cannot escape us. If Harper and Miss Sabbatini are not the entire gang, they are at least two of its leading members.'

'What is more,' said the inspector indignantly, 'I have complied with your request, Mr Holmes, that nothing concerning the letter or the envelope should be made public. I have done so against my better judgment.'

Holmes had been listening with eyes closed and fingertips pressed together.

'I should find it hard to conceive of a more certain way of making those items public than by detaining a suspect within hours of receiving them.'

Again I came to Lestrade's defence.

'Dash it all, Holmes, anything less than arrest or surveillance and the birds might have flown. The woman first and her friends in short order. It was the best move on Lestrade's part to bag one of them and keep another in his sights.'

He only seemed to sink further into gloom.

'The bird or birds, as you so felicitously term them, have either flown already or are even now testing their wings. My dear Lestrade, I daresay you will recall my second request—that I should be allowed to put certain questions to your suspect before she was invited to make a statement or was charged?'

'And that undertaking is now to be honoured, Mr Holmes.'

My friend nodded. When he looked up, his eyes were brighter but he scarcely appeared like a man who has lost a penny and found a shilling.

'Then, if you please, we will have the lady brought in so that I may speak to her.'

Lestrade stepped outside and I heard him giving orders to one of his officers. There was a pause of some minutes and presently he came back, following a demure young woman of warm complexion, raven hair, and slim figure. She was modestly but finely dressed in a pale grey walking-gown, a matching hat and a light veil which she now put up. Lestrade brought a chair for her and she sat down. Holmes looked at her for a moment, then said, 'Miss Sabbatini, my name is Sherlock Holmes. It is possible that you may have heard of me.'

'Oh, yes!' she said eagerly, as if his was the first friendly voice that had spoken to her since her ordeal began. 'Yes I have.'

'Very well. I am not employed by the police. In any case, you are under no obligation to answer my questions or theirs. However, if you are willing to tell me what I want to know, it is possible that I may be able to save you a good deal of trouble.'

'Yes,' she said again, though her hands gripped the arms of her chair until her knuckles whitened, 'by all means, Mr Holmes.'

'In that case, Mr Lestrade, may we have the letter written to Mr Frederick Smith MP and the envelope addressed to Dr Neill?'

He stood up and these were handed to him. He held the black-mail letter to Mr Smith before her.

'Did you write this letter, Miss Sabbatini?'

It took only a glance before she said eagerly, 'Yes. Oh, yes. I wrote that.'

'A letter blackmailing Mr Smith . . .'

'Yes, but I did not mean to . . .'

'We will leave that for a moment, if you please. Is this also your writing on the envelope addressed to Dr Neill at 103 Lambeth Palace Road?'

'Of course. It is the same. It is how I always write.'

'And you are, I believe, sole beneficiary under the will of Dr Neill?'

This startled her, for she did not see how Sherlock Holmes could know such a thing. Nor did Lestrade.

'You have evidently discovered a good deal about us, Mr Holmes. However, you are correct. I am the sole beneficiary under his will. Why should I not be? We are engaged to be married!'

It was now the turn of Sherlock Holmes to look surprised but he quickly composed himself. Such engagements, after all, are easily made and easily broken on the part of the lady.

'How long have you known Dr Neill?'

'A year or so. We met in America when I was there with my parents.'

I confess that this demure figure, answering his questions so frankly, was not at all how I had imagined the blackmailer of my client. However, the bomb that had been ticking quietly under us all was now about to be detonated.

'You admit that you wrote the letter to Mr Frederick Smith. Why?'

'Why should I not? I wrote it because Dr Neill was too busy.'

'Too busy? Busy with what?'

Now she turned away from Holmes and looked at Lestrade.

'It is possible that you know something of this, Mr Lestrade, being a policeman. Dr Neill has a great reputation as a pathologist. He was retained some months ago on the advice of the Commissioner himself, Sir Melville MacNaghten, to advise the police about the poisonings in Lambeth.'

Lestrade looked as thunderstruck as any of us had been.

'Pray continue, Miss Sabbatini,' he said, now trying to look as if he had known about the Commissioner's recommendation all along.

'Dr Neill was extremely hard-pressed to discharge all these commitments, in addition to his work at the hospital. Documents came to him from the police and were then passed on by him to the coroner's office. It was essential that he should make copies of them for reference. There was a very great number. We were in Hertfordshire together, you understand, and they were to be posted to London as a matter of urgency. To help him, I copied out several in my own hand. The letter to Mr Smith was one of them.'

'You have told me what I suspected from the first, Miss Sabbatini,' said Holmes gently. 'We will leave it there for the moment, if you please. I shall confer with Inspector Lestrade upon your answers to my questions. However, I should be very surprised if your troubles are not at an end by this evening.'

Lestrade got up and escorted Miss Sabbatini to the door. As it closed, Holmes turned to me.

'Your client, Watson! By now Dr Neill is probably on his way back to America, where he will no doubt find safety!'

Lestrade stood with his back to the door.

'Safety from what, though, Mr Holmes?'

Holmes swung round on him.

'Blackmail! Blackmail at least. Very possibly murder, though we do not yet know that he resembles the suspect or that he could have been in the place where any murder was committed. Who ever heard of such a gang of blackmailers? Was it not obvious from the first that this was a single-handed criminal? What had he to do but persuade other men and women to copy documents for him? To do so on the pretext that he was a medical consultant to Scotland Yard is, I confess, a nicer stroke than I should have thought him capable of.'

'Not so fast,' Lestrade interrupted, 'Miss Sabbatini might do it for love. How could he depend on the others?'

Holmes looked at him in despair.

'Do you still not see it? Give me pen and paper, send me out into Lambeth, or Bermondsey, or the docks. There are communities from all over Europe and Asia who scarcely speak English, let alone write it. There are scribes who take down their letters for them but to whom English is almost or completely a foreign tongue. A man of moderate resource and intelligence could have any document copied for him by such a person, who would not understand more than a word or two of what it contained. I could bring you back confessions of my guilt in the Lambeth poisonings by this evening in a dozen different hands. Would you believe me then?'

Lestrade shifted uncomfortably in his chair. Holmes continued imperturbably.

'If I were Dr Neill and I wanted to incriminate a man for my offences, I should choose such a one as Walter Harper. Unless he is much maligned, that young gentleman has used his father's money to live high upon the hog, as they say. I should wait my chance, enter his room, and purloin his notepaper for a few hours. I would take it to one of my dupes who would indite a blackmail demand to the young man's father. I should hope that the current rumours of Walter Harper's involvement in the deaths of two young women would lead the police to search his rooms. There they would find the same undoubted evidence of his complicity in blackmail as I have done. You see? Who better placed than Dr Neill to accomplish this? He knew Harper well, could follow his movements, and had access to his rooms.'

'Very well, Mr Holmes. Then Dr Neill and he alone is our blackmail gang. Perhaps he is also our murderer.'

Holmes pulled a face.

'As to that, my friend, the evidence in your hands points rather away from Dr Watson's client than towards him. I daresay, however, that we may congratulate ourselves on the prospect of seeing him go to prison for the next fourteen years on charges of attempted extortion.'

Lestrade looked brighter than at any time since our arrival. But Holmes had not done with him.

'May I remind you, however, that such a prospect diminishes with every minute that you sit here? Should Dr Neill evade us, it would not look well in the annals of Scotland Yard, when 103 Lambeth Palace Road is scarcely twenty minutes' walk away.'

XV

The behaviour of Sherlock Holmes on that spring day continued to veer between the unpredictable and the erratic. Had I not known him so well, I might have detected a taste of sour grapes as he wished me well with my case, and washed his hands of it. If proof of this were needed, it was surely provided by his positive refusal to accompany Lestrade and myself with half a dozen uniformed officers, in our descent upon Lambeth Palace Road.

'My dear fellow,' he said humorously, 'you will manage it well enough between you. And if you cannot, then I am sure my presence would make no difference. I shall return to Baker Street, to Mrs Hudson's admirable tea and cakes.'

'Holmes! We must catch this fellow before it is too late.'

'So you must, Watson. For me, however, the call of tea and cakes was ever irresistible.'

With that, he waved down a cab on the Embankment and was driven away. Lestrade looked after him in blank astonishment. So it was that I alone followed the inspector with his search warrant into the solid suburban terrace, while the uniformed men stood at the front and back to prevent an escape. There was not the least difficulty in entering Dr Neill's rooms for such apartments within a house are seldom locked when men live *en famille*. Of the fugitive, there was no sign. His possessions appeared to be in place, though Mrs Sleaper could not lay hands upon a Gladstone bag that was usually in the wardrobe. She had thought nothing of it when her 'charming Dr Neill' had gone out that morning and she had heard him hail a cab for Charing Cross.

'Which can only mean the boat-train for France, I suppose' said Lestrade gloomily, drawing out his watch. 'I daresay he'd be there by now. They won't send him back neither, they never do. Sailing out of their ports, he could be anywhere tomorrow. And, of course, we can't stop their ships. Act of war.'

The search did little credit to Dr Neill, revealing as it did some disgusting photographs of young women, but neither did it produce evidence against him. There was a salesman's sample-case of medicines of the most ordinary kind. One drawer yielded several unfilled gelatine capsules, far more commonly used in America than in England for administering evil-tasting medicines. As for blackmail or murder, there was nothing.

'We'll go through it with a toothcomb,' Lestrade said wearily, 'carpets and boards up, furniture apart. Still, it looks to me as if we've lost him.'

As the search continued, I was apprehensive that the maid-of-all-work, Maisie, might recognize me as the gas company inspector of the other day. The one stroke of fortune in all this was that it proved to be her afternoon off, during which this good girl invariably walked with her 'young man' in Battersea Park.

An hour and a half had passed in a fruitless ransacking of Dr Neill's rooms. I was about to follow Holmes to Baker Street, when I heard a commotion in the street. I went to the sitting-room window and saw that a cab had drawn up. Two unspeakable ruffians, who looked as if they had never in their lives until now ridden in a hansom, got out and slouched off. Then through its open doorway, very slowly, emerged the frock-coated and silk-hatted figure of Dr Neill. Behind him came Sherlock Holmes, holding at his side what looked very like my service revolver. So much for tea and cakes!

Dr Neill saw before him two uniformed police officers. With an inspiration born of terror, he turned and took Holmes by surprise, knocking him flat and diving back into the cab. From my vantage point, I saw Neill burst out of the far door and race across the road towards an alley between the opposite houses.

'He won't get far down there,' Lestrade said confidently. A few minutes later, a dishevelled figure reappeared between two uniformed men, the handcuffs on his wrists.

I truly thought 'this case of mine' was at an end. How mistaken I proved to be!

For the moment, Sherlock Holmes was as smug as the cat who has had the cream.

'I quite anticipated, Watson, the capital error of which you and Lestrade would be guilty. Great heavens, man! Since the papers appeared this morning, Dr Neill has known that Miss Sabbatini was arrested yesterday. Chapel Street, Berkhamstead. What more need he be told? He guessed that she would, however innocently, speak his name to the police and reveal his part in the letters. Did you suppose he would still be waiting for you in his lodgings at three in the afternoon? He fled, it would appear, almost empty-handed, which suggests a fine state of panic, does it not?'

'Where else were we to start our search? And where did you find him?'

'My dear fellow, the criminal investigator must hold in his mind certain data. He cannot, to be sure, carry the timetable for the entire railway system of Great Britain. At a minimum, however, he must have in his head such items as the departure-time of the boat-train from Euston to connect with the Transatlantic sailings of the White Star Line from Liverpool. You tell me that Dr Neill hails from Chicago. That would be his quickest route home, would it not? I grant that you might send wires for the arrest of Dr Neill—but I shall eat my hat with pleasure if that proves to be more than a *nom-de-plume*.'

Lestrade gave a start at this and Holmes continued.

'I was already present at the great terminus of the North-Western Railway when Dr Neill's cab arrived in good time for the five o'clock train. Two friends of mine, whom you saw decamp from the cab just now, and whom, in deference to their own desire for anonymity, we will call "Cats-Meat" and "The Groundsman", made a rendezvous with me there at the cab-rank. Dr Neill could not arrive too early, of course, for that increased the risk of his being spotted at such an obvious location. Once we saw him draw up, it was a simple matter. My two friends and your handy little revolver persuaded him to step back into his cab rather than out of it. Charing Cross? To be sure, he would take pains to let Mrs Sleaper hear him shout "Charing Cross" to the cabbie this morning, the better to put us off his trail.'

In the sequel to this, Dr Neill was taken to Bow Street police-station, whither Holmes, Lestrade and I accompanied him. He was brought before the desk-sergeant and charged with demanding money with menaces, contrary to the Larceny Act 1861. He seemed not the least concerned.

'You have got the wrong man, of course,' he said genially, 'but fire away. What I asked Miss Sabbatini to assist me with was all done for Mr Walter Harper, for some work of his. He it was who claimed to be devilling for his tutor who, in turn, was a police surgeon of some sort. Of the other letters I know nothing. There you have it, gentlemen. If he will murder girls in Stamford Street, he will hardly stop at blackmail. I was a fool, I suppose, not to twig him from the first.'

After that, he declined to say another word.

'At the worst,' said Lestrade doubtfully, 'I must release him as an innocent dupe.'

'At the worst,' Holmes muttered, 'he is the Lambeth poisoner.'

The evidence of that seemed to fade by the hour. Lestrade tried him by asking how it was that the blackmail demands relating to Ellen Donworth and Matilda Clover could have been written other than by the murderer, a day before anyone knew the first girl had been poisoned and almost a fortnight before the second one had died.

'I guess,' said Dr Neill good-naturedly, 'you would have to ask the man who gave me the letters to have copied. Walter Harper.'

That young man could no longer be left out of it. During the evening, Lestrade gave orders to what Holmes called his 'minions' to bring Walter Harper to Bow Street.

'For it amounts to this,' the inspector said grimly, 'we may never convict Dr Neill of blackmail unless we first convict him of murder.'

So it was that on the following morning Dr Neill took his place in a line of men who stood the length of a wall in Bow Street yard. He was among twenty or thirty men, all dressed in suits and hats, the tallest at the centre of the line and the others falling away to either end, as if it had been a group photograph. Three witnesses attended. There had been time enough to bring Mrs Phillips from the house where Matilda Clover lodged. Lestrade's men had also found Sally Martin and Jenny Frere, two of those who 'hunted in the same pack' with Matilda Clover. Unlike her friend Lucy Rose, they had been out with her every night for a week or two before she died and had seen the man she was with on the last night of all.

Sherlock Holmes still had an air of patient endurance, the courteous man who considers his time is being wasted but who is too well-bred to speak of it. He stood with Lestrade and two uniformed officers in a far corner of the sunlit yard. Mrs Phillips, like a galleon under sail, made her stately way down the line. She scarcely looked at Dr Neill but passed on and touched the shoulder of a shorter man almost at the end of the line. Sally Martin and Jenny Frere followed her. One by one they passed by Dr Neill, though Sally Martin paused and looked quickly at his boots. Then they walked on and touched the shoulder of another man. When they had gone Holmes favoured Lestrade with a look of worldly wisdom. For all three women had walked past Dr Neill and touched the shoulder of Walter Harper.

When we were alone together, while Lestrade left his office to give instructions for Harper's continued detention, Holmes turned from the window and said quietly, 'You know, my dear fellow, that I would not for the world offend you?'

'I daresay you would not intend to do so.' It was the best that I could manage.

'All the same, I wonder if you would permit me to lend you a little assistance in this case of yours. You have managed it admirably to this point in many respects. Now, however, I cannot help observing that the threads of your evidence appear remarkably tangled. You would not sleep easily, I know, if you were instrumental in assisting Lestrade's blockheads to get an innocent man hanged.'

'Once and for all,' I said irritably, 'it is not my case—it is our case. And you may do what the devil you like with it!'

'Capital,' he said with a smile. 'Then we will return, if you please, to this matter of the talking corpse.'

XVI

For the whole of the next spring day we followed the arteries of pleasure lying just south of the river, a warren of streets and alleys where the mild sky was dulled by smoke and the tin thunder of trains echoed from every bridge and tall archway. Holmes began at Westminster Bridge, where the entrance canopy of Astley's Amphitheatre and Circus extends over the pavement. We followed the walls of the Canterbury Music Hall and Gatti's Palace of Varieties, whose blue and red placards boasted Head Balancers and Acrobats, Minstrels, and Performing Horses. We searched streets of brick terraces, darkened by soot and decay, upper floors painted with advertisements for cigars, confectionery, embrocation, and Old England Snuff. In the little windows of tobacconists' shops, the covers of the week's *Tit-Bits* and the *Police Budget* had yet to placard the news of Dr Neill.

It was early evening when we paid for our entrance to the Canterbury, whose interior was a domed oriental palace with gold-painted stucco adorning the boxes and galleries. Its speciality was the 'Fish Ballet' performed by ladies in silver fleshings behind a thin gauze curtain drawn across the arch of the stage.

On his rare visits to the music hall, Holmes showed little interest in the performance. Life for him was at the rear, along the promenade bar, which looked on to the stage in front but whose windows at the back surveyed the streets below. The chatter and laughter, the clatter of glasses, the oysters served with brown bread and butter were all the entertainment he required.

It would be foolish to pretend that the majority of strollers in the Canterbury's Long Bar were other than counting-house clerks masquerading as top-hatted swells and discreetly-painted street-girls in cloaks and bonnets. Holmes and I sat with our plates of oysters and glasses of hock at a round marble-topped table while we watched the passing show. Hour followed hour and I was suddenly aware that we were sitting through the stage performance for a second—or perhaps third—time. Then he stood up, smiled, and to my dismay accosted one of the girls. To me, she looked indistinguishable from the rest.

'Happy birthday, my dear!' he said jovially. 'Happy birthday, Lucy Rose!'

'Beg your pardon?' She swung round upon him, not best pleased, but Holmes continued to smile in sheer amiability.

'We are a week early but our wishes are no less sincere! Happy birthday, Lucy Rose! Or perhaps I should say, happy birthday, Louisa Harvey!'

This brought me to my feet, which was just as well for the girl swung round and then was about to run. Finding me in her way she stopped and Holmes took her by the arm.

'Have no fear, Louisa! We mean you no harm.'

'What the devil is this?' I said to him with some little spirit, 'You swore she was in Lambeth Cemetery!'

'And so she was, were you not, my dear? Standing with the idlers by the railings, watching in dread as poor Mattie Clover's body was brought up.'

The keenness of his eye, in picking out a face from a crowd, was legendary but my astonishment must have been all too visible.

'Watson, Watson!' he said softly. 'How much the world owes to Somerset House and its register of deaths, which we have all been searching! But how much more to its register of births, where I alone have spent my leisure hours. 4 April is the young lady's birthday, if you recall. Now, there is no Lucy Rose born on that day, if the records are to be believed. But seventeen years ago, Louisa Jane Harvey uttered the first notes of a career which has brought her to where we find her now.'

He held her so gently by one arm but she might as well have struggled against a steel trap.

'What d'you want with me?'

'The truth,' he said a little more sternly. 'The truth you have kept to yourself too long. The truth you owe to Matilda Clover. The truth about Dr Neill.'

There was no more resistance in her now. She sat down at the little marble table as suddenly as if her legs might not have supported her. She said nothing. Holmes snapped his fingers at the waiter for three glasses of sherbet.

'Come,' he said, sitting opposite her, 'tell the truth and he will never more be free to harm you. Keep it hidden and he will be set at liberty to find you.'

She breathed deeply for a moment, then said, 'I was so frightened!'

'You were with Matilda Clover when the two of you met him, of course.'

Louisa Harvey, as I must now call her, nodded.

'As I supposed,' Holmes said. 'This man thought he had murdered both of you. But Matilda was alive two weeks later. And you escaped him. How?'

'It was the Alhambra in Leicester Square,' she whispered, 'the long bar, like this one. He asked my name and said he came from America and was working at the hospital. I was to spend the night with him off Oxford Street, a hotel in Berwick Street. Later we went to the Northumberland public house near the Embankment and Mattie was there. He wanted us both. He said he had special stuff that made it more frisky. Something he got through being a medical man. He gave us each two long pills. I pretended to take mine but switched them to the other hand and then threw them behind me. He made me open my hand to show I'd swallowed them. But I was rid of them by then. Mattie slipped hers in her pocket. He promised to meet us later at the hotel, saying he'd got an appointment at the hospital first. I waited but he never came.'

Holmes gave a long sigh.

'He is, I daresay, certifiably insane. It will not help him, of course, for the law has its own very peculiar definition of insanity. I do not doubt, however, that the great Dr Maudsley would find his brain most instructive, when our prisoner has no further use for it himself.'

'I was so frightened!' the girl exclaimed, not listening to him. 'I kept to the house and never went out. Then I walked out one night, and in Stamford Street I saw him again. He didn't see me, I think, being too far away. Later I heard that two girls died there and I was so scared he might find me at Ma Phillips's. I ran off to Brighton and worked at the bar in Mutton's. I'd been there ever since, until yesterday. Yesterday I came back, thinking perhaps he might be gone to America by now. When I heard your voice behind me, saying my real name like that, I nearly died of fright, thinking it might be him.'

'Let us hope,' said Holmes reassuringly, 'you will not need to die of anything at all for many years to come. It is plain to me that your poor friend Matilda kept the two pills he had given her and later, perhaps for a lark after she had drunk that half-bottle of whisky, she took them. But her murderer could not know that she had kept them so long or that you had never taken them at all. So he accused one of his dupes of killing you both, when you were still both alive.'

He turned to me and I was surprised to see his face relax in a smile.

'Tell me, Watson, does not our young friend make a very charming corpse?' The girl gave a start at this but he went on, 'Louisa is the talking corpse whom I promised would sooner or later provide the solution to our case.'

I was about to ask how long he had known all this and kept it from me. But I was so relieved to hear him refer to 'our case' at last that I let the matter drop.

At Bow Street, after we had relinquished charge of Louisa Harvey to a police matron, Lestrade was waiting for us. He was not quite pacing up and down but his difficulty in avoiding such exercise was plain.

'Another letter!' he said furiously. 'Postmarked in Holborn last night at 10 P.M. and therefore sent at least four hours after Dr Neill was taken into custody!'

Holmes read the sheet of paper, chuckled, and then handed it to me.

'Very good!' he said merrily. 'Very good indeed! Is it not, Watson?'

> Dear Sir,
>
> The man you have in your power is as innocent as you are. I gave the girls those pills to cure them of their earthly miseries. Others might follow Lou Harvey out of this world of care and woe. Lord Russell had a hand in the poisoning of Clover. If I were you, I would release Dr T. Neill or you might get into trouble.

Yours respectfully Juan Pollen, alias, Jack the Ripper.
BEWARE ALL! I WARN BUT ONCE!

'I fail to see, Mr Holmes, what is good about an event of this kind.'

'Only, Lestrade, that there are so many explanations of the message that it hardly merits thought. Oh, very well. If nothing else will do, Mr Slater hears a rumour of the arrest and the crime, then enjoys a little revenge on the Lambeth constabulary. A dozen malcontents might do it. Set it aside, my dear fellow.'

So, next morning, Louisa Harvey looked from a window into the Bow Street yard where the men were drawn up again. Unlike the previous witnesses she confessed herself too terrified to confront her would-be murderer face to face.

She picked out Dr Neill at a glance.

'And is there no other man in that line whom you have ever seen before?' Holmes asked gently.

She shook her head. He directed her attention to young Walter Harper.

'Not that one?'

Again she shook her head.

'No. He is quite like a boy that goes with the girls here in London, and down at Muttons in Brighton. All the same, he ain't the one.'

'Then you identify only Dr Neill?'

'Dr Neill? Oh, no! I don't see any Dr Neill.'

Lestrade uttered a gasp of dismay, audible to everyone in the room.

'Just now, you picked out one of those men as Dr Neill, miss!'

A third time she shook her head, more emphatically.

'Not as Dr Neill.'

In that instant my spirits also sank, as our carefully-wrought solution to the Lambeth murders seemed to disintegrate. Then a miracle occurred.

'You never asked,' said Louisa Harvey reproachfully. 'You only asked if I'd know his face. That's him. But that's not his name.

'Least not the one he told me. He's Dr Cream. Funny sort of name, Cream, the sort you'd remember. He showed me a letter he'd had from America. Addressed to him at Anderton's Hotel in Fleet Street. It had Dr Cream on it. No doubt of that.'

Holmes turned slowly and accusingly to Lestrade.

'He arrived at Euston the other day with no luggage. Whatever he took with him must have been deposited and was waiting there. I take it your men have by now searched the cloakroom at Euston for any article belonging to Dr Neill?'

The inspector's face was, to coin a phrase, an arena of conflicting emotions.

'A Gladstone bag was missing from his rooms, according to Mrs Sleaper. That has been sought for in the cloakroom and the lost-property office . . .'

'And not found,' said Holmes patiently. 'Perhaps they would be better employed searching for a Gladstone bag whose ticket-holder is Dr Cream.'

A little after nine o'clock that evening, Scotland Yard became possessed of a Gladstone, containing the passport and personal effects of Dr Thomas Neill Cream. Long before the first police dossiers crossed the ocean, the bound notebooks of Sherlock Holmes yielded several entries from the Chicago press, recording suspicious deaths among Dr Cream's female patients and a prison sentence imposed for the death by poison of a male patient, Daniel Stott, of Grand Prairie, Illinois.

XVII

Such was the conclusion of the Lambeth poisonings, thanks to Sherlock Holmes and his 'talking corpse', who had survived such a villainous design against her life. Holmes himself seemed little surprised that there were such degenerates as would put their victims to an agonizing death as a matter of entertainment. He would shrug and talk again of Roman emperors, Renaissance princes, the Marquise de Brinvilliers at the court of Louis XIV, as if they were the most common thing in the world. However, he spared me the observation that when a doctor went wrong, he was the worst of criminals.

Yet, after all, this was not quite the conclusion. Once the name of Dr Cream was revealed, a good deal else followed. He was not American by birth but Scottish. So far as he had a medical speciality it was in the trade of abortion. His dealings were with women of the streets in Chicago and from one of these he had contracted a disease which affected his body and mind alike.

As soon as Holmes heard this, he needed no other explanation. Dr Neill, or Dr Cream, or Dr Neill Cream as he was now generally known, was a man with the fury of an avenger, the inspiration of a demon, and the skill of a torturing fiend. All the murder and all the blackmail had come from that one perverted genius, which lay disguised behind the shallow geniality of his mild manner. There are men who commit crimes as terrible as his, to the astonishment of those who know them. How can a man so amiable and self-effacing be the murderer of half a dozen young women? In his case, however, once the truth about him was known, it fitted a pattern that had been half-visible all the time.

Sherlock Holmes, though he seemed to wash his hands of the investigation, had not taken his eyes from it for one moment. It exhibited to him a degree of human depravity which Professor Moriarty or Colonel Moran, or even Charles Augustus Milverton the arch-blackmailer, could scarcely have matched. Dr Neill Cream, as I now call him, was mad as well as bad, to an extent which these other villains had never been.

A man in his middle years, however evil his course of life may have been, will generally show some development of character. The Lambeth murderer offered not the least sign of remorse, never a murmur of repentance during his weeks in the death-cell of Newgate gaol. We were assured by Lestrade that the poor wretch sang and danced and capered like a music-hall clown to while away his last hours. When he conversed, it was merely to boast of his amorous conquests and to claim the murder of still more victims. It was

· 544 ·

as if his mind had been driven into one narrow and terrible track by the very exposure of his guilt. He no longer made any attempt at geniality or gentility, nor did he show the least fear at the prospect which he faced.

Sherlock Holmes was of the opinion that Dr Neill Cream should have been reprieved, in order that this specimen of morbid psychology might be investigated by the alienists. He was mad, of course, by the standards of psychopathology. However, the English law takes its definition of insanity from a period fifty years before when either a man must have been unable to know what he was doing or, if he did know, he did not know it to be wrong. The cold-blooded destruction of the victims in this case made nonsense of such a plea.

In those days, of course, there was no Court of Criminal Appeal. A prisoner's only hope was a recommendation by the Home Secretary for a reprieve from the gallows to life imprisonment.

A week or two went by. I woke one November morning to find that a thick yellow fog had settled upon London. It was scarcely possible from our windows in Baker Street to see the outline of the opposite houses. A greasy, heavy brown swirl of vapour drifted past us and condensed in oily drops upon the glass. Sherlock Holmes pushed back his chair from the breakfast table and gazed at the weather which promised to keep him immured for several days to come. Then he glanced at his watch and his mood lightened.

'I had almost forgotten, my dear fellow.'

I put down the paper.

'Forgotten what, Holmes?'

'That client of yours, Watson. They hanged him at Newgate a full two hours ago. I cannot claim that I have always given full satisfaction to those clients who have been good enough to consult me, but I do not think that I have ever contrived to get one of them hanged.'

Notes

The Two 'Failures' of Sherlock Holmes

i. Marshall Hall's view of the Crippen case is given in Edward Marjoribanks, *The Life of Sir Edward Marshall Hall*, Victor Gollancz, 1929, pp.277–84. Marshall Hall believed that, had the defence been entrusted to him, 'Crippen would have been convicted of manslaughter or of administering a noxious poison so as to endanger human life.' Such a course, however, might have imperilled Ethel Le Neve's defence. 'Crippen loved Miss Le Neve so tenderly and whole-heartedly that he wished her to escape *all* the legal consequences of his association with her. He had, indeed, brought the tragedy upon her, but to ensure her complete scathelessness he was willing to die for her.' Marshall Hall's great rival, F. E. Smith, Lord Birkenhead, wrote of Crippen, 'He was, at least, a brave man, and a true lover.'

ii. Both George Lewis and Oscar Wilde's friend Robert Ross considered that a prosecution of Lord Queensberry for a criminal libel on the playwright was ill-advised. Lewis's view was that Wilde should tear up the insulting card and forget about it. However, goaded by Lord Alfred Douglas and encouraged by his solicitor Charles Humphreys, Wilde swore out a warrant for Queensberry's arrest on 1 March 1895. Cf. Richard Ellmann, *Oscar Wilde*, Hamish Hamilton, 1987, pp. 411–13.

Wilde's purloining of other men's epigrams is described in G. M. Young, *Victorian England: Portrait of an Age*, Oxford University Press, 1960, p. 163n.

The Case of the Racing Certainty

The career of Harry Benson and William Kurr as international swindlers is combined with the exposure of corruption at Scotland Yard in George Dilnot (ed.), *The Trial of the Detectives*, Geoffrey Bles, [1930]. The book contains a transcript of the 1877 trial. Following this scandal, the Detective Police of Scotland Yard was restructured as the Criminal Investigation Department, or C.I.D. A Special Branch was also created, principally to counter the threat from Sinn Fein, as well as an independent power of prosecution in the office of Director of Public Prosecutions.

The Case of the Naked Bicyclists

A full account of the case appears in F. Tennyson Jesse (ed.), *The Trial of Samuel Herbert Dougal*, William Hodge, 1928. In her finely intuitive introduction, Fryn Tennyson Jesse remarks of the nude bicycling that Dougal liked 'a touch of an orgy' in his activities. 'What a picture in that clayey, lumpy field, the clayey lumpy girls, naked astride that unromantic object, a bicycle, and Dougal, gross and vital, cheering on these bucolic improprieties.'

The Case of the Sporting Major

Though the case against Alfred John Monson was found 'not proven' under Scottish Law, Edward Scott, *alias* Sweeney, was never brought to trial. When he did not appear to answer the charges of murder and attempted murder in 1897, he was outlawed by the High Court of Justiciary in Edinburgh. The year after Major Monson's trial, Scott was discovered to be appearing as assistant to a music-hall magician. Curiously, no proceedings were taken against him and the decree of outlawry was eventually rescinded.

The Case of the Hygienic Husband

George Joseph Smith (1872–1915) served three prison sentences, totalling three and a half years, for larceny and receiving. Between 1898 and 1915, he also contracted eight marriages, seven of them bigamous. Three of these wives, Bessie Mundy, Alice Burnham, and Margaret Lofty, were drowned by him in their baths. Smith was an amateur musician and, having left Margaret Lofty dead in the depths of her bath, he took advantage of a domestic harmonium in the next room to give a farewell rendering of *Nearer, My God, To Thee*. His principal motive in the drownings was mercenary but he had no conscientious objection to murder. He was tried only for the killing of Bessie Mundy, for which he was hanged. A transcript of the trial is included in Eric R. Watson (ed.), *The Trial of George Joseph Smith*, William Hodge, 1922. The editor remarks on the familiar truth that psychopaths of Smith's type find it easiest to attract victims from the educated and articulate middle class, 'be it governess or lady's companion, or young lady in business'. In this view, Smith the ex-regimental gymnastic instructor and petty thief, had a knack of detecting 'fires of repressed passion' in outwardly-conventional young women of the professional class.

The Case of the Talking Corpse

On the gallows trap, Dr Neill Cream is said to have made a last-second confession, 'I am Jack—' Billington pulled the lever before the name was completed. According to the records, Cream was a prisoner in Joliet Penetentiary, Illinois, until 1891 for having poisoned Daniel Stott. Could he have committed the Whitechapel murders in 1888? In *The Times* on 12 March 1985, Donald Bell, a Canadian journalist, offered evidence that anonymous letters from Jack the Ripper and others known to be by Neill Cream were in the same hand. Though Cream should have been in Joliet in 1888, it was alleged that in nineteenth-century America a convict with money could pay another man to serve part of his sentence for him.

A further curiosity is that Marshall Hall went into court during Neill Cream's trial and recognized him as one half of an ingenious double-act. Two men, whose appearance was near-identical, had worked a system by which they gave one another alibis. One of them had been Marshall Hall's client in a case of bigamy and the lawyer recognized him as the man now in the dock under the name of Thomas Neill Cream. On the other hand, Marshall Hall considered Neill Cream's claim to be Jack the Ripper as no more than the characteristic vanity of the professional criminal. Cf. Edward Marjoribanks, *The Life of Sir Edward Marshall Hall*, pp. 47–8.

III

The Execution of Sherlock Holmes

For my parents

Justin Melville Gwyn Thomas 1900–92

Doris Kathleen Thomas, *née* Serrell, 1906–55

Contents

Acknowledgments

I am most grateful for information kindly provided on Johann Ludwig Casper and Carl Liman by Ms. Helen D'Artillac Brill of the University of Cardiff and on respirators of World War I by Mr Martin Boswell of the Imperial War Museum, London.

The Execution of Sherlock Holmes

PROLOGUE
by John H. Watson, M.D.

Before setting out on my story, I must say something of the late Charles Augustus Milverton of Appledore Towers, Hampstead. Those of my readers who have read the story of that title may recall a little of what follows. Though dead for three years, the ghost of this scoundrel threatened greater harm to Sherlock Holmes than Professor Moriarty himself had done.

Charles Augustus Milverton! My friend called him the worst man in London, more repulsive than fifty murderers with whom we had dealings. A reptile, said Holmes, a slithery, gliding venomous creature with deadly eyes and an evil, flattened face. This king of blackmailers lived in luxury by bribing treacherous valets or the maidservants of men and women in a high position. The most virtuous soul need only be guilty of a trivial error of conduct, no more than a mere indiscretion. Once in Milverton's hands, a single thoughtless letter or even a note of two lines had been enough to ruin a noble family.

Once or twice his fame as a poisoner of reputations reached the columns of the sporting magazines. I recall Sherlock Holmes pointing out to me a couplet in *Turf Life in London*.

559

A viper bit Milverton—what was his plight?
The viper, not Milverton, died of the bite.

Such was our enemy. As Holmes remarked, that round smiling face concealed a heart of marble. Milverton squeezed his victims little by little, by holding a threat over them and a false promise before them. One or two more payments and the poor wretches thought they would be safe. They never were. Only when no more was to be got, or in two cases when the victim retired to his dressing room carrying a revolver loaded with a single bullet, did this villain's prisoners gain their release.

Milverton's last extortion was to be £7,000 from Lady Eva Brackwell, shortly before her marriage to the Earl of Dovercourt. This was the price asked for several imprudent letters written by the young woman a year before. These were addressed to a country squire, ending a fond childhood friendship which had briefly blossomed into romance. Unfortunately for her, it was an easy matter to cut off or otherwise alter the date on some of these notes. The 'warm friendship' was thus represented as continuing secretly long after her betrothal to Lord Dovercourt. A dishonest servant of the squire's, amply rewarded, placed the papers in Milverton's hands. Unless young Lady Eva paid the price, Milverton swore the Earl of Dovercourt would receive this correspondence a week before the wedding. He insisted to her ladyship that he always carried out his threats. To weaken would destroy his reputation and profession.

To any decent mind, the conduct of such a villain is so monstrous that there is a temptation to think it cannot be true of any man. From the evidence of my own eyes and ears, I know it to be true. I was present at our Baker Street rooms in January 1899, when Milverton adjusted his cravat with a plump little hand and said to Holmes in a voice like soft but rancid butter, 'You may be assured, my dear sir, that if the money is not paid promptly by the fourteenth, there will certainly be no marriage on the eighteenth.'

How supple and skillful a blackmailer is! How knowing in his choice of victims! Many a bridegroom might forgive a past flirtation, and Holmes suggested as much to our visitor. But Milverton was accustomed to choose his prey with care and to infuse his own peculiar venom into the falsehood and rumour that attended the cancellation of an engagement in high society. A year earlier Captain Alexander Dorking had defied him over jewellers' receipts and hotel bills relating to a long-dead liaison with a fast woman. Two days before the captain's wedding to the Honourable Miss Clementina Miles, an announcement in the *Morning Post* informed the world that the marriage would not, after all, take place. The bride's forgiveness of the groom was not enough to repair the damage caused by the incriminating documents. Milverton had also insinuated a tainted gossip into the clubs of Pall Mall so that it might reach the ears of the young lady's family and society in general. This hinted at a loathsome disease, contracted by the captain ten years earlier in an act of undergraduate folly. In January 1899, Lady Eva well knew the sort of tales that would circulate if she called Milverton's bluff. There could be no marriage to any man after that.

Sherlock Holmes had reluctantly agreed to act as intermediary on the young woman's behalf, offering the scoundrel her little fortune of £2,000. Milverton laughed in his face and would take nothing less than the £7,000 demanded. He suggested that her ladyship might easily raise an extra £5,000 by taking the family jewels inherited from her grandmother and exchanging them for imitations done in paste. Even had she done so, Holmes warned her that the reptile would return for more. So long as a penny remained in the victim's purse, there was never an end to blackmail. This was one of few occasions when Holmes and I resolved to do wrong in order that right should prevail. There could be no compromise. A viper's nest can be cleared in only one way.

A week later we set out for Hampstead on a blustery winter's night, carrying what Holmes called his 'up-to-date burgling kit with every modern improvement which the march of civilization demands.' We judged that Milverton would be in bed by the time we made our way through the laurel bushes of the extensive garden. It took only a few minutes to find the weak point in the defences.

Holmes's diamond-tipped glass cutter silently removed a circle from a pane in the conservatory door. By turning a key on the inside we passed into the drawing room, our identities concealed by black velvet masks, like a pair of Limehouse footpads. Ahead of us, the study was sufficiently illuminated by a well-banked fire for Holmes to work on the tall green safe without turning on the electric light.

He would leave no trace, no scratches on the steel mirrors of the lock. With the skill and accuracy of a surgeon he used his instruments upon the somewhat antiquated Milner device. His strong yet delicate hands showed the quiet competence of a trained mechanic. After twenty minutes, the lock clicked. He drew the door of the safe half open to reveal a score of packets, each labeled and tied with pink tape, like a lawyer's brief. At that moment a door slammed somewhere deeper in the house and we heard footsteps approaching us. Holmes closed the safe, though without locking it, and we drew back behind the long velvet curtains drawn across the windows. The door to the inner room opened and the snick of an electric switch filled the air with a harsh brilliance.

He was visible through a crack in the curtains! Not a shadow of suspicion touched his features as Milverton in his claret-colored smoking jacket sat down in a red leather chair with a cigar in one hand, a document in the other, and began to read. The back of his broad grizzled head with its patch of baldness was towards us. My fingers tingled at the thought of how easily a blow to the skull from Holmes's jemmy might rid the world of this genteel blackguard. But that would not serve our purpose. How long we might be trapped behind the velvet drapery was therefore impossible to guess. I noticed, however, that our unwitting host looked at his watch with growing frequency and impatience. He was clearly expecting something—or someone. Presently there was a footfall on the veranda and we heard a gentle tapping. He got up, crossed the room, and went out to open the door.

I heard little of the conversation at that distance beyond recognizing his quiet visitor as a woman. As they turned to come in, I heard him say, 'Half an hour late!' and 'Made me lose a good night's sleep!' Then a little more clearly, 'If the countess is a hard mistress, this must be your chance to get even with her. Five letters which compromise the Countess d'Albert? You want to sell and I want to buy. It only remains to agree on the price.'

They were both in the study now, she a tall, slim, dark woman with a veil over her face and a mantle under her chin. Milverton was saying, 'I should want to inspect the letters, of course.' She had her back to us, but presently I could see her making the gestures of raising her veil and dropping the mantle from her chin. He turned to her and looked startled at first; then he seemed about to laugh. There was no hint of fear in his voice. 'Great heavens, it is you!'

'The woman whose life you have ruined!' she said without the least tremor in her voice. 'The wife whose husband broke his gallant heart and died by his own hand!'

'You were so obstinate,' he said softly, wheedling her almost as if offering a caress to console her. 'I put the price well within your means. Yet you would not pay.' Then his face changed, as if he had seen something concealed from us. 'I warn you that I have only to raise my voice, call my servants, and have you arrested!'

She turned a little and I caught the suggestion of a smile on her thin lips. There was a crack, no louder than the snapping of dry wood. He stared at her, as if turned to stone, but did not fall. The sharp sound cracked again; her arm was stretched out and now the muzzle of a small silver revolver was not two inches from his shirt front. A third and fourth time she fired. He remained motionless for a moment longer, as if the shots might have been blanks. Then he fell forward, coughing and scrabbling among the papers on the table. 'You've done me!' he gasped and at once lay still.

The woman dropped the gun and hurried into the darkness of the veranda. Holmes strode from behind the curtain and turned the key in the door that connected us with the rest of the house. There were now several voices and sounds of movement. Without a word he flung open the safe door. In two or three armfuls he carried the packets of papers across the room and dropped them onto the banked coals of the fire, which blazed up in sudden brightness as it consumed them. Finally he scooped up the silver revolver and said, 'This may be useful, Watson. I rather think there are two shots left.'

With that we raced for the brick wall dividing the garden from its surrounding heathland. Even as we sprinted across the lawn, we were illuminated, for shafts of white electric light shone suddenly from every uncurtained window of the house. Several pursuers were almost at our heels. They so nearly caught us that one of them snatched and held my ankle as I went over the top of the wall. He might have brought me back into their grasp but Holmes chose this moment to fire over their heads the two last shots from the little gun. They flung themselves down, and a run of two miles in the darkness across Hampstead Heath took us clear.

The beautiful assassin, though still unknown to me, was picked out by Holmes a few days later from an Oxford Street photographer's display of the beauties and celebrities of the previous London season. As for the silver revolver, I never saw it again. When I asked him what had become of it, he said, 'I tossed it away, just after we cleared the wall. It was empty.'

'It may be found!' I protested.

'I do hope so, my dear fellow. Do you not see? The lady who rid the world of that reptile stood in danger. In her confusion, she dropped the weapon on his carpet and that might have been her undoing. It was plainly the gun that had killed him and, if it were traced to her, might have put her life in peril from the law or from the criminal underworld. Now she is safe, and so she deserves to be after suffering so much at his hands. They will hardly think she was one of the pair who scrambled over a six-foot wall and sprinted across the heath.'

'The villains may trace the gun to you instead.'

'I hope they may,' he said, lighting his pipe from a long spill. 'They will find me well prepared for them.'

Such chivalry was characteristic of my friend, but, as you shall see, he was to pay dearly for it.

THE DISAPPEARANCE

Three years had passed since that windy January night on Hampstead Heath and I had long ago assured myself that we and the world had heard the last of Charles Augustus Milverton. How mistaken I was!

There are few greater horrors in life than when a constant companion, a husband, wife, or child, sets out from home in the most usual way and never returns. It is surely worst of all when there is no message, no report of a death, injury, derangement, or desertion. I had not even seen Sherlock Holmes set out from our Baker Street rooms on a spring morning in 1902, though the sound of his feet on the stairs and his shout to Mrs. Hudson told me he was going.

He did not return that evening. I was used to his mysterious absences for several days when he had an important investigation in hand. We had recently been occupied in 'The Case of the Naked Bicyclists,' which led to the bizarre circumstances of the Moat Farm Murder.* Yet there was nothing in this investigation to take Holmes away so unaccountably.

All the same, I waited. After a few days longer, I began each morning by running my finger down the small 'wants' and 'offers' in the personal column of the *Morning Post*. This was our regular means of communication in such emergencies. The codes we used were known only to each other and might be seen in the press by millions of readers who would be none the wiser. Each of these little announcements was prefaced by the two letters NB for 'nota bene.' To the uninitiated, they appeared to be mere puffs for well-known products or services, unusual in a column of this kind but without being exceptional. NB marked them out.

The signal that invariably opened our communication was 'Rowlands Antimacassar Oil.' Since one example saves many words, let

---

* For an account of this adventure see 'The Case of the Naked Bicyclists' in Donald Thomas, *Sherlock Holmes and the Voice from the Crypt*, Carroll & Graf, 2002.

me suppose that Holmes had gone suddenly to a secret address in London and wished me to join him. After the antimacassar oil advertisement, the next NB would name a city or county. In this case it might be '"London Pride" Pipe Tobacco. Threepence an ounce.' So much for that day's column, which gave me 'London.' Next day NB might add 'Grand Atlantic Hotel, Weston-super-Mare. Preferential Rates Available.' Knowing already that he was in London, I would merely count the letters of this second message and make a total of 60. From our folders of London maps I would draw sheet number 60 of the Ordnance Survey's invaluable microcosm of the capital. As those who use it will know, sheet 60 covers the Paddington area from Hyde Park in the south to the Regents Park canal in the north and from Chepstow Place, Bayswater, in the west to Seymour Place in Marylebone. Further down the column might be a second NB announcement. 'Bisto Makes Tasty Soups.' That would be all. Counting the letters in each word I would find 5 +5 +5 +5.

We had divided the vertical and horizontal edges on our maps into 100 equal lengths. Therefore 5 +5 and 5 +5 would stand for 55 by 55. On this basis I would take sheet 60 and measure 55 from the east, along the bottom of the map, and 55 from the north, down its left-hand side. Using a ruler, I would discover that the two lines from these points would intersect on the west side of Spring Street, almost within the shadow of the great railway terminus at Paddington station. The invaluable Ordnance Survey marks each dwelling house, though no more than a millimeter in size. For whatever reason, in this example Holmes would be found at 8, Spring Street, Paddington, to which I must make my way.

It was rarely indeed that we had recourse to such secret and unbreakable codings, which covered not only locations but a variety of necessary information. By this time, I had been Holmes's companion and colleague for more than a dozen years. You may imagine that we had planned for most contingencies. Yet no one outside an insane asylum could have anticipated the horrors which beset us in the spring of this fateful year. The days passed and the *Morning Post* personal column bore no messages.

A week went by, ten days, a fortnight. I inquired after those 'found drowned,' after victims of road accidents, the subjects of inquests from murder to suicide. I visited mortuaries in Lambeth, St. Pancras, and Chelsea. It was to no avail. I put aside my aversion to my friend's addictions, and gained entry to dockside lofts and cellars frequented by the opium smokers of Limehouse and Shadwell. I half mentioned my fears to our friends at Scotland Yard, saying that Holmes had gone off I knew not where. Lestrade and Gregson pulled wry faces, chuckled, and suspected that Mr. Holmes was 'up to his old tricks.' After all, what could they do with such information as I had to offer them? I did not think he was up to any tricks.

If you have read my account of his final encounter with Professor Moriarty in 1891, the dreadful struggle on the brink of the falls of Reichenbach, the plunge into the swirling waters, you may recall that this was preceded by weeks—perhaps months—of anticipation. Holmes would close the shutters on entering a room, as if against an assassin's bullet, saying, 'It is stupidity rather than courage to ignore the danger when it is close upon you.' This was so unlike his usual self-assurance that I worried, all those years ago, if he was well. He looked even paler and thinner than usual.

Then, on a single day in the course of that year, there had been three attempts on his life. In the morning, as he walked the short distance from our rooms to the corner of Bentinck Street and Welbeck Street, a two-horse van was driven straight at him, full-pelt. He sprang for the footpath and saved himself by a fraction of a second as the van disappeared. Within the hour, walking down Vere Street, he escaped death by an even smaller margin when a large brick from one of the house roofs shattered at his feet. The police were summoned but concluded that the two-horse van was driven by a madcap and that the wind had blown the brick from a pile of materials waiting to be used in repairing the upper storey of the house. That very evening there was a direct attempt against him in a dark street, when a ruffian with a bludgeon tried to knock his brains out. The fellow found to his cost that he was knocked cold instead by his intended victim and given in charge to the police.

By contrast, there had been nothing of this sort in the present case. Just then my friend was still engrossed in the matter of the Moat Farm murder. Nothing in that afforded a reason for attempted assassination! Yet at the time of the earlier threats—and often since then—Holmes had talked of the great criminal conspiracies underlying crimes that might appear separate and unconnected. He called it 'some deep, organizing power which for ever stands in the way of law, and throws its shield over the wrongdoer.' The men who wielded such power would surely give all they possessed to eliminate Sherlock Holmes. He claimed that he had felt their presence even when the mystery of a case had been solved—and in other cases in which he was not personally consulted. When Professor Moriarty had been unmasked, Holmes thought at first that he had beheaded the monster of criminal conspiracy. Instead, like the Hydra, it had lost one head only to grow many more.

Moriarty was dead, there were no two ways about that. Yet I now began to speculate on the names of men who had particular cause to wish the destruction of Sherlock Holmes or, as was often the case, had paid with their lives but had left behind others who might be no less passionate for his downfall. In the recent past he had been the means of sending to prison for fifteen years Herr Hugo Oberstein, the international agent in the case of the secret Bruce Partington submarine plans. He had protected and exonerated those who rid the world of Giuseppe Giorgiano of the Red Circle, a fiend who had earned the nickname of Death in southern Italy. Oberstein was behind bars and Giorgiano was dead, but the one had a foreign government loyal to him and the other a gang of cutthroats sworn to vengeance. I confess that, at this stage, the name of Charles Augustus Milverton had not so much as crossed my mind.

After three weeks there was one person whose assistance I had not sought and to whom I must confide my fears. Mycroft Holmes, of Pall Mall and the Diogenes Club, was now the government's chief interdepartmental adviser. He must be told of his younger brother's disappearance. 'Not only is he an adviser to the British government,'

Sherlock Holmes had once said to me, 'on occasion he *is* the British government.' All the same, I did not see what Brother Mycroft could do now. It was a terrible thing to admit to myself, but after a few weeks instinct assured me that I should never more see him whom I have always known to be the best and wisest of men.

If you have the patience to read what follows, you will find that I was wrong, though in what condition I saw him was another matter. By then Sherlock Holmes appeared as a man who has the shadow of the hangman's rope upon him. You will also understand why this narrative could not have been made public at an earlier date. Even now, I have wondered from time to time whether it would not be best to burn all the notes and the evidence, to let the tale die with me. It was never one that we discussed often in the future. Yet I hear that voice again in my mind. 'If you are an honest man, Watson, you will set this record against my successes.' It may be that, in this case, posterity will judge that Sherlock Holmes succeeded to an extent he never equaled, either before or since.

THE TRIBUNAL

'William Sherlock Scott Holmes! You stand charged that you, with other persons not in custody, did willfully murder Charles Augustus Milverton, at Hampstead in the County of Middlesex, upon the sixth day of January in the year 1899. How say you? Are you guilty or not guilty of the charge wherewith you have been indicted?'

Holmes had known from the first that they meant to murder him, come what might. The semblance of a trial continued during the evenings of three days, but these preliminaries to his execution had been devised solely to make his death more gratifying to them. When the ritual was over, the memory of the proceedings haunted his sleep every night in the time they allowed him before he was to be hanged. Every night, in that well-ordered mind, the nightmare took a precise form.

'The dream,' as he afterwards called it, began invariably with a jolt, like a great heartbeat of warning or fright, which brought him from the depths of unconsciousness to the mists of a drugged hyoscine sleep. Then there began the calling of his names and the indictment.

In his dream, he struggled to repudiate the two self-appointed judges who sat beyond a sunburst of arc light. Except for the brief moments when they seated themselves or left their places, he had seen them only as an actor sees the rows of an audience through a haze of limelight. In the nightmare of light, his mouth moved but his throat remained silent and impotent to answer. During his waking ordeal, a week previously, he had said simply and clearly, 'It is a matter of fact that I killed Charles Augustus Milverton. I did so to rid the world of a noxious villain. I did it alone. I would do it again and think my own life not too great a price to pay.'

'Your gallantry in protecting your friend Dr. Watson is commendable,' the voice said sardonically. 'It is wasted, however. It will not prevent him from standing where you stand now. You fled in his company and were seen to do so. The matter of a young woman on the premises is also under our investigation.'

'You are in error. Charles Augustus Milverton died by my hand and I required no assistance.'

'Guilty or not guilty!' the voice rapped out. 'Make your plea!'

'A man does not plead to gangsters and impostors.'

'Then you shall be entered mute of malice, as if pleading not guilty,' said the voice behind the arc light, 'and your trial shall proceed at once.'

He could have sworn he recognised the voice of this presiding 'judge.' Yet it had belonged to that man whom he had seen most efficiently shot dead at Appledore Towers, Hampstead, by a young woman's silver revolver three years earlier. Indeed, we had read the report of the inquest on Charles Augustus Milverton in the *Times* with its verdict of 'murder by person or persons unknown.'

Two dimly defined figures faced him from behind a broad oak table. Beyond them stood a man in a prison warder's uniform of some kind, a person whom they addressed as Master-at-Arms. He was to guard and, if necessary, subdue the handcuffed prisoner.

Holmes, seated on an upright wooden chair, had been weakened by the hypnotic that had kept him unconscious for many hours. He might have been a lone prisoner at the far end of the earth for all that he could tell.

As the voice behind the light talked on, in its mockery of the judicial process, he strove to calculate how long he had been kept in a drug-induced coma. The opening of his 'trial' was the first day of full consciousness. Even then, his coldly rational intellect was at work behind the fuddled eyes. Holmes had no memory of how he came to be there, apart from recalling a taste in his mouth. Yet that taste was everything to him just now. It had been sweetish, partially disguising something salt and harsh. That was his first clue. He knew that the sweetness was merely sugar of milk, universally employed to make medicine palatable. The harshness that it veiled was surely hyoscine hydrobromide, an hypnotic that can wipe from the patient's mind all memory of events heard, seen, or felt during the period of its operation.

Sherlock Holmes the analytical chemist, with his extensive apparatus in our Baker Street rooms, had tested hyoscine once or twice with a fingertip taste. The memory of it was as securely catalogued in that invincible mind as if it had been entered in the files of St. Mary's Hospital or the Radcliffe Laboratories. He knew better than any man how powerful a weapon the narcotic might be in the hands of the criminal world. Those who had drugged him evidently knew no more than that it would erase the memory of subsequent events and had made the mistake of believing that the memory of tasting and taking it would be lost as well. Meanwhile, Holmes confronted them behind their shield of light. He must first discover who these enemies were, where he was, and how they had brought him there.

In the course of his 'trial,' he understood that it was not their plan to kill him at once. Others who sought revenge upon him had been invited to watch him die. In the meantime the men who sat in judgment would break his spirit, so that the witnesses of his death might see him kneel for mercy and plead for his life as he was dragged to a beam from which the heavy rope of the gallows dangled. The story of Sherlock Holmes as a coward and a weakling in the end would do more to exhilarate and encourage this criminal brotherhood than any other coup.

Every night they gave him a choice as he lay on the wooden bed in his condemned cell. He might either drink the contents of the medicine glass, which would render him unconscious until morning, or be held down while a hypodermic syringe sedated him. He drank from the glass, if only to determine the drug they used. One touch on the tongue was enough.

His captors took no chances with him. A steel anklet and a light, five-foot steel chain locked him to a ring and a wall plate, whose four screws were deeply set into the stonework of the cell wall. This chain was just long enough for him to reach a small alcove with a basin and a drain behind the head of the wooden bed and too short for him to reach the guard who watched him while he was waking or sleeping. The anklet, almost tight to the skin, scraped flesh and bone whenever he moved.

As for his surroundings, the door from the cell to the passageway and the door to the exercise yard outside were both locked and barred. In the corridor sat two more guards who would enter immediately to their colleague's assistance at the first sound of a disturbance and who, meantime, scrutinized the length of the cell through a glass spy hole every ten or fifteen minutes. For good measure, there was a bell within the guard's reach. If pressed, it would bring immediate assistance from the men who sat outside.

It seemed useless for a man to fight against the effects of a nightly potion of hyoscine. Holmes knew this well enough. Yet after the first dose he knew something more. A sweet vegetable taste on his tongue suggested that hyoscine had been reduced and mingled with another drug. In order that it should have a more powerful effect, they had fortified it with an opiate. It was precisely in making doubly sure he was in their power that they gave Sherlock Holmes his first hope of defeating them.

I believe I was the only man on earth who knew of my friend's pernicious addiction to narcotics at times of idleness, a secret compulsion that is now common knowledge to those who have read of him. So long as he was alive this was never revealed to another living soul. Much has since been made of his use of cocaine and the hypodermic syringe, somewhat less of his use of opium. It was opium which took him to those dens of Wapping or Shadwell, of which I have already written elsewhere. Medical men will know, if others do not, that the use of opiates habituates a man to them. It is notorious that the greater the use, the less potent the effects. It would have been absurd to suppose that, even then, he could have fought off the effects of such a dose as they administered each night. Yet even before his 'trial' ended, by an effort of subconscious will and as the hours of the night wore on, he was able to rouse himself to the level of 'twilight sleep,' the effect of hyoscine alone.

My friend confessed to me that the labour of this partial awakening was atrocious. Each time that he attempted to rise from the drugged depths of consciousness, he went through a period of delusion. It seemed that he was manacled to a monstrous engine of some kind, whose wheels or piston rods he was forced to turn with more pain and effort than he had ever known. At last he overcame the resistance of the mechanism and gained a momentum through which he floated free of his labour. Then, with a thump of the heart, his dream would begin again.

As in the repeated showing of a film or the constant rehearsal of a play, his accusers took their seats in his dream. A curiosity of his twilight sleep was that Holmes began to see details hidden from him in conscious reality. It seemed that the effects of the narcotics forced upon him had dulled part of his waking brain during his trial. Only in this hyoscine sleep did he identify his 'judges' from the shadows beyond the arclight brilliance. As these accusers took their seats on the previous evening, Holmes now recalled that he had made out a smooth-shaven moon face, the features veiled from further identification by the brilliance of light. In the world of a waking dream, his subconscious mind endowed this blank moon with a fixed smile that conveyed malign cruelty. Imagination added hard gray eyes behind gold-rimmed glasses; memory recalled spite in a voice that was smooth and suave. Among the wraiths of semi-consciousness he heard the man address him. Holmes could not tell at first whether the words were an invention of his own fancy or whether he had heard them in the drugged torpor of his ordeal.

'You think us impostors, Mr. Holmes. Yet no men alive have a better right to demand the forfeit of your life. Charles Augustus Milverton, whom you murdered, was my elder brother. I am Henry Caius Milverton, and you might have verified my existence had you chosen to do so. Do not deny your crime, I beg you. The silver revolver, caliber .22, was found. It was child's play to compare the fingerprints upon it with those upon several objects obligingly but unwittingly handled by you.'

Holmes strove after the reality of the voice. Was he merely deducing the identity of Henry Caius Milverton from a dream? He knew instinctively that the words were real, spoken to him and blotted out by the next onset of hyoscine. In his mind he turned a little from the glare of light, trying obliquely to see beyond it. The voice continued, introducing a second judge.

'My colleague Captain James Calhoun, denounced by you as the head of a murder gang in Georgia, was not lost at sea, as you supposed. Because the sternpost of his ship's boat was found floating in mid-ocean after a severe gale, you thought him drowned. Had you been as clever as you would have the world believe, you would have seen at once that the debris was deliberately set adrift where it would be found. The Lone Star, for whom your minions waited at Savannah, entered Bahia three weeks later, unremarked, as the Alcantara. A lick of paint, Mr. Holmes, was sufficient to defeat you.'

'You have the conceit of clever men, Holmes'—the well-fed drawl was Calhoun—'but you were watched as soon as you accepted the case against me, even when you were reading ships' registers and insurance files at Lloyd's of London.'

Henry Milverton chuckled at the colonel's pleasantry and resumed.

'Somewhere beyond these walls,' the voice continued, 'is Colonel James Moriarty, who is detained for the time being over matters relating to a family heirloom. Unusually, he bears the same first name as his brother, the professor whom you sent to his death at the falls of Reichenbach eleven years ago. It is a long time, is it not? And yet no doubt, Mr. Holmes, you are familiar with the old Italian proverb. Revenge is a dish which persons of taste prefer to eat cold. Before the melancholy conclusion of your history, Colonel Moriarty will demand certain satisfactions for his brother's death— satisfactions which you will be in no position to deny him.'

The voice uttered a rich chuckle, as if in appreciation of its own consummate wit, and then proceeded.

'Consider the matter of the Greek interpreter. On the basis of a newspaper cutting, you believed Harold Latimer and Wilson Kemp, whom you sought for murder, had stabbed one another to death in a railway carriage near Budapest. You should not, Mr. Holmes, believe all you read in the papers. These gentlemen and others will be invited to watch you dance your last half hour in the noose.'

'Mr. Latimer is a knave,' said Holmes mildly, 'one who tortured and murdered the brother of the girl he had promised to marry, in order to extract from him the family fortune.'

'So you say, Mr. Holmes.'

Sherlock Holmes endured this banter in the world of a dream, but his mind was elsewhere. Scrutinizing the architecture of his 'courtroom,' drawing out the half-remembered details with an effort that approached physical pain. Despite the central glare of light, he had seen that it was not a room but a vaulted space, the meeting of four massively built and stone-flagged passageways. Each was faced by a gothic arch. Nothing in the shadowy perspectives told him whether he was in England or in Europe, in a remote fastness or at the centre of a great city. Piece by piece, he reassembled the image of it. He woke next morning with the central enigma unraveled in his mind. The key to it had been a name, Henry Caius Milverton. He repeated that name over to himself silently, as if fearing that another sleep would wipe it from his mind.

During several days, whenever the 'court' was not in session, he was to remain in the cell, his last refuge until they led him out to the gallows. It was a bare whitewashed room with a slightly arched brick roof supported on iron girders and tunnel-like in shape. At one end, behind the head of his bed, was the small, open alcove with its basin, a gutter, and running water. He was watched day and night by one or other of Milverton's 'warders.'

His furniture consisted of the solid wooden bedstead about nine inches in height from the floor, with a thin mattress and a single blanket. There was a table and a wooden upright chair by the bed and another table and chair at the farther end of the cell for the use of the warder. The table and chair by the bed were removed at night, as if for fear he might make some use of them to escape. The cell was lit on its long outer wall by two iron-grated windows with small panes of opaque fluted glass. Its floor was laid with red polished tiles. His food was already cut up and brought to him on a white tin plate, without cutlery. No doubt they feared he would cheat them by using a knife to escape or to make away with himself before the appointed date.

Holmes had taken measurements with a sure eye. The cell was almost nineteen feet long by eight feet wide and seven feet tall at the lowest point, where the roof and walls met. The long wall adjoining the corridor was blank, apart from the plate to which the anklet and chain were attached and a double gas bracket for illumination after dark. The narrow wall at the far end, facing the bed, had a door leading at right angles to the corridor. On the other long wall were the two narrowly barred windows and a door to a yard. This wall was also lit from a double gas bracket. The narrow wooden bed with its rough prison-issue blanket and a canvas pillow stood along the wall adjoining the corridor at the far end from the door.

The light anklet chain, when stretched at full length, allowed him to reach the basin in the alcove behind him. In the opposite direction, he could stretch to a point almost halfway down the length of the cell. It stopped short of the door to the yard and the wooden chair with its table where the guard sat. As well as the guards in the corridor, two men took it in turns to watch him within the cell. With the chain on his ankle he could not have reached them, even if an attack would have made escape possible. Such food as he was brought was put on a plate just within his reach and then the guard drew back. It was made plain to him that he would never leave this cell, except for sittings of the 'court,' until the morning when they took him out to the gallows shed in the yard. It was equally plain to them that no one could save him, least of all Holmes himself. This belief he considered to be their greatest weakness.

Even at night as he slept his drugged sleep, there was a guard in his cell, as well as the others in the corridor outside, within easy call. Yet night and his dreams offered him hope. Though he was required to drink the glass of hyoscine hydrobromide, it must have seemed to his guards a superfluous precaution. He could scarcely move from the bed. Both doors were beyond his reach, and though he might stretch out an arm to touch the nearer barred window with his fingertips, he would be seen and heard at once.

With such precautions, it mattered little to his guardians whether he swallowed the hyoscine hydrobromide or not. All the same, they were instinctively obedient to Milverton and would make him do it. Holmes understood that he had been given the sedative merely so that he should not be troublesome in the hours of darkness by arguing or pleading. He was careful to give no trouble. After a couple of nights they took less interest, and the man who brought the glass sometimes glanced away if distracted by sound or movement. It was possible for Holmes to tip a little from his glass so that it fell upon the woolen socks covering his feet while he sat crossed-legged. The man who came to take the empty glass away would lean toward him, perhaps to smell the sweetness on his breath. It was always there, and this seemed to satisfy them that they had reduced their captive to obedience. They would not risk giving him an overdose without Milverton's authority, and it seemed that Milverton was usually elsewhere.

After he had spent several nights battling against the drug's effects, the upper level of what he called his twilight sleep became easier to attain. In this state, Holmes knew that he had once heard the rumble of a man's breath. With their prisoner helpless, the guards usually spent the night sleeping on the wooden chair. This item of intelligence began to form the basis of their captive's plan. A night or two later, lying half-conscious, he heard something more. It would have meant little to most men, but to Sherlock Holmes it made clear a large part of the mystery of his abduction.

At first he was not quite sure, in the fog-like vapours of hyoscine, that he had truly heard it. Yet he knew that if it were real, it must come again. It seemed like the boom of the dreadful engine to which he was attached as he struggled to consciousness. He now heard it again, four times in quick succession. It was no engine, but a large clock. If it had struck four, he would wait until five to judge its direction. Yet, to his surprise, the four booms came again in much less than a minute. This time it had a deeper tone and, almost at once, he heard it four times more in a note higher than either of the other two. Holmes, the musician, composer, and author of a critique on the motets of Orlando Lassus, enjoyed the gift of perfect pitch. He had only to hear a sound in order to pick out its equivalent on a keyboard.

That night he had heard E natural four times, B flat in the octave below, and then G natural in the octave higher. No man ever knew the streets of London and their great buildings as he did. In campanology, those three bells and those intervals between them occur only in the striking of St. Sepulchre's, St. Paul's Cathedral, and the descant of St. Martin's-le-Grand. He woke next morning with the exultation of a child at Christmas. What might have been inaudible in the remote 'courtroom' or when the streets were crowded could be heard in the silent hours between the last drunkards shouting their way homeward and the carts at dawn making their way to market. He knew, as surely as if he had drawn lines of triangulation on a map, that he was in the grim and disused limbo of Newgate prison. The vaulted space forming the 'courtroom' was at the meeting of the four great passageways, like aisles and transepts under a cathedral tower.

Until a few months before, as my readers may recall, Newgate had been the most feared and fearful gaol in England's history, filled with many of the worst specimens of mankind. It was a detentional prison where they were held during their trials. Those condemned to death or corporal punishments remained until the dates of their executions or whatever form of penalty had been ordered. A corridor with fifteen death cells and the execution shed in the yard outside had a simple motto on its archway: 'Abandon hope, all ye who enter here.' Holmes now had not the least doubt that it was in one of these cells that he was held prisoner. No one in the world outside would think of searching for him in this disused fortress of despair.

His enemies had timed their revenge with devilish precision. Parliament and the City of London had resolved to pull down the ancient prison in Newgate Street and build the court of the Old Bailey on its site. The last man in the condemned cells had been hanged in 1901, as had the last woman, Ada Chard the baby-farmer. Other prisoners were transferred to nearby gaols. The building and its contents passed from the prison board to the city corporation. For several months, prior to demolition, it stood empty, 'in the hands of the contractors.' A supply of gas to the lamps was maintained and the unused gallows of the execution shed still remained in working order.

How easy it must have been for the contractors to pass the custody of the empty building to subcontractors in those last weeks. Henry Milverton and his accomplices had devised a poetic extermination for Sherlock Holmes, a warning to others who might interfere with the workings of a mighty criminal empire. Yet Holmes was not naive enough to believe that all this had been done merely to destroy him, when they might as easily have run him down in the street or dropped a boulder on his head. His death delighted these men, but it was a mere pastime that coincided with some greater plan. Behind the charade of a court and a Newgate hanging lay a criminal enterprise that might shake the entire world. It was something that perhaps only he had the power to prevent. Whatever the plot might be, it depended on a criminal gang having possession of the prison for some weeks or months. What the objective might be, Holmes could not at the moment deduce. But he swore to himself that he would find out.

The most curious aspect of his plight was that when sentence was pronounced upon him on the following day, he felt lighter in his heart than he had done since the nightmare began. It came as no shock to him, not even a surprise, to hear the ritual words in Henry Milverton's oily tones. 'You are to be taken back to the place whence you came and from thence to a place of lawful execution. And there you shall be hanged by the neck until you be dead.' Any other man chained to the wall of the condemned cell, with guards outside and within, far from help and with the gallows waiting in the yard, must surely have given up hope. Yet Holmes put his faith in one indisputable fact. The power of his mind, the strength of his reason, the observing and analytical machine that he became at such times, were stronger than all his captors put together.

The man whom they called the master-at-arms, a burly and grizzled fellow, led him away in handcuffs from the last act of the trial. This time he was not immediately returned to his cell, but taken in an opposite direction. The prisoner and his escort came to an iron-faced door topped by steel spikes. The master-at-arms produced a heavy key and opened the largest Bramah lock that Holmes had ever seen, drawing back its bronze bolt with a massive rumbling. They crossed the paved floor of a somber high-roofed lodge, from which it was possible to hear the sound of traffic in the street, and passed through a doorway leading to what had evidently been the prison governor's office. The walls were still hung with notices by the Court of Aldermen forbidding liquors to be brought into the prison or setting out rules for clerks and attorneys who were visiting their clients.

In a well-lit anteroom, where descriptions of prisoners were taken, an open cupboard displayed the irons worn by the notorious burglar, highwayman, and prison-breaker of a century before, Jack Shepherd—iron bars an inch and a half thick and fifteen inches long. Holmes noticed irons for the legs, about an inch in diameter and clasped with strong rivets. On the wall of the office there still hung two old paintings of the penal colony at Botany Bay. Yet his attention was held by three rows of faces arranged along the top of a low cupboard. They were the death masks of men and women who had been hanged at the prison for a hundred years past.

Henry Milverton was behind him now, pointing out a prize specimen among the masks. 'There, Mr. Holmes, is Courvoisier, publicly hanged more than sixty years ago for the murder of Lord William Russell. You will see that the brow is low, the lower part of the face sensual. The upper lip, like that of most of the group, is abnormally thick. As your lip will be, Mr. Holmes, for it is conges-tion caused by the process of hanging—or rather of strangling. You will observe that some, like Courvoisier, have died with their eyes open and some with them shut. Those whose necks are broken by the drop have their eyes closed, those who drop short and choke to death have them open, as yours will be, Mr. Holmes.'

Holmes said nothing, but he noticed for the first time a weighing machine in one corner of the room.

'You will oblige us,' said Milverton, 'by standing upon the scales. Your weight is of importance to the master-at-arms, so that the end may be as we wish it to be. Many people, Mr. Holmes, have looked forward to this spectacle and it would never do for your final appearance to be too brief. You must expect us to have some sport with you after you have put us to so much trouble. A short drop and a long dance for you, I fear, Mr. Sherlock Holmes.'

Holmes stood upon the metal plate of the machine but still said nothing. The grizzled brute, whom they called the master-at-arms, fiddled with the bronze disks of the weights—first he added one, then replaced it with a smaller one—until the metal arm of the balance oscillated slightly and was still. Milverton pretended to busy himself with some papers but as soon as the weighing was over he looked up.

'Good-bye, Mr. Holmes. We shall not meet again until the morning of the great occasion. It is the custom, is it not, to allow a man three clear Sundays before his execution? That we cannot do. However, it will be a week or more before some of our friends are here, so you may make whatever peace you can in that time with whatever gods you think may spare you their attention. There will come a point, however, when you will wake each morning not knowing whether this is—or is not—to be your last. A morning when you are merely allowed one more day to live will make you think yourself the luckiest man alive. Fancy that, Mr. Holmes! At such times, as your despair becomes unendurable, you will consider us as your dearest benefactors for allowing you one more brief day! You have no idea how well we shall get on!'

Holmes fixed the man with his sharp but steady gaze. Milverton held his eyes for a moment, then smirked and looked down at his papers.

The way back to the condemned cells was not by the route they had come. It led down an ill-lit corridor and over a covered bridge. There was a glimpse of four galleries of cells under a glass roof, all deserted and silent. Holmes and his escorts passed through an iron gate and along a small passage, paved with slate, beside an exercising ground that he calculated must border on Newgate Street. There was not an inch of that short journey that was not catalogued in his mind. I daresay he could have told you the number of paving slabs they had crossed, how many were chipped, and where the cracks were.

He noticed, a little beyond the bridge and the glass roof, a side opening with several sets of clothes or uniforms hanging upon wall-hooks. Next to it was a recess with a sink, three razors and brushes, a hand-mirror face-down upon a stone surface. At such moments, I had often observed, he became an invincible brain without a heart or the tremor of a nerve or a pang of affection. Perhaps it was as well for him that this should be so. As they came out under a covered arch he saw for the first time what lay beyond his opaque cell windows. It was a yard beyond reach of the sun with the cell block on one side. Its walls rose sleek as marble to what Wilde, the prisoner-poet, had called 'that little tent of blue which prisoners call the sky.'

Abandon hope. . . . The builders had chosen an apt text for the condemned block. Even a man who could free himself from the chain at his ankle, render himself invisible to the guard in his cell, open the prison locks on the outer door, spirit himself from the cell into the yard, might just as well have surrendered to the hangman. The smooth expanse of the great walls was almost unbroken. In the northwest corner, halfway from the ground to the summit was an old water tank, neglected since the days when it had provided the first water supply to the buildings below. Above it, just below the top of each wall ran a stout wooden axle set with sharpened steel wire. A man who attempted it would find that he could scarcely hang by as much as a finger without encountering the savage metal.

Holmes walked slowly between his guards, as if it were a great effort to move his legs in time with theirs. They did not hurry him. There was surely a satisfaction in showing him the hopelessness of his situation. He could only guess what part such men had played as common criminals before they put on the livery of Milverton's prison officers.

Along one wall of the yard, the paving had been dislodged by the sinking of the ground. There were single letters engraved on the stone at intervals, A G, an L, and an M and another G. Holmes did not need to be told that he was walking over the graveyard of men and women who had been hanged at the prison and whose bodies, mouldering and rotting in quicklime, caused this subsidence in the ground. If his escorts smiled as they passed, it was with amusement at the famous Sherlock Holmes now walking over his own grave. At one end of the yard he noticed a shed, like a small stable. Through its open doors he glimpsed a black platform on wheels. Thirteen steps led up to its top, which was large enough for several men to stand upon. Though no rope was coiled on the beam above it, this was plainly to be the means of his death. Holmes glanced at it and knew what the way ahead must be.

While he sat on the bed in his cell, one of the escorts locked the anklet to the links that chained him to the wall, removed his hand-cuffs, and left him to his own contemplations. There was no mirror in the cell. Holmes knew only by touch that a beard had begun to establish itself on his face and that his hair was unkempt. Such things mattered nothing to him just then. As he sat on the edge of the narrow wooden bed, his thoughts were far away. His formidable intelligence was tuned only to victory over his adversaries. Without intending it, they had now shown him a path to freedom. It was not a certain path, but it was the only one. Even before he could begin upon it, there was a battle to be won.

He took up his usual position, sitting cross-legged and silent at the head of the bed, his gaze concentrated upon whichever guard sat at the table in the far end of the cell. The man who kept watch was beyond the range of Holmes' capable and efficient fists but never beyond the reach of those unblinking and penetrating eyes.

THE CORPORAL OF HORSE

There were two men who took it in turns to watch him as he woke or slept. They had divided their duty so that each kept vigil for two days and then two nights alternately. At night they slept in the wooden chair, beyond the range of the chain that held his anklet.

Holmes gathered that the name of the first man was Crellin. He was tall with a lantern jaw, dark hair piled on his head like an old-fashioned courtier's wig, and a look of brutalised cunning. A movement of his mouth seemed at first to promise a skeptical smile. It was no more than a misalignment of the lips. Crellin might laugh, but he never smiled.

The other man was more slightly built, his complexion so deeply reddened by the sun, the skin so tight and shiny on the bones of his face, that he looked as if he had been boiled. Holmes heard him referred to as Mac. At a glance, this smaller man seemed the less pugnacious of the two. Holmes decided to put the matter to the test. It was not necessary that he should defeat all his captors. One might be enough.

He had once remarked that from a single drop of water the logician could infer the existence of the Niagara Falls or the Atlantic

Ocean without ever having seen either. It now seemed that by knowing the nickname of one jailer Sherlock Holmes proposed to find a path to freedom from the condemned cell of the most closely guarded prison in the world. The thing was so utterly impossible that not even Henry Milverton would feel that he needed to protect himself against it.

From the moment the warder who was his daytime keeper entered until the man left at dark, Holmes was the hawkfaced, cross-legged idol whose eyes drilled into the guard's mind and thoughts, scattering them like ninepins. I had seen him confront a practised trickster or a hardened scoundrel and with this same unblinking stare fix the unfortunate wretch for perhaps thirty seconds. None of them ever endured it longer. Some, like Professor Moriarty, tried to turn it to laughter, but the flame scorched them. To be burnt like an insect by such unblinking and brilliant fire for an entire day would beggar description! On the first occasion, Crellin glared back at the steady glitter of those eyes. He growled a threat, as if that settled the matter, and looked away. The eyes gave him no rest. Chained as he was, Sherlock Holmes pursued the sullen bully into the dark shadows of his mean soul.

Yet it was a waste of time. Crellin might squirm, but he would not squeal. He had taken Milverton's shilling and must do as he was told. After an hour he growled threats of coming to do for Holmes with his heavy fists, but he never dared to set foot within reach of the prisoner's chain.

Mac was a different case. The line of the mouth was far more sullen, but it was the self-doubting sullenness of the uneasy child. Perhaps, when he took the same shilling, he had not bargained on being the instrument that would prepare an innocent man for the hangman's noose. Not that Mac would compromise his own safety or risk his own skin to save him, but he squirmed far more readily than Crellin. The cross-legged inquisitor gave him not a moment's rest from the steady eyes. At first Mac pretended not to notice, but in the confined dimensions of the cell he could not help it. He got up and stood at the opaque window glass, for all the world as if he could see through it and admire the view. He turned his chair and sat sideways to the man he was guarding. He pretended to read. He clasped his hands behind his back and with head lowered paced an absurd eight-foot sentry-go across the cell and back, as if in deep thought. And then he turned to Holmes and shouted,

'Look somewhere else, will you? Look somewhere else, blast your eyes!'

But the man whom he must help to kill spoke not a word from Mac's entry at morning until his departure at evening. After his first two days it was plain that Mac dreaded the cell. Holmes had found a weakness in their scheme, not in chains or locks, or in hyoscine. It existed in the man they called Mac. The man's flaw was a tender conscience, and the poor devil dreaded that any of the others should detect it. Holmes could tell this by the way he loudly and unevenly, with his fellow jailers before entering the cell, laughed for Holmes to hear him and know that he cared nothing. Once inside, before the keen-eyed inquisitor, it was a different story.

Sherlock Holmes, for all his fame, was a mortal man. Neither I nor any other living soul was ever to know what terrors he may have felt in these long hours. Yet not by a word or the blink of an eyelid did he betray them. There are those who will scoff and tell you that all this was the bravado of a schoolbook hero. It was nothing of the kind but, rather, his inner concentration on the nub of a plan formed in a mind that was hard as a diamond and by thoughts clear as perfect crystal. He must judge to the minute when the silence was to be broken. There would be one chance and one chance only. The moment came on the fourth day, in the middle of a long afternoon. His words were spoken loudly but not too loudly. The tone, however, was sharp as the crack of a circus whip and Mac jumped at the sound of them.

'Listen to me, McIver!'

Perhaps it was the sound of his own name, spoken by a man who could never have heard it used, that broke the fellow's composure. Cross-legged and still, Sherlock Holmes spoke again. His voice was too soft to be heard beyond the cell, and it now seemed intended to comfort the man who had been set to keep watch on him.

'I think, Corporal McIver of the 21st Lancers, that it is time for you and me to exchange a few words.'

The reddened skin grew tight as a mask on the cheekbone, and the elongated eyes looked straight at Holmes, stilled by fear, like a rat before a basilisk.

'I understand entirely,' Holmes continued. 'The first thought in your mind is that Mr. Milverton—or by whatever name your master calls himself—will cut your throat once he knows that you have revealed your identity to me. You are, or rather were, Corporal McIver of the 21st Lancers, a veteran of the cavalry charge against the Sudanese rebels at the Battle of Omdurman, lately discharged from the Army as the victim of a distressing medical complaint— Egyptian ophthalmia. All you wish now is to marry your childhood sweetheart. But that is not easy, is it?'

Holmes had softened him up carefully over many hours. Now the mesmerised incomprehension in McIver's eyes turned to outright fear.

'You cannot have set eyes upon me until you saw me in this place,' he said in a stage whisper, fearful of being heard by those outside the cell, 'and I know nothing of you. You cannot tell me who I am.'

'Quite so,' said Holmes soothingly. 'However, let me assure you I know enough—if not all—about you. The 21st Lancers, the Battle of Omdurman, your discharge from the Army on medical grounds. The woman you had hoped to marry. I know more than enough to have left a hidden message already, scratched somewhere and somehow—in the plaster of a wall perhaps. When this building is dismantled, as it soon will be, such a message including your name would lead the police straight to you. It has even been known for a prisoner in this very gaol—Benson was his name—to leave a dampened paper message on the floor where one of the guards would tread on it unwittingly and just as unwittingly lose it on the dry pavement outside these walls. Have no fear. I am sure you have been warned against such tricks. There are far better ones than that, believe me.'

'Mr. Milverton knows of all your tricks,' said McIver hastily.

'Not quite all of them, I think,' said Holmes amiably. 'What Mr. Milverton does know, however, is that once in the hands of the police, you would betray him and his entire conspiracy. And you know perfectly well, Corporal McIver, that were I to say as much to him as I am saying to you now, you would be dead before this evening's sun had set.'

'What can you tell?'

'Enough to end your life even before mine. If your master knew that I had identified you and had already taken measures to pass on that knowledge, you would not live the hour. He would not dare allow it. Whether I inform him or not is a matter for you.'

The eyes that had fled from Holmes's scrutiny before could not bear now to leave his face. In a sudden flood of panic, the discharged soldier had fallen victim completely to Holmes's precept that 'What you can do in this world is a matter of no consequence. The question is what can you make people believe that you have done.' He had not half finished with the wretch, while McIver struggled to imagine how a total stranger could have known so much about him.

'When you were invalided home from Egypt,' Holmes continued, 'and discharged from your regiment, you were thrown upon your own resources. Had you held the rank of sergeant, a pension might have been procured for you. Yet a sergeant is, shall we say, *rara avis in terra*—a rare bird. If I am not mistaken, a cavalry troop consists of some sixty troopers plus six corporals and one sergeant. You were not he. It is not to be wondered at that you have failed to find regular employment since your return. Your malady sits plainly upon you.'

As Holmes was talking, McIver's face showed the contending emotions of a man who feels himself ever more securely snared and yet hopes that the snare may break and set him free.

'You may guess, Mr. Sherlock Holmes,' he said, mingling scorn with trepidation, 'but you cannot know. Mr. Milverton would see your tale for what it is.'

'I do not guess,' said Holmes mildly. 'I never guess. Mr. Milverton knows that, to his cost. You appear to forget that while you have watched me in the past few days, I have also watched you. You are a mere prison guard, but it is my profession to observe. Your name was easy to discover. Indeed, at my arrival I heard distinctly one of your accomplices call you Mac.'

McIver got up from his chair and stood as if he might advance upon his prisoner. 'That is nothing!'

'In itself. . . .' There was something like steel in Holmes's voice that made the man sit down again. 'In itself it is nothing. However, I have had ample opportunity of observing you, even when you were out of earshot. I had a distinct view on the second day, as I was led back down the corridor. The man I believe you call Crellin stood behind you and spoke. You turned to him. He had spoken a name—or a word—to make you turn. I assumed it was your name and, of course, lipreading is necessary in my walk of life. Indeed, I have written a little monograph on the production of sound from labial distortion. From the chuckle to the scream.'

McIver was staring at him now, as if he dared not miss a word.

'Well, now,' Holmes went on, 'I had no doubt that the first syllable of the word spoken by Crellin was 'Mac.' I would expect that anyway, for I had heard you called by it. Try forming it for yourself. There is a characteristic compression of the lips followed by a sideways opening of the mouth. Crellin's lips then made the shape of an 'i.' This is easily read, being the letter which opens the mouth higher and narrower than any other. Quite unmistakable. Then his upper teeth touched his lower lip harder than they would to make an 'f.' Therefore, the sound could only be a 'v.' Finally, the lips protruded in a flute-like way and the skin on his throat was strained a little tighter. To the trained eye, this could only be 'er.' It was not difficult.'

'Very clever!' The man was shaken but still scornful.

'And then there are your boots,' said Holmes.

'What of 'em?'

'Army boots,' Holmes said, 'still worn by you after your discharge.'

'Any man could buy boots like these. Workmen's boots, more like than army ones.'

'Indeed,' said Holmes indulgently. 'However, such boots are made of black pimpled leather and are worn as such by civilian workmen. Yet consider this. Any man who has been a soldier knows that the first command to the unfortunate recruit is to take a hot iron and to iron out the pimples of the toe caps so that they are perfectly smooth. They can then be polished for the parade ground until, if you will forgive the cliché, the poor recruit can see his face in them. Your boots are not those bought by a civilian worker. Rather, they are boots worn by a man who has lately been a soldier and can afford no others.'

For some reason, the revelation about his boots shook McIver more thoroughly than the discovery of his name.

'Why are you not afraid?' he asked Holmes suddenly. 'I do not understand it.'

Holmes smiled at him, the lips thin and hard.

'If I were afraid, not you or any man should know it. For fear merely begets fear, and that would never do. Allow me to proceed. Boots of that kind are not worn by a sergeant, whose footwear gleams all over and is of an easier type. Therefore, you could only be a corporal or a private trooper. Oh, do not ask me how I knew you were a horseman. Merely watch the way you walk, when next you pass a plate-glass window. You have recently done some years of foreign service. Your complexion tells one at a glance. I deduce that you went with Lord Kitchener's expedition to reconquer the Sudan six years ago. A soldier who suffers, as you do, from Egyptian ophthalmia can scarcely dispute that. All the other mounted regiments of that force were Egyptian levees. Any man who reads his morning newspaper knows that the 21st Lancers were drafted in to lead the charge at Omdurman and that they were the only British mounted regiment sent for that purpose.'

It was with some gratification that Holmes saw the man bow his head and stare at the floor of the cell to hide his confusion.

'Solar discoloration of the epidermis is a phenomenon essential to the work of the criminal expert,' Holmes assured him quietly. 'In your case, the effects of the Egyptian sun have been prolonged and have hardly begun to fade. The inner surfaces of your wrists remain white, as does a thin margin along the hairline of your forehead, which was covered by your helmet. There is a marked degree of permanency in the burning elsewhere. I judge that this would not have been acquired in less than five or six years, which approximates to the departure of the 21st Lancers for service in the Sudan campaign. You are evidently a man of some capability, and such a man does not usually serve in a single posting for six years without rising to the rank of corporal or, at any rate, of acting corporal. There are significant losses among a regiment overseas for six years, more from sickness than from battle, and significant vacancies for promotion. In either rank you would be referred to as Corporal McIver. Your modest advancement suggests to me a satisfactory character as a soldier and that you have lately turned to crime from particular necessity and not from mere viciousness.'

The unhappy wretch looked up at him again, desperate now to prove his tormentor mistaken on any point at all. If he could knock down one of Holmes's deductions, perhaps the rest would follow like skittles.

'You cannot tell why I came home. You are no doctor.'

'Indeed not,' said Holmes in the same quiet and sympathetic voice. 'Yet you bear unmistakable marks of a disorder upon the lids and rims of your eyes. For many years the contagion known as Egyptian ophthalmia has been brought back by soldiers who have served in that country and have had the misfortune—or imprudence—to mix there with certain forms of low company. Moreover, I have observed that when your duty is to guard me at night, you take a white tablet from each of two bottles, evening and morning. They are plainly homeopathic powders, which are customarily compressed into tablets for convenience. My eyesight is not deficient, and in passing I have read the labels on the bottles.'

By looking at McIver now, it was evident the fight had gone from him.

'*Argentum nitricum* and *Hepar sulphuris*,' said Holmes, 'are each admirable treatments for a number of complaints but are seldom combined, as the good Dr. Ruddock tell us in his "Vade Mecum," except in the treatment of this ophthalmic condition or of an ulcerated throat. It seems obvious that you do not suffer from the latter, and therefore it follows, from simple observation, that you are a prey to the former. Soldiering has been taken from you as a result of your complaint and you have been returned to your native country.'

He paused and McIver said nothing. Holmes continued his explanation.

'For some reason you have felt obliged to turn to villainy, a profession to which it seems you have proved to be singularly ill-suited. It cannot be from destitution, for you showed a good character as a soldier and your indisposition is not such as to preclude you from all employment. What is the thing that most often makes a man of your age and condition act, contrary to character, in return for the promise of a substantial sum of money? Why, surely, the most common reason is to provide for a future with a woman whom you love. You have not long returned and have had little time to find a partner for life. This suggests that you knew one another before you sailed to Egypt and that she has waited faithfully for you during your absence. Now, how long do you suppose she would be safe if Milverton settled accounts with you?'

That last thrust went home. There was silence for a full minute. Holmes had said all that he proposed to say and did not break it. At last McIver looked up.

'What will you do?' he asked, and his voice shook. He no longer doubted that if Holmes spoke to Crellin or Milverton, he would most certainly be dead before sunset, perhaps after such retribution as should make that death itself a blessing. Holmes was in no hurry to reply. He waited a moment longer. The cross-legged graven image sitting at the head of the bed lacked only the curled pipe that he used to smoke in this posture in our Baker Street rooms.

'No,' said Holmes at length, 'I believe the question is, Corporal McIver, what will you do?'

The man had stumbled into a quicksand of panic and knew not how to get out.

'I cannot save you, Mr. Holmes. How can I? I am searched every time I leave and enter. For days I am not allowed to leave at all.'

'I do not suggest you should save me. In any case, I do not fear my death. Yet I might ask for those dignities and comforts that are the right of any man, even one under sentence.'

He told me that there was no mistaking the relief on McIver's face. The man was far more weak than wicked and now saw that he might escape, whatever the fate of his prisoner.

'What comforts?' he asked, suddenly eager to know the price.

'Water,' said Holmes, 'a glass of water that is free from any drug, a glass which stands upon your table and which you will bring me to drink from when I require it.'

'You shall have that, by all means. You might have had that anyway, by merely asking.'

'And then,' said Holmes thoughtfully, 'confined as I am, held by a chain and deprived of movement, I feel it a toll on my physical well-being.'

'I cannot free you from that chain, Mr. Holmes!'

'I would not ask it. So far as you are my friend, I am yours, and I do not willingly put my friends in danger.'

At this, he half thought McIver might kneel and say, 'Bless you, Mr. Holmes,' or some other stage nonsense.

'I feel a dreadful lethargy,' he explained. 'Food sits on my stomach, kills my appetite, and I sense a great lassitude.'

McIver was far out of his depth as he stared back.

'What is it that you want, sir?'

'More than anything,' said Holmes slowly, 'I should like the most ordinary remedy in the world. I have no means of escape and you cannot set me free. Yet for as long as I am permitted to live, I should like a packet of charcoal biscuits every day. You may obtain them at any pharmacy or any druggist. I believe they would do me great good.'

After what had passed between them, this request appeared so trivial that McIver seemed to doubt his good fortune. How could a condemned man who nonetheless held the corporal at his mercy ask for so little?

'Is that all?' he said hesitantly.

'For the moment,' said Holmes. 'There may be other little things. Rest assured, I shall not put you in danger. What should I gain by that?'

McIver almost laughed with relief as he spoke.

'Of course I shall bring a store of charcoal biscuits, a supply for a week or two. That is nothing. I can bring them as if they were for my own use. You shall have water whenever you want it.'

Then his face darkened a little.

'How do I know you will say nothing of what you have discovered?'

'You have my word,' Holmes said icily. 'I have never broken it yet, for good or evil, not even to Professor Moriarty and his kind. Besides which, to betray you would not save me. So long as you are obedient in these little matters, you shall be safe.'

That night, before he left, McIver brought the glass of water, unseen by the others. Crellin, knowing nothing of this, followed a few minutes later with the hyoscine solution. Holmes took that glass in his hand while the bully moved the bedside chair and table from his reach. Then Crellin turned and, standing over his prisoner, watched him drink down the glass. No one who had seen Holmes's sleight-of-hand with far more difficult objects could doubt that the contents of the glass he had drunk was water. The hyoscine, no more than half a glass, had been disposed of under cover of the blanket.

That night, after the gas had guttered and the glow of the mantel had dwindled like a dying sun, it was Crellin who slept, the man's bulk against the table, while the oil lamp spluttered and faded. Almost silently in the darkness, Holmes felt for the seams and the threads of the cheap mattress. Before dawn, with teeth and nails, he had made an opening no more than a few inches long and well concealed in the fold of the canvas beading. Even had they found it, the rent he had made in the material might have seemed like wear and tear. Yet they never searched. He had begun to depend upon this. After all, he was a prisoner whom they saw chained to the wall, drugged by night, with the eyes of his guards constantly upon him, in a cell that was locked, inside and out, by keys always beyond his reach. Nothing was passed to him but food and drink. Even the food was first cut into pieces so that he need not be allowed the use of a knife or a fork. What could he have that would be worth searching for?

When the work was done, Sherlock Holmes lay back and thought of the mountain he must climb. To escape from the cell was only a beginning. There was no way out through the prison building with the first guards a few feet outside the cell door and many more beyond them. The sixty feet of smooth granite that rose from the yard were his only hope. His enemies knew much of Sherlock Holmes the public man, but his private life was as secret as only he could make it. His adversaries knew little of Sherlock Holmes and his chemical researches and nothing whatever of Sherlock Holmes the disciple of Paganini and scholar of polyphonic music. Nor did they know of him as a mountaineer who had attempted the so-called Widow-Maker glacier of the Matterhorn. He had yet to conquer it, but he was one of few who had come back alive from the attempt.

It was not in any of these accomplishments that he now placed his hope, but in another area of expertise. No man in the world was as well-informed in the minutiae of sensational and criminal literature as Sherlock Holmes. His extensive library, shelved on the walls of our Baker Street rooms, would have been so much dry reading to those who sought his destruction. Yet he knew and could recall every page that was of interest to him.

Somewhere in all those pages were two or three devoted to Henry Williams, a childhood chimney-sweep and an adult burglar, sixty years ago. Holmes had read of him and visited the old man on his deathbed. There it was that Henry Williams, whose adventures grace the twentieth chapter of the *Newgate Chronicles*, imparted to my friend the secrets of his craft. For Henry Williams, all those years ago, had lain in the death cell of this same great prison when burglary was still a hanging matter. And Henry Williams had escaped the gallows by becoming the one man who had scaled those fearful walls of Newgate Gaol.

QUIET AS THE GRAVE

It was only the moral insanity of Milverton and his accomplices that had allowed Sherlock Holmes a lease on life until the 'witnesses' of his murder should arrive to enjoy a gallows tableau of vengeance. Brief though the time left to him might be, and however urgent the necessary action, he knew that he must wait until the conditions were exactly right for what he intended. Once again, he would have one chance—and one chance only. He required a night when Crellin was the warder in his cell after McIver had carried out his evening duties and withdrawn. Holmes wished the corporal of horse no harm. McIver had been essential to him, the one man over whom he could exercise command. Whatever this ex-trooper suspected, he dared not report it to Crellin or Milverton, for fear of the story that Holmes had to tell. Captive and captor were indissolubly bound by their pact.

Two days later a half-caught murmur from one of the guards in their purloined prison board uniforms suggested to Holmes that Henry Milverton himself was in Newgate that night. If Milverton was there, the master-at-arms and the execution shed might have been prepared for the next morning. Holmes knew that this night was the only one on which he could count. He would be free or he would die in his own way. If death was the choice, he would take with him Milverton and as many of his accessories as possible. Nine years earlier he had faced Professor Moriarty with the same resolve at the falls of Reichenbach. He remarked then that his own life was an easy price to pay for the destruction of such evil.

McIver had done his duty in the cell by day and was to be one of the two men to keep watch in the corridor that night, sleeping by turns but ready to assist Crellin in the cell if need be. Just before the change of guards, the corporal brought a glass of the sweet and oily hypnotic.

'The water, if you please,' said Holmes quietly. 'I find the taste of this draft quite as abominable as its effects.'

The man's nerve withered in his presence. He could not meet the dark and penetrating gaze, perhaps knowing that murder was intended in the morning. He turned away to fill the water glass. For the benefit of anyone else who might chance to see him, Holmes raised the glass of hyoscine to his lips, then threw back his head as if to swallow the contents and be done with it. Before McIver could turn, in one flowing downward movement of his arm to suggest exhaustion, he had tipped the eggcupful of fluid between the wall and the bed. The sickly mixture had merely wet his lips to give off its sour-treacle odour. McIver brought the glass of water. Whether he suspected what had become of the drug, Holmes never knew. Yet, with the prisoner chained and watched in a locked cell, what did the sleeping draught matter? It was intended to prevent a condemned man from giving trouble.

Holmes had been careful never to give trouble.

'My time is short and I think we may not speak again,' he said softly to the corporal, handing back the glass. 'You are a weak and foolish man but not, I think, a wicked one. From now on you must follow your conscience. I daresay I shall never be in a position to help you, but, should it happen, you may depend upon it that I will do my best to set you free.'

McIver's eyes betrayed his helplessness and he murmured even more softly in his turn.

'You must not speak to me now, sir. You must not, if you wish me well.'

Holmes smiled. It was the second time that McIver had called him 'sir,' the instinctive deference of the old soldier to his commander. Given a few more days, he might have turned this jailer into an ally.

'One more thing,' he said quietly. 'On no account enter this cell tomorrow morning before others have done so. Mind you see to that.'

It was as much as he could do for the frightened corporal of horse. Perhaps it was because they had heard something about the hour of his death that the others seemed a little more careless with him that night. It must have seemed to them that they had only to keep an unconscious man safely in his cell for another eight or nine hours. Perhaps soon after dawn, in the presence of Milverton and his criminal associates, three warders and the master-at-arms would drag their half-conscious captive to the execution shed twenty yards away across the exercise yard.

Crellin entered to find Holmes already lying on his side with the upper blanket drawn over him. The man locked the door with his bunch of keys, returned it to his belt, and made a perfunctory search of the prisoner. An oily sweetness of the drug hung in the close air and the jailer's nostrils could detect it. Neither man spoke. For his part, Holmes sensed the customary odour of drink on this ruffian's breath. Crellin inspected the manacle on the left ankle of his prisoner and pulled hard against the fastening on the wall to check its strength. He crossed the room to the wooden chair on which he had sat during every night of his vigil, in profile, with his back to the wall, his right arm resting on the bare wooden table beside him.

Sherlock Holmes had calculated his reach as a matter of simple mathematics. It was too short to touch Crellin. The chain allowed him five feet, enough to reach the little alcove behind him with its washing basin and drain. In the other direction, by lying flat, he could add a further six feet and at least two feet more for his extended arms. Measuring the paving tiles beside his bed by rule of thumb and allowing for the width of the floor, he had calculated that he would be almost two feet short of the chair on which Crellin sat. Henry Milverton did not make the mistake of underestimating his captive. The jailers would always be beyond his range.

Crellin lit his warder's night lamp, which Holmes had identified at first sight as the 'Hesperus' model made by Jones & Willis of Birmingham. It was lit or extinguished without any need to remove the glass chimney. The reservoir when full might last for several hours, but on previous nights it had guttered and faded after no more than two. As on all those other nights, Crellin now came closer and shone the lamp on the sleeping figure of the prisoner. Satisfied by what he saw and sure that it was safe to sleep, he went back and set the lamp down on the tiles beside his chair. Before sitting down, he went through the usual ritual of crossing the cell and pulling down the draw chain beside the gaslight on the opposite wall. Behind the three glass fishtails of its shade, the double flame dwindled to a dying glow. Without a glance at the sleeping figure under the blanket, he went back and stood by his chair to extinguish the second double gas lamp above him. He turned down the wick on the Hesperus oil lamp and positioned it beside his chair again, perhaps eight inches away. The cell was in shadow, no better lit now than by the gentlest nursery nightlight.

Sherlock Holmes lay motionless, waiting impatiently rather than fearfully to begin his work. Unless he could extinguish the low flame of the conical burner, his hopes were at an end. Twice in the next hour one of the men outside shone a lantern through the spy hole of the cell. The path of light missed Crellin, nodding on his chair, but illuminated the prisoner's bed and the upper half of the little alcove behind it. There was no sound from the passage, and during the half hour that followed, the light did not appear again. If ever a man possessed his soul in patience, it was Sherlock Holmes in the depth of that night. Twice more, far beyond the prison walls, the bell of St. Sepulchre's tolled and the deeper notes of the great cathedral followed it.

He knew to the inch and to the minute what must be done. Like all drunkards, Crellin would fall at first into a deep sleep that would leave him insensible for half the night. Then he would become restless and, finally, would wake suddenly and without warning. During the first of these phases the plan must be carried out. As Holmes listened, he heard the breathing grow slower and deeper, almost dwindling into silence. The man's head remained pillowed on his arm, which in turn still rested on the table beside him.

During his first hours in the cell Holmes had reckoned its dimensions as nineteen feet long, by eight feet wide and seven feet high. One thousand and sixty-four cubic feet. Some of that capacity was taken up by furnishings and fittings, notably a solid three-foot-square stone table at the far end and the wooden bed. The total space remaining was about a thousand and fifty cubic feet. He had even estimated the capacity of the wooden chair, now removed beyond his reach for the night. It seemed designed for the death cell, its joints being carefully dovetailed, without a single nail that might be used as a key or the condemned man's means of self-destruction.

As for the fittings, the four fishtail gaslights, a pair on each of the long walls, were of the common type with a Sugg-Letherby's No. 1 burner. Each of the four would be fed by ten cubic feet of gas an hour. A slight odour of spirit as they were lit had assured Sherlock Holmes that they were fed by that cheaper type of fuel known as water-gas, commonly used in public buildings. If released unlit, its high concentration of carbon monoxide would be enough to poison almost all the air in the cell by the end of sixty minutes. Those who breathed it might not be dead at the end of the hour, but they would never regain consciousness unaided. Yet even had his enemies thought Holmes capable of reaching the draw chains of the burners, they knew that he must be the first to die.

Among the volumes frequently taken down from his Baker Street bookshelves by my friend were the varied works of Dr. Daniel Haldane of Edinburgh, including *Haldane on Poisons*. Newgate prison, like most such institutions, tendered for the cheapest sources of fuel. These included this old-fashioned water-gas piped from a mains supply. It had once been produced by the decomposition of water, now often replaced by the use of petroleum as its origin, which gave it that spirituous odour on lighting. Its economic brightness was caused by the high concentration of carbon monoxide. Its use was more easily and carefully regulated in old and ill-ventilated public buildings than in private homes. It was seldom supplied to private citizens because of a greater danger of explosion if it should be misused.

It was the duty of the two guards in the corridor to shine a lamp through the spy hole of the cell door from time to time to make sure that all was well within. Holmes had noticed in the past night or two that they did this every half hour or so to begin with and then, as they took their chance to sleep, they seemed content to shine the beam on the prisoner's bed at intervals of an hour or more. He waited until one of the men outside had shone the lamp through the spy hole. It was past midnight and he judged that it would be the best part of an hour before they did that again.

No man ever moved as silently and with such economy of movement as Sherlock Holmes. With no more sound than a shadow he stripped off his shirt and held it in one hand. In the other hand he carried the light steel ankle chain clear of the floor so that it made no more noise than a silk rope. At the limit of the chain he stared down at Crellin, several feet away. The man, now palefaced from drink, was sleeping so deeply that his breathing was scarcely audible. There was a sickly perspiration on his forehead and his mouth sagged open. Holmes knelt silently and then measured his length across the cold paving of the tiled floor, reaching his arms at full stretch toward the Hesperus lamp by Crellin's chair. The bully heard no more sound than if a bird had glided overhead.

My friend's calculations were correct. The lamp stood about a foot beyond the tips of his fingers. Using the buttons of the shirt cuffs to link the arms together as a lasso, he held the garment by its tails and cast it like a frail noose. It hit the glass chimney silently but slithered down without effect. For the first time the measured and controlled beat of Sherlock Holmes's heart began to quicken. He cast again and this time saw the cotton arms snag on the top of the lamp's glass chimney. Controlling his breath, as if for fear of waking the guard, he shook and worked the loop of cloth gently until he saw it slide down the far side of the glass to encircle the lamp at its base.

His remarkable hearing was tuned to every nuance in Crellin's breathing. He knew that he must now draw the lamp toward him without rousing the sleeping warder. The Hesperus lamp had been constructed so that the oil and the wick sat in a smooth metal bowl that formed its base. Yet to drag smooth metal roughly toward him would cause a rasping on the tiled floor that might wake the sleeper.

Crellin gulped air into his throat and Holmes stopped at once. He waited until the sound of the man's breathing was regular again and then tilted the lamp a little by pulling on the cotton noose. Only the smooth and rounded edge of its metal base now touched the tiles as it ran in a series of three brief crescents, as if on the rim of a wheel. It made no more sound than the feet of a rat hurrying across the dark yard outside. Once only in the next ten minutes did Crellin shift against the table with another heaving breath.

Holmes eased the lamp quietly toward him and still there was no further movement from his guard. Presently his fingers touched the warm metal of the lamp base. As he drew back to the darkness of his bed, he held in his hands a treasure greater than the wealth of kings.

Without hesitation he carried the lamp silently into the little alcove with its basin and drain, where he turned down the wick as low as he dared without extinguishing the flame. Then he heard the movement of the metal cover on the spy hole and had just time to slip back and draw the blanket over him on the bed before a tunnel of watery light illuminated the cell. He thought that he had little more to fear from this hourly inspection. Two men in the corridor guarded the cell door that night. One was McIver. The other was either the brutal master-at-arms or one of his assistants. When two men performed such a duty, it was the weaker who was given the chore of an hourly inspection while the other slept. He had no doubt, in this case, that the weaker was McIver.

In the faint light that illuminated the cell from the alcove, he moved toward the draw chain controlling the supply of gas to the fishtails on the far wall, just on the near side of Crellin's chair. The chains were closer to him than the lamp had been, but higher on the wall. The ankle chain was too short for his purpose, but by turning his body sideways he could reach a point a foot from the wall and a foot short of the metal pull. With a quiet breath he flicked the cotton noose of the shirt at its full length until he caught the chain and started it swinging like a pendulum against the wall. Keeping the metal links free of the wall, he flicked it harder, so that it swung further away from him and came further back.

The extent of its nearer swing was eight inches short of his stretched fingers, as he measured it by sight, then six inches as he flicked it again, then four. Four inches would doom him as surely as four miles. Then the thin metal links brushed his fingertips, but he lost them again. And then, as it came swinging back, he snatched with all the energy of his being and just held it. Now he had only to draw gently on the thin chain. A moment later, he heard the first whisper of escaping gas issuing from the double jet above Crellin's head as he slept.

The two fish tails on the nearer wall were more easily within his range, but it had been necessary to make sure of the more distant ones first. With a single flick of the cotton shirt he caught the swinging links. Silently he pulled at this chain controlling the burners behind the fishtails. The whisper of water-gas became a rush. Much was still in the hands of fate but now only one path lay ahead of him, for better or for worse. Stripping the rough canvas cover from the prison pillow, he arranged the under-blanket and the pillow to give some semblance of a sleeping figure beneath the thin upper layer. Enough to satisfy McIver. Then he groped in the thin mattress for the packets of medicinal charcoal that the corporal had brought him.

Lighter than air, the whispering gas was filling the upper layers of the cell and time was beginning to run against him. The length of the chain at his ankle allowed him to move into the alcove with its basin and drain, where the flame of the oil lamp still wavered. In a few moments he must extinguish it. Holmes knelt down where the waste pipe ran into a gully that led to the grating of the drain outside. However faint and tainted, it was the one supply of air. Using the canvas pillow cover, he worked quickly to form a hood that might be worn like a surgeon's mask, tied by its tapes behind his head. It was common knowledge from his own experiments that charcoal was the best air filter, absorbing the poisonous compounds of gas. How much it would absorb or with what effect, only the next hour would tell. As he was making his preparations the bell of St. Sepulchre's tolled three times, as if hurrying on the dawn.

Now I must break a confidence that is no longer of great matter. Sherlock Holmes contributed much to chemistry and science in general but did not care to do so under his own name. He intended that his enemies should have no idea of these interests. The world did not know that under the name of the chemist Hunter he had contributed a paper, 'On the Effects of Pressure on the Absorption of Gases by Charcoal,' to the *Journal of the Chemical Society* in 1871, where the world may still read it. In his study of history he had been much taken by the startling proposal of Lord Cochrane in 1812 to defeat Napoleon three years before Waterloo by an invasion of France under cover of 'sulphur ships.' To effect this, however, the attackers must be protected by a mask of some kind—and there was none. However, my friend had corresponded with the late Dr. John Tyndall in 1878, following that great man's invention of a respirator. This enabled firemen to breathe for thirty minutes or more in smoke that would otherwise have killed them, and allowed coal miners to survive who must otherwise have been suffocated by gas.

Dr. Tyndall's respirator consisted of a hood attached to a metal cylinder or pipe, packed with charcoal, surrounded by a layer of cotton wool, moistened with glycerine, and fitted with a piece of wire gauze at the end to hold the pad and the charcoal in place.

Holmes turned down the wick and took the extinguished Hesperus lamp. He removed its glass lantern. Working with the deft fingers of a craftsman, he found the two buttons of the screw heads that tightened the metal wick holder to the base and shielded the reservoir of fuel. He undid them and carefully drew the metal sheath from its base. It tapered to a hole at the top, round which he could just measure forefinger and thumb. It was enough. Further down was a slot that admitted air to the base of the wick.

Though time was short, Holmes worked characteristically, always with haste but never in a hurry. Within the metal cylinder of the wick holder he formed a lining of loosened woolen padding from the mattress. Though he had no pure glycerine, it was a principal ingredient of the soft soap allowed him. He used the soap and a palmful of water to moisten the cotton waste at the open end of the metal cone and the lower air slot, sufficient to catch grosser particles of carbon in the air. The broken biscuits of Mostyn's Absorbant Medical Charcoal, like small pebbles, then filled the metal cone through which he must draw breath.

Using the water jug again, he moistened the canvas pillow cover and formed it into a hood about his head. His mouth and nostrils were enclosed in the larger end of the conical wick holder, the wet canvas about his head forming a crude seal against contaminated air. Then he lay on the chill stone of the tiles, the tapered end of the metal wick holder directed to the waste-pipe hole at the end of the gutter that ran from the basin. Whatever air reached him from the yard outside would lose some of its impurities in his makeshift filter. So would the gas that began to fill the cell. He held fast to the hope that the floor of that alcove was almost the last area that the silent and swirling deadliness of the carbon monoxide would reach.

If it were my purpose to make a fine hero of Sherlock Holmes, I might say that he lay on the cold tiles, breathing steadily but economically through the device he had fashioned, and that he prayed. Yet one had only to be in his company for five minutes to recognise in him the most perfect reasoning and observing machine the world has ever seen. He was not devoid of faith or human warmth, but at that moment, if ever, only cold reason and critical observation would save him.

Once he had told me that logic alone would lead a man to the deep truths of religion. Then, again, he asked what is the meaning of this circle of misery, violence, and fear in which we live? It must tend to some end, or else our universe is ruled by chance, which is unthinkable. But to what end? There, he said, is the great outstanding perennial problem to which human reason is as far from an answer as ever.

How long he lay there, the cold striking like a steel blade to his bones, I never knew. He heard St. Sepulchre's deep notes twice more, at least, and the cathedral bell that followed. He saw a flickering reflection beyond the alcove, a lantern shining through the spy hole. But he had calculated the risks with his customary inhuman precision. Whoever looked through the spy hole would see a shape under the blankets and, knowing that Crellin was keeping guard, would also know that the shape must be that of the prisoner. Had there been no guard in the cell, they would have looked him over thoroughly at short intervals.

In the iron chill of that night Holmes waited for the pale yellow lantern light to play again on the wall by the alcove. But he had seen it for the last time. He waited and listened. As he did so, if he is to be believed, Sherlock Holmes soothed his nerves by rehearsing in his mind a book that had shaped much of his character since he first read it at the age of ten. It was no fairy story of giants or goblins but the *Prior Analytics* of Aristotle. 'A syllogism is a form of words in which, when certain assumptions are made, something other than what has been assumed necessarily follows from the fact that the assumptions are such. . . .'

Cold reason told him that the plan must work, but reason may fly away or be flawed in the lonely dark hours of such a night. An undetected current of air might draw the gas astray from Crellin and toward the alcove. Holmes had calculated, as surely as any hangman, the direction in which his victim's body would fall. When the muscles no longer held the frame, Crellin would slide from the chair. He could not fall to his right, because the table would stop him. If he fell to the left, his body lying on the floor with the keys at its belt would surely be within the prisoner's reach. It was most likely that Crellin would do neither but would fall forward. In that case, if the fall was forward and slightly to the left, Sherlock Holmes might be saved. If it was somewhat to the right, he was certainly destroyed. In the gas-filled cell, he would have become his own executioner. It was not a matter of cold reason, after all, but the spin of a gambler's wheel.

Such precision of thought would have been preposterous in any other man who lay perspiring on the cold tiles with a fear that at any moment he might scent the faint rotting smell of water-gas seeping through the suffocating wad of charcoal. If Crellin had not fallen by then, Holmes was as good as dead. Yet Holmes was not any other man. He was surely the only one alive who might have escaped from such captivity. St. Sepulchre's tolled again and then he heard a thud, easily audible in the alcove but not in the corridor beyond the thick walls and stout door of the cell. At that moment, he who had breathed so economically in the past hours stopped altogether and held his breath as he waited for the louder clatter of the chair. But there was no clatter. Crellin alone had fallen. After lying immobile for so long, Holmes moved with the speed of a cloud crossing the moon.

Only the reflection of the night sky through the uncurtained window glass lit the cell. He took the deepest breath of air his lungs would hold and crossed the threshold. Through the swirling spirit odour of gas, he saw the dark shape of Crellin's body. The man might still be alive or already dead. Had he fallen toward the table, the keys on his belt would be far out of reach. Then there was nothing but the hope that prisoner and jailer might die together in a blast that would shake Newgate Street. The odds were finely balanced. Yet on this occasion, Fortune and mathematics had favored the brave. Crellin's body had toppled away from the table to the left, toward Holmes, head and shoulders within reach of the ankle chain and the extended arms.

With aching lungs Holmes held his breath and drew the heavy burden of the body further toward him until he could reach the half-dozen keys on the ring at Crellin's belt. The keys to the corridor and the yard outside would surely be there. Unless the game was to be lost, the key to the metal cuff round the prisoner's ankle must be with them.

With his throat compressed and veins swelling, logic and probability fighting the weight of fear, Holmes touched the keys in the darkness and knew that three of them were too big to fit the steel anklet. The image of a fox gnawing through its leg to escape the trap flashed like fire behind his eyes. He tried the first of the other three keys and felt it jam in the lock of the leg iron. While fighting against the beating in his skull and the pain at his breastbone, he slowly and judiciously eased it clear. The second was far too loose a fit. That left only one more.

But in the darkness he had started at the wrong end of the row of keys and now, as he tried the last of all, the lock moved. For the first time since his arrival in that place, the steel fell away and his leg was free of the anklet. The first of the three larger keys failed in the lock of the door to the yard. The next turned the lock, and he took the handle in a strong but noiseless sweep. To his dismay, the unlocked door stuck fast and, in his bursting chest, he felt a chill of incomprehension. A bubble burst from his throat; he took in a mouthful of poisoned air, and he forced it out again by naked willpower. As his throat closed, choking, a part of his mind that seemed far removed from the agony told him that he had not yet drawn the door bolts free. Holmes snatched for them, drew them carefully and silently back, gently freed the door, and stumbled into the cold night air of the yard, muffling the convulsions of his throat in the pad made from the canvas pillow cover. Yet this was not his escape. It was a mere chance of escape, a chance that most men would have contemplated— and despaired.

HENRY WILLIAMS'S LEGACY

How long he lay outside the yard door he did not know, nor whether the jailer who had fallen from his chair was alive or dead. When he opened his eyes, the door to the cell had swung shut under its own weight. Sherlock Holmes pulled himself up and tried the handle. The lock had not closed again. He covered his mouth and nostrils with the wet canvas of the pillow cover and went into the darkness. With the door open, the air began to clear. A first predawn lightness was in the sky, enough to make out the lineaments of furniture and other objects.

The shape of Crellin was lying facedown by the chair in the place where Holmes had left him. It seemed evident in an oblong of reflected moonlight that the guard must be dead. His head lolled stupidly to one side, the eyelids half open and half shut. Dixon Mann's *Forensic Toxicology* was as familiar to Sherlock Holmes as the English dictionary was to others. From what he could see in faint light from the yard, Crellin's cheeks were a healthy cherry pink. The lips were moist, no doubt from a froth that had dispersed when breathing ceased. The eyes, as he raised the lids, were wide and staring. He did not need to look for a pulse in order to know that carbon monoxide poisoning had killed Milverton's bully stone dead long before the prisoner had made his escape into the yard.

Though the open door had cleared the air immediately around it, the water-gas floated sluggishly in the rest of the long cell. It had saturated the air and the fabric. Holmes stepped out into the yard, drew a hard breath, and closed his smarting throat. Back in the cell, he dragged the body across to the bed. It took all his strength to lug Crellin onto the hard surface and cover him with the blanket. Then he went back through the door to the yard, closed it, and locked it from the outside. In the cell the gas still bubbled from the four unlit jets. Having warned McIver to let the others enter first, Holmes was prepared to let them take their chance. They had carried out their inspection every morning before it was fully light, lamps in hand. There was so little daylight in the deep well of the prison yard that the cell needed light long after sunrise. The blast from a gas explosion, touched off by the flame of their lamps, might make the body on the bed and those of the intruders conveniently unrecognisable. His enemies would not know whether he was one of the victims. Nor could he be certain at once which of them might have perished. As a final touch, he had locked the anklet round the leg of Crellin's corpse. An inspection lamp shining through the spyhole of the door would show them a figure lying under a blanket with a crown of dark hair visible and the chain in place.

Presently Sherlock Holmes stood in the cold mist of the morning by the locked outer door of the cell. If he got no further than this, then despite all his ingenuity he would be caught and killed before the sun lit the great cathedral cross half a mile away. In his white shirt, dark trousers, and socks, his shoes tied together by their laces round his neck, he prepared to test the truth of Henry Williams's story.

This was the moment of predawn greyness, half an hour before the watery gold in the east and the first long shadows of the early spring sky. In a far corner of the yard he could make out the low elongated shed with its beam above the gallows drop. On three sides, Newgate's walls rose above him, high and sheer, smooth and deadly with a patch of a pale cloud far overhead, still touched by late moonlight. The fourth side of the yard contained the condemned cells with three rows of barred windows above them. The roof of this structure was a dozen feet lower than the tops of the walls on the other three sides, but Holmes turned his back on it. At roof level, a thin metal canopy extended a dozen feet along its entire length. It was designed to trap a climber beneath it, being too frail to take a man's weight. The wall face, as Henry Williams had promised him, was the only way.

He glanced up at the polish of a blank wall, laying his hand on it and touching an icy smoothness. It was useless to look for crevices that might bear the pressure of a foot or the grip of fingers. The weight of stone blocks pressed them so tightly together that even a gap in the mortar would scarcely have given lodging to a fingernail.

Holmes was better versed in prison lore than any other man. His copy of the *Newgate Chronicles* commemorated a number of felons whose time had come and who tried in their last hours to climb these walls by studs or hessian on their shoes. One or two had started well, only to fall back into the yard. They were supported on the trap and hanged on time.

The old iron tank was high above him on a bracket in the angle of two walls. A rusty stain of water down the stonework below showed where it had overflowed from time to time. Above the metal cover of the tank and a little to one side of it, the wooden axle set with sharpened wire ran round the three walls that enclosed the cell block. It was this device which would throw the climber downwards, if his fingers lost their grip on the steel wire.

When they brought him back from his tribunal, Holmes had made a passing and surreptitious study of this device. The prison authorities had not supposed that any prisoner could gain such a height or that, if he did, he would keep a grip on such a vicious deterrent as the axle. At the best, he might hope to dangle there if he chose, at a dizzy height above the paving of the yard unable to climb up or down. Milverton's men had not prevented my friend from studying such defences. Nothing would have pleased them more than to watch him calculating the hopelessness of an escape and breaking down from weariness, Sherlock Holmes pleading for his life at the end.

If he sometimes showed little mercy to others, it was certain that he now showed none to himself. He would not fear to go where the humble chimney-sweep had gone before. Crossing to the angle of the wall in which the now disused iron tank had been installed, high overhead, he touched the surface of the stone again. It was beyond reason that they could have raised an object of such weight and bulk as a metal tank to so great a height, and fixed it there, without using scaffolding and thereby defacing the masonry in that angle. There were certainly no convenient crevices for the hands or feet, but Henry Williams had described to him how the broken face of the stone might prevent a hand or foot from slipping if the pressure of the climber's body could hold him in place. Like a sweep's boy or an acrobat, Sherlock Holmes now stood barefoot in the cold morning and prepared himself for an assault on the towering wall. Williams had never mastered the art of the chimney-sweep or the prison fugitive more surely than Holmes, his last apprentice.

It was, the old man had told him, a matter of lodging in the corner and working your hands behind you 'like a crab,' braced by the feet where the two walls came narrowly together. The dying sweep boasted of having worked to the top inside a great factory chimney. 'And keep yer boots and stockings orf,' he added. 'That's what does for most that tries it.' Immediately after this conversation, my friend had been intrigued enough to try the method and found that with practise, it could be made to work. Without that practise, it is doubtful that even Holmes could have accomplished such a climb. In the angle behind him, however, he could feel that the stonework was 'rusticated,' as builders call it, that is to say broken and ridged from the devices of the water engineers. With his back to the icy wall, he now prepared to put the old man's wisdom to its final test.

As yet there were no sounds from the gaunt prison building. A guard who shone a light through the spy-hole of the cell door would still see a dark-haired figure asleep under the blanket and would have no reason to enter. Crellin's chair was to one side of the spies' field of vision. They would assume that he was still sitting there. Where else should he be?

Putting the danger of pursuit from his mind, Sherlock Holmes took up his position. It required both hands against the surface behind him and one foot across the narrow meeting of the walls to brace himself. Yet it was a trick that a thousand sweeps' boys learnt before their childhood was over. He drew up the other foot and used it as a lever across the angle. The soles of his feet felt the slight contours of the stone and for a moment he clung motionless, clear of the ground.

The art was to move the hands, as the old man had told him, like the claws of a crab. Wedged in the angle, the purchase of his feet holding him, his palms and fingers now worked alternately upwards. It was a game that children might play to the height of a few feet. It could also carry a man like Henry Williams to sixty feet, if his nerve was strong. He glanced up as a thin drift of river cloud darkened the early dawn.

With a patience that he showed only in extreme peril, Holmes moved himself cautiously, an inch at a time, as the early mist became a faint grey light. He held his body in the angle, feeling skilfully for the furrows of the surface that gave purchase to palms and fingers. As if through instinct, he did not put a hand or a foot wrong, though the urgency of escape quickened his blood as full daylight began to penetrate somewhere beyond the yard. His hands pressed the broken surface until it tore at his skin, yet he breathed long and slowly, as though with the inhuman indifference of a machine.

Sometimes it was difficult to find a corrugated patch of stone behind him. Once he lost his hold and his hand slipped, though he saved himself on the chipped corner of a block an inch or two lower down. Then he stopped and breathed slowly, never looking down at the death that waited in the yard below if he were to fall from the height he had now reached. From time to time, he turned the palm of one hand a little, just sufficiently to wipe sweat or blood on his shirt or trousers.

At length the flat and rusted underside of the tank was close above him. Sherlock Holmes used to say, modestly, that he was stronger than most men, but the truth was that he was not strong in a conventional way. It was in his sinewy arms and legs that he had such power. I had seen him not merely bend a poker into a semicircle but straighten out one which had been recently bent by a threatening visitor. Had all else failed him, I daresay my friend could have made his living as Hercules at a fairground. Such power served him well in moments like these.

Two hundred feet from the little shops housing mapmakers and ships' chandlers, he fought for his life on the prison wall. Where the iron angle supporting the tank was fixed, the stone had been coarsened by damage and he found a better hold. He reached and caught the metal strut. The purchase of his feet against the wall levered him. Praying to whatever gods might be that the bracket was not rusted through, he snatched again and hung by both hands, his feet dangling as if from the summit of a church tower.

The long reach of his arms and legs proved to be his salvation. He swung until he could kick out with both feet and find leverage across the angle of the walls once more. With one hand gripping the bracket, he stretched upwards and sideways with the other, found a metal bar for one foot and hoisted himself, facedown on the cover of the tank. The worst of the climb was over, and the ordeal of the sharpened wire lay ahead.

The length of a long wall separated him from the rooftop that led the way to freedom. Yet with the self-confidence which irritated so many of his rivals, Sherlock Holmes never doubted that what he had just done, he could do again. Now he had only to stand upright and stretch to one side, in order to touch the wooden axle with its sharp metal wire where it ran along the wall. It was the only link to the first rooftop above the street.

His shirt or whatever cloth he might wrap round his hands to protect them from the sharpened wire would weaken the sureness of his grip on the wooden axle. 'The blades may hurt you,' Henry Williams had said, 'but they won't kill you. Not unless you let 'em. What you must do is make up your mind, tell yourself there's a hundred feet to get past. P'raps it ain't so many. Then you hang on for dear life and count. After ten, there's only ninety to go, after forty there's only sixty. You'll do thirty and you're more than halfway to fifty, so you mustn't give up. You do fifty-one, and you've got less to go than you've done already, having come through so much. You're nearer the finish than the start. So you ain't going to give up and drop now, are you? Not having come through all that and with less to go! That's common sense.'

For a brief moment, Holmes stood on the metal surface high above the yard and smiled at the old man's wisdom. He said aloud to himself for the second time that morning, 'Fortune favours the brave.' Though he never boasted of it, he knew as he prepared for his ordeal that to fail now would very probably make my own life forfeit to Henry Milverton and, possibly, that of the young woman whose silver revolver rid the world of the villain's elder brother.

Each change of handhold would bring him six inches closer to his goal. At every change, as his weight hung from the axle, he might shed blood from his hands. Whatever the pain, it was not an eternity. Perhaps no more than a few minutes. Closing his mind, as if all this was happening to another man in another world, he gave his concentration to counting the changes of grip, measuring what must still be endured, and seeing in his mind the dwindling numbers ahead. When he passed fifty, he heard the old man's voice again, 'So you ain't going to give up and drop now, are you? That's common sense.'

Working hand over hand along the axle, he thought only of the roof he must reach. Far from the pain in his hands he continued to count the growing number of wounds that were past and the dwindling number to be endured. At last he hung above the abandoned cell block, the flat roof a dozen feet below him. There was nothing for it but to release his grip on the end of the wooden axle. Most of those who met him found Sherlock Holmes physically languid rather than agile. Only when circumstances required did he exercise his phenomenal dexterity. He had the suppleness of a cat, and nothing less would have enabled him to drop so accurately and without injury to the rooftop below. He landed squarely on the flat lead of its surface. It was the first prison block, whose roof led towards the street.

He knelt for a moment, then pulled himself upright and listened. There was no light in the yard below. The voices which he could hear at a distance were surely those of market porters setting out their street-stalls, nothing more than the men talking as they walked to and fro with baskets on their heads.

By keeping below the parapet of the roof, he would be hidden from the street. It would not do to come this far and then be taken for a rooftop burglar, seized and delivered to the prison gate by hopeful reward-hunters. The flat roofs of the prison and the street lay ahead of him in succession, with several alleyways below. It was now that he took the greatest care. Somewhere, the old sweep had told him, there was a low brick wall belonging to a bookbinder. It marked the first rooftop beyond the prison. Two men who had followed Williams in his attempt to escape the gallows had made the mistake of coming down before they reached this wall. They had found themselves trapped in the old press yard behind the prison wall, where reluctant suspects had once upon a time been pressed to death, if necessary, with increasing iron weights on their chests to make them give evidence.

The voices below him, whoever they had come from, were now silent. He crawled forward, close to the parapet with his head well down, taking cover in the angle of deeper shadow which the early sun had not as yet dispersed. Time might be against him, but Holmes was a man of exceptionally acute hearing and he still heard no sound of alarm or pursuit. Instead, he looked up a few minutes later and saw, across the flat roof, a dividing wall no higher than his waist. It was painted with white letters, 'Bindery.'

He made his way to the roof-hatch, put on his shoes, and slipped quickly and unnoticed through the bookbinder's premises. Assuming the purposeful air of a journeyman, he crossed the street below and was lost among the sooty tenements of the city. Just then, in the yellow light of the new day, there was a brief lightning flash behind him, reflected in the sky ahead. The cold air and even the paving under foot shook with a monstrous roll of thunder, rattling the glass of the shopfronts. A deep and resonant roar sounded across the rooftops, as if the sound had taken a second or two to catch up with the tremor of a blast. Then all around there was a pattering like hail, as fragments of stone rattled down from the sky. From somewhere else came a clatter of glass broken by the force of the detonation. The carters and the costermongers at their stalls looked up, as if waiting for a sequel and a gathering of storm clouds. But the single shuddering roar fell to a rumble and faded. There was silence, a caustic stench of burnt fabric, and then the unmistakable flickering and lapping sounds of flame.

As the ill-clad figure of the fugitive made his painful way, slow and stooping among the market traders in the shabby streets, he calculated that the lantern flames of the execution party had ignited more than a thousand cubic feet of water-gas with a detonation like a howitzer shell.

BROTHER MYCROFT

Having given you the account of Sherlock Holmes's ordeal, as I later heard it from his own lips, I must now return to the circumstances of my own life during his curious disappearance.

To most of those who recall that spring of 1902, it was a time of celebration. A little more than a year earlier Victoria, the great Queen Empress, had gone to her reward, after sixty-four years on the British throne. Few people had ever known what it was to be alive except when she reigned over them. That New Year had been a time of solemn pomp, a great funeral, and commemoration. Now the flags flew in the bright spring air among the preparations that went forward for the coronation of her eldest son as Edward VII in August.

Such public jollity made my own despondency all the deeper. The columns of the *Morning Post* had brought me nothing, and in the circumstances, I cared very little for flags and bunting, for crowned heads and fireworks.

A further week or so passed, after I had spoken to our friends at Scotland Yard about the strange disappearance, and still I heard nothing of Holmes. Even if I went back to Lestrade or Gregson and told them that he was still missing, what could they do? Worst of all, I now faced the disagreeable task of informing Mycroft Holmes that some accident or villainy had surely overtaken his younger brother. By the middle of April, the matter could no longer be put off. We were to lunch together at his club, the Diogenes, in Pall Mall. All that I knew—or rather did not know—must be put before him. Yet what he or the entire government could make of it was beyond me.

During this time, I had gathered no positive evidence of being spied upon—and yet I felt sure it must be so. If Holmes was right in believing that a wide criminal conspiracy was at work in London, my enemies would arrange matters so that I should never see the same shadow twice as they followed me about. There would be enough of them for one to watch me for a mile or an hour at a time and then be replaced by another. For this reason, I gave up hansom cabs and had taken to traveling by the new electric underground railway. A man may be followed easily in a cab, but I had mastered the art of getting on a train as it pulled in and getting out at the last minute to see if any other passenger did the same, thus forcing my follower to reveal himself. Sometimes I was quick enough to do this and still board again if the coast remained clear. At other times I waited alone on the platform for the next train or the one after. Yet another of my shadows might be waiting at a station further on and I should be none the wiser.

Sometimes I would come up into the daylight from the underground station and perhaps notice that a man who had been reading his newspaper by a lamppost now folded it and walked in the direction that I had taken. Of course, it was a hundred to one that he was an honest fellow who had stopped to check the price of gilt-edged stock or the odds offered on the favorite in the 2:30 at Epsom races. How, in any case, could a spy know that I would leave the train at this place? Yet there are only six stations on the line from Baker Street to Waterloo, and they could set a dozen men after me, if they chose, so that one waited at each stop of the train. If Holmes was right in describing the extent of such a criminal conspiracy—and if it mattered enough to them—they could watch me day and night, even from other premises in Baker Street.

I had lived like this for a few weeks, trusting no one and looking everywhere about me. At first I took it for granted that those who shadowed me would be men. Then one day I had the thought— what if one or more of them was a woman? I had been entirely unprepared for that. I wondered whether I should challenge them when there was a policeman standing by to see fair play. Once I saw a fellow coming after me as I left the street door in Baker Street. My blood was up. I turned to confront him and damn the consequences. Moreover, I had a vague recollection of seeing that face and figure before! At the last moment I recognised him as Fothergill, a medical student at Cambridge and Barts Hospital, who had been scrumhalf for Harlequins half a dozen times when I played rugby football for Blackheath.

In the end I knew this would not do. I must assume that they were always watching—and make the best of it. On an April morning I left the train at Trafalgar Square to keep my appointment with Mycroft Holmes. I went up the steps and into the open sunlit space with Admiral Nelson on his column far above the chestnut trees in bud.

Pall Mall is surely the home of the gentleman's club. I left the square by Cockspur Street and passed the Regency grandeur of the Royal United Service Club with its full-dress portraits of Crimean generals seen through long Georgian windows. I passed the intellectual elegance of the Athenaeum with its philosophers and men of letters, the Travellers Club, and last of all the Reform with its air of literary periodicals and Liberal statesmen. Yet our times have changed and not much for the better, as it seems to me. The air of the wide avenue from Cockspur Street to St. James's Palace was raucous to a point that would have shocked Sir Robert Peel or Lord Palmerston. An organ-grinder, of all things, was rolling out the favorite of the music halls, 'Rosy, you are my posy. . . . You are my heart's bouquet.' Worse than that, a uniformed constable was standing by amiably and listening, as if giving the performance his blessing.

Three times, in that promenade of taste and decorum, I was accosted by beggars. One thrust himself in my way, the smell of beer upon his clothes, and complained of a wife and three little ones to find a living for. I dismissed him with the injunction to find work at the dockside hiring yard in Wapping or Shadwell. The second complained of needing a sub until Saturday, which was as good as to say he had drunk his week's wages already and had a tidy sum due for payment on the slate at some tavern in Lambeth or Clerkenwell.

Finally, there was a one-armed beggar sitting against the wall between the Reform Club and the Diogenes. I am not a medical man for nothing, and I could see plainly that his second good arm was carefully concealed by his coat. He rattled a tin cup and complained of being an 'old sojer wot lorst a limb' at Maiwand in the Afghan campaign. If you know anything about me, you will know that Maiwand was the battle in which I sustained a wound which ended my career as an army surgeon. If this fellow had ever been nearer to Maiwand, or Afghanistan, or India, than Clapham Junction, I would eat my hat.

I do not as a rule see red, but I did so now. How could I not, when I thought of fallen comrades exploited by this mean cheating? I thundered at him that he was a disgrace to the nation, a wretch who sullied the name of honours won in that campaign—and that I should do such things—I knew not what they were, but they should be the terror of such as he! At this point, in his sly and insinuating manner, he said, 'You'll have to speak close, guv. I don't hear so well as I used.'

It was almost more than flesh and blood could stand. I leant into the unwashed odour of him, the ginger hair and slobbered beard, the crafty gaze of those eyes, the nose that scented easy money.

'I shall certainly . . .'

Before I could add what it was that I would certainly do, he spoke softly.

'As you value both our lives, Watson, give me in charge to that policeman just beyond you. The fellow standing opposite us at the St. James's Square turning has had me in his sight for the past half hour. Let the club porter do it for you.'

How I kept my composure after all that had happened, I cannot tell you. Yet to hear his voice was to know that every word was in earnest. I straightened up and said loudly, 'You are no soldier but a common scoundrel. Bread and water is too good for you!'

I strode up the steps of the Diogenes Club and gave my instructions to the hall porter. He looked from the doorway and saw at a glance the scene I had described. The policeman was still listening to the barrel organ. The 'old sojer' from Maiwand was still sitting disconsolately against the wall of the Reform Club, holding out his enamel cup to passersby. Opposite the St. James's Square turning, a man in a long coat that was too heavy for the spring warmth was pacing slowly and glancing at his watch from time to time, to give the impression of one who was kept waiting at a rendezvous.

The porter crossed Pall Mall and began to walk towards the policeman. Behind me, the voice of Mycroft Holmes said, 'My dear Dr. Watson! Why do you come alone? Is not Sherlock with you?'

Curiously, both children had been given the first name of William, which was why neither used it. William Mycroft Holmes was tall and portly, in so many respects the antithesis of his younger brother. In the matter of clothing, he must have been the despair of Savile Row. The suit that a careful tailor had made for him looked as if it had been wrapped round a miscellaneous bundle rather than a measured body. The face was round, while his brother's was aquiline. Yet the gray eyes had that same penetrating gaze, and the forehead, unusually wide, was crowned by the flat and shortcut hair of a schoolboy. If the body was absurd, the head, without being in the least handsome, spoke of double-firsts in mathematics at Cambridge or in classical languages at Oxford—or both. He was, I had heard from Sherlock Holmes, a Fellow of All Souls and traveled to Oxford every week to dine at that college among the nation's intellectual elite. Mycroft had won his fellowship by a brilliant contribution to classical grammar in a competitive essay on 'The Resolution of Enclitic δε.' Yet to the nation, he was virtually unknown. Sometimes fun had been poked at him, but you may be sure he never saw the point of it. Sherlock Holmes assured me that this paragon, as a Balliol undergraduate, had been the target of satire in the famous book of college rhymes.

My name is William Mycroft Holmes,
A giant among little gnomes.
You've lost your Greek optative verb?
I'm thinking, kindly don't disturb.

'Where is Sherlock?'

There was no time for explanations. I led him to the window of the Diogenes Club. The barrel organ had fallen silent and we were just in time to see the constable crossing Pall Mall. He stooped and spoke to the derelict who looked up from his sitting place.

'I do not understand,' said Mycroft Holmes simply, as the constable took the beggar's arm and encouraged him to his feet. They began to walk away towards Vine Street police station.

'That is your brother.' I noticed that the loiterer near St. James's Square gave one more look at his watch, for the sake of verisimilitude no doubt, and then walked away in the other direction.

'My brother? Sherlock? That beggar?'

I nodded. The shock of the past ten minutes after weeks of terrible anxiety had drawn the energy from me.

'That is your brother.'

'Masquerading as a beggar in Pall Mall? But why? Does he not see how he might embarrass me?'

'You shall hear everything, so far as I know it.'

Mycroft Holmes was not mollified by this. He looked down at me from his considerable height. There was a mixture of incomprehension and reproof in his expression, which now gave him something of a sulky air. He shook his head slowly.

'I have tolerated his frolics and farces, goodness knows,' he said plaintively, 'but this is quite beyond everything. On my way here I stopped and heard the story of his dreadful injury. I was so taken by it that I gave the fellow half a sovereign. I do call that the limit!'

THE HOMECOMING
1

It was enough for the time being that I had seen him alive. I still could not say he was safe if the stranger who stood across the street from the Diogenes Club was what I suspected. Yet I knew that if Holmes were to survive, he must be left to his own devices. When the mysterious beggar was led away by a police constable, the watcher on the opposite pavement ended his vigil, and I believed Holmes had won the first hand in the game. Had I embraced the vagrant as my friend, we might both be floating in the river with our throats cut by now.

Communication between us appeared to be impossible. How easy it would be for our opponents to intercept a letter addressed to me by bribing a dishonest postal sorter or, more likely, by planting their own man to work at the sorting office by means of a forged reference. A message scrawled on the morning newspaper pushed through our letter box, or slipped inside its pages, would also be read.

My thoughts ran upon a message added to a newspaper or a letter. No doubt the thoughts of our enemies followed the same path. Only one who knew the workings of that indomitable intelligence would understand that Holmes might transmit the most detailed and vital messages invisibly, by means of what was missing rather than by what was added. I recalled the mysterious incident of what the dog did in the nighttime. But the dog did nothing in the nighttime, I protested. Precisely, said Holmes, that was the mystery.

The morning after the Pall Mall encounter, I unfolded the newspaper which awaited me on the breakfast table and saw that there had been a mistake. It was not the *Morning Post* but the *Times*, and it was dated the day before yesterday. Looking at the front page, it was distinctly marked in pencil '221b Baker Street.' It had frequently happened that the wrong paper was delivered by a careless newsboy. That it should be two days out of date was no mere error.

Those who have read our Lauriston Gardens mystery in *A Study in Scarlet* or *The Sign of Four*, may recall the 'unofficial force' always at the disposal of Sherlock Holmes, his Baker Street Irregulars. He need only send Mrs. Hudson's Billy for them. Ten minutes later, accompanied by a wail of dismay from our landlady, naked feet would patter on the stairs as with a loud clatter of voices a dozen dirty and ragged little street arabs burst in on us. Yet in the presence of Sherlock Holmes they were as smart and obedient to command as they had just been ragged and disrespectful.

These young scamps had often been our eyes and ears, once showing themselves better able to keep a log of Thames river traffic than any division of Scotland Yard. How easily might one of them insinuate himself into Baker Street newspaper delivery. How easily might a villain who tracked Sherlock Holmes be tracked in turn by twenty pairs of eyes following every movement and manoeuvre. It is a truth that the most consummate villain, or the most widespread yet tightly controlled criminal conspiracy, is helpless against one thing—the will of the people. In our case it was not only the prospect of half a sovereign for work well done that attracted these little brigands but the adventure of working with the most famous detective in London.

I opened the paper again, no longer wondering who had sent it or how it had got here. But there was no message, nothing written on any page except the address of our rooms on the first. I stood up and shook the pages, one by one. Nothing fell out. I sat down again, went through it more carefully, and noticed that there was a page missing. It would scarcely have been noticed by anyone checking to see if a message had been written in the margin or hidden between the pages. Nowadays a single page of newsprint is sometimes added to supplement the folded double pages and this was how the mutilated one appeared.

Without stopping to finish my breakfast or even my coffee, I called a cab from the rank at Regents Park and went straight to my club—the East India in St. James's Square. The East India takes in every morning and evening paper from the capital with quite a few of the better-class provincials. I turned to the missing page of yesterday's *Times*. The major item, a continuation of Home News under the Cricket columns, was not in doubt.

THE ELECTRIC STORM
Another Electric Explosion In The City

Fresh details have emerged from the City of London concerning the electric explosion which occurred early in the morning of Thursday last. It is the latest in a series of such accidents to the electric supply affecting the Newgate Street area. On the last occasion, our readers will recall from our report of 6 January, a series of the electric conduit boxes opposite St. Sepulchre's and in Newgate Street itself were seen to issue smoke and shortly afterwards exploded with a burst of flame. In the present case, it is reported that a far larger explosion occurred within the disused buildings of Newgate prison.

Contrary to first reports, there was no injury or loss of life. We are grateful to know that this misunderstanding has been clarified. The contractors' men had not yet arrived for their day's work. It is thanks to this, rather than to any vigilance on the part of the electric supply company, that serious injuries, indeed fatalities, were avoided. Several windows in Newgate Street were cracked by the blast and one window display in the direct path was wrecked. A column of smoke was seen to rise above the high walls of the exercise yard of the deserted prison. Any person at the centre of the explosion, where happily there were none at this hour, must infallibly have perished.

It had been supposed that the supply of electricity, an amenity which reached only certain wards of the prison, had been disconnected some time ago. This was evidently not the case. A supply of commercial water-gas was also continued by the Aldgate Coal and Coke Company. An electric spark appears to have been the cause of the explosion. Disconnection of their supply has now been undertaken by the Charing Cross and City Electric Light Company from the company's Newgate Street conduit box.

It is stated on behalf of agents to the subcontractors that no serious damage was sustained beyond a small area within the prison which had in any event been prepared for demolition in a few weeks' time. A small fire which had begun was brought quickly under control without requiring the attendance of the London Brigade. There is nonetheless a cause of severe misgiving as to the safety of the Charing Cross Electric Light Company's mode of supply and the wisdom of allowing a flow of highly volatile water-gas to continue in such ancient and ill-ventilated premises as these. A report of the Cripplegate Ward Fire Committee is to be presented to the next meeting of the ratepayers. The matter is also to be debated next week at the monthly meeting of the Court of Common Council to be held at the Guildhall on Wednesday.

Only when I heard the complete story of my friend's escape did I understand that he was coming down to freedom from the roofs of Newgate Street as the lighted lantern flames touched off the gas filling the condemned cell. The whole truth, to which the newspapers did not have access, was that the door and windows of the condemned cell had been blown clean out into the exercise yard, along with several feet of its wall. Even as I read the newspaper report, it told me a hundred times more than it might have conveyed to any other reader. As a medical man with some experience of injuries from explosion in battle, I could not believe that anyone in that cell itself—or many of those in close proximity—would have survived the ferocity of a blast that did such damage.

As I sat on the library sofa before the log fire, I knew this was a veiled account of how Sherlock Holmes had escaped from the tightest corner he was ever in. Had all his enemies been destroyed? It seemed at least one might still be tracking him, to judge by the incidents in Pall Mall. Could they tell whether Holmes had perished in the blast or not? Knowing the man they were dealing with, they would not be fools enough to take the explosion for an accident.

Had my friend thought his time had run out and had he striven to take them all with him—only to make a lucky escape?

I flatter myself I came close to the truth, even before hearing his account. As a medical man, I knew an eruption of highly explosive water gas would leave human debris in the ruins. Whether any belonged to their captive would be hard to say. I did not yet know my friend had taken the precaution of locking the metal cuff round the ankle of his dead guard. There was a chance that Crellin might pass as the body of Sherlock Holmes burnt beyond recognition.

I could only make my way back to Baker Street and await further communications. The next morning brought another copy of the *Times*. It was two days old, but there was not a page missing.

Clearing aside the breakfast things, I spread the paper on the table and began to go through it minutely. There was no item of news that could be of the least relevance. I was reduced to running my finger down the first of the Deaths columns and when I reached the foot of it, I felt as if my heart took a final leap and stopped. The corner of the page was torn away. To a casual glance, it might seem that this was damage inflicted by the sharp edge of the letter box or by carelessness. The complete copy of the paper in the club library told me otherwise.

> Milverton. Suddenly at Claremont, Cape Town, on the 14th inst., Henry Caius Milverton of The Borders, Windlesham, Surrey. The interment of ashes and a memorial service will be held at St. George's Church, Windlesham, on a date to be announced.

In all our dealings with the criminal underworld, there were perhaps half a dozen names never to be forgotten. Milverton was one of them, though which Milverton this might be I had as yet no idea. However, as I read the announcement, the message from my friend could not have been plainer. One other thing I knew from it, whoever Henry Caius Milverton was, he had died a good deal nearer to home than the Cape Province of South Africa! The announcement was clearly intended to appease the curiosity of those who would otherwise wonder how their acquaintance had—more literally than they would guess!—vanished into thin air. Of course, I could not even begin to prove it, but I felt to a certainty that Henry Caius Milverton had been blown to smithereens in that Newgate explosion.

Next evening I had an unexpected visit after dinner from Mycroft Holmes. His mood was partly one of annoyance at the game his brother seemed to be playing with us all and partly a real concern for the safety of that brother's life.

'I had it out with Inspector Lestrade this afternoon,' he said aggressively, throwing off his coat and sitting down by the fire. 'He and his people are subordinate to us in the hierarchy of government, which is sometimes rather useful. All the same, in my position it does me no good, you know, to have Sherlock playing the fool all over London.'

He was plainly very agitated and got up at once. Pacing round the room, he paused to wave a hand at the chemical table, sadly unused in recent weeks.

'Why can he not settle to something worthwhile? What does he see in all this trumpery? You will find one day these escapades will land us all in chancery.'

'I wish he was here so that I could ask him what he sees in it,' I said sadly.

This seemed to mollify him. He poured himself whisky from the decanter, added a dash of seltzer, and sat down again.

'I came tonight, Watson, because Lestrade told me something this afternoon. It sounds to me like a tale from a schoolboy's magazine, but you ought to hear it.'

'I should like to.'

'Very well. Lestrade spoke of some business a few years ago. Three men were killed in England, all from the same family. Name of Openshaw.'

'The case of the five orange pips.'

He pulled a face.

'Call it what you like. Rumour says, according to Lestrade, that each of them received an envelope containing five orange pips.

This was to tell him he had been chosen for assassination. A boys' magazine story, pure and simple!'

'But what of it?'

'A criminal gang came from the United States, from the state of Georgia. Its members belonged to what is called the Ku Klux Klan and its leader was Captain James Calhoun.'

'Quite correct,' I said helpfully. 'Calhoun escaped from England after the murders, but his ship, the *Lone Star*, went down in an Atlantic gale that autumn. The sternpost was found floating, all that remained of the vessel.'

'No!' He slapped his knee.

'I fear you must explain that,' I said cautiously.

'According to Lestrade, that was what the world was meant to think. Captain James Calhoun was not dead then—but he is now.'

'I don't understand that.'

Mycroft Holmes sighed, as if despairing of me.

'Lestrade has it on the authority of an American treasury agent with whom he has had professional dealings. Whatever you and my brother may think, the U.S. Treasury never believed Calhoun was lost at sea. A sternpost! The whole thing was only too easy to arrange. Calhoun has operated since then under assumed names, closely protected by his criminal organization. A treasury man working incognito was able to attend a grand council, or whatever it may be, of this Ku Klux Klan. He identified Calhoun as being present.'

'But Calhoun is dead now?'

Mycroft Holmes stretched his feet toward the fire, a mannerism he shared with his brother.

'He is dead now, quite recently. But the curious thing, according to Lestrade's information, is that he is said to have died in England.'

I seemed to hear the voice of Sherlock Holmes cautioning silence and said only, 'An odd story.'

Mycroft Holmes laughed, a thing he seldom did. Then he poked the fire irritably.

'Odder than you suppose. According to Lestrade's story, Calhoun was killed in London—murdered, presumably—and yet there is no body.'

There is no body! I thought of Henry Caius Milverton, for whom there was also no body, merely a jar of ashes. Once again I kept this to myself. However, I offered a lame explanation.

'Your brother merely presumed that Calhoun had gone down with his ship. He did not regard it as proven fact.'

Mycroft Holmes raised his flourishing eyebrows.

'Merely presumed, did he? It is not like Sherlock merely to presume. He is so damnably sure of himself as to be insufferable. When you see him, you had better pass on the information. Tell me, Doctor, are you sure that you know nothing of my brother's whereabouts?'

'Quite sure,' I said humbly.

He lumbered to his feet.

'It really won't do to have him acting the goat all over London as he seems to do at present. A one-armed beggar! You can tell him; it seems he listens to you. He will damage reputations other than his own. What's more, it doesn't do for him to be always hobnobbing with men further down the hierarchy, Lestrade and the like. Tell him when you see him.'

'You may be sure I will.'

With that, he plodded down the stairs to the cab, whose horse and driver had waited patiently throughout his visit. And so Brother Mycroft began his stately progress back to that little world of his own, where the sun rises each morning over the Palace of Whitehall and sets every evening behind St. James's Street. Beyond that, for him, lies outer darkness.

If two such men as Henry Caius Milverton and James Calhoun had died without a body between them, there was surely much more to the story of Newgate. On the following morning there was no copy of the *Times*. The *Morning Post* appeared as usual. I read it over my coffee and toast, folded it, and laid it down. Only then did I notice that where the penciled address '221b Baker Street' should have been, someone had written '23 Denmark Square, EC.'

From my days as a medical student I knew Denmark Square, just off the City Road where it runs down toward Finsbury Pavement.

It is not the most salubrious part of London—shabby terraces with a dusty patch of grass and a few stunted trees at its centre. I took sheet 53 of the Ordnance Survey map of London from the shelf and confirmed that 23 Denmark Square was the southernmost house of the terrace forming the eastern side of the square. On the reverse of the sheet are lists of those businesses that occupy premises on the map. At 23 Denmark Square, on the ground floor, was James Pocock & Son, pianoforte action makers and repairers of musical instruments.

It seemed I now knew where I might find Sherlock Holmes. But was he hiding there, held captive, or merely awaiting my arrival? Surely it was better to go at once than to delay and find that I had come too late. An hour later, I took the Metropolitan Line from Baker Street to Liverpool Street, through smoky tunnels and in such crowds that I could not tell if I was being followed or not. The carriages rattled along a deep canyon with embankments of brick on either side. Above us were blocks of warehouses, a gasworks with tall chimneys like minarets. The fiery mouth of an open retort glowed like the crater of a volcano.

The City Road is lined with dirty unpainted buildings and choked by heavy drays and baggage carts. Ramshackle oyster bars and little drinking shops with grimy uncurtained windows were well patronized by early morning. I turned into Denmark Square. The decaying houses were tall enough to have accommodated at first the prosperous families of a lawyer, a bill broker, a merchant of India rubber or Norwegian timber. Now the handsome terraces were sooty tenements with a different family in every room above the ground-floor workshops.

At the centre of the square was an area of grass worn brown by the crisscrossing of footsteps and two chestnut trees not yet come into leaf and looking as if they never might. I took my seat on a bench at the centre of this dusty isolation. I had not seen anyone following me—but then I did not suppose that I should.

I took out a paper and began to read. The rumble of carts, cabs, and twopenny buses from City Road was constant. Scales and arpeggios rose from the premises of the piano action manufacturer. Repairing violins is a considerable part of such trades, and a craftsman began to tune and play, simply at first and then with flowing confidence.

As I sat there, I lost interest in my newspaper, my thoughts filled by the nobility of such sounds in a place as desolate as this. But what was the music? I would guess the composer was Bach. A theme wove and interwove a rich tapestry of sound that became an advancing wall of sublime melody in counterpoint. I had no doubt who was playing that gimcrack violin, and I thanked heaven Holmes kept his musical accomplishments secret from enemies and allies alike. This was not his beloved Stradivarius, but Holmes could conjure celestial harmonies from a tinker's fiddle. The performance was not intended to ease my mind or lift my spirits. When my friend was engaged upon an inquiry, everything pointed to one end.

A simple theme had begun this majestic fugue. Now, as it wove in and out of the music, I half recognized it. I almost snatched hold of it, only to feel it slip away. I knew it, I could swear I did, but I am not knowledgeable enough to tell one of Bach's fugues from the other. Perhaps I had heard it in company with Holmes at a St. James's Hall recital.

The great tapestry of sound mellowed and softened, gathering for the grandeur of its conclusion, sunset clouds weaving together, dissolving and combining in sonorous triumph, a minor key moving into position for a final sublime chord in the major. Very softly the elusive theme was stated alone and I knew what it was. Indeed, I sang it softly to myself as I listened.

> *Half a pound of tuppeny rice, half a pound of treacle,*
> *That's the way the money goes, pop goes the weasel!*

Who but Holmes could make something so splendid out of material so simple? But there was more, to remind me of the second verse of the old nursery rhyme.

Up and down the City Road, in and out the Eagle . . .

The Eagle! That famous tavern in the City Road was close to where I sat. As a medical student at Bart's, the oldest hospital in the City of London, I had known the promenade bar with its music hall, garden orchestra, magic mirrors, French ropedancers, and infant prodigies! The nursery rhyme figured in our boisterous singsongs. I had often reminisced to Holmes about those days.

I got up, as if I had been merely sitting to pass the time, and took a roundabout route to Shepherdess Walk and the tavern, all yellow London brick above and gold paint on black at eye level with handsome plate-glass windows. The tiled entrance lobby and the pale green marble pillars led to long bars and ample space. There were customers at the tables, but not one who might be Sherlock Holmes. Just then, someone stood up and walked away from a table where he had sat alone.

He was a stout, florid-faced man, his red hair somewhat darkened by age. I did not recognize him as he passed me, and for that I give thanks! I should surely have greeted him instinctively and given the game away. He was some years older than when I had last seen him, and it was something in his eyes rather than in his face that prompted my recollection. Mr. Jabez Wilson!

In the scrapbooks of our investigations, which I have compiled over the years, Mr. Jabez Wilson brought us one of our first cases, the affair of the Reheaded League. That league proved to be a cover for the most ingenious and ruthless gang of bank robbers. Sherlock Holmes had saved Jabez Wilson from being unwittingly implicated in the crime and had earned him a modest reward from the bank's insurers. Mr. Wilson had professed eternal indebtedness to his benefactor. It was not the least surprising if he had given shelter to Sherlock Holmes at 23 Denmark Square in his present hour of need.

We passed as if we were strangers. I sat with my glass of ale and listened to the barroom piano playing 'Daisy, Daisy, give me your answer do.' On the buttoned leather of the seat beside me lay a discarded copy of the *Racing Times*. I glanced at it without picking it up. It had been folded open at a page on which someone had underlined a horse for the 3:30 at Cheltenham. The horse was Noli Me Tangere and I had no doubt that the underlining was Mr. Wilson's.

Noli me tangere: 'Do not touch me,' or in the famous regimental motto, 'Do not come near me.' Thus I received my instructions. I finished my glass of ale, drew out my watch to check the time, and walked down the City Road with the air of a man who has an appointment to keep. Presently I came to a doorway. Its brass plate promised an oculist. In the waiting room I inquired whether a member of the practice might be free to give my eyes an examination. Half an hour later and a guinea the poorer, I came out into the street again.

As I walked past the steps of Wesley's Chapel with its statue of the great founder himself, I noticed an orphan flower girl with the last of her day's offerings laid out on the cold stone, violets and wallflowers, roses and carnations, forced in hothouses for early sale. Her dark print dress was plain but not torn, and her shoes had seen better days. I judged she was about fifteen, and the barefoot child who hung about her, no doubt her sister, about eleven. Such children often share a single room with two or more other families in the Drury Lane tenements. The elder came forward, towards me, crying out, 'Flowers! Pretty flowers! Here's spring to a certainty! Twopence for a buttonhole! And it shall be twopence for my night's lodging, not a dram of gin!'

I did not doubt her, but she was upon me before I could reply, touching my face.

'Feel my hand, how cold it is.'

Without more ado, she began to pin a white carnation in the buttonhole of my lapel.

'Only be careful how you undo it,' she said, almost laughing now.

'Take this, my poor girl.'

I drew my hand from my pocket and pressed a sovereign into her outstretched palm. She stared at it and cried, 'The heavens be your honour's resting place,' then turned to her young sister. With such treasure, they could shut up shop, certain of a warm meal and bed.

Only be careful how you undo it! Most of the Baker Street Irregulars had sisters or female cousins as destitute as they. If this was not one of them, I thought, may I be shot.

I reached Baker Street and, despite my impatience, walked up the stairs from the sooty air and blackened brick of the railway as if I had all the time in the world. No one followed me, but one pair of eyes would surely be trained on our front door as I walked toward Regent's Park. Once inside our sitting room, I closed the curtains, put up the gas, and drew the white carnation from my buttonhole. The stem was protected by a twist of silver foil. When I unwound it, the foil was lined by a slip of paper. On this, in diminutive letters, was a message.

It was the first direct news of Holmes since his disappearance.

> My dear Watson, I write this with gratitude to our red-headed friend. The events of my captivity and escape are such as you may now guess. Henry Milverton and James Calhoun perished at the hour they had chosen for my own death. Two underlings have survived. Beware the disgraced Petty Officer Alker, Master-at-Arms, a naval hangman. Most important, kindly address to me by first collection tomorrow a shoe box wrapped in brown paper, tied with blue string, and sealed with wax. 'Poste restante, City Road Office, London EC1' will find me. Make no secret that you are sending it to me. Our lives remain in danger. Noli Me Tangere.

2

I slept little that night as I pondered how to send a parcel by mail to ensure that our enemies saw the address upon it but without letting them know that I wished them to see it. At such moments I missed the presence of my friend beside me. What if the spies had found me unproductive and had ceased to spy upon me? I might have reassured myself. Until Sherlock Holmes was in their grasp again, I was the most likely person to lead them to him.

There was a warm summer wind and a scent of blossom as I set off down Baker Street with a wrapped shoe box under my arm on the following morning. I had as yet attached no label to the parcel. The coronation of our new king, Edward VII, was to be the spectacle of the season. Every window of the stationers and trinket shops offered mass-produced cards for sale, looking like the largest and most splendid playing cards you ever saw. Each displayed a crowned figure in full coronation robes of crimson or royal blue braided with gold, be it King Edward or Queen Alexandra, the Prince or Princess of Wales. A coronation ode by Dr. Benson of Eton College set to music by Sir Edward Elgar was thumping out from the regimental bandstand in the Regent's Park, and was soon to be taken up by massed choirs the length and breadth of the land.

> *Land of hope and glory*
> *Mother of the free . . .*

In the post office I took a gummed label from a packet and wrote in large capitals the poste restante address my friend had given me. I was at one of the wooden tables provided, and before I could finish the final line, a fellow pushing through the crowd jogged my elbow suddenly and—I could almost swear—deliberately. My pen flew across what I had just written. I swung round on him. He was a stout, florid-faced man, his red hair somewhat darkened by age. Mr. Jabez Wilson of the Redheaded League treated me as a total stranger once more. Raising his hat, he said, 'I do beg your pardon, sir, indeed I do. Entirely my fault. I really am so sorry.'

He went on his way, struggling through the crowd. I saw that Holmes had opened a door for me, and I knew exactly what to do. Muttering to myself, I screwed up the label, made a great display of irritation, and tossed the crumpled paper into the wire container of the basket in the corner of the room. I took a fresh label, and at length I handed the package to the clerk. I turned to the door and made my way out onto the steps.

Sunlight over the eastern rooftops was turning the day from spring to summer, warming the walls and terraces. I stood there for a moment, as if I had forgotten something. Turning abruptly, I made my way back to the counter. There I bought a dozen creamlaid envelopes embossed with a blue stamp and asked loudly, as if to reassure myself, whether a parcel handed in at 9:30 that morning would reach the City Road post office before the end of the afternoon. I was promised that it would. Then, as if finding the easiest way out through the crowd, I edged round past the wire basket into which I had thrown the first crumpled label. At such an early hour the basket had contained only that label, two folded sheets of paper that someone had discarded previously, and a messenger boy's apple core. The folded sheets and the apple core were still there. The crumpled label with Holmes's address upon it, which had been resting on top of them, was gone.

Dressed in a country suit and hat with a pair of optician's horn-rimmed spectacles containing plain glass, I passed an hour after the postal delivery ruining my digestion with cups of coffee at the refreshment stall that fronts the corner of the City Road and Denmark Square. On that corner stands the City Road post office, also in line of sight from 23 Denmark Square, across its dusty central lawn.

Customers pushed their way in by the door marked 'push' and came out through the door marked 'pull.' I did not look for customers, however; I watched for the shoebox parcel tied with blue string. Whoever carried that was my man or, indeed, woman. Mr. Jabez Wilson was surely the most likely, unless Alker or one of our opponents tried to pass himself off as the recipient and collect the item from the counter.

I waited in vain until almost five o'clock. Then, to my dismay, I saw Sherlock Holmes striding confidently from Denmark Square towards the post office door. He wore a dark suit and hat, as if to advertise his presence. Why, after such careful concealment, had he now given himself away so completely and defiantly? I did not approach him, for that would have made matters worse.

I sat at the small metal table under the tin canopy of the stall, where I was hidden by the crowd of drinkers standing or sitting around me. Presently, Holmes reappeared with his parcel. He did not return to Denmark Square, but began walking down the City Road in the direction of the Metropolitan underground railway at Moorgate. It was that time of day when the commercial streets of the City begin to fill with shopworkers and office clerks pushing their way homeward.

I stood up, but even before I could step out from the canopy I saw the man who, I swear, was the master-at-arms. He did not look precisely like the fellow who had kept vigil in Pall Mall when Holmes was playing at being a military beggar. Yet there was enough about him to suggest that he was the same. Now I observed him in more detail. There was a broad face with the look of a smile at the mouth until you reached the eyes and saw that he was not smiling at all. He was heavily built, though not tall, and the strength in the arms suggested how easily he had pinioned those poor wretches who had struggled to gulp down a few moments more of breath and life. If his reputation is to be believed, he had adjusted the noose round the throats of seven murderers and three mutineers of the Pacific Squadron, as well as innumerable Chinese and Indian rebels. Though the afternoon was still mild, he was wearing a dark overcoat with the collar turned up.

My attention was briefly caught by a red-faced and bandy-legged little lounger who got up from a table near me. He, however, went off in another direction and was evidently not involved in the matter. Nothing in that bustling street of trade and traffic can have suggested to Holmes that he was now being followed. He did not so much as glance in Alker's direction. My friend seemed in mortal danger, and yet I knew by instinct that I must not frighten off his pursuer. I had my revolver in my pocket, but it would have been impossible to fire it in such a place as this without the danger of hitting an innocent bystander. On the other hand, how easily might Alker, in the growing pressure of the crowd, draw level and slip a knife between the ribs of Sherlock Holmes.

Thanks to the jostling crowd, I was able to take up my position about ten feet behind Alker and follow him as he was following Holmes. Even had he caught sight of me, he might not have recognized me; but, in any case, the master-at-arms had eyes only for his quarry. As we crossed between the lumbering wheels of carts and wagons, towards the station, I became certain that he had come on his own.

Alker was not much more than a brute, but he had something of a brute's simple cunning. He positioned himself so that in the press of passengers towards the train he was able to push his way into the carriage next to the one that Sherlock Holmes had entered. From time to time Holmes had made a movement at the last minute, as a matter of precaution, but never dextrously enough to outwit the patient hatred of his unseen adversary.

I had not the least idea what my friend's destination might be. On these occasions one can only take a ticket for the longest journey and alight at whatever station may be necessary. As Alker sat in one carriage next to that of Holmes, I sat, or rather stood, in the carriage beyond it. By now I was as determined that Holmes should not see me and give the game away as I was that I should outwit Alker.

If our destination was Baker Street, we had surely taken the longest and slowest route, by way of Tower Hill, Westminster, Kensington, the bleak suburbs of West London, Paddington, and Marylebone. I consoled myself by believing that Holmes knew what he was doing and that he could scarcely come to harm on the train with Alker in a different carriage. At every station I moved to a point where I could see who got off the train. It was at Kensington that I saw the tall, gaunt figure of Sherlock Holmes step down to the platform and walk slowly away. Kensington, it seemed to me, had no connection with the case at all. Perhaps it was a blind, as they say. He did not even look round as Alker went cautiously after him. I let several passengers precede me and then took up the pursuit.

The whole business had an element of farce, and yet, as events were about to show, it had death at its heart.

It was not difficult to keep track of Holmes and his shadow, by using the rounded bulk of the Albert Hall and the Albert Memorial. Then Holmes, unaware of how close danger and death had come, made the worst mistake of all. With the sun below the horizon and dusk setting, he turned through Alexandra Gate into the vast unlit territory of Hyde Park. By the time that we reached the far side and the streets that led home, the trees, bushes, and grassland would be in darkness, the perfect terrain for an assassin.

Already the parkland seemed deserted. A photographer was wheeling out his black canvas booth through the gate; ribboned children and their governess were carrying off the toy yacht they had been sailing on the Round Pond of Kensington Gardens. Alker continued to shadow Holmes with consummate ease among so many trees and the bushes of laurel or rhododendron. The way led parallel with Kensington Gore for a while. Then Holmes turned, as if to cross Rotten Row and leave all safety behind him. He walked unhurriedly, without once looking back, still carrying his parcel and deep in thought. He was offering himself for the kill.

I drew the revolver from my pocket, but kept it concealed. Beyond the tops of the furthest trees, where the great Park Lane terraces show their upper floors, there were lights in several windows. It would soon be too dark to shoot. There was nothing for it but to attack or accost Alker. He was in the open some forty yards behind Holmes and I was about as far behind him again. We had reached the wide earthen carriageway of Rotten Row, lined by chestnut trees on either side, where 'pretty little horse-breakers' of the 1860s broke more hearts than horses. Even now the Sunday morning 'church parade' of open carriages, with drivers and grooms in livery and silk hats, makes it the parade of gallantry, no less than the mounted regiments galloping in the weekday dust.

What followed was so rapid and so unreal that I can still scarcely believe I was a witness. Holmes turned suddenly and shouted in a tone of anger, 'Watson! You had really better leave all this to me!'

As if that were a signal, there was a drumming like a boxer's gloves on a canvas training bag. A fine bay horse with its head down, pulling against the bit, came pounding over the bare earth of the Row as it gathered speed. I stood still, stricken by astonishment. These is no other phrase for it; the whole thing was like an apparition. On the horse's back was a figure in regimental uniform of some kind. It was growing dark, but not too dark to make out a scarlet jacket, brass buttons, and a cavalry trooper's cap on his head.

Alker stopped as well, for he had been about to cross the hardened earth of Rotten Row in pursuit of Holmes. Now he was prevented from doing so by the approach of the horse. The trooper was riding as if a pack of hellhounds might be after him, and even from where I stood I could hear the snorting breath of his mount.

Alker took a step or two backwards, as if to keep clear of the galloping horse whose hooves were now showering earth to either side. I could see that the rider was leaning forward, his chest along the horse's neck. He appeared to be performing some trick in which he would whisk something from the ground as he sped by. Then I saw that what he held in his hand was a cavalry saber. Suddenly he held it out sideways. It did not flash, for there was too little light, but I could swear that I saw a pale gleam. It cut the air with no more than a whisper and then there was a sudden whistling sound as the air left Alker's body through his severed neck while his head bumped along the dried earth.

I was unable to move from the spot in my terror and fascination—even though this might have been some madman who intended to kill us all. I saw that Alker's headless body remained upright for several seconds before it crumpled to the ground, as if some lingering message from the missing brain was still controlling the dying limbs. I had heard of such grisly wonders in cavalry engagements.

I need not have worried about the rider's intentions. He looked neither to right nor to left, never slackening his speed. The hoof-beats grew gentler until dusk veiled the identity of the man whom I was to hear of as the corporal of horse.

Sherlock Holmes appeared to be unmoved.

'A weak man, perhaps, but not a wicked one,' he said calmly. 'Now he may live without fear. I shall not betray him to our friends at Scotland Yard if you do not. If I calculate correctly, he is the only one remaining of those with whom I had dealings during the weeks of my captivity. Others were to have been there but were prevented for one reason or another. I fear it is not impossible that we may yet hear from them. However, let us be thankful that we have purged the world of the majority.'

I did not reply. The shock of what had happened deprived me of the power of motion for a few minutes, but I did not sleep all that night and I was physically incapable of speech until late on the following day. Whether the corporal of horse contrived on his own to rid the world of the one conspirator who might kill him, or whether he and Holmes planned the whole thing together, I do not know. I may say, however, that my friend did not betray him and nor did I.

3

The papers were full for many days of the 'Headless Man' mystery in Rotten Row. Yet the nine-days' wonder passed. Before it was over, we received a visit from our friend Inspector Lestrade, to whom we told nothing of what we knew. Scotland Yard had concluded that the murder was done with a cavalry saber, but they had concluded little more. Alker was known to them as a man of fifty-five who had ended his naval career at forty and then found a place among such dealers in female flesh as Henry Caius Milverton. It must have cost our Scotland Yard a good deal to say, 'We should value your views upon the case, Mr. Holmes.'

But Sherlock Holmes was capable of seeing nothing in a case as easily as he could see a great deal. He listened to what our visitor had to say of the evidence in the murder and then sighed. 'I fear, Lestrade, that I cannot make bricks without straw.'

My friend felt that he owed Corporal McIver a debt of honour and that the debt had been paid. When we were alone, he put the entire adventure from his mind.

He sat quietly for a moment and then with a new eagerness changed the subject of our conversation.

'You will recall my little composition, an improvised prelude and fugue for the violin upon the nursery rhyme "Pop Goes the Weasel"? You heard it while I was concealed in the house of Mr. Jabez Wilson in Denmark Square.'

'I recall it. I thought it very clever.'

I was about to add that it seemed clever as a pastiche, but happily he cut in ahead of me.

'I have never before thought of setting down my compositions on manuscript paper and offering them to a music publisher. I am tempted to make an exception in this case. I propose to solicit the attention of either Peters in Leipzig or Messrs. Augener, who have once or twice inquired of me whether something of mine might be available to them.'

'But you cannot become Sherlock Holmes the composer! The world knows you as Sherlock Holmes the consulting detective. Would it not cause confusion?'

He took the pipe from his mouth and contemplated the plaster ceiling rose of the electrolier.

'True. I should have to assume a nom de plume of some kind, to compose, as the French say, *sous le manteau*—and that would belittle the composition. I might suggest instead that it is a discovered fragment from the past, by one who was a master of counterpoint. I could not masquerade as Johann Sebastian Bach; that would be absurdly overweening. I think, though, I may fairly lay claim to one of the great man's sons. I believe that would meet the case. I shall perhaps be Carl Philipp Emanuel Bach. Yes, I think so. That would not be excessive in this instance.'

'You cannot possibly do that, Holmes! All the world knows "Pop Goes the Weasel."'

'You underestimate the cultural *snobisme* of the age, my dear old friend. They will know it, to be sure. But will they dare to admit to one another that their minds run upon such lowly things as they sit in the Wigmore Hall or some other recital room?'

He put down his pipe and stood up. He opened the case, drawing out his Stradivarius and bow. Protest was useless. There would be no stopping him now.

The Case of the Greek Key

1

If Sherlock Holmes devoted all his energies to defending the honour of a humble chambermaid on Monday, he was as likely as not to be engaged in saving a peer of the realm from disgrace on Tuesday. He had a voracious appetite for humanity, its foibles and its failings. Indeed, he often put me in mind of that Latin tag that I had been made to learn at school. 'Homo sum, humani nihil a me alienum puto': 'I am a man and nothing human is alien to me.' I once quoted this to him, in part to see his reaction, adding that it was one of the wisest comments of the great Roman orator, Cicero. Holmes stared at me, drew upon his pipe, and then said, 'I believe you will find, Watson, that Cicero said no such thing. The comment, if you wish to attribute it, comes from a very tedious Roman playwright. Should you care to verify it, you will find that he lived two centuries later than your great orator.'

Yet my judgment of Sherlock Holmes was not in error. After his death it was my duty as the executor of his will to list the rough copies of his correspondence still lying in his old tin trunk, which remained in the Baker Street attic. There were many letters or notes to the poor and the desperate for whom he had worked without fee, rather as great defenders in the criminal courts will take poor persons' defences without recompense of any kind. When he was once asked why he did this, he replied that he believed—as Francis Bacon had done—that every man is a debtor to his profession and must make some return.

Yet there was another extreme in his work. Among his posthumous papers were three rough drafts, much revised, of letters that began with a formal but imposing phrase, 'Mr. Holmes, with his humble duty to Your Majesty. . . .' What follows is an account of how one of these came to be written. The paper on which it is set out appears a little yellowed and brittle with the passage of time. Those who now read the circumstances of the case will understand at once that an earlier disclosure of the events might have put the very safety of the nation in peril.

To begin the story, I must go back to an October morning in 1908. It was not long after dawn, and the scene was an area of sloping downland above the cliffs of St. Alban's Head in Dorset. Several groups of figures, some of them in the topcoats and uniforms of senior naval officers and others in formal dress beneath their winter coats, stood looking out to sea. Though a morning mist still veiled the further distances of the English Channel, a thin sunlight already touched the pale green waves.

By his own choice, Sherlock Holmes and I stood at a little distance from the others, as if to show that we were there as guests and not as of right. In his close-fitting cloth cap and gray travelling cloak, he stood apart in more senses than one. Behind us, more than a mile inland, the little lanes and paths that ran from the village of Worth Matravers were closed and guarded by parties of Royal Marines. They had orders to let no one through under any pretext for the next hour. You would have looked in vain for a naval attaché from the great European embassies in Belgravia or Eaton Place. Not one had been invited.

As we stood silently, a throb of powerful engines sounded across the calm water, growing presently to a heavy beat of turbines in the stillness, like the drums of an ancient war god. A newly built leviathan was coming in from the Western Approaches to the start of a measured mile, returning to Portsmouth Dockyard after sea trials in the Atlantic. The main trials had been held in the remoter areas of the ocean. The performance on this October morning was as much as the illustrious spectators were allowed to see. Presently and quickly the ship materialised from the sparkle of October mist, the brightness of veiled sky shining on her flanks of pale grey steel. From the groups of senior officers and Whitehall dignitaries came the murmuring of a single word: '*Dreadnought!*'

Sweeping past us through the gentle tide, the length of the most powerful and best-armoured battleship the world had known sliced the water with the grace of a cruiser. Even Sherlock Holmes stood in silence, admiring the clean lines of her hull. The decks were clear of the conventional clutter of a capital ship. Before and aft of the two modern funnels, the deck areas held a series of gun platforms able for the first time to sweep through arcs of fire not much less than 360 degrees. A tripod mast gave a commanding view to the control platform and its gunnery officers. The mighty gun barrels themselves were ten and twelve inch, enough to destroy any other ship afloat at a distance of six miles or more and to riddle the thickest armour plate at three miles.

I witnessed this speed trial thanks to the friendship between Holmes and Admiral Sir John Fisher, First Sea Lord and architect of the new Royal Navy. Fisher was known for his maxim 'Hit first, hit hard, and keep on hitting.' A close friend of King Edward, he was rumoured to have urged the sovereign to 'Copenhagen' the Germans at Kiel, as Nelson had done the French, by striking at them first and without any declaration of hostilities while England still held the naval advantage. The king was horrified, the cabinet outraged, and Fisher lamented to his friends that the country no longer had the leadership of a William Pitt—or even a Bismarck.

Holmes and Fisher had been friends since the assistance that was given to the First Sea Lord in the case of 'The Naval Treaty.' Since then, Holmes would never hear a word spoken against Sir John, whom he described as having 'not an inch of pose about him' and to whom he gave the motto 'Sworn to no party—of no sect am I. I can't be silent and I will not lie.'

As we looked on, *Dreadnought* seemed to turn on her heel at the end of the measured mile—18,000 tons moving with the precision of a torpedo boat—gathering speed again towards Portsmouth Dockyard. I just made out the wake washing away behind her stern, until the mist hid her once more. The distinguished spectators stood in silence. Here and there a pair of field glasses was buttoned into its case once more. Yet there was no cheering and no jubilation at the sight of such power, merely a sense of awe. Beside me, Holmes quoted Rudyard Kipling in a soft but ominous tone.

> *A-down the stricken capes no flare—*
> *Nor mark on spit or bar,—*
> *Girdled and desperate we dare*
> *The blindfold game of war.*

'Mark my words, Watson, the blindfold game of espionage must be played first. Grand Admiral von Tirpitz and his Ministry of Marine in Berlin will see to it.'

We turned away to the carriages that had brought us from the railway.

'All the same,' I said, trying to cheer him, 'Jackie Fisher has got Tirpitz snookered. There are five of these monsters building in yards on the Clyde and the Tyne. Tirpitz has not one. If he had one, he could not use it without deepening and widening the Kiel Canal to get from the North Sea to the Baltic, and dredging the approach to every dockyard. If he deepened those sea lanes, our thirty-three battleships could sail in and bombard him at close range.'

Holmes stamped impatiently over the downland.

'It will not end there,' he said firmly, 'mark my words.'

In this, he was right. Kaiser Wilhelm and his Grand Admiral spent many millions of pounds deepening and widening the Kiel Canal for the new High Seas Fleet, as well as dredging the sea routes to naval bases on the North Sea. The keels of their first Dreadnoughts were laid: A submarine fleet was under construction. Fisher's battleship had bought him time but not victory in the race. A new advantage must be sought but, for the present, the matter rested there. I heard no more from Holmes than the venomous insults exchanged between the First Sea Lord and Admiral von Tirpitz.

Tirpitz began putting about a story that Sir John Fisher had deliberately engineered a German naval scare in England in order to get increased naval estimates passed by Parliament. Indeed, Tirpitz claimed that Fisher had admitted this to the German naval attaché in London. On hearing this, Fisher sought out the attaché at an evening party, at which both were guests, and told him, 'Tell Tirpitz—using the immortal words of Dr. Johnson—"You lie, sir, and you know it."' Not another word was spoken. Such was the unhappy state of relations between the two great naval powers.

I now move forward to the point where these powers became antagonists in a period of preparation for a great European war. How tragic it seemed to those of us who remembered England and Germany as close allies during the reign of our great Queen Empress, Victoria. At her deathbed, King Edward and Kaiser Wilhelm had knelt in prayer together, as they were soon to walk behind her coffin, the one her son and the other her grandson. All this was put aside as the war hounds of Europe growled ever more menacingly across the narrow seas.

2

It was an afternoon of early autumn, when the trees in the park had lost very little of their summer green. The air of Baker Street was as warm as June and the shops still had their striped awnings pulled out above greengrocers' baskets and booksellers' tables. By instinct, Holmes and I could now tell when a cab or a carriage slowed to a halt outside the door of our lodgings. On the present occasion, however, I rose from my chair with a feeling that this vehicle lacked the cheerful harness rattle of the cabs that usually brought our visitors.

Through the net curtains I saw a twopenny bus on its way to Marble Arch, the sides placarded with advertisements for Old Gold Virginia Tobacco, Van Houten's Cocoa, and a new production of *The Rivals* at the Haymarket Theatre. On the far side of the street, hidden from view until the bus had passed, was a closed carriage. Its black coachwork gleamed, its brass lamps were immaculately polished, and a horse fit for the Ascot Gold Cup stood patiently between its shafts. A liveried coachman held open its door. Two men stepped down and prepared to cross the street. My attention was caught by a small discreet gold crown emblazoned on the black gloss of the carriage door panel.

There was no mistaking the first man as he came across the street. He had taken the precaution of wearing mufti, but even without his uniform Sir John Fisher was known to thousands from his photograph in the picture papers and his caricature in *Vanity Fair*. It was an open, honest face with a dour humour in the lines of the mouth and a quiet merriment in the pale eyes. The dark hair was short and neat, the complexion sallow, for he had been born in Ceylon. His enemies murmured that his mother had been a Cingalese princess—hence his wicked cunning and duplicity.

When I saw the man behind him, I understood the gold crown on the door panel. These two men had been friends for more than twenty years, since Viscount Esher supported Fisher in demanding a modern Royal Navy for a modern world and in reforming the Committee for Imperial Defence. It was believed that no two public men in England held such power. Twelve years earlier, Lord Esher had been appointed by the prime minister, Mr. Balfour, as permanent secretary to the Board of Works. Behind this banal title lay the reality of such influence behind the scenes as only a gray eminence can exert. Lord Esher's task was to superintend and maintain the homes, comforts, and ritual of the royal family. He had the ear of the monarch to an extent that most prime ministers would envy. He had installed the lift at Windsor Castle for the ailing Queen Victoria and had pushed her bath chair when she expressed a wish to see once more her childhood home at Kensington Palace. In 1897 he had staged the dazzling imperial pageant of her Diamond Jubilee, and persuaded his 'Dear and Honoured Lady' to extend the route of her procession south of the River Thames, so that she might be seen and applauded by her poorer subjects. Small wonder that in the new reign, Esher remained the intimate of her son, Edward VII.

'Hello,' said Holmes, standing behind me. 'It seems they mean business. I suppose Jackie Fisher or Reggie Esher alone might suggest a pleasant social visit. Two of them together can only mean trouble of some kind.'

Presently there was a knock at the door and Mrs. Hudson, more flustered than was customary, ushered in our two distinguished visitors. There was a cordial babble of greetings, in the course of which I was introduced to Lord Esher, whom I had already recognised from his photograph in the *Illustrated London News* of the previous week. Then, from the depths of the armchair in which my friend had installed him, Fisher said: 'My dear Holmes, I must come to the point of our visit with somewhat indecent haste. In a moment you will understand why. So far, the full details of this matter are known only to Esher and myself—and to one other person whose identity you will readily guess.'

'Not Mr. Asquith, I think,' Holmes interrupted sardonically.

Esher shook his head.

'No, gentlemen. Not even the prime minister is privy to the entire story. We are here with the knowledge and approval of King Edward himself. It seems that he reposes a good deal of confidence in the name of Sherlock Holmes.'

I thought that Holmes sounded a little too suave in his reply.

'I was able to render His Majesty a small service some years ago in the so-called Baccarat Scandal. A most disagreeable affair of an officer and gentleman cheating at cards in his presence. It came, in the end, to a trial for libel. The Prince of Wales, as His Majesty then was, had been required to give evidence.'

Fisher turned a little and stared at him directly.

'Cast your mind back to certain other cases that came your way at the time. The affair of the Naval Treaty, the blackmail of a crowned

651

head by Miss Irene Adler, and, perhaps especially, the disappearance of the secret plans for the Bruce Partington submarine.'

'Naturally I still have the papers relating to every case.'

Fisher's impatience was a driving force of his character. He turned to Holmes.

'Never mind the papers. Did you—then or at any other time—acquire information relating to the ciphers of the German High Seas Fleet?'

'Or any German system of codes, come to that,' added Lord Esher quietly.

Holmes looked at them for a moment as if he suspected a trick. He had filled his pipe but, perhaps out of deference to our guests, had not yet lit it.

'The Imperial German Navy has had nothing to do with any case of mine,' he said presently, waving a match to extinguish it. 'So far as I am aware.'

There was no mistaking the disappointment in the faces of our two visitors.

'However,' he continued, 'a practical working knowledge of coded messages is certainly necessary in my profession. I have deciphered the hieroglyphics of the Dancing Men and the riddle of the Musgrave Ritual. As you are no doubt aware, my solution in the Musgrave case led to the recovery of the ancient crown of the kings of England, lost by the Royal Stuarts after the execution of Charles I. You may also care to take away with you a small monograph of mine on the use of secret communications in the war of Greece against Persia during the fifth century BC. Despatches from Athens to Sparta were sent as meaningless strings of letters on a strip of cloth. When the strip was wound round a particular wooden baton, in a spiral and at precisely the angle known only to the sender and the recipient, the random letters formed themselves into words.'

'Very interesting, Mr. Holmes,' said Lord Esher, who looked as though he did not find this story interesting in the least. 'The question is whether, from your experience or your researches, you can break the German naval code—and do it within the next fortnight.'

'If it is to be done, by all means let it be done quickly,' Holmes replied with that languid air of self-assurance that so irritated both his adversaries and Scotland Yard. 'I daresay any fool could do it, given time. A fortnight sounds like a generous allowance for a man of moderate intelligence.'

'I have to tell you,' Fisher interposed, 'that our best cryptographers at the Admiralty have tried for two months without success.'

'That does not surprise me in the least. Pray tell me what, if anything, is known about these most interesting ciphers. What are they used for?'

The First Sea Lord and Viscount Esher looked at one another and, by the slightest change of expression, seemed to agree silently that they must reveal more than they had intended.

'Our instructions . . .' Fisher began.

'From His Majesty, I presume?'

'Our instructions are to tell you all that you may need to know in order to accomplish this. You will also understand why it must be done. It seems that we have a spy at the very heart of Admiralty intelligence. He has apparent access to warship design, speed, gunnery performance, and the devil knows what else. Let us not be self-righteous about it. I may tell you in strictest confidence that we have our own man in Berlin. He makes his reports to our naval attaché at the embassy.'

'I should have been surprised had it not been so,' said Holmes equably.

'According to this source, information is being passed by the traitor in our ranks to an enemy agent in this country. The encrypted messages are then transmitted by Morse code over a relatively short distance. We must assume that they are picked up by a German naval vessel in international waters, perhaps no more than five or ten miles from Dover or Harwich. The coded transcript then goes to the Ministry of Marine in Berlin, to the Wilhelmstrasse. Our man there has no official access to decoded messages and has seen only two, at considerable risk. Both related to Royal Navy gunnery signals. He has seen a number of transcripts, still encoded, and provided us with sequences of letters. These match certain sequences in Morse transmissions that our monitors have intercepted. It has been impossible to decipher more than a few words in all. Even that is mere luck. It seems plain that the code not only differs in every transmission; it differs from word to word in a single message.'

'His Majesty is determined,' added Esher, 'that the turncoat in our service shall be hunted out and put behind bars in the shortest possible time. He regrets only that in time of peace the scoundrel cannot be hanged or shot.'

Holmes raised his eyebrows.

'Have a care, my lord! With my humble duty to His Majesty, he must do no such thing as hunt the rascal out and expose him to the world. Do you not see? In this game, the turncoat is your most valuable piece upon the board. If you can pick him out and leave him be, all may yet be well. If he is clapped behind bars, Tirpitz will close down the entire business and you will have lost the only thread that guides you through the maze. Let well alone.'

I do not think Lord Esher, to judge from the expression on his face, relished returning to his royal master and telling him that Sherlock Holmes thought his instructions mistaken.

'If time is at a premium,' said Holmes enthusiastically, 'may we have sight of these unusual documents?'

Sir John Fisher cast his eyes round the room. The disagreeable truth was that there was no surface large enough to display the transcripts except the worktable of Sherlock Holmes. This disreputable piece of furniture was stained by overzealous chemical experiments, while a medical scalpel lay in a butter dish, near a dismantled Eley revolver and a blood-stained nightstick peeping from its newspaper wrapping. Unabashed by this, Holmes all but swept the contents of the table to the floor in his eagerness to have the coded messages before him.

We arranged four chairs round the table. Admiral Fisher opened his briefcase. A folder containing fifty or sixty transcriptions of intercepted transmissions was laid before us. If I describe the first, it will do for all the rest. There were no words, merely blocks of fourteen letters at a time. The first line may suffice.

WTRYILJGDVJNLS DDPYUGSHMKRWEX CNBJJUSDTINCRL

How on earth such drivel could contain details of warship design, gunnery trials, speed at full steam, diesel consumption, and armored plating was beyond me. Fisher looked up at us.

'You may save yourselves the trouble of trying to substitute one letter of the alphabet for another. Our cipher clerks have run the entire gamut in the past few months.'

'I should not dream of such a thing.' Holmes stood and walked across to the window in easy strides. He turned and came back towards us. 'The message may elude us at the moment. The nature of the code can scarcely be in doubt.'

'Can it not?' asked Esher skeptically. He was in no mood to let Holmes play the prima donna at such a time as this.

Holmes sat down again. 'If your information is correct, it is quite plainly a looking-glass code.'

'Perhaps you had better explain that,' said the First Sea Lord uneasily.

Holmes looked from Sir John to Esher.

'As sender and recipient, you would each have a copy of the same piece of plain text. It would probably be a page from a book, a novel, or the Holy Bible perhaps. That would be the key to the cipher. Let us suppose that you wish to send Lord Nelson's famous signal at Trafalgar, "England expects." Let us also imagine that the first words of the cipher key in the hands of each of you are "In the beginning." Now, line up the two phrases. Your signaller will not want to transmit for longer than necessary. Therefore, for speed and convenience, you may construct a grid of the alphabet beforehand, running *A* to *Z* across the page and *A* to *Z* down the left-hand margin.' Sherlock Holmes's long bony fingers worked deftly with pencil and ruler on a plain sheet of paper.

CIPHER KEY: IN THE BEGINNING

SIGNAL: ENGLAND EXPECTS

```
A B C D E F G H I J K L M N O P Q R S T U V W X Y Z
B C D E F G H I J K L M N O P Q R S T U V W X Y Z A
C D E F G H I J K L M N O P Q R S T U V W X Y Z A B
D E F G H I J K L M N O P Q R S T U V W X Y Z A B C
E F G H I J K L M N O P Q R S T U V W X Y Z A B C D
F G H I J K L M N O P Q R S T U V W X Y Z A B C D E
G H I J K L M N O P Q R S T U V W X Y Z A B C D E F
H I J K L M N O P Q R S T U V W X Y Z A B C D E F G
I J K L M N O P Q R S T U V W X Y Z A B C D E F G H
J K L M N O P Q R S T U V W X Y Z A B C D E F G H I
K L M N O P Q R S T U V W X Y Z A B C D E F G H I J
L M N O P Q R S T U V W X Y Z A B C D E F G H I J K
M N O P Q R S T U V W X Y Z A B C D E F G H I J K L
N O P Q R S T U V W X Y Z A B C D E F G H I J K L M
O P Q R S T U V W X Y Z A B C D E F G H I J K L M N
P Q R S T U V W X Y Z A B C D E F G H I J K L M N O
Q R S T U V W X Y Z A B C D E F G H I J K L M N O P
R S T U V W X Y Z A B C D E F G H I J K L M N O P Q
S T U V W X Y Z A B C D E F G H I J K L M N O P Q R
T U V W X Y Z A B C D E F G H I J K L M N O P Q R S
U V W X Y Z A B C D E F G H I J K L M N O P Q R S T
V W X Y Z A B C D E F G H I J K L M N O P Q R S T U
W X Y Z A B C D E F G H I J K L M N O P Q R S T U V
X Y Z A B C D E F G H I J K L M N O P Q R S T U V W
Y Z A B C D E F G H I J K L M N O P Q R S T U V W X
Z A B C D E F G H I J K L M N O P Q R S T U V W X Y
```

He worked with such intensity that I swear, for the moment, he had forgotten any of us was there. Then he looked up.

'I do not find such a grid essential, but few people are trained to encode messages in their heads. Very well, then, gentlemen. "England expects" and "In the beginning." Take the first letter of each. If you will follow my pencil tip, you will see that a downward line from E on the top horizontal line and an inward line from I in the left-hand vertical column will meet at M. The first letter of our encoded signal is therefore M. Following the same process with the second letter of the signal and the cipher, N and N meet at A. Perhaps you will take it from me that if you follow the remaining letters and note where their lines meet on the grid, ENGLAND EXPECTS is encoded as MAZSEOH KFCRKGY.'

It seemed to me, as the saying goes, that our two guests were trying to hang on to his coattails. Holmes remained composed and self-assured.

'You will understand the simple advantages of this system at once. The message is transmitted as MAZSEOH KFCRKGY. The normal tools of decoding are useless. It will not do for your Admiralty cryptographers or their unseen adversaries to puzzle which letters stand for A, B, C, and so forth. Nor will it help you to look for the frequency with which letters appear, assuming that the most common letter in almost any language is E, the next most common T, followed by A. In my example, our original message contained the letter E three times. When encrypted as a looking-glass cipher, however, the first E appears as M, the second as K, and the third as R. As for frequency, the only encoded letter which appears more than once is K, which stands for E on the first occasion and C on the second. T never appears and A only once.'

There was a profound silence, broken at last by Lord Esher.

'Put as you put it, Mr. Holmes, the whole thing sounds quite ghastly.'

'In other words,' said Fisher quickly, 'you tell us that the code cannot be broken.'

'I did not say that. It is necessary to know or deduce what text is being used as the key.'

'But if that text may lie anywhere, in thousands of books and millions of pages, in dozens of languages, the code cannot be broken. Surely that is what it amounts to? Our own people are only able to say that the same groups of letters are sometimes repeated. As you describe it, these may be repetitions of the same words or differing words that appear in the same letters by chance.'

Holmes shrugged.

'A code may be broken in only two ways,' he said patiently. 'It may be possible to penetrate it a little, at least sufficiently to deduce the principle of its construction by internal evidence. More likely, it must be a matter of trial and error. The code-breakers of His Majesty's Admiralty have tried and it seems they have erred. It remains to be seen whether I shall do better. I have the advantage, at least, of recognising what sort of code it appears to be.'

It need hardly be said that as I sat there I felt increasingly uncomfortable in the final stages of this encounter. Once or twice I caught the exasperation in glances between Admiral Fisher and Lord Esher. Yet, as in his dealings with Scotland Yard, Sherlock Holmes hardly bothered to disguise his belief that incompetence at the Admiralty had caused the predicament our visitors now found themselves in. This was to put a considerable strain on his friendship with the First Sea Lord. Yet Sir John Fisher was realist enough to know that Holmes was the one man in England who might help him. The transcripts of the intercepted signals must remain where they were—on the shabby worktable in our Baker Street rooms.

For three days Sherlock Holmes scarcely moved from that stained table on which the transcripts were laid. He worked in his purple dressing gown and, for all I know, his pajamas underneath. From first to last he went at his task in a silence that almost forbade anyone in the room to move or breathe. His efforts were broken only by the sound of another sheet of crumpled foolscap hitting or missing the wicker of the wastepaper basket. He looked up, without expression but with evident reproof, every time I tried to turn a page of the *Morning Post* without rustling the paper. I was so obviously a hindrance that I thought it best to leave him to himself. I went for walks nearby in Regent's Park, where the first yellowed leaves blew and scuffled about the broad avenues of trees. I lunched at my club each day, where at least I could be sure of conversation. Finally I dined there, alone.

Coming back to our rooms as the evening mist of an October night began to gather, I found no welcome fire dancing in the grate. Mrs. Hudson's timid housemaid had been told not to interrupt 'the gentleman' by laying one. No meals were set out on our dining table. Holmes picked at the food like a gypsy from a tray beside his writing pad. He took little nourishment, unless shag tobacco could be counted as such. On the first day he went to bed very late. On the second, as I came into the unaired room at breakfast time, it was plain that he had not moved from his writing chair all night. By any description, he looked white and haggard, like a man who has lost a stone in weight.

'This really will not do, old fellow,' I said gently. 'You will crock yourself up. That will be the end of it. What good will that do?'

He glowered and said nothing. I ate my bacon and eggs, trying not to clink the cutlery. The rustle of butter or marmalade being spread on toast seemed unthinkable. All that day he might as well have been in a trance for what I could get out of him. He sat at the blotter with a few books at his side and covered page after page with scrawled figures, letters, calculations, variations of words in half a dozen languages. Once again, only the light crunch of discarded paper aimed at the basket broke his absolute concentration. He glared at the work before him.

It was just as I was going to bed that I noticed a sudden brightening in his face, shattered though he looked. He glanced up from the folio page before him.

'Before you turn in, Watson, have the goodness to hand me the third book on the right from the second shelf down.'

I took down a slim red volume, lettered in gilt, its cover tarnished somewhat by frequent reading or reference. My only interest was in going to bed and I did not bother to read the title. I noticed, as he opened it, that the flyleaf bore a neat but faded inscription. 'To Mr. Sherlock Holmes with the author's best wishes and sincere thanks.' I thought nothing of this. There were a few dozen volumes on our shelves presented to him by their grateful authors, whom he had helped out of one fix or another. He peered into its pages, his sharp features contracted in a frown. There was no sound now but the hiss of the white gas lamp that illuminated the table.

At last I said quietly, 'I beg you to put away these things until tomorrow and get some sleep. This cannot go on without detriment to your health or your concentration and ruin to your eyesight.'

'Yes, yes,' he said impatiently, 'good night.' After that I might as well not have been in the room.

Though I had taken no part in his day's labours, I fell asleep at once. The next thing I knew, my shoulder was being tugged violently. I sensed that this had been going on for some time in an effort to rouse me.

'Watson!' I saw that his features were alive with excitement; even the sleepless pallor had gone. 'Get up! I need your immediate assistance. I believe I have it, but you must help me.'

'Holmes, it is pitch dark. What time is it?'

'A little before four o'clock. I must have your help in this, old fellow. I need you to listen and tell me whether I am right.'

From the comfortable darkness of my bed I moved slowly downstairs to the tobacco-fogged gaslight of the sitting room. I could not see how on earth he had broken such a code as he described. As I entered the room, Holmes threw down on his table the book I had handed him before going to bed. I picked it up and glanced at the title. *Through the Looking-Glass and what Alice found there.*

'I deserve to be shot,' he said triumphantly. 'Where else should the answer to a looking-glass code be, except in Alice?'

By his chair lay the graph-paper grid of the alphabet that he had drawn up for our visitors. Beside it was a sheet of paper with a single line of writing at the top. He handed it to me with the grid, so that I could follow him. He was as close to exultation as I had ever known him.

'Put these two together, my dear fellow, and that is the answer. At least in this case.'

I looked at the grid. It was, after all, nothing but the letters of the alphabet written horizontally across the top and vertically down the righthand side, the squares filled in accordingly. Then I studied the first line of the coded message he had been working on. It was in the familiar blocks of fourteen letters each.

PRPMUQAKENUJQR BNAVQPNVABTLLZ TQSLLAMCZSLKWG
JPSOOSLBYPYVCK WGJHXHYABCDHSF

I could make absolutely nothing of this gibberish, nor could I see what help was required. In short, I was not a little irritated at having been woken from sleep to be confronted by it.

'You may see something in it,' I said wearily, 'but I do not. There is a sequence of A, B, C, D toward the end, and that is about all.'

He took up the children's storybook and read aloud the first lines.

'One thing was certain, that the *white* kitten had had nothing to do with it—it was the black kitten's fault entirely.'

'Holmes! It is past four in the morning. Whatever this nonsense about kittens may be, tell me and let us have done with it. I should like to go back to bed!'

He pushed another sheet of paper across the table. In this case, he had written three entries across it, one beneath the other, seventy letters in each case.

1. WHAT IS THE KEY? *One thing was certain, that the white kitten had nothing to do with it—it was the black k*
2. WHAT IS THE ENCRYPTION OF THE SIGNAL? *prpmuqak-enujqr bnavqpnvabtllz tqsllamczslkwg jpsooslbypyvck wgjhxhyabcdhsf*
3. WHAT IS THE MESSAGE CONTAINED IN IT? *Belt nine inch; Main six inch; Upper amidships six inch, five inch, four inch; Forward fiv(e)*

As I reached the third of these questions, I knew at once that there would no more sleep for either of us that night.

'I deserve to be shot,' he repeated happily. 'Where else should one find the key to a looking-glass code but in that supreme authority—the work of the Reverend Charles Lutwidge Dodgson, known to the world as Lewis Carroll? I was prepared to try the beginning of every paragraph against every signal in these transcriptions. It is not a long book, little more than a hundred pages, but it would have taken us a week or more. Yet sooner or later there is always a stroke of luck in these matters. One does not count upon it, yet one expects it. The key to the cipher in the fifth signal was in the opening lines of the story! How crass I have been! Yet it is all the fault of these Admiralty people and their invariable knack of missing the point.'

'And the message? What is being measured?'

'I have got a little further than the line you have seen.' He picked up the paper on which he had been working, and began to read once more. 'Belt, nine inches main; six inches upper. Amidships, six inches, five inches, and four inches. Forward, five inches and four inches. Aft, extending sixteen feet above and three feet six inches below the load waterline. Bulkheads four inches, forward and aft. Barbettes, that is to say gun turrets, nine inches and eight inches. Gun shields, nine inches. Conning tower, ten inches forward, two inches aft. Communication tube, four inches and three inches forward. Four-inch battery, three inches. Before I woke you, I was able to identify references to light protective plating of a mere inch over the ammunition magazines.'

'But what does it amount to?'

'It amounts, my dear friend, to a complete inventory of the armour plating on our latest Dreadnought battle cruiser, faster than yet as powerful as any battleship, but sacrificing armor for speed. Twenty-eight knots, to be precise. Unless I am much mistaken, this is the top-secret legend of particulars for HMS *Tiger*. All her strengths and weaknesses are here. Von Tirpitz would sell his ears and whiskers for such information. Were I an enemy captain or submarine commander, I should now know where a lucky shot just below the waterline or aft of the funnels and abreast of the magazines would blow a battle cruiser of twenty-eight thousand tons to Kingdom Come.'

If this were true, the Royal Navy had been dealt a near-mortal blow and did not even know it. No longer in a mood to sleep, I sat down in my chair. This secret, revealed to the walls of our curtained sitting room in the small hours of a foggy autumn morning, was surely the most momentous that had ever been uttered there. In the hands of a future enemy, it could lose us a major naval battle in the North Sea or the Atlantic. It might well cost us a war.

3

'The blindfold game of war,' said Holmes quietly. 'All Europe seems to be at peace under sunny autumn skies. Yet the four of us are now engaged by the enemy as surely as if ultimatums had expired and ambassadors had been withdrawn. The battle of smoke and mirrors begins.'

A warm morning light filled the sitting room, from which the last odours of a heartily eaten fried breakfast had not quite faded. Holmes had sent his wire to Fisher with strict orders that the First Sea Lord was to travel in mufti and by hansom cab. Fisher from Whitehall and Lord Esher from Windsor had arrived simultaneously, suggesting that they had convened a hasty conference before meeting us. Esher looked relatively composed at what he now heard, but Sir John Fisher's complexion was drained and white as candle wax.

'What is to be our first step?' His question was directed at Esher, but it was Holmes who intervened.

'Do nothing, Sir John. Allow the traitor continued access to secret documents and to think himself secure. Let the transmissions continue. Only see to it that the most vulnerable documents are replaced by copies that contain as much false information as possible. Give away only what you think the enemy may know already and what he might gather from public information. Apart from that, feed him falsehoods, if you can. Tirpitz has no reason, presumably, to know that your man in Berlin has discovered what is going on. Here is your chance to lead the grand admiral a dance.

It is all you can do. Follow that one gleam of light. A single arrest will leave you in darkness.'

This time it was Sir John Fisher who got up and crossed to the window. With one hand in the palm of the other behind his back, he gazed down at a file of children being brought home from play in the park.

'We cannot change course,' he said at length. 'So long as we had five or six of the Dreadnought class of battleship and Tirpitz had none, we were ahead. If I had had my way, we should have followed Lord Nelson's example and Copenhagened the High Seas Fleet and the Kiel Canal, with fifteen thousand Royal Marines ashore, but the king would not have it. Now Tirpitz has his Dreadnoughts—and his submarines. Make no mistake, my dear Holmes, the game has changed. We can outdo him only by faster ships carrying the same armament. That, gentlemen, is the rationale of the Dreadnought battle cruiser, of which we have a dozen and he has none. Speed rather than armor plate is its protection. Last month, two ships of the class, *Inflexible* and *Invincible*, were steamed at full speed, seven thousand miles to the Falklands. There was not the slightest hitch in their water tube boilers or their turbine machinery. They would be upon the enemy before he could know it. But an enemy who had the secrets of their design, particularly areas less endowed with protective armour, would know exactly where to put a torpedo or a shell through these weaker points.'

The First Sea Lord turned from the window.

'You must not intervene,' Holmes insisted in the same calm voice. 'Information must continue to flow. The Morse code signals must be allowed to go out as usual. The best you can do for the moment is to let them carry falsified legends of ships' particulars or misleading figures of turbine and boiler performance.'

Fisher pulled a face.

'It will be difficult. We may cause confusion in our own ranks.'

'Nevertheless, it must be done,' said Holmes patiently. 'There is no other way.'

A dozen times in the next few weeks a plain envelope arrived 'by hand of messenger,' usually a young Royal Navy staff officer in mufti bearing details of the intercepted signals. Once again Sherlock Holmes worked day and night. This time not a sentence, not a phrase, in *Through the Looking Glass and what Alice found there* matched the garbled blocks of fourteen letters. Perhaps, as a matter of routine, our enemies had switched to another text as their key. Holmes grew more gloomy as the October days drew in and November took its turn.

'They cannot suspect anything amiss,' I said, trying to reassure him. 'After all, their signals are still being sent out.'

He did not seem to be much reassured beyond sighing and saying, 'It means we are left with trial and error, Watson. Brother Mycroft and the advanced mathematicians are apt to refer to certain numbers so vast that they are "beyond computation." Such are the odds against us now.'

He sat one afternoon with a dozen transcripts before him. Jackie Fisher was at him every day, insisting that until one more signal was deciphered there was no way of knowing whether our spy had been deceived by the falsified documents.

Presently, Mrs. Hudson brought a tray of tea things and set the silver teapot down beside him on the table. As the good lady went out again, Holmes turned to me and said, 'This is all wrong. It cannot be done.'

I was shaken by his remark, for it was the only occasion on which I had heard him use such words. Then he paused and corrected himself.

'It cannot be done in the way that we are doing it now. The key may be in any book in the world or in a single word used over and over. We are being led by a ring in our noses. Our mistake, Watson, is that we are beginning at the beginning, when we should be beginning at the end.'

'How can we begin at the end? We need the key first to decipher the message.'

He shook his head.

'We shall never fathom the key. That is what they count upon. At a guess, it would take a length of time approximately equal to the present age of the universe. Let us ignore the key and, instead, try to guess correctly even a small part of the signal sent. We shall try to work backwards from the letters of the encrypted signal to the letters of the code. Once we have part of the code, we may work forward to the rest.'

Having no better suggestion, I let him have his way.

'However elusive the key to the code, my dear Watson, we may be sure of certain words in the messages sent. Remove their disguise and you have part of the key.'

'Such as?'

'Given the events of the recent past, it is inconceivable that 'Dreadnought' should not be among the words in the signals. May I be shot if one block of fourteen letters does not contain that name. The secrets of that class of ship is the prize they seek.'

'Dreadnought is eleven letters, not fourteen,' I said cautiously.

'Very well. Let us allow for Teutonic formality. 'HMS DREADNOUGHT' will give us fourteen letters.'

He gathered up the transcripts and we prepared to work through the night. It was a little after two in the morning when we were working on a recent signal. The fourteen grouped letters were still gibberish—KQSUDIMUUCFSLL.

'Once again,' said Holmes patiently, 'suppose that these letters signal 'HMS Dreadnought,' what will the cipher key be?'

Carefully, he began to trace the sequence back. We had tested hundreds of these groups against the reading 'HMS DREADNOUGHT' in the hope each time that this was their message—but without success. One by one he followed the present string of letters to see whether they might yield a key. Two minutes later we stared at the result. It was a key and a message in one.

'DEAR ME, MR HOLMES'

I felt the shock like a blow to the chest. The thing was impossible, and yet, as we had worked through the night, it now seemed as if our distant and invisible enemies had been thinking our very thoughts for us. We got up and went in silence to our usual arm chairs. After so much work, my despair was all the greater.

'Well, that is the end of it,' I said miserably. 'How the devil could they know?'

Holmes knocked his pipe out against the fireplace and refilled it. For a moment he said nothing. Then he lit his pipe and turned to me.

'I believe they could not know. Therefore, they did not know. If I am right, this is in every sense a lucky shot, a shot in a thousand. It has a ring of heavy Germanic facetiousness. You will recall that several of my adventures, such as they are, lie in the hands of the public, thanks to your gift for romanticized narratives. I should find it remarkable if they were not read by such men as these. This was a phrase of the late Professor Moriarty's and has circulated widely. We must proceed on the assumption that it is pleasantry among our adversaries and no more.'

'Can we do that?'

He seemed remarkably unruffled.

'You will observe that several signals were sent after the date of this one. That surely would not have happened had they thought the hunters were on their trail. You will also recall that when our visitors have come here, I have surveyed the street from time to time. I do not think that they were followed or watched. All the same, it may come to that. I think it is as well that we should hold future discussions with Sir John and Lord Esher away from public scrutiny.'

I was far from reassured. On the following afternoon a private room of the Diogenes Club was secured for us by Mycroft Holmes. We had thrown off any pursuers by taking a twopenny bus from Baker Street to Oxford Circus, alighting, then getting on again after the waiting passengers had done so. Anyone following us would have had to get off and on as well. None did.

Furthermore, Sir John Fisher assured us that the Morse code transmissions had continued. Two signals were intercepted in the previous week. Had the signallers believed that their codes had been deciphered and that they themselves were in danger, they would have fled before then. It seemed as if the use of 'Sherlock Holmes' in their key was, after all, merely a joke among those who thought themselves superior even to the famous detective.

Yet my relief was short-lived, as Sir John spread before us the latest transcripts. I expected the usual groups of fourteen letters. What I saw was quite different.

72-48-03-61-74 | 82-30-42-13-06-53 | 29-71-46-22 | 38-72-49-17 |

The First Sea Lord looked up at us.

'They have abandoned Morse for a two-digit code. Our monitors now hear two series of short pulses from one to ten. A pause. Two more. Then a long pulse, no doubt to signal the end of a word. It is something entirely new. At any rate, our people have never come across the like of it. What do you say to it now?'

Holmes stretched out his long legs and touched his fingertips together.

'Never fear, Sir John. I believe you are wrong in supposing this device to be new. Something tells me that it goes back many centuries. Moreover, the fact that the signals are still going out confirms, as you say, that their reference to me was mere whimsy inspired by Watson's turn for romantic fiction. In that, as so often in such matters, it seems I have been proved correct.'

4

Further precautions were taken. There was no more post 'by hand of officer.' Intercepted signals were to be relayed direct to us from the rooftop mast of Admiralty Arch. Pride of place on his worktable went to an 'ink-writer' devised by Holmes some years earlier. From a wire aerial it could take down messages in Morse. Rescued from the attic, this contraption worked on an accumulator battery. I saw only a square glass jar filled with sulphuric acid and distilled water. By means I did not comprehend, an endless strip of white paper moved slowly above the inkwell as a message was received.

A stylus attached to the mechanism kept pace with the signals of each transmission, drawing dashes or dots in time with it. Holmes assured me that it required only an electric current from the battery to pass through a magnet. A lever would then lift a small ink wheel into contact with the paper.

'The length of an ink mark depends upon how long the current flows,' he said, not for the first time. 'Dots or dashes are determined by the duration of the current. By this means, our friends at Admiralty Arch can transmit to us in Morse code. In the case of the new code, however, they will transmit dashes for digits of ten and dots for single numerals, making up the pairs of numbers that our adversaries now appear to prefer.'

'Black magic!' I said uneasily.

He laughed and shook his head.

'Not in the least, my dear Watson. Have you noticed, by the way, that each pair of numbers in the ciphers appears to stand for something like a letter or a syllable? Taken together, they must certainly equate to an alphabet in some form. In every one of the ciphers the double digits run from one—with a nought before it—to eighty-seven. Now consider this. That is far too few for a system like the Chinese, where each ideogram stands for a word and many thousands of symbols are required. At the same time, it is rather too many for a purely alphabetical system as we know it. Our alphabet has only twenty-six letters, after all, and the Greek has only twenty-four.'

'Very well, then eighty-seven symbols cannot be an alphabet.'

He chuckled.

'Not as you or I think of it, Watson. However, I would bet a good deal that what we are looking at is a code written in syllables rather than letters, though based upon an alphabet. That should narrow down our hunt considerably.'

'I wish I could see how. As yet we do not even know which alphabet it may be. This is worse than your looking-glass nonsense.'

Before he could reply, there was a knock at the door and Mrs. Hudson came in.

'Mr. Lestrade and a lady to see Mr. Holmes, supposing it might be convenient.'

I would have suggested it was anything but convenient. Holmes beamed at her.

'By all means, Mrs. Hudson. It will be a sad day when we are too busy to see Inspector Lestrade.'

Our landlady withdrew, and after several measured steps upon the staircase her place in the doorway was taken by Lestrade, our small but wiry bulldog as I thought of him. The lady in his company seemed not the least remarkable. She looked very much what she proved to be, a widow of sixty obliged to take in lodgers, dressed on this occasion in a dark red hat, a brown travelling-cloak and a fox fur of uncertain quality about her neck.

'Good morning, gentlemen,' said our Scotland Yard friend. 'Allow me to introduce you to Mrs. Annie Constantine of Nile Street, Sheerness.'

Holmes bowed as if before a duchess.

'My dear lady, my dear Lestrade, you are both most welcome. Please take the chairs by the mantelpiece and tell us to what we owe the honour of this visit. I confess I have been expecting something of the sort for two or three hours.'

Lestrade did not look best pleased by this. When Mrs. Constantine had been arranged in a chair by the fireside and fresh tea had been ordered, he sat down opposite Holmes and said: 'Expecting what exactly, Mr. Holmes?' His eyes widened and he looked more than a trifle put out. 'I do not see how you can have been expecting something you knew nothing about.'

Holmes laughed merrily but there was no merriment behind his eyes.

'Allow me to explain. Several days ago it was arranged that Superintendent Melville of the Criminal Investigation Department at Scotland Yard should be informed by his inspectors of any unusual entry by beat constables of the London area in their station Occurrence Book. Not crimes, you understand, but anything out of the ordinary that was reported—the results were to be conveyed to me. Special attention was to be given to the Thames estuary.'

'Ah, then you were not being so very clever just now, were you, Mr. Holmes?'

My friend ignored this snub.

'I said to myself at the time, if there is anything worthy of note, it will be an officer with the capacity and shrewdness of Inspector Lestrade who recognizes it and acts at once.'

There was a pause while the morning tea tray was set down and then Holmes began to pour.

'Perhaps I had better hear what this good lady has to tell us,' he said genially, handing her a cup.

Mrs. Constantine looked at Lestrade, as if for permission to speak, then turned to Holmes.

'As you mayn't have heard, Mr. Holmes, I keep a lodger. Usually a young single gentleman that has the first floor back. I breakfast him, but otherwise he does for himself. Last year Mr. Henshaw came to me, Mr. Charles Henshaw, a very genteel young man. He teaches French, not at school but to professional young men with examinations to pass. They come to the house and he has the use of the downstairs drawing room to give them lessons. Otherwise, the upstairs is his domain.'

'Really?' said Holmes indifferently, though for reasons I could not see he was missing neither a word nor an inflection of her voice. 'A nice young man?'

'Ever so nice. Regular at the Congregational chapel on Sundays. And I don't mind telling you that if I'd known there was to be so much trouble as this, I'd have acted otherwise on Monday morning.'

'What trouble precisely, madam?'

'Well, Mr. Holmes, it was the middle of this last Monday morning and everything in the street was as quiet as you could wish. Nothing but Mr. Lethbridge the constable, that lives two roads away, coming down on his beat. Then it happened.'

She sat back and folded her arms, as if the matter was at an end.

'What happened, Mrs. Constantine?'

'The bang, Mr. Holmes. I was at the back, where the maid was taking out the clothes from the washhouse to dry on the line. I was just tipping out ashes from the grate of the copper. Then there was a flash that lit up the window of the upstairs back room—Mr. Henshaw's study—brighter than day and a bang that rattled every windowpane in the street. My first thought was the gas fire had gone up. Seeing Mr. Lethbridge patrolling the street, I rushed out and called him. He ran back and went up the stairs first and I went up behind him. I half expected to find poor Mr. Henshaw stone-cold dead. But there he was, sitting on a chair, just looking a bit shocked. And the strange thing was—after such a bang that might have wrecked the entire house, not a thing in the room seemed harmed.'

'Curious,' said Holmes gently.

'It was curious all right. Ever so sorry, he was. Went to light the gas fire and it somehow blew back. Only thing is, Mr. Holmes, there was no match that had been struck, the fire wasn't lit, and there was no smell of gas. But there was a horrible smell of something else. Till that moment I never really thought about it, but I think I smelt it up there before, from time to time, only not so strong. Anyway, that was the end of it. Mr. Lethbridge went back to his beat and I suppose Mr. Henshaw went back to reading French. Then, last night, there was a knock at the door and I'm told I'm wanted at Scotland Yard today.'

If my friend felt any excitement at this, he concealed it admirably under an appearance of casual interest.

'Tell me about the flash, Mrs. Constantine. Did it at all resemble the bright flash you see when the metal poles of a tramcar cross a connexion?'

'Now you mention it, sir, it was just like it. That hadn't occurred to me.'

Holmes stood up and walked past the worktable to a jumble of books, papers, bottles, and implements on an old sideboard. He came back with a small six-sided clear-glass bottle and drew the stopper from it.

'Will you tell me, Mrs. Constantine, whether the smell that you say was not like gas was anything like this? You need not get too close to it, just enough to be able to smell. Just smell and do not inhale.'

He held it at a little distance and waited until the fumes drifted across to her. Mrs. Constantine gave a slight cough, screwed her face up, and exclaimed, 'Ugh! Nasty, beastly stuff! What he wanted with it I do not know. But that's it, sir.' She took a long sip from her cup of tea.

'Perhaps, Mr. Holmes,' said Lestrade, 'you might let us into your little secret.'

'I have no secret, Lestrade. What Mrs. Constantine could smell was sulphuric acid.'

'What's he doing with sulphuric acid?' the inspector asked suspiciously.

'What's he doing short-circuiting a battery, Lestrade, and a fully charged battery at that, on a Monday morning? Tell me, Mrs. Constantine, does your Congregational chapel have electric light?'

'I think its Sunday school hall does. That was only built three or four years back.'

'Then I daresay that is how he charges his accumulator battery—and why it was fully charged on Monday morning. Tell me a little about this nice young lodger of yours. Does he travel much, for example? Abroad, perhaps?'

She laughed at him.

'Lord bless you, Mr. Holmes, I shouldn't say he'd been further abroad than the end of Margate pier. No. He does go to Oxford every week or two, on a Saturday, to buy books for his French.'

'Rather odd, is it not, that he should not buy them in London, so much closer?'

'Well, you see, Mr. Holmes, I was given to understand that he has a friend he meets in Oxford. They take tea together.'

'Ah,' said Holmes, 'that must be it. One more question, dear lady. From what part of the country does he come?'

Mrs. Constantine looked troubled and then replied,

'I don't know that I could say, Mr. Holmes. Not from round our way, I should think. He talks quite like a gentleman, that's all.'

'Very good.' My friend looked thoroughly satisfied. 'One more word, Mrs. Constantine. I am quite sure you have nothing to fear from the young gentleman. The police are merely looking for unusual occurrences over a very wide area—is that not so, Lestrade?—and that is the sole reason you have been troubled. This is clearly nothing more than a trivial domestic mishap. You will continue to allow him to lodge with you, shall we say for the next six months? He seems, after all, an admirable tenant in every other way.'

'I can't say as I know about that,' she said with a slight coloring of indignation.

'I do not believe you will have further cause for complaint, but I must have your promise upon this. Nor must you say a word to him or anyone else about our conversation. I must have your solemn promise upon that, too.'

She hesitated and I intervened.

'Perhaps you have a sister or a friend with whom you might care to stay for a few weeks, until the upset of this has worn off. Provided the maid could look after Mr. Henshaw.'

'I might, sir. However it may be, you shall have my promise for the next six months. As to what has passed between us here, mum's the word.'

To meet Mrs. Constantine was to know that the promise would be kept. She was the type to sweep Napoleon and his invaders out of England with a broom and a bucket. As our visitors left, it was only Lestrade who seemed in a fit of the sulks, piqued that he was not to be let further into the secret.

Holmes was jubilant. He was not a man much given to wine, but that evening we shared a bottle of Dom Perignon, one of six dozen presented to him several years before by a client and as yet untasted.

The next morning there was no sign of him. He was not an early riser, and until I inquired of our landlady's maid-of-all-work, I had supposed he was still sleeping. His room was empty and my day passed idly but agreeably, a day chiefly remarkable for the autumn's first flurry of snow. At six o'clock I heard his shout to Mrs. Hudson on the stairs. He was back.

'I thought you had gone missing,' I said, half joking.

He flung down his hat and stick on the chair; his cloak followed. 'My dear Watson, I have spent the day in that most admirable of institutions, Somerset House. In painted halls and palatial apartments, enjoying unrivalled views of the river steamers on the Thames, one may study the records of births, marriages, and deaths to one's heart's content.'

'Whose birth, marriage, or death?'

'No one's. There is a far smaller section where those who have changed their names by deed poll are obliged to register the fact. I confess that the name Charles Henshaw sounded to me like—what shall we call it?—a light adaptation of something else. I was not entirely surprised to find that at Chatham Registry Office—not a million miles from Sheerness—it was adopted several years ago by Karl Henschel.'

'A German?'

'I confess, I should have thought so. In this case, when he changed his name, he was already an Englishman, or rather a German who had become a naturalised Englishman on a visit to Australia. You could hardly bury a secret much deeper than that.'

'But Mrs. Constantine has not the least doubt that he is English, through and through.'

'He is a linguist, my dear chap. A German linguist, particularly, will often speak more correct English than an Englishman born and bred. As for teaching French to English youths—or English to French youths—what better cover could there be? You might suspect him, perhaps, of being French by birth or sympathies. If he were German, you might say, the last thing he would do is to teach French in England.'

'And his Saturday visits to Oxford, what about those?'

'We shall be at Paddington tomorrow for the early train. On my way home, I paid a brief visit to Scotland Yard. Whitehall and the Embankment looked quite charming in the snow, quite like a Camille Pissarro sketch in oils. Superintendent Melville has deputed Inspector Tobias Gregson to shadow Herr Henschel, as we had better call him now. Gregson is one of the best men at the game. Even were Henschel to suspect that he was being followed, he would see that Gregson had slipped away from him in London. At Paddington I shall look for Gregson on the platform for the Oxford trains. He will tip us the wink, as they say, and identify Henschel. I have our man's photograph this afternoon, taken without his knowledge yesterday. Then, my dear Watson, Gregson will be on his way and the game will be in our court again.'

5

'You may as well pack your razor and a clean collar,' said Holmes at breakfast. 'I have wired ahead to engage rooms at the Mitre Hotel. I daresay it may prove an unnecessary precaution, but it is as well to be prepared. Your army revolver you may bring if you please. I cannot suppose it will be necessary on this occasion.'

Saturday morning had dawned bright and cloudless as midsummer, giving the lie to 'drear November.' Under his travelling cloak, Holmes wore a dark suit with a gold watch-chain over the waistcoat. This formal attire was scarcely what a lounger would choose for a weekend. As our cab rattled along the Marylebone Road toward Paddington station, I could not help wondering what our spy might look like. Would Karl Henschel be the bearded agent of romance or merely a young man who might be mistaken for an insurance clerk? One thing seemed certain, he could not be the traitor in the Admiralty. Sir John Fisher had assured us that there was no Charles Henshaw on their records.

At Paddington the concourse of the great railway station was bustling with weekend travelers crowding about the bookstall, the flower-sellers, and the cab ranks. Columns of smoke rose to the high curve of the glass roof from several green-liveried engines of the Great Western Railway waiting to depart. There was no train at the platform for Oxford and only a handful of passengers waiting by the leather trunks and wicker hampers, neatly piled for the luggage van.

It was hardly twenty minutes later when I recognized Gregson in his pale gray topcoat and bowler hat, keeping well back from his quarry. He scarcely needed to 'tip us the wink.' From where we stood it was quite plain to see who his quarry was. I should have taken the young language teacher for an army subaltern on weekend leave, neatly turned out in a belted Norfolk jacket and twill trousers, a black leather bag at his side. Slightly built, clean-shaven and with short-cropped hair, he had an air of peremptoriness about him.

The young man's back was to us as Holmes looked Gregson in the eyes at a distance of several yards and inclined his head an inch or so. Our Scotland Yard friend in his gray topcoat walked past us as though we had been strangers and disappeared on the far side of the bookstall. We made our way to the further end of the platform, which would bring us close to the exit when the train reached Oxford.

It did not seem that Henschel was accustomed to spend the night in Oxford but would return to Sheerness by a train that would leave for London in the late afternoon or early evening. At our destination, however, we had already arranged for a hotel porter to take our travelling bags from us and carry them to the Mitre Inn.

There was no difficulty in finding a compartment to ourselves on the journey. A dreary hour of West London was followed by enchanting views of the Thames valley running among the winter woods of the hills with flooded water-meadows to either side. It was not yet midday when we saw from the railway line the spires and towers of the ancient city.

The station approach at Oxford was lined by luggage wagons and cabs, but Henschel crossed the road and began making his way toward the centre of the town on foot. We kept well back, walking separately, until he turned up the wide thoroughfare of Beaumont Street with its plain but handsome houses. The creeper-covered windows and archway of one of the colleges faced us from the far end. I was as sure as I could be that our man had no idea he was being followed. He did not once look back or make any manoeuvre to suggest that he was trying to throw off a shadow. Our only risk was that an accomplice lay further back, trailing us in turn. Yet there was no sign of such a man, and he would have been astute indeed if he had been able to shadow Sherlock Holmes unobserved!

I was conscious that every stretch of open street or pavement increased the danger of Henschel spotting us. I need not have worried. At the top of Beaumont Street he turned into the wide courtyard of the Ashmolean, the university museum, which was raised on a plinth with its Grecian portico, pillars, and statues, a sculptured goddess sitting high above a classical frieze. As the corner concealed us briefly, I drew level with Holmes and said, 'For all we can tell, he may have come like any other tripper to see the collections. It seems more than likely.'

We separated again, two visitors dutifully and individually making our tour of the exhibits. The museum was admirably laid out for the purposes of tracking our suspect. Tall display cases running across the galleries make admirable cover for the hunter, yet one step beyond them gives a wide view ahead and behind. To begin with, from our concealment among the displays of classical sculpture on the ground floor, we watched Henschel go up the grand staircase leading to the galleries above.

Holmes waited until the young man had turned the corner to the second flight of steps and then walked slowly after him. I saw my friend pause and begin studying a dark van Eyck landscape on the half-landing. He had his back to the flight of stairs up which Henschel had gone to the floor above. Yet as Holmes stood there, I could see that in the palm of one hand he held a small round pocket mirror, reflecting the stairs behind him and the gallery above.

I followed cautiously up the staircase, well lit by its roof lights, to the wide and airy exhibition hall of the first floor. Before me lay a vista of Italian Renaissance art, to which we and our quarry were the only visitors just then, except for two ladies talking quietly together and a middle-aged gentleman on his own. There were display cases ranked in the center of the gallery and paintings along the walls to either side. I am no expert in such matters, but the small brass plates on each frame identified for me two Botticelli sketches of nymphs in woodland and a dimly lit papal portrait by Fra Lippo Lippi. How such things could be connected with espionage and naval codes defied explanation.

Holmes had disappeared from view. However, I became aware that Henschel was paying very little attention either to the paintings or to the Florentine ceramics and silverware that filled the glass display cases between them. He walked to the far end of the gallery and there helped himself to one of the small green canvas stools that filled a metal rack. These stools are commonly supplied in the great museums and art galleries for those amateurs who choose to spend a day sketching or copying some work by a master. The Ashmolean is next door to Mr. Ruskin's School of Drawing and Fine Art, which provides an ample supply of pupils. You will see such students busy every day in the galleries, as if they might be in the Louvre or the Uffizi.

Yet Henschel did not sit down to sketch any of the paintings. He held the folded green canvas of the stool in one hand and his black bag in the other as he walked through a side turning into a set of smaller exhibition rooms. This area was devoted to archaeological displays and, once more, the tall glass cases afforded ample cover. Each of them was layered with shelves on which were set out fragments of pots, amphorae or pithoi, small votive objects, here and there what appeared to be a rusted blade or implement.

Karl Henschel passed 'Mesopotamia,' 'Ancient Egypt,' 'Anatolia,' 'Ancient Cyprus,' and stopped at a display of cases along the far wall marked 'Ancient Crete and the Aegean.' There he opened out his little stool of green canvas and sat down. From his leather bag he took a small copying board to which was clipped a pad of paper.

I believe he had not the least idea that anyone else was there and probably he did not care. Why should he? He got up and walked away, into another room. He must have opened his pocketknife, for I heard him sharpening a pencil into a basket that had evidently been provided. The polished boards of the wooden floors acted as an excellent soundboard and I knew I should hear him coming back the moment he moved. While the coast was clear, I strolled past the case where his stool was parked and paused like a casual visitor to see which display meant so much to him that he had come from Sheerness to make a sketch of it.

I would not have crossed the road to copy what I now saw before me. Imagine, if you will, a few dozen scraps of old clay tile. Most were the colour of slate, a few looked like dark terra cotta, rather the colour of burnt sealing wax. Some were roughly square and a smaller number were oblong but sandy-colored and tapering at one end. None of them was more than five inches square. There was also a small ornament that I noticed was labelled as a seal ring.

This entire collection was described on its plaque as 'Linear B' tablets, most from the ruins of the Minoan palace at Knossos on the island of Crete. I remembered, from my schooldays, that this was the location of the labyrinth where Theseus slew the Minotaur in the famous legend. A small printed card informed the visitor that these clay tablets dated from a time before the Trojan War, probably about 1500 B.C. They had been found during the past ten years by Sir Arthur Evans, in his excavations of the site.

There were marks upon these baked clay tablets. A few were single downward strokes, which looked like some method of counting. For the rest, imagine tiny representations of an axe head, a five-barred gate, a wigwam, a fish, a star, and so forth. Such was the writing of Linear B. A further display card attempted to describe the pronunciation of certain words. I learnt that 'at-ku-ta-to' signified ten working oxen and 'at-ku-do-nia' fifty of the same beasts. Then I heard a movement in the next room and walked quietly but quickly away, behind the screen of another case. I took a glance presently and saw that Henschel was now sitting before this curious display and making small neat sketches of the tablets.

For the next three hours, taking turns, we kept up our scrutiny. It was not difficult since we had Henschel bottled up in the set of smaller exhibition rooms. He could not come out except by returning through the displays of antiquities and then down the avenue of Renaissance paintings to the grand staircase. From where he sat, he could hardly be aware that we were, at varying levels, always within sight of that exit route.

Holmes even equipped himself with one of the canvas stools and chose the portrait of an amiable Venetian courtesan by Carpaccio, before which he became the model of concentration. He sat with his notebook and pencil as other visitors came and went. Presently, a thin elderly man with pince-nez, walking stick, a rather rusty frock coat, and a neat gray beard took a stool from the rack and sat before a Piranesi sketch of the Coliseum. He paid no attention to anyone but, after almost an hour of noting and sketching, he stood up, polished his pince-nez with a blue silk handkerchief, dabbed his watery eyes, and returned his canvas stool to the rack. Holmes sketched angles and features, lost to the world in Carpaccio's portrait, until the old man had shuffled past him on his way out.

At the instant that the tapping of the old scholar's walking stick reached the half-landing of the staircase, Holmes sprang up and approached the rack of stools in a dozen quiet strides. I followed him as he added his folded stool to the rest. His eyes scanned the metal frame rapidly and came to rest on the four metal tubes that were its corner posts.

'As I thought!' he breathed sharply. His forefinger entered the nearest of these upright supports and screwed out a coiled piece of paper, no more than a single sheet of manuscript. As he unrolled it, I had just time to see:

57-09-83-62-15||19-80-05 . . .

His finger was to his lips as he returned it to its hiding place. Though his voice rose no higher than a whisper, its urgency was never in doubt.

'After him, Watson! He is not agile enough to have got far!'

'Henschel?' I gasped.

'Leave him. It is best that he should not see us again.' He strode to the staircase and went down it, two at a time, closing on the hobbling frock-coated gentleman with his stick, who was just going out into the museum courtyard. Then my friend slackened his pace and sauntered a dozen yards behind him, like a casual visitor once more. We took up our vantage point behind one of the stone pedestals and watched the old man walking across Beaumont Street and turning down it the way we had come. Then, to my surprise, he suddenly drew a key from his pocket, slid it into the latch of a white-painted door beside him, and disappeared into one of the handsome plain-fronted houses.

Sherlock Holmes was triumphant.

'And that, Watson, is how they do it! Now let us have no more of this until Monday morning. We have done all that is required of us for the time being.'

It seemed to me that we had done nothing of the kind. However, Holmes was in no mood to listen to argument. He insisted that we should not hurry back to London at once, or indeed the next day. Monday would be time enough. That evening we dined in the lamplit parlour of the Mitre with its low beams and memories of the coaching inn it had been until half a century before. Holmes pronounced the food and wine excellent. He talked of archaeology and the stupendous discoveries at Mycenae by the great German Heinrich Schliemann. How three gold-masked figures, warriors of the Trojan War, had been unearthed and how, when the masks were removed, their perfectly preserved faces had been recognizable for some minutes before they crumbled into dust.

'"Today I have looked upon the face of Agamemnon,"' he recited with a chuckle. 'No wonder Herr Schliemann sent that telegram to the King of Greece. Now, one pipe before my bed, my dear fellow. Sufficient unto the day is the evil thereof.'

We retired to the sitting room that he had reserved for our use, while the groups of tall-hatted undergraduates began returning to their colleges before lockup and the life of the university passed by in the lamplit street below us. Great Tom began to toll his hundred strokes from Christ Church tower, at the end of which time the porters would shoot the iron bolts across to close the main gates and those who were not inside their colleges must face the justice of the dean or the proctors on Monday morning. Only now were we solitary enough to discuss the afternoon's events.

'That old man was not our Admiralty spy,' I said incredulously. 'He cannot be!'

Holmes laughed and lit his cherrywood pipe from the fire.

'No, my dear fellow. The game is played in three moves, not in two. There is the spy who passes information. There is the old man who encodes it. Then there is Henschel who transmits it. Perhaps Henschel is also useful in formulating the language of the code.'

'A language that no one has used for more than three thousand years?'

'Precisely. In the present case, its rarity is what makes it unique. Almost nothing was known about Linear B until Sir Arthur Evans discovered the first tablets at Knossos. The meaning of the language is virtually unknown today. A string of meaningless ciphers. What better code could there be? It is not necessary to know its ancient meaning in order to give it a new one for purposes of espionage. It is the last thing in the world that anyone would think of!'

'But the code is written in numbers.'

'Quite right, Watson. On Monday morning I propose to put that difficulty to someone who can answer with rather more authority than either the Admiralty or Scotland Yard.'

On Sunday he was content with a riverside stroll round the circuit of Addison's Walk, where that famous essayist of the *Spectator* used to take his constitutional as an undergraduate at Magdalen. I noticed, however, that after breakfast he had withdrawn to the hotel writing room and penned a note. As he handed it to the page boy I was able to read the address: 'J. L. Strachan-Davidson, Esquire, The Master's Lodging, Balliol College.' On our return, as the river mists began to halo the lamps of the street, Holmes inquired of the concierge and was handed a small neatly written envelope in reply.

On Monday morning we set out to walk a few hundred yards down 'The Turl' in search of our adviser. I knew little of the Master, as I must now call him, except as a younger man, 'the lean, unbuttoned cigaretted dean.' He was a tall and angular Scot of luxuriant eyebrows and formidable reputation, an authority on Cicero and Roman criminal law. Holmes assured me that I should find all I needed to know of him as a tutor in one of the famous college rhymes.

> *Take a pretty strong solution*
> *Of the Roman constitution,*
> *Cigarettes not less than three*
> *And mix them up with boiling tea.*
> *Then a mighty work you've done,*
> *For you've made Strachan-Davidson.*

'I was once able to do the Master a small service concerning a scrape that one of his undergraduates was in—a nasty but petty blackmail. As you know, I do not expect favor returned for favor. However, he is good enough to write to me that he welcomes the opportunity to renew our rather slight acquaintance.'

Once inside the lodgings on the college's Broad Street front, we were shown up immediately to the Master's sitting room. The door stood open and from within came the sounds of a tutorial in progress. Two young men were sitting in arm chairs and Strachan-Davidson, his back to the fireplace and his arms stretched out at either side along the mantelpiece, was in full flow on the subject of Sparta's invasion of Athens during the Peloponnesian War.

'Do come in!' he said enthusiastically. 'Lord Wroughton and Mr. Sampson are just construing for us book four of Thucydides. Find chairs, if you can.'

We found them among the comfortable disorder of the room, books piled here and there, papers gathered untidily.

'Now, my lord, if you please.'

Lord Wroughton was a dark-haired and fresh-faced young man with the embarrassed look of one who had spent the previous evening dining not wisely but too well, when he should have had Thucydides as his sole companion.

'*Tou de-pe-gig-no-menou therou,*' he muttered, '*Peri sitou ek-boleen* . . . 'In the following summer, when the corn was in full ear.'"

'Yes, yes,' said the Master with Scots impatience, 'and when was that?'

'It was . . . that is to say, Master, I believe. . . .'

Sherlock Holmes took pity on the unfortunate young nobleman and intervened.

'I believe, Master, that we are safe in dating the expedition of the Syracusans against Messina as 1 June 425 B.C.'

The Master's eyebrows rose.

'Really, Mr. Holmes? After two and a half thousand years in which even the season has been a matter of debate, you are able to tell us the precise day?'

'It is really very simple, Master. Climate and season of every kind are necessary subjects upon which the criminal investigator must be informed. In this case, given the dates of ripening corn in Attica lying between 20 May and 10 June, the corn in full ear would scarcely be before the end of May. No reference is made to harvest, however, which suggests that the date of sailing was well before the end of the first week in June. Though I would allow a little latitude, I believe you will find that the tides necessary for embarking and landing the invading force would give very little alternative to 1 June. The coastline is not an easy one for shallow draft.'

'Dear me,' said our host genially. 'Well, if Thucydides is to become a matter of criminal investigation, perhaps we had better leave him there. Lord Wroughton and Mr. Sampson, I shall be pleased to receive you both at the same time next week, in the hope that the first five chapters of book four will be firmly in your minds by then. Good morning to you.'

As the two young men excused themselves deferentially to Holmes and myself, the Master shut the door and turned to us.

'My dear Mr. Holmes,'—only now did he shake our hands— 'though it is a great pleasure to make your acquaintance again, I confess I have been puzzling what use Linear B could have for you. One moment and I will put the kettle on.'

Holmes stretched his dark-suited legs before him.

'Every possible use, Master. The matter is in strict confidence, of course.'

'Of course. I imagine you would not be here otherwise.'

'You are a collector of seal rings and coins from the ancient world, I believe.'

Strachan-Davidson turned round with the kettle in his hand, beaming at us.

'You have heard of my winter journeys to the Middle East, I imagine. A numismatist in a dahabeeah, as my young men call me here, a coin collector in an Egyptian sailing boat. I have one or two seal rings. You may still pick them up from market stalls in Cairo and in western Crete, you know.'

'And Linear B?'

'I have followed the work of Sir Arthur Evans with great interest. A good many of the texts were published lately in his book *Scripta Minoa*. Unfortunately he is still in Crete, so you cannot very well consult him.'

Holmes nodded.

'The question is a simple one, Master. Could Linear B be used as the basis of a code? I beg you to consider the question most carefully.'

The Master's ample eyebrows rose once more.

'Oh yes, indeed. Linear B *is* a code, Mr. Holmes. Nothing else. It is a code so remarkable that no one has yet resolved it. A few decipherments here and there but very few and amounting to very little. Much of the rest of our understanding is guesswork. A school of thought, to which I am inclined to belong, believes these symbols to be early forms of classical Greek. From that there has been an attempt to evolve pronunciation. There is far to go.'

'Deciphered or not, its structure might form a modern naval or military code?'

The Master handed us tea in silence.

'The subject matter is the palace of Knossos, particularly its ships and arsenal. However, to draw each pictogram would be laborious. Nor could you print them, for no printer's type would be available.'

'How do scholars make texts available to each other? I imagine that must often happen.'

'Indeed, Mr. Holmes. The problem has been solved by certain scholars in Etruscan and Babylonian by reducing ancient symbols to modern numerals. Each symbol is given a number, as a kind of shorthand.'

'Could each Linear B symbol be a letter of an alphabet expressed as a number?'

The Master shook his head.

'No, Mr. Holmes. It is early days but, it seems, each symbol is a syllable rather than a single letter.'

Sherlock Holmes let out the long sigh of a man who is vindicated after all.

'Thus,' Strachan-Davidson continued, 'a modern message in Linear B would consist of several double digit numbers in groups, each double digit representing a syllable or whatever unit the code-maker chose and each group making up a word. It could serve for whatever message you wished to send. You would not have to decipher Linear B to use its signs as such a form of communication, though you might choose to do so.'

Holmes was in his familiar attitude, listening with eyes closed and fingertips pressed together.

'One further point, Master,' he said, now looking up. 'What advantage would this system have to distinguish it from any other form of code?'

Strachan-Davidson looked surprised.

'Only one, Mr. Holmes. Every other form of code, in letters or numbers, is adapted from something commonly understood in its uncoded form. It may be a word, a book, a numerical formula. However disguised or distorted, common knowledge lies behind it. In the case of Linear B, very little is known. Even that little knowledge is shared by only a handful of men throughout the world. The rest of mankind is excluded from the game, so to speak.'

'Precisely,' said Holmes quietly, 'how many of that handful live in Oxford?'

The Master thought for a moment.

'Sir Arthur Evans, but he is in Crete. There are two of his assistants, but they are with him. There is the keeper of antiquities at the Ashmolean.'

'And no others?'

'Dr. Gross is not a member of the university. He was deputy keeper in the department of antiquities at the Royal Museum in Berlin. He retired and has lived in Oxford for a year or two.'

'An elderly man with pince-nez who lives in Beaumont Street, I believe?' Holmes inquired innocently.

'Then you are familiar with him?'

'A passing acquaintance.' Yet those who knew Sherlock Holmes well, medical men above all, would have detected a quickening beat at the temples accompanying such a lucky shot in the dark. We took our leave presently. Holmes did not ask the Master for a pledge of confidentiality. Anyone who had been in the presence of Strachan-Davidson for any length of time would know that such a request was quite unnecessary.

6

By that evening, we were before our own fireside again in Baker Street, though not before Holmes had insisted upon a detour to the St. James's Library, of which he was a member and from which he carried off that imposing volume which bears upon it the name of Sir Arthur Evans and the cryptic title *Scripta Minoa*.

We had just finished our supper of 'cold fowl and cigars, pickled onions in jars,' as the poet has it, when Holmes filled his pipe again with the familiar black shag tobacco and crossed to his worktable. He laid a pile of blank paper and the intercepted signals on one side of his wooden chair and placed the *Scripta Minoa* on the other.

He selected a fresh nib from the box for his Waverley pen, then sat down with a cushion behind him, as if for a prolonged study of the puzzle.

There would be no more conversation that night. I made the best of a bad job, selecting a volume of Sir Walter Scott from the shelf and retiring to my own quarters. I do not know at what hour, if at all, he went to bed that night. He was sitting at the table next morning, the air once again as thick with smoke as a 'London particular' fog, *Scripta Minoa* at his side. There was no weariness about him but the exhilaration of the hunter at the chase.

'We have them by the tail, Watson,' he said triumphantly. 'In the past hours, I am convinced I have learnt Minoan arithmetic from Arthur Evans's drawings. A single vertical stroke is a one. A short horizontal dash is ten. A circle is a hundred. A dotted circle is a thousand. A circle with a horizontal bar is ten thousand. There are eighty-seven known syllabic signs in Linear B, but the double digits of the good Dr. Gross number ninety-two. There can be no doubt that those five extra double digits represent the means of counting.'

For the next two days and a good part of their nights he worked his way through intercepted signals that had previously been meaningless strings of double digits. Most of them remained so. Yet here and there he swore he was able to decipher numbers in the messages. Our sitting room bristled with his gasps of frustration and self-reproach as he failed to reclaim anything more. Elsewhere, sets of numerals were repeated, but it was not yet clear what they meant. It was on the afternoon of the second day that he thumped the table with his fist and uttered a loud cry.

'Eureka! I believe we have it!'

Even now he could not decode the alphabet or syllables represented by the double digits of Dr. Gross's cipher. Yet on the previous day he had identified five separate double digits as the Mycenean system of counting. That was all he needed. In the scanning of the present document he had decoded sequences of such numbers, though the letters of the alphabet and all its words still eluded him. The numbers he had decoded began with the sequence, 685,

3335, 5660, 120 . . . Even though the adjacent words remained a mystery, these numbers struck a chord in the formidable memory of Sherlock Holmes. He had encountered them before, in one of the Admiralty plans.

He unlocked a drawer in the table and took out a thick folder containing a sheaf of papers entrusted to him by Sir John Fisher. These were copies of Admiralty documents. Holmes had requested them as being the most likely to attract our antagonists. Already, he had spent more than a day and a night working on these copies. Now a needle glimmered somewhere in the haystack.

We worked together. Holmes read out sequences of figures from the naval documents and I checked them silently from a list of numbers he had drawn up as he had worked on the German signals over the past few days. After more than two hours, none of the numerical sequences in the signals had matched any in the Admiralty papers. I lost count of our failures as we came to yet another paper. Still the double digits that stood for an alphabet in the German code meant nothing. Only the ancient system of counting, which Holmes had deciphered after several days' study, might help us.

He read out a sequence of almost fifty numbers from the present document. As I checked them against the list he had made from the code, I held my breath. We read again to check for errors, and, I confess, my hand holding the paper trembled. There was no mistake. Call it luck, but from first to last, every number in the coded signal matched its equivalent number in the Admiralty document. It was soon evident that this entire coded paper must be an exact copy. Having got the numbers, we could now read the adjacent code for the objects to which they referred. The weariness left the voice of Sherlock Holmes as he grasped the key that would unlock Dr. Gross's enigma.

'Six hundred and eighty-five! Three thousand, three hundred and thirty-five! Five thousand, six hundred and sixty! One hundred and twenty! . . .'

I knew, not for the first time, that my friend had done the impossible. This was Sherlock Holmes at his best and most invincible, doing something that no other man on earth could have done. He stood with his back to the fireplace as he read out the list. When we came to the end, he sat down again and spoke as if he feared it was too good to be true.

'Those numerals, Watson! Identical and in the same sequence throughout the cipher and the document! It is thousands to one against mere coincidence.'

'But what is the Admiralty document you have been reading figures from?'

'The design calculations for the latest and most powerful battle cruiser of all, HMS *Renown*. By the pricking of my thumbs, I knew they would be after information such as this!'

He sat at the table for a moment and then turned to me again.

'Look at this dockyard manifest. It is a list of weights when the battle cruiser is fully loaded. All the tonnages in the right-hand column correspond to the numerals in Henschel's signal. An entire sequence of fifty! It must be the same document. Very well. If that column of figures is correct, then each of Henschel's double-digit code words on the left-hand side must describe the item whose weight appears on the right. See here. We have our decoded numerals for weight on the right. They stand opposite two unknown words in Henschel's code, the first being 46-24-47. The word in the Admiralty list at this point is "General" in "General Equipment." Therefore 46-24-47 in Henschel's code surely stands for "General," in whichever language. You see?'

I began to see but he was not to be stopped.

'And here again. Against the entry for "3335 tons," the word in the Admiralty document is "Armament." Henschel encodes this as 25-80-13-24-59. We know that the Ashmolean Museum can put sounds to Linear B syllables. In English, these five double digits must sound something like "Ar-ma-me-n-t." Thus five of the eighty-seven syllables of the alphabet are revealed! The syllables before "5660 tons" must match "Machinery." Before "120 tons" the numerical syllables, if one may call them that, must encode "Engineer's Stores."'

By evening, ignoring the tray that Mrs. Hudson brought, Holmes had broken what secret Admiralty files still refer to as the Linear B code. Dr. Gross had not translated his ciphers into German but simply encoded whatever he received. No doubt an elderly scholar of ancient languages may quail before engineering terminology. Holmes had deciphered every numerical sign for weights, the load calculations for HMS *Renown*. Matching the words of each item to its known tonnage, he pieced together the German code of Dr. Gross's ancient Mycenaean 'alphabet.' He found that 80-41-24-53 must stand for 'MACHINERY,' so that 24 stood for 'NE.' He confirmed it in the next line where 18-46-24-27 must be 'ENGINEER,' for 24 was 'NE' in both cases. It was the same throughout the document and, indeed, in all the other coded signals. Our enemies had never varied the basic Linear B code, so sure were they that it could never be overcome.

By next morning Holmes had equivalents for seventy of the eighty-seven letters of the word code, as well as all the numerals. Whether the learned Dr. Gross exactly copied the symbols of King Minos five thousand years ago—or varied them to suit his masters' purpose—Sherlock Holmes had him by the tail as surely as Theseus ever had the Minotaur.

As if to confirm this, the next transcript to reach us from the Admiralty contained a page opening with the familiar sequence of double digits 57-09-83-62-15 ‖ 19-80-05. I checked the pencilled note I had made at the time and found that it was identical to the opening of the cipher written on the paper that Dr. Gross had left in the stool rack of the Ashmolean Museum. This time the message had nothing to do with armaments but, rather, with the time required to gather Class A Naval reservists at Chatham and other ports of the Thames estuary, in the event of general mobilization and impending war.

7

Not many months after this, on a hot summer day in the far-off dusty Balkan town of Sarajevo, two bullets from the gun of a

Bosnian student shot dead the Archduke Franz Ferdinand of Austria and his duchess. It was well said that the bullet that killed the heir to the throne of Austria-Hungary was a shot that echoed round the world. At the time, I confess, I could not have believed that this Balkan outrage, shocking though it was, would precipitate a war unparalleled in human history. Yet there was no longer any doubt that the blindfold war that Holmes and I waged against unseen adversaries was in earnest. Our Baker Street rooms resembled more and more a battlefield. Several times that summer, during the remaining weeks of peace, Sherlock Holmes was absent for the entire day on a visit to the Admiralty. His business was with a mysterious group of people known only as Room 40.

In the wake of our Linear B discoveries came Superintendent Alfred Swain of the Special Branch. That branch was created at the time of the Fenian explosions in the 1880s and had originally been known as the Special Irish Branch. Before long it concerned itself with every kind of threat to the security of the nation. One afternoon, when Baker Street was a trench of white summer fog and the street lamps popped and sputtered at noon, was the first time that this Special Branch officer was our guest. The clatter of a barrel organ serenaded us from the opposite pavement with 'Take me on the Flip-Flap, oh, dear, do,' as coins rattled into the grinder's cap

The Special Branch may consist of hard, resolute men well able to take care of themselves, yet Superintendent Swain was a tall, thin figure, neatly but plainly suited. He spoke quietly and, as he sat down, he turned an intelligent equine profile and gentle eyes toward us. Inspector Lestrade had warned us scornfully what to expect from a man who read Lord Tennyson's *Idylls of the King* or Mr. Browning's translation of the *Agamemnon*—or even Tait's *Recent Advances in Physical Science* and Lyell's *On Geology*. There had been a movement among his colleagues to get rid of Alfred Swain by posting him to the Special Branch. He was thought by his CID superiors to be 'too clever by half.' He certainly gave the impression of a man who would rather have come to tea to discuss the novels of Mr. George Meredith—one of Sherlock Holmes's unaccountable enthusiasms. Holmes took to him from the start. As his grey eyes studied my friend intently, Swain picked his words carefully, almost fastidiously.

'Mr. Holmes, it must be said at the outset that you have lately performed a service to your country such as few men have done for many years past. Thanks to you, we now have Dr. Gross and Herr Henschel where we want them.'

Holmes looked alarmed.

'Not under arrest, I hope? I have had Sir John Fisher's word on that.'

Swain shook his head.

'No, sir. The First Sea Lord has kept his word. Indeed, you have given us an invaluable advantage in this. We are now reading their coded signals. But before we can take the matter further, we must identify the third member of their conspiracy, presumably at the Admiralty. When that is accomplished, we shall endeavor to turn their stratagem against them, rather than throw them into prison. Thanks to you, we have the means in our hands to save the lives of hundreds of our soldiers or sailors in the event of war, even to save our country from defeat.'

'I am relieved to hear it,' Holmes said, indifferent to such flattery. 'And what have you done to identify the traitor in the Admiralty?'

'Both Dr. Gross and Henschel are closely watched. From their method of procedure, it seems that Henschel probably knows nothing of the spy's identity. It is possible that neither of them does. Henschel appears to be a mere technician who transmits whatever is given him. Each man works, as it were, in a watertight compartment. None of them, if he were caught, could betray any part of the conspiracy but his own.'

'But you have connected their movements together?'

Swain sat back in his chair and folded his hands across his waistcoat.

'We have had Dr. Gross under observation. He uses no telephone. He has sent two wires, both of which we have read. They were directed to the librarian at the British Museum, requesting certain books to be brought up from the stacks for Dr. Gross's visit. He also receives a small amount of post, three communications in the past five weeks.'

'You have opened those envelopes, Mr. Swain?'

'We are aware of their contents, sir,' said Swain evasively. 'Apart from Henschel and Dr. Gross, there is the man whom I will call the naval spy. There appear to be twenty-four people at the Admiralty, from senior officers to junior clerks, who might have taken the design calculations of HMS *Renown* from the building in order to copy them. We have had them all under observation for some weeks and they have made no evident contact with either Dr. Gross or Mr. Henschel. Yet during that time, in the present international tension, the coded German signals have been transmitted almost nightly. We do not believe that Henschel can be transmitting from his rooms. Yet the signals are going out from somewhere near Sheerness, no doubt to a German naval vessel or trawler in the North Sea.'

At this point Swain took a notebook from his pocket and began to read a list of the information transmitted in the past few weeks.

'Particulars of Armament: *Indefatigable* Class. Particulars of Anti-Torpedo Boat Guns, 4-inch and 6-inch. HMS *Princess Royal*: replacement of nickel steel, armour diagram. Comparison of Boiler Weights and Performance in HMS *Inflexible*, boiler by Yarrows, Ltd., and HMS *Indomitable*, boiler by Babcock & Wilson. I understand, gentlemen, that Yarrow boilers are lighter and would allow *Indomitable*'s six-inch armor to be increased to seven inches without affecting her speed.'

Alfred Swain paused, then added.

'That is a sample of the technical information passing to our adversaries. More recently there have also been manoeuvre reports, gunnery ranges, torpedo matters, fire control, and signals. Last week, for the first time, there were answers to questions that Henschel must have received. Which parts of the fleet have been in the Firth of Forth since the beginning of May—the First and Eighth Destroyer Flotillas or any ships else? Have there been mobilizing tests of flotillas or coastal defences? What numbers of the Royal

Fleet Reserve Class A reservists are called in for the yearly exercise?' Swain paused and looked at us. 'All these are details vital to the other side in any immediate preparations for war.'

Holmes crossed to the window, drew aside the net curtain, and looked down into the thin summer fog. It was possible to see across the street, and no doubt, though the barrel organ was still rattling out its tunes, he satisfied himself that the movements of our visitor were not under observation by our enemies.

'Tell me about Dr. Gross, Mr. Swain.'

Swain looked a little uncomfortable.

'There is little to tell, sir. He was an archaeologist as a younger man, with Schliemann at the discovery of Troy, and then deputy keeper of antiquities at the Royal Museum in Berlin. He has lived quietly as a retired gentleman in Beaumont Street for the past two years. He goes out either to the Ashmolean or to work in one of the libraries. He takes lunch at the Oxford Union Society, of which he is a member. That seems to be his only social contact. He retires early to his rooms until the next day. In the past five weeks he has visited London each Monday and stayed for one night at the Charing Cross Hotel. He leaves each morning after breakfast and walks up the Charing Cross Road to the British Museum.'

'Who watches him?'

'He works all day in the North Library, Mr. Holmes, where I have kept him company—at a distance. He speaks only to the assistants and leaves at five thirty. He dines early at an Italian café in Holborn, then walks back to the hotel by eight P.M. One of my colleagues is already dining at the café when he arrives. Dr. Gross speaks only to the waiter and returns direct to the hotel. Whoever the spy in the Admiralty may be, it seems he does not write to Dr. Gross, or speak to him, or communicate by telegram or telephone. We have watched the old man every minute, so far as we can. There appears to be no dead letter box except the hollow frame of the rack of camp stools in the Ashmolean Museum. Dr. Gross uses that only to leave the encoded messages for Henschel. It is possible that Henschel does not know the code and, though a member of the conspiracy, does not know precisely what the signals contain when he transmits them.'

Holmes sighed deeply.

'I ask myself, if I were Dr. Gross, how would I manage it? Easily enough, I believe. There are so many ways! I daresay I would receive a letter at the Oxford Union Society. I understand it is run like a gentlemen's club, where there is a very large green baize board next to the porter's desk, crisscrossed with wire. Any letter through the post or a message by hand may be inserted there and left until the member collects it. The place is reserved to members only and you might keep observation outside for a month of Sundays without knowing what goes on inside.'

Swain looked a little embarrassed.

'One of our plain-clothes officers has walked through that corridor and scanned the letter board every morning. There is never a letter for Dr. Gross.'

'He may use another name and collect the letter even so.'

'Mr. Holmes,' said Swain quietly, 'there are dozens, scores, of letters sent there every day. We cannot open them all, under every name, without giving the game away. In any case, he might as easily receive a letter at the Charing Cross Hotel, under any name.'

Holmes seemed to change tack.

'Precisely. Then it must be a matter of observation—the most tedious of occupations. Yet it seems evident that Dr. Gross receives his information in London. Communication evidently does not take place between the time he leaves the hotel and the time he returns, unless something is slipped between the pages of a book on a British Museum shelf and he obtains it from there.'

'I think not,' said Swain quietly.

There the matter rested until three days later. At breakfast, Holmes said cheerfully, 'I trust you have no engagements this evening, Watson?'

'As it happens, I have not. Why?'

'Because it is Monday and Dr. Gross, being a creature of habit, will spend the night at the Charing Cross Hotel.'

'He may not.'

'He will. I took the precaution of calling there yesterday and asking if a message might be left for him. It might, though I did not leave one. What shall we say? Eight o'clock precisely.'

'How long for?'

'My dear fellow, if I knew that, I should hardly need to go at all! All night if necessary, though I think that unlikely. It seems that the contacts Dr. Gross makes in London must take place during those hours at the hotel. I have also considered Swain's suggestion that something is slipped into a volume at the British Museum. The reader inserts a message between the pages, hands the book in, the book goes back to the underground stocks. It is then ordered by another reader who retrieves the paper. I confess, I think that an unlikely method. There is the risk that it might be ordered by a third reader between those two or that the message between the pages might be noticed or even lost. Moreover, any investigation would instantly identify two members of the conspiracy rather than one. The Charing Cross Hotel seems altogether more probable.'

So it was that our cab carried us to the great lamplit space of Trafalgar Square and then into the Strand to the Charing Cross Hotel, next to the continental railway terminus. We made our way along soft carpets, down an avenue of gilt-columned mirrors and pillars of raspberry-coloured marble, to the First Class Lounge. The deep blue velvet arm chairs with a polished table next to each were reserved for those first-class passengers of the Southern Railway who awaited trains, at all hours of the day or night, to take them to the Channel ferries and on to Calais, Ostend, Paris, Berlin, or Milan.

Holmes selected a chair by the wall and pressed a small electric bell. A moment later it was answered by a 'buttons,' a youth in a page-boy's tunic and trousers with a matching forage cap in chocolate brown. The brass buttons of the tunic had been polished until they almost dazzled the sight. At a second glance, I recognised his face as one of those young rascals who formed what Holmes called his Baker Street Irregulars and who had been our eyes and ears on so many occasions. In this case, the lad had grown out of childhood by a year or two but remained on what Holmes called his 'little list' of informants.

'Been and gone, sir,' he said, even before Holmes could ask the question.

'Already?'

'Yessir. Your gentleman that usually comes back from reading his books at eight o'clock must have missed his dinner tonight. He was back here at seven. Calls from his room at half past and gives me half a crown to fetch his package from the station cloakroom for him. He give me the cloakroom ticket and I come back with a little attaché case. Locked. Couldn't say what was in it. Give me the other half a crown when I got back. A good night's pickings, Mr. Holmes.'

'A little attaché case,' Holmes repeated thoughtfully. 'Well done, Billy. Well done, indeed.' His hand went into his pocket and a gold half-sovereign glinted as he discharged it into the waiting palm. 'That will double what the other gentleman gave you. Now you may bring us two glasses of single malt and a jug of hot water.'

'Not soda, Mr. Holmes?'

'I am not accustomed to ruin a single malt with seltzer, Billy. Now, cut along.' As soon as the lad was out of earshot, he turned to me. 'Watson, we have them! Or we will have them by next Monday. Monday is the clue. A man who abstracts confidential papers on Friday evening knows that they will not be called for until Monday morning. He has the entire weekend to copy them. The maximum time and the minimum risk. On Monday morning he leaves the attaché case in the station cloakroom; inside it are the copies he has made. No doubt he then enters this hotel, seals the cloakroom ticket in an envelope, and leaves it as a message to be collected by Dr. Gross, on his arrival from Oxford later that day.'

'By Jove,' I said, half admiring these scoundrels, 'and all that Dr. Gross must do on Monday evening is to give the boy the cloakroom ticket. The case is fetched for him.'

'Just so. On Tuesday morning Dr. Gross gives the boy the empty case to deposit at the station cloakroom, and the boy brings back a new cloakroom ticket. Dr. Gross then puts the ticket in an envelope and posts it in the hotel letter box, so that it reaches his man by Wednesday, in time for the attaché case to be taken by this friend to his Admiralty office on Friday. Or he may summon a page to his rooms and send the lad to post it outside. The Special Branch would see nothing out of the ordinary. And so the game goes round.'

'Indeed,' I said, improving on this. 'And when he sends the attaché case back to the cloakroom, it may not be empty. Gross would surely leave instructions in it, as to the documents to be copied that weekend. The Admiralty spy collects them on Wednesday evening at the latest, in ample time for this.'

'Admirable, Watson! No doubt you were about to add that our Admiralty spy may also find in the case an envelope of banknotes, the wages of treachery.'

Billy returned with two glasses and the jug of hot water. Once he had gone, Holmes resumed.

'Dr. Gross returns to Oxford on Tuesday and encodes the information, in time for Henschel's visit to the Ashmolean on Saturday. And so the circle is closed. I should wager that none of the three men has ever seen either of the other two.'

Sherlock Holmes was proved correct in almost every particular. By the following Tuesday the Admiralty spy was revealed as a young man by the name of Preston, a naval draftsman. Those who knew him called him diligent, solitary, a man of impeccable moral character and strict conscience but with few friends. He lived in a modest house in a South London street where he nursed an invalid sister.

Only a search in the Criminal Record Office files revealed that Preston's brother-in-law, an attorney's clerk married to this invalid sister, had sought her cure by plunging heavily into the stock market with money borrowed from the firm's client account. As usual, he had hoped to replace the 'loan' and take the profits it had made for him. As is often the case, his desperate investments had failed him. When he went to gaol, his wife who was Preston's sister had taken poison. However, she misjudged the dose. The poison did not kill her but left the invalid now crippled and imbecile. Preston had cared for her thereafter. Whether her tragedy bred in him some hatred of his nation or of mankind in general, both of whom had turned their backs upon her and driven the husband and the brother to their respective crimes, who can say?

8

Under the authority of Superintendent Swain and the Special Branch, the railway police at Charing Cross were enlisted. With their assistance and the authority of the Home Secretary, the attaché case was removed from the cloakroom once it had been deposited on the following Tuesday morning. It contained the instructions, as Holmes had guessed, and the banknotes, as I had suggested. They were £5 notes and the banks have a habit of listing the names to whom they are issued. One had been in a German Embassy draft, while the other had circulated in Germany itself. Within an hour the case was returned to await collection.

Now the blindfold war took a new form. Every Tuesday the attaché case was opened and the list of information required by Dr. Gross or his masters was copied. For the next two days, however, in Room 40 of the Admiralty Building, two draftsmen drew up bogus inventories and plans, details of manoeuvres and gunnery, signals and mobilisation. It was these that Preston was allowed to purloin and that sowed error in the finely worked espionage of our adversaries. Ranges were understated, locations of shore batteries revised, movements and manoeuvres misreported. The armor belt diagrams of our warships were sometimes thickened or extended, sometimes diminished in extent. The High Seas Fleet of Admiral von Tirpitz, which had previously been trained to destroy a precise target, would now shoot at random—or, worse still, in error.

Sherlock Holmes was a frequent visitor to the famous Room 40 of the Admiralty cryptographers during the war that was to come. Yet his greatest service to the nation's cause was performed before a shot had been fired. Thanks to my friend's machinations, as the last glorious summer of peace darkened across the continent, Dr. Gross was no longer to be seen at the Charing Cross Hotel. The Great Northern Hotel was his lodging and the railway termini at Kings Cross and Liverpool Street became his promenade. As for his confederates, the Special Branch acted on advice it did not entirely understand and paid out still more rope for the spies to hang themselves.

At the Admiralty, a secret signal was decided upon. It was to be broadcast to all ships of the Royal Navy as soon as a state of war with the German Empire and its allies was declared. That signal was to be 'England Expects.' Upon receiving it, ships' captains would open their secret orders, discover their meaning, and act accordingly in the war of which they were now informed. Yet this signal was not so great a secret that Preston could not get his hands on it. During the last weeks of peace it was encoded by Dr. Gross, transmitted by Karl Henschel, and filed by the Senior Intelligence Officer of the German Ministry of Marine in the Wilhelmstrasse.

The coded signals from Henschel, received by a destroyer of the High Seas Fleet riding an oily swell somewhere off the Thames estuary, continued to carry information on Royal Navy gunnery and ship design. Increasingly these reports were supplemented by reports direct from Dr. Gross. From personal observation the elderly scholar was gathering details of mobilisation and troop movements as the prospect of war drew nearer. Trains from Liverpool Street were carrying Royal Marines to Harwich and Hull, hardly convenient for a campaign in France but essential for an attack upon the North Sea coastline of Germany. Fort Codrington, near Felixstowe and the eastern coast, had become their transit camp. The Fifth and Seventh Destroyer Flotillas were seen off the Wash, moored as if to escort troop transports.

Three weeks before the day on which that most dreadful of all wars began, Dr. Gross was able to inform his masters that the British Admiralty had placed an immediate order with the Stationery Office for 1,200 copies of charts and land maps covering the Danish west coast of Jutland from the Skagerrak at the northern tip to the Frisian

Islands and the German frontier in the south. It seemed that Sir John Fisher was to get his wish to 'Copenhagen' the enemy and seize the Kiel Canal, perhaps without declaration of war.

Though the landing would be on their territory, there was little doubt which side the Danes would support. They had lost their provinces of Schleswig and Holstein to Germany in the war of 1863 and smarted to recover them. If the Royal Navy put 15,000 Marines ashore on friendly Jutland, these troops would be scarcely a hundred miles from the Kiel Canal, and thus poised to sever Germany's link between her Baltic and North Sea coasts. Such a spearhead would become a dagger pointed at the heart of Prussia and even at Berlin itself. Indeed, it would be a dagger at Germany's back as she faced France and Britain on her Western Front.

On the last night of peace in August 1914, as the minutes passed and Berlin ignored each ultimatum from London and Paris to withdraw its invading army from Belgium or else face war, Holmes and I were at Scotland Yard. Neither Preston nor Dr. Gross had been arrested, though both were closely watched. Karl Henschel sat before us, for he alone had been detained and his confederates knew nothing. In the green-walled office above the Thames, with its wooden cupboards, bare table, and hat rack, Alfred Swain interviewed the young man while Holmes and I sat to one side. Henschel seemed indifferent to his fate.

'I did nothing unlawful,' he said repeatedly. 'I was given signals to send and I sent them. Why should I not? I could not tell what was in them. I did not know and it was never explained to me.'

'Listen to me carefully,' said Superintendent Swain, leaning forward across the table towards the young man like a true adviser. 'By your own choice, you became a British subject. Now, it appears, it would have been far better for you to have remained a German. As an alien, you could not commit treason against the King of England.'

'It was not treason! To send messages!'

'Please believe me, if war comes, you will be tried for treason as a British citizen. That you will be found guilty is a certainty upon such evidence. Three weeks later you will be taken from your cell at eight o'clock in the morning, a rope will be put round your neck, and you will hang by it until you are dead. No one will notice your death among so many, and no one will care, least of all your paymasters in Berlin. To them you are no more than their post boy.'

'No one has ever been hanged in England for such a thing as I have done!'

'Quite right,' said Swain encouragingly. 'If you were sentenced this minute, it would be for a breach of the Official Secrets Act. You would probably go to prison for four or five years. I daresay you would be released after three.'

'Well, then?'

'Once war begins, what you have done will not be regarded as a breach of Official Secrets but as treachery under the Defence of the Realm Act. For that you will be hanged. The ultimatum is running out for you, Mr. Henshaw, as surely as for your masters in Berlin.'

'My true name is Henschel, not Henshaw!'

'Alas,' said Swain, shaking his head, 'no. You may wish it was so but it cannot be. You changed it of your own free will, as you became an Englishman of your own free will. And so you will be hanged as Charles Henshaw, the English traitor. If you nourished dreams of being a hero, you may safely forget them. You will have no memorial in your own land. If you are truly fortunate, you will be shot rather than hanged, tied into a kitchen chair on the rifle range of the Tower of London. And that, Mr. Henshaw, is all that you have to look forward to in this world.'

I do not know why but this, of all things, broke his nerve. He trembled and he could not speak. He was, after all, a petty figure in the conspiracy—an impoverished teacher of languages, who now found himself terrifyingly out of his depth. Sherlock Holmes intervened, for all the world as if he were 'prisoner's friend,' as they call it at courts-martial.

'It will be too late once war has been declared, Herr Henschel. It is neck or nothing for you—here and now. You had best decide at once between prison and the hangman. Indeed, you may yet decide between prison and freedom, but you had best be quick about it.'

Henschel could not reply until he had taken a drink from his glass of water.

'How can I choose? What is done is done.'

Holmes shrugged.

'By continuing to do what you have done for several years. Transmit the signals that are given you to transmit. They will mean nothing to you, as you say, but they may save both your life and your liberty. The choice is yours. Life or death. Captivity or freedom.'

The choice, of course, was nothing less than betrayal of his paymasters, and I do not know who had given Holmes the authority to suggest it—possibly Alfred Swain himself. Henschel had a certain value. I am no expert, but I have heard that those who are experienced listeners can identify the very finger of the operator on the Morse code button! How long such a deception might be kept up, I could not tell. Yet every transmission that put the Germans in error was worth its weight in gold. At that moment the great bell of Big Ben, on its parliamentary tower, began to strike eight in the evening. The tolling was close to us and the reverberations long, loud enough to interrupt conversation. It came like a funeral knell for Karl Henschel. If he was not broken already, this broke him. He looked down at his hands in his lap and said:

'Tell me what to do.'

There was a sudden relief in the room and we breathed more easily, for it is a terrible thing to send a young man to his death in such a way. Holmes crossed to the window and opened it a little for air in the warm August evening.

'You may demonstrate your expertise for us,' he said coolly. Though it sounded casual enough, this was what he had been working for.

That night, even before the ultimatum to Germany expired, Henschel tapped out a brief message, repeated several times. I swear that he thought it a mere demonstration and had no idea that it was transmitted through the darkness to his friends in Berlin. Though it was encoded, I read the cipher and saw 'ENGLAND EXPECTS.'

Six weeks earlier, among the falsehoods passed off on Preston and Dr. Gross, this had been the masterstroke of Sherlock Holmes. Admiral von Tirpitz's intelligence officers had been informed by their spies, who knew no better, that 'England Expects' was the signal for launching Sir John Fisher's 'Copenhagen,' the attack on Kiel by way of an invasion of Jutland with 15,000 Royal Marines. Now, on the third floor of Scotland Yard, above the Thames and the street lights of the Embankment, Karl Henschel tapped out that message. Far worse for Grand Admiral Tirpitz and the Kaiser's High Seas Fleet, the same message was echoed openly in a few hours time when war was declared and it was broadcast to the entire Royal Navy. Ships' captains opened their sealed orders and read its true meaning—merely that war had begun. Yet to those who listened in Berlin, it seemed that the air was alive with immediate orders to launch or support 'Copenhagen' and the seizure of the Kiel Canal.

In the circumstances, what followed is scarcely surprising. It is a matter of history that not a single Royal Marine landed on Danish soil. Most of the 'Marines' reported by Dr. Gross at Liverpool Street station were mere barrack-duty veterans dressed for the part on their train journey to the East Coast ports, to give the impression of an army on the move. The destroyers seen on the horizon were ships that passed in the night. It is also a matter of history that Helmuth von Moltke kept back from the Western Front 20,000 of his best troops in Schleswig-Holstein to protect Germany's Danish flank from this mythical attack. A month later, for want of those 20,000 troops at the Battle of the Marne, the great German advance on the Western Front was halted and beaten into retreat only twenty miles from Paris.

'Charles Henshaw' tapped out the signals given him for the rest of that great war. For how long those who listened believed him it is impossible to say. Dr. Gross was briefly interned and then allowed to live at liberty in Oxford. Outrageous though this might seem,

Sherlock Holmes insisted that it was the best policy. Preston, the spy in the Admiralty, was suddenly alone and without understanding why. He knew only that the instructions and the money that had awaited him every week at Charing Cross cloakroom ceased to appear from the moment of the war's beginning. He might have inquired of Dr. Gross or Karl Henschel, but, thanks to the ingenuity of the German espionage system, he did not even know their names, let alone where they might be found. Frightened and bewildered, he went on with his work as a naval draftsman, watched by those he never saw. His disloyalty in peacetime would lie within reach of the gallows if he continued it in wartime. The temptation to be a spy had gone forever. Once again, Holmes insisted there must be no arrests, no headlines to tell our enemies that their agents had been unmasked. Only by this means could Karl Henschel be used as the means of undermining German intelligence with his false reports.

What the full consequences were, who can say? It is certain that the diversion of 20,000 troops from the Battle of the Marne saved Paris and France, if not England. The battle cruisers of the Royal Navy suffered considerably at the Battle of Jutland in 1916. How much greater their losses would have been had the secret documents concocted by Sherlock Holmes and Jackie Fisher not found their way into the hands of Tirpitz and his staff is a matter of conjecture. Certain it is that my friend was absent for an entire afternoon at Windsor soon after the outbreak of war. He returned and would say little. After a little while he took from his pocket a fine silver cigarette case. Presently he handed it to me.

'In all the circumstances, old fellow, I should like this to be yours.'

The sterling silver was engraved with a crown and a single royal name followed by 'R' and 'I' for 'Rex' and 'Imperator.' In addition, as if this were intended for a recipient of exceptional merit, the case was further engraved on the back with the words 'ENGLAND EXPECTS.'

The Case of the
Peasenhall Murder

1

Sherlock Holmes was not a man much given to holidays or to any form of travel for its own sake. I once made the mistake of assuring him that the Taj Mahal and the treasures of the Nana Sahib would merit a journey. He answered me in the words of Samuel Johnson to James Boswell, who had promised his friend that the Giant's Causeway was worth seeing.

'Worth seeing,' said Holmes with a sigh, 'but, alas, not worth going to see. Life is too short to allow of making mere excursions.'

Apart from his professional visits, he was generally content to remain in London and, indeed, in Baker Street. The only exception he allowed was in his pursuit of archaeology and antiquity. The isles of Greece and the great sites of Troy or Mycenae were too far distant, but the Dark Ages of his own land held a fascination for him. During one of these expeditions, it was my own calling as a medical man that involved us in the strange mystery of the Peasenhall Murder.

Holmes had conceived a taste for the history of East Anglia with its flat landscapes running to the sea and its wide horizons above fields and waterways. Here the noble Saxons of Mercia had fought unavailingly against the Danish invaders twelve centuries before.

It was, he said, unspoilt rural England at its best. Our visit was arranged for the first half of June. We were to make our headquarters for ten days at the Bell Hotel in Saxmundham, a grey brick structure adjoining the Town Hall. The Bell was a well-appointed hostelry, built just before the coming of steam, in the last days of horse-drawn mail coaches.

The train from Ipswich deposited us at a little station where one feels the fresh breeze from the North Sea hardly more than five miles distant. No sooner had we finished lunch than Holmes must be up and doing, as the saying goes, carrying out his inspection of the ancient parish church that stood close by. In his impatience, he was for all the world like a major-general reviewing a summer camp.

It was a bright afternoon when my friend introduced me to the ancient tower of Norman stones and flint. It rose beyond the great trees that lined a steep path from the town. Within the nave, there was a fine old hammerbeam roof and a charming mediaeval font carved with emblems of the Evangelists and supported by two dwarves carrying clubs. I noticed, however, that my friend stood longest by a grave in the churchyard that was marked with a skull and crossbones. Its inscription was carved in memory of Joel Eade, 'whose soul took flight in 1720.' The macabre suggestion that the poor fellow had been carried off by devils was precisely of the kind to attract Sherlock Holmes.

The rest of the day was uneventful, though the sight of the sky gave me some uneasiness. There had been rain the night before, and the dark clouds across the fields promised worse to come. As we sat down to our dinner in the comfortable hotel, the gathering winds outside assured us that a true storm was blowing up. It was an apt prelude to the horrors of the following day.

Until four o'clock next morning, the rain fell as if it never meant to stop, the wind driving against the windows of our rooms. By breakfast time, the gale had blown itself out and the rain had dwindled to a fitful drizzle. We had just risen from the table when our landlady bustled across the room; she was followed by a stranger in police uniform. It was the constable who spoke.

'Dr. Watson, sir? Police Constable Eli Nunn. May I speak with you, Doctor?'

There followed a most vexing conversation. A medical man, like any other, wishes to take his holiday leisure without interruption. However, a young woman had been found dead that morning in the nearby village of Peasenhall. She had been six months pregnant, with no father to her child, and it was believed that she might have made away with herself. It was imperative that a doctor should attend before the police could move the body to a mortuary. Dr. Lay, the regular medical practitioner, was out on an urgent call, but some convenient busybody had noticed the name of another doctor in the list of guests at the Bell Hotel, Saxmundham! If I would be so good as to attend for a few minutes, it would then be possible for the police to proceed in their business.

It promised to be a most tiresome errand, but, in the circumstances, I could scarcely refuse. Nor, I believe, would Sherlock Holmes have permitted it! A pony and trap waited outside. Constable Nunn whipped up the horse and we bowled along the little Suffolk roads in a thin sunlight, which now followed the storm. Had I known what awaited me, I believe nothing would have induced me to climb into that trap.

The distance was greater than I had expected. We went through the charming village of Sibton with its ruined abbey and cottages in pink and cream, before coming to the more remote and workaday settlement of Peasenhall. I could not help wondering whether Eli Nunn's choice had fallen on me because someone at the hotel had let slip that I was in the company of the famous Sherlock Holmes.

Presently, Constable Nunn reined in the horse outside Providence House, a well-built residence in the main street of Peasenhall, a village that seemed little more than a single long street. We were escorted to the back and entered by a rear conservatory, which in turn led into a small kitchen, about ten feet by eight. A narrow flight of stairs led upward from one corner, so that the servants might reach their attics without appearing on the main staircase.

Someone had draped linen over the only window, which cast a further gloom on the scene.

The moment I stepped into the kitchen from the conservatory, I smelt a strong odour of paraffin and a nauseous taint of burnt flesh. Then I looked down and saw the body of a girl lying across the floor on her back. She was wearing her stockings and a nightdress that had been partly charred, as had one side of the body itself. The cause of her death was never in doubt, for there was a wound extending from under the angle of the right jaw across to the left jaw, completely severing the windpipe. Another wound below the angle of the right jaw ran upward underneath the chin. Either of these injuries would have been fatal, but there was also a puncture wound near the breastbone. I also noticed that the door of the little staircase had been thrown back with such violence, presumably in a struggle of some kind, that it had broken a bracket of the narrow wall shelf.

How anyone but a thoroughgoing village idiot could imagine that this was a case of suicide defied explanation. If the poor girl had inflicted either of the throat wounds upon herself, she would certainly not have lived long enough to carry out the second. Indeed, the blood that had spurted from the wounds had splashed the little stairway to the second step. It needed no examination to tell me that she was dead, but I satisfied myself that she was almost cold and that rigor mortis was well-nigh complete.

'She has been dead for at least four hours,' I said, turning to Constable Nunn, 'and possibly for much longer, since a body will cool more slowly in summer temperatures.'

The worst aspect of all was that the murderer—for this was murder if ever I saw it—had apparently tried without success to set fire to the place. In the event, the body and its linen were only charred on one side. A broken paraffin lamp lay on the floor, where it had presumably fallen at the moment of her death or a little before. Perhaps the oil from this had caught fire, but it would probably not have been enough to cause such damage to the body or the clothing as we now looked upon it. Where the rest of the paraffin had come from, I could not say.

My presence at the scene made very little difference. A few minutes after our arrival, Dr. Charles Lay, the village physician, returned from his visit to Sibton, and I handed the investigation to him with considerable relief. Though one grows accustomed to the horrors of medical life, there was much about the death of this poor young girl in so brutal a manner that shook me more than I would have expected. Sherlock Holmes stood quiet as a statue and said nothing. However, he accompanied me when I stepped out into the back garden to confer with Dr. Lay. He stood apart a little as we held our conversation and then approached me.

'There are two curious pieces of evidence in this matter, Watson. I fear they may yet lead the Suffolk constabulary far from the truth. Did you not observe them?'

'I can't say that I did,' I replied rather impatiently, for the whole thing seemed plain enough to me.

'There was a newspaper folded under the young woman's head and it had been charred a little in the abortive fire. It was a copy of the *East Anglian Times* for the day before yesterday. We must assume that the murderer put it there—but why? There were also fragments of a medicine bottle scattered on the floor. One of them included the neck of the bottle with the cork so well jammed into it that it appears immovable. Another fragment of the bottle had a label with writing upon it. Unless I am much mistaken, it read 'Two or three teaspoonfuls, a sixth part to be taken every four hours—For Mrs. Gardiner's children.' The ink had run a little but I believe that was the inscription. I gather the name of the owners of this house is Crisp, not Gardiner.'

'Perhaps it contained paraffin to add to the blaze,' I said a little irritably. 'Mrs. Gardiner may have something to answer for.'

Holmes looked across the little garden towards the rear door of the house.

'Were I to commit a murder and attempt to burn the body,' he said thoughtfully, 'I do not think I should wedge the cork so tightly in a bottle of paraffin that I could not withdraw it quickly at the critical moment. I would, at the very least, make sure of that.'

I was too much affected by what I had just witnessed to pay much attention to my friend's forensic niceties.

During the remaining ten days of our stay at the Bell Hotel the murder of Rose Harsent, as her name proved to be, at twenty-three years old seemed to pursue us. It had seemed natural to me that the little community of Peasenhall should prefer a verdict of suicide by a poor girl who was six months pregnant with no father to her child rather than that one of its own members should stand accused of both the paternity and the murder. The facts made nonsense of this, however. So, at least, the coroner's jury found.

For the next week our good landlady at the Bell Hotel lost no opportunity to bring us the latest gossip. I cannot dignify it by the name of news. What neither Holmes nor I had realised was that what the newspapers now called 'The Mystery of the Peasenhall Murder' had been preceded a year earlier by 'The Great Peasenhall Scandal.' Our hostess described this earlier sensation with more relish than seemed quite decent.

She told us that two Peasenhall youths, George Wright and Alfonso Skinner, belonged to that unsavoury class of Peeping Toms, whose amusement it is to spy on courting couples and the like. This pair of scoundrels let it be known that on the evening of 1 May, they had witnessed grossly indecent and dishonourable conduct between Rose Harsent and William Gardiner, a married man who was father of six children and who had risen to the position of foreman at Messrs. Smyth's Seed Drill Works in the village.

The alleged incident had taken place at a building in Peasenhall that they call the Doctor's Chapel, a Congregational chapel presided over by a local worthy, Mr. Crisp of the ill-fated Providence House. Rose Harsent was a servant at the house and it was part of her duties to clean this nearby chapel. Hence she had need of the chapel key from time to time. William Gardiner and his family lived two hundred yards further down the main street, at Alma Cottage. This industrious foreman was also a leading light of the Primitive Methodist connection at the pretty village of Sibton a couple of miles to the east. Rose Harsent sang in the choir at Sibton.

Once the scandal reached his ears, William Gardiner denounced it as a disgusting falsehood. He confronted his two slanderers, as he called them, who scornfully stood their ground. Gardiner then asked the superintendent minister of his congregation, Mr. Guy, to hold a chapel inquiry into the allegations. This was done, his accusers were heard but disbelieved, and Gardiner was exonerated. The minister and his elders thought the accusation 'trumped up,' nothing but 'a tissue of falsehood,' and reinstated Gardiner, who had resigned as a matter of honour from his positions as steward, choirmaster, and Sunday school superintendent when the story first reached him.

He now went to a solicitor and began proceedings for slander. Unfortunately, he then dropped these proceedings. His explanation was that Wright and Skinner had no money, that even if he won he must bear all the costs. He had no funds for this. On reflection, he also thought Rose Harsent would not be 'strong enough' to face the ordeal of the witness-box and cross-examination. Innocent or guilty of the scandal, her reputation must be indelibly tarnished.

All the same, it looked bad for William Gardiner when he withdrew the slander action. It seemed halfway to an admission of guilt. His wife Georgina never believed the charge, for she said her husband had been at home with her during the time when he was alleged to have been with Rose Harsent at the Doctor's Chapel. Rose had been the friend of Mrs. Gardiner and continued to be so after the scandal, an ally who came regularly to the house, and a coreligionist at Sibton chapel. Throughout the entire affair, however, Georgina Gardiner's evidence, true or false, was ridiculed by spiteful locals as that of a wife protecting her husband, herself, and their six children.

Naturally, Gardiner became the first suspect in the subsequent death of Rose Harsent. Worse still for him, various 'evidence' or tales now emerged from the year when the gossip ran riot before the murder. I recalled that Holmes had seen the name Mrs. Gardiner written on the label of the broken medicine bottle beside the body. Yet Mrs. Gardiner explained that she had given Rose the bottle, which then contained camphorated oil for a throat complaint. No doubt it might later have held paraffin, used by the intruder in the attempt to start a fire.

A Methodist preacher, Henry Rouse, claimed to have seen Gardiner and Rose walking together between Peasenhall and the chapel some weeks after the scandal. He had written a letter to Gardiner, warning him against indiscretion. Unfortunately, for reasons he could not explain, Mr. Rouse sent the letter anonymously and in his wife's handwriting. It was subsequently proved that this old man had been the instigator of slander and author of anonymous warnings in another village, from which he had moved to Peasenhall at short notice.

Gardiner himself had to admit sending two letters to Rose during this time, although when read in public they contained only the most unobjectionable account of the measures he was taking to seek justice for them both. The most damning letter, said to be Gardiner's, was an anonymous lover's assignation note. This came to Rose Harsent by post not many hours before her death. The writer asked her to leave a candle in the window of her attic room at ten P.M. that night. If this signal told him the coast was clear, he would come to her at midnight, by way of that back kitchen, where her body was afterwards found. The great courtroom expert, Thomas Gurrin, held that this note and its envelope were in Gardiner's writing. Two humble bank examiners of suspect signatures swore that the script was not Gardiner's. It seemed to me, as they say, six of one and half a dozen of the other.

Undeniably, it was a case of the most sordid kind. Holmes and I seemed well out of it. All the same, I was not the least surprised that it made headlines in the local papers or that before the end of our visit William Gardiner had been arrested and charged with the young woman's murder. The evidence, such as it was, pointed only at him. Holmes said little or nothing about it, contenting himself with the antiquities of Suffolk.

On the last Saturday of our visit, however, my friend suggested that we might make a railway excursion to the nearby coast and enjoy a little sea air. Great Yarmouth was the destination chosen for our day by the sea. It was a pleasant enough place, though inclining a little too much toward a resort for trippers, in my view. That need not have mattered, had Sherlock Holmes not noticed a gaudy placard on the promenade for a beach sideshow. It was a fly-by-night affair in a canvas booth, and it promised a tableau of 'The Dreadful Peasenhall Murder.'

Poor Rose Harsent had not been dead a week, and the man accused of her murder had been arrested only a few days ago. Already some rascal was taking his profit from their misfortune. All the same, Holmes must visit this disgraceful display. It was evident that the proprietor of the waxwork had never heard of laws relating to contempt of court or indeed the presumption of innocence. Neither the setting nor the persons of the display resembled reality, of course. Yet there before us was a makebelieve Rose Harsent in the pose of having her throat cut by a makebelieve William Gardiner—all in wax. The whole thing was a trap to fleece idlers and muckrakers.

Holmes said not a word as we stared at this outrage. I am pleased to say that the police had already been informed. The exhibition was closed down and the proprietor taken into custody a few hours later. It was only when we had left the booth and walked a few yards by the sea that my friend turned to me and remarked:

'Unless I am very much mistaken, Watson, we shall hear more of this wretched matter. As yet, we know far too little to judge the case. Curious, is it not, how so many ignorant people believe that creating a scandal will draw the veil from some hidden truth? In reality, scandal obscures the truth more effectively than anything else. For the present, however, William Gardiner may thank his lucky stars that the law of Judge Lynch does not yet operate in the fair county of Suffolk.'

2

Why Holmes or I should hear more of this hateful business was beyond me. The trial of William Gardiner for the murder of Rose

Harsent came on before Mr. Justice Grantham and a jury at Suffolk Assizes in Ipswich, and neither of us received any summons to appear as a witness for either the prosecution or the defence. I had not even been called to give medical testimony at the inquest. Dr. Lay could say all that had to be said about such matters. It was Holmes who brought up the case six months later, after breakfast in Baker Street, on a dank November morning.

'I trust, Watson, you have no pressing engagements for the next few hours. I believe we are about to have a visitor, and I should greatly appreciate your company.'

'Oh, has someone made an appointment? I thought the day was free.'

'No appointment has been made. Indeed, I and the gentleman in question are complete strangers.'

'Then who the devil is he to come here in such a manner?'

'His name is Mr. Ernest Wild and he is the author of a successful operetta, *The Help*, and a widely praised volume of verse, *The Lamp of Destiny*.'

'My dear Holmes, perhaps you would tell me why in thunder this librettist and versifier, unmet by either of us, is to descend upon us unannounced. If he is to descend at all!'

My friend chuckled.

'Because, Watson, Mr. Ernest Wild is also a young barrister of the Inner Temple and defence counsel to William Gardiner of Peasenhall in his trial for the murder of Rose Harsent. The famous Marshall Hall should look to his laurels, for Ernest Wild has already defended thirty murder cases and saved twenty-seven clients from the gallows.'

I was impressed by this and said so.

'He did not, of course, obtain acquittals in all twenty-seven cases but, at the very least, murder was reduced to manslaughter and his client lived to fight—possibly to kill—another day. Mr. Ernest Wild is what they call a coming man.'

'And why should he visit us?'

'For a reason known to all the world but you, old fellow. I was up unaccustomedly early this morning and have had the advantage of reading the *Morning Post* long before you came down to your breakfast. Two trials of William Gardiner have come and gone. The result is that two juries could not agree upon a verdict and he must be tried again. The worst is that at present eleven jurors would hang him but one held out. Even that man did not think Gardiner innocent. However, he has a conscientious objection to capital punishment and has written to the paper to say so. Had I not a distaste for puns, I should say it is only thanks to that one man that Gardiner's life still hangs by a thread rather than by a rope. Ernest Wild knows very well that the likely outcome of another trial will be the hanging of his client. As a defender, he has done almost everything within his power and it has been too little. Where else should he look for assistance?'

'Yet how can you be sure he will come to us?'

'Wait and listen!' he said softly.

We did so for several minutes and heard nothing. Then, as I was thinking what nonsense the whole thing was, there came the unmistakable jangle of the Baker Street doorbell.

'Voila!' said Holmes with a smile of insufferable smugness.

It seems he had advised Mrs. Hudson of this likely visit. The door of the sitting room opened and with 'Mr. Wild to see Mr. Holmes, sir!' she ushered in a dark-haired man in his earlier thirties. His wide-boned face, strong features, the firm line of his mouth, and the penetrating gaze of his pale eyes gave him a look of solemnity and determination. Yet the line of the mouth and the hard gaze of the eyes could turn in an instant into the most charming and boyish smile. At present, there was no occasion for a smile. He shook hands with us both, took his seat almost without waiting for an invitation, and came straight to the point. He nodded at the *Morning Post* which lay on the table, a little the worse for wear after Holmes's attentions.

'Gentlemen, it is good of you to receive me at such short notice. I observe you have read the morning paper. No doubt you have seen the outcome of the murder trial at Ipswich yesterday. William Gardiner has evaded the hangman briefly by virtue of a single juror's whimsy. Unfortunately, he has not escaped for long, if the Crown persists in trial after trial.'

'As they will most certainly do,' said Holmes, reaching for his pipe with a weary gesture. 'They cannot do otherwise, if eleven jurors are already of one mind.'

'Just so. All he has gained is three more months in a squalid prison cell. He eats, sleeps, and breathes next to the room where he will be hanged. The gallows remain so close to his bunk that, were it not for the wall, he might reach out and touch them. Mr. Holmes, I speak as a man and not as a lawyer. I believe William Gardiner to be innocent, upon my life I do, while most of Suffolk prefer him to be guilty. He will never be found innocent at Ipswich assize court in the face of such prejudice and insinuation as he now faces.'

'Surely,' said Holmes, drawing his pipe from his mouth, 'surely he is fortunate in his defender.'

Our visitor smiled awkwardly and shook his head.

'No, Mr. Holmes. I have taken on more than I should in a case like this. Gardiner needs more than a junior barrister; at the least his case requires a man who has taken silk and is a King's Counsel. That was why I came straight to London last night after the verdict and called upon Sir Charles Gill and Sir Edward Clarke. If either of them would lead for the defence of Gardiner at a retrial, I should be honoured to act as their junior counsel.'

'And they will not?' Holmes raised his eyebrows, though scarcely in surprise. 'There again, Sir Charles and Sir Edward are two of the busiest men at the bar. I see that Sir Charles is leading counsel in the Marylebone Railway inquiry and Sir Edward Clarke leads for the defence in the Dunwich by-election petition. As for Sir Edward Marshall Hall. . . .'

'Mr. Holmes, the retrial will come on in a few weeks. Such men are fully booked, as they say, for many months and cannot alter their arrangements. They say that they could not give Gardiner's defence the time and attention it deserves, nor could they get up the facts of the case as thoroughly as I have already done. Yet, as you will know, a junior counsel without a leader carries less weight with a jury and far less weight with a judge.'

Holmes laid down his pipe and nodded sympathetically.

'Mr. Justice Lawrence had no business to make those interjections of his during your speech to the jury yesterday. However, I do not see how I can be called to the bar and equipped with a knighthood as a King's Counsel before the retrial of Gardiner takes place.'

Wild folded and unfolded his hands.

'No, sir. Yet it remains within the power of the solicitor-general to call a halt to the prosecution of William Gardiner. In other words, to enter a writ of *nolle prosequi.'*

I saw Sherlock Holmes tighten his nostrils, one of those small gestures of skepticism.

'I cannot believe that the solicitor-general will abandon a case in which eleven men out of twelve have found the accused guilty of murder—a murder that was little less than butchery. Suppose for a moment that Gardiner was the murderer and is now set free—and murders again?'

Wild shook his head.

'My hope is that Gardiner may be judged in a tribunal quite different to that which he has faced so far. One that may persuade the solicitor-general to stay his hand. The case against this man is based entirely on a mass of circumstantial evidence and scandal. There is not a shred of direct evidence that connects the accused man with the murder of Rose Harsent. Yet circumstantial evidence has been fueled by a previous scandal. That is enough to prejudice any jury and carry the day against him. Even his own good character may destroy him.'

Holmes contracted his brows sharply.

'But is not your defence based, in part, on the fact that Gardiner is a man of principle and morality, a man of religion who is assistant steward, Sunday school superintendent, and choirmaster in his Methodist congregation?'

'Precisely,' said Wild, bringing his hand down on his knee. 'A rogue would be easier to deal with! Among the malicious, his nickname in the village before the scandal was Holy Willie, and I can see why. When Gardiner is in the witness-box, he is almost master of the courtroom as a revivalist preacher might be. That is the problem. He believes he is master and will endure no insinuation. When I questioned him in the witness-box about Wright's story of the alleged misconduct with Rose Harsent at the Doctor's Chapel, Gardiner fairly rounded on me and told the court it was a vicious lie from beginning to end. Very well. I daresay it was. Then I asked him about the evidence of Mr. Rouse, the preacher who said that he had seen Gardiner and Rose Harsent walking quite innocently along the road to Peasenhall together. "A downright lie!" he said. His neighbour recalled that Gardiner had lit a fire in his washhouse the morning after the murder. "A deliberate lie!" snaps Gardiner.'

He paused and then resumed.

'You see where this leads, Mr. Holmes? He will brook no contradiction. Gardiner will never say that a man or woman may be in error, that his neighbour must have mistaken the day on which the fire was lit in the washhouse, for example. The village folk are all downright or deliberate liars when they contradict his account. Small wonder if he was unpopular. But imagine the effect of all this on a jury.'

Taking the pipe from his mouth, Holmes began quietly to play act a courtroom scene of cross-examination. As I listened, I thought, not for the first time, what a ferocious antagonist my friend might have been, had he chosen a career at the criminal bar.

'"I see, Mr. Gardiner," says the cross-examiner gently. "So all these other witnesses are liars, are they, including some who have been your friends in the past? Tell me, what reason have all these good people for telling lies about you? You cannot name a single reason—and yet they are all liars! You alone are telling the truth? And you ask my lord and the jurors to believe that?"'

Holmes put down his pipe and then continued in the voice of an imaginary prosecutor.

'"Unlike those whose evidence is against you, the truth that you alone tell has hardly a shred of corroboration? And you ask my lord and the jury to believe that?"'

He paused again, for effect, and then concluded in the same voice.

'"All these people, some of whom, like Mr. Rouse, have supported you in the past, now combine together to tell lies about you for this mysterious reason that you cannot name? And you also ask my lord and the jury to believe that, do you?"'

Mr. Wild winced and Holmes inquired sympathetically, 'It goes something along those lines, I suppose, Mr. Wild?'

'It goes like that almost word for word, sir.'

'Of course it does,' said Holmes with a sigh.

'The facts of the case, sir, are becoming lost in slander and innuendo—and I almost fear that I may become lost with them!'

The facts of the Peasenhall murder! Such as they were, they became our constant companions in weeks to come. Indeed, there were now embellishments of the original story, all of them to William Gardiner's prejudice. Skinner had claimed he went to a hedge near the Doctor's Chapel with Wright and had listened to a couple engaged in an immoral act. He now remembered that the man and woman had jokingly discussed passages from the Book of Genesis, which may have a lewd interpretation in certain minds. He and Wright had already recalled that, as they waited, they saw quite plainly Rose Harsent come out after some time, followed by Gardiner a little while later. It was not only the voices of the guilty couple, but their appearances as well, to which these wretched youths were prepared to swear.

Whatever was believed in court, the 'truth' that circulated in the neighbourhood, through the little villages, seemed to be unquestioned. The Peeping Toms were believed. Gardiner had been the girl's lover. She had conceived a child by him, and, in order to conceal his guilt and avoid a paternity summons, he had murdered her in the most brutal fashion. This also carried the comforting hope that if William Gardiner could be made to bear the guilt, the rest of the neighbourhood would breathe freely again.

I have put the facts that Mr. Wild gave us into a nutshell, for it took him a good hour and more to explain the entire case. When he had finished, he sat back in his chair and looked at each of us in turn. Sherlock Holmes got to his feet, crossed to the sideboard, and refilled his pipe from the tobacco jar.

'I sympathize entirely, Mr. Wild. I see the threat of a great injustice here, though I am not convinced of Gardiner's innocence. I do not entirely see, however, what it is that you would like me to do.'

The young man looked him straight in the eyes.

'I would ask you to fight a duel, Mr. Holmes.'

Despite the solemnity of the case, my friend threw back his head and laughed as he took his seat once more.

'Would you have singlestick or pistols for two?'

Ernest Wild did not smile.

'I do not believe that William Gardiner can receive justice at the assize court where he now stands, though it is heresy for me to say so. His only hope must lie in another arena.'

'Of what possible use would that be?' I interposed.

The young lawyer turned to me.

'Dr. Watson, William Gardiner's last hope may lie in the Crown withdrawing the prosecution because they see that the man is innocent. It is in their power to do that, whatever local prejudice may say.'

I almost gasped at the audacity of it.

'The Crown has won eleven of the twelve jurors to its side and might have got the other had he not been an eccentric! Why should they withdraw from the case?'

'One moment,' said Holmes. 'Tell us, if you please, Mr. Wild, a little about this other arena, where it seems I am to fight my duel.'

The young advocate let out a long breath, as if he knew that he had won my friend to his side at last.

'Mr. Holmes, it is no secret that you count among your associates—if I may call them that—some of the best men at Scotland Yard.'

'They would not have to be so very good to be the best of a bad bunch. No matter. Pray continue, sir.'

'Let their best man be chosen. Let the two of you sift the evidence and the witnesses, free from all slander, prejudice, intimidation. Work together if you wish, fight it out if you must. When that is done, your findings shall be presented to the Director of Public Prosecutions or the solicitor-general, or the Home Secretary himself for that matter. If you can carry the day, your reputation is such that I believe a plea of *nolle prosequi* may be entered by the Crown and the agony of William Gardiner brought to an end. No less than that, the agony of his wife and children too.'

'And if I do not carry the day,' said Holmes nonchalantly, 'my reputation and much else shall end in the mud. And I must warn you that if I investigate the evidence, you, Mr. Wild, may not get the answer you are hoping for.'

'Whatever fee you may think fit shall be paid. I have undertakings as to the expenses of the case from two newspapers, the *Sun* and the *East Anglian Times*.'

It seemed to me that Holmes bridled a little at this.

'A man does not take money for seeing that justice is done. Before I move a single inch in this matter, however, I must take sight of William Gardiner. Even then, I do not suppose that Scotland Yard or the solicitor-general will look favorably on what you propose.'

Ernest Wild looked a little awkward.

'Sir Charles Gill and Sir Edward Clarke were unable to accept a brief in the case. However, both men sit in parliament, and they have assured me that in the circumstances they will urge Sir Edward Carson, as solicitor-general, to permit such an investigation, independent of the Suffolk constabulary. These two are men of great influence at the bar and well known to him. Sir Edward Clarke was solicitor-general before him and afterwards led for Oscar Wilde against the Marquess of Queensberry in the notorious trial. Carson led for Queensberry with Sir Charles Gill as his junior. You see? I think Carson will not lightly dismiss advice from two such learned friends. Meantime Gardiner cannot be released, of course. If you must see him first, I will obtain a visitor's warrant and you may travel down to Ipswich Gaol.'

'To the ends of the earth, if necessary,' Holmes said quietly. His voice was so soft, as he stood gazing at the drizzle of rain and soot falling across the roofs of Baker Street and beyond, that I was not quite sure if there was irony or resolve in his tone. Only when he turned round could I see that his eyes were bright with a strange chivalry of justice.

3

As the train carried us north from Liverpool Street to Ipswich three days later, I asked my friend how he knew that Ernest Wild would come to us so promptly.

'I have deceived you again, Watson,' he said, drawing up the strap and closing the carriage window against the draft. 'I have followed the events of this case in the papers. I thought it might come to such a point as this. The night before we entertained our visitor, I received a note from Sir Edward Clarke, just before dinner. He informed me he had been unable to accommodate Mr. Wild but that they had discussed such an arrangement as is now proposed. Sir Edward too had misgivings about this case. He asked me to see the young man. I replied at once and suggested an early hour next morning. After the first case at the assizes, I rather thought that the defence would get itself into a scrape. Once again you have trusted me too far in supposing that I can perform miracles.'

He gazed out across the damp ploughland north of London, and added without prompting:

'I have disliked this business from the start. Gardiner may be the murderer of Rose Harsent. It seems someone in the village surely is. Yet here is a man who has raised himself by his own efforts, acquiring the arts of reading and writing on the way. He is surrounded by many who have done nothing to improve their minds or skills, some of whom are no doubt envious clodhoppers. Of course, I do not think such jealousies make him innocent of murder. He is a man of resolve and so perhaps he has the resolve for such a crime. To be sure, he is a man of religion. Primitive Methodism, as I understand it, is a faith of the poor and the simple. It has no charms for me, Watson, yet I honour those who embrace it. But too many men of religion have committed murder. Therefore I cannot suppose that a sense of self-righteousness makes him innocent either.'

The train jolted to a halt at the signal for a country crossing, and we sat in a silence broken only by the long escape of steam. Then we jolted forward again, and Holmes resumed.

'Yet, Watson, what better target for the rustic voyeurs and scandal-mongers than a serious-minded man, an industrious worker who professes to be devout? People love to sniff out hypocrisy, perhaps in the hope of drawing away attention from their own, for it is a universal vice. You saw for yourself that within hours of Gardiner's arrest, his guilt was being proclaimed in a waxwork display on the seafront at Great Yarmouth. The evidence alone must determine his fate.'

Sherlock Holmes had seemed to blow this way and that until I had no idea what was in his mind.

'From all that we know so far, can you not decide whether you believe him guilty or innocent?'

He pulled a face at the trees and fields of Hertfordshire beyond the carriage window.

'As to that, my dear fellow, I will tell you when I know him a little better.'

Mr. Wild and his instructing solicitor, Arthur Leighton, were waiting for us as the train pulled into Ipswich station. The horse and trap outside carried us through the streets of the country town to its prison gates. As there is a sad similarity to the fortress-like appearance of provincial gaols, so there is a common odour within them of sour humanity and despair. We were shown into a room where prisoners facing trial were permitted to consult their legal advisers. Inspector Lestrade of Scotland Yard, the burly rival of Holmes, stood beside a former military man who was now the prison governor. It was a dismal place, in reality a meanly furnished cell with a single barred window high in its opposite wall. A table and half a dozen wooden chairs were all the comforts that it contained. Even at noon, on this winter day, the white gaslight sputtered in lamp brackets along the pale green lime-washed walls.

Once the introductions had been performed, the governor addressed us.

'Gentleman, the prisoner Gardiner and whatever other witnesses you may care to see shall be brought before you. I will grant you such privacy as I may. You have Inspector Lestrade with you, so I think we may dispense with a guard in the room itself. Two prison officers will be on duty outside the door. In the circumstances, however, Gardiner must remain handcuffed while he is with you. I respect your need for confidentiality and shall withdraw as soon as the arrangements have been made.'

He left the four of us—Wild, Lestrade, Holmes, and I—and went to order the escort to fetch Gardiner. The Scotland Yard man turned to my friend.

'Well now, Mr. Holmes, this is a favour I should not have done for any man except yourself.'

Holmes gave him a quick and humourless smile.

'My dear Lestrade, it is I who have undertaken to pay a favour and the recipient is the English legal system. Favour or not, let it be in respect of a man who deserves to hang if he butchered that poor girl but shall not go to the gallows when he is innocent. My mind is as open as I trust yours is. I must draw such evidence from witnesses and circumstances as will convince you that Gardiner did or did not murder Rose Harsent. You will inform your superiors or the solicitor-general accordingly. That is all I ask.'

'The whole thing might be far better done in a court of law,' said Lestrade with a tired shrug. He drew up one of the plain wooden chairs to the table and sat down with his notes spread before him.

'I would trust this man's life to you rather than to a jury,' said Holmes quietly. 'That is the extent of my confidence in your love of justice.'

This seemed to catch Lestrade on the hop, as they say, and he sat there without speaking a word for the next few minutes. Holmes,

Wild, and I had taken our seats next to him with one chair on the far side of the table for our witnesses. Almost at once the door opened and we heard the bustle of a large man being led between two escorts. Before us, in handcuffs, stood the accused whose life was now in our hands. William Gardiner was a finely built man of thirty-four with clear eyes and hair so black that he might have been of Spanish origin. His descent was, as I soon learnt, from those hard-working Huguenots who had sought refuge in Suffolk from religious persecution in France two centuries earlier.

It had been agreed that Ernest Wild should abandon his role as examiner to Sherlock Holmes and Lestrade. My friend looked up at the tall prisoner with his raven-black beard and said quietly, 'Sit down, if you please, Mr. Gardiner.'

There was a pause and I saw the emotions contending behind the prisoner's quiet demeanour. It must have been many months since anyone had done him the courtesy of addressing him as 'Mr.' Gardiner. Though he was wearing prison handcuffs, he managed the chair easily enough. Holmes looked him directly in the eyes and Gardiner held his interrogator's gaze. His manner was not hostile, but utterly confident.

'My name is Sherlock Holmes. To my right is Inspector Lestrade and on my left is my colleague Dr. Watson. Mr. Wild is already familiar to you. You know who we are and why we are here?'

'I do, sir,' said Gardiner in that strong, quiet voice that seldom wavered except under the emotion of questions respecting his wife, children, or religion. 'I know all that, and my gratitude to you is unbounded.'

Holmes sat back in his chair, a little brusquely as it seemed to me. 'We are not here to earn your gratitude, but to serve justice. If you are innocent, we shall do all in our power to demonstrate it. If you are guilty, that shall also appear.'

'Then we are at one in our purpose, sir,' said Gardiner in the same firm but quiet voice, 'and if the truth shall indeed shine through all this, I have nothing to fear.'

Only then did his eyes cease to search those of Sherlock Holmes and look down at the table. Sitting in that drab and tainted cell, I thought that the power of Gardiner's personality seemed at times almost to dominate Holmes and Lestrade. Either this was a man whose piety and decency were an example to us all, or one of the devil's own breed in his cunning and dissimulation. The next two or three days would tell.

Holmes took him through the course of his life, eliciting how one of nine pauper children born in the workhouse had by dint of hard work become foreman carpenter at Smyth's Seed Drill Works in Peasenhall. He had taken a loving wife from the Primitive Methodist congregation at Sibton, two miles away, and accepted salvation through its faith. He rose through the ranks of the chapel as he had done at the works. At thirty-four, this pauper child was assistant steward, Sunday school superintendent, choirmaster, and organist, though the choir was a mere dozen voices and organ-playing little more than an accompaniment of chords on the harmonium. It was in this Methodist chapel that William Gardiner, the married man, had met Rose Harsent, who was twenty years old at the time. It seemed that she had been brought to the primitive faith by her former suitor, though their courtship had now ended. Miss Rose had been a member of Gardiner's little choir and had asked him to teach her the harmonium.

Among his other accomplishments, he could read well and write passably, though his penmanship lacked a number of refinements. His reputation with his employers was such that two years earlier he had been sent to manage the firm's stand at the Paris Exhibition and had written several letters to them reporting on the event. It was said among some of his more envious neighbours that he had 'done well for a workhouse brat.'

'Very good then,' said Holmes, when all this ground had been cleared. 'Now let us come, if you please, to the night of 1 May, thirteen months before the murder. It was the evening that gave rise to so much talk about you and Miss Rose Harsent, was it not?

Tell us what you did and where you were between seven and nine o'clock.'

Gardiner held his gaze once more.

'That is easily done, sir. I had been driving Mr. Smyth on business that afternoon, over to Dunwich. He will vouch for it that we were late back. We came to the drill works again just after seven that evening. I rubbed down the horse, which is my job, and gave him his feed. Yet the animal would not take the bait to start him eating. I thought I should leave him a while and then, if he still would not eat, I must report the matter to Mr. Smyth. Home I went and had my tea at seven thirty, as my wife will tell you. The walk is a quarter mile or so and not more than six or seven minutes.'

'At what time do you usually have your tea?' asked Holmes.

'Normally, sir, I have my tea at six. On this occasion, it was a little before eight when I finished the meal and about five minutes after that when I was ready to go out again. Then I went back to the drill works to attend to the horse, to see if he had eaten. I found that he had. I would have reached the works very soon after eight o'clock, I daresay not much more than five minutes past. I came out again about eight fifteen. It was then that I saw Miss Rose Harsent standing by the gate of what we call the Doctor's Chapel, which she cleaned every week. I did not see Wright hanging about then. If he was there, he was concealed from me. Rose was in service with Mr. and Mrs. Crisp at Providence House. That chapel was Congregational. Mr. Crisp being one of the deacons, cleaning it was part of Rose's duties.'

'You went across the road to her?'

'No, sir. She called me over and said that she had finished her cleaning but could not get the chapel door to close, so that she might lock it. She had been a friend to Mrs. Gardiner and me for a few years, so naturally I went to help. The door was an old one and I found that the rain had swollen it at the bottom. I caught hold and gave it a good slam, enough to close it so that it might be locked. We came back down the path together, for the chapel stands back thirty yards from the road. That is the distance they have now measured. We walked together a little way to Providence House, a few minutes, half of my way home. We talked of chapel matters as we went, choosing hymns for the anniversary and so on. I left her at the corner, saw her go into Providence House, and walked the rest of the way home, just a couple of minutes more. And that was all there was to it, sir, no matter what they may say. My wife will tell you that I was home before half past eight.'

Inspector Lestrade had been fretting to get his own question in.

'What of the young man, George Wright, who tells a different story?'

'I saw him twice, sir. When I left the Seed Drill Works and went home to my tea, just before seven thirty, he was hanging about the gate of the works. He was there, still hanging about, when I went back about half an hour or so later. I knew him, of course, for he is a labourer at the works, but I never stopped to say more than a word as I passed.'

'And that is all?'

'And that is all, sir.'

'Not quite,' said Lestrade ominously, 'for this is not a court of law and the suspicion still stands against you. What do you say to the allegations of Wright and Skinner? Please do not tell me that it is all a lie from beginning to end, for that will not do in this room. William Wright swears on his oath in court that he saw Rose Harsent enter the Doctor's Chapel about seven thirty that evening. He saw you follow her a few minutes later. Contemptible though it may be, he then went to fetch his young friend Alfonso Skinner to have some fun, as he put it, by spying on you and the young woman. At about eight o'clock these two youths crouched down behind a hedge, on a high bank near the southwest window of the chapel. They have sworn in court that they heard your voice and that of a young woman, whom they later saw to be Rose Harsent. They heard the sounds of an act of gross indecency. . . .'

Gardiner's face was tight as canvas under full sail and dark as indigo.

'It is. . . .'

'Kindly do not interrupt me,' said the Scotland Yard man calmly, 'and in your own best interests do not tell me again that it is a foul lie unless you can show that to be true. These two young men heard the two of you clearly enough. Your voices were plain enough for Skinner to make out the exact passage from the thirty-eighth chapter of the Book of Genesis which you and Rose Harsent used to describe your misconduct. Wright left his friend for about ten minutes during the time that you were in the chapel with the girl. He came back and stayed another fifteen minutes. He was in time to hear the rest of your conversation and to see you both leave. From where they were hidden, they were able to see the girl leave first and then to watch you following her.'

Gardiner would keep silent no longer.

'It is an abominable falsehood! By all I hold sacred, it is! A libel on holy scripture as surely as on my reputation! Why should they do such a thing to me? I never in my life wished them harm.'

Sherlock Holmes intervened.

'One moment, Lestrade. Is it said that Mr. Gardiner and the girl left the chapel together?'

Lestrade turned over several pages of his papers.

'According to Skinner, Rose Harsent left and Gardiner followed a few minutes later. The girl went on ahead to Providence House, he says, while Gardiner came out, tiptoed across to the other side of the road, and took the same direction. Skinner followed him in turn. I daresay, Mr. Holmes, your cases are in a superior class to this kind of thing. For your information, however, guilty parties in conduct of this kind seldom leave the scene of their amours together.'

For some reason that was not plain to me at that moment, a look of relief appeared on the face of Sherlock Holmes. Before he could speak, however, Gardiner burst out again.

'Those two young men say they hid behind that hedge about twenty minutes after eight. I was on my way home from the chapel by then. Skinner says they were there about an hour, and Wright too, except for the ten minutes he was away walking about the road. I was at home before all that. He says he was there for an hour and

Wright was there three-quarters of an hour. As my wife will tell you, I was with her all the time that this wickedness was supposed to be happening at the chapel. She knows it, and for that reason she never believed a single word that these slanderers spoke.'

'So she has said,' Lestrade remarked coldly. Gardiner stared at him.

'Will you believe these two foul-minded rascals or her? I never saw Rose Harsent at all that evening except when I came out of the works at about quarter past eight. I went to the Doctor's Chapel and slammed the door so that she could lock up. I never so much as set foot inside the building beyond that. When I heard what was said about me by those two young men, I started an action for slander.'

'And withdrew it,' Lestrade said quietly.

'Only because the attorney told me that those two had nothing and I must pay the costs even if I won. I had not the money to pay costs. After that, there was always two of those wretches to back each other up. I had only my wife, who is disbelieved because she is my wife, and Rose, who might have spoken for me too. But I could not put that girl through such an ordeal as an action for slander.'

Holmes leant forward a little and took up the questioning.

'Mr. Gardiner, tell me this. It is a very simple question. Let us suppose it was only slander or malice on the part of Wright and Skinner, perhaps a vicious sense of fun. Why would these two youths stick to their falsehood after Rose Harsent had been murdered and your life was at stake in a murder trial?'

I quite expected Gardiner to act a dramatic part over this, but he became very quiet.

'Because, Mr. Holmes, they are evil through and through. That is the simple answer to your simple question, and I will tell you why I make it. They saw that if they told the truth and admitted their falsehoods about me after Rose died, I should certainly be acquitted on the charge of murdering her. There would be nothing to connect me with this young woman in an immoral way and their lies would be turned against them. They feared that when I was set free, I should find the money to sue them in earnest for their slanders. I would have the decision of a jury behind me. And they knew very well I should win. Worse than that, for them, they might be indicted for perjury and sent to prison for many years. What worse perjury can there be than trying to swear a man's life away? Rather than risk prison, they would see me hanged. It was the only way they could be safe. I never said any of this when I was in the witness-box, for it would be no evidence in the case. My only witness to the truth, Rose Harsent, was dead. But as you ask me, Mr. Holmes, that is the depth of their evil. Those two are a hundred times more likely to have murdered her than anyone else I can think of.'

It was an argument that might have gone against him in court, when he was cross-examined. Spoken in that prison room, as he spoke them, the words carried a terrible probability to my mind, though not to the Chief Inspector's.

'It is easy enough, Gardiner, to call men evil,' said Lestrade sharply, 'but of little use unless you can show them to be so. These are two witnesses who submitted to the chapel inquiry, which they were not bound to do, and have never refused to cooperate with the law.'

'I can show you what they are!' said Gardiner quietly, and for the first time his dark eyes glittered with malice. 'Suppose, sir, you had seen filthy behaviour of the kind they allege, seen it between a young woman you knew and a married man who was also of your acquaintance. What would you have done?'

Lestrade colored a little at this.

'You are not here to ask questions, Gardiner, but to answer them!'

'All the same, Lestrade,' said Holmes gently, 'it may do no harm in this one instance.'

Lestrade glared at him, I can use no other word. Reluctantly, he gave way.

'Very well, if I knew the fellow, I should take him on one side and speak to him.'

'Just so,' said Gardiner gratefully, 'or, sir, if that accomplished nothing, you might speak to his wife. You would not ignore the man and his wife but spread dirty stories of him behind his back, among all those who knew him. Among his neighbours and friends. There, sir, is the difference between the good and the evil man. Whether you believe me or them, I leave you to judge of what kind these two witnesses show themselves to be. Evil tongues.'

'The tongue can no man tame,' said Holmes thoughtfully, 'it is an unruly evil.'

'Full of deadly poison,' Gardiner took up the quotation. 'The General Epistle of James, Mr. Holmes, sir, chapter three, verse eight.'

By the time that Holmes and Lestrade had finished questioning Gardiner over the allegations of his conduct with Rose Harsent, it seemed to me that a long couple of hours had passed. So great had been the intensity of these exchanges that it was only when we stepped out into the dark prison courtyard that I looked at my watch and saw that four hours and a half had gone by.

Darkness had fallen before we stood in that yard with a winter drizzle falling. The oil light was reflected in pools on the smooth paving of the yard and on the rough stonework of its walls. The burly figure of Lestrade in his travelling cloak confronted Sherlock Holmes as we waited under the light of the stone porch for Arthur Leighton and the cab that was to take us to the White Horse hotel.

'Well, Mr. Holmes,' said the Scotland Yard man rather huffily, 'I don't see how all that has got us much further. I don't believe your client stands an inch further from the noose.'

'He is not my client,' said Holmes patiently. 'Mr. Wild is my client, so far as I have one. I am prepared to find Gardiner guilty or innocent, as the evidence presents itself. Yet if you believe that what we have heard gets us no further, I shall be sadly disappointed in you.'

'I say only that we have wasted our time this afternoon.'

Holmes rounded on him.

'This allegation of misconduct in the Doctor's Chapel is the only sinister link between the accused and Rose Harsent prior to the murder. She was a member of the Primitive Methodist congregation, a friend of Gardiner and his wife who visited their house regularly. She continued to pay these visits after the scandal broke. That could hardly be the case if Mrs. Gardiner believed her husband to be the girl's lover. The world has seen that good lady twice in the witness-box. Is it likely that such a woman would have welcomed Gardiner's mistress under her roof—as the companion of her six children? Gardiner denies the truth of the scandal, his wife denounces it as impossible because he was at home with her at the material times. If it were not for the story told by Wright and Skinner, Gardiner's name would have no connexion with the murder nor, indeed, with the pregnancy of Rose Harsent. I do not think, Lestrade, that we have wasted our time.'

'Then you had better have a look at these, Mr. Holmes.'

Lestrade put his hand in his pocket and drew out an envelope, from which he took two photographs. They had been taken by a police photographer and were reproductions of two sets of hand-writing. The first showed a pair of single-page letters carried to Rose Harsent by her young brother, telling her that Gardiner proposed to sue Wright and Skinner over 'some scandal going round about you and me going into the Doctor's Chapel for immoral Purposes.' Gardiner had signed both letters. The handwriting was firm and rounded, but the phrasing was laboured, as might befit a self-educated man. The writer also showed a tendency to use a capital 'P' and 'R' in the middle of his sentences to begin certain words, where a small, lowercase initial letter would have been usual.

'And now this,' said Lestrade confidently. The second photograph showed an assignation note for the night of Rose Harsent's death, written by a lover who was surely her murderer. It was accompanied by the envelope in which it had been posted, addressed to 'Miss Harsent, Providence House, Peasenhall, Saxmundham.' I read the note, whose dreadful appointment the poor young woman had kept.

'Dear R, I will try to see you tonight at twelve o'clock at your
Place if you Put a light in your window at ten o'clock for about
ten minutes. Then you can take it out again. Don't have a light
in your Room at twelve as I will come round the back.'

'Well now,' said Holmes quietly, 'it seems you have the better
of us all, Lestrade. And this is the evidence on which the famous
Mr. Thomas Gurrin, handwriting expert extraordinary of Holborn
Viaduct, proposes to swear a man's life away? I fear, my friend, that
he will have to do better than this.'

'You deny the resemblance, Mr. Holmes?'

'Oh, no!' said Holmes at once, 'The resemblance between the two
letters is quite remarkable. Perhaps a little too remarkable. What I deny
is the authorship of the murderer's note. In the first place there is the
literary style, which I know is not a matter of handwriting. The first two
letters to Rose Harsent, signed by Gardiner and admitted by him, are a
little awkward. They are the work of a man not born to letter-writing.
Look where he says 'I have broke the news' and 'she say she know it is
wrong.' Then there is a sentence eleven lines long but with hardly any
attempt at punctuation, which was still beyond him. By contrast, the
unsigned assignation note, which we may assume was the work of her
murderer, has a confidence and a precision. I do not think its author
would write, as Gardiner does, 'you and me' rather the more correct
form 'you and I.' A small matter, but significant.'

'I don't see that,' said Lestrade gruffly.

'Do you not?' Holmes now held the two photographs side by
side under the light of the porch. 'Then let me help you a little in
the matter of the handwriting. In the unsigned note, presumably
from the murderer, there is much play of using incorrectly a capital
initial 'P' or an 'R' in the middle of a sentence. It occurs three times
in seven lines. In the two signed letters by Gardiner, the first is eighteen lines long and the curious capital 'P' occurs only once, the 'R'
not at all, though there were four opportunities. The second letter
is more than thirty-six lines long and no error of the sort occurs
whatever.'

737

'Which signifies what, precisely, Mr Holmes?' There was no mistaking the skepticism in Lestrade's voice.

'Which signifies, my dear fellow, that someone has taken an occasional eccentricity of handwriting, imitated it, and turned it into a regular feature of the script. And then there is the accuracy of the script. It is Gardiner's style but more rounded and regular than Gardiner could ever be. Many a bank forger might be caught if our experts were alive to a single fact: It is very difficult for any man or woman to sign his or her name identically on every occasion. Where it appears to be identical, time after time, it has very likely been counterfeited with great care.'

'Which gets us where, Mr. Holmes?'

'To the point, Lestrade, of acknowledging that the unsigned assignation note is written in Gardiner's style, but a style more polished than Gardiner ever attained. And then there is the envelope in which the unsigned note was posted.'

'You don't deny that the unsigned assignation note and the envelope are written in the same hand and by the same person?'

'Not in the least.' Holmes wagged the photograph a little. 'Yet look at the address.'

Lestrade read slowly, 'Miss Harsent, Providence House, Peasenhall, Saxmundham.'

'There you have it,' said Holmes triumphantly, 'and the postmark on the envelope is Yoxford—which is also the postmark for Peasenhall itself. This letter was surely posted in the box opposite Hurren's post office in the main street of Peasenhall and collected by the postman. It was franked at Hurren's and delivered. To add Saxmundham is superfluous. Saxmundham may be the largest village between here and Ipswich but the note would never have gone there. This is as redundant as if you were to address a letter to London, England, when you posted a letter in London to be delivered in London. A man who has lived as long in Peasenhall as William Gardiner would not address a Peasenhall letter to Saxmundham.'

'Unless he wished to disguise his intent,' Lestrade replied.

Holmes laughed.

'Unless he wanted to draw attention to himself. If he wished to disguise its origin, better by far for him to walk to Saxmundham and send the letter with a Saxmundham postmark on it. When we began our labours this afternoon, I was quite prepared to find that Gardiner was the murderer. You, my dear fellow, have helped to bring me to the near certainty that he can only be innocent.'

This caught the inspector on the raw and he became a little snappish.

'Be that as it may, Mr. Holmes, my time grows short. At the risk of trespassing on your hospitality, I should be grateful if we could deal with Gardiner's murder alibi after dinner this evening. The facts are known and it hardly requires an inquisition or further witnesses. I cannot stay in Ipswich for ever.'

'Good God, man! You have only been in the town for a few hours!'

I was not surprised that there was general silence in the cab until we drew up in the half-timbered yard of the White Hart. The old low-beamed hotel was busy that evening with barristers on circuit for the assize court at the Shire Hall. The White Hart is where the bar mess meets for dinner during these weeks, though Mr. Wild absented himself in order to keep us company. The ice was broken a little, as the saying is, when the four of us sat round our table in the panelled dining room. By an unspoken agreement, we avoided all mention of the case, which was soon to occupy us into the small hours.

4

As usual, Holmes had engaged a private sitting room adjoining our bedrooms. With Lestrade and Mr. Wild we took our ease in armchairs, a decanter of whisky and a jug of hot water with a plate of lemon on the table between us.

'Let us clear the ground,' said Holmes, looking about him. 'Certain facts are plain. On 31 May last, Rose Harsent received an anonymous note from her lover, asking her to put a light in her attic window at Providence House at ten P.M. and promising to come to the back door at midnight. It is disputed whether that note may or may not be in Gardiner's handwriting.'

'It is his handwriting,' said Lestrade hastily. 'Mr. Thomas Gurrin has said so on two occasions in court. He is the greatest expert we have.'

'Or the greatest charlatan,' said Holmes equably. 'However, let us return to the night of 31 May. Rose lit a candle in her window that remained there for ten minutes or so. Gardiner and his neighbours were standing in their doorways or in the street watching the storm. Had Gardiner stood in the middle of the road, he might have seen the candle in the window, two hundred yards away. All other evidence apart, Rose Harsent was certainly alive at ten P.M. and dead at eight A.M. next morning.'

'Let us say four A.M.,' I added quickly, 'and quite possibly two A.M., according to postmortem evidence of rigor mortis.'

'So it shall be.' Holmes put down his glass and glanced at the sheet of paper before him. 'Gardiner and his wife were asked by a next-door neighbour, Mrs. Rosanna Dickenson, an ironmonger's widow, to keep her company because she was afraid of the storm. Mrs. Gardiner arrived at Mrs. Dickenson's house at about eleven thirty P.M. Gardiner had said that he would look to see that the children were sleeping. He then followed his wife about fifteen minutes later, let us say eleven forty-five P.M. Gardiner was described by Mrs. Dickenson as 'calm and collected.' He was wearing carpet slippers and not dressed for going out, even in fine weather, let alone in the storm that was still in full force. The couple stayed with Mrs. Dickenson until one thirty A.M. and left together. I see that Mrs. Dickenson was not cross-examined at the trial, so I take it we may accept the truth of her evidence?'

Our Scotland Yard man took the pipe from his mouth.

'I think we may.'

'Very well. Mrs. Gardiner then describes how they walked straight home and went to bed. She recalled that the first predawn light began to appear in the sky just before two o'clock. Remember that this was 1 June and almost the earliest sunrise of the year. As they got into bed at two twenty A.M., she said to her husband, 'It is getting quite light.' Furthermore, the walls of those cottages are thin and their neighbour, Amelia Pepper, heard Mrs. Gardiner's voice and her tread on the stairs at about two A.M. Mrs. Gardiner tells us that she had a pain in her body and did not sleep until after five A.M., when she heard the clock strike. Her husband was in bed with her all that time. If this is true, then he cannot have murdered anyone after eleven forty-five P.M., unless we disregard his wife's evidence.'

'Which we should be well advised to do,' said Lestrade quickly. 'It is completely uncorroborated after two A.M.'

Holmes looked at him without expression.

'I think, Lestrade, that a little common sense will suffice. If you check your diary or your almanac, you will find that the sun rises at that time of year at two forty-five A.M. and that it lights the sky from below the horizon somewhat before then. Were I Gardiner intent upon murdering Rose Harsent, it would be a deed of darkness. I should not walk down the main street in broad daylight where a wakeful neighbour or an early riser might see me from a window or even meet me on the way. Peasenhall is not Park Lane or Baker Street. Country people rise with the sun, not several hours after it. Added to that, the medical evidence cannot place the crime later than two or three o'clock, four o'clock if we accept Dr. Lay's unsupported guess.'

'That is certainly true,' I said before Lestrade could intervene again. 'In any case, Miss Harsent was in the kitchen when she was murdered, and the candle in her bedroom had been put out. If her lover failed her at midnight, she would surely have gone to bed and not sat up in the kitchen for two hours and more in her nightclothes.'

Lestrade turned round to us all.

'This may be very a very amusing game to you, gentlemen. To me, it is something else. The young person may have been murdered as late as four A.M., according to Dr. Lay. If that was the case, then she had indeed sat up waiting or gone to the kitchen at that hour, however unreasonable it may seem to you. Remember she was wearing night attire and may have gone downstairs in answer to a knock or signal. Let that be enough.'

'Enough for suspicion and innuendo, far too little for guilt,' said Holmes quietly. 'If I were you, I should place the murder at a time before the Gardiners went to Mrs. Dickenson and not afterward. That would put it before eleven forty-five P.M. on the previous evening.'

'Time enough, Mr. Holmes.'

Holmes stared into his glass.

'Is it, indeed? Rose Harsent was seen alive by Mrs. Crisp who said goodnight to the girl at ten P.M. It was ten fifteen when Mrs. Crisp went to bed and to sleep. She woke somewhen during the night and heard a thud, followed shortly after by a scream. She said at first it was at midnight; now she is not sure of the time, but it was dark. No matter. We have a period between ten fifteen and eleven forty-five, less than that if Gardiner was the murderer. He had to be at Mrs. Dickenson's in his carpet slippers at eleven forty-five, so let us say between ten fifteen and eleven thirty.'

'Long enough,' said the inspector decisively.

'What about the blood with which he was covered when he arrived at Mrs. Dickenson's?'

'What blood?'

'Precisely, my friend. There was none. Gardiner is said to have cut the throat of this young woman during a struggle in the kitchen. There was a struggle, of course, since Mrs. Crisp heard first of all a thud and then a cry soon afterwards. The thud, no doubt, was the staircase door banging back against the wall and the cry was the poor girl's last utterance.'

'I don't entirely follow you, Mr. Holmes.'

'I quite see that, Lestrade. The kitchen of Providence House is a small one, some ten feet by eight. The blood had spurted to the second step of the staircase. A man who grappled with his victim while he cut her throat, in a space as small as that kitchen, would have been covered by it. His shoes would have trampled it all over the kitchen floor. Forensic examination shows that there was not a speck of blood on Gardiner's shoes or clothing, neither the clothing that had been washed nor that which was waiting to be washed. All his clothing was examined by Dr. Stevenson of the Home Office, a man who can not only detect blood on clothing that has not been washed but the remains of blood on clothes that have been washed. There was not a drop.'

Lestrade said nothing, for Sherlock Holmes now held the floor.

'What there was, however,' my friend continued, 'was a copy of the *East Anglian Times* under the girl's head. Why? Is it likely that Gardiner would bring a paper to which he subscribed and the Crisps did not in order to leave it under her head? Then again, there was a medicine bottle with a label 'For Mrs. Gardiner's children.' Is not that the first thing he would have taken away? Might it not be the first thing that another man would leave there to incriminate Gardiner? In which case the crime was committed by someone known to him, well enough known to be informed that the Gardiners of Alma Cottage subscribed to the *East Anglian Times*, rather than the *Chronicle*, which was taken in by the Crisps at Providence House.'

'You tell me nothing I have not heard already.'

'Then how can you hear it and still believe that Gardiner was the murderer of Rose Harsent? It can only be because no case has been built against any other man. That is not a good enough reason to deliver any poor devil to the hangman's mercies.'

Lestrade hung on like a plucky terrier to a thief's coattails.

'Gardiner had ample time to burn a bloodstained shirt before his clothes were taken for examination three days later. If murder was his purpose, he might have gone barefoot into that kitchen and wiped away any prints as he left. Mammal's blood, possibly human, was found in a crevice of his pocketknife. . . .'

'Rabbits!' said Holmes furiously. 'Have you never heard of hulling rabbits? There is not a countryman who does not use his knife regularly to prepare them for the pot. I should find it far more incriminating if his knife was perfectly clean.'

But Lestrade would not be stopped.

'He has no alibi but for the time spent with Mrs. Dickenson. The Gardiners' neighbour, Amelia Pepper, swears only that she heard the voice and step of Mrs. Gardiner after two A.M., not her husband. Rose Harsent may have met her death as late as four A.M. If she died the evening before, Gardiner had time to kill her at eleven P.M. and be back in Mrs. Dickenson's sitting room forty-five minutes later.'

'Then his wife is necessarily a liar.'

'Not necessarily, Mr. Holmes, but she is his wife. There is not an insurance company that would take a wife as sole witness in a husband's claim! If Gardiner killed that girl, he killed that girl. Not all your clever theories, Mr. Sherlock Holmes, can alter that!'

'Very well. Then if he killed her, he must have had good reasons.'

'He had good reasons, indeed,' said Lestrade triumphantly. 'He had such reasons as being the father of her unborn child and being determined to protect himself, his family, and his reputation by putting an end to it!'

'Which brings us back to the Doctor's Chapel and the scandal again,' said Sherlock Holmes thoughtfully.

'So it does.'

'Well then, Lestrade? Had we not better have an understanding between us? We have done enough sitting about in chairs. Let us take this matter of the chapel *au serieux* and fight the battle there, at the scene of the scandal. Shall we do that as soon as the principals can be gathered? I believe we shall have you back in London in no time at all.'

'We might do that, Mr. Holmes. I will go this far. If you can disprove absolutely the scandal of the Doctor's Chapel, you shall have your way. For then the motive of the murder falls to the ground. I do not see how you can do it, but I will go that far to meet you.'

'There must be sound tests of what, if anything, can be heard behind the hedge.'

'They have been tried.'

'They must be tried again. And there must be an examination of the two youths who claim to be witnesses of immoral conduct between Gardiner and Miss Harsent.'

'That has been done. Wright and Skinner have said all that there is for them to say.'

'Nonetheless, Lestrade, I shall require George Wright, Alfonso Skinner, and Mr. Crisp, who was deacon of the chapel and who with his wife employed Rose Harsent.'

'Mr. and Mrs. Crisp? What have they to do with it now?'

Holmes let out a long sigh, which may have been of satisfaction or relief.

'You see, my dear fellow? It seems they have not said all they have to say. I believe, Lestrade, this is another of our cases in which you and Scotland Yard will live to thank me for my assistance.'

5

The rain had cleared before midnight, and by dawn the clear sky had laid down a frost to accompany our visit to the Doctor's Chapel at Peasenhall. For the number of us who were to gather there, we might have hired a charabanc. Peasenhall consists of the main road, which they call the Street, and a road running south from it at the midpoint, which is Church Street. The Doctor's Chapel is two hundred yards down Church Street, reached through a narrow iron gate on the south side. Beyond this lies the equally narrow path that runs along by the building, overlooked on the other side by a tall bank topped with a hedge and a hurdle fence.

The chapel itself is a small structure with the appearance of a single-storey thatched cottage. It has three square windows and a plain door on this southern side. I doubt if its pews would accommodate fifty worshippers. It is surrounded and overhung by trees which give way to open fields a little distance beyond. Such was the scene of the scandal, upon whose proof or disproof the fate of William Gardiner must now depend.

Waiting for us by the door were PC Nunn, with a face of the severe but thoughtful type, Mr. Crisp, with an ear trumpet and walking stick, and his wife, who was, as they say, a stout body of fifty or so. We were introduced to them. The other two witnesses present were the Peeping Toms of the scandal, merely indicated to us as they stood apart sullenly. William Wright and Alfonso Skinner now wore their Sunday best.

I confess that I did not like the look of these two from the start.

Wright was a sallow, even swarthy young man who looked entirely out of place in a suit and cravat. His heavy jaw and the morose stare of his dark eyes gave him a mingled look of malice and Neanderthal stupidity. Skinner was quite the contrary, a more dangerous antagonist. He had a sharp, impatient manner, hair closely cropped, and narrowed eyes that stared without emotion. I swear that those eyes would watch suffering with indifference, would look on without either anger or compassion. In all my experience with Sherlock Holmes, I had seldom had the sense so strongly of men who would crush their victim as a matter of habit, hardly caring whether they did so or not. If it was necessary for William Gardiner to be hanged in order that they should be safe from prosecution over their perjury, I wager they would send him to the gallows as readily as they would order a chicken to be slaughtered for Christmas.

If Gardiner's life was in the hands of Sherlock Holmes, I was never so grateful for my friend's reputation. It seemed plain from the two scowling figures that PC Eli Nunn had given Wright and Skinner little choice as to whether they attended this interrogation or not. A request from Holmes had been as good as a bench warrant from a High Court judge.

I stood with Nunn and Holmes a little apart from the others, while we discussed how the experiment was to be carried out.

'I must tell you, sir,' said Nunn apologetically, 'that we have already carried out a test of our own. On 28 July last, I stood behind the hedge up there, where these two young men claimed they were hiding on the evening of the alleged incident in the chapel. For the purposes of the test, Wright and Skinner went into the chapel, the door was closed, and, as I had instructed them, each in turn read out the first ten verses of the thirty-eighth chapter of the Book of Genesis, the story of Onan.'

'Thank you,' said Holmes, interrupting him. 'I am familiar with his story.'

'Then I must tell you, sir,' said Nunn reluctantly, 'I could hear every word.'

My friend was remarkably unruffled by this.

'You do not surprise me in the least. Which other officer was in the chapel with these two when they read from the Book of Genesis?'

'None, sir. There was no need. I saw fair play by making sure the door and every window was shut.'

'But not by having an official witness in the chapel, where these two scoundrels could read or shout as loudly as was necessary to make their voices carry to you? Nor by choosing some other passage with which you might be unfamiliar but one whose words you expected to hear?'

Nunn was a decent fellow, I felt sure, and I was sad to see him cut down like this. I would have preferred him as an ally rather than an antagonist, for I cannot believe he liked Wright and Skinner any better than we did.

'No matter,' said Holmes reassuringly, 'we will return to these things later. For the moment, let us carry out an examination of the *locus in quo.*'

He handed me his travelling-cape and walked once round the outside of the little building. Then he began to inspect the door, windows, and ventilation. The white-painted door was unlocked and opened easily as he knelt down and studied the lower edge, where Gardiner swore it had stuck fast on the night when Rose asked him to slam it for her.

'You see, Watson?'

'I see nothing.'

'Precisely. You see nothing because this door has been repainted. It is now eighteen months since the night of the alleged scandal, and the state of the paint suggests to me that it has yet to see a single winter before this one. In other words, it has only been painted after the murder. No doubt that was done to conceal something else that had been done to it before. Now, if you will be good enough to run your hand down the edge of the door where it meets the frame, you will feel that the upper stretch is smooth because the new paint is built upon a previous coat. Down here, however, you can feel the grain of the wood quite easily. In other words, at the bottom of the door someone had planed away the swollen surface so that it would close and lock more easily. After the murder, someone else painted the door, concealing what had been done. It may have been by chance, but it made a liar out of William Gardiner when he first told the story of slamming the swollen door because it had stuck—told it when his only witness was now dead and buried.'

'Those two wastrels have something to answer for!' I said angrily. Sherlock Holmes straightened up from his inspection.

'Let us not jump to conclusions. On its own, this does not mean that Gardiner has told the truth in every respect. However, in his story of the swollen chapel door, it seems he has spoken the entire truth and that someone has tried to make him appear a liar.'

'Of course! Skinner described himself in court as an odd-job man for Mr. and Mrs. Crisp. Surely that would make him the odd-job man for the chapel as well, would it not? He planed the door to make Gardiner seem a liar and then painted it to conceal what he had done.'

'No doubt, if it can be proved.' My friend was busy with the three square windows, each made up of small leaded panes.

'You will recall the words of Skinner at the trial, "We heard rustling about and the window shook."' Holmes turned to me. 'Be so good as to shake that window, if you please.'

I was not sure quite what he had in mind, but there was no way of causing any vibration, except by vigorous contact with the glass or the glazing bars. The window frame was set solidly in the wall and nothing else would do. Holmes looked through it into the interior of the little building.

'The only way to shake the window from inside would be to strike directly at the glass, preferably at about the level of the windowsill. Yet there is a fixed seat running just beneath it on the inside. That would make it almost impossible to hit the window accidentally while standing up. Sitting down, one would almost have to hit it with the back of one's head. Tell me, what else would produce such an effect?'

I lost his drift for a moment and he laughed.

'Come, Watson! Surely, a servant girl doing her duty, cleaning the chapel with vim and vigor—including its windows! That is something they may have heard and adopted it for their story. If anything moved that window, it was Rose Harsent and her duster!'

He had not done with the small leaded panes.

'Consider these little panes of glass. Seven up and five across. There are thirty-five of them in a space the quarter of our sitting-room window in Baker Street. They do not suit a chapel, where all should be light and airy and delicate. Where else would you find such things as these? I will tell you where, my dear fellow. In the grim walls of lunatic asylums and prisons. In those unhappy places from which it is judged best that no sound of grief or frenzy shall be heard. What, then, of the lowered voices of a man and woman in intimate conversation?'

He turned from the window and looked at a small and narrow flap of metal, angled downward from the wall, level with the middle of the window and a few feet from it. For the first time since our arrival, I heard him chuckle and guessed that all might yet be well.

'See here, Watson. This is an old friend. The ventilator system. How extraordinary that a few months ago the mysterious death of the great novelist Emile Zola from charcoal poisoning should have taken us to France to examine just such forms of apparatus as this! Because there could be no proper intake of air through their windows, the good Congregationalists of Peasenhall installed a form of tube. I know it well. Devised by Mr. Tobin of Leeds. This model made by a rival is known as the Hopper.'

He pressed the metal flap that projected downward from the wall and I heard it click, as though it was now shut. Taking the lip of metal, he then opened it again.

'A small catch inside does the trick. Within this flap is a draft-proof boxed-in ventilator. Imagine it as a square drainpipe on a larger scale. It is made of perforated zinc but lined with wood. The air passes from the outer world though this inlet and so through the wall. It then turns a corner downward, drawn by the warmer air within the building, which naturally rises upward in the room. At floor level the incoming air turns again and is released into the interior. It may be assisted by a fan of some kind, though I think not in this case.'

He closed the outside flap again with the same click.

'Now, my dear fellow, with the ventilator closed, the door shut, and with windows that cannot be opened, no conversation in a normal voice could be heard distinctly—if at all—even where we are standing. Those two louts were six feet above us and nine feet further away, crouching behind a hedge. Even an exclamation or a casual cry would be so indistinct that its location would not be certain at such a distance. With the ventilator open, it might be possible to hear voices without being able to detect what they were saying. I doubt even that, since the sound would have to enter the tube low down on the inside wall. It must then pass along deadening wooden surfaces, against the flow of air, and round two corners before it reached anyone outside. Even if it was audible when it did so, the flap outside would direct it downward, not upward to the bank and the fence.'

'Then we have them!' I said exultantly.

He shook his head.

'Not as securely as we need to or as surely as I mean to have them when they are brought in to be questioned.'

6

Once again it was Holmes and I who sat with Lestrade and Mr. Wild at a table, this time inside the Doctor's Chapel. Its interior suggested the plain and humble devotion practised there. The walls were merely whitewashed over, and it was evident that they had been built of simple cob, as country folk call their mixture of clay, gravel, and straw. Sherlock Holmes sat at the center of our 'inquisition.' If he had been the patient inquirer at Ipswich gaol, he was now the avenger, seeking justice for William Gardiner. He knew the truth, but it was another matter to prove it.

Mr. and Mrs. Crisp came in first. Conversation through the ear trumpet of old 'Tailor' Crisp, as they called him, was almost impossible. It was his wife who submitted to the courteous but direct questioning of Sherlock Holmes.

'Tell me, Mrs. Crisp, I presume you do not leave the chapel unlocked at all hours?'

'No, sir. It is always locked when not in use.'

'And you—that is to say you and your husband—have the key?'

'We do, sir.'

'How many copies of the key are there?'

'Two copies, sir. We hold them both. The one in use is with other keys in a drawer of the desk, kept locked, and a spare key is kept in the safe. That is in case the first should be lost.'

'Rose Harsent would be given the key from the drawer when she went to clean the chapel on Tuesday evening and would hand it back it to you when she had finished?'

'Exactly so, Mr. Holmes.'

'Always on the same night?'

'As soon as she got home from the chapel or a very little later.'

'Why was the chapel cleaned on a Tuesday, Mrs. Crisp? I should have thought it might have been more likely to be cleaned on a Saturday, ready for Sunday service.'

'Saturday is a busy day, sir, and the chapel deacons hold their meeting on Wednesday. I like to have it cleaned on Tuesday, for the deacons next day, though the work is not always done as late as the evening. First thing on Wednesday morning, about half past eight, Mr. Crisp and I go down Church Lane and satisfy ourselves that everything is in order and the place properly cleaned for the evening meeting and prayers. By going early, it gives time to have anything put right that needs putting right.'

'And when you went to the chapel first thing on the morning after the alleged scandal, everything was as you expected? The chapel had been cleaned?'

'It had, sir. Even the numbers on the hymn board had been changed as usual and the hymn books put in order.'

'And you are quite sure that you entered by using the key that was in the desk drawer?'

'It was the only one we had ever used, sir. The other had never left the safe. Naturally, it was where I put it the night before, when the girl handed it back. I can't say exactly what time that was, for I had no reason to remember until the murder. It might have been as late as nine o'clock that she gave it me, because she was sometimes back and busy in the kitchen before I came in. Not later than nine, though. If it had been later than about nine, I should have wondered where she was. She was a good girl and dependable, except for whatever put her in the family way.'

'Very well,' said Holmes. 'The time of her return is of great importance, Mrs. Crisp. However, you must not let us persuade you to say anything that you do not accurately remember. There is one thing more. When she returned that evening, was her dress as it normally might have been?'

'Indeed it was, sir. By the time I saw her, she had put away her shawl, and of course she would not wear a bonnet to go so short a distance.'

After Mr. and Mrs. Crisp had withdrawn, Wright and Skinner entered together. Whether Eli Nunn had sent them both at once or whether they had insisted upon this, in case one might contradict the other in his absence, I could not tell. A meaner-looking pair of bullies I had never seen. I do not say they would lie in wait to garrotte a man for his purse, but, I thought as I looked at them then, they would blast the reputation of man or woman without a second's thought. Skinner, I think, was the worse of the two.

One by one they told their stories again. Wright, who was loitering in Church Street, had seen Rose Harsent go up the path to the chapel at seven thirty that evening, and Gardiner had followed her at about seven forty-five. Wright had gone to Skinner's lodgings about eight o'clock and urged him to come and watch some fun. They arrived outside the chapel at eight fifteen or eight twenty and crept up along the raised bank until they might crouch behind the hedge. From there they could look down at the southwest window of the chapel. Skinner had remained in position for about an hour. Wright had been absent for about ten minutes during this time, but they had both been there when the couple in the chapel went their separate ways home.

Skinner gave the more complete version of what he alleged had happened in the chapel, though both agreed that it was getting too dark to see distinctly through the window. Skinner heard a woman's voice, which he could not recognize, say 'Oh! Oh!' At that point Wright went away for about ten moments. Skinner heard the woman say, 'Did you notice me reading my Bible last Sunday?' The man, whose voice was allegedly that of Gardiner, said, 'What were you reading about?' 'I was reading about like what we have been doing here tonight. Chapter thirty-eight of Genesis. It won't be noticed.'

'You may save yourself the trouble of being coy with us, Skinner,' said Lestrade. 'Onan spilling his seed upon the ground, you mean?'

To my astonishment, Skinner blushed.

'That is correct,' he said. '"And Judah said unto Onan, Go in unto thy brother's wife and marry her and raise up seed to thy brother."'

'You are to be congratulated on your knowledge of Holy Writ'—the voice of Sherlock Holmes had an edge like a freshly honed razor—'especially since you say you are not a church-going man. And was that all you heard?'

'Later on the female said, "I shall be out tomorrow night at nine o'clock but you must let me go now." George Wright had returned by then and was with me when that was said.'

Wright nodded his head but without looking up at us.

'And that was all?' Holmes inquired gently.

'All that I remember, sir.'

'You had known this young woman for years, had you not, Skinner? By your account, you did what you call odd jobs at Providence House. You tell us that you heard her talk of Bible-reading in chapel on the previous Sunday. Since you heard everything so plainly, how is it possible you could not know her voice after an hour of listening to it, but only recognized her when you say she came out of the door?'

'She talked low.'

'And yet you heard her so plainly?'

Skinner scowled at his shoes and said nothing. My friend exchanged a glance with Lestrade, as if it was time for some prearranged ceremony to take place. Then he turned to the two young men again.

'Wright and Skinner, you will please go outside with Dr. Watson and Constable Nunn to the fence behind which you say that you crouched. You will crouch there again. I shall stay here and Chief Inspector Lestrade will see fair play. This time, I shall be the one who recites the thirty-eighth chapter of Genesis. You will be able to demonstrate to Dr. Watson and Constable Nunn that you are able to hear the words.'

'It is not a fair test!' said Wright scornfully.

'Fairer by far than the test to which you have put William Gardiner!' Holmes snapped. 'The ventilators will be open, which they may not have been that evening. You will have as good or better chance than then of hearing what is said.'

They would have wriggled out of this, I swear they would, but for the presence of PC Nunn and a Scotland Yard man. With Nunn and the two youths I went up to the bank and crouched behind the fence. At a signal, Holmes began to read. With the ventilators open, I could just hear the murmur of a man's voice but not the words. The ventilator flap was at least twelve feet away from us and the sound would have had to travel round two corners in a muffled tube. It was impossible, of course, to say that a younger witness with exceptionally acute hearing might not pick up something. With the ventilators closed, I could hear nothing. All the same, there was nothing to prevent Skinner with a young man's sharp ears telling the court of what he alleged had taken place. We returned to the little chapel and I took my place at the table again. Eli Nunn stood behind the two witnesses.

'Well, now,' said Holmes to the two young men, 'let us decide whether you have been truthful witnesses or willful perjurers before the King's justices. How much did you hear?'

'Some of it,' said Wright sullenly. 'It was in the evening then, not the afternoon with the drill works going.'

'Same here,' said Skinner.

The eyes of Sherlock Holmes glinted very slightly with triumph.

'It is a quiet afternoon. If you can hear any sound of the road at present, please tell us. As for the machinery at the seed drill works, that is silent at my request.'

Skinner glared at him, but Sherlock Holmes had got him on the run. Before long, this malevolent lout would be fighting for his life.

'You tell us that you heard some but not all of that passage from Genesis,' said Holmes courteously. 'Let me tell you, gentlemen, that I would not profane this little chapel or dignify you by using Scripture for such a purpose. Inspector Lestrade will read out the words I used and to which he was a witness.'

Lestrade glanced down at a small sheet of paper before him and looked more self-conscious than I had ever known him before. He read slowly and solemnly.

'Hey! diddle-diddle, the cat and the fiddle, the cow jumped over the moon, the little dog laughed to see such craft while the dish ran after the spoon.'

'Quite.' Holmes looked again at the two witnesses. 'I repeated the verse twice to give it sufficient length.'

'It is nothing but a filthy trick!' said Wright angrily, while Skinner's eyes narrowed with fury.

'Oh, no'—Holmes shook his head slowly—'the trick was yours. A trick that may yet have William Gardiner, who has never done you the slightest harm, dangling at the end of the hangman's rope. Constable Nunn, be good enough to lock the door and oblige me by arresting these two and charging them if they should try to leave before they have answered fully.'

He stared at the two witnesses.

'Let us come to certain questions that you have never been asked in court and for which you may be less prepared. You have both sworn that you saw Rose Harsent leave the chapel, followed a little later by William Gardiner. How did you see them?'

Skinner hesitated, but Wright had the answer.

'We were above them looking down. The hedge is about ten feet from the chapel and perhaps we were six or seven feet further along it. Not more. Easy enough to see anyone in the dusk.'

'How did you see them?' Holmes repeated. 'In your evidence, you told the court that when you reached the chapel it was eight fifteen and getting dark, so that you could not see clearly what was happening inside. If you are to be believed, the man and woman did not leave until nine fifteen or nine twenty. When you verify the fact in your diary, you will see that the sun had set at seven fifteen. It may still have been getting dark, as you swore was the case, when you both reached the chapel at eight fifteen. By nine fifteen it was not dusk but pitch dark and had been so for up to half an hour.'

There was silence in the little chapel for a moment before Holmes continued in the same level voice.

'Anyone coming from the chapel into the path that runs beside it would be in a canyon below the hedge. That path is unlit, the road beyond has no street lighting, the seed drill works would long ago have been in darkness. Further along, the road might be illuminated by the reflection from the windows of the houses, but near the chapel there are no houses. Even had there been a glimmer of light, every man that I have seen in Peasenhall—and in numerous photographs of Peasenhall—wears a similar cap, large and round. Every woman wears either a hat or a shawl—she wears the shawl over her head after dark. Identification might not have been easy in full daylight, yet you ask us to believe that it was simple, through a hedge, in complete darkness. I may have some say in what happens to you both as a result of the evidence you have given. Do not try my patience.'

'They might have had oil lamps,' said Wright desperately, 'I do not recall.'

Holmes nodded as if he accepted this, but Skinner could hardly restrain himself from glaring at his companion for the stupidity of the suggestion.

'I see. You do not recall it but they might have had oil lamps, might they? You have given evidence at the coroner's court, the magistrates' court, and twice at the assizes. Neither of you has mentioned a single oil lamp until now. Let that pass. They had oil lamps, did they? Yet rather than light them, they spent an hour in the chapel in total darkness, did they? They must have done so, for you took your Bible oath four times that it was too dark for you to see inside the building. Mrs. Crisp tells us that, next day, the chapel had been cleaned and even the hymn books put in the correct order and the numbers of the hymn board changed. A remarkable accomplishment in total darkness. Indeed, if you are correct, Rose Harsent had a lamp. Rather than light it, she did all this in darkness.'

Neither of them answered him. Sherlock Holmes sat back in his chair and continued without mercy.

'If they had lamps, when did they light them?'

'I don't recall they did,' said Skinner grimly.

'That is something else you do not recall.' He was the quiet assassin now. 'But they would have lit them before they left the chapel, surely. Why else carry them?'

'I suppose so.' Skinner gave up the struggle.

'If you have spoken a word of truth between you, those lamps must have been lit long before. If your story is to be believed, Rose Harsent said of some mishap that might have stained or disfigured a surface, 'It won't be noticed.' How could she tell what would be noticed and what would not if she could not see it?'

'I don't know.'

'If they lit lamps, you could have seen what was happening. You swear you could not. Therefore they did not have lamps and you could not have seen who it was that came out through the door.'

Wright had given up and was staring at his feet. Skinner struggled in the net. I do not think, in all my experience of Sherlock Holmes, I had ever seen such a mixture of fear and anger as in the eyes of this young rustic. He was not done for yet.

'You do think yourself clever, Mr. Holmes, the Baker Street detective! Perhaps if you'd spent a little less time in London and a little more in the country, you might have learnt a good deal.'

'I am always ready to learn,' said Holmes humbly.

'Well then, look at the sky at night! You talk about it being pitch dark. That sky ain't pitch dark all the time. Moonlight and starlight show a good deal.'

'I hardly think starlight would have illuminated the sunken path, hemmed in by shadow as it is.'

'I daresay not, but moonlight would. With a clear sky and the moon almost at the full, as it was.'

'You say the moon had risen?'

Skinner relaxed, as if he had sprung a trap on his victim.

'Of course it had risen, or we wouldn't have seen Rose and Mr. Gardiner, would we?'

'Dear me,' said Holmes, 'a perfect example of *petitio principii*, better known as begging the question. Do go on.'

Skinner went on.

'Three nights before, on the Saturday, a dozen of us went rabbit-catching. We do that when the moon is full sometimes. I can give you the names of witnesses enough. We went off early, about seven or eight, seeing that was when the moon come up and crossed the southern sky, as it generally does. That night, the moon would have shone almost directly onto that chapel door, the path, the gate, and the road beyond. It rises always a few minutes later every night, don't it? We all know that. But not so much later as to make much odds only three nights after, when we saw what we saw at the chapel. Don't tell me what we could and couldn't have seen, Mr. Holmes. We were the ones that were there.'

'Very well,' said Holmes meekly, 'then let me ask you one more thing and we shall have done.'

My heart sank. Was this all? It seemed as if these two wretches might be almost safe in their tale of 'seeing' Rose and her lover together at the chapel. Safe enough to hang William Gardiner. Skinner squared his shoulders confidently for the one more question. He truly seemed to think that he had beaten Sherlock Holmes at last.

'All right,' he said magnanimously, 'what do you want to know?'

'Who locked the chapel door?' asked Holmes in the same meek voice. 'Mrs. Crisp and her husband found it locked as usual when they went there at half past eight on the following morning. You have both sworn that a woman left first on the evening before, Rose Harsent, if it was she. You did not follow her but waited for the man, William Gardiner, if it was he. You understand?'

'Well enough, I should say.'

'Who locked the door that evening, for locked it was and locked it was found the next morning?'

Wright joined in.

'Gardiner must have done that. He was the last to leave. It can't have been anyone else, can it?'

'It cannot,' said Holmes in the same subdued voice. 'And you followed Gardiner, did you not? According to your evidence, Skinner caught up with him almost at once. Let me see. Here we are: "I walked level with him for about twenty yards." You then stood at the crossing and watched him continue home down the main street of Peasenhall, which is simply called the Street? Is that correct?'

'Of course it is,' said Skinner with a slight laugh at the absurdity of it all. Sherlock Holmes changed his manner in a split second. He came in, as they say, for the kill.

'Kindly do not laugh, Skinner; a man's life depends on our conversation this afternoon. So does your liberty for the next seven years and that of your foolish friend. All this was at nine twenty, you say?'

'I have said so in court. It was nine twenty or perhaps by then nine thirty.'

'Mrs. Crisp was able to tell us this afternoon that long before nine twenty, let alone nine thirty, the key to the chapel was safely locked in a drawer of her desk. Gardiner could not have used it to lock the chapel door.'

'Then he did not lock it!'

'Mr. and Mrs. Crisp found it securely locked the next morning. According to your sworn testimony, you watched Gardiner walk home from the Doctor's Chapel. Rose Harsent was nowhere around. You did not follow her when she left and had gone on ahead. Gardiner, also according to your evidence, did not approach the door of Providence House. To use your own words in court, he walked straight past it.'

'Then. . . .'

'I am there before you, Skinner. Then, perhaps, Gardiner returned in the middle of the night, burgled Providence House, ransacked the desk, forced open the drawer, took the key to the chapel, and locked it? Or Rose Harsent got up in the middle of the night, broke open the desk, and took the key for the same purpose. By a fairy's magic wand, all trace of breaking and entering vanished before Mrs. Crisp went to her desk the next morning. And all this happened at a time when neither the man nor the woman in your story had any idea that they had been watched—and therefore they had no reason for doing it. In any case, they would have thought that early next morning would do just as well for locking the chapel.'

'It must have. . . .'

'Do not tell me what must have happened, Skinner. Had you been a little more skilled in falsehood, you would have invented a story in which Gardiner caught up with Rose and handed her the key before he went home. If there were a word of truth in anything you have sworn to, Gardiner could not have given the unlocked chapel door a second thought and it would have been still unlocked next day—which it was not. Had he been uneasy, he would have hurried after Rose Harsent, got the key, and gone back to lock it then and there, which you swear he did not. My only regret in all this is that public flogging has been abolished for willful perjury.'

It was a masterly cross-examination. He had them by the throat as perhaps only Sir Edward Marshall Hall might have done in a court of law. Neither of these surly young fellows could muster an answer, for they had expected only a repetition of the more kindly questions asked at the assize court. But still he had not quite done with them.

'Before we are rid of you this afternoon, I will add one brief lesson in astronomy. The moon's orbit is somewhat more eccentric than that of the earth round the sun, where sunset and sunrise have a more regular principle. In the autumn, the time of the moon's rising will scarcely vary from one night to the next. Therefore, when it rises just after dusk, it is good moonlight to make hay by, the so-called Harvest Moon. In October it is Hunter's Moon. Unfortunately for you, the springtime month of which you speak is one when the differences in the moon's rising are far greater from day to day, sometimes more than an hour and often fifty minutes between one night and the next. The fact that the moon rose conveniently for you at seven thirty P.M. on Saturday means that it would not rise three days later until after ten o'clock. At nine twenty, in the darkness of that alley below the hedge, you could not have seen a single thing by moonlight to which you have sworn in court, even had those things taken place.'

They hung their heads, but still he had not done with them.

'Every item of your evidence taken together is now exposed for what it always was—a tissue of vindictive lies. At first you told these falsehoods for motives of malice, to ruin the lives of an innocent man and woman, a man whom you despised as "Holy Willie." Then murder was done, and you dared not confess your slanders.'

In the matter of his reputation, William Gardiner was triumphant. Sherlock Holmes had fought the two bullies to a standstill, and they stood silent before him.

He spoke once more before Eli Nunn led them out.

'Repeat your vicious allegations in court once more and you will find that you have gone to sea in a sieve. I will myself lay an information against you with Inspector Lestrade as my witness. I will seek a warrant for your indictment on charges of willful perjury, for which you may be sent to penal servitude upon conviction for a term of seven years. Think on that.'

There was a silence in the chapel as the door closed upon them. Even Lestrade and Ernest Wild sat in awe. Presently Wild turned to the Chief Inspector.

'I cannot anticipate what you will say to the solicitor-general, Mr. Lestrade, but I must tell you this. If there is a third attempt to try William Gardiner for murder, after all that you have heard and he has suffered, I do not think the Crown will offer those two scoundrels as witnesses on its behalf. However, I promise you that I shall subpoena them for the defense, as hostile witnesses, and treat them as Mr. Holmes has treated them this afternoon.'

Lestrade got to his feet and shuffled his papers together. His bulldog gruffness had softened and he almost smiled.

'It is not in my gift to decide such matters, Mr. Wild, only to make my recommendations. However, after what we have seen and heard this afternoon, I do not think you will be called upon to do anything of the kind.'

7

Whatever Lestrade's failings as a detective, the inspector was a man of honour. He had given his word that his recommendation to the Metropolitan commissioner of police, and thence to the Director of Public Prosecutions, should be based upon the evidence. He was not to be influenced by the local prejudice that had brought William Gardiner so close to the gallows trap and the unmarked grave by the prison wall. My own part has been to reveal, for the first time, the role played in the famous Peasenhall case by Sherlock Holmes.

The world knew in a day or two that William Gardiner would not be called upon for a third time to stand trial for the murder of Rose Harsent. Yet innocent though he was, he and his family were punished by public opinion. He was forced to leave his home in Alma Cottage and take his wife and children to London, where their future lives were hidden in its twenty thousand streets.

At dusk on the day when the end of the prosecution was announced, as a soft January snowfall began to cover the stretches of Baker Street beyond the window, Holmes stood looking out at the smoky sky, from which the large flakes were falling slowly through the first yellow flush of lamplight.

'*Fiat justitia, ruat coelum*,' he said thoughtfully, drawing the velvet curtains and turning to the firelight. '"Let justice be done, though the heavens fall." The heavens are certainly falling at the moment, rather pleasantly, and justice has been done to William Gardiner in ample measure.'

He sat down and began to fill his pipe with the black shag tobacco that he habitually kept in a Persian slipper, a souvenir of some long-forgotten adventure.

'Tell me,' I said, 'did you ever believe the man to be guilty? Was your promise to Lestrade of being willing to find him innocent or not anything but a blind, as they say?'

He looked into the crackling logs of the fire and sighed.

'You see, Watson? You are too quick for me, as usual. I decided at the outset that I could not appear to be a counsel for the defence, for that would have turned Lestrade into the prosecutor as well as the judge. It was obvious from the start that the slanders that Wright and Skinner spread about the poor fellow were false. They were demonstrably false upon common sense and deduction. It really mattered nothing whether one believed Gardiner and his wife. The importance attached to her evidence and his was the red herring in the case. It was the one crucial error committed by Ernest Wild that he made so much seem to depend upon it.'

'It was not thought beside the point in court.'

He waved this aside like the smoke of his pipe.

'It was why the jury nearly convicted him, all but one man. The whole thing was settled in my mind by the impossibilities in the slanderers' stories. Such people can rarely spread lies without giving themselves away. Mr. Wild did not quite appreciate the extent of this. He is good and we shall hear more of him, but after all he is not Sir Edward Marshall Hall and never will be. He never even suggested, I think, that Gardiner could not have left the chapel last and yet the door was found locked next morning. He did not point out that two hours after sunset it was pitch dark and yet Skinner claimed to identify two people, seen in total darkness through a hedge, on a path below him and a little distance away.'

'It has been pointed out now,' I said quietly.

'When they were cornered, of course, they said there must have been a lantern and that was when I knew we had them! The whole story was an impossibility.'

'And they were wrong about the moon.'

He paused a moment.

'There, Watson, I must confess a small subterfuge. I do not know when the moon rose that night, though the nightly intervals of its rising are certainly far longer at that time of year, more than an hour sometimes between one night and the next. I did not know that it was pitch dark rather than moonlight at the time they claimed to have seen such goings-on. Yet, faced with the challenge, nor did they. For me, that was the final proof of their malice, dishonesty, and stupidity.'

'You used a trick?'

'A trick if you care to call it that. What is in a name? Our friend Professor Jowett used to say much the same of logic. Logic, he said, is neither an art nor a science. Logic is a dodge.'

Having had enough of this, he reached for his violin case.

'While you were out yesterday, I made some small improvements to my prelude and fugue on the theme of "Pop Goes the Weasel." It is, I believe, now ready for Messrs. Augeners' attention. Ah! I see from your expression that I have played it to you before, I think?'

'Just the other evening.'

'Nonetheless,' he said happily, 'you might care to hear it again.'

764

The Case of the Phantom Chambermaid

1

It was a cool midsummer morning, during the week in which the Poisons Bill was before a House of Commons select committee. After a glimpse of early sun, a thin mist had gathered over the pale blue Baker Street sky, even while I read a summary of the previous day's proceedings from the parliamentary columns of the *Times*. I folded the paper and was about to say something to Holmes concerning the deficiencies of the new law, when he rose from his chair, stooped to the fireplace, took a cinder with the tongs, and applied it to the bowl of his cherrywood pipe. The red silk dressing gown made his tall, gaunt figure seem even taller and gaunter in the faint sunlight. Puffing at the pipe and staring down into the grate with his sharp profile, he spoke thoughtfully.

'The season is passing, Watson, and it is high time we got away. Everywhere else the sun must be shining. In London, it might as well be February. Do you not feel it? Even the footpads of the East End will have deserted us for Margate sands. Life has become commonplace, the newspapers are sterile, audacity and romance seem to have passed for ever from the criminal world.'

I was well used to these periodic outbursts of self-pity.

'We might take lodgings for a week or two at one of the Atlantic resorts,' I said hopefully, 'Ilfracombe or Tenby, perhaps. There is also a standing invitation from the Exmoor cousins at Wiveliscombe.'

He turned a tragic face to me and groaned.

'One of those unwelcome summonses that call upon a man either to be bored or to lie.'

I thought it best to ignore this passing dismissal of my family. I said, rather brusquely, 'Once the matter in hand is dealt with, you have no further commitments. You may travel where you please and for as long as you please.'

He groaned again.

'The matter in hand! Oh, Watson, Watson! The Reverend Mr. Milner, Mrs. Deans, and her daughter Effie. A girl who was, I understand, a chambermaid at the Royal Albion Hotel in Brighton and was, I also understand, dismissed because someone saw her enter the room of a gentleman during the night. Really, Watson! Why should I care if a hundred chambermaids enter the rooms of a hundred gentlemen—or whether they are discharged from their employment or not? No one suggests that anything was stolen from this room—from any room, indeed. Merely that this young woman was seen entering during the night. That such a case should attract the least attention attests to the triumph of the banal in our society.'

'You have often remarked, old fellow, that it is the banal and the commonplace that are the hallmarks of major crime.'

'Well, well,' he said grudgingly, 'that, at any rate, is true.'

He went off to his room and for several minutes I heard him banging about, making a quite unnecessary disturbance. When he returned he had changed his dressing-gown for a black velvet jacket.

'The Royal Albion Hotel.' He sat down and sighed. 'I smell the tawdry odour of its brown Windsor soup from sixty miles away.'

It was half past ten when a cab stopped below our windows and there was a sound of voices. When the Reverend James Milner had wired to make his appointment, he informed me that he and two members of his Brighton flock would take an early train from their seaside homes and be with us by eleven o'clock. He was, I gathered, superintendent of the Wesleyan Railway Mission in the town, ministering to the workers and families in the little streets that cluster round the lofty terminus of the London Brighton and South Coast Railway. Mrs. Deans and Effie had brought their trouble to him. In a most quixotic gesture, he had decided to announce the child's trouble to the famous Sherlock Holmes.

They were an odd trio. Mr. Milner in his black cloth suit and tall white clerical collar lacked the more exotic qualities of other clergy and could only have been a plain Methodist minister. His sleek hair was prematurely gray, but his spectacles gave him a youthfully studious look. Mrs. Deans, in a flowery summer dress, came up our Baker Street staircase like a cruiser under full sail. Her round face and porkpie bonnet gave her the air of one who could hold her own. I could imagine this doughty person with her sleeves rolled up to drub the washing in its bowl or give what-for to anyone who exchanged cross words with her. When I heard that the terrace of cramped little houses in which the Deans family lived was called Trafalgar Street, I saw her at once as one of those formidable women who had sailed on HMS *Victory* to Nelson's famous battle and had loaded the great guns for their menfolk to fire.

Effie Deans, the subject of this consultation, was probably no more than fifteen or sixteen, a chubby or cherubic girl with a cluster of fair curls under a blue straw boater. In the circumstances, it was not surprising that her prettiness was clouded by apprehension.

'Gentlemen,' said Mr. Milner, once Holmes had sat us all down, 'what may be a matter of sport to the rest of the world is life and death to the honor of Miss Deans and her mother.'

Mrs. Deans nodded emphatically. The minister continued.

'Effie Deans has been dismissed from a post that she had held for almost two years, sent away without a reference or a character, for an offence which she cannot have committed. The gentleman in question made no complaint against her—indeed, it seems he was not even questioned. A hotel porter claims that he saw her enter the room during the night. He reported the matter and she was dismissed next day, despite her most positive denials. I have known her as a good, honest, and truthful girl, who attended the Wesleyan Mission Sunday school every week of her childhood.'

Holmes had been staring at him with a curiosity that was discourteous, if not hostile.

'Unfortunately, Mr. Milner, what you know her to be is not the issue. Let us keep to the facts. If Miss Deans is as bad as Jezebel, it matters nothing so long as she was not there and did not enter that room. If she was there and did enter it, she may be as good and truthful as you like, but she was guilty of the fact and was properly dismissed. Let us have no more of Sunday school, if you please. It will not get us very far.'

Holmes was in an unfortunate mood. He should never have mentioned Jezebel, to judge by the look on the face of Mrs. Deans and the flush that rose from her neck to her cheeks. No Baker Street detective was to say such a thing of her daughter. Before Milner could add a word, she let fly.

'See here, Mr. Holmes! It's not just that my Effie is a good girl and wouldn't have done it. She was at home all night and *couldn't* have done it!'

He admired her spirit.

'Excellent, madam! You have, if I may say so, an unerring grasp of the laws of evidence. Pray continue.'

The Reverend Mr. Milner was out in the cold now.

'Well, sir,' Mrs. Deans went on, 'she come home as usual close on half past eight that evening. Don't take my word for it. We had the Todgers.'

'Todgers, madam?'

'Them that live next door. Had them in for a hand or two of whist and Beat-Jack-out-of-doors, also a glass of shrub and a pipe.'

I swear I saw in my mind Mrs. Deans smoking her pipe with the rest.

'I assume they were not with you until two in the morning?'

'Near midnight. They saw her all the time. Then we went to bed. She went to her little room in the attic. To get out, she comes down through the room where Alf and I sleep. I laid awake an hour and more with my stomach after the shrub. How could she come down and I not see nor hear her? How could she unbolt the downstairs door and go out without I hear her—or without Alf seeing it when he gets up at three? Which he must do to go on early turn at the railway goods yard at four. And don't tell me, Mr. Holmes, that I can't prove what I say. Do I look the sort that'd let her daughter go out on the streets at one or two in the morning and never say a word?'

'No, madam,' said Holmes uncertainly, 'indeed you do not. In any court proceedings, however, you will be asked the following question: Why should this porter, whoever he was, say that he saw your daughter entering a guest's room at one or two o'clock that morning, if he could not have done so?'

Her eyes narrowed as she looked at him.

'Yes, Mr. Holmes! Oh, yes! I'd like him asked that question! I'd like him asked good and proper, in such a way as he wouldn't forget being asked for a very long time!'

If ever a woman had captivated Holmes in a quarter of an hour, it was Mrs. Deans. The Reverend Mr. Milner had given up. His parishioner was doing his job far better than he could have done it for himself. Holmes stretched out his long thin legs, and when he looked up, his eyes were brighter than I had seen them for a long time.

'It seems,' said Mr. Milner hastily, 'that the night porter said he recognized her in part by her uniform, the black dress, white apron, and white cap. Of course, that might have been worn by someone else, though it is not clear why anyone else wishing to enter the room should have bothered to put the uniform on. Whoever did so can hardly have expected to do it without disturbing the occupant.'

'Quite so,' said Holmes thoughtfully. 'What do we know of the gentleman who occupied the room? He was alone, I take it?'

'He was talked about in the town during the weeks since he came there.' Mrs. Deans had once again got in ahead of the Reverend Mr. Milner. 'A spiritual gentleman. Always seeing ghosts, he said. Something to do with the Society for Cyclical Research.'

'Society for Psychic Research,' Mr. Milner said quickly. She stared at him, then turned back to Holmes.

'They say he saw that many ghosts, he had to put himself to sleep at night with clarasomething from a smelling bottle. My girl could still smell it next morning. And he had a rumpus with the showfolk at the Brighton Aquarium. Professor Chamberlain and Madame Elvira that do tricks with ghosts and guessing. He thought he was superior to all that tommyrot. The Brighton papers wouldn't print his letters nor theirs for fear of being took to court.'

I looked at Holmes. An extraordinary change had gradually come over his face during these exchanges with their hints of ghosts and fraud. His eyes were shining like two stars with a hint of enthusiasm ill-contained. His hands gripped the arms of the chair and I almost thought he might spring from it. The Reverend Mr. Milner got in his twopenny-worth at last.

'The gentleman in question is a spiritualist,' he said quickly. 'Mr. Edmund Gurney is a scholar and a gentleman who resents the cheapening of his beliefs by the mind-reading entertainments, mesmerism, and trances at the Aquarium, as do all those who take a sincere interest in such matters. His own work for the Psychical Research Society is at a far superior level. He is, I understand, a classical scholar of Trinity College, Cambridge, a friend of Dr. Frederick Myers and his circle. He is certainly a musicologist and has written upon the theories of sound. His particular interest appears to be in what are called phantasms of the living. That is to say, the possibility that we may have a vision of those we know or love at a crisis in their lives, not infrequently at the moment of their deaths. It is the case of a man who sees at the end of his garden path the figure of a friend whom he had believed to be still in India. He then hears that the friend was, indeed, still in India and that he had died at the moment of the apparition.'

Holmes had listened to this last revelation with eyes closed and fingertips pressed together. He now looked up.

'Mr. Edmund Gurney sounds an admirable gentleman. I cannot believe that it is any of his doing that Effie has been dismissed. Indeed, if what you say is true, Mrs. Deans, it seems that he sleeps with the aid of a soporific and may well not have known anything of this incident. This is a curious and, indeed, intriguing inconsistency. My dear Mr. Milner! My dear Mrs. Deans! My dear Miss Effie, if I may so address you. You may count upon this difficulty of yours receiving my fullest and most immediate attention. This enigma is almost more than I had deserved!'

'You will take the case?' Milner asked nervously.

'Mr. Milner, I could not do otherwise. Indeed, you may depend upon Dr. Watson and myself being in Brighton by this evening. You yourselves must return there forthwith. I shall ask Mrs. Hudson to summon the boy. A wire must go to the post office at once engaging rooms for us.'

Milner eased his starched clerical collar with a forefinger.

'In the matter of your fee, sir. My friends are scarcely in a position. . . .'

'We will not talk of a fee, if you please. Some things, my dear Milner, are more than money to me.'

'Then where shall we find you? Where will you stay?'

Holmes, mystified by the question, looked at him.

'Where else should we put up but at the *locus in quo*?'

This stumped all three of them.

'Why,' said Holmes blithely, 'at the Royal Albion Hotel, Mr. Milner. We may even learn to relish its cuisine.'

The change that had overtaken Sherlock Holmes since his sullen mood after breakfast would hardly have been believed by those who did not know him well. He had pined for adventure and challenge. Now that this had presented itself, if only in the form of a dismissed chambermaid, he was transformed by an excess of energy. Though he sometimes used to talk of retiring to the Sussex downs and keeping bees, I swear he could not have endured it for more than a fortnight.

That afternoon we took tea in the Pullman car of the express that whirled us to Brighton, the sunlit fields and downs of Sussex spinning away from us, the sun glittering on the sea ahead. The light was in his eyes again. He hummed or sang quietly some battle hymn of his own throughout the journey until our train drew into Brighton and we felt a light ocean breeze on our faces.

2

So it was, upon my friend's impulse, that we had left the comforts of our quarters in Baker Street for an indefinite spell of indifferent cooking and the sound of breakers on shingle carrying to our ears at the Royal Albion Hotel. Within two hours of leaving London, we had moved into our suite, a spacious sitting-room with our bed-rooms to either side. Its windows enjoyed a view across the busy esplanade to a broad expanse of waves that stretched between us and the coast of France sixty miles way. At this time of year, the edge of the sea was a promenade for mothers in full skirts, blouses, and straw boaters, fathers in their best suits and hats. Children gathered excitedly before the puppet booth of the Punch and Judy show on the beach when its little trumpet announced each performance.

We soon accustomed ourselves to the daily round. Each morning, several ponies drew the wheeled cabins of the ladies' bathing machines down to the water's edge and pulled them back up at sunset. The regimental band of the Coldstream Guards played briskly every afternoon at two P.M. on the far end of the old Chain Pier, while bearded fishermen mended their nets on the lower esplanade. Fishing boats and yachts lay drawn up on the shingle, except for a few jolly little craft like the *Honeymoon* and the *Dolly Varden*, which bobbed and twisted in the swell with their apprehensive passengers.

Within an hour of our arrival, we were sitting down to an early 'theatre' dinner provided by these seaside hotels for patrons who have booked seats at some theatrical performance. Holmes, in one of those infuriating moods which took him from time to time, would say nothing beyond remarking, 'There is not a moment to be lost.' On the contrary, I thought, we seemed to have all the time in the world. He withdrew behind the *Evening Globe* while the waiter attempted to serve us *turbot a la mayonnaise*. The Royal Albion was a large, solid building, now past its best, which qualities were reflected in its menu. Holmes ate rapidly but in silence, evidently turning over possibilities in his mind. Even before the coffee was served, he pushed back his chair and stood up.

'Come, Watson. I think it is time we were on our way.'

As we came out into the evening sunlight of the esplanade, I was about to ask him what our way might be. Before I could do so, he very pointedly drew a deep breath, swelled out his chest, tapped his cane sharply on the paving of the esplanade and said, 'How good it is to breathe sea air again after a winter of London fogs. What was it that they called this town in the days of the good King George III? They nicknamed it Doctor Brighton, I recall. And not without reason.'

'I daresay I should breathe a lot more clearly if I knew where the blazes we were going.'

He looked at me in astonishment. 'But you must have known, my dear friend. You heard the tale told this morning, of second sight and phantasms of the living. Where should we go for entertainment on our very first evening in Brighton but to the lecture-room of the Aquarium, apparently disapproved of by Mr. Gurney, for a display of Professor Chamberlain's magical accomplishments with the talented Miss Elvira. Their names are on the bill over there.'

So that was it. Why such vulgar entertainment should be of the least use to our defence of Effie Deans was quite beyond me.

If you have ever visited Brighton, you will know that the Aquarium has less to do with sea creatures than with popular entertainment. It stands under its famous clock tower just at the landward end of the Chain Pier with its strings of colored lanterns. We paid our sixpences and passed through the turnstiles to a land of fairy lights and fireworks. Among the shows and exhibitions advertised, its theatre offered Madame Alice Barth's Operetta Company in the Garden Scene from *Faust* and 'Dr. Miracle,' a one-act piece never performed before. Holmes led the way to the plainer fare offered by the lecture theater which was placarded by 'Professor Chamberlain's Experiments in Mesmerism and Thought-Reading.'

At the door, a newspaper review was displayed under glass. It was a cutting from the *Brighton Herald*, praising the excitement of last Saturday's performance, when 'Dr. Mesmer' had hypnotised a youth and a girl. The youth was subjected to kickings and prickings, the girl to abuse and mockery. When brought back to consciousness, each of the dupes smilingly acknowledged the applause and confessed to having no memory of the ordeal. A heckler in the front row who had denounced the display loudly as a 'put-up job' was thrown out of the hall by several members of the large and excited audience. I cannot pretend that this was the entertainment I should have chosen for my first night in Brighton.

Across a bill advertising the show was a more recent banner still damp with paste. It announced that Professor Chamberlain and his medium, Madame Elvira, had been retained by other managements to provide 'select high-class seances for the popularizing of phenomenal science.' In consequence, this week must be the last of their present season in Brighton. It seemed that they had been in residence at the Aquarium during most of the summer so far.

We paid a further shilling and were ushered to seats near the front of what was not so much a lecture hall as a music hall or a palace of varieties. It seemed less crowded than on a Saturday night, but the buzz of excitement was still unmistakable. Professor Chamberlain, playing the role of Dr. Mesmer with an electrical magnet, first invited several victims onto his platform and made some magic passes over them. They then submitted to a few blows without apparent resentment. Among roars of approval from the onlookers, they also performed as though they believed themselves to be dogs or cockerels, infants at feeding time, or soldiers at drill. They finally woke up at the snap of their master's fingers, remembering nothing.

For half an hour we endured this sort of thing. Nothing would have been easier to counterfeit.

Chamberlain was a broad-shouldered young man with a flop of pale gold hair aslant his forehead and penetrating blue eyes. He was, I suppose, the type who might be handsome to a shopgirl or a maidservant, perhaps because there was a common look to him that brought him within every female's grasp. Yet the more one looked at him, the more his youthfulness came into question. He was like a modern French painting, best seen from a distance, since cracks and crevices appear on closer inspection. As I studied him during his performance, I thought that after all he was not so much a young man as the ideal of what an indulgent old woman might think a young man should be. In this, at least, I was to be proved right. Quite probably he would never see forty again and must have spent some time each day concealing the fact. Perhaps his appearance alone would not have mattered quite so much had it not been for his voice, or rather its confident twang. It was not so much an accent as a distortion of his speech, which might equally well have been acquired in the stockyards of Chicago or the dock-side of Liverpool. It seemed to me that he had no real voice at all, merely a self-confident nasal bray.

Presently the audience fell silent, as if it knew that we had come to the serious business of the evening. Whatever flippancy had been evident in Chamberlain until now, he became as solemn and as insinuating as the Reverend Mr. Milner could ever have been in the pulpit of his Wesleyan Railway Mission.

We were introduced to Madame Elvira, a shrewish little person with ginger hair. She was wearing a dress of electric blue with white ruffs. It seems that she was blessed with gifts of many kinds, including 'second sight,' which may have been the least of her accomplishments, if Professor Chamberlain were to be believed.

'Madame Elvira was born in the Middle West, where her ancestry included Indian blood from the tribes who fought at Fort Duquesne a century and more ago. She lived many years of her childhood as a friend of those tribes with the most happy results. By long practice and sympathetic attention she has attuned her spirit to those of the dead warriors and chiefs by whom messages from the beyond are so often brought to us.'

'Which is to say,' remarked Holmes softly, 'that Madame Elvira has very probably never been further west than the terminus of the Hammersmith railway.'

The professor explained that a man whom Madame Elvira had never seen nor heard of might write his name upon a card. The card would then be handed to the professor, who would stare at it long enough and hard enough to fix the image of the signature in his mind. Twenty feet or more away from him, Madame Elvira would sit at a typewriter with her back to him. She would be blindfolded by volunteers from the audience. The image in the mind of the professor would then be transmitted to that of his protegée, before our eyes. She would type it correctly on a sheet of paper without removing her blindfold. Rarely in the past had she been mistaken and even then only in a syllable or so.

The professor called for several more volunteers to do the blindfolding and see fair play. He was down among the audience now, handing out several dozen blank cards to those of us in the front rows. On these we were to write our names and individual seat numbers. When the cards had been gathered in, he invited a woman in the first row to stand upon the stage and shuffle them like playing cards so that there could be no question of any prearranged order. Then he sprang back behind the footlights. Madame Elvira sat patiently at her table before the typewriter. Her back was toward Professor Chamberlain and the audience as she clenched and stretched her fingers, no doubt in preparation for her task. Two other women were still blindfolding her to their satisfaction.

The professor in his swallowtail evening coat addressed his public in his confident twang.

'Thank you very much, ladies and gentlemen. In a moment we shall come to the highlight of our evening and our seance will begin, as soon as the two good ladies who have volunteered to ensure that my partner cannot by any means see me or any clue

I might give her have completed their task. We have all heard of cheats in the thoughtreading profession who signal to one another, haven't we? Eyes right for hearts, left for diamonds, up for clubs, and down for spades. One wink for an ace, two for a court card. We know all about that, don't we? Of course we do! And we aren't having it here, are we? Of course we aren't! What you see before you now is genuine second sight, authentic mindreading. It may succeed, it may fail. One thing you may depend upon, ladies and gentlemen, is that it is entirely genuine.'

He had all the panache of a man who sends you a dishonored bill with a note to say that payment is guaranteed.

'I have here fifty cards, ladies and gentlemen, each with the number of a seat and the name of a customer. I shall look at each in turn because, you understand, in order that second sight may operate it is necessary that another person should first see them and transmit them. But I shall do more than that. It is when thoughts are transferred in this way that the mind is most open to messages from the spirit world. For that reason, I shall also repeat to you whatever messages come to my mind as I hold the card before me. I cannot promise you there will be such messages, of course. I am in the hands of those beyond the veil who transmit them. What vulgar people call ghosts. However, whatever messages I have for those who have written these cards shall be relayed to them.'

Beside me I heard Holmes emit a despairing sigh. Professor Chamberlain had not finished.

'Blindfolded though she be, Madame Elvira has a magic touch with a typewriter. On that machine she will print out the name from each card as it appears in her mind. A copy shall be given to the lady or gentleman whose name and seat number appears upon it, thus putting her performance beyond any suspicion of trickery.'

He was staring at the first card, as if to fix it in his mind. He closed his eyes.

'I address the gentleman who wrote this card—for it is a gentleman in this case. Now, sir, while Madame Elvira sees in her own mind the very image that has just left mine, my thoughts are wandering, open to whatever message may be waiting for you in the world of the spirits. That world is infinite and we, in our finiteness, may not easily interpret its signals. . . . I have something. I do not say I understand it, but the letters of the message begin to form in my mind. I see the word 'Death.' What follows? Now it comes to me. *Death is but some means of reawakening.* . . . Wait, there is more! *Think nothing joyful unless innocent.* . . .'

'Intolerable rubbish!' said Holmes *sotto voce.*

Chamberlain opened his eyes. It was possible to hear the brief rattle of the typewriter keys, the ting of its bell, and the whiz of the paper being drawn clear. A volunteer from the audience who had helped to blindfold the girl brought the writing to him. Chamberlain came forward to the footlights.

'The number of the seat is twenty-four and the gentleman sitting in it is Mr. Charles Smith. The messages from another world are also typewritten upon the card.'

There was a murmur of expectation. Chamberlain stabbed a finger dramatically through the limelight, towards seat twenty-four.

'Am I right, sir?'

I could just catch a murmur and a nod.

'Have I ever met you before, air? Are we known to one another?' Another murmur and a shaking of the head.

'Do you understand how the message applies to you?'

A briefer, less certain nod. An assistant or runner carried the piece of typed paper to the man who had been named, as if it were a prize. This seaside entertainment began to intrigue me. Holmes affected boredom. We went through a dozen names, each embellished by strange 'messages' from the hereafter that combined the impenetrably obscure and the blindingly self-evident. If it was a trick, I could not make out how the devil it was done. The girl could see nothing and yet she was never wrong.

The minutes passed and now he had taken another card at which he was staring. I heard him say, 'A message is coming clearly to me but from very far off. I beg you will keep silence, ladies and gentlemen. . . . Perhaps it is directed to a professional gentleman, a man of learning. It is in two parts . . . or even three. . . . I hear the first one. *Knowledge protects its opposite.* . . . And then, *Experience brings understanding.* . . . Wait, there is one more! *Time precedes oblivion.* . . . Ladies and gentlemen, the meaning of much of this is hidden from me, but I have faith that it will be clear in some way to the recipient.'

'That experience brings understanding is clear enough to a baboon!' said Holmes quietly beside me. 'And unless I am much mistaken, my dear Watson, you are about to win a prize in a monkey show.'

The typewriter rattled and the paper was brought back.

'The number of the seat is thirty-one and the customer is Mr. John Watson! Am I right, sir?'

'Yes!' I called back abruptly. 'And I have never met you before.'

'Congratulations,' said Holmes acidly. 'Why is it that I am the only one to see how the trick is done?'

This rigmarole continued on the stage. Then, without warning, Holmes began to mutter each correct name even before Madame Elvira could begin to type it. I was alarmed that he might be overheard and that we might be identified as spies. Presently, however, we received another instruction from the hereafter. *Triumph in false strife makes power destroy itself.* This was followed at once and even more dramatically by *I pledge my name for truth.*

'The seat is number thirty-two and the occupant is Mr. Sherlock Holmes.'

His name meant nothing to the performers or their audience, I think, though I believe I heard a laugh from someone who perhaps thought him to be a wag playing a joke on the professor.

'Am I right, sir?'

'Indeed you are,' said Holmes in his most charming manner, 'and, of course, I have never had the pleasure of your acquaintance until now.'

The scrap of typing was brought and he thrust it into his pocket.

The rest of the performance was a variant of this game. Cards were drawn from a pack and correctly guessed at. Once or twice Madame Elvira even pronounced in advance which card a volunteer would draw. Yet in all this there was nothing much beyond the manipulation of a deck of cards as a skilled poker cheat might have done it. The deck was torn from a manufacturer's wrapper each time, but that would not prevent it being tampered with. The whole thing reeked of the gaming saloon.

All the same, the audience seemed well pleased. Yet the second-sight act had soon become what they call 'dead lead' to them. A moment later they were noisily applauding the return of the mesmerized when young men stooped, were kicked, and turned round to thank their assailant, as 'Dr. Mesmer' had commanded them in advance, or young women barked like dogs and scuffled on all fours. This was far superior to messages from 'the beyond' that sounded as if they might have a profound meaning and yet tortured the brain unendurably in any attempt to draw common sense from them.

I was ready to leave long before the end of the show, but Holmes seemed determined to see it through to the finish. Afterwards we took a final stroll along the deck of the Chain Pier while a crescent moon formed a thin path of pale glittering light all the way to Boulogne. I took the scrap of paper with my name typed upon it, screwed it up, and was about to throw it over the rail into the water.

'No!' said Holmes sharply. 'That is our first trophy of the battle.'

'A trophy of a wasted evening!'

He chuckled at this.

'A trophy of time well spent. You really could not see how it was done?'

'I suppose there was a trick,' I said grudgingly. 'All I saw was the fellow staring at a card, mumbling so-called philosophical remarks about knowledge, power, and staking one's soul for truth. Then the girl typed out the answer—the name on the card and the messages.

Professor Chamberlain cannot have been a muscle-twitcher, that much is evident, for she could not see him. As for those spoken messages, how could there be a meaning in all that foolish babble?'

'Very easily, my dear fellow. In the first place, he talked a great deal, but only the messages from the spirit world were important.'

'Did you hear mine? Knowledge protects its opposite. Experience brings understanding. Time precedes oblivion.'

'Quite so. The kind of gibberish that seems to the simple-minded to be the wisdom of the ages. It quite occupies one in trying to decipher it while the real trick is pulled. Our Professor Chamberlain is a clever fellow, make no mistake of that. A clever fellow, although a ruffian and a fraud.'

'Then there is a message in the gibberish?'

He threw back his head and laughed.

'Oh, there is, Watson! Indeed there is. Try the first letter of each word in your own message. Knowledge protects its own. Experience breeds understanding. Time precedes oblivion.'

'K-P-I-O. X-B-U. T-P-O. It makes worse gibberish than ever.'

'I confess that it took me until the third attempt to work it out. All the same it is a commonplace device. Now, replace each letter with the one in the alphabet which precedes it.'

'J-O-H-N. W-A-T-S-O-N.'

'Just so. John Watson. She could not see him, therefore it had to be a spoken code. Even then, the girl could not possibly have deciphered his endless verbiage; therefore, the clue must be contained in a few of the words. What else could provide it but those messages from the beyond? She is, I imagine, a simple soul, therefore the method must be consistent. The first letter of each word seemed likely. As I listened, I realized that it was not the first letter but that the number of words in the spirit messages exactly matched the number of letters in the customer's name. Ten in your case. Chamberlain did not, you observe, choose long names. I believe mine was the longest. Interesting, by the way, that it appeared to mean nothing to him. I daresay he has been abroad or in the colonies.'

'And then?' I inquired.

'Quite. I deduced that it could not be the first letters of the words after all. That would have been too obvious to anyone in the audience with an ounce of sense. However, it would not be difficult for the girl to transpose each letter in the alphabet by one place. That would do it. Most of those people would give up after finding the initial letters did not work. For the rest, Chamberlain could alter the system a little each week during the weeks of their engagement. To be sure, he and the girl would probably be caught out in the end if they remained in one place long enough. That, however, they did not propose to do.'

'He called me a man of learning.'

'And so you are. We will not go into the matter of the way in which the brushing of your medical stethoscope wears away the nap of your waistcoat as it dangles there. Chamberlain is not clever enough to observe that. However, look at you against a sea of cockneys and yokels in such a place. Why, Mrs. Hudson's cat would appear a figure of learning in such company.'

'With whom we have wasted an entire evening!'

He stopped and lowered his voice.

'Watson, our time has not been wasted. It is plain to me that our two pigeons are about to take wing. I should give a great deal to know why.'

'Indeed?'

'You will have observed that there was scarcely an empty seat in that auditorium. They cannot be taking flight for lack of custom. Had they arranged another engagement, they would have known long before now and there would be no need to paste an urgent sticker across their advertisements. They have every reason to remain here. Moreover, why such haste to be gone? Today is Tuesday and it now seems they are obliged to close on Saturday.'

'They must close somewhen and must announce it.'

'Precisely but why was the paste on the closure stripper across their bill still wet? They are leaving a successful run with a minimum of notice. If you ask me, that has the mark of two people doing a bunk.'

We reached the pier turnstile again and crossed the esplanade toward the hotel. In the lobby, Holmes went to the desk and began negotiations with the night porter. A large cream envelope embossed with a post office stamp was produced. A few coins changed hands. Holmes, dipping the pen in the white china inkwell, wrote a brief message on hotel notepaper and addressed the envelope. The night porter beckoned an infant pageboy who took the envelope, received a further coin, and disappeared into the night at a run.

When Holmes came back across the lobby, I noticed that he no longer carried the theatre program for Professor Chamberlain's antics, prefaced by photographs of the performer and his medium, the 'professor' looking a good deal younger than he appeared in reality.

'Where has it gone?' I asked. He knew exactly what I was talking about.

'Little Billy, or whatever his name may be, is running for the midnight post from the railway station. I have every hope that by tomorrow morning those two most interesting faces will be on the desk of Inspector Tobias Gregson at Scotland Yard.'

We withdrew to our quarters where we settled ourselves with whisky and tobacco. Holmes still kept up an irritating pretence that I had been taken in by Chamberlain's performance, merely because I had not at first seen how the tricks were done.

'Surely, my dear fellow, you did not believe that a common young fellow and girl like that were capable of reading one another's minds.'

'I had not given the matter much thought,' I said a little irritably. 'It seemed scarcely worth it.'

'Let us be thankful that it is not,' he said, yawning. 'If men and women up and down the land became capable of reading the thoughts in one another's minds, murders would be as common and disregarded as sixpenny coins. We, my dear fellow, might be looking for some other means of livelihood.'

'And what of Miss Deans in all this? That poor child has lost her employment.'

'You may be sure that I have not forgotten the plight of our young Miss Effie Deans. If I am to help her, however, I now require what our legal friends call further and better particulars. Let us turn our attention next to the mysterious Mr. Edmund Gurney to whom she is said to have made advances. A man whose life is devoted to phantasms of the living rather than voices of the dead and who seems to be that most interesting person—a chloroform addict who is either an eater or an inhaler. It is said that the girl was seen trying to enter his room at an unseemly hour. I should greatly like to know why the accusation was made, and, I daresay, the answer lies within that room. I believe that our next task must therefore be to search Mr. Gurney's room and his possessions quite thoroughly but without his knowledge. We should lose no time in doing so.'

3

'The thing is quite impossible,' I said, for the fourth or fifth time. 'There is no suggestion that Gurney has done anything criminal or improper. You cannot simply burgle a fellow guest in a respectable hotel! Even if a chambermaid entered his room during the night, that is the affair of the management. For its part, the management appears to feel that the question is settled. You may be sure that they will not let you in there.'

'Burglary by night and housebreaking by day,' he said, his eyebrows drawn down as if in deep thought. 'It would, I suppose, be termed breaking and entering on premises such as these—were it not for the fact that you, my dear Watson, are the man to do it.'

You may imagine that I was appalled by the suggestion.

'I shall do no such thing. Whatever you think we might find in there. . . .'

'I have no precise idea what we might find. However, let us drop the matter of burglary and consider the peculiar self-anaesthesia of Edmund Gurney.'

I made no immediate answer to this, but the matter remained fixed in his thoughts. Presently he tried to revive the topic.

'It is a matter to interest a medical man, Watson. Mr. Gurney appears to be an habitué of chloroform, very probably an addict by this time. Oh, very well, let us put it more kindly and say that the poor fellow suffers from neuralgia. The anaesthetic dulls his pain sufficiently for him to enjoy a night's rest.'

'What then?'

'The practice may nonetheless be lethal,' Holmes insisted.

'It is foolish in the extreme but also difficult to prevent. Once a man is habituated to sleeping under the influence of chloroform, he may find it impossible to do without it.'

'Precisely. If memory serves correctly, anything over two fluid ounces swallowed or inhaled is liable to prove fatal. The quantities are very small—so is the difference between life and death. In the hands of a layman, it must be a threat to life under any circumstances.'

I began to see what was coming as he leant back in his chair.

'If someone approached you, Watson, and told you that there was a very strong smell of chloroform coming from a room where a man was sleeping, you would be prepared to investigate, as you would if there were an odor of escaping gas or a smell of smoke.'

'I daresay. But who is going to tell me that?'

'The hotel manager, once I have had a word with him. You may be sure that he will not risk having one of his guests found dead in the morning. He is, after all, not the owner of the hotel and I fancy he would not keep his job long after an incident of that sort. Mr. Gurney, I have no doubt, lies sedated by fumes. He will be your patient for a few hours, if that seems reasonable. We shall both keep him company and I shall look around me.'

I confess that I was filled with curiosity. What Holmes had first proposed now began to sound less heinous. Any medical man must thoroughly disapprove of these amateur experiments with anaesthetics, however great the discomforts of neuralgia. Such misuse will lead to addiction and the victim will never break himself of it. I might still have jibbed at what Holmes suggested. However, it would certainly give me the authority to have a straight talk with

Gurney over the folly of these practices and a chance to put him on the proper path for treatment. That at least was in keeping with a doctor's Hippocratic oath. Moreover, Holmes's intention of merely looking around him seemed to fall far short of burglary.

So it was that on the following night, just after eleven o'clock, Holmes went to the hotel desk and alerted the manager to a strong smell of chloroform in the corridor outside Gurney's room. He voiced his fears of a tragedy but added that a doctor of consider-able experience was his companion on this visit. Unless he was a complete fool, the Italian restaurateur who had been appointed by the owners to manage the hotel must have realized that his guest practised something like self-anaesthesia. Five minutes later the three of us stood in that corridor and I allowed myself to be persuaded that I could detect a sickly sweetish whiff of chloroform in the enclosed air, sufficient to suggest that a man breathing the enclosed air of the room was in danger.

The manager tapped lightly at the door, but Holmes had watched Gurney go up to his room after dinner and had timed his report accordingly. By now, I suspected, the foolish fellow was in the arms of Morpheus. Of course he was not anaesthetized as deeply as a patient would be for a surgical operation, but nor would he be easily roused within the next hour or two. I was not surprised when there was no response to the knock. We both looked at the manager, a Milanese of lean and cadaverous appearance, as if to imply that should there be a mishap, he was bound to be held accountable. To me, he looked more than ever like some mournful bird of prey.

He motioned us back, then slid his passkey into the lock and pushed open the sitting room door. In truth, there was an odour but it was suggestive of operating theaters generally and not over-whelmingly evident as chloroform. We waited. As many of my readers will be aware, Brighton was the first town in England to have a supply of electricity under the Electric Lighting Act of 1882, so that the manager had only to turn a switch in order to illumi-nate the sitting-room. It was furnished with a pair of armchairs, a table with two upright seats at it, and a bureau. To one side was the bedroom door, which had been closed but not locked. Within that was a further division with separate doors for bedroom and bathroom.

When the first inner door was opened, there was a definite odour of chloroform, so strong that I opened the bedroom door in fear of what I might find. The dose had been potent enough for Edmund Gurney to succumb to sleep even before he could turn off the light. Yet nothing had prepared me for the grotesque spectacle that I now saw. He lay on the bed in the stark electric glare, wearing his nightshirt, the upper part of his body propped against the headboard. His body had slumped at an angle and his head was almost entirely encased in a rubber sponge bag, which he had drawn down far enough to cover his nostrils and mouth. His practice was evidently to soak the rubber bag in a measure of chloroform and then draw it over his head as he lay down to sleep. It was dangerous and foolish in the extreme, for he had no means of controlling the amount he ingested. He was a perfect subject for 'The Hypochondriac's Tragedy.'

First of all the sponge bag must come off. As I pulled it clear, he hardly stirred and I prayed that, this time, he had not gone beyond recall. His face was deathly pale, the countenance of a tall, lanky, big-boned fellow, perhaps forty years old. His blue eyes were a fraction open, but I am sure he saw nothing. The moustache was lank and the hair combed like thatch down either side of his head. I took his wrist and felt a pulse, which was stronger and steadier than I had feared. Perhaps, like so many habitués, his constant use had hardened him to the effects of the fumes. Holmes meanwhile had opened the window and fresh air began to drift into the room. I turned to the manager, who was hovering over us. There was no need to use deceit, for what I told him was the perfect truth.

'You had better leave him to me for an hour or so. His life is not in immediate danger from the chloroform, which will pass off slowly. However, it may sometimes act as an emetic. If that were to happen when he is deeply asleep, there is a risk that he might choke on his own vomit without waking.'

I did not add that it was a remote risk. All the same, had such a thing happened after I had abandoned him to return to my room, matters would certainly not have gone well for me at an inquest. The manager's relief was tinged with apprehension.

'You do not ask for an ambulance or a doctor from the hospital? There will be no police?'

'It would serve no purpose. He must be watched for an hour or two. That is all.'

In his gratitude, I thought he might seize my hand and kiss it. He had, of course, dreaded the publicity that hospitals and ambulances—let alone the police—bring to an establishment like his. Holmes and I did not appear to him as the types who would tell the story round the streets of Brighton.

'Mr. Holmes has some experience in medical matters,' I said to him reassuringly. 'He can watch for me if I should be out of the room at any time.'

I did not add that my friend's experience in medical matters, such as it was, usually concerned those who were already dead. Indeed, the manager with his thin, stooping gait and black clothes might have graced an undertaker's parlour. He now withdrew in a fusillade of thanks and assurances while promising to be at beck and call if he were needed.

Holmes closed the door as the man left and came into the bedroom.

'Well done, Watson! A first-rate performance!'

I looked at Gurney; I was convinced that I could have fired my revolver into the ceiling without waking him.

'It was no act, I assure you, Holmes. His pulse is a little above normal. In the case of poisoning by chloroform, the rate may rise to one hundred forty or more, at which it is fatal. If it should increase now, I shall indeed summon whatever assistance is needed. He has taken a dose sufficient to put him to sleep. At least he is not one of those chloroform-eaters who prove to be suicides.'

'Or victims of murder,' said Holmes casually. 'You will find at least three recent cases in Caspar-Liman's *Handbook of Medicine*.

Let us hope we can prevent anything of that kind. If someone were able to enter this room, think how easily they could pour a further thimble or two of chloroform over that sponge bag with the poor fellow already unconscious and knowing nothing further. You know how little coroners and coroners' juries are to be depended upon. The whole thing would be put down to the dead man's folly.'

He withdrew to the sitting room and I could hear him moving about. I left Gurney for a moment and went into the bathroom to find the chloroform. It was necessary to calculate, if possible, what dose he might have taken. I opened the cabinet and undid the top of a dark green bottle to smell the sweet and colourless contents. A fatal dose would probably have been between four and six ounces. Not more than an ounce or two had been used from this bottle altogether, some of it perhaps on a previous night. That, at least, was a welcome discovery.

From what little I knew of the man, I was not surprised that the rest of the cabinet contained an array of patent medicines and quack remedies. Carter's Little Liver Pills, Beecham's Powders, and the respectable potions of their kind rubbed shoulders with the Patent Carbolic Smoke Ball Inhaler, guaranteed to prevent influenza, Kaolin-and-Opium for the dysenteric, Propter's Nicodemus Pills or 'The Old Man Young Again,' Klein's Opening Medicine by Royal Appointment, Chocolate Iron Tonic, and goodness knows what. Holmes appeared in the doorway.

'What have you found?'

'Only that the poor wretch has turned his digestive tract into a druggist's waste pipe,' I told him. 'At least he has not taken anything like enough chloroform to kill himself.'

'Come in here,' he said peremptorily. 'I believe we are a little closer to knowing a useful fact or two about Professor Chamberlain. The hotel bureau was absurdly easy to open. Not least because Gurney had simply left the key to the top flap under a sheet of paper in the drawer beneath. I have always maintained that those who lock away their papers and valuables are far less fearful of thieves who may find the key than that they themselves will lose it or, more often, forget where they have put it. In this case there were no valuables in the upper section but a correspondence file and a series of letters.'

The flap of the bureau was down, supported on the two runners that Holmes had pulled out. On the table at the centre of the room was a long cedar-wood letter box in which a series of papers had been filed in order of date. It was characteristic of Gurney's punctilious and scholarly mind that the letters sent to him had not only been filed in order but had their envelopes pinned to them with the date of receipt written in pencil upon them. Holmes took one letter from the file, put the cedar-wood box back in the top of the bureau, and closed the flap without yet locking it again.

I was still uneasy at the manner in which he had made free with Gurney's possessions, but my friend had anticipated this.

'It had to be done, Watson. There is a dark plot in these papers, unless I am much mistaken. What a fastidious fellow he is! Every letter kept and filed. These relate to his residence here and go back only a few weeks. When I think of my own unanswered correspondence, transfixed by a jackknife to the center of the mantelpiece in Baker Street, I become aware of deficiencies in my way of life. Look at this!'

He laid before me a typewritten envelope addressed to 'Edmund Gurney, Esq., The Royal Albion Hotel, Brighton.' It was postmarked with a date several days earlier and was one of the most recent to be received. Gurney had noted its receipt in pencil with a date one day later than the postmark.

'What of it?'

'Now look at this.' It was another typewritten letter also bearing the date of the postmark and a pencil date of receipt by Gurney a day later. It bore the address of 'Marine Parade, Brighton,' and was signed 'Professor Joshua D. Chamberlain.' I read it without waiting for any invitation from Holmes.

> *My dear Mr. Gurney, I write to thank you for your generous letter and to express my delight that all differences between*

us have been resolved. I now see that they were never more than misunderstandings, for which I must hold myself entirely responsible. I should have made it plain that my performances, however much they may overlap your own more serious interests, were never meant to be more than entertainments of the kind offered by Jasper Maskelyne or the Davenport Brothers at the Egyptian Hall in London and elsewhere. You, for your part, are a well-respected investigator of second-sight phenomena and apparitions of the living. Though I maintain that Madame Elvira has remarkable abilities in respect of the former of these, I see that I must have caused you offence and for this I am truly sorry.

I am gratified that we may now be partners rather than adversaries. It would give me great pleasure if, as you suggest, we were able to undertake a tour together in the eastern cities of the United States. Whether we should appear under the same billing, or myself as entertainer and you as the true scholar and investigator, is a matter we might discuss. The interest in your book Phantasms of the Living *would be intense and I believe you would find yourself acclaimed there as perhaps you have never been in your own country. As you know, the work of Madame Elvira and myself in popularizing psychic inquiry has been nominated for an award by the Psychic Research Society of Philadelphia, though without our prior knowledge or consent. We would be honoured if it were possible for us to withdraw that nomination and to put your name forward in our place.*

My partner joins me in sending our sincere and cordial greetings.

I looked up at Holmes.

'A quite extraordinary letter. The fellow was still claiming his psychic powers last night.'

'Yes, yes,' he said impatiently. 'But I did not ask you to read it, Watson. Look at it! Do not read it! And look at the envelope.'

I could see nothing. The date on the letter and the postmark were the same. Both bore a pencil date a day later, when Gurney had noted them, a few days ago.

'The typing, Watson!'

Those who have followed our adventures will recall that Sherlock Holmes quickly developed an interest in the new invention of the typewriter. 'I think of writing another monograph some of these days,' he had said, 'on the typewriter and its relation to crime. It is a subject to which I have devoted some little attention.' He believed, as he said, that 'a typewriter has really quite as much individuality as a man's handwriting.'

In the present case, he took a magnifying lens from his pocket and handed it to me as I studied the black carbon lettering.

'Had this correspondence been set in type by a printer, Watson, the level of the printed letters would be straight as the edge of a rule can make them. However, one can see immediately that this note was typed by bar-end letters. That is to say, capital and lowercase of each letter are at the top of a thin bar. The bars stand in a semicircle above the ribbon of the machine. When a key is pressed, the chosen bar comes down, hits the ribbon, and imprints the letter on the paper.'

'There is no doubt, I assume, that this letter and the envelope were typed upon the same machine that Madame Elvira used in her performance?'

'None whatever, though that is not the most significant feature. If you consult the paper that you were about to throw into the sea, you will observe certain similarities between it and these two items. Place a ruler under this line of type, the letters *e*, *s*, *a*, and *t* drop slightly below. Whereas *h*, *n*, and *m* rise slightly above. The letter *c* drops when it is in lowercase but rises when it is a capital. That is caused by a minute variation in the metal casting of each bar that carries the capital and lowercase characters. So many parts are produced by machinery alone that any bar arm will vary minutely from the average setting. It is also evident that letters that drop are on the left-hand side of the keyboard and those that rise are on the right. That is not uncommon.'

He looked up at me quickly, lips lightly compressed in a panto-mime of calculation.

'Forty bar arms carrying two characters each, each arm subject to slight variation. A further variation in casting eighty characters. The odds are easily half a million to one against two machines of the same make being identical. Add to this the wear caused to the machine by the individual user. A criminal who disguises his own handwriting has a better chance of escape.'

It seemed to me a good deal of fuss about nothing very much.

'Since Chamberlain signs the letter, it is presumably his machine. For the life of me, Holmes, I do not see what the dispute is about.'

He stared at me.

'When this matter comes before the Central Criminal Court, as I have no doubt that it will, there may be a good deal of dispute. It will not do to say that the machine is presumably his. It must be his without question. By then it may have vanished. The piece of paper that you so nearly threw into the sea may be all that will tie Professor Chamberlain to this letter and, therefore, perhaps tie him ready for the gallows.'

'The gallows?'

'Unless we look about us very smartly indeed. Do you not observe something psychopathic about his manner of speech? There is a man who would smile and smile—and be a villain. Now will you look at that letter and that envelope. Do not read—look!'

I looked and still thought only that the letter and envelope seemed to have been typed on the same machine. I said so, but this was not what he wanted. At last I made the only comment that seemed warranted.

'The letter is clearer than the envelope.'

'Clearer? How?'

'The letters are more distinct, blacker I suppose.'

'Well done, Watson! The ribbon that typed the envelope is well worn. The ribbon that typed the letter is significantly less worn, though not new. It would seem that the letter and the envelope, though bearing the same date, were typed days apart—or more probably a week or two apart.'

'Gurney has penciled the same date of receipt upon them.'

'Such a jotting would be easy enough to imitate.'

'The letter and the envelope may have been typed on the same day. The envelope was typed first, then a new ribbon was used to give the letter a smarter appearance.'

'My dear Watson, I will wager you a small sum that not more than one in a hundred people usually type the envelope before the letter. Moreover, they would change the ribbon for both the envelope and letter—or for neither. In any case, this letter was not written with a new ribbon, merely a ribbon that was much less worn than when it was used for the envelope. You may depend upon it, this letter was written well in advance of the date now typed upon it. Indeed, if you will take the glass and look closely, you will see that the date, as it is typed, has a somewhat blurred appearance compared with the rest of the letter. I recognize the machine as a product of E. Remington & Sons of Ilion, New York. It is an admirable make of machine on which one may move backwards by one space and type a character again, if it has been rubbed out for correction. The date on this letter has been typed over two or three times on a worn cotton ribbon to give it super-ficially the same appearance as the rest of the writing done with a newer ribbon.'

'Why should he write an undated letter admitting his fault to Gurney, withhold it for a week or two, then date it and send it?'

Holmes returned it to its envelope and placed the envelope in the bureau again.

'Because this letter was never sent.'

'And the envelope with its stamp and postmark?'

'The envelope originally contained a quite different communica-tion, something innocuous and not ostensibly from Chamberlain. Why, then, the substitution?'

'Why could Chamberlain not simply have sent the letter we have found?'

'My dear Watson! This letter is utter nonsense! With our own eyes we saw Chamberlain practicing his old frauds some days after it was sent. This message of reconciliation was not intended to be read by Gurney. It was to be found by others when Gurney could no longer contradict it.'

'Found by whom and when, if not by Gurney?'

'His executors, no doubt, or perhaps the police authorities. This whole scheme depends upon the near certainty that once Gurney has filed away his post bag he is unlikely to consult this item again in the next few days or hours merely to reread—what shall we say?—some innocuous and dreary cutting from last Saturday's paper.'

'And then?'

'And then it will not matter, Watson. In this scheme of things, the next few days are all that Edmund Gurney has left to him.'

I could not see murder in all this and, for the moment, dismissed it as melodrama. We looked again at the drugged and unconscious figure on the bed. He was in no danger now, but I was reluctant to leave him just yet. Holmes had opened the medicine cupboard and was going through the contents. Inspecting the pills and powders, he called out names from time to time and asked me to identify the ingredients. We went through the list, from the Carbolic Smoke Ball remedy to Propter's Nicodemus Pills. Holmes gave a short sardonic laugh at the promise by the latter to make 'The Old Man Young Again.'

'And by what means is that to be accomplished?'

'Chicanery and imposture,' I said, coming into the bedroom for fear of waking Gurney. 'I have had patients who take these and many other cure-alls. They are ineffective but usually harmless. You will see that Propter's Nicodemus capsules contain a tonic dose of arsenic, but you could eat an entire box of them and not suffer the least harm. They have a pinch of aphrodisiac cantharides, but not enough to make the old man any younger than he was before.'

Holmes drew an envelope from beside the bottles. It contained slips and receipts from the firms that had supplied Gurney through the post with the nostrums of the hypochondriac. He had no doubt kept these scraps of paper so that the addresses were to hand for his next order. 'The Carbolic Smoke Ball Company begs to assure its clients that £100 has been deposited with the City and Suburban Bank to be paid out to any who shall suffer influenza for six months after using the smoke ball three times daily before breakfast during four weeks.' 'Learmount's Patent Chocolate Iron Tonic is best taken in warm water upon rising. A further tablespoonful may be administered before retiring. It is entirely safe for children at five years of age.'

Kaolin-and-Opium of Hackney Downs and Propter's Nicodemus Pills of Fortess Road, Kentish Town, both contained a leaflet of praise from various invalids throughout the country whose health, if not their lives, had been saved by resorting to these concoctions. Propter's added a circular to long-established clients, accompanying a complimentary box of twenty 'improved' capsules, 'designed to prevent the nighttime restlessness that may previously have been consequent upon their use. To obtain this effect, it is of the utmost importance that the capsules should be taken in the order indicated, twice daily.'

'At any rate,' I said, looking into the box, 'he can come to no harm from these, for he has taken eighteen of the twenty already and there is another box unopened.'

We went back to the sitting room and occupied the two armchairs. It was close to the hour when Gurney might safely be left to sleep off the remaining effects of the chloroform. I proposed to read a lecture to him in the morning on the folly of meddling with anaesthetics.

'As for that last letter of Chamberlain's,' I said to Holmes, 'we can hardly discuss it with Gurney, unless you choose to confess to having broken open his bureau.'

'There was no breaking,' he said indifferently. 'However, as you say, it is not a matter for discussion. I think we must take the fight to the enemy. Tomorrow morning we shall have Chamberlain's lodgings at the Marine Parade apartments in our sights and we shall not lose him from that moment on. I require to know everything about him—where he goes, what he does, who keeps him company. For that, I shall need your assistance. It is too easy for a man to give the slip to a single pursuer. Chamberlain is a most dangerous, I would almost say pathological, villain. I do not believe that he would stop at murder, if it truly suited his purposes. Do not tell me, Watson, that I am neglecting Miss Effie Deans. I swear that the solution to that poor girl's difficulties lies somewhere in all this.'

It was almost two o'clock in the morning before we summoned the manager to assure him that Edmund Gurney was in no danger and might safely be left. The courteous Italian was effusive in his thanks and assured me that whatever was in his power by way of obliging me for my help should be done. Prompted by Sherlock Holmes, I said there was one thing. On no account must Mr. Gurney be asked to leave the hotel until I had had the chance of a serious discussion with him. I undertook that I would settle the matter before the following night and would, I trusted, put paid to his pernicious habit of self-anaesthesia. I think the gaunt *maitre d'hotel*, with his pale features and black suiting, was a little uneasy at this, but he assured me that everything should be done as I instructed.

4

Holmes and I returned to our suite at the Royal Albion a little after two in the morning. I had earned a night's rest and wanted no assistance in dropping off into a profound sleep as soon as my head touched the pillow. It seemed to me that this had lasted for no more than an hour or so when I was roused by a sudden tugging at my shoulder. I woke to find the electric light full on and Holmes standing over me, his face shining with energy. Before I could ask him whether Gurney had taken a turn for the worse, he said:

'Come, Watson! It is gone six o'clock and we must be up and doing! If the game is being played as I suspect, our birds will have flown before long.'

He was talking about Professor Chamberlain and Madame Elvira, of course. Despite the ungodly hour, he had already been downstairs, roused the night porter, and sent a further telegram to

Inspector Gregson at Scotland Yard, to follow his letter as soon as the post offices should open.

'We ourselves cannot wait for such offices to open, my dear fellow. We must be on the Chain Pier as soon as its gates are unlocked for the seven o'clock steamer to Boulogne.'

'They surely cannot be going to Boulogne. Their last performance is tonight.'

'I have just taken the precaution of walking a little distance down to the theatre billboard. Another flyer was pasted across it late last night or early this morning. There is to be no more mesmerism nor mindreading. The Aquarium management regrets that tonight's performance is cancelled in consequence of the indisposition of Madame Elvira. If they attempt to take the steamer, we shall catch them. More to the point, the deck of the pier looks diagonally across to those apartments on the Marine Parade. They cannot leave without our seeing them.'

I was wide awake now and soon ready for the pursuit of our suspects. A little before seven o'clock, we were at the pier, where the steamer for Boulogne was alongside and the first passengers were filing aboard over her paddlebox. It was a fine cool morning, the mist still clinging over the sea and a band of pale sun along the eastern horizon. None of the passengers was recognizable as Chamberlain or Madame Elvira. Presently the ropes were thrown off, the gangway was pulled aboard, and the paddles of the *Sea Breeze* churned the green channel water to a hissing froth as she went astern and swung round towards the French coast.

Holmes and I were the first to take deck chairs on the pier that morning. I had with me my neat Barr & Stroud precision field-glasses in their military leather case, with which he could almost have read a newspaper headline on the promenade. We waited, under the pretext of reading our copies of the *Times* and the *Morning Post*, as the sunlight grew warmer and the first promenaders appeared on the esplanade. I was about to say pessimistically that we might sit there all day and see nothing, when Holmes exclaimed quietly,

'There he is! And so is she! I would say that she looks worried but not indisposed.'

He handed me the glasses. I saw that Chamberlain and the girl had come out of the doorway of the apartments and were standing on the pavement in earnest conversation. Holmes snatched the glasses back and adjusted the focus a little.

'He is going, I think, and she is staying. Let us be thankful there are two of us. She is giving him a pair of books.'

'I daresay he will find a chair in the sun and spend the day reading.'

'No, Watson, no! One book might be for reading. If he has two, the odds are that he is taking them somewhere.'

'At this hour of the day? The libraries will not be open, nor will the bookshops.'

'Then his destination is evidently a place where such institutions will be open by the time of his arrival. There is, I think, a label pasted on the cover of one book. An orange oval with black writing. We have him!'

I was intrigued by this, but still far from understanding how we had him!

'The St. James's Street Library, in the shadow of the great palace, founded by John Stuart Mill and his friends for the public good almost fifty years ago. A treasure house of learning and the arcane, a scholar's paradise. For many years I have been a member. So it seems has friend Chamberlain, though I imagine he has only temporary privileges there. You may depend upon it, Watson, he is going to London—and so are we.'

It was hard to realise that we had only left London two days before. Yet every instinct told me that Holmes was right. Chamberlain was opening a Gladstone bag and adding the two books to whatever else it might contain. Then he swung round, striding toward West Street and the long climb that leads to the railway station at the top.

'Watson! Quick as you can! Cut through the little streets to the side, past the Royal Pavilion! Book two first-class returns to London before he can get to the railway ticket office and see you. I doubt whether he will recognise us among so many of his audience, but we must not take the chance. I shall follow him, in case he should have other plans, but I swear that Gladstone bag has the look of the London and Brighton railway about it.'

I did as he asked, Holmes following the fugitive westward while I strode at my best pace past the lawns and Georgian houses of the Steyne, the oriental onion domes of the Prince Regent's palace by the sea. My years of playing rugby for Blackheath have served my constitution well. I cut through quickly by way of the little streets where our client Mrs. Deans and her family lived. I came out at the lower level of the station, the smoky air leaving a gritty deposit of soot between the teeth. The booking hall was empty when I arrived and took our tickets for London. I had beaten Chamberlain to it! I saw him approach up the long slope of Queens Road, and by loitering I overheard him take one single ticket for London. Holmes was right. Professor Chamberlain had no intention of coming back to Brighton. What of Madame Elvira?

There was no sign anywhere of Holmes as the pursuer. Only when I walked toward the departure platform did I hear a quiet voice behind me.

'The ticket, if you please, Watson. We shall travel as strangers and meet at the far end in an hour's time.'

And so it was. I chose a compartment on one side of Chamberlain with Holmes on the other. He could not leave the train without being seen by us both. As our train crossed the Thames below Chelsea Bridge and began drawing into Victoria Station, our quarry was on his feet, the bag in his hand, ready to be one of the first to alight.

Then the chase began, though it was one in which we must not allow our fugitive to suspect that he was followed. Chamberlain had commandeered the only hansom cab just then upon the station rank. By the time that another had arrived and we swung ourselves aboard, his had turned away down Victoria Street and taken the corner into the long curve of Grosvenor Place. Holmes lifted the little trap in the roof and shouted to our driver, 'Follow that fare in front! As hard as you can go down Grosvenor Place! Five sovereigns for you if you still have him in sight when he reaches his destination!'

Happily for us, we had a sportsman on the driver's perch. Wrenching the horse's head round, he drove it at a hand-gallop after the receding hansom. He slowed briefly as the observant eye of a policeman glanced in our direction, then picked up speed as we turned the corner. We were nearly done for at the next junction, as a lumbering railway van pulled out in front, but we carried on round the stern of it. Then we were bumping and bouncing over the cobbles towards Hyde Park Corner. Unless Chamberlain looked back, for which there was no occasion, he would have no idea of our cab swaying and lurching in his wake.

We seemed to be in a mad stampede, in and out of the vehicles as we careered round the busy crossing of Hyde Park Corner with the grand park trees and handsome terraces to either side. Once or twice in our zigzag course the horse's hooves slipped on the greasy cobbles, but we came to no harm. Once a man, taking the horse for a runaway, tried to grab its bridle. Then a bread delivery van came out of a side street. But now we were in Piccadilly. If we were blocked in among the traffic, so was our quarry. For a moment I thought we had lost him, but our driver shot through a gap, almost grazing the pole of an omnibus. As Chamberlain turned into the Haymarket, we were very nearly on his tail. His cab stopped at the bottom, opposite the Duke of York's Place, and I went after him on foot while Holmes emptied seven golden sovereigns into the cabman's palm and I heard the cry of, 'You're a toff, sir, you are! A real gent!'

Unaware of all this, Chamberlain had entered the offices of the Messageries Maritimes, whose vessels link metropolitan France with North Africa, Indo-China, Southampton, and New York. Holmes gestured to me to enter, while he remained outside. Under the pretext of consulting the company's timetable, I was able to hear Chamberlain claiming the ticket that he had booked for the next day's sailing from Southampton to Cherbourg and New York.

As he emerged, Holmes and I observed our usual routine for keeping a fugitive in sight without alerting him. I do not think I had been recognised by Chamberlain but, in any case, I now hung back, and it was Holmes who kept pace at a steady distance behind him as we moved westward down the handsome avenue of Pall Mall towards the ancient brickwork of St. James's Palace at the far end. Chamberlain still carried his Gladstone bag.

Our little procession went the entire length of Pall Mall and then turned into St. James's Street. About halfway up, Chamberlain stopped, looked about him, and then went up the steps of the St. James's Street Library. Holmes followed him discreetly. Through the window, I saw Chamberlain standing in the vaulted entrance hall, which might have graced one of our larger banks, and handing a clerk the two volumes from his leather bag.

He came out and walked away down the street. What was Holmes doing? Why were we not in pursuit? Presently he appeared on the steps and looked at the disappearing figure.

'We can find him when we need to,' he said quietly. 'Our first task must be to save Edmund Gurney.'

I then noticed that he had, under his arm, a volume borrowed from the library on whose steps we stood. It was a slim book in royal blue cloth stamped with gold, which Chamberlain had handed to the library clerk a few minutes before. The author's name meant nothing to me at first. Comte Henri-Gratien Bertrand. Then I remembered dimly that he had been an aide-de-camp of some kind to the Emperor Napoleon. Even in the labyrinthine world of Sherlock Holmes's scholarship, this seemed far removed from the matter in hand. I saw the title: *Journal Intime: Recueil de pieces authentiques sur le captif de Ste.-Helene.* I was none the wiser, beyond gathering that Bertrand had kept a private journal as a companion of the emperor in his last years of exile on St. Helena. Abstruse works of this kind were meat and drink to Holmes. Among other readers, I doubt if one in ten thousand had heard of the Comte Bertrand.

Then he opened the pages and I saw a slip of paper with writing on it. It appeared to have been left there inadvertently by a previous reader of the book and so, presumably, was Professor Chamberlain's. 'Pages 464 & 468. The whole worth reading twice. 19A + 1C. 19th to the 28th June.' The pages referred to were toward the end of the book and presumably described the emperor's last days. The 28th of June was today's date.

'19A + 1C. 19th to the 28th of June,' Holmes murmured. 'To obtain this effect, it is of the utmost importance that the capsules should be taken in the order indicated, twice daily. Watson, we must go at once! Let us pray we are not too late.'

'Back to Brighton?'

He looked at me as if I had lost my senses and hailed another cab as it came sailing down from Piccadilly.

'To Brighton? By no means! To Kentish Town, driver! Fortess Road! As fast as you can go!'

If the race to follow Chamberlain had been a madcap drive, this was worse. We flew down Dover Street, across Oxford Street to the Euston Road, up the Hampstead Road, through Camden Town, and presently drew up in Fortess Road. Throughout the journey Holmes had been muttering to himself, as if for fear that he might forget, 'It is of the utmost importance that the capsules should be taken in the order indicated, twice daily.'

We had stopped outside the North London Manufactory of Propter's Nicodemus Pills. It was a drab redbrick building whose signboard was visible through a veil of soot. Holmes led the way, demanding to see the proprietor upon a matter of life and death and uttering threats of prosecution before the fact upon a charge of attempted murder.

The proprietor was not there, or if he was he had taken shelter. We were shown into the office of the manager, a room that had a good deal to do with ledgers and invoices but little with the healing of the sick. It was just the accommodation I had supposed that vendors of quack medicine would inhabit.

Holmes ignored the invitation to take a chair. He stood before the manager, the aquiline profile now hawk-like and the eyes burning, as it were, into those of his adversary. He did not even inquire the man's name.

'Listen to me,' he said quietly, 'and think very carefully before you reply. Unless I have the truth now, it is very probable that you may face a charge of attempted murder and not impossible that you may be tried for murder outright. This is my colleague, Dr. Watson of St. Bartholomew's Hospital. He will recognize any attempt at evasion or imposture, and in that event you will be in very serious trouble.'

The manager looked at first as though he thought Holmes was an escaped lunatic of some kind. After the brief introduction of my name, however, he began to appear gratifyingly frightened.

'I am Jobson and I have done nothing!' he said.

'Very well, Jobson who has done nothing, listen to me. Have you at any time in the past few months sent to your regular customers a complimentary sample of an improved version of Nicodemus Pills?'

Jobson looked as if this might be a joke or a trick.

'No,' he said at length, 'of course not. We don't send out complimentaries.'

'Let me give you the wording. The box of twenty improved capsules is 'designed to prevent the nighttime restlessness that may previously have been consequent upon their use. To obtain this effect, it is of the utmost importance that the capsules should be taken in the order indicated, twice daily.''

'I never heard of such a thing.' To look at Mr. Jobson was to believe that he spoke the truth.

'What are the principal ingredients of your Nicodemus Pills?'

'The largest is milk sugar, then liver salts, cream of tartar, liquorice, arsenic in homeoepathic dose, cantharis similarly, coffee, sarsaparilla. . . .'

'Calomel?'

It was evident from Jobson's eyes that he had not the least idea what this was.

'A substance derived from mercury,' I said quickly, 'used as a rule for laxative purposes.'

'Never,' he said earnestly. 'That would never do.'

'Nor do you use gelatine capsules for your potions?'

'The price,' he said, 'would be too high. Our powders are compressed into tablet form.'

Holmes looked at me. His eyes were gleaming with triumph.

'Very well,' he said, 'our cab is waiting for us. You may expect, Mr. Jobson, to hear from Scotland Yard. I daresay Inspector Tobias Gregson will want a word with you in the course of his investigations.'

Holmes stopped the cab at the first post office and wired again to Gregson, instructing him to meet us at all costs upon our return at the Royal Albion Hotel, Brighton. If that was impossible, he was to send the 'most competent' of his men on a matter of life and death.

We cabbed it direct to Victoria and then caught the Pullman to Brighton. Even so, it was six o'clock by the time of our arrival and the summer sun was already declining across the tract of sea beyond the canyon of Queens Road and West Street below us. We reached the Royal Albion as the early dinner guests were sitting down to their meal. Among them was the sad, dishevelled figure of Edmund Gurney who, presumably, still knew nothing of my ministrations to him during the previous night.

Holmes watched him like a falcon through the open door of the dining room, though what he was waiting for was not yet plain. If there was such danger, why did he not go and speak to the man? We took armchairs in a corner of the lobby, by a dwarf palm growing in a copper tub. Gurney was coming to the end of his dinner. He poured a glass of water from the carafe, opened a little tin on the table beside him, and took out a gelatine capsule, which was the last of the complimentary set of Propter's Nicodemus Pills. My own view remained that if the others had done him no harm, there was no reason why this one should.

Holmes sprang from the chair beside me, crossed the dining room in a few swift strides, and with a blow of his arm knocked the tin and the capsule from Gurney's hand. The invalid Gurney sat ashen and quivering with shock at the sudden attack. Other guests were motionless and silent, all staring in one direction. It was a complete study of still life, the lean and menacing figure of Holmes included, as he leant forward towards his victim. The shock was broken by a voice from the hallway behind me.

'Mr. Holmes, sir! Mr. Holmes!'

I turned and saw Inspector Tobias Gregson in his three-quarter topcoat and carrying his hat in his hand.

5

As the three of us sat together in our room later that evening, Inspector Gregson put his glass down and said, with a further shake of his head, 'It was an assault, Mr. Holmes. It was as surely an assault upon the man as any that I have ever witnessed.'

'Gurney held death in his hand, Gregson, as surely as if he held a bomb that was about to explode.'

'And how can you say that, when you do not know what might be in the capsule?'

Holmes held a flame to his pipe.

'I have no doubt, my dear fellow, as to what is in that capsule, none whatever. When it is analyzed it will be found to contain calomel. At a guess, I would say about ten grains of calomel.'

'Well, ten grains of calomel would not kill him,' I said reluctantly. 'At the worst, it would upset his digestion.'

Holmes ignored this, refusing to rise to the bait. In the silence that followed, it was Gregson who began to tell a story that at first seemed to have little to do with the events we had witnessed.

'As to Professor Chamberlain and Madame Elvira, Mr. Holmes. Upon receiving your wire and the theatrical program with the photographs of the two performers, I made one or two inquiries. Forewarned is forearmed, gentlemen. Madame Elvira's photograph meant nothing to me, I must confess. Professor Chamberlain, however, I recognized. Indeed, we have our own photograph of him in the Criminal Record Office. Nothing to do with second sight, I assure you, but everything to do with forging two letters of credit on the Midland Counties Bank. He served six months for that, but he almost escaped us before the trial by taking passage for North America. He was brought back from Quebec at our request.'

'Then I trust your men will also be in Southampton early tomorrow morning,' said Holmes quietly. 'It would not do for Chamberlain to elude you a second time in that manner.'

'Two of my men will be watching the liner *Bretagne* from the moment she docks until the moment she sails again for Cherbourg and New York. He will not get far on this occasion.'

'Then you had better watch out for his accomplice,' my friend interposed. 'His partner in crime may already be aboard the *Bretagne*. I have no doubt that Madame Elvira slipped across the Channel to France today and that she travelled by train to Cherbourg. She is either waiting for him there or possibly has boarded the *Bretagne* already for the outward crossing to Southampton.'

By little more than a flicker, Gregson's eyes betrayed that he had taken no precautions as to Madame Elvira. He sipped his whisky again and then resumed.

'Yesterday afternoon, gentlemen, I also spent an hour at the Pinkerton bureau in London inquiring as to the American antecedents of Joshua D. Chamberlain. Though he is an Englishman born and bred, he has spent a considerable amount of time in the United States. I was told a most interesting story. While there, a year or so ago, he made a profound impression on Mrs. Marguerite Lesieur of Philadelphia, the middle-aged widow of the railroad builder. He persuaded her of his powers of communicating with the dead when assisted by a medium. This was Madame Elvira, who proved to be his sister. Mrs. Lesieur was generous in return and promised greater rewards to come. Chamberlain is clever. He demurred at first and returned to England, pursued by her letters at every post. In the end, Mrs. Lesieur set up the Psychic Research Society of Philadelphia and made it the means of offering him a handsome reward.'

'And then he was unmasked in England?' I asked.

It was Holmes who now took up the tale, looking at me and shaking his head.

'Not quite, I think. It is evident that he and his sister took to the stage. They were ignored at first by those like Gurney and Myers whose interests in psychic phenomena were sincere. When Gurney came to Brighton for a month's convalescence, the performances of Professor Chamberlain were drawing crowds of holidaymakers for the fun of the thing. Gurney, however, at once saw the man as a charlatan and all he stood for as a mockery of true interest in unexplained psychic phenomena. We know that there was a bitter and probably libelous exchange of letters sent to the local newspapers. Chamberlain dared not sue, of course. He would have been proved a liar, and news of that must sooner or later have reached Philadelphia. Rumours of his quarrel with Gurney would inevitably reach occult circles in London. From there, they might easily cross the Atlantic in letters to like-minded spiritualists in Philadelphia and elsewhere. As a result of his cheap and demeaning vaudeville acts in Brighton, Chamberlain stood to lose everything that Mrs. Lesieur had promised him.'

Holmes paused, reached for the whisky decanter, and refilled Inspector Gregson's glass.

'Matters had gone almost too far for Chamberlain to retrieve his position, unless. . . .'

'Unless, Mr. Holmes?' Gregson asked.

'Unless Edmund Gurney were to recant and confess his belief in these frauds. Chamberlain might say that Gurney had recanted. He might announce it all over Philadelphia, but of course Gurney would deny it and reveal him as a liar as well as a charlatan. It was necessary for Chamberlain that Gurney should recant and then be in no position to deny it.'

'Because he had taken calomel?' I asked skeptically.

'No, my dear Watson. Trickery is Chamberlain's trade and he was more diabolical in planning Gurney's death than in contriving any of his stage effects. Whether he learnt this art of murder from the Comte Bertrand's account of Napoleon or whether that merely refreshed his memory, I cannot tell you. Certain it is that he had that nobleman's account of the St. Helena poisoning with him for the past six weeks—borrowed from the St. James's Library. The dates are stamped in the two volumes.'

'I have lost you, Mr. Holmes,' said Gregson, 'with the Comte Bertrand and Napoleon.'

'Very simply, inspector, if the Comte Bertrand is to be believed, the Emperor Napoleon was murdered on St. Helena. Probably it was done at a distance by the command of his enemies in Paris. He was given arsenic in his medication over a period of time. It was not enough to kill him, indeed it may have stimulated his system a little. Yet arsenic in such doses very often produces both restlessness, as in Gurney's case, and constipation. One night the Emperor Napoleon was prescribed a remedy for these afflictions. Ten grains of calomel to be taken with a glass of wine and a biscuit. After a night of severe sickness, he was dead the next day. None of these facts is in dispute.'

'But he did not die from calomel, surely?' I persisted.

'No, Watson, indeed he did not. The secret that our modern judges at murder trials have so far prevented the press from reporting is this. The effects of arsenic, given in moderate doses over a period of time, are of questionable benefit but not fatal. Let us suppose, at the end of a few weeks, the victim is then given a single but sufficient dose of calomel—ten grains would be ample. The chemical reaction with arsenic in the stomach will create mercury cyanide, which kills quickly. Not only does it kill quickly, it also removes the traces of arsenic and is almost impossible to detect on postmortem examination by methods at present known to us. Hence the continuing debate as to the proximate cause of the Emperor Napoleon's death.'

Gregson and I looked at him in silence. Holmes drove his argument home.

'This devil Chamberlain worked it to a nicety. From London he sent the complimentary box of Propter's Nicodemus Pills in capsule form. He had, of course, bought a box of the pills and substituted gelatine capsules, nineteen filled with a moderate dose of arsenic and the last with a heavy dose of calomel. They were to be taken in order, so that the calomel would be swallowed last. To take capsules in a prescribed order is so common nowadays that the victim would think nothing of it. Chamberlain had also ordered a printed slip from a jobbing printer, who would not think twice about an apparently innocent prescription of this sort. The empty capsules themselves were readily available from any pharmacy, as was the calomel. Even the arsenic will present little difficulty until the new Poisons Bill becomes law. No alarm would be raised until tonight, when Gurney took the last capsule with its calomel—or rather until tomorrow morning when his body was found. By then Chamberlain and his sister would be far away. Moreover, the overwhelming probability is that death in his case was likely to be attributed to an overdose of chloroform. Such a pernicious habit was the perfect cover.'

So that was it! The last piece of the puzzle which Holmes's conduct had presented to me in the past few days had now fallen into place.

When we were alone together, my friend added an explanation which was not for Inspector Gregson's ears.

'As for the letter of apparent reconciliation from Chamberlain to Gurney,' he remarked, 'it required only a girl dressed as a chambermaid to enter the room while Gurney slept or was elsewhere. Whether she or Chamberlain himself carried out the exchange of papers, it was simple to take the key from the bureau drawer—the first place that any thief would look. It was then only necessary to replace whatever document was in that envelope with the letter that we found the other night. It required only the commonest black dress and white apron, purloined from an unlocked servants' cupboard on the landing, for Elvira Chamberlain to impersonate a hotel servant if she was challenged. In the dim light of an internal corridor, at midnight, the night porter saw a chambermaid, or rather a girl in a chambermaid's livery. The only girl who served these rooms was Effie Deans. Therefore, the fellow easily persuaded himself that he must have seen what Mr. Gurney might call a phantasm of the living—in the shape of Miss Deans.'

'They appear to have found entering such rooms and opening bureau drawers rather too easy,' I said with a trace of skepticism.

Holmes laughed.

'We may never know how, or when, one of them purloined the key to Gurney's room and made a wax impression. I swear that Chamberlain the burglar reconnoitered his victim's rooms at the start, saw the Nicodemus Pills and the way to be rid of his antagonist. Perhaps Elvira was able to do everything else with a passkey. However, I may tell you that with my burglar's kit at hand, I could open any of these old bedroom locks in a twinkling. At some point, I have no doubt, the sister replaced some ephemeral piece of correspondence by the effusive thanks that is in Gurney's correspondence box now and that Chamberlain marked with whatever date of receipt he pleased. In consequence, the world, including Mrs. Marguerite Lesieur, was intended to hear that the two men had made up their quarrel and that Chamberlain's reputation was restored. Had the villain's scheme worked, his benefactress would also have heard that the psychic investigator Edmund Gurney had, tragically, been found dead in a Brighton hotel bedroom from misuse of chloroform.'

'Does all this make Madame Elvira a murderess?' I asked.

'I suspect she is no more than her brother's dupe in the matter of the letter and that she knew nothing of the poison. That will be for a court to decide when the pair of them are tried for attempted murder. I have no doubt that if Chamberlain also entered Gurney's room at some point, which on the face of it seems almost certain, his principal intention was not to exchange the two letters but to inspect that counterfeit tin of Propter's Nicodemus Pills and to satisfy himself that Gurney was taking his prescribed doses of the capsules.'

Not all of this was revealed at the Central Criminal Court a few months later. Chamberlain was proved to have been previously convicted of a number of petty offences of dishonesty before the forgery of two letters of credit from the Midland Counties Bank, which had sent him to Pentonville prison for six months a few years earlier. The jury in the present case found him guilty of attempted murder by 'arsenical poisoning,' but all mention of calomel was omitted. He went to penal servitude for seven years. Madame Elvira was not proved to have known of his intention and was found guilty of no more than breaking and entering the hotel room. She went to Millbank prison for six months.

As for our client, Effie Deans was taken back by the manager of the Royal Albion Hotel on the positive insistence of Sherlock Holmes. To be sure, the manager had reason to be grateful to us. However, the matter did not rest there. The owners of the establishment undertook that upon her seventeenth birthday, not that many months away, Miss Deans was to be promoted to the position of assistant housekeeper. This, in itself, was the first rung of a ladder to higher things than she or her parents had dreamt of.

Needless to say, we never saw the remote delights of Ilfracombe or Tenby with their respectable families building sand castles or riding the local donkeys. We were, as Sherlock Holmes was soon reminding me, far too busy for that and much too occupied to visit the Wiveliscombe cousins.

Yet for the man I believed we had saved, the drama did not end happily after all. A year or so later I picked up the *Times* one morning after breakfast, as wheels and harness rattled up and down the length of Baker Street. I was turning the pages of the newspaper when my eye was caught by a brief obituary column.

> We regret to announce the sudden death, by misadventure, of Mr. Edmund Gurney, Joint Secretary of the Psychical Society, author of *The Power of Sound* and other works. Mr. Gurney, who was born about 1847, was the son of the Rev. Hampden Gurney, late Rector of Marylebone. He received his education at Trinity College, Cambridge, of which he became a Fellow after taking his degree as Fourth Classic in 1871. Mr. Gurney was the author of *Phantasms of the Living* and had published two volumes

of essays. He suffered from obstinate sleeplessness and painful neuralgia, and succumbed to an overdose of chloroform, incautiously taken last Friday evening when alone at the Royal Albion Hotel, Brighton, whither he had gone for a night on business.

I passed the paper without comment to Sherlock Holmes. He was sitting in his black velvet jacket while very precisely dividing the leaves of a cigar butt in the butter dish with the aid of a small surgical knife, in pursuit of a case of robbery with violence. He made no immediate reply as he read the newspaper notice.

Presently I said, 'My warnings about chloroform, such as they were, seem to have done him little good.'

He put the newspaper down, picked up the scalpel, and resumed his inspection of the cigar butt. Without looking up, he said, 'Had it not been that Chamberlain is still serving seven years in Pentonville, I should have been haunted by the spectre of the professor crossing the threshold of that hotel room and dripping chloroform remorselessly onto the face of the sleeping victim until respiration ceased. I hold no very high opinion of coroners and their juries, as you know. You might murder half of London and they would bring in a verdict of natural causes. In Gurney's case, I assure you, they would have called it misadventure. Not suicide, you observe, and certainly not murder. The poor fellow's weakness was the centre of all that passed. Without that, Chamberlain would have got nowhere.'

'I fear my advice to him was ill judged, for all the good it did,' I said quietly.

Holmes frowned at the work upon which he was engaged.

'Then make amends now, my dear fellow, by warning the world against such pernicious habits. When you come to write up this little adventure of ours, which I fear will probably happen, play up the dangers of the practice and give it some such title as 'The Mystery of the Brighton Chloroform-Eater.''

As the reader will observe, I declined Holmes's advice in the matter of the title.

The Queen of the Night

It was not often that Holmes and I had a client whom we served twice, in quite different matters. Yet such was the case with Lord Holder. The events of this second inquiry followed at some little distance the Newgate Adventure, as my friend described it, early in 1902. More than once they hinted at the great criminal enterprise, frustrated by Sherlock Holmes on that occasion, which had involved the great but deserted prison as a command post of the underworld.

It was on a morning not long before the coronation of Edward VII that Holmes first mentioned Lord Holder. I confess I did not recognize the name of our intended visitor and said so. Holmes folded his newspaper and said,

'You would know him better as Mr. Alexander Holder, of Holder & Stevenson, bankers of Threadneedle Street. He is now both a peer of the realm and an alderman of the City of London.'

At once my mind went back to the Case of the Beryl Coronet, one of our earlier investigations. Mr. Holder had been approached by an illustrious client whose name was of the noblest and most exalted. As security for a short-term loan, this client deposited a coronet of thirty-nine fine beryl stones, pale green shading into yellow and blue. It was one of the most precious public possessions of the Empire.

The sequel requires few words. While the coronet was in Mr. Holder's possession, there was a robbery—three jewels were broken from their settings and stolen. Suspicion fell on his son. Holmes proved the boy innocent, a youth of generous instincts, one of whom any father should be proud. Since then, the banker had been ennobled for his services to the nation, not least to patrician families who raised money in difficult times by pledging jewels and works of art.

When he entered our sitting room, I still recognised Lord Holder as our client in the former case. Though now about sixty, he remained a man of striking appearance. His figure was tall, portly, and imposing with a massive, strongly marked face and commanding figure. He was dressed in a somber yet rich style: black frock coat, neat brown gaiters, and well-cut pearl-grey trousers.

After we had talked a little of his son, who had risen to become private secretary to Lord Milner in Cape Colony, he came to the purpose of his appointment.

'Gentlemen, the matter at issue is a delicate one. May I ask what you know of the imitating or, indeed, counterfeiting of sapphires and Brazilian diamonds?'

Holmes took the pipe from his mouth and frowned.

'They are two very different things, my lord. A good reproduction of sapphires may be obtained by using cobalt oxide. The process is similar to the imitation of rubies and often more successful. A Brazilian diamond of the first water would be impossible to imitate with any success. Even a close examination by a retail jeweller would reveal the fraud at once. A casual glance need not betray, certainly not in some lights. However, the deception could not be kept up for more than a short period of time and certainly could not be depended upon.'

I turned to our visitor.

'Why do you ask, my lord?'

Our visitor looked distinctly uncomfortable.

'Since I know that everything said here will remain in confidence, I shall try to explain my unease. You are, I imagine, aware of the Earls of Longstaffe?'

I laughed at this.

'Anyone who reads the racing papers or the gossip columns could not be unaware of them.'

'Our firm has for many years been bankers to the family, most recently to the present Lord Adolphus Longstaffe, as we were to his father, Lord Alfred, before him. There has frequently been occasion to advance money against security until such time as funds could be raised by the sale or mortgage of a further portion of the Longstaffe estate.'

'A sale more often than a mortgage, I fear,' said Holmes, gazing at his pipe.

'The Longstaffe family suffered greatly from the depredations of the late Lord Alfred. It is common knowledge that his way of life in the German spa towns, not to mention Paris and Biarritz, left the estate crippled by debts and claims against him in the courts. He died in Baden-Baden, I believe, at the gaming tables with a hock and seltzer in one hand and not a single lucky card in the other. I fear that his successor, Lord Adolphus Longstaffe, has continued in much the same way,' he continued.

'I fear so, Mr. Holmes. We customarily hold certain family jewels for safekeeping and, when necessary, as security until the value of land can be realized. Among these is a splendid royal clasp, the so-called Queen of the Night, bequeathed by William IV to his favorite, the young Lady Adeline Longstaffe, seventy years ago.'

'I am aware of the Queen of the Night,' said Holmes in a quiet voice. 'When the clasp was shown in the Paris Exhibition, the catalogue gave a specification of its extreme dimensions as three inches laterally and vertically.'

His long, slender fingers drummed on the arm of his chair absentmindedly.

'I fear I am a stranger to this treasure,' I said frankly. Lord Holder turned to me.

'Lord Adolphus Longstaffe as the senior member of his family is herald to the Prince of Wales, or to any heir-apparent to the throne. It is a ceremonial rank only. The neck of the robe covering his lordship's tunic on great occasions bears this clasp, the Queen of the Night, whose value is perhaps greater than most state jewels. As with so many priceless ornaments, even the Koh-i-Noor diamond in the royal crown, the gem is not large. You might hold it on the palm of your hand, but not quite in it.'

'I am still not entirely clear what it is, other than a clasp at the neck of his cloak.'

'A fine Brazilian diamond, Doctor,' said Lord Holder patiently, 'a twelve-sided rhombic dodecahedron, set among sapphires of the deepest blue. There is also a small silver clip. This enables the diamond to be detached and worn alone, if so desired. The great Koh-i-Noor—the River of Light in the royal crown—is said to weigh one hundred eighty-six carats, though there has been some dispute of late. Estimates of the Queen of the Night may also vary, but it cannot be less than one hundred forty carats. The entire clasp is a work of art, a brilliant star among midnight blue, as well as a jewel. Like any treasure of that nature, the workmanship makes it almost impossible to put a realistic value on it. It is, quite simply, beyond price.'

'From where did it come?'

Holmes intervened.

'You may believe if you choose, Watson, that the star came from the looting of the Portuguese vice-regal palace by European mercenaries during Brazil's wars of independence. It is said to be the ransom paid for the viceroy's life and the vicereine's honour. I prefer the tale of it, being wagered and lost against a woman's affections, during a game of faro played between a royal brother and a future prime minister in the presence of the Prince Regent at Carlton House.'

'You are admirably informed, Mr. Holmes,' said Lord Holder with a faint smile.

'However, why should it be the cause of trouble now?'

His lordship shook his head.

'It is not yet the cause, but I fear it may be. In a matter of weeks, we shall begin the ceremonies attendant on the coronation of His Majesty Edward VII. Lord Adolphus Longstaffe must play his part as herald to the Prince of Wales, and the Queen of the Night will be the clasp at the neck of his robe.'

'Where is it at present?'

'Just so, Dr. Watson. At present it lies in a velvet-lined box, within a safe of two-inch steel, inside the strong-room of our bank. That is where it is usually kept, except on ceremonial occasions or when securely on display.'

'Why should it be at risk on this occasion if not on others?'

Lord Holder folded his hands uneasily.

'The Queen of the Night has appeared in many places. It has been photographed, exhibited here and in Paris, and is well enough known to jewellers and connoisseurs. There is hardly a book on *bijouterie* in which it does not make its appearance.'

'I see no harm in that.'

'Nor I, Dr. Watson. Yet such photographs and displays give ample scope to counterfeiters. I have it on good authority that in the past three months, since the date of the coronation was announced, a jeweller in Brussels has been commissioned to produce a passable imitation of the Queen of the Night. It is such a commission as a thief might offer, particularly at a time like this.'

'Raoul Grenier et fils is the firm in question,' said Holmes calmly.

Lord Holder sat suddenly upright in his chair.

'Mr. Holmes! There are only two or three men in the City of London who know that! It has been held in the strictest confidence! How can you possibly know?'

'Because,' said Holmes thoughtfully, 'it was I who gave the order.'

The silence in the room had the quality of the stillness that follows the explosion of a shell or a grenade.

'You, sir? The thing is impossible!'

'It is not only possible, Lord Holder, it is the truth. I must ask you to trust me. It is plain that I should not have done this with dishonest intent, for if that were the case, I should not have told you now.'

'But if an imitation is produced, you make the task of a thief all the more easy!'

'On the contrary, my lord. In my opinion, what I have done is the sole means of saving the precious clasp from being lost for ever. I need hardly remind you of your own words just now. Much of the value lies in the workmanship. Moreover, this is not the Koh-i-Noor diamond, which stands alone. The Queen of the Night might be broken up and its recut stones sold for a small fortune.'

'But why should you care about the Queen of the Night? You are not commissioned to guard it, surely?'

Holmes shook his head.

'I care nothing for it, sir. It is a matter of no importance to me whether it is stolen or not. I play a larger game. In that game, the diamond and its sapphires are no more than pawns. Beyond that, you may summon Inspectors Lestrade or Gregson from Scotland Yard so that I may be handed over to them. Or you may trust me and say not a word to anyone of what has passed between us this morning.'

'And that is all?'

'That, I fear, is all, my lord. There is no other course.' It was hard to say whether our guest, who made his way down the stairs half an hour later, was more shaken or shattered. Had it not been for the service Holmes had done him in proving his son's innocence all those years ago, I really believe that Lord Holder would have summoned Lestrade and Gregson, and told them to do their duty.

2

'Holmes! What the devil was all that about?'

He raised his hand to silence me and went off to his room.

When he came back, he was holding a large buff-colored envelope. He sat at the dining table, laid the envelope before him, and looked up.

'What was it about? It was about matters that I cannot reveal to anyone but you, my dear fellow, not even to a loyal and impeccable servant of the Crown like Lord Holder.'

'Has this something to do with the matter of your disappearance some months ago?'

He smiled.

'Dear old Watson! There is no pulling the wool over your perceptive eyes, is there?'

'I should hope not!'

'Then you will recall the proceedings of the criminal tribunal that condemned me to death in Newgate. I described to you how hyoscine wiped many of the details from my mind. With some effort, fragments of them came to me in sleep. I recall a remark of the late Henry Caius Milverton about Colonel James Moriarty, the surviving younger brother of my ancient enemy, the late professor. Milverton apologized for the fact that Colonel Moriarty had been temporarily detained over a dispute relating to a family heirloom. You will recall my saying that the colonel had been looking forward to my ropedance, as they called it, having cut me to pieces beforehand.'

'I should not have thought the finances of such a family as the Moriartys would run to an heirloom to dispute about!'

He smiled again at this.

'It was not their heirloom, I assure you. The Moriartys are consummate thieves, Watson, and I concluded at once that the heirloom in question belonged to somebody else. Then, quite lately, I was invited to the Grosvenor Hotel, Victoria Station, at the behest of Monsieur Raoul Grenier.'

'The jeweller from Brussels?'

'The same. He had come over by ferry from Ostend to Dover and so to London, for no other reason than to consult me. The matter was so delicate that it was confided to me on condition that I divulge it at that time to no one, not even to your good self.'

'Nor Lord Holder?'

'Lord Holder and the entire world were suspects, to Monsieur Grenier. He knew of the forthcoming coronation, of course, and he well knew that it is a time when the jewels on display are at their most vulnerable. Even the crown jewels of England must leave the Tower of London, where at all other times they are guarded day and night by a regiment of the Foot Guards. I concluded that was assuredly the thought behind the Newgate conspiracy. Grenier himself, incidentally, has been retained by two crowned heads of Europe to alter the ceremonial headgear to fit the skulls of a new generation. It is sixty-four years since our late queen was crowned.'

'This Monsieur Grenier sounds to me like a very fortunate and prosperous fellow.'

'Scarcely. He told me that he had been visited by a certain Count Fosco. The count had commissioned him to make a glass replica of the Queen of the Night. My mind went back to that remark of Henry Milverton's about an heirloom. My nostrils scented a Moriarty.'

'But surely Count Fosco was a name in a novel, assumed to disguise a member of an Italian secret society.'

'It was that which brought Grenier to me. He guessed that the name was a mere cloak, and yet he dreaded to turn away the man, for fear that a secret society lurked behind him. He could not believe the imitation was required for any honest purpose. It is not uncommon for the owners of such treasures to have high-class copies made so that they may be worn on less important occasions, while the originals are held safely in a bank vault. There are also foolish people who cannot afford such originals but whose vanity is satisfied by an artificial resemblance. Grenier's visitor was neither of these. To use the poor fellow's own words, the man who came to him reeked of dishonesty. Our jeweller knew very well that the original of the clasp belonged to the Longstaffe family—and feared the worst. Either the so-called count proposed to steal the original and substitute the imitation—or the last of the Longstaffes planned to perpetrate a trick of some kind upon his creditors.'

'Surely not!'

'I think not. Yet it must be conceded that Adolphus Longstaffe, like his father, has a rackety reputation. Much of the Caversham estate in Suffolk has been sold and the great house at Pickering Park in Sussex with all its lands has been at risk.'

'Not to mention Portman Square in London and most of Marylebone!'

'Exactly so.'

'Mind you, if Lord Adolphus Longstaffe were to go smash, the whole world would hear it.'

'Quite correct, Watson, and when a man of that sort faces ruin, there is no knowing what he may do. It might seem a mere peccadillo to place the imitation as surety with a bank, while breaking up the original and selling its stones.'

'But what of Grenier?'

'I asked him as a great favor to me, for he once received a favor *from* me, to make a cheap imitation of the clasp. Such an insult to his professional reputation! He was to tell no one. At the same time, he must wait until it was too late for our friend Count Fosco to have one made elsewhere before the coronation. Then he would regretfully inform this bogus nobleman that, under such pressure of work as the coronation demanded, he could not fulfil Fosco's commission for several more months.'

'Then you put Grenier in danger!'

'I think not.'

He opened the envelope and drew out a number of photographic prints.

'Count Fosco is a made-up name. There are Italian secret societies to be sure, but not in this case. That part of the trick was a bogey to frighten the dupe. But Grenier is no dupe.'

'What are these?'

He spread the photographs before him.

'You will recall our friend Colonel Piquart, to whom we were able to render a service during the deplorable Dreyfus affair in Paris.* He became thereafter Minister of Defence in the government of

---

* 'The Case of the Unseen Hand' in Donald Thomas, *The Secret Cases of Sherlock Holmes*, New York: Carroll & Graf, 1998.

Georges Clemenceau and director of military intelligence. It was the work of a day for him to establish that the address given by Count Fosco in the Boulevard Saint Germain was merely an office where letters had been collected for several months on behalf of Colonel Jacques Moriarty of the Rue des Charbonniers in the slums of Montmartre. Inquire in Montmartre and you will probably find that this domicile is as elusive as the first one. The more accurate Christian name of its lessee is, of course, James, rather than Jacques. See for yourself. I do not think Monsieur Grenier need greatly fear the threats of Count Fosco and the assassins of the Red Circle. This is single and single-minded fraud.'

The photographs showed a man in outdoor clothes striding towards, or from, an ill-painted door in a dark courtyard of some kind. It was plain that these were images obtained secretly, perhaps from a passing vehicle, of a man who had no idea that he was the object of interest. The quality of the prints suffered a little from the conditions under which they were taken.

Several of them gave a clear view of a man who was dark-haired and a little stooped, though with something of a military bearing. He had a withered look to him, beyond his years. In my own medical practice I often connect this last symptom with foreign or colonial service. There had been a good deal of that as France acquired her colonies along the Mediterranean coast of North Africa. From what I could see of him, he looked little enough like a count or, indeed, an Italian assassin.

'It is incredible!' I said as I stared at the monochrome portraits.

'Not in the least. Even after all my captors were accounted for, I thought we might hear from one or two of their friends. For me, this is not a matter of jewels and baubles, Watson. Let us call it a contest to see whether Colonel Moriarty shall live in peace and safety. It is plain that neither he nor I can do so while the other remains alive. That is what will bring him to London. Once in London, of course, he will not resist the Queen of the Night, even without a counterfeit to switch for the real clasp.'

'Can you be so sure?'

He looked at me thoughtfully.

'You will recall, Watson, the matter of the tie-pin.'

'I cannot say that I do. Which tie-pin is that?'

'It is a green emerald tie-pin, in the form of a serpent of Aesculapius. Professor Moriarty was wearing it on that late afternoon in the mist at the falls of Reichenbach. When at last he fell to his death, for one of us must fall to end that long struggle, the weight of his body as he went backwards ripped it from his shirt and it came off in my grasp. Even before he hit the rocks in the torrent, so many hundreds of feet below, I had slipped it in my pocket.'

'Where is it now?'

'That is the point, my dear fellow.'

He pushed towards me another item from the envelope, a cutting from a newspaper, *Paris Soir*, dated some weeks ago. The column carried a small announcement in English that if Colonel James Moriarty of the Rue des Charbonniers would call at the Banque de l'Orient in the Avenue de l'Opera, he would find something to his advantage.

'He has it now?' I asked.

'For some weeks past. I asked to be informed when it was collected. You may depend upon it, he will recognize what it is. I admit the device is less picturesque than throwing down one's gauntlet in the days of chivalry. Yet he has determined to exact vengeance from me and I can do no more than offer myself. You may depend upon it, he will be in London when the new king is crowned. I would go so far as to say that he will put up at the Dashwood Club in Curzon Street.'

'Named after Sir Francis Dashwood of the Hellfire Club in the 1760s!'

'That tells one of its reputation, does it not?'

3

By the evening, I was in a solemn mood. The thought of Colonel James Moriarty evoked all the old fears and perils from which we had so lately escaped. After supper, however, my friend pushed back his chair, got up from the table, and crossed to the fire-place, where he stood with his back to it, hands clasped behind him.

'My dear fellow, there really is no cause for such gloom. The game will be won by he who has knowledge on his side. I have devoted a little time to repairing the gaps in our acquaintance with a man who must now be our prime adversary. Colonel Moriarty, as his name suggests, was once a military man and a member of the gentry. To this day he is curiously but legitimately the lord of the manor of Copyhold Barton in the county of Dorset. Unfortunately, behind this grand hereditary title he owns not a square inch of land in Copyhold Barton or elsewhere. He has fallen so low that he haunts the worst districts of Paris. His habitation is among the apache street robbers of Montmartre and the ladies of the twilight in the Avenue de Clichy or the Parc de Monceau. That is his true manor and in it he is lord, under the law of the fist and the razor.'

He scraped at the bowl of his pipe for a moment, then he looked up.

'The world knows little of him. Therefore, he is a man of presumed good character in the county of Dorset. His grandfather was obliged to sell the estate—but not the title—and nothing is known to the grandson's discredit. His grandfather had acquired that title for a mere fifty pounds to add respectability to a dubious business of promoting foreign railway shares.'

'But surely the present Moriarty is a proven criminal and something can be done about him?'

He shook his head.

'There is not a single criminal conviction against him. He is not, as they say, known to the police. Were I to associate him with my captors and make accusations of attempted murder a few months ago, he could take me to court and recover punitive damages. I have nothing but my unsupported word against his.'

'Then who were his family, other than the late professor?'

Holmes sighed, sat down, and stared at the fireplace, unused just then and covered by a silk Chinese screen in the summer warmth.

'The lordship of the manor is not worth a penny piece, but it confers certain ancient ceremonial privileges. For five hundred years its owners have enjoyed burgage tenure. That is to say, they had the right of a mediaeval burgess to represent that part of Dorset at coronations, the opening of parliament, the trooping of the color, and other royal ceremonies. Two of them are grooms of the chamber to the Earl of Dorset. To be sure, they are mere servants of a greater servant of kings, but they have bought a place in a greater man's retinue on these occasions.'

'And that is all we know? Why, the scoundrel may be present at the coronation!'

Holmes smiled and leaned back in his chair.

'While enjoying the hospitality of Mr. Jabez Wilson, I made use of Somerset House, the census returns, registers of births, marriages, and deaths for the past forty or fifty years. I consulted the annual Army Lists. The name of Moriarty is not common and the entries were few. It surprises me that my enemies had not gone to greater lengths to conceal their secrets.'

'They imagined you would be dead by now.'

'True. The titular father of the professor and the colonel was Major Robert Moriarty. According to the Army Lists, he served in India and died there of a fever. His wife, Henrietta Jane, was a creature of too delicate health for the Indian climate. She is listed in the 1851 census as living throughout his absence in rooms near Hyde Park Gate. The land registers show a lease purchased by Lord Alfred Longstaffe just before her arrival.'

'A kept woman!'

'You have such an ear for the bourgeois cliche, Watson. A kept woman, if we must call her that. The reason for her sudden removal to Hyde Park Gate, where she was previously unknown, became evident when I put the census of births and the Army List together. When Professor Moriarty was born, Major Robert Moriarty had been serving in the China Wars for at least eight months. When a still younger child, a blameless station master now deceased, first saw the light of day, the major had left for India a year earlier and had now been dead two months. You may recall from the Roman history lessons of your schooldays a sardonic comment by the historian Suetonius on such misalliances.'

'"How fortunate those parents are for whom their child is only three months in the womb."'

'Precisely.' Holmes lit his pipe and shook out the flame. 'Only the elder boy, the colonel, was his father's son. Imagine the scene when the unmarried Lord Alfred Longstaffe refused Henrietta Jane's demand that he should accept the two natural sons as his own. If the census of 1861 is to be believed, she was obliged to settle for a small allowance and genteel poverty in the charming cathedral city of Wells.'

'The future Colonel Moriarty, as the eldest son, would inherit the title of lord of the manor.'

Holmes nodded.

'In the Army Lists, that eldest son was also a junior captain in South Africa and the Transvaal during the 1870s. If he has a genuine title to his colonelcy, it is by purchase of some kind in a frontier force. Diamond-mining in Kimberley was in its first buccaneering phase. Fortunes were made in the mines and lost at the card tables. So the military Moriarty came back richer than he went out.'

'What of his criminal conspiracy with Milverton and Calhoun?'

'Captain Calhoun and Henry Caius Milverton had a common interest in the sea. Calhoun was a mere pirate. Milverton was a partner in the London-to-Antwerp line that bears his name, among others. Their signboard still faces the Thames, above the dock gates at Shadwell. Yet this Milverton was quite as vicious as his brother. He escaped notice in the 1885 exposure of what the penny-a-liners call 'the white slave trade.' Yet the public denunciations by the Salvation Army and the *Pall Mall Gazette* put an end to those activities for a time. His part was to transport young women from this country to France and Belgium, while bringing those from France and Belgium to the streets of our own cities. By such means, in whatever country they found themselves, they were far from home, having only so-called protectors to depend upon.'

'Had you encountered Colonel Moriarty before you and I met?'

'Only by reputation. I was able to assist the father of a young girl and in so doing to secure the conviction of Mrs. Mary Jeffries, a keeper of houses of ill repute in Chelsea and the West End. After the 1885 newspaper outcry over the protection of young girls, London became too warm for Colonel Moriarty, and he made his way to Paris. We may assume that his income still derived from the trade in female misery practised in partnership with Henry Milverton.'

He smoked in silence for a moment and then resumed.

'To tell you the truth, Watson, I never believed that Milverton and Calhoun had gone to such trouble over the ruins of Newgate Gaol merely to murder me. They would have murdered me with great relish, of course, but a barrowload of bricks tipped from a rooftop onto my head in Welbeck Street would have done the job. Yet there was more to it. My death was to be a bonus, a mere entertainment. There was a greater coup with a well-organized criminal conspiracy behind it. You know how at the time of a coronation there is loose talk about the crown jewels?'

'You cannot believe that!'

'I do not disbelieve it. Newgate Gaol is at the heart of the City of London and secure as the Bank of England. Yet there could be no better bolthole in the aftermath of robbery, which is when even the most ingenious villains are liable to be caught. Who would dream of searching a prison—not the likes of Lestrade or Gregson, you may be sure! I believe that with a network of foreign accomplices and a team of bullies, the thing could have been done. With such resources, I know I could certainly do it.'

'I still say the whole thing is a fantasy! In any case, with Calhoun and Milverton dead, there is an end. Colonel Moriarty alone would not attempt it.'

He looked at me patiently.

'That is why he will confine his interest to the one treasure that was his goal from the beginning. Of course he cannot walk off with the crown or with the royal orb and scepter. I doubt if he ever wanted them. He could not sell such treasures for profit, least of all among the apache gangs and the throat-slitters of Batignolles or Belleville. He is a dedicated maniac, prepared to take a man off the streets of London and strangle him privately in the execution shed of Newgate Gaol purely for pleasure.'

'And what is his mania now?'

Holmes leant towards the fireplace and concluded his history.

'By the time they grew to manhood, the two elder Moriarty brothers were plainly fired by resentment. Yet they lacked the opportunity to revenge themselves on the Longstaffe family, most of all upon the Longstaffe father who had disowned two natural sons and consigned them to beggary, and upon the half brother, Lord Adolphus, who had usurped them. When the mind of a Moriarty is warped into criminality, a single gem will suffice.'

'And that is the reason behind today's playing at fox-and-geese with Lord Holder?'

My friend was unmoved by skepticism.

'The loss of the Queen of the Night would disgrace the Longstaffe family utterly. It would bring criminal suspicion and rumours of complicity upon such a spendthrift and prodigal as Lord Adolphus himself. To lose the appointment as royal herald after several hundred years would be ruin to family honour. Such is the vengeance that I believe Colonel Moriarty seeks, in addition to a handsome souvenir.'

Among the coronation postcards and placards for sale in the shop windows of Baker Street, I had noticed one which showed the Prince of Wales with his retinue. Royal blue was their colour, their robes lined with white satin. I had noticed one of them whose blue velvet cloak was fastened at the throat by a clasp of night-blue jewels set round a blazing white star. Such postcards are mere caricature exaggerations, but the design was plain enough. The memory of this determined me.

'We must see what Lestrade has to say tomorrow.'

Holmes got up and began to interest himself in his chemical table.

'We will leave Lestrade out of this, if you please, and Brother Mycroft too. I have a more important matter to settle with Colonel

Moriarty, and no man shall come between us. If either he or I would live in safety, a duel to the death must decide which of us it shall be. The same thought has surely crossed his mind, for he will know by now that I survived the Newgate blast. Besides, if you truly wish to see the last of the Queen of the Night and the rest of the crown jewels, to bring in Scotland Yard is quite the best way to accomplish it.'

Then he slipped into silence and stood over his chemical table in deep thought until he straightened up to withdraw for the night. As he went, he turned to me.

'You may rest easily, Watson. I have deduced everything about this robbery—where it will happen and when, as well as the name of the man who will carry it out. It is only his method that still eludes me.'

'I call that a pretty large exception!'

'Not at all. If Colonel Moriarty proposes to steal the Queen of the Night, it is of the first importance that we should dictate the method to him.'

Naturally, he did not explain to me how that could be done.

4

It was most unfortunate that at this juncture Mycroft Holmes should have muddied the waters by certain conversations with Inspector Lestrade, whom he was apt to regard as his luggage porter or bootblack, and whom he was also apt to chivvy or bully as though it were a sport. From his lofty perch as the government's chief accountant and interdepartmental adviser, Brother Mycroft now raised the matter with Lestrade of security at the coronation festivities, as it affected the crown jewels and those of visiting royalty. He then suggested to the Scotland Yard man that Sherlock Holmes might be retained to supervise or implement whatever security seemed advisable.

Inspector Lestrade, who hoped one day to be Superintendent Lestrade or even Commander Lestrade, was aware of the considerable influence exercised in such promotions by Mycroft Holmes. So the inspector spoke to his superintendent, who spoke to his commander, who spoke to the Commissioner of Metropolitan Police, who spoke to the Home Secretary, who, in his turn, spoke to his interdepartmental adviser, Mycroft Holmes, who commended it as a capital idea—and so the message was relayed all the way back down again.

As a result, Mycroft Holmes and Lestrade paid us a visit soon afterward, on an otherwise sunlit afternoon, to inform us of the decision that had been taken. The inspector was already briefed and prepared to discuss the particular arrangements for Coronation Day, 2 August. In what manner did my friend think he might best protect the jewels of the state at Westminster?

'By sitting here in my chair with my pipe and reading the death-chamber memoirs of some criminal of rare distinction, I daresay,' Holmes replied without a glimmer of humour. 'A French Bluebeard would promise something more in the way of style than our own marital assassins.'

Lestrade went red in the face, but Brother Mycroft was not to be denied.

'This will not do!' he boomed at his fractious sibling. 'On the subject of your protection of the regalia, I have given my word!'

'But not mine,' said Sherlock Holmes humbly.

'Why, for heaven's sake? Why will you not do it?'

'Because I should dance attendance to no purpose and that is something I decline to do. There is a great and most interesting robbery in prospect. The papers will be full of nothing else if it happens. Yet it has nothing to do with Coronation Day. I have seen that for myself.'

'What have you seen?'

'Only what you or anyone else might have noted, with a little care and a modicum of common sense. I know that there will be an attempt. I know the item to be stolen and I know the name of the man who will steal it. That is nothing. Any fool might guess at it. Unlike any fool, however, I now know how it is to be done and where. I know the time of the theft to within five minutes.'

'Five minutes!'

'Oh, very well, let us be generous and say within ten minutes. There remains merely the question of whether the thief can screw his courage to the sticking point when it comes to the moment. I cannot be answerable for his nerve. However, I think you and Lestrade had far better leave the whole thing to me.'

'Then at least tell me where, when, how, and by whom!'

'No.'

I knew he was talking about the Queen of the Night but did not dare to say a word. Mycroft Homes seemed to swell beyond his normal size.

'Then, I am to take it, you do not trust your own brother!'

How I wished I had been somewhere else just then. I had a vivid impression of their nursery tantrums in days long gone by

'I trust my own brother implicitly,' said Sherlock Holmes evenly.

'But you do not trust him sufficiently to prevent this criminal outrage, whatever it may be.'

Sherlock Holmes stared at him and then spoke very quietly.

'You have understood nothing, Mycroft, if you believe that. I do not wish to prevent what you call an outrage. In fact, I would encourage it, if I could. There is a personal affair that must be settled and this theft is the occasion of it but no more. It cannot be resolved in any other way.'

Mycroft had evidently heard something from Lestrade about his brother's subversive political outbursts, for now he asked, 'This is not some trumpery, I hope, which involves stealing the crown jewels and giving them back to the princes of India?'

Sherlock Holmes shook his head.

'No. If it were merely that, I should tell you everything and invite you to join me in the venture. I have already pledged my word to Lord Holder in the matter of securing the Lord Mayor of London and the Mansion House during the festivities. What you propose would create the most flagrant conflict of interests.'

This was news to me. I did not know that he had seen Lord Holder again.

'I cannot see it, Sherlock,' said Mycroft Holmes ominously.

'I daresay not.'

It was, as they say, the last straw that broke the camel's back. Mycroft Holmes swept from the room without another word, Lestrade at his heels, and was driven away into the summer dusk. That was as far as anyone could get with my friend.

After they had gone, I tried to soothe Holmes by reverting to the Queen of the Night, in whose safety he had a real interest. I thought this might please him. In the course of conversation, I said:

'It seems extraordinary, does it not, that all this magnificence was created just to button the neck of a man's cloak?'

He had just picked up the evening paper and glanced at it. Now he threw it down again and got to his feet, striding restlessly across to the window and turning back.

'Just so, Watson. Magnificence and flummery. Whether flummery is the price one must pay for magnificence or whether magnificence is the cost of flummery, I should not care to say. Let it suffice for the moment that I swear Colonel Moriarty means to have the Queen of the Night and I care for nothing else. To be sure, he has money enough, the reward of human bondage. To him, I daresay, theft is a way of vengeance against those who have wronged him and his martyred brother ever since birth. I am one of the guilty. You might call it a matter of justice by his own perverted lights, against the Longstaffe family and society as a whole.'

'He will be caught.'

Holmes sat down again and shook his head.

'Not by Lestrade and his kind. Colonel Moriarty is that most dangerous type, a criminal who is not known to be one and who works alone. Curiously, it is a species encountered often in what Professor von Krafft-Ebing calls lust murders. Because he works alone, there is no one to betray him, which is far the commonest method of detection. He works in utter secrecy, deep in the bomb-proof shelter of his skull.'

One of my most uncomfortable evenings drew to an end at this point. For the next few weeks, however, during his visits to us

Lestrade became slyly witty in a manner that was most provoking. He would refer, with a wink at me over the rim of his glass, to the value of the jewels on display at the ceremony in Westminster Abbey and the dangers they must be exposed to. Then he would add that the humble efforts of Scotland Yard might prove sufficient to keep them safe without the assistance of a higher intelligence. It was galling in the extreme, and I feared there must be an explosion.

Holmes kept himself in check for longer than I had expected. However, when these pleasantries were repeated for the fourth or fifth time, he remarked casually, 'I do not imagine that the disappearance of the royal jewels would be regarded as theft by those Indian princes from whom they were looted by British power in the first place. Indeed, if I could be quite sure that they were stolen only to be returned to their rightful owners, I daresay I should be ready to put my meagre talents at the disposal of those who perpetrated such a robbery.'

Lestrade's bluff laughter in response to this had a false note about it. I believe that he had been truly shocked by the utterance of these subversive comments, whatever their intent. The anarchic and radical element in Holmes's character was one with which our visitor could never get to grips. We heard no more from him on the subject of the royal regalia. However, when the inspector left us that night, Holmes burst out in anger.

'It is quite obvious now, if it never was before, that Lestrade and his crew are utterly unsuited to dealing with a threat of this kind. I lose all patience with such people! Thank God I have never mentioned Colonel Moriarty to Lestrade. One might as well hand over the Queen of the Night to the robber and be done with it!'

A day or two later, he was absent from morning until evening. On his return, he revealed that he had spent the day with Lord Holder. Despite his outburst to Mycroft Holmes and Lestrade, my friend so far relented as to permit his lordship to conduct him upon a tour of the coronation routes and to introduce him to those buildings where the great jewels of state and their wearers might be gathered. Apart from the royal apartments of Buckingham Palace, which neither Colonel Moriarty not any other thief would get near, these consisted of the ceremonial area in Westminster Abbey, as well as its antechambers, and the robing-rooms of the House of Lords. As a chamber-groom to the Earl of Dorset, our adversary would have brief and limited access to these. In company with Lord Holder, Holmes had examined these rooms and their adjacent reception areas. Here, if anywhere, a surreptitious theft might be possible or a sudden attack might take place on Lord Adolphus Longstaffe as the Prince of Wales's herald. But Holmes came home disgruntled and sat in his chair biting a thumbnail with vexation.

'Contrary to the urgings of Brother Mycroft and Lestrade, it is out of the question that there will be an attempt to steal the Queen of the Night during the coronation.'

'Then the treasure is safe?'

In the frustration of the moment, he cried out:

'Good God, Watson! This scoundrel was prepared to murder me to gain his ends! Do you not understand that if there is no attempt at robbery during the coronation, it will be made in some other manner? That is our certain hope!'

'Or perhaps the entire story of the theft is a fairy tale.'

He looked at me more calmly but sadly, as if I had failed to listen to a word.

Next morning he went again to Lord Holder, who had been created an alderman of the City of London the previous year and had now been accommodated by the Lord Mayor with a room at the Mansion House for the course of the celebrations. The coronation itself was only the first of several occasions at which the royal regalia and state jewels were to be worn. A monarch who is crowned in the City of Westminster must also take possession of the City of London a few days later. The second processional route would lie through the districts of law and finance. At noon a grand luncheon was to be held in the great Egyptian Hall of the Mansion House, where the Lord Mayor of London would play host to His Majesty and where Lord Holder would have much to do with the arrangements and the custody of the jewels.

'Since you are already acquainted with Lord Holder,' said Holmes to me next morning, 'you may find it instructive to see for yourself the areas of the Mansion House that must be guarded.'

An hour or so later we stood in his lordship's room, which looked through a round-arched window towards the river and London Bridge. Our host then indicated a slightly built man who had just come in, an individual in a brown suit that was almost a match in color for his luxuriant mustache and eyes.

'It would have given me great pleasure, gentlemen, to show you the banqueting hall and the anterooms myself. Unfortunately, I am sitting in the Lord Mayor's court this morning. Therefore I must leave you in the capable hands of Inspector Jago of the City of London Police.'

'Inspector Jago and I are old friends,' said Holmes graciously. 'I am sure we shall get along admirably.'

The inspector extended his hand to each of us in turn,

'It is a year or two since then, Mr. Holmes. A matter of the Bank of England, as I recollect, robbed handsomely by three enterprising young American gentlemen.'

He took us straight to the Egyptian Hall, lofty as a cathedral nave, whose plan had been based upon an Egyptian chamber of the ancient world. Inspector Jago opened the double doors and waved us in, as if he were the owner of the place. Two tables, each a hundred dinner places long, ran down either side with a high table across the far end. Side screens of lofty Corinthian columns supported a vaulted roof and framed the great classical arch of the west window. I was quite unprepared for such magnificence as this. The niches between the columns at either side were filled by sculptured groups or single figures in the manner of Grecian antiquity. Royal banners and shaded flambeaux hung before each alcove. Gilt chandeliers on triple chains were suspended at intervals from the roof down the entire length of the hall. Here the newly crowned King Edward would take lunch.

'Four hundred guests at a time, gentleman,' said Inspector Jago quietly, for all the world as if we were in church. 'Even this will be too little for His Majesty's visit. We shall be using the Venetian Parlour, Wilkes's Parlour, and every hole and corner. In short, we shall hardly know what to do with everyone.'

I glanced at Holmes, hoping he was not about to denounce flummery again. He merely inquired, with a little impatience, 'And what of the other offices appointed for the day?'

Inspector Jago touched his forehead briefly, as if to indicate a lapse of memory.

'Quite right, Mr. Holmes. Follow me and you shall see what we have by way of robing-rooms and the like. With space so tight, it would never do for our guests to be seated at luncheon in their robes! We have provided the most secure accommodation for cloaks, robes, and insignia. This way, if you please.'

We followed him up a broad flight of marble stairs and a little distance along a wide passageway. He stopped outside a double door of stout oak panels furnished with an impressive selection of locks and bolts.

'Here, gentlemen, are the rooms always set aside by the Lord Mayor as robing apartments for ceremonial occasions. Royalty and majesty, of course, have apartments of their own. At other times we use these as aldermen's committee rooms of the Common Council. They run along this side of the building and look down into the courtyard at its center. This door is the only way in. On the day of the royal visit, it will have a guard of two sergeants and two reserves from the Provost Marshal's Corps under the command of a senior captain. Once the rooms are locked after disrobing and the guests have gone down to lunch, no person will be permitted to enter until the function is over and the robing begins again.'

He took out a key, unlocked the oak doors, and led us into a spacious oblong room. This was the area where each courtier in turn removed his robe with the assistance of his attendants and put it on again after the luncheon. Three tall sash windows along the left-hand side looked down into the courtyard. A large table at the centre, equipped with upright chairs padded by black horsehair, certainly had the air of a committee room. At the far end a second locked door led into the room where the robes were to be kept after they had been taken from their wearers. All furniture had been cleared from this second room and it was now occupied by three ranks of tailor's dummies in pale brown canvas set out as precisely as soldiers on parade.

'Here we have a second room almost identical to the first,' said Jago reassuringly, 'occupied at other times by the filing staff of the Clerk to the Common Council. There is no access but by the way we have just come. A mouse could not get in or out on the great day without authority.'

'It is not a mouse that concerns me,' said Holmes mildly. 'A rat, perhaps, but a rat bearing such authority as you and your men might defer to without a second thought.'

Jago laughed as uproariously as he could manage.

'Well and good, Mr. Holmes, if you say so. I am sure we must all be guided by you in this matter. In this second room, the cloaks will be mounted on these dummies; they will be safe as in the Bank of England. It is divided from the first room and the room beyond by doors securely locked.'

'In the light of the case upon which you and I were engaged so many years ago,' said Holmes coolly, '"safe as the Bank of England" appears to me an unfortunate choice of simile.'

The thirty or forty tailors' dummies consisted of stuffed canvas bodies, from neck to hips, mounted on black-painted iron poles. Inspector Jago had bounced back from Holmes's rebuke with the aplomb of a rubber ball. He brushed his moustache confidently on the edge of his hand and beamed proudly.

'This, gentlemen, is what our frog-eating friends on the far side of the English Channel would call the *garde-robe*. Because, indeed, it is where the robes are guarded.' He spread his empty hands like a conjurer performing an impossible trick. 'Once again, there is no access except by the way we have come, which will be guarded as tight as the Tower of London. Safe as the Tower itself!'

'Do you really think so?'

'I think so, Mr. Holmes. I believe I am entitled to think so.'

'And what of the third room beyond this?'

'You may see that, if you please, sir. Of course you shall. It is not in commission just now—quite *hors de combat* and locked up, in fact. For it is the post-room. Not much to the purpose, except when the clerks are here. But you wish to see it, sir, and so you shall. Not much to the purpose on the great day, we may safely say, but you shall see it indeed.'

'I doubt very much,' Holmes replied caustically, 'if you may safely say anything.'

Jago slipped his key into the Yale lock and opened the door. Here was a room about half the size of the first two, a dead-end with no entrance or exit but by the way we had come, as Inspector Jago hastened to assure us. There was only a single sash window. The further wall, an exterior wall of the building, was filled by cupboards floor to ceiling. For further security, these were built some way into the wall itself. The cupboards appeared to be locked, perhaps by a single key that fitted the entire suite. Holmes surveyed them in a long single glance.

'I think we have seen enough,' he said, 'except for the matter of the windows.'

'The windows?' For the first time, Jago lost a little of his bounce.

'The windows,' Holmes repeated. 'You have done so thorough a job, Inspector, creating a strong room from these three offices, ensuring that the only access—and, indeed, the only exit—is by way of a heavily guarded exterior door. Come now, you have surely seen that the only remaining weakness can be the windows. You were teasing us—or testing us—by not mentioning them, were you not? Putting us to the proof!"

This caught Mr. Jago nicely, on one leg, as it were. It was plain he had never given a thought to the danger of attack at such a height by way of the windows which were on view to the courtyard. However, to admit that now would demolish him.

'I have had the windows in mind, Mr. Holmes,' he said uneasily.

'To be sure you have,' replied Holmes consolingly.

'I did not, however, consider them the most likely approach.'

'Did you not? Surely they are the only approach, once your guards are in place.'

'I was about to mention them, however.'

'To be sure you were. I did not suggest the possibility of an attack down through the ceiling or up through the floor, for I was quite certain that you must have taken precautions against that too.'

'Indeed so,' said Jago hastily. 'Police constables are to be posted in rooms above and below.'

'Excellent! In that case you can have no objection to assisting me in a small experiment with the windows. Would it be possible for one of us to go down into the courtyard and maneuver a small weight attached to a piece of string?'

He drew from his pocket a ball of thin cord, to the end of which a one-pound scale weight with a hook had been attached.

'It would be possible, Mr. Holmes, only. . . .'

'Only your instructions are to trust no one, not even Dr. Watson and myself. You must not leave us alone up here to wander about at will. Equally, you could not send one of us alone to roam the building on our way down to the yard. You are quite right, you have thought of everything, and you have passed the first test—loyalty to those in command of you. I should not dream of compromising you. Indeed, I insist that if you would be so good as to go down and manipulate the weight as I shall instruct you, you must lock us both in here and, if possible, one of your constables should keep surveillance upon us. However, it is imperative that I should have this assistance with my little experiment, and I would prefer not to involve anyone but the three of us.'

In the end, as Holmes had foreseen and contrived, Jago went down to the courtyard after locking us in, with a pantomime of reluctance. As soon as he was gone, my friend said:

'Quick about it, Watson. That wretched fellow is worse than Lestrade. If we leave it to them, there will not be a jewel left in the entire royal collection. I must make a survey of the rooms. Open the window over there and lower the little weight on the cord—as slowly as you can. That will occupy him for a moment.'

I pushed up the window and began to pay out the cord. While doing this, it was not easy to watch what Holmes was up to, but he was striding about the anteroom, the garde-robe, and the post-room while pausing briefly from time to time. Once or twice I heard a tiny rasping sound of metal on metal. Then he appeared at the window beside me and began to shout instructions at Jago, thirty feet below. I cannot bear to repeat them all, for some were so idiotic, but at last he called down:

'Take the weight! See how far it will swing side to side, along the wall. If our man comes down over the roof, he may gain a window ledge by descending to one side and swinging across. We must take measurements of that possibility.'

'But the windows can be locked, Mr. Holmes.'

'With a small steel jimmy, he can wrench them from their frames.'

'In the City of London and in broad daylight, Mr. Holmes?'

'He may carry a cloth and pail and masquerade as a window-cleaner.'

'During His Majesty's visit?'

'Or he may enter by night.'

However low Jago's opinion of my friend's detective skill, it was lower still by the time the inspector returned to what he called face-tiously his garde-robe. He must surely have suspected something from this farce but he could not see, let alone prove, anything amiss. I had been a little put out when Holmes made his tour of Westmin-ster Abbey and the House of Lords without me. Now I wished that I had also spent the day of the Mansion House visit at home.

4

The world knows that Coronation Day came and went without the loss of a single jewel. This enabled Lestrade to be still more witty at our expense, ruminating over his evening whisky and water at the manner in which the bumbledom of the Scotland Yard force had triumphed without the assistance of a detective genius. Sherlock Holmes remained unruffled, favouring him only with a quick humourless smile that was more than anything a grimace of impatience.

My thoughts still turned from time to time to Colonel Moriarty. Though Holmes and I knew of his criminal intent, he had surely missed the boat now that the main coronation ceremony was over. Even Holmes himself, when he sent a final refusal to stand guard at the coronation itself, remarked, 'The whole alarm over the coronation and the jewels is a fuss about nothing.'

'You cannot know that,' I said. 'No one can.'

'You will recall my reply to the wretched thief in the Case of the Blue Carbuncle, as you chose to call it. "My name is Sherlock Holmes. It is my business to know what other people don't know."'

So it came to the week of the Lord Mayor's luncheon. The street banners and loyal flags that had decorated the West End on Coronation Day now appeared in the great commercial streets of the City of London, around St. Paul's cathedral, on banks and insurance offices, at commodity brokers' and stock dealers'. Little rows of bunting also adorned the close-packed houses of the adjacent East End, as well as the docks of Wapping and Limehouse.

The behavior of Sherlock Holmes had created a dilemma for me. He would say nothing more, yet he appeared sure of everything. He had long ago left Lestrade and Brother Mycroft high and dry. Even my loyalty was put to the test. Had he got the wrong end of the stick, as the saying goes? All men are mortal, even Sherlock Holmes. It was not beyond possibility that he was in error over some vital detail. He had admitted errors in certain past cases.

How could Holmes know from the start that it was not the coronation but the Lord Mayor's luncheon that would be the occasion of a sensational theft? Unless the colonel was to knock down the wearer of the Queen of the Night in full public view, the only opportunity must be while the robes, cloaks, and their insignia were locked away in the garde-robe during the official luncheon.

Unless our opponent had a team of labourers with pick-axes to break through a twelve-inch stone wall, the only approach to that room was by double doors securely locked and bolted, guarded by armed sergeants of the Provost Marshal's Corps. Within the anteroom, the communicating door, which led into the garde-robe with its rows of tailor's dummies, was also locked. There were the windows down one side, overlooking the courtyard thirty feet below. However, since Holmes had made such play of these to Inspector Jago, police guards in the courtyard were to keep constant surveillance to frustrate any attempt at the casements. The smaller post-room at the end would also be locked but its own cupboards, large enough for a cat but not for a man.

The integrity of the Provost Marshal's Corps was unquestioned. Even if an intruder could hide himself in these rooms during the royal luncheon, any theft would be discovered once the minor courtiers and their attendants returned to assume their robes for the rest of the ceremonies—while the thief must still be there. The disappearance of the Queen of the Night would cause any suspect to be stripped to the skin—however discreetly. Then, if nothing was found, he must be free to go. Yet he would go without his trophy. Every room or cupboard would be taken to pieces, floorboards taken up. No one would be permitted to return, certainly not a thief who might have hidden his booty there.

Suspicion must fall primarily on the two unfortunate sergeants at the door of the garde-robe, who entered it alone when they collected and handed out the robes after lunch. Or perhaps it might fall upon a chamber-groom who assisted his master to disrobe and robe again. Holmes had calculated how such a crime might be carried out. If he could calculate it, so might someone else.

If ever there was a mystery in a locked room, this must be it, and I am not a great believer in such riddles. Colonel Moriarty would take one look at the provost sergeants and abandon his plan—if he ever had one. This would not suit Holmes, who intended a final encounter with his adversary, but Colonel Moriarty was not there to suit Holmes.

That evening after dinner I watched Holmes cautiously from behind my newspaper as he sat at his worktable. He unwrapped a chamois leather and took out what might have been the Queen of the Night, had the famous ornament been nothing but a Christmas-tree decoration or a glass fancy-dress trinket. Perhaps he hoped to trick Colonel Moriarty into stealing a mere gewgaw rather than a Brazilian diamond set among indigo sapphires. In the heat of the moment the colonel might be deceived, though I doubted it. In any case, a counterfeit may be of use to the thief. I could not see what help it would be to those who hunted him. I opened my evening paper, certain that this trumpery, as Mycroft would call it, seemed unlikely to warrant the duel to the death that Sherlock Holmes had set his heart on. I was wrong—but I could not know it then.

5

The sunshine on the Lord Mayor's day of glory showed that first mellowing that comes with the turn of summer into autumn. Holmes and I were at the Mansion House by early morning. Lord Holder and Inspector Jago left us much to ourselves, his lordship believing we knew best and the inspector regarding our presence as unnecessary. We both wore formal court dress of black frock coat and white tie, striped trousers, and silk top-hat.

Four hundred of the noblest were to sit with King Edward, Queen Alexandra, the Prince and Princess of Wales, the Lord Mayor, and Aldermen of the City of London in the grandeur of the Egyptian Hall. Lesser chamberlains, heralds, and those who could not be accommodated in such splendour were to take lunch either in the Venetian Parlour or Wilkes's Parlour. Lower still were those officers and officials who would be accommodated with little more than a buffet.

'You would do me the greatest service,' said Holmes as we made our itinerary of the upper floor, 'if you were to take up your position in Lord Holder's room. From there, you will have a direct view across the courtyard into the windows of the garde-robe and a room to right and left. That is to say, the anteroom on the left, the garde-robe, and the post-room on its right, as we saw them on our tour of inspection. On Lord Holder's desk you will find a pair of field-glasses with Zeiss precision lenses. Train these on the opposite windows. Leave nothing unobserved.'

As an afterthought, he added, 'No matter what you see, remain there until the appointed time. You may observe what looks like a crime in progress, but it may be nothing of consequence.'

'It would help a good deal if I knew what I am supposed to see.'

'I anticipate there will be a crush in the anteroom when the royal procession from Buckingham Palace breaks up in the courtyard and the minor nobility enter to disrobe for lunch. That will dwindle, everyone will leave to go down to the Egyptian Hall, and the doors will be locked and secured by the provost guard. The rooms will remain quiet for an hour or more during the royal lunch. The two armed sergeants and the captain of the Provost Marshal's Corps will stand guard on the only door giving access, with two more sergeants in reserve. Jago and several of his men will be in the courtyard. A blue-bottle fly, I suggest, will not get in or out during that time.'

'And you, Holmes?'

He shrugged. 'I shall await events and keep my eye on Colonel Moriarty throughout lunch. He with his co-chamberlain will attend in the robing-room as grooms of the chamber to Lord Dorset. Then he will be seated in the Egyptian Parlour. Lord Holder has placed me there as well, with a convenient pillar between us. When the meal is over, you will make your way to the doors where the provost sentries stand. The keys are guarded by the Lord Mayor's chamberlain. He will hand them to the guard commander, who will open the doors and stand back for the minor courtiers to enter. The two sergeants will unlock the garde-robe, enter, and hand out the robes to the attendants in a strict order.'

'And you?'

'I shall be there. You have your revolver with you and it is loaded?'

'Of course. All the same, I cannot see that there is the least opportunity for Colonel Moriarty to lay hands on the Queen of the Night!'

'That is precisely how he would wish it to seem. You understand your instructions.'

'Such as they are.'

'Capital! We may have every confidence that this will end well.'

I had not the least confidence of any such thing. I had no clear idea of what Colonel Moriarty looked like except from shadowy photographs of a tall black-coated man coming and going in a dingy courtyard. As one of the grooms of the chamber to the Earl of Dorset, he would be dressed in a scarlet tunic with a little gold piping, but almost every man in the building would be wearing one of those. He would have no robe of his own, being merely a servant of the earl.

I calculated that the distance across the courtyard was about eighty or ninety feet. My field-glasses were rather of the Barr & Stroud pattern with precision-ground lenses. They brought the opposite windows sharply into view and gave me a clear enough image beyond them for the canvas texture of the naked tailor's dummies to be plainly visible. As yet there was nothing to observe. I remained in position until I heard the deep bell of St. Paul's in the distance, striking noon. Presently the buzz of conversation from Inspector Jago's men in the courtyard gave way to the first rumble of carriage wheels.

Briefly, I trained my glasses on the arrivals below: King Edward and Queen Alexandra in an open brougham, she graceful and he majestic; the Prince and Princess of Wales, he in royal blue as befitted the occasion; Lord Longstaffe behind him with the Queen of the Night—the cause of all the trouble!—at his throat. I brought it into focus. There was no mistaking this as the genuine article when the August sun flashed upon it. Surrounded by its cluster of twelve sapphires, the twelve planes of the great stone glittered and dazzled alternately. A sapphire may vary from pale blue to indigo, and generally the lighter cornflower blue fetches the highest prices. In this case, the effect of stones of the deepest blue was far more dramatic. As Lord Holder had remarked, what might be lost in price was made up for by the value of the clasp as a work of the jeweller's art. Behind the stout figure of Lord Longstaffe, I made out princes and princesses, several crowned heads, the shah of Persia, ambassadors and diplomats. Though less grand than the coronation ceremony, it was in some ways more lavish.

Turning the field-glasses to the windows opposite, I saw the locked double doors of the anteroom swing open. The royal party and its distinguished guests were disrobed elsewhere. In the anteroom, as Jago called it, the lesser aristocracy—heralds and chamberlains—presented themselves to the dressers who drew off each robe and entrusted it to a uniformed provost sergeant at the doorway of the garde-robe. It was carried through and arranged on its allotted tailor's dummy. There was an air of slow ceremony and none of that rush, disorder, or confusion that enables a thief to snatch a treasure and run.

After fifteen minutes at the most, the last of the lords and ladies-in-waiting had left and the three rooms opposite me were quiet, as Holmes had prophesied. The garde-robe itself had undergone a transformation. Its forty or so canvas dummies were now a glittering parade, robes of scarlet and gold, blue and gold, green and silver, adorned with clusters of brilliants. Black cocked hats, some gold-braided and some not, sat upon the round canvas polls of the heads, uniformly tilted forward to secure their balance. Yet these canvas figures reminded me not so much of court splendour as of carcasses strung up for dissection in an anatomy theatre.

For half an hour I scanned the three rooms through my glasses with little idea of what I might expect to see. Once I fancied that I caught a movement. It startled me almost as much as if a corpse had winked at me during an anatomy class. There was nothing more. Surely a thief would not choose to be trapped with two burly provost sergeants guarding the only door and police under the windows.

I settled down for a moment and then—there it was again! Just a fleeting sight of red moving among the rows of dummy torsos which obscured most of the view. One thing was certain: if anyone was in the garde-robe, he would be in full view the moment he came out into the antechamber. But how would he have a key to let himself out? Perhaps I was only seeing what I feared to see. Possibly a provost sergeant had been left to patrol the room. Holmes had told me the garde-robe would be quiet. He did say it would be empty or unoccupied. Who knows what last-minute instructions had been issued?

I had taken up my position so as to have a full view of the garde-robe, a three-quarter view of the anteroom to the left, and perhaps a quarter view of the post-room to the right, which contained only drawers for stationery and was not involved in the present arrangements. In any case, that was also locked. I tried to locate the royal-blue cloak of Lord Longstaffe, the Prince of Wales's herald, among the files of those mounted on the dummies. In the spaces between the first ranks I caught glimpses of dark blue, scarlet, emerald-green, and gold on the figures behind. Of the rear two ranks I could see little or nothing. Through one gap there was the left shoulder and lapel of a dark, blue cloak. It might have been one of a dozen, but beyond question the blue nap of the velvet was bare of any ornament. Either it was not Lord Longstaffe's cloak, or else the Queen of the Night had been removed.

For what seemed like an age but was probably no more then thirty seconds, I was torn between unease and the fear of making a monumental fool of myself by getting into a panic over a cloak that never carried an insignia in the first place! Through the field-glasses, I studied as much of the gold braid on the epaulette as I could see. It was no great help, because all these robes and cloaks had gold-braided epaulettes of some pattern. Even if this was Lord Longstaffe's cloak, perhaps the diamond and its sapphire cluster had been laid in a locked drawer for further security.

I could see three or four inches of the upright collar and a gold-embroidered frieze upon it. I looked again. Just within my range of vision and no more than an inch high, the gold embroidery formed a motif of three feathers—beneath, in letters so tiny that I could not be sure of them, I swear were the two words '*Ich dien.*' You may believe that this is the 'I serve' motto of the King of Bohemia, slain by the Black Prince at Crecy in 1346, or the Welsh '*Eich dyn*'—'Behold the man'—with which Edward I presented his son to the people at Carnarvon. In either case, it was the Prince of Wales's motto and his emblem of three feathers on the tunic of its herald! And where the Queen of the Night should have sparkled and glittered, there was only bare blue velvet! My heart and entrails sank with panic.

Still dreading that I had somehow made an utter fool of myself, I bolted out of Lord Holder's room and raced for the main doors of the garde-robe where the two sergeants and captain of the Provost Marshal's Corps were on duty. In one of Holmes's famous exhortations, there was not a moment to be lost. But what was I to do? The provos would not open the oaken double door at my mere request. Almost certainly they would not have been entrusted with the key to do so. To denounce Colonel Moriarty as a thief who was ransacking the rooms would expose us to him completely, if the figure I thought I had seen proved to be somebody else.

I had the sudden thought that I must flush him out—whoever he was—and as I came within sight of the provost guard I thought I knew how to do it. I now see that I had little time to consider the wisdom of my action. Yet one thing was certain. If Colonel Moriarty was in the garde-robe he could not be simultaneously eating lunch in the Venetian Parlour or any other venue. I confronted the young provost captain.

'It is imperative that I should speak at once to Colonel Moriarty, chamber groom to the Earl of Dorset. He is at lunch, I believe, in the Venetian Parlour.'

If he was in the garde-robe, this would betray him. The young captain coloured a little.

'If Colonel Moriarty is at luncheon, it is impossible for him to be called away.'

'I am Dr. John Watson, surgeon-major of the Northumberland Fusiliers. It is imperative that I should speak to the colonel at once! The matter cannot wait!'

The truth was I had been regimental surgeon-major fifteen years ago in Afghanistan. I was so no longer. The white lie seemed a forlorn hope, but I had the most prodigious stroke of luck. As a medical man, I am used to reading from their facial expressions the thoughts of those who learn what my calling is. The young captain plainly sensed a medical emergency. He inquired no further.

Striding to the corner of the passageway, he barked out a name. A young trooper came to attention before him, received his command, and doubled away. As I followed the captain, I saw in a shadowy alcove to one side three Martini-Henry rifles stacked wigwam-style. The defenders of the realm and the monarch were taking no chances!

For a minute or two I paced the marble balcony above the broad staircase until I heard the sound of distant footsteps. My heart sank. It seemed plain that Colonel Moriarty had the unshakeable alibi of having been at lunch in the Venetian Parlour during every minute of the time that I had been telling myself stories about the Queen of the Night.

I drew back. He came up the first flight of the staircase, the rear view of his scarlet tunic and dark trousers marking him out as what he was. The plain cocked hat, left off in the Venetian Parlour, was now on his head again. I knew not what to expect as he came up the second flight to the level of the balcony, his head bowed. As he turned towards me, I strode forward, displaying far more confidence than I felt. He looked up and my heart almost stopped dead. I found myself staring into the face of Sherlock Holmes!

6

'Congratulations, my dear fellow,' he said sardonically. 'Your inability to follow the simplest instructions is, happily, something I might have depended upon. You have very nearly ruined everything.'

'Where is Colonel Moriarty and why are you wearing that uniform?'

'This is not a uniform, merely an ordinary military tunic, borrowed for the occasion. Colonel Moriarty is, I trust, in the process of robbing the nation of the Queen of the Night. Indeed, I imagine that by now the gem must be on its way to its destination.'

'On its way? The outer door is still locked and guarded by the provost sergeants. The door between the anteroom and the garde-robe is still locked, so for that matter is the last one between the garde-robe and the post-room. Anyone in there is still there—trapped.'

Then I saw the certain answer.

'Is our man in his place at the luncheon-table?'

'There is no doubt of it. Indeed, he has not been out of my sight since before the garde-robe was closed and locked.'

'Then what the devil is going on?'

My friend merely chuckled.

'Poor old Watson. I fear you would never make an international jewel thief—let alone catch one. I have not the least doubt that Colonel Moriarty has somehow had the run of the garde-robe and the rooms either side of it at some time in the recent past. Perhaps long before the coronation, when no one was paying attention to them. Indeed I have been counting on this, and I have kept his secret for him. As to the diamond and sapphires, I imagine they are on their way to Paris.'

How this was possible, or why Holmes made light of it, was beyond me.

'Why are you in that tunic?'

'Despite the pillar between us in the Venetian Parlor, it is best to be inconspicuous. The best way is to dress as most people here are dressed. Lord Holder was kind enough to arrange it.'

'Then who is at lunch?'

'With Colonel Piquart's assistance, I went to some trouble over the photographs he was kind enough to send me. I observed that each was marked with the date on which it was taken. One of those dates was no other than the day on which Colonel Moriarty paid his call upon our jeweller, Raoul Grenier, in Brussels. Therefore the man in the photographs could not be he. I had doubts about it from the first. On Colonel Piquart's recommendation I applied to that most useful organisation in Paris, the Deuxieme Bureau. They were able to identify the man in the photographs as an accomplished swindler and fluent linguist, known in their records as Colonel Lemonnier. In his line of business, he naturally has a number of pseudonyms. Perhaps he sometimes calls himself Colonel Moriarty—I doubt it. Perhaps Colonel Moriarty sometimes calls himself Colonel Lemonnier, I doubt that too.'

'And Lemonnier, no doubt, was one of the lesser breeds for whom a champagne buffet was provided and where no one would notice if a man was missing or not!'

'Excellent, Watson. As for appearances, Colonel Moriarty has seldom been in England for the past seventeen years, since the so-called white-slave scandals. Few people would have much recollection of what he looked like. Fewer still would care to be his friends.'

'But the theft has not been prevented. That seems the long and the short of it.'

Holmes sighed and leant back against the marble balustrade.

'I have said, until I am weary of saying so, that I have no wish to prevent it. If it is prevented, Colonel Moriarty goes to prison for a short term. If it is committed, he and I may settle matters in our own way.'

He now drew out his notebook and laid upon it three tiny wafers of steel, unfolded from tissue paper. The metal was dark and pliable, speckled by bright dust.

'The other day, while you assisted our friend Jago by swinging a weight from his garde-robe window, I made a quick but meticulous survey of that room, the anteroom, and the post-room, whose doors were conveniently open. These wafers are magnetized steel. The powder is metallic dust, easily attracted when a delicate magnetized probe is inserted into a keyway. I obtained it by using one steel wafer in the Yale lock on the door that passes from the anteroom to the garde-robe, a second on the door between the garde-robe and the post-room, a third in the locks on the post-room cupboards until I found one which produced a similar result. It was the work of a minute.'

'What is the dust?'

'Bright steel with a low carbon content. The low content makes it easier to work in the construction of Yale-pattern locks. This is the residue from an attack on the mechanism of the three locks. The weapon was almost certainly a very fine diamond-head drill. The brightness of the dust confirms that the attacks were recent, no doubt while the rooms were still being used as offices and without a special guard. Even today, the post-room has no part in the ceremonial.'

He folded the metal wafers into his notecase again.

'The Yale works on a novel principle. Other locks open by the key lifting the levers that hold the bolt in place. Unless the outline of the key matches the position and shape of the levers, it will not lift them. In a Yale, the entire lock turns, provided the contours of the key match those of the interior. Otherwise the key may not even thread the lock. With other locks a burglar may use two or three picks simultaneously. In the narrow Yale keyway a thief can only insert one pick, which makes the method almost impossible.'

'You presume that Colonel Moriarty prepared these locks in advance?'

'There would have been no metal dust in the keyways otherwise. The interior of a Yale is a series of steel pins. Drill them all and there is no obstruction to a key of that make. It will turn the lock. For every pin you drill, the more likely that any other Yale key will turn it. Drill them all and there is no resistance to your key, but the lack of resistance would betray you. The trick is to drill two or three pins and work a fourth with a single pick. The two pins remaining provide to make it seem the lock is in order, moving easily as if freshly oiled.'

'Every lock, surely, is different.'

'Very few keys and locks are unique. Each firm has quite a small number of patterns. The odds that your door key will open another particular one are many thousands to one. You would not know which to try. That is of no use to a criminal. Yet every pin removed shortens those odds. When three have been removed and a fourth can be manipulated with a needle-probe, a man with a hundred keys of general stock pattern could probably open a lock. Indeed, the latchkey of 221b Baker Street came within an ace of moving the lock that separates the anteroom from the garde-robe.'

Behind us, on the stairs rose a hubbub of voices as the minor courtiers returned to be robed. The Lord Mayor's chamberlain in black breeches and buckles, lace cuffs and collar, passed us with Inspector Jago in uniform and a City of London police superintendent. The chamberlain presented a key to the captain of the provost guard. The captain unlocked the oak double doors, than pushed them inward and wide to either side. The first dozen dignitaries whose cloaks or robes were mounted on the tailor's dummies made their way into the anteroom, among them the tall and dignified Lord Holder and the stout gray-mopped figure of Lord Adolphus Longstaffe. The two provost sergeants who were to unlock the garde-robe at the far end and hand out the garments followed them respectfully.

Holmes motioned me onward, while he hung back. I kept to one side, in a corner of the anteroom by the window. The sergeants had unlocked the next door and now brought forward the robes, one at a time, and handed them to the chamber-grooms who would assist their patrons to put them on.

There were still fifteen or twenty minor courtiers in tunics and breeches, awaiting their cloaks or robes. To one side stood a belted earl and two attendants in scarlet with black braid. One of them caught my attention, as I watched from a little behind him and out of his present range of vision. He was tall, thin, no more than fifty, but with a dry look to him and the skin-texture of a wrinkled prune. It was not this that held my gaze, but rather the way his reddened forehead seemed to curve outwards, the look of his sunken eyes, and his manner of letting his head turn slowly from side to side, as if in time to some inner music or the demands of a deep intellectual problem. I had seen such movements before and knew that they betrayed concealed agitation. They had been a compulsion of the late Professor Moriarty, whose bulging forehead and sunken eyes I seemed to see before me now. There was only one man in that room who could be Colonel Moriarty.

How easy it would be for Colonel Lemonnier, whom nobody knew, to masquerade at lunch as Colonel Moriarty, whom nobody knew either, while there was one guest fewer, unnoticed, in the crush of the champagne buffet. I turned away, sure that he had not noticed me, and went to find Holmes, who was standing next to Jago. I noticed that the inspector's color was rather high, his moustache appeared to bristle, and he had withdrawn into a dignified silence.

'Thanks to official incompetence,' said Holmes to me behind his hand, 'Lemonnier left the Venetian Parlour unobserved, before luncheon was over, and has disappeared. Nonetheless we will wait here, if you please, and be ready to move quickly. If you wish to witness my *pièce de resistance*, keep your eyes on Lord Holder.'

Lord Holder stood an inch or two taller than anyone in his immediate vicinity. He was walking towards us, smiling contentedly, and the little crowd of courtiers drew back a little before his regal person. He was escorting the bowed figure of Lord Adolphus Longstaffe. The whole appeared to have been staged so that among the front rank of onlookers was Colonel Moriarty. As if by instinct, my fingers closed on the cold metal of the revolver butt in the pocket of my black morning coat. What followed took only a few seconds and seemed like a lifetime.

Lord Holder and his protégé came on, their heads and necks visible above the others. As they drew closer, their epaulettes and then their lapels came into view. When I stared at Lord Longstaffe, I felt the wonder of a small child witnessing the first miracle of a birthday conjurer. There, on his left lapel, blazed a white diamond fire and a deep indigo of surrounding sapphire. The outline of the Queen of the Night, an irreplaceable treasure that Holmes had assured me was on its way to Paris, shone brilliantly among us.

My gaze swung to the gaunt but inflamed face of Colonel Moriarty, whom I quite expected to draw a gun and tear the gem from Lord Longstaffe's breast. But if my face reflected utter astonishment and disbelief, the colonel's betrayed only the deepest horror. He did not reach forward to snatch the jewel but recoiled at the sight of it.

At that moment Sherlock Holmes beside me doffed the black cocked hat of the uniform that he had borrowed and made an exaggerated and eye-catching gesture. Colonel Moriarty, with a stony fear still flooding his sunken eyes, for all the world as if Don Giovanni's devils were dragging him down to hell, turned his heavy head and saw us. He knew well enough who we were. Beside us he saw the unmistakable figure of Inspector Jago in his ceremonial uniform, flanked by a superintendent of the City of London Police. My revolver was halfway out of my pocket before our adversary could reach for his. I did not doubt that he was carrying a gun, but, to my surprise, he made no attempt to reach for it. Instead, he turned and ran, pushing aside those behind him, and disappeared down the marble corridor with Jago and the superintendent in pursuit.

'Jago!' Holmes's voice rang out like a parade-ground command. 'Let him go but lay a trail for us!'

My friend now pushed through the crowd of astonished onlookers. In a few strides he was through the anteroom and the garde-robe, swooping into the post-room, opening a cupboard with a key that Lord Holder had given him. The cupboard contained a machine of some kind, a cast-iron box with a brass-framed, air-tight lid, inset with a glass panel. To one side of this rose a white porcelain handle, like a small beer pump. Inside the box I saw through the glass a three-inch bell-mouthed opening at one end, an incoming air pipe at the other. Lightweight envelopes of black rubbery gutta-percha in felt covers lay to hand, ensuring that each exactly fitted the tube.

Thought I had never seen such a thing before, I knew what this apparatus must be. This was a house tube connecting the office in the Mansion House with the pneumatic dispatch system—the system that carries telegrams and small post through forty miles of London's underground postal system. The pipe at one end of the box would exert a pressure of some ten pounds to the square inch on sending, or a vacuum of six pounds on receiving. It could transport bundles of seventy-five telegrams in a gutta-percha envelope, and would cover a mile through a three-inch tube in about two minutes. The diamond and the surrounding sapphires, unclipped, would be light enough to fit into two envelopes.

Sherlock Holmes checked the list of possible destinations framed on the inside of the cupboard door.

'I hardly think he will have communicated with the Houses of Parliament, Buckingham Palace, or Scotland Yard. I prefer Charing Cross Station! That is quite another matter. I will bet a pound to a penny on the next ferry train to Paris.'

He scrawled a message on a dispatch form, inserted it into a fold of gutta-percha, and addressed it. Over his shoulder, I saw the words, 'Lestrade. Scotland Yard.' All this, which takes so long to tell, occupied less than a minute in reality!

'I have had my doubts,' I gasped as we raced down the stairs to the courtyard, 'but I confess them ill-founded. The manner in which you have duped this last Moriarty rivals the best you have done. I shall never forget his face when he stared at Lord Longstaffe's lapel and knew he had stolen the fake that you planted for him!'

He stopped dead at the turning of the staircase and looked at me.

'Have you understood nothing? That bauble on Longstaffe's lapel was the fake! The Moriarty family knows a counterfeit when it sees one plainly. However, in the half-light of the passageway, he could not tell. He thought he saw the very thing he had stolen half an hour before, as a murderer sees a ghost. It shook him! By God, you saw how it shook him! Then he turned his head to find the two of us and two policemen staring at him. After that, it mattered nothing whether the bauble was a fake or not. Your revolver was half out of your pocket and he knew he was almost caught.'

We flew through the doorway into the courtyard and Holmes shouted at a constable for a closed brougham to follow Inspector Jago. As we clattered out of the courtyard, he turned to me more calmly.

'I will borrow your revolver, old fellow, if I may.'

I handed him the cold butt of the gun.

'Charing Cross?' I said.

'Think of it. Moriarty easily contrived to be locked in the anteroom or garde-robe, and quite possibly hid himself in the postroom, when everyone else had left. Colonel Lemonnier represented him in the Venetian Parlour. Within five minutes, the colonel came out of hiding and removed the Queen of the Night from the lapel of Lord Longstaffe's cloak, unclipped the diamond center from the sapphires, and dispatched two small envelopes in the pneumatic tube. When the minor courtiers returned, what was easier than for the thief to stand back against the wall behind the open doors or step out from the concealment of a long curtain when the coast was clear and mingle with them. Up to that time, there was no cause for alarm. When that alarm was raised, there would not be a shred of evidence against him.'

'The hunt would be up as soon as the theft was discovered.'

'Those cloaks were brought out one by one. Half the people there would have drifted away. Colonel Moriarty would have ample time to slip away before Lord Longstaffe noticed his loss. He might prefer to stay. The Queen of the Night would not be found on him, whereas any one of the twenty or thirty people who had left might have it. Colonel Lemonnier would be the first to reach Charing Cross. Have no fear, his freedom is important to our plans.'

'And our colonel?'

'He must bolt for home, among the apaches of the Place Pigalle and the street women of the Avenue de Clichy. You may be sure that his rooms at the Hellfire Club are deserted—and the bill unpaid! The next ferry train for Folkestone and Boulogne, I think, Watson.

He need only collect two small and unremarkable packages from the telegraph office, assume the style of a boulevardier, and dine tonight beyond the reach of the English law, while Jago and Lestrade are still searching the Mansion House!'

We were pelting downhill toward Ludgate Circus, the great dome of St. Paul's and its pillared portico at our backs.

'The game is altered for him,' Holmes said grimly. 'He believes he has seen the very jewel he stole and dispatched half an hour before. It could not by any means be where he saw it now unless he was betrayed. In his place, how would you respond to that?'

'I should go straight to wherever I expected it to be—to see what trick had been played upon me.'

'Exactly.'

Our driver, a uniformed constable, saw ahead of him a barrier across Fleet Street and the Strand, routes reserved that afternoon for the royal procession.

'With any luck,' said Holmes softly, 'our fugitive will have been delayed by that.'

We swung right towards Blackfriars Bridge. In a moment we were racing along the Embankment towards Westminster, the river sparkling on our left, penny steamers trailing banners of black smoke; on our right, the trees and lawyers' chambers of the Temple. We swung again, up the narrow canyon of Villiers Street, Charing Cross Station on a vast undercroft of sooty brick rising massively above us.

Holmes was out of the carriage first, racing for the departure platforms. We found Inspector Jago, still in black uniform with gold piping, pacing the concourse, studying the passengers who filed past the ticket-collectors. I saw Holmes signal to him and they drew back cautiously behind a corner of the bookstall, where they could keep watch on the post and telegraph office.

As I joined them, Holmes was saying earnestly, 'Twenty past two. There is a ferry train at three and calculate the packages were collected from the office half an hour ago. You may be sure the name on them will not be Moriarty. It may be Lemonnier. It may be anyone.'

He strode across the busy concourse in full view and entered the office while Jago and I watched. I saw him at the counter, confronting the manager, a man of middle age, no doubt accustomed to dealing with postal fraud. Their conversation continued until I saw Sherlock Holmes shout something at the unfortunate guardian.

There was a pause during which the man may have replied. Then he very slowly raised his hands in the air. I guessed that Holmes had drawn—or threatened to draw—my revolver from his pocket. There were moments of passionate anger in him when he might certainly be capable of shooting a postal official who obstructed his investigation.

Fortunately, Inspector Jago was looking in the other direction just then, watching the crowds who pressed homewards from their day of celebration along the royal route. The postal manager stepped to one side. Holmes had him covered with the gun in one hand and was rifling the rows of wooden pigeonholes in which messages and small packages awaited collection. He drew them out by handfuls, glanced at them, and threw them on the floor. Finally he shouted at the terrified postal official, received a reply, threw open the door, and strode in our direction again.

'For God's sake, Holmes!'

'I am told that I have seen every telegram or package that is awaiting collection. Not one! Not one item here that is bulky enough to be what we seek. Someone has got them!'

'Not Colonel Moriarty,' I said reassuringly. 'He could hardly have been here long enough before we arrived to enter the office and leave again. Lemonnier, under whatever name they have agreed, is another matter.'

Inspector Jago had evidently paid little attention to what Holmes was saying. He now spoke without turning to us.

'Well now,' he said quietly, 'there's a thing!'

The minutehand on the large four-sided clock on the girders above us approached the half hour. We followed his gaze.

'Now there is a curious thing,' he said. 'That grizzled man wearing a livery cape coming towards the steps down to the washrooms—he has a Robert Heath livery cape, just as a cabman might. No harm in that. But where it hangs open, see if that isn't a silk surplice shirt underneath, such as only a gentleman would wear. He doesn't try to look a gentleman, to be sure, and yet he happens to be carrying a Jenner & Knewstub leather travelling-bag. A most expensive item with compartments for clothing, shaving brushes, and all else that a real toff might require.'

'One thing certain,' said Holmes peremptorily, 'he is too short and too well-set to be Colonel Moriarty. Meantime, we must keep watch here. For the moment you have your curious acquaintance bottled up, if you need him.'

The minute-hand on the large clock above us touched the next Roman numeral. Half past two. We were within sight of the ticket-barrier for that platform which served the ferry train. None of the passengers who had filed through showed the least resemblance to our prey.

'And behold!' said Inspector Jago presently. 'Our man has come up again with his livery cape still on, his surplice shirt, but without his expensive travelling-bag. Unless I am mistaken, he is making for the cab rank. I think, however, he is not a cabdriver but a passenger in a hurry.'

Jago turned and looked hard at two men reading newspapers on a passengers' waiting bench. I had not noticed them there when we arrived, nor had I noticed them arrive since, so unobtrusive were their movements. Now they rose separately and set off in the wake of the livery cape.

Holmes, Jago, and I watched the iron-railed space within which the steps led down to the steam and marble of the washrooms. There was a cloakroom for the deposit of luggage down there, and the explanation of Jago's curiosity might be as simple as that. I waited for the first sign of a red tunic, but I waited in vain. It was Holmes who moved first. His target was a man in black city coat and trousers with a silk hat and silver-knobbed ebony stick. It was only at a second glance that I saw that he carried a Jenner & Knewstub overnight bag in his left hand.

I should not have known him as Colonel Moriarty, though he was of the same height. The silk hat disguised something of the bulging forehead; a pair of heavily rimmed spectacles gave him a studious air that somehow brought forward the deep-set eyes. He had a dark moustache and was walking in a curiously determined manner.

At the top of the steps from the underground cloakrooms, he swung away from us rapidly and approached the revolving door of the Charing Cross Hotel. We took up the pursuit, striding at a little distance behind him. As the door turned slowly, we were just in time to see him enter the ground-floor lift. The lift-boy pressed a button. Holmes sprang up the stairs, striving to keep level with our fugitive, while I stood guard at the ground-floor entrance. Jago was to take the second lift to the top of the building so that our man should be cut off from above. Then, to my consternation, the first lift, which had been ascending, began abruptly to come down from no higher than the second floor. The man must still be in it. The result was that my two companions had overshot the mark without knowing it and I must face this maniac alone. My hand went to my pocket. Then I stopped and recalled that Holmes had my revolver.

I braced myself for the struggle, grateful that I had not forgotten all my tactics from years of playing rugger for Blackheath. As I watched and listened, the lift rumbled to ground-floor level and then, without a pause, continued to descend. We had completely misjudged our levels for it was now dropping to the lower side entrance of the hotel, coming out into Villiers Street. Our man had stranded the three of us. Yet I was still sure he had not seen us. This charade was a final precaution in order to throw off the scent anyone who might be tracking him unobserved.

The next point where he might be caught was at the entrance to the platform for the three o'clock ferry train to Folkestone. The race began once more. It was now twenty minutes to three and the three o'clock ferry train must be preparing for departure.

'Leave all this!' Holmes shouted to me, as he came back down the stairs, gesturing at the cream and raspberry decor of the grand hotel.

As we came out into the station concourse, I said, 'We shall catch him at the platform for the Continental Ferry Train.'

'No! That is what he will expect us to do!'

'What then?'

'Every train from here crosses the short distance across the river bridge to Waterloo Station and stops before it goes on elsewhere. He still has time to catch a suburban stopping train in five or ten minutes, alighting a few minutes later at Waterloo, while we are left guarding the platform here. Then he may take the ferry train from Waterloo—or any other train that will carry him to Folkestone or Dover. We should still be waiting here. Or at Waterloo when it is too late. We must catch him now.'

'But there will be police at all the stations.'

'Good God, man! From Waterloo, he can get to any station in London or the rest of the country.'

'There will be police everywhere by now, surely.'

He heaved a sigh, drawing breath.

'At this moment, there are perhaps half a dozen people in London who know the Queen of the Night is missing—and three of them are here. The entire Metropolitan police force is probably still guarding His Majesty's ceremonial route.'

By now Jago had come up with us. Far away, at the shabbiest platform of Charing Cross Station, stood the shabbiest train, a collection of ancient carriages destined for a modest suburban itinerary that would wind slowly to New Cross, Lewisham, Blackheath, and the stations of Southeast London. Passing the ticket-collector at the barrier, I noticed a tall athletic man in a brown tweed overcoat, carrying a leather Jenner & Knewstub bag.

How easily a reversible coat can change from City black to the brown tweed of a racing man on his way home! Holmes took off at a sprint, Jago and I a little behind him. The iron gate was closed now and a whistle had blown. Jago shouted a command at the ticket-collector as the train began to move forward slowly across Hungerford Bridge, the brown tide of the river turning silver in the afternoon sun. Holmes hurdled the gate and raced ahead of us, but it seemed we had lost sight of our man. Then I heard a crack, rather like the detonation of a lifeboat maroon. The revolver, whatever type it might be, was a heavier gun than mine. I calculated that it had been fired at us from the forward carriage of the slowly moving suburban train.

There was no time to run back and communicate an urgent message to the railway police at Waterloo, for the train would arrive there and leave again before the signal was received. If we lost him now, Colonel Moriarty might alight at any station among the homeward crowds, drop down to the track far from anywhere, and be in London, in England, in Europe—for that matter, in Timbuctoo.

Holmes had jumped from the platform and was running along the track at the rear of the train. He was sheltered at this angle from the aim of the marksman, but then, as the wheels gathered speed, he was exposed once more to two further bullets from Colonel Moriarty's revolver. The sound of the shots was hardly audible above the iron rumbling of the wheels, but one passed close to Jago. If I heard correctly, three shots had been fired so far and three more live rounds would probably remain in the chambers of the gun. If the colonel could kill, maim, or even drive us back, he had the world before him and a racing start.

The several carriages of the train, with a fussy-sounding little engine at their head, rolled forward across the ironwork and planking of the river bridge. In the sunlight, Waterloo Bridge to our left was heavy with road traffic; Westminster Bridge to the right was still decked with red, white, and blue bunting for the royal occasion. I knew we should never find Colonel Moriarty in such crowds as besieged the platforms at Waterloo by this hour. If we failed, I thought, no one else was even looking for him.

Just then a metal signal arm on a tall gantry, which had so far been pointing earthward, rose to the horizontal with a heavy clang, and its light changed from green to red. The train slowed down with a jangling of buffers and a squeal of iron wheels on steel. It halted almost in the center of the long bridge in a long silence. Whether it was waiting for an empty platform at Waterloo or whether the signalman in his box had noticed three of us on the line, I had no idea.

With Sherlock Holmes in the lead, my revolver in his hand, we moved forward, our backs almost pressed against the coachwork to give the smallest angle of fire to our adversary. There was a shout from the engine driver.

'Get off the track!'

It was not directed at us, but at someone on the far side of the train. From ahead of us, though out of sight, came a sound of feet on gravel.

'He's making a run for it!' Jago called out.

'Not with a fully loaded travelling-bag in his hand,' said Holmes quietly.

We skirted round the rear coach to take our enemy from behind. As we came out from cover, I was prepared to throw myself down to avoid a bullet from Colonel Moriarty. Yet there was no sound of gunfire or even of a voice. The summer afternoon was as quiet as if we had been on some remote beach or mountainside. No train came in either direction, and for the first time I realised that someone must have seen us and ordered all traffic across the bridge to be stopped. I now saw a most extraordinary sight. The tall figure in the brown tweed coat was standing at the parapet of the bridge, facing downstream. The black leather travelling-bag was in his hands. Or rather, he was holding it open and turning it upside down. I had a brief glimpse of shaving brushes and soap-stick, clothes-brush and razor, a pajama case and a tight wad of clothing tumbling helter-skelter into the current of the river below.

It might have been an act or surrender or probably the quickest way of discarding the bag that weighed him down. He took the gun from his pocket. As he raised it, I jumped for cover of the stationary carriages. But he had turned toward the far end of the bridge ahead of us and fired. Why had he not fired at us?

I need not have worried. He swung round almost at once and there was another crack. A bullet chipped the woodwork of the carriage door about two feet from my head. Then I saw the reason for the previous shot. From the far end of the bridge, where the track ran into Waterloo station, a dozen men were working their way slowly in our direction, keeping their heads down and ready to throw themselves flat. All but two of them wore blue serge tunics and trousers with the tall helmet and silver star marking them out as officers of the Metropolitan Police. In the lead, a man in grey sidled along the parapet. In front of him, wearing a short summer-weight overcoat and a bowler hat, walked the cautious figure of Inspector Lestrade.

It was impossible to see whether any of these men carried guns. I could see none. Whether they did or not, Colonel Moriarty would hardly have bullets enough to kill them all. In any case, he would surely be overpowered while he tried to reload. He now looked at them and then threw the black leather bag after its contents. Had the Queen of the Night gone the same way? If it had, there was an end of the evidence that might prove a charge of theft!

His way back was as securely blocked as his way forward so long as Holmes had my revolver in his hand. If I was correct, Colonel Moriarty had one live round in his gun and Holmes had all six. On both sides, the colonel's captors moved forward, hemming him in. What followed was the work of a few seconds. He jumped onto the wide iron ledge of the balustrade and looked downstream toward Waterloo Bridge. His gun was in his hand. No one could have said what use he might make of the final bullet.

Lestrade and the men behind him stopped. Much as they wanted their man, they wanted the contents of his pockets still more, if these should include the splendid Brazilian diamond and its clusters of sapphires. Sherlock Holmes paced slowly forward, the gravel of the track shifting and grating under his steps, his aquiline features calm in the presence of a glare of pure hatred from the last Moriarty. He held the borrowed revolver at his side, pointing at the ground from his right hand as he walked. Deliberately and slowly he strode into the range of the colonel, the last of those men who had planned his ritual murder in the execution shed of Newgate Gaol.

The tall figure of the colonel was motionless. He was surely judging the moment when his antagonist would be close enough for the remaining bullet to find its mark. No one else moved. Holmes had wished for a final settling of accounts and it seemed that his wish had been granted. If Moriarty should miss him, the bullet that was fired back would settle the matter. Standing against the sky, the colonel presented the clearest possible target.

Holmes was about thirty feet away when his antagonist raised his arm. My friend took one more step, the revolver still pointing at the ground, and then our hearts jumped with a sense of sickness as Moriarty fired. Holmes swayed, not as if he had been hit but as though he had heard the bullet coming and had moved out of its way. Then he took another step and moved slowly on. I do not know what the phrase 'mad with terror' customarily implies, but to me it described the expression of Colonel Moriarty's features to the last detail.

The only sound now in the warm afternoon was the distant hiss of escaping steam from the boiler of the little engine and the measured sound of gravel at every stride that Sherlock Holmes took. At about ten feet he raised the gun. Moriarty spat out some curse or expletive that I could not distinguish at the distance separating us. At the same moment, the revolver in Holmes's hand jerked briefly. Colonel Moriarty went forward at full length, toppling and then cartwheeling through the air into the current below.

Even so, I could not tell whether the last of Sherlock Holmes's would-be executioners fell with a bullet in his brain or threw himself to his death in defiance of those who had cornered him at last, casting the Queen of the Night into the oblivion of the deep river mud. His body was never found—or rather, if it was found, it was never identified. Among the poor wretches found drowned in the following weeks, two or three had been terribly mutilated by the steel paddles of passing river steamers or other accidents. Some had been carried far down the broad estuary and been given to the sea. I choose to believe that the colonel was one of them.

Even after that, fate had been crueller to him than any contrivance of our own. While Holmes faced this final duel, two of Jago's men had arrested Colonel Lemonnier in his cabman's cape as he left Charing Cross. Lemonnier protested his innocence of any crime, beyond having changed places at the Mansion House lunch at the request of an acquaintance he had known for only a few days. He had never heard of the Queen of the Night, and offered no resistance. In his pocket, however, lay two small packages containing the two portions of the famous jewel, the unclipped diamond and the sapphire clusters. By what means he had robbed Colonel Moriarty of these in the final exchange of the traveling bag was never revealed. Lemonnier insisted that the colonel had given him the packages as a parting gift and that he understood them to be mere paste, intended as a *pourboire* for an obliging street girl in Piccadilly.

On the evening of that memorable day, Inspector Lestrade was our guest in the Baker Street sitting-room.

'You see, Mr. Holmes?' he said genially. 'We're always there when we're needed. Why, now, if I hadn't used a bit of policeman's plain common sense, we wouldn't have had that bridge cordoned off as it was. And in that case, gentlemen, I needn't remind you that the late Colonel Moriarty would have reached Waterloo Station on the far bank of the river. Once he was there, he might have been on a train to anywhere in a few minutes. By now—who knows?—he might have been sitting in Paris, admiring his trinket—as Lemonnier insists it is.'

Holmes muttered something but kept his peace.

Lestrade leant forward in his chair.

'And you'll both recall that case, gentlemen, when you were both walking through the park a little while back and happened to see a man get his head cut off by a galloping soldier. Well, do you know what?'

'I have not the least idea what, Lestrade, but you are no doubt about to enlighten us. You were not fortunate enough to identify the assassin, I suppose?"

The inspector sipped his whisky and water, then leant forward again.

'No, Mr. Holmes. I was fortunate enough to identify the owner of the head, despite his efforts to remain anonymous by having nothing in his pockets.'

'My felicitations,' Holmes closed his eyes. 'Pray continue.'

'Alker was his name. A former petty officer of the Royal Navy provos, identified almost by chance during a visit to the pathological laboratory where the head rests in a jar of formaldehyde. On several melancholy but necessary occasions of overseas service, the records tell us, Alker acted as a military and even a civil hangman. What do you say to that, now?'

'At least, Lestrade, you may be certain that he was not murdered in revenge by someone he had hanged. Beyond that, I do not think I can assist you.'

Lestrade puffed himself up a little at our lack of appreciation.

'I may say that I have sent a few criminals to the gallows,' he said portentously, 'but I can't say I've ever met a hangman at work.'

'No,' said Holmes dryly. 'No more have I. With or without his head.'

Notes

p. 587 E. Harris Ruddock, *The Homoeopathic Vade Mecum*, Roericke & Tafel, 1889, discusses the treatment of Egyptian ophthalmia at page 373.

p. 621 'The Resolution of Enclitic δε' was a problem in classical Greek grammar to which the subject of Robert Browning's poem 'The Grammarian's Funeral,' like Mycroft Holmes, had devoted his energies.

p. 628 'The Five Orange Pips' appeared in *The Strand Magazine* for November 1893.

p. 632 Examples of those who rivaled Sherlock Holmes in building fugues upon popular themes and nursery rhymes include Alec Templeton in the Benny Goodman number 'Mr. Bach Goes to Town' and Sidney M. Lawton, Music Master of Queen's College, Taunton, England, in his ingenious fugue upon 'Twinkle, Twinkle, Little Star.'

p. 633 'The Red-Headed League' appeared in *The Strand Magazine* for August 1891.

p. 641 The phenomenon of the body remaining upright after decapitation was witnessed by hundreds of onlookers when Captain

Nolan remained upright in the saddle for some time after his head was taken off by a Russian shell, before the ill-fated 'Charge of the Light Brigade' at Balaclava on 25 October 1854.

p. 645 *'Homo sum, humani nihil a me alienum puto.'* Sherlock Holmes was, as always, correct when he ascribed this to the Roman play-wright Terence in *Heauton Timorumenos* I, i, 25.

p. 647 Nelson's attack on the 'armed neutrality' of Copenhagen, on 2 April 1801, was the occasion on which he put his telescope to his blind eye and refused his commanding officer's signal to withdraw, saying to his subordinate, 'You know, Foley, I have only one eye—I have a right to be blind sometimes. . . . I really do not see the signal.'

p. 647 'The Naval Treaty' appeared in *The Strand Magazine* for October and November 1893.

p. 652 The case of Irene Adler was the first story in *The Adventures of Sherlock Holmes*, 'A Scandal in Bohemia,' which originally appeared in *The Strand Magazine* for July 1891. 'The Bruce-Partington Subma-rine Plans' appeared in the same magazine for December 1908.

p. 688 'Cold fowl and cigars, Pickled onions in jars' was the mid-night feast offered by a London tavern known as the Magpie and Stump. The poet recalled by Watson is by R. H. Barham, whose verses, 'The Execution: A Sporting Anecdote,' appeared in *The Ingoldsby Legends* (1840).

p. 703 By the Peace of Vienna in 1864, after the British and French failure to support Denmark against Prussia, Christian IX renounced his claim to Schleswig and Holstein, first occupied and then annexed by the Prussians.

p. 763 *'Fiat justitia ruat coelum'* was pronounced by William Murray, 1st Earl Mansfield (1705–93), Chief Justice of the King's Bench, in overturning the sentence imposed on John Wilkes in 1768 for publishing an antigovernment newspaper. Four years later, in a momentous judgment, Mansfield freed a slave, James Somersett, who had set foot on English soil during his master's visit to London. 'Every man who comes to England is entitled to the protection of the English law, whatever oppression he may heretofore have suffered, and whatever may be the colour of his skin, whether it is black or whether it is white.'

p. 788 In his comment on murder by chloroform, Holmes is evidently thinking of Carl Liman's 1876 edition of *Practishes Handbuch der gerichtlichen Medicin* by Johann Ludwig Casper (1796-1864), a pioneer in forensic medicine.

p. 791 John Nevil Maskelyne (1839–1917), born in Cheltenham, England. A stage conjurer at sixteen, he was lessee of St. George's Hall, London, and exposed the stage magic of the Davenport Brothers' so-called Cabinet and Dark Seance. He appeared at the Egyptian Hall, Piccadilly, 1873–1904. His techniques were employed to great effect in the art of camouflage during both world wars.

p. 795 Propter's Nicodemus Pills were made famous by Edward Lear in his poem for children, 'Incidents in the Life of My Uncle Arly.'

> *Like the Ancient Medes and Persians.*
> *Always by his own exertions*
> *He subsisted on those hills;—*
> *Whiles,—by teaching children spelling,—*
> *Or at times by merely yelling,—*
> *Or at intervals by selling 'Propter's Nicodemus Pills.'*

p. 824 'The Final Problem' appeared in *The Strand Magazine* for December 1893.

p. 824 Sir Francis Dashwood (1708–81), politician and rake, Chancellor of the Exchequer and Postmaster General. As organizer of the Hellfire Club from 1755, he was reputed to have staged orgies with other 'monks,' including John Wilkes and the poet Charles Churchill, first among the pastoral ruins of Medmenham Abbey on the bank of the Thames and then nearby in caves on the estate of his fine Palladian mansion at West Wycombe.

p. 842 'The Adventure of the Blue Carbuncle' appeared in *The Strand Magazine* for January 1892.